THRONE OF DARIUS:
A CAPTAIN OF
THEBES

The fight against Alexander the Great: Book I

MARK G. MCLAUGHLIN

Contents

Author's Preface   vii

Part I
Thebes

1. Thebes   3
2. Pelion   9
3. Thebes   15
4. The Enclosure of Iolaos   21
5. The Enclosure of Iolaos   29
6. The House of Pindar   35
7. Alexander's Camp   41
8. The Palisade   45
9. Thebes   55
10. Pindar's House   65

Part II
Athens

11. The House of Demades   73
12. The Port of Piraeus   79
13. The Port of Piraeus   85
14. Piraeus   93

Part III
Ephesos

15. Ephesos   103
16. Ephesos   107
17. Miletos   113
18. Dascylion   119
19. The Meander River   129
20. The Hellespont   133
21. The River Granicos   137
22. The River Granicos   147

23. The River Granicos 155
24. The Long Hill 167
25. Behind the Macedonian Line 173
26. The Hill 179
27. Slavery 187
28. Alexander Moves South 195
29. The Slave March 199
30. Sardis 205
31. The Hellespont 211
32. Ephesos 215
33. Ephesos 221

Part IV
Miletos

34. Miletos 227
35. Miletos 233
36. Miletos 239
37. Miletos 245
38. The Island of Lades 251
39. Miletos Harbor 259
40. Miletos Harbor 263
41. The Necropolis 269
42. Old Citadel Hill 277
43. Miletos Acropolis 283
44. Miletos 293
45. Memnon's Claw 301
46. Miletos 307
47. Miletos 313
48. Miletos 319
49. Mycale 327
50. Miletos 335
51. Miletos 341
52. Miletos 347
53. Miletos 353
54. Miletos 363
55. Miletos 371
56. Miletos 375
57. Miletos 381
58. Miletos 387
59. Myndos 393

Part V
Halicarnassos

60. Halicarnassos	401
61. Alinda	409
62. East of Myndos	415
63. Halicarnassos	421
64. Into the Interior	427
65. Halicarnassos	431
66. Outside Mylasa	437
67. Outside Halicarnassos	443
68. East of Mylasa	449
69. Halicarnassos	455
70. In the Interior	461
71. In the Interior	467
72. Bogdan	473
73. Bogdan	479
74. Halicarnassos	485
75. Bogdan	491
76. Diospolis	499
77. Halicarnassos	505
78. Diospolis	513
79. Halicarnassos	521
80. Outside Laodikea	527
81. North of Myndos	531
82. Diospolis	535
83. Halicarnassos	543
84. On the Coast near Halicarnassos	549
85. Halicarnassos	555
86. The Island with a View	565
87. Outside The Tripylon Gate	571
88. The Long Island off Halicarnassos	579
89. Halicarnassos	585
90. The Long Island	589
91. Halicarnassos	593
92. The Long Island	601
93. Halicarnassos	607
94. Halicarnassos	615
95. The Royal Citadel	621
96. The Island of Cos	627

Epilogue: Cos

97. The Island of Cos   635

A Note from the Author...   651
Acknowledgments   653
About the Author   655

Author's Preface

Throne of Darius is not just another pikeman in that massive phalanx of novels glorifying Alexander of Macedonia, known to history as "the Great." It is, instead, a tale dedicated to those who fought against him. Of Greeks, who, as the Theban lyric poet Pindar wrote of other heroes, *"have taken strife as their bride, and are faithful until death."*

As Alexander marched on with his Macedonians, not all Greeks followed. Many stood up for their honor, their cities, their families, their faiths, and their freedom. History is of course written by the victors, but the vanquished, too, have their stories to tell. This is one of them.

It IS Greek to Me…

Many wonderful and talented authors writing tales of Alexander's times sprinkle or even flood their stories with Greek or Persian words for military units, weapons, buildings, and titles that are, for lack of a better term, "foreign" to most contemporary readers. Some of these are so obscure or ungainly that even those of us who drink deep from the cup of history have to pause to ponder their meaning or go look them up on our bookshelves or online.

Rest assured, dear reader, that this author knows his *sarissa* from his *taxeis* (the one a very, very long spear, the other a body of men carrying them), but feels no compulsion to give constant proof of such knowledge. Instead, this author has sought to limit the use of such language and to write in such a way as to allow the reader to move ahead without the need to slow down for such verbal speed bumps. So, too, will there more often be yards, miles, and pounds instead of *pygons*, *parasangs*, and *minae*.

I have "but little Latin and less Greek" (at one time a thoroughly damning insult, especially among the previous generation of those who, like me, were fortunate enough to receive a classical education). Thus have I chosen to write in American English and not Greek-inflected, -affected or -afflicted English, for the first is my mother tongue, as I suspect it is of most of those who will open the cover and turn the pages of *Throne of Darius*.

I might add that the Greek terms, names and locations have been verified with my editor, for whom Greek is her mother tongue. As per her recommendation, however, for ease of reading, Alexander remains Alexander instead of the more correct Alexandros, and the Persian king of kings remains Darius rather than the more proper Darios, as most readers are more familiar with them by those versions of their names. Otherwise, all names and locations are left in Greek.

The sack of Thebes – 335 B.C.

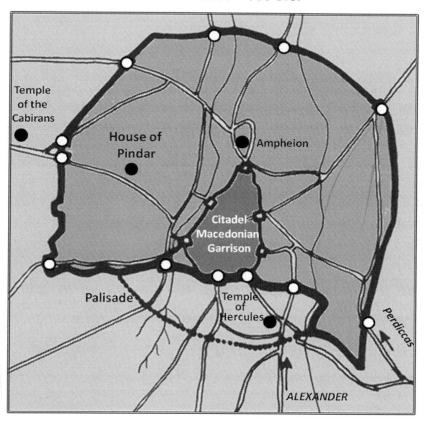

Asia Minor during Alexander's Era

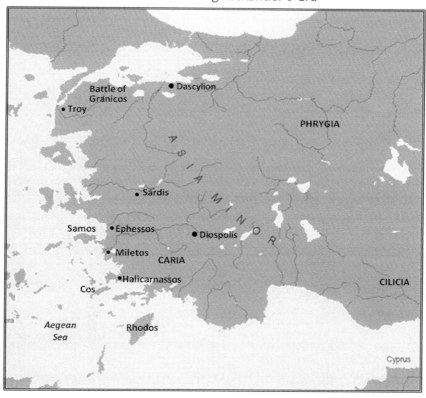

The Battle of the Granicos River – 334 B.C.

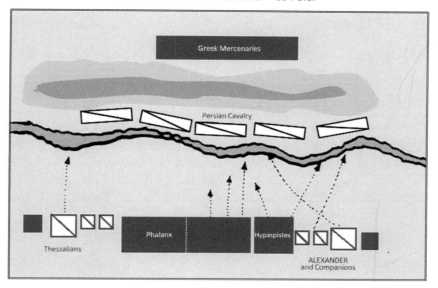

The Siege of Miletos – 334 B.C.

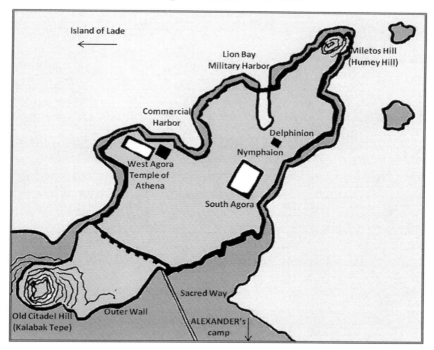

The Siege of Halicarnassos – 334 B.C.

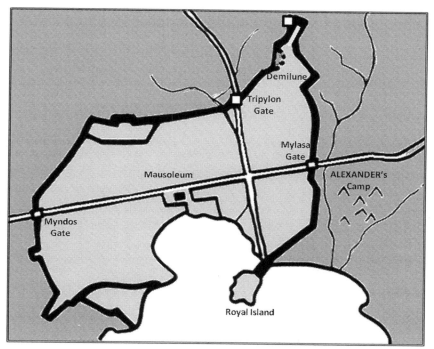

PART I

Thebes

CENTRAL GREECE

Year Two of the Reign of Alexander of Macedonia

Thebes

NEAR THE CADMEA - THE FORTRESS ON THE THEBAN ACROPOLIS

"**A**lexander is dead! Alexander is dead!" howled the boy, his voice part joyful scream, part clarion call to bloody murder. "Rise up, Thebans! Rise up! The day of delivery is here!"

To punctuate his cry of rebellion, the scruffy, excited lad drew a small, notched blade from inside the folds of his short, tattered and dirty tunic and jabbed it into the neck of the first Macedonian soldier he spied. Not much older than the boy and possessing little true Greek, the guard did not fully comprehend what the youth was saying – at least not until he felt the jagged blade plunge into his throat.

By then, it was too late for the soldier, the spear he had been lazily leaning on clattering to the stones as he clutched his bleeding neck with both hands. It was his last conscious act on earth. Other carving knives, drawn from other dirty tunics, came slashing down behind the armored greaves on his legs. Still more blades found the open spots between breastplate and underarms, cutting at and into every vulnerable part of his once lean and now horribly mutilated form.

The young soldier died, as did scores of his comrades throughout the occupied city. Only the lucky few went quickly. Most died horribly and all were put down violently – taken by surprise, alone or in small groups, on the streets, in the market, and even in their beds.

Some few, some very, very few, managed to form a semblance of a phalanx – that bristling shield wall for which first Greece and later her Macedonian overlords were famed. Secure in their thorny armored shell, the soldiers cut their way through the ever-thickening mob back to the citadel, that mighty stone fortress called Cadmea – only to find its massive doors shut tight.

Trapped at the foot of the long steps leading up to the fortress, the spearmen braced themselves against the rough granite. Hundreds of frenzied citizens pushed, and pressed, and hurled themselves like waves pounding the beach, only to crash and break upon the Macedonian shields. Nearly overborne by numbers, the Macedonian spearmen never faltered, never tried to flee. Each to fall went to his death as a soldier – stabbing, thrusting, and slashing with spear, sword, and knife into the howling mob. Brave as they were, their numbers continued to shrink. Slowly, step by blood-spattered, slippery-stone step, they gave ground, making the Thebans pay a toll in blood for each stair the soldiers gave up in their retreat toward the citadel.

Theban flesh met Macedonian iron and bled, but it, too, did not yield. Forward the men of Thebes not so much charged but raced, and raced headlong to hurl themselves at the hated occupiers. Women threw stones, clay pots, dishes, and even food in an overhead barrage, forcing many of the soldiers in the second rank to raise their shields high. At their feet, other soldiers were busy fending off the little boys who were squirming beneath the hedgehog of spears to prick, and cut, and even bite at their ankles. The Thebans came on as a people drunk; intoxicated on a heady mix of blood, liberty, and revenge; a concoction made more potent yet by remembered visions of their city's ancient glory.

Although the city was swept by this human maelstrom, a few of the Macedonian patrols escaped back to the steps of the citadel, the phalanx opening ever so slightly to let them in. Their lives were bought with those of their comrades in the ever contracting, slowly retreating but never collapsing phalanx.

As these soldiers fell back to the citadel, their comrades within, too, were beset.

Just before dawn, a handful of assassins slipped into the sleeping chambers of the fortress commander. The battle cry of 'Alexander is dead' then but a whisper on their lips, the raiders seized general Amyntas and the leader of the Macedonian collaborators, Timolaos. They murdered them, and in a manner so vile only those who strike in the name of vengeful patriotism can rationalize.

The first, a Macedonian war hero, much beloved by his men who nicknamed him "Abrutes" (or eyebrows), they hung on a hook like a pig and sliced his throat as if butchering a hog. His killers cheered as the general's life's blood drained away. Amyntas' second in command, Alexiades, tried to save his general, but to no avail. The Theban assassins bound up Alexiades hand and foot and threw him from the wall by the city's Ismenian Gate. His bones broken, unable to move, the Macedonian captain was left for the wild dogs and wolves to dine on at night.

As for Timolaos, a Theban who had sold out to the Macedonians, his death was even more unpleasant. To the killers, whose homes and property Timolaos had seized and whose relatives and friends he had driven into exile, the Theban politician was no mere foreign occupier but a native-born traitor to his people and to his city. Viewed as a man who had chosen Macedonian barbarians over Theban Greeks, Timolaos died a traitor's death, given over to the women of the families he had betrayed, robbed, imprisoned and humiliated.

These deaths were but the clarion call, the prelude to the mass uprising, but old soldiers do not die easily. Veterans all, the Macedonians rose from their beds, grabbed swords and shields before even donning their tunics, and, fighting naked, regained control of the Cadmea from the invaders. Enraged by the cowardly murders of their general and their captain, the soldiers took some slight solace in knowing that their officers did not go to Hades alone, as many of their killers soon followed.

Once they had scoured the Cadmea clean, the garrison put on their armors, broiled out of their barracks, and went about the grim and bloody business for which they were trained. Set-jawed, steel-eyed Macedonian soldiers methodically cleansed the citadel's interior of the

5

Thebans - all Thebans. With jabbing spears and slashing swords, they mowed down not just the armed intruders but also workmen, cooks, shopkeepers, slaves, casual interlopers, whores, and camp followers, sparing neither women nor children in their cold rage.

Murdering their way from the barracks through the courtyard to the citadel gate, the Macedonian garrison regained control of the entry way to their fortress from the inside. Only then could they unbar the massive doors and start to bring in what few survivors remained of the city patrols. As the gates swung open, a mighty rush of Thebans came on again, the promise of death in their fiery eyes, only to be skewered on the spears and pikes of the now reinforced and doubly ferocious phalanx.

Back and forth the mass of flesh and wall of shields contended. On one side, grim soldiers in bronze armor; on the other, a great wave of humanity intent on spending itself upon the unyielding barrier. The press of bodies pushed the phalanx back, step by slow step, forcing the Macedonians ever backward, one booted foot at a time until they filled the gateway. There the phalanx paused, its spear points the teeth of the aping maw of a blood-splattered monster.

One by one, men in the back ranks found safety within the Cadmea, their home since placed there by the Macedonian tyrant Philip a few scant three years ago.

For many hours, the Thebans repeatedly launched themselves at the shrinking phalanx. The mob eventually fell back, only to give way to athletic young men with slings, and bows, and javelins. These youths rained a heavy barrage upon the Macedonians. Few missiles found a lethal mark, yet under this steady nuisance the soldiers could not lower their shields or fall back to close the gate again, lest the boiling crowd pounce and overcome them.

While the young men kept the Macedonians pinned, a one-armed man climbed into the bed of a cart, stood and addressed the crowd, many of whom were looking for a way to quietly escape from the scene of the battle.

"Friends, fellow citizens of Thebes! You know me! I am Coroneos! One of the very, very few survivors of the Sacred Band. I left my right arm on the field of Chaeronea, and had-I not fainted from loss of blood and been carried off, the rest of me would be out there still, beneath that mound of earth that covers my brothers."

Cheers and salutes from several in the mob encouraged the wounded veteran. Emboldened and heartened by their reaction, the old soldier spoke on.

"Today you have given me a chance to avenge my brothers, and to once again fight for our freedom! Not just freedom for Thebes, but freedom for all of Greece! Let all who love freedom come with me now! Up those steps, where we shall strike the first blow to destroy the tyranny of Macedon's kings over Greek democracy! Screw your courage to the sticking point, my fellow citizens, and follow me up those steps – to freedom!"

Swapping men in and out of the shield wall, the watch commander had kept the citadel doorway open to those few soldiers who managed to straggle back to the fortress, yet still blocked to the mob. With each wounded man he pulled back, he prayed to Zeus for night - and with it for a respite from missile fire so he could recover the last of his men and close that bloody gate.

With his prayers still floating up to Olympus, he heard the one-armed man exhorting the crowd to action. That wild man in the lead, on came the Thebans once again. Despite their frenzy, they were still but a mob and could not break his shield wall. Once again, like the tide going back out, the crowd fell back, dragging their wounded with them.

The respite the Macedonians earned did not last long, as once again they heard cheers and shouts in the square. The next attack came moments later. But it was not the mob this time, nor the young slingers and bowmen and javelin-throwers either. It was the hoplites: the citizen soldiers of the city, heads fully encased in plumed helmets, steely eyes peering through narrow slits. Their strong, muscular breasts protected by cuirasses of bronze, their powerful legs girded with greaves, they bore great, heavy, full-body shields strapped to their necks and shoulders, leaving hands free for their long, sharp spears. Sons and grandsons of fighting men, these were descendants of the army that had won fame half a century earlier for beating that once most unbeatable of all Greek armies – the Spartans.

The Macedonians knew this was no rabble. Like themselves, these men of Thebes were soldiers, heirs to the legend built by Epaminondas and Pelopidas, raised on the gloried remembrances of victories at Haliartos, Coronea and Leuctra. Many were veterans who still rankled at their defeat by Philip and his son Alexander at Chaeronea three years ago. These men, sons, and grandsons, and great-grandsons of the dragon-sown men of old, came forward in grim silence. Like the fabled warriors of bronze who had painted the club of mighty Hercules on their shields, these common men of Thebes marched into the square, the crowd parting as a curtain upon the stage. In measured step they came, seeking not just to spill blood but also to reclaim their honor.

In that narrow gateway, phalanx crashed into phalanx. Spears and pikes shattered on shields. Swords battered helmets and sliced at feet. Daggers sought for the slightest of openings in the great armored barriers – and where daggers failed, hands and fingernails and teeth bit and tore.

A new wall formed, one built of the dead. Theban and Macedonian corpses were its stones, and their blood the mortar. Behind that horrible barrier the garrison eventually found desperately needed succor. The barricade of corpses blocked the path gateway just enough, just barely long enough, for the Macedonians to take one last step back. It allowed them the moment they needed for the great gates to be shut and barred, thus for the time being robbing the Theban hoplites of their final revenge.

Or at least delaying it, for then began the siege of the Cadmea, a fortress within a fortress, a garrison surrounded by a city, a band of soldiers alone, waiting for salvation from a dead king – their cherished Alexander.

2

Pelion

ON THE BORDER BETWEEN EPIRUS AND
ILLYRIA: (175 MILES NORTH OF THEBES): THE
KING'S TENT

"I told him that a king should lead and that he should command – but to charge up those heights, pike in hand like some common soldier, that was never my lesson!"

"Langaros, do not blame yourself. Philip's son was always head-strong. Remember that charge of his at Chaeronea, when he slaughtered the Sacred Band of Thebes?"

"Aye, Philotas, the gods know he should have died that afternoon, the young fool, fighting at the front of the cavalry as he did. Philip was so proud of his boy that day."

"He would have been no less so this day, urging forward your Agrianian light infantry on one side of him and my phalangites on the other. We both did our best to guard him. Oh, King Langaros, what else could we have done?"

"Had I been but two steps closer, General, perhaps I could have stepped between him and that Dardanian javelin…"

"…and then it would have been your body here on the pallet for the priests to cleanse."

"So it should have been, Philotas, so it should have been."

"At least we have the field – and the heights. Alexander bought us those with his life. Now we have Cleitos shut up in the town, and we can begin a proper siege."

"To what end, Philotas? To what end? The king is dead. The army shaken, the commanders already bickering and scheming among themselves, each dreaming of marching back to Pella to take the crown for himself."

"Parmenion will never allow that. Nor will Olympias."

"Hah! Parmenion is old, a companion of one dead king, and now what, general to another royal corpse? The soldiers may respect him but that is all. As for the queen, Philip had already set her aside. If not for the sake of Alexander, they'd have killed the witch!"

As the king of the Agrianian hillmen spat out that last word, a cold wind kicked up, nearly snuffing out the torches by which the apparently lifeless body of Alexander was illuminated. The whistle of the wind masked all other sounds, giving way only to the rustle of silk and the slight footfall of a woman entering the company of the mourning warriors.

"King Langaros, think you I would die so easily?" said the woman, her accent thick and her tone as deadly as it was seductive. "The blood of the gods courses through my veins, as it does through those of my son."

"Majesty," said the hill king, surprised, embarrassed, and wary at the sudden appearance of the storied mother of the young royal whose body lay still yet beautiful on the pallet. "We thought you in Pella, at court."

"What good would I do my son there?" replied the queen regally, gently folding back the hood of her cloak. "Alexander is at war, and boys who play at war oft have need of their mothers."

"I am afraid, my Queen, that your son is beyond such need."

"Why do you say such nonsense, Langaros? Look, here he is, sleeping sweetly before your eyes, waiting for me to wake him."

"Majesty," interjected the general, his voice choked with sorrow, "he is not sleeping. He is dead. Even now the priests are preparing the bier so the army may pass in review, and the soldiers pay their last respects to their king."

"You are as much a child as ever, I see, my dear General," chided Olympias. "You know nothing of me or of my son, let alone of his destiny or of the power that lies within us. Look upon his body with a more discerning eye and you will see that though his chest does not move, his color is not like that of a man whose soul has departed. I say he is not dead but merely asleep. Alexander has not left this world; he is still with us, dreaming of victories yet to be won, and of honors and glories soon to be showered upon him."

"Olympias," sighed King Langaros gently, moving closer in an attempt to offer some comfort. "It is a great sadness to lose a child, but denying it will not undo the loss. Come, we shall find suitable quarters for you in the camp. Leave the priests to complete this last task for their king."

"No, Langaros," replied Olympias calmly, yet with a forceful majesty in her voice that made Langaros quake. "It is these ignorant priests who must go. Have these charlatans leave me and my ladies in waiting to our task. General," the queen added as she addressed Philotas, her voice royal and commanding, "have your men remove my son and place him in the royal pavilion. Surround it with a wall of men in armor, pikes held high and backs to the tent. Let none enter but me and my women."

"Majesty..."

"You have your orders, General. I give them to you as your queen, not merely as the mother of Alexander. King Langaros, if ever you loved my late husband or my son, I ask that you, too, do the same. Protect the camp and the pavilion, and keep those bumbling, foolish priests away. Will you do this for me, and if not, will you at least do so for my son?"

The king and the general looked at each other, both uneasy at their charge yet neither willing to further confront the chillingly beautiful and coldly calm woman who stood so imperially before them.

"It shall be as you command, my Queen," replied Philotas with a sigh.

"My men, too, shall do as you ask, Olympias," consented the Agrianian king.

"Thank you both. Now go about your tasks as my women and I go about ours – and again I caution you, for your own sakes, see that we are not disturbed."

The pavilion into which the body of Alexander was carried was not overly large or richly appointed. It was the tent of a king but of a king at war, and of a young king at that, Spartan in its furnishings as would become a soldier more eager for battle than for comfort. Olympias lovingly daubed the now naked body of her son with scented oils, taking special care around the raw, reddish gaping mouth of a wound from which a deadly javelin had been pulled.

"There, there, my sweet boy," she murmured soothingly, tracing serpentine patterns on his arms and chest with first one oil then another from a chest of tiny vials. "Sleep while you can for now, for come the dawn you will never need sleep again."

As Olympias continued her ritual, her women began their appointed tasks, the younger ones stripping naked and writhing slowly, dancing methodically to music only they could hear. Other, older women brought forward baskets from which they coaxed snakes and serpents of varying sizes and hues. These they directed to the pallet upon which Alexander lay, guiding the larger to coil around his ankles, knees, wrists, elbows, and shoulders. The smaller, thinner snakes they helped to his mouth, to his wound, and to other openings and orifices, assisting them to slither on, around and into his now oddly warming corpse.

Again and again the women went to the baskets, bringing forth more and more of the slithering monsters to cocoon and encapsulate the body in a glistening, moving shroud. Upon this quivering mass of man and monsters, Olympias drizzled yet more oils and slathered greasy unguents from small twisted jars, all the while chanting beneath her breath in a language neither Greek nor Macedonian. Sometimes singing, sometimes murmuring, but always speaking, she worked to draw life from the serpents back to her son.

Slowly, steadily and methodically did the Queen of Macedonia work her magic, invoking names of gods and heroes and powers from ages long thought passed. As the moon crested in the night sky, she signaled silently to three of the young virgins of her party, each of whom then left the tent only to return moments later, leading three charges.

The first led three black rams. The second led three young girls and the third, three young boys. All seemed oddly calm, dazed, and drugged as they were, their eyes rolling, their voices silent. Each woman motioned for her followers to kneel, as other matrons came forth with golden cups and knives, knives they used to open the veins of boys and girls and rams alike.

As the cups filled, the young women handed them one at a time to the queen, who slowly poured the contents of each over the snake-encased body of the boy king. Over and over again did the women and the queen perform this ritual, until not a drop remained in any cup or sacrifice. The handmaidens removed the nine corpses just as the sun began to rise. Others of the ladies in waiting to Olympia then opened the eastern flap of the tent to allow the rays of the sun to enter and strike the writhing, slithering, blood-soaked mass that covered the boy king's body.

As the bright spears of the dawn's light struck, the serpents slithered away, seeking the warming rocks outside the tent.

"Bring water, fresh, clean, clear water," commanded the queen, no weariness but only certainty in her voice. As her women brought forth the great jars, the queen emptied yet more vials into them, swirled them about, and directed her ladies to bathe the body, cleansing it and the pallet of all traces of blood. As they finished, all could see Alexander's chest rise and fall, and his eyes move behind their closed lids.

"He lives, my queen!" cried one of the handmaidens joyfully. "You have brought him back from the edge of the abyss!"

Olympias allowed herself to shoot an uncharacteristic smile at the girl. Let the girl believe what she will believe, the queen thought to herself, and let her spread the tale far and wide. With each telling the legend will grow. They will think me powerful, and will come to fear me, and will think twice about challenging a woman who can bring a man back from death. Like Achilles reborn, they will believe him invincible, and to be both beloved of and protected by the gods – if not a god himself.

"Now, my son," said the queen sweetly, quietly and lovingly, "awake, and sleep never more."

3

Thebes

THE HOUSE OF ARISTOPHANES

"What do you mean, Alexander still lives?" demanded young Aristophanes of his captain. "Demosthenes of Athens himself sent us the news – confirmed news – of the boy king's death! I heard it from a trader in the marketplace! He even brought forward an eye-witness, a runaway Macedonian soldier who saw Alexander fall to a barbarian blade during a battle up north!"

"Well…" sighed Dimitrios, a captain of Thebes, as he came through the doorway into the drab, dimly lit, and nearly bare of furniture dwelling, "it seems that somebody got it wrong. And yes, there are still men in the agora who swear that Alexander truly is dead, his blood watering some Illyrian field. They say it is a different Alexander who wears the crown, a lesser Alexander, the son of Aeropos, a kinglet from Lyncestis or some other Macedonian pig-sty with delusions of city-hood. Others claim it is Antipatros or some other noble or prince who has taken command. But they seem too desperate to believe in their own lie – not that it matters. Whoever is leading that army, no Macedonian is going to take it kindly that we murdered their soldiers. They are going to want something for that insult, and my guess is that gold and apologies alone will not do it, nor will any excuses about being lied to by Demosthenes."

"Well, even if Alexander is alive," said Aristophanes as he poured some cool water from a cracked earthenware jug into a chipped clay cup, "his army is stuck fighting those tribes, and it will be months or even a year before he can mount a major campaign on this side of Thermopylae."

"If only that were true, my friend," said the captain.

"What do you mean?" said Aristophanes, perplexed as he sat down on an old wooden chest, and bid his guest take his ease on a simple wooden stool, one of the few pieces of furniture in his small home in the center of Thebes.

"Not only isn't Philip's curly-haired young pup dead in the north like some want to believe," continued the captain – "he's moving south – moving like Zeus' own lightning. Whether he beat down or bought off the Illyrians, no matter how he did it, that war is done. And as for Thermopylae, well, our scouts report that he's already cleared their hot springs. Alexander will be here within the week – and he won't be alone. Word from Thessaly is he's got Perdiccas' with him…"

Aristophanes could not help but shudder, spilling the water as he set the jug down on an uneven shelf. "Philip's general? That means the Companion Cavalry, the royal guard pikes, and the hypaspistes, those nasty buggers, – the veteran infantry of the old tyrant's army."

"Yes," agreed the Theban captain, as he sipped gingerly from the cup, wiping away a dribble. "The same men who beat us before, at Chaeronea…"

"Don't remind me, I was there on that sad field…"

"Aye, Ari, so you were. Even if you were too young to stand in the line, you were there doing your bit – and so were a lot of our friends… your father and brothers among them, the gods have mercy on their souls."

"Many of them still lay out there," Aristophanes interrupted, "those whose bones were trampled under the hooves of Alexander's Companion Cavalry. Wasn't even enough of them left to bury – or burn."

"Yes, right brutal bastard that Philip, he was, that old one-eyed gimp. Beat us right proper, he did. Then made us swear to recognize him as – what did he style himself – Hegemon of all Greeks. Imagine, a Macedonian barbarian claiming not only to be a Greek but also the embodiment of all that is Greek."

"Yes," agreed the younger man, "and then as if that was not enough, he robbed us blind and stuck an army of occupation in our own citadel, on our own acropolis, just to make sure we did not forget our humiliation. I am glad somebody put a knife in the old bastard last year. Wish it had been me, or that I'd been there to see that."

"Well, it's not the old lion we have to worry about now, but his son," replied the captain. "But he's brought with him that superb war machine his father built. A machine that has trampled the liberty of all Greeks, that has forced proud city states to kneel and pay homage to... to...to a bunch of unlettered sheepherders one generation removed from pure barbarism."

"And now it's our turn, again?"

"That is precisely why our elders have called us to arms," Dimitrios replied, the sounds of such a gathering rising in the distance, in the street outside the humble house of Aristophanes.

"Well at least we won't be alone," said Aristophanes with confidence. "They say in the market that Demosthenes of Athens has put out the call to all of Greece to rise up against the tyranny of these foreign barbarians. I heard a rumor that he sent five talents – five – of his own money to pay for new arms and armor for our men."

"That will barely make up for what we lost after Chaeronea, especially after the elders take their cut..." snarked the captain, who took another sip of water. Aristophanes nodded in agreement with his captain's assessment, gave out a big sigh, and stood up to pace about the single room that was his family's home.

"So how close is Alexander?" asked Aristophanes of his friend.

"Well," murmured the captain, pausing to scratch his head and to sift through the many rumors that had washed over him, "a fisherman from Lake Copais, up near Onchestos, brought his catch to the market this morning. He says there were some strangely attired horsemen poking around there yesterday – 'foreign looking' he said they were, with javelins, and shields, and…"

"Lake Copais! Onchestos!" remarked Aristophanes, jumping upright with surprise. "That's six miles from here – a morning's stroll, even for an army of heavy infantry!"

"Which are no doubt close behind those scouts. We've already doubled the force holding the palisade…"

"You think that little hasty wall of dirt and stakes south of the city will stop Alexander?" asked Aristophanes rhetorically. "It was built to seal off the southern gates of the Cadmea, to keep what is left of the besieged garrison in, not to hold off a relief force coming from the outside."

"That's why we need to strengthen it – and for that we need time," Dimitrios explained. "That's why I've come for you. I need you to spread the word, gather the rest of our company together. The general has already mounted up the cavalry and sent them out on the road to Onchestos. The light infantry are about to set after them, and at a run. We and a few other companies of heavy infantry are to follow. Add some punch to their little jabs, says the general. Or give them a base of support to rally back on, cover their withdrawal if they meet any serious opposition…"

"You mean like a phalanx, with those 18-foot-long pikes of theirs…"

"Yes, Ari, or anything else the light troops can't handle…"

"Well, Dimitrios, I suppose it had to come to this eventually. But even if Alexander is alive, and even if he has brought the whole of his father's army, what will it avail him?" chortled Aristophanes confidently. "All Greece is with us! I hear Athens is on the march!"

Captain Dimitrios only sighed more deeply. Rising from his stool, he put a big-brotherly like hand on Aristophanes'shoulder, looked his much younger comrade in arms straight in the eye, and dissuaded him of his illusions.

"Athens is not coming."

"What! But Demosthenes promised…"

"Well, promises are easy, and cheap. A few wagon loads of spears and helmets, some money too – that is all that Athens has sent. But what else could we expect? No love lost between our two cities. But of course those wagons were accompanied by yet more stirring words of glory and praise, exhortations about us standing up for 'liberty', and 'autonomy', and 'democracy', and all other manner of tripe from that silver-tongued-liar Demosthenes."

"But surely the other cities…"

"No," said the captain, shaking his head. "No other cities are coming to our aid. Even our neighbors have failed us – and worse, the Plateans and Phoceans have joined up with Alexander. Seems they want to settle some very old scores, back from the days of the Persian wars, when our ancestors took money from the Medes, stood with the Great King and burned Plateai to the ground. You would think that after a century and a half they would forget…"

"I guess not," interrupted Aristophanes. "It appears that there are many in Greece who have not forgotten – or forgiven us – for the folly of our forefathers."

"Sadly, so it seems."

"Then we are truly alone?" gulped Aristophanes.

"Well, no" laughed the Theban captain, "not quite alone. We've got plenty of company coming – unfortunately they're coming with Alexander."

4

The Enclosure of Iolaos

ON THE ROAD TO THEBES

The Theban cavalry came upon the Macedonian scouts at a place known to locals as the Enclosure of Iolaos, not far from Onchestos on the shores of Lake Copais.

Men of Thrace, these scouts or *prodromoi* as they were called for their posting at the head or rather in advance of the army as it marched, were little better than freebooters. Wild men of the frontiers, they were led by equally wild Macedonian officers drawn from stake holdings on the border of those untamed lands. To these hard men, loot and pillage were things done not just for sport or spite, but also to supplement their pay. Living off the land, they roamed like a wild, angry herd, half-men, half-beasts, the centaurs of Alexander's army. They ranged far, and wide, and fast, untethered and independent of command – or of conscience.

It was while in the process of doing what came naturally to these scouts that the Theban horse came crashing down upon them – scattering the Thracians as if they were wooden toys kicked about by some angered toddler. Little did the Thebans know that scattering came natural for the *prodromoi* – for these men were bred to scout, and raid, and run away, not fight. For that job, especially in Alexander's army, there were many, many others whose training, skill, and demeanor made them better suited for drawing blood.

The Theban horsemen, however, saw this overhasty flight of the Thracian scouts as something quite different. They cheered their own temerity and jeered at the fleeing Thracians, seeing in their hasty retreat a reaffirmation of the puffery propaganda circulating the markets and taverns as to the cowardice of the Macedonians. It was well known, they told themselves, of how under the boy king these men of the north had lost that courage and taste for battle that Philip had so drilled into them.

Thus it came to pass that as the Theban horse were celebrating their easy success, they too in turn were hit unawares – and hit hard.

First to slam into the Thebans was an ilai, or squadron, of Pharsalians. This force of some 150 veteran horsemen from Thessaly oft served as personal bodyguard to Parmenion, the oldest, wisest, most cautious yet also most combatively stubborn of Philip's old generals. The Pharsalians cut through the Thebans and came through the other side. As they reigned up, reformed, and made ready for a second pass, two other squadrons hit the Theban horse, one from their right, the other from their left.

The fourth and final squadron of the Thessalian regiment dealt the killing blow, banging head-on into the disorganized mass of Thebans. As the Thebans had scattered the Thracian scouts, so now were the Thebans themselves broken apart. But while the Thracians had gathered themselves back together, the Thebans could not. Their confidence as shattered as their formation, gripped by fear, and with enemy horsemen all around them, the Theban cavalry did not merely cease to be an effective fighting force – they simply ceased to be at all.

The erasure of their cavalry screen left the Theban javelinmen, and the slingers and archers who had come up at a run behind them, in a difficult situation. Some of the more enterprising and more eager of these skirmishers had run past the Macedonian horse to pick away at the thick columns of enemy infantry clogging the roads. Others had wandered even a bit farther afield, to snipe at the drovers and drivers of the Macedonian supply train. Their cavalry shield gone, however, these plucky young fellows had little choice other than to fall back. Unlike their mounted comrades they kept together. Like the Thracian centaurs, the Theban light infantry knew how to scatter with purpose. These farmboys, goatherds, and street rats knew how to use cover to their benefit so they could live to fight another day.

It was while scurrying back across the fields and through the woods toward home that the lightly armed troops descended upon, swarmed about, and eventually trotted past two companies of hoplites, the second of which fell under the command of Captain Dimitrios.

"What do you suppose spooked the javelinmen so?" Aristophanes asked of his captain. "Surely they're not running away from a few scouts?"

"Well, friend," jibed a ranker, "maybe we had better catch one of those boys and ask him, although you'll not outrun him encased in armor as we are. Best try and trip one up with your spear, or knock one down as he runs by!"

Aristophanes, taking the suggestion to heart, did just that, and down tumbled a slinger, the hoplites' spear tangled up in his legs.

"What the hell did you do that for, you damned idiot!" shouted the fallen skirmisher, rubbing his leg where he'd hit the spear shaft hardest. "We're on the same side, or did you think I was some Macedonian pig-farmer!"

"Sorry, friend," Aristophanes said apologetically, a difficult thing to do with a straight face considering the laughter and jeering of the file of spearmen behind him. "My captain just wanted to get one of you fellows to stop, and to tell him why you're running away – and from whom?"

"From the damned Macedonians, that's who!" the youngster spat back testily as he rose up and dusted himself off. "Hundreds of them, and that's just the cavalry. There's thousands more behind them, down the road just a piece by the enclosure. The whole damn Macedonian army, pikes and all!"

"What?" interrupted Dimitrios, coming over to examine the scuffle. "What do you mean? Where's our cavalry? They're supposed to be out here protecting you!"

"Well, damn poor job they did of that, thank you very much," quipped the skirmisher, standing up and managing to walk off a limp. "They got chased off pretty quick by the Macedonians. Hardly put up a fight at all, if you ask me, least not from where I was standing. No sir, damn rich boys on their fancy horses – they took off at the first charge!"

As if on cue, the sound of hoofbeats – scores of them – drowned out their conversation. A cloud of panicked Theban cavalry came streaming by. They were followed close at heel by the Thessalians, many hurling insults and javelins or screaming war cries and slashing out at the frightened and defenseless Theban horsemen.

"Form phalanx! Form phalanx!" shouted Dimitrios, hurrying to put his men into order. "Prepare to receive cavalry!"

Unfortunately for the company ahead of them on the road, their captain was not as quick to react as Dimitrios. Caught in column of march, gear wrapped about or dangling from their shouldered spears, their shields still in the carts that followed them, the first company fell to pieces. The luckier of its members raced off to follow the retiring skirmishers and fleeing cavalry. Others were skewered or trampled as they broke ranks before the enemy horsemen, whose merciless laughter grew louder with every poor soul they stabbed, lassoed, trampled or decapitated.

Some few of the first company managed to form up and fall in behind Dimitrios and his men. Like the soldiers of the second company, those that had kept their weapons in turn firmly planted the iron butts of their spears in the ground, the sharp points angled forward, and set a booted foot on the base. Even the most rash and excited of the pursuing Thessalians caught themselves up short of that bristling porcupine – or rather, their horses did it for them. Smarter and less prone to excitement than their riders, the warhorses of Thessaly knew better than to impale themselves on a hedge of iron spearpoints.

But the Thessalians did not run away – they merely pulled back, began to reorganize and to move about the flanks and rear, looking for that tender spot to charge home.

"Orb! Form orb!" shouted Dimitrios, giving the order for all-around defense. Within minutes, the arrow-straight line of spearmen transformed into a hollow circle, spears pointing out in every direction, safe and protected from attack from any quarter – but also now completely incapable of movement in any direction. If the company of hoplites felt invulnerable to attack by cavalry, it was also now entirely immobilized – trapped as surely as if it had fallen into a pit.

"What do we do now, Dimitrios," asked Aristophanes a bit nervously. "We can't go forward, we can't go back – they've got us surrounded."

"Aye," added another soldier. "They've got us penned in. Only a matter of time before they bring up their slingers and archers, then the javelin-throwers. Whittle us down, pick us off – and then they'll bring in the pikemen to finish us off."

"Quiet!" barked Dimitrios. "Quiet in the ranks! There'll be time enough for talk later on in the barracks, or the tavern. Hold your tongue and save your breath!" shouted the captain, who then mumbled "you'll need it all, and soon."

For hours, or what seemed like hours, the stalemate persisted. The Theban band, its farmers and tradesmen wearing the battered armor of their fathers or of their own earlier campaigns, were hardly a frightening or uniform sight. Their spears varied greatly in length and thickness. Some wore bronze greaves on their shins and sturdy hob-nailed boots on their feet. Others wore only sandals, and while some had fitted bronze or leather armor, others had but thickly padded linen vests, if that about their chests. Officers like Dimitrios had bright, tall plumes adorning solid bronze helmets that protected the head, nose, neck, and cheeks, while others had what appeared to be nothing more than beaten metal chamberpots pushed down about their ears.

All but those who escaped the decimation of the first company, however, had shields – the great, round, wood, and leather, and bronze hoplons from which their hoplites ancestors had drawn their name. Others carried the older, infinity-shaped version of that shield, preferring its cut-out sides and length to the more modern form. Many bore the symbol of the club that the demi-god Hercules had wielded, for it was Hercules who had married the Theban princess Megara and so blessed their city (before he was made mad by the gods and slaugh-tered Megara and their children, but that was another story). Others had the heads of animals, the likeness of laughing men or some symbol of their profession, guild or family painted on their shields. The only thing that was uniform about them was that each man held his shield to protect the man to his right – and would give their own life before putting their shieldmate at risk.

The Thessalian horse knew what these men could do, and were in no hurry to put the Thebans to the test. The cavalry formed into wedges, formations pioneered by Alexander to break into enemy lines, but kept back. Ever watchful, ever threatening, they kept silent watch over their prey. Even their horses refrained from neighing overmuch. Content to hold the Theban band where it stood, the Thessalians waited for their support troops to come up. In the meantime, a few Thracian horsemen trotted about to hurl the odd javelin or two at the Theban infantry. They took turns to prick, and whittle, and taunt, and snipe away at the hedgehog formation, just as Aristophanes' comrade had predicted.

As mid-day dragged to late afternoon, the Macedonian skirmishers made their appearance. Among them were the corps of archers, the *toxotes*, their long bows normally of little note to a solid shield wall, but the Thebans were not arrayed to face archers, but cavalry. Shields facing out all around, many men had their backs and heads exposed to plunging fire from the bowmen. Some men in the center raised their shields above their heads, but others in front dared not, lest the cavalry charge in upon them.

Under steady, constant fire from all directions, the company could not help but take losses. A man down with an arrow in his neck here, a javelin in his back there, or struck by a bullet from a slinger as he tried to cover a fallen comrade with his own body, the orb closed in upon itself, ever shrinking. After a few hours of this, fully half of the company were down, while many of those still standing did so only with great difficulty, holding their spot in the ranks despite their wounds. Aristophanes was among those walking wounded, a strip torn from his cloak now a makeshift tourniquet to stop the flow of blood from where his leg had been pierced by an arrow.

The Thebans were tired beyond exhaustion, their arms aching from grasping their long spears, their necks and shoulders sore from the straps of their heavy shields. Baked in their armor by the mid-day sun, choked by the dust kicked up by the circling cavalry, they badly needed rest but could take none. Whenever a man let his shield slip even a fraction, one of the circling cavalrymen would dash forward and hurl a missile into the ranks.

The enemy horsemen and light troops, however, had no intention of closing in for the kill. Their job was to keep the Thebans penned in, softening them up for the death blow by the heavy infantry. The Thebans did not have to wait overlong for their coming. As the afternoon drew on, in the distance could be seen the gleaming speartips of the Macedonian pikemen – the true native Macedonians of an army gleamed from many other lands.

For Dimitrios and Aristophanes, it was no longer a matter of life or death – but of how death would come.

"Well, old friend," asked Aristophanes, struggling to remain on his feet and barely holding back the quiver in his very dry throat, "what now? Do we form up and charge and take a few of them down with us, or do we stay here while the arrows rain down, the pikes crash into us and the cavalry ride down the rest?"

"Quiet! Ari!" mumbled Dimitrios. "I'm thinking."

"Well, Captain, think quick. I don't think you have much time to debate the question. Any minute now…"

A trumpet blare cracked the air, loud as thunder and as unexpected. Again came a blast of music – a single brash note meant as a call to attention. Gain the attention of the hoplites it did, many turning around or looking over their shoulder to see what it was all about. From behind the ranks of Thessalian cavalry rode a single figure, two tall, black and red feathers rising high from his helmet. Despite the bright armor and obvious richness of his cloak, it was not the rider, however, that fixed the gaze of the soldiers. It was the horse he rode.

And what a horse. It was a massive monster of a horse, larger than any mount the Thebans had ever seen. Its coat was as dark as midnight, blacker than a starless night sky. Solid and unbroken was that blackness – save for a white mark on the forehead, a mark reminiscent of a star or an oxhead. Then there were the eyes. The piercing steady eyes, and one of them – blue? Never had men of Thebes seen such a horse. The beast came closer and closer, all the while showing no fear, no hesitation, as it kept prancing on steadily, only to stop but a whisper's breadth from the hedge of spears.

"Men of Thebes!" proclaimed the rider, who only by so speaking broke the trancelike attention the hoplites had focused on the horse. "Men of Thebes! I salute your steadfastness, your courage! And for that I would spare your lives this day – and the lives of your citizens, if you would but hear me and take a message back to your leaders!"

A grumbling arose from the Theban ranks. "Who are you, fellow, to address us in such a manner," demanded Dimitrios.

"I am my father's son. King after his passing by right of succession. Hegemon of all Greece by agreement of the League of Corinth. Commander of the army by acclamation. I," he paused briefly, drawing in a big breath before continuing, "am Alexander."

5

The Enclosure of Iolaos

LATER THAT SAME DAY

The appearance before them of a man they had been told was most assuredly quite dead sent a collective shiver through the otherwise steadfast ranks of Theban soldiers. This was no ghost addressing them, yet he might as well have been a hoary specter breathing frozen mist, skewering them with the icy gaze of cold, dead eyes. What a rain of arrows, a storm of javelins and a hailstorm of stones could not do, this boy king did: shook the armored men to their core.

"I am Alexander, King of Macedonia, Hegemon of the League of Corinth, Strategos of all Greece and, by right of conquest, your sovereign lord and master," announced the young warrior king, his voice loud, measured yet with a strong hint of chastisement to come quite evident. "All of that am I to you, Thebans," said Alexander strongly, "yet here you stand before me, armored head to foot, bearing shield and spear, the blood of my soldiers and their commanders barely dry upon your hands. Pray, Thebans," added Alexander quizzically, "what grievous offense have I given to cause you to abuse me so?"

A light breeze raised some dust and caused Alexander's cloak to flap, but for many painful moments no other sound could be heard on the field. No soldier so much as coughed, nor did the king's mount snort or scuff with a hoof, in such control of him was Alexander.

"Well?" asked Alexander again, "surely there must be some reason for all of this rage, and murder, and rebellion? Or have the men of Thebes become so phlegmatic that they are moved to slaughter by whim?"

The Thebans remained silent, yet there was some movement in the ranks as a soldier from the middle files pushed his way to the front.

"We have good cause to be in arms, you murdering bastard," came a voice from the ranks. "We fight for that most sacred right of all Greeks – freedom!"

"Freedom? Freedom from what? To do what?" scoffed Alexander.

"From foreign rule, your honor," came the reply, "from the rule you and your late father imposed upon us against our will."

The reply seemed to perplex the Macedonian king, causing even his great dark mount, Bucephalus, to fidget briefly. "Our rule is not foreign, Theban. It is the necessary joining of all Greeks under one banner, to stop fighting among ourselves so we may march forward, together, for a greater cause!"

"And what cause is that" came another voice from the Theban ranks. "To enrich Macedonia at our expense? To be slaves to you and your nation of shepherds and pig-keepers?"

A roar of approval mixed with nervous laughter sprung from the phalanx, its sound rushing toward Alexander and breaking upon him, as a wave crashes into a rock on the shore. Some hoplites banged spear on shield in approval; others stamped their spear butts into the ground, or hooted in agreement with their comrade's brave response.

Alexander, only made more resolute by this outburst, gripped the reigns of his war horse, clicked his heels and made the mighty Bucephalus rear up, its hooves but a hair's breadth from the shields of the front rankers. "Are you so small-minded and so lacking in vision that you cannot see beyond the boundaries of your tiny city?" screeched the young ruler, his composure gone and his blood rising. "Ours is a holy cause, a righteous path to punish the Persians for the desecration of our temples, the murder of our citizens, the burning of our cities! Greeks! We have 150 years of Persian wrongdoing to avenge!"

Alexander paused to see if his words took root among the Theban band, but sensing only confusion, indifference or scorn, quickly changed his tack. "Or perhaps I am speaking to the wrong people. Perhaps you are no longer Greek. Perhaps that Persian gold your fathers and their forefathers took was not merely a hiring price for mercenaries, but was solicited as your neighbors say by a people so enamored and in awe of Persia as to be more Medes than Greeks? Are you indeed the traitors in our midst, the vipers in our beds that the Phoceans and Plateans tell me you are? By the gods, seeing you before me, I half believe that you truly have been seduced by the Medes – or at least their gold!"

"Better Persian gold than Macedonian iron!" came the retort from the phalanx.

"I see, I see," huffed Alexander, visibly angered and struggling to control his temper. "If I believed that, I would order my men to cut you down where you stand, to so disfigure your corpses that even Hades himself would not recognize your shade when it passed over the river into his realm. But I will not act in haste, or in the heat of the moment. Thebans!" shouted Alexander, his voice as thunder, "I give you your lives – and one day! March back to your city. Call your elders together! I give them until tomorrow at dawn to surrender the leaders of this traitorous conspiracy – Phoenix and Prothytes I believe they are called. Surrender these murderers and instigators to murder to me! Tear down the palisade opposite the Cadmea, open your gates, and raise the siege of the citadel! Do this, and all shall be forgiven – for what is a king if he cannot show mercy to his children?"

Alexander made Bucephalus rear up again, this time noisily striking the shield of a front ranker with his mighty hooves. The king then spoke once more, and with no hint of charity in his voice.

"Do as I ask, or I shall do it for you. And if I do, look to your city. Look to your wives, to your mothers, and to your fathers, and to your sons and daughters. For by night fall tomorrow they will submit or their bodies will be skewered on pikes and your homes will be naught but ashes."

The march back to Thebes seemed to take ten times as long as the march from the city. The smoke from the wild fires that burned in the turf islands in the swamps of Lake Copais seemed to foreshadow the impending fate Alexander had promised for Thebes. Despite the threatening cloud of Thessalian horsemen hovering about, the hoplites kept a measured, steady, and unhurried pace, not giving their escort the satisfaction of believing the men of Thebes to be unduly concerned. Still, Alexander's words and the earlier rout of the Theban cavalry and light troops made most of the soldiers uneasy, and when soldiers are uneasy they grumble.

"Who does he think he is, some god to stand in judgment of us like that!" spat one old veteran.

"Actually, I think he does believe himself a god, or at least the son of one, or so I hear," jibed another. That drew a round of mumbled laughter from his fellows.

"Should have just skewered him where he stood, him and that big lumbering mountain of his he calls a horse," mumbled another. "One quick thrust and our worries would all be over."

"Yeah, well, who was stopping you?" came the reply from the back ranks.

"That'll be enough!" shouted the captain. "Silence in the ranks! You are hoplites of Thebes, men of the phalanx! Not a bunch of whimpering stable boys or churlish layabouts! Be quiet! There are too many foreign ears about!"

The captain's command, however, was quickly ignored.

"We should have fought, I tell you!" grumbled one old warrior. "What will they think of us back home, marching back like this, with hardly a shield shattered or a spear bloodied!"

"Aye, and being herded home, like goats, by the likes of them on their shaggy ponies!" commented another soldier, pointing his spear for effect at the Thessalian escort. "It is humiliating, I tell you! By the gods, so humiliating!"

"Enough, I said!" commanded Captain Dimitrios, far more emphatically than the last time, but still ignored by his soldiers, just as before.

"And what's this about turning over our elders?" remarked another soldier. "He thinks they're just going to say 'oops, sorry my King,' tug at their forelocks, bow down like some Persian boy to his master, and give themselves over to his vengeance? For that is what it'll be, mind you, vengeance – bloody vengeance! And then to tear down the palisade and throw open the gates? I suppose he'll expect us all to turn around, bend over, and pull up our..."

"I said enough!" boomed Dimitrios. "Next man who so much as coughs I'll put my foot down his throat! I said silence and I mean silence! We march on, steady and proper, and without a grumble! There'll be time enough for talk when we get back. The assembly is going to want a full report, and what we do next is up to them!"

"You don't mean you think we're actually going to surrender to that little piss..."

Before the soldier could finish his sentence, the captain, true to his word, swept his spear across the man's knees, brought him to the ground, and kicked him in the teeth.

"I said 'silence!'" shouted Dimitrios, red with exertion and rage. "I will have discipline in the ranks, or so help me by all the gods I will split the next man who crosses me from throat to balls! I'm in a killing mood, lads, a real killing mood, and Hades take me if I'm not as good as my word on this!"

Their discipline restored, as much by their captain's fury as by knowing he felt the same as they, the column of spearmen marched on. Steadily, quietly and with men holding their gear close so as not to make any undue sound, the hoplites reached the palisade by the southern gate. Their Thessalian escorts peeled off as the column marched past the Temple of Heracles, but watched menacingly as the Theban guards moved the barrier that blocked the road toward the Elektrian Gate. Dimitrios and his men marched proudly into the city, just beneath the watchful gaze of the guards on the towers on either side of the gate. Other eyes were on them as well from the citadel. From those walls, what remained of the Macedonian garrison could be heard jeering, taunting, and hurling all manner of crude insults at the returning hoplites.

Those jeers turned to cheers soon enough, however, for from their high vantage point the garrison could spy the tips of the forest of sarissas, the 18-foot-tall pikes of the Macedonian infantry, as Alexander's army came within sight of the city.

Succor – and revenge – were at hand.

6

The House of Pindar
THEBES

The pain in Aristophanes' leg, though crippling, was slight when compared to the pain he felt for his city. Hobbling back from the shores of Lake Copais after he had been wounded had not helped. The wound festered, just as did that left by the incomplete revolt begun but two weeks past – that particular open sore being the decimated yet grimly determined Macedonian garrison holed up atop the acropolis in the Cadmea. Two weeks of siege had weakened the dwindling defenders of the citadel, but now the besiegers were themselves besieged: Alexander had come, and with him, the hosts of Macedonia.

While Captain Dimitrios and the remaining able men of the company stood to arms on the walls, Ari was being cared for by the captain's family. A descendant of the lyric poet, Pindar, Captain Dimitrios and his family were treated as literary royalty – or at least as royal as those of the *demos* who ruled the city would allow. The House of Pindar, as it was known, was better appointed than almost any other in the city, for it was part home, part library, and part shrine to the famed poet, dead now for just over a century.

While no one in the family had taken up the stylus (for how could they dare compete with their ancestor), all of the men, and even most of the women, were well learned – a rare and quite scandalous situation as the education of women was thought to be folly, or worse, throughout most of Greece. The captain was no poet either, but a canny merchant when not called to duty. His brother, Klemes, fortunately for Ari, was one of the most respected physicians in the city. It was he who attended the wounded soldier, whom Dimitrios had brought to the House of Pindar rather than leave him to the tender mercies of some itinerant medicine man in Ari's home neighborhood in the Ampheion section of town.

"Why should we bow to a mere boy, Philip's son though he be?" sputtered Klemes, spit flying from his angry mouth barely missing dripping onto the wound he was dressing. "Um, sorry about that," apologized the physician, dabbing away the spittle. "I was taught to irrigate a wound, but not in such a manner" he added in a rare attempt at humor.

"Perhaps because he is a king – and a soldier," replied Aristophanes, grimacing as Klemes poked, and prodded, and squeezed, and sniffed about the oozing gash in his leg. "Of that last your brother and I know firsthand. He stood in the ranks at Chaeronea when the young Macedonian lion came down upon us. I was out on the flank with the rest of the slingers and javelin boys when Alexander charged. I never would have thought cavalry could be used like that – to crack a phalanx like a mason's wedge splits stone. And he almost did it again to us out by Lake Copais."

"Aye, I recall Chaeronea. I was there, too," mumbled Klemes, "but not in the line of battle like my brother. Yet I saw plenty of Alexander's handiwork, back in the tents treating the wounded. Even our Sacred Band, our finest of the fine, could not withstand his charge."

"Yes," interrupted Dimitrios, as he entered the room, noisily tossing his helmet onto its stand. "Wheat has more chance against the whirlwind than our spearmen had that sad day. And here we are again," sighed the captain to his brother, "again the wheat, again the whirlwind."

"But this time we have our walls – the strongest and thickest in all the Greek lands – if not the world!" replied the physician. "Oh, 'Seven-gated Thebes,' the jewel of 'Solid Greece,' with walls of solid rock..."

"They're not quite all that solid, brother," corrected Dimitrios. "The base is solid enough, and too deep for anyone to tunnel under without hitting bedrock, but the walls themselves are made up of two thinner layers of stone blocks, faced with brick and with rubble in between."

"God damnit, Dimitrios, I'm a physician, not an engineer. I only know what I've read and what I can see for myself," said Klemes, annoyed at being corrected by his brother.

"Don't worry, doc," said Ari, through gritted teeth, "we'll defend those walls and the seven gates, just like the seven champions..."

"Which is only half of the *Thebiad*, as you should well know," Dimitrios interjected. "A generation later the city was destroyed..."

"...but rebuilt, and even stronger than ever, isn't that right, doc?"

"Ari has you there, brother," said Klemes, very pleased at having his know-it-all brother taken down a peg.

"That's right," continued Ari. "And we will beat this king just as Epaminondas turned back the king of Sparta – and then maybe follow the Macedonians back to their lair, just as we did to the Spartans!"

"Things are a little different now, my friend," said Dimitrios as he poured himself some wine mixed with water, and nibbled on a bowl of olives. "The Spartans were poor horsemen, and ours were better. Alexander's, however, are better still, as you saw at Chareonea a few years ago, and again out at Lake Copais..."

"Let Alexander try to break stone with horse!" shouted Ari, his passion almost letting him forget the pain in his leg as Klemes worked away. "I'd like to see him try!"

"Oh, Ari, he will try. Of that I am certain. He's a hot head, that son of Macedonia."

"I hear he believes himself the son of Zeus..." noted Ari with a disapproving snort.

"So I suppose he'll call down thunderbolts from daddy to shatter our walls, is that it?" harrumphed the physician. "Or perhaps change himself into a swan, or an eagle, or a wisp of smoke and fly over the battlements, and take us in the night like the great seducer himself?

That's how Zeus impregnated Alexander's mother Olympias, or so goes the tale, plowing Philip's queen after some Dionysian bacchanal."

"He came to her with a clap of thunder and a bolt of lightning as I heard it – and you're mixing up your gods again, Klemes – Dionysus or Bacchus, which is it?"

"Sorry, it's from those years I spent across the western sea. Those fellows from Rome call the god of wine by that later name. Half-barbarians yet, those lads from the Tiber, afraid they won't much amount to anything. Now the Syracusans and the Tarentines – those are proper Greeks all, even if most were born on the wrong side of the sea."

"Klemes," sighed the wounded soldier, "I envy you your travels."

"Oh, you will see enough of the world someday, even if you have to limp your way through it," said the physician, trying to lighten his patient's anxiety while his medicines and skills did their work.

"Not as long as Alexander's army surrounds the city, my dear brother," said Dimitrios . "There must be 20,000 men out there. They waste no time, and already have dug in deep outside each of the city's seven gates. That is not all; they have started on another even longer line opposite the palisade – the wall we built to seal off the outer gates of the citadel, around the temple of Heracles."

"Well, let the Macedonians dig. A little honest work in the dirt will do those northern sheepherders some good," quipped the physician. "May their hands blister and their backs ache, and may they all burn to a crisp in the summer sun. Serves them right for coming down to Boetia. This is our land, Theban land, and the sooner they realize they can't pry it from us, the sooner they'll give up and go back to their miserable cold mountains!"

The fervor with which Klemes spoke translated to his hands, unfortunately for his patient. Try as he might, Aristophanes could not hold back his scream of agony as the physician squeezed the wound in his leg.

"Ahhhh!" sighed Klemes with evident satisfaction, despite Ari's scream. "That's it! Look at that pus! Good, good – and now blood! Clean, honest blood! Perhaps now this leg of yours will heal. I'm going to let my maggots munch on the dead flesh, set my leeches to clear the wound, and then I can stitch it. Or perhaps you'd prefer I cauterize it? Depends on what kind of scar you'd like on your thigh."

"Scars are all the rage with the ladies these days," quipped Dimitrios, as he poured himself some cool water to swish about the bottom of his wine cup. "You know, especially those ladies who loll about the temples. They give special discounts for war heroes, especially those that can show where they've been cut."

"Really?" said Ari hopefully as he sat up, the pain forgotten as his thoughts turned to more amorous musings.

"You should be more concerned about being able to walk again," scolded Klemes, "than about getting a bargain from some flowery tart because you have an especially ugly scratch."

"How long before I can put some real weight on this leg, before I can get back into the ranks and take my place in the line?" asked Ari. "When Alexander tries to come through or over our walls, Thebes will need every one of her sons, and I don't want to miss out on the fun!"

Klemes did not respond immediately – he did not have to; his eyes and his breathing said it all.

"My friend," began the physician in that tone a father takes to tell a son a beloved pet has been run over by a cart in the street, "the wound was very deep, very deep. It severed muscle, scraped bone, and tore flesh going in and coming out. There are splinters from the shaft of that spear floating about that may never come out – and digging at them is beyond my skill, and will do more damage than good. And my oath as a physician, you recall…"

"Something about doing no harm, yes, yes, I remember" grumbled the wounded soldier.

Klemes paused, swallowed hard, and breathed deep, holding it overlong until finally expelling the air in a great bubbling sigh. Placing his hands on Aristophanes' shoulders, the physician gave him the speech – the same speech that has been spoken a hundred thousand times and more by physicians from the Pillars of Hercules to the deserts of Bactria – and beyond, to whatever lies inside the great river that encircles the world.

"Your days as a soldier are over, Ari. You will never stand in the ranks again. With time, and prayer, and good fortune, you will walk and walk unaided – but haltingly, at least at first, and with a noticeable limp."

"But didn't Melon, the hero who killed the Spartan king at Leuctra and saved our city years ago, didn't he have a limp? That did not stop him!"

"Well, Ari, I am not quite that old as to have known Melon, let alone to have been his physician. I do not know how serious a limp he had, if he truly had one at all, but I know what I see here."

"So what now?" shouted Ari, angry and frustrated. "Do I shave half of my head and beard like some trembler, some half-man who won't do his duty? Who won't do his duty as a man or a citizen and stand shoulder to shoulder with his brothers, feet firmly apart, gritting his teeth, and shouting defiance to our enemies?"

The physician shook his head gently, sighed, and looked the young man squarely in the eyes.

"Ari. You may ride a mule or perhaps even a horse again someday, and you will be able to walk, but with difficulty and always with pain. You did stand, and stand with honor, and you shed blood for our city, but," he added with conviction and sympathy, "this war is no longer yours to fight."

7

Alexander's Camp

OUTSIDE THE ELEKTRIAN GATE OF THEBES

"You offer them mercy and they insult you this way!" shouted Perdiccas angrily. "Did I not tell you they are nothing more than Persian-loving scum! These Thebans are not worthy of your forgiveness, my King," the Macedonian general shouted, gesticulating wildly for effect. "How much more proof of their treachery do you need! Unleash the army, Alexander; let us tear down this city and cleanse the world of this stain upon the honor of Greece!"

Perdiccas took a moment to compose himself, then, like a teacher berating a student, proceeded to lecture the young king.

"I caution you against showing clemency, Alexander. Show these Thebans mercy, let them get away with killing our men, and you will lose the support of the army. You know what your father's answer to such rebellion would have been."

Alexander listened in earnest to his father's old general, a valiant, much-scared, and well-respected officer. Perdiccas was the son of a minor noble from the lake district around the Orontes, a commander who rose through the ranks because he led quite literally from the front rank of the phalanx, pike in hand.

"I understand, good Perdiccas," smiled Alexander slyly, "but I believe these insults to my good offices are but the mewling of a few hot heads. Their leaders are men who took Persian coin not just from the old Great King, but most certainly from his successor. Darius is as new to his throne as I am to mine, but he is already playing the old game, to keep us fighting each other at home so we cannot go east."

"Besides, my teacher Aristotle long ago advised me to treat the Greeks as a leader, not as a master. They are family, he told me – contentious, stubborn, and difficult – but family. You've spent too much time fighting barbarians," added the king. "Now those, those we can treat as if they were no better than animals – but not the Greeks. I have other plans for them, as you will see when we go to face the Great King."

Alexander paused and motioned for a slave to bring him a cup of wine, then walked over to a map of Greece splayed out on a camp table. "But Darius is not the only one behind this uprising. The Thebans most certainly were also swayed by the seductive promises offered by Demosthenes…"

"That Athenian rabble-rousing pederast!" spat the older Macedonian general. "He prances and prattles before the mob, like, like some, some…actor on a stage!"

"Now, now, Perdiccas," teased Alexander. "Some of my best friends are actors – you've seen how entertaining Thessalos and Athenodoros can be, especially when they do one of those plays by Euripedes. Damn, how I love his stuff."

"Well, well..." grumbled the general. "Demosthenes is a worse actor. Worthless windbag! I say once we finish here, we march on Athens and hang him upside down, naked, swinging from the Parthenon itself!"

Murmurs of agreement, sprinkled with muttered jibes and muted laughter filled the command tent as Perdiccas, his face reddening with every word, continued his diatribe on the perfidies, despicable personal habits, and dubious parentage of the noted Athenian orator. Alexander allowed this to continue until Perdiccas, his spleen sufficiently vented, appeared to run out of insults to hurl at what some in Greece believed to be the very embodiment of Athens and its democracy.

"One chastisement at a time, good Perdiccas, one chastisement at a time. That vile Athenian who spins lies like a spider spins a web, will be dealt with in turn," said the king with a smile like that of a cat contemplating a mouse for his dinner. "He is one of those few Greeks over whom indeed I must be the master, rather than the leader. Besides, the rest of the army has not yet come up. There are seven gates leading in and out of this city, and most we have covered by no more than a few companies of light troops and some hasty trenches. We need more men if we are to threaten Thebes with siege and sack, and show them how fruitless their rebellion is."

"My battalion is here!" replied Perdiccas proudly. "My men alone are enough to beat these soft-living city dwellers, just as they did at Chaeronea three years ago!"

"And mine are ready, too, majesty" piped up another battalion commander, Amyntas, son of Andromenes. "The Plateans are ready as well my King. For 150 years they have longed to avenge the wrongs done by their neighbors from Thebes, when those traitors sided with Xerxes the Persian and burned Plateai to the ground!"

"If they have waited that long, then what is a few more days?" replied Alexander calmly. "Believe me, good friends, my anger at Thebes is no less than your own. My wrath will be like that of Zeus himself should the Thebans not come to realize that they have been duped into this act of rebellion. General Parmenion is already across the Hellespont with the advance guard, and I long to join him and begin our own war of vengeance on Persia."

"Besides," added Alexander with a smirk, "Theban gold and Theban men would be valuable additions to our forces, and I would not waste what men we have with us in fighting fellow Greeks, not even Thebans. They can pay for their treachery with the blood of their soldiers when we invade Persia. I can trust you to put them in the very front, right, Perdiccas," he added with a knowing titter.

"So, for now, return to your post and maintain the guard. Take no action on your own, not unless you hear from me directly."

"Aye, young lord," grumbled Perdiccas unhappily. "If that is your command, but if those Theban bastards keep up their taunting from the walls and towers..."

"I understand, General. But you have your orders, so…"

Before the Macedonian King could finish, his words were drowned out by the sound of trumpets, one after the other, followed by the shouting of hundreds of voices.

"What is going on out there? Ptolemy," said the king, addressing one of his close companions, "go find out what the noise is all about."

Within minutes Ptolemy, son of Lagos, boyhood friend and trusted staff officer of the boy king, was back inside the command tent, nearly breathless.

"They're attacking, my King!"

"The Thebans? Are they coming out of the city?" asked a startled Alexander, reaching for his armor and helmet.

"No, my King," replied his aide and friend, "it's not the Thebans."

"Then who is attacking?" asked Alexander.

"It seems we are!"

8

The Palisade

THEBES

P erdiccas was not alone in his eagerness to get at the Thebans. His men shared that desire. Without his commanding presence to hold them back when the Thebans hurled yet another set of insults at them, there was nothing for it but for the Macedonians to attack. Grabbing ropes, ladders, and a tree trunk to use as a battering ram, the men of Perdiccas' battalion rushed to the southeastern gate of the city, just north of where the Ismenion bastion jutted out into the plain. Few made it up the walls, let alone to the gate, as the defenders rained javelins, arrows, and stones down upon them in a crossfire from the tall circular towers to either side. Thebans in the Ismenion fired into the left flank of the charge, causing further casualties – casualties that only seemed to inflame the angry Macedonians to further exertions. Yet still the gate held – but even the torrent of rocks, and arrows, and javelins could not dissuade the Macedonians from coming on again, and again, and again.

As water naturally flows toward the path of least resistance, so did the Macedonian attack. Large groups of men sloughed off to the left, around the corner bastion toward the city's southern side – and attacked the palisade of stakes the Thebans had erected there to seal off the Elektrian Gates beneath the citadel.

"Here they come, lads!" roared Captain Dimitrios, for it was his company – or what remained of it – that had been sent down from the walls to thicken the line at the palisade. "Lock...shields!" He commanded his men, as did other company commanders to his left and right.

"I know some of you are afraid," he shouted honestly, "but your fear is forgiven as long as you hold the line!"

The Macedonians came on in a wild, savage rush, the battle madness bringing their barbarian heritage to the fore, erasing the discipline that the old king had drilled into them. Many in the Theban line were visibly afraid, as were those in the small squadron of horse who stood behind them, between the hoplites and the gate.

"Present...Spears!" Dimitrios ordered, as his men and all of those along the line of stakes lowered their eight-foot long weapons, their front bristling with a hundred razor sharp, broad, flat leaf-shaped tips. The Macedonians obligingly came on, only to become entangled and disorganized amidst the maze of sharp stakes. As they struggled to cross the barrier, gaps opened in their ranks, and into these openings Captain Dimitros and his men thrust their spears, sticking them hard to the Macedonians and inflicting great, bloody wounds.

"Hold the line!" shouted the captain. "Hold the line!" And hold they did, these hard men of Thebes, their spears jabbing out through the scalloped openings on the sides of their shields, which resembled an infinity sign turned sideways. These protected them in the attack far better than the standard, round hoplon, the original shield from which these traditional soldiers of Greece got their name.

"Eleleleu! Eleleleu! Eleleleu!" shouted the Thebans, roaring out the battle cry that had led them to victory over Sparta nigh on three-score years past. As much to taunt their foe as to boost their own spirits, the companies to either side of Dimitrios' took up the cry, until, like a wave, it rolled across the length of the battlefield and along the ramparts of Thebes.

Still the Macedonians came on. Their first and second ranks, gutted and slashed by the Thebans, were barely down before the third rank broke upon the shields, bashing and battering them in an effort to tear out the living hearts of the dragon-born men of Thebes.

It was here, at a point not far from Alexander's tent, that Perdiccas rejoined his command. Had he any intention of obeying Alexander's order to restrain the troops, however, Perdiccas quickly threw aside that notion. Seeing his men falter after their initial repulse, the old scrapper did what he did best. Grabbing a pike from a surprised soldier, Perdiccas roared his own battle cry and exhorted the men to form ranks like proper soldiers and then follow him.

And follow him they did, through a storm of arrows and javelins at, into and over the palisade. Fired up with righteous anger, the Macedonians tore at the barrier. Cutting at the stakes with swords and daggers, pulling down the palisade with their bare hands, they ripped a breach in the barricade through which first Perdiccas' own battalion, and then that of Amyntas poured. Amyntas had heard Alexander's orders, but upon seeing Perdiccas breaking through the barricade, he too was driven to follow.

The two battalions of Macedonians tore into the Thebans at the palisade as lions into a pride of lesser cats. Captain Dimitrios and his Thebans fought hard and bravely, but were sorely pressed to withstand the sheer madness of the Macedonian onslaught.

At first the Thebans merely recoiled, falling back slowly, a half step at a time, back among the scattering of tombstones in the cemetery of Kastellion, in the area behind the now shattered barricade. As with all Greek cities, there was no room inside the walls to bury the dead, so families interred the remains of their loved ones outside the walls. Many of those ancient tombs and monuments dated from before the time of legends, back before Oedipus and his sons Eteocles and Polyneices reigned, their inscriptions long worn down to be beyond reading.

Many of the ancient tombs were waist high or higher. Several dozen Theban soldiers climbed up on them. These elevated stones provided a platform for the light troops, the peltastes, to stand on to hurl javelins, and fire slings, and arrows over the heads of their own hoplites at the advancing

Macedonians. Others from the rear ranks of the hoplites line climbed up all the better to spear down into the Macedonians. The Macedonians followed their example, and the two groups began firing and jabbing at one another from rival tombs, while the spearmen battled in the mud below.

Captain Dimitrios and his men had never trained for this kind of fighting. Hoplites battles were strict, formal affairs where two blocks of iron and bronze collided head on in an open field. The battle among the tombs was not the typical scrum of two shield walls grinding against each other with which the heavy infantry in each army were familiar. Instead of solid lines a hundred meters wide and four to eight ranks deep, the Thebans were forced to form into small bands between the larger stones. At least the tombs gave some protection to their flanks, as the struggle devolved into something akin to a score of fierce street fights.

At first the Thebans had the better fortune, with the peltastes on the stones pelting the Macedonians from above while the hoplites held fast in the alleys below. What had been a slow retreat, face to the enemy, became an unflinching defense. As spears broke and shields shattered, men began swinging about the broken spears, using the hard iron butts as clubs. Others drew their short swords and daggers, and dove in and under the shields to slash at calves, and thighs, and ankles. Faced with such determined resistance, the Macedonians started to recoil.

"Who are the men of iron now!" shouted a Theban soldier.

"That's it, run, run back to your mountains and to your goats," yelled another. All along the line, Theban soldiers, exhilarated at seeing the Macedonians falling back, shouted insults and taunts...but all to the opposite of the intended effect.

Amyntas brought up more missile troops to provide covering fire, but as their heavy, accurate fire cut down more and more of the exposed Thebans, other Macedonians took heart. As the Theban archers, slingers and javelinmen were swatted from their perch on the tombs, the Macedonians became encouraged, and now it was the Theban hoplites themselves who began to give ground. Exhausted, they looked for a second line to come forward as in a relay, to give them a breather – but no second line came out of the city. Weary beyond imagining, these citizen-soldiers, these farmers and shopkeep-ers, masons and blacksmiths, could take no more. They broke, with dozens fleeing in panic back toward the city. Captain Dimitrios tried to rally some of his men, but with their friends running in fear on all sides, even the captain's best men threw down their spears, unstrapped their shields and ran for their lives, sweeping the captain back in the flood.

As the Theban cavalry came forward to try to stem the Macedonian tide before it reached the still open gates, Captain Dimitrios again tried to rally his men – and any men whom he could grab. A small band gathered hesitatingly around the brave captain, but as they turned about and steeled themselves against the wave of Macedonians to their front, they heard screams from behind. Screams of "save yourselves! Run for your lives!" caused even the captain to turn around, and what he and others saw broke whatever courage they had left.

Heartened by the charge of Perdiccas, which they could see from atop the acropolis upon which the Cadmea stood, the garrison in the citadel opened their own gates and exploded forth. They swept aside the few Thebans who were stationed there to pen them in, and swarmed out to attack the gate from the rear. In moments, they had joined up with the advancing battalions – and in so doing trapped hundreds of Theban soldiers in a killing zone just outside of the city wall.

Few Theban soldiers kept any semblance of order, and that small band that had coalesced around Captain Dimitrios was not one of them. The captain sorely missed having his friend and fellow hoplites, Aristophanes, beside him, to protect his right side with his shield. Yet though alone now in a stream of panicked soldiers, he kept his head, searching for some island of resistance to break the Macedonian tide.

One company of old men – white-haired grandfathers considered too long in their years to stand in the front line of battle – had been kept in reserve. To them fell the task of holding the Heracleion – the temple of Heracles situated outside the southern gates, in the ground between the city gate and the palisades, both of which were now in Macedonian hands. A sunken road running parallel to those walls of stakes provided this company to which Dimitrios gravitated with some advantage of ground – and a concealed area, out of view from most of the advancing Macedonians. There the old men stood, the battle swirling around them.

The Macedonian attack pressed forward, but the confusion of the fighting and the intermingling of companies from separate commands left the attackers disorganized – and vulnerable to a counterattack. From the gates to either side of the Cadmea poured just such a punishing reprimand – the phalanxes of Thebes marching in serried ranks, spears at the level, shields locked. Perdiccas, his blood up, waving a now broken pike in one bloodied hand and a sword in the other, charged like a madman, frothing at the mouth, into the Theban's iron hedge.

Such valor spurred other Macedonians to similar bravery – and a similar fate. Cold and collected, the Thebans brushed off the disorganized charge and kept advancing. From his vantage point at the Heracleion with the old guardsmen, Captain Dimitrios raised a deep-throated cheer, as did the men around him. He cheered even louder when he spied that Perdiccas, desperately wounded, was carried from the field, still shouting hoarsely to his soldiers to press forward for the glory of Macedonia and its young king.

Behind the Macedonian lines, Alexander tried to make some sense of the confused battle, relying on his close-knit group of friends and aides to relay orders and receive reports from the front. One of those, Ptolemy, rode up and, barely pausing to catch his breath, reported: "Perdiccas is badly wounded my lord, but Amyntas has taken charge of both his and Perdiccas' battalions. They have linked up with the garrison – but the Thebans have sortied, and our men are hard-pressed."

"Those impetuous fools! I told them not to attack until we gave the Thebans time to surrender!" raged Alexander. "Ptolemy, go find Eurybotas the Cretan, tell him to take his archers forward to support what is left of Perdiccas' battalion. Find Attalos as well, have him send forward his Agrianian tribesmen – let's see how the Thebans like being showered by their javelins, and by Cretan arrows. I'll bring up the

Hypaspistes in support, and if their spears aren't enough I'll order in the Companions..."

"Damn bad ground for horsemen, my King..."

"Then I'll dismount the Companions if I have too! Now go!" ordered Alexander firmly. "Perdiccas and that fool Amyntas got us into this mess, so we had better make the most of it. Damn those Theban bastards! If they want a war, then so be it – and it will be the last they ever make!"

True to the command of their prince, the archers and javelin throwers of the Macedonian advance guard rushed forward, and poured through the gaps the heavy infantry had torn in the outer palisade. They began a covering barrage, hurling their spears and firing arrows over the heads of their comrades – all in full view of Dimitrios and the elder hoplites hidden in the sunken road by the Heracleion.

"Up and at them, lads" shouted Dimitrios. "There's easy meat for the taking!"

With a howl, the company of older hoplites roared out of the sunken road, moving to as full a charge these old men could manage as soon as they hit level ground. The lightly armed and quite unprotected archers and javelin throwers neither had time nor distance to react as they would on a battlefield. Trapped between the advancing Thebans and the palisade, dozens were cut down and the rest fled in every direction. Eurybotas the Cretan tried to rally a few of them to stand, but a Theban spear through the throat silenced him – forever.

Dimitrios was in the forefront of the charge, but his elation was as short-lived as the Thebans' victory. No sooner had they regained the line of the palisade and chased the light infantry away than they were blinded by the glare from a thousand brightly polished shields. Forward, in grim determination, Alexander himself at their head, came the Hypaspistes, the elite of the elite royal guard, the most experienced and most deadly of the heavy infantry of old Macedonia. With Nicanor, son of Parmenion, the late King Philip's most trusted general, in their front rank, these hardened veterans moved ahead in perfect step and in deadly silence, the glare of death in their eyes even brighter and more piercing than the sun's rays which reflected off their gleaming shields.

Dimitrios and his small elderly band tried to hold a breach in the palisade, but they were as driftwood swept aside by a tide. With so many of the old men down, their commander and a few of the others still remaining upright fell back, trying to drag the wounded back to the city. The captain and a handful of the rest covered their backs as they retreated. It was only with great difficulty, and often by slashing at fellow Thebans who also were racing back to the gates, that Dimitrios finally cut a path back into the city – with what seemed to be the entirety of the Macedonian army close at his heels. Even those who had come out to throw back Perdiccas were caught up in the tide of frightened men, men who had spent all the coins of courage they had brought to the field.

The gates to either side of the Cadmea still open, and the citadel garrison itself now pouring out to join the fray, no barrier remained to the Macedonian army. Organized resistance collapsed. Small groups of soldiers tried to form up and block some of the key streets while their families fled before the invaders. Others tried to make a stand in the agora, but Macedonians poured in from all sides of the open market-place, catching them in the flank and rear. Deep into the city they drove, past the Spring of Ares and into the city's beating heart.

Some brave Thebans sought to staunch the flow of invaders, but, as with the fight in the marketplace, such engagements were brief and bloody. Wherever a group of Thebans formed ranks, they were soon either outflanked from a side street or overborne by the sheer weight of numbers – and by the blood rage of their attackers.

Fighting devolved into house to house and even room to room as the battle dissolved into thousands of individual combats. Here the professional soldiers of Macedonia had the advantage over the part-time citizen soldiers of Thebes. Men more familiar with their olive groves and fields of barley proved little match to men who spent their days on the drill field. Women and children barricaded themselves in back rooms while men too old or weak for war struggled to break through the walls leading to the houses behind, hoping to escape the rampaging Macedonians. Behind the Macedonians came an even more brutal wave - their allies from Plateai, from Phocea, and other cities and towns that had over the years suffered humiliation, enslavement, and ruin at the hand of Thebes. For them, this was payback time; and their grudges ran old and deep.

Alexander, himself now covered in blood and given over to a red rage, did nothing to restrain them. To the contrary, he let slip that army from his leash. So began the death rattle of ancient Thebes.

9

Thebes

ALEXANDER'S TENT

"**B**etter a small city on a rock, governed by free men, than an empire of splendor filled with slaves," or so the people of Thebes had boasted when they had overcome the Spartans. But that was 60 years ago, before the age of the newer, even deadlier Spartans – for so terrible had the soldiers of Macedonia become. And they demonstrated that terror with almost mechanical, even Spartan precision as they swept over the small city on the rock and crushed it flat beneath their hob-nailed boots.

Occupying a tongue of land between two streams, the Boetian Plain to its north and the swampy ground of Lake Copais to the south and east, Thebes was not easily navigated. No planned colony of Ionia, this ancient city built, shattered and built up again on the broken bones of the first, was no stranger to tragedy. What befell Thebes that day, however, was nothing less than an apocalypse, and the name of that apocalypse was Alexander.

Whatever lessons he had learned from Aristotle about how to treat the Greeks had been washed out of his memory once his blood was up. Seeing Theban cavalry trampling their infantry as they fled in panic, Alexander threw off the cloak of command and rode to the chase, like some mercenary savage from the horse tribes of the steppes, instead of a king and the son of a king.

His soldiers were no better. As the mad spree of murder and revenge intensified, so did the looting, the raping and the burning. Fires broke out all over the city. Some by accident, most set by victorious soldiers from the outlying towns out of spite – or for sport. An old city, the timbers holding up its roofs were dry and caught fire easily. Buildings collapsed, burying those hiding within. Flames spread through the agora, swept through the crowded slums, and leaped across the narrow alleyways and even the streams. In fire, the city died, much to the delight of Macedonia's boy king.

Some who were there swore they saw the Keres, the monstrous part woman, part carrion bird daughters of Nyx, goddess of the night, sweep down into the flames to carry off and feast upon the dead. Others swore they saw their father, Erebos himself, in the dark, oily clouds of smoke that rose above the dying city.

But there were other demons and monsters about, mortal ones, their hands red with blood and gore, and their packs overflowing with the spoils of war.

Yet there were some among the Macedonian horde that had retained their humanity and had kept both their heads and their honor. One of these was Alexander's favorite childhood companion, Hephaestion, a slender man of such beauty and grace, he was one of the few able to calm the young king when the rage came upon him. But even Hephaestion had his limits.

Alexander had gone battle-mad, much as he had done when leading the pursuit of the broken enemy on the field of Chaeronea. Inflamed by the fighting, he had given himself to the passion of war, forsaking the responsibility of command for the adrenal rush of personal combat. Halted in his pursuit only by the exhaustion of his inexhaustible steed, the king, his eyes glazed over and his armor covered in blood, seemed to be in another plane of existence when his friend finally caught up with him.

"Alexander, my King, my Lord, my friend," spoke Hephaestion gently, as he rode up behind Alexander, removed his helmet, and placed a comforting hand upon the king's shoulder. "Enough. Call an end to this. It is enough."

The touch of he whom Alexander loved above all others, even almost above himself, did much to cool the king's battle ardor. As the red rage cleared from his eyes, and the adrenaline rush of combat dissipated, Alexander once again began to breathe normally. After a few gasping breaths, he become calmer, and started to feel the blessed release, the exhaustion that, like a lover spent, comes once the battle is finally done.

"Alexander, put a stop to this. For the sake of your own honor, if not in the name of mercy," pleaded Hephaestion, "make it stop. Look, see here, I have brought some old men from Thebes to speak with you, to plead with you. I beg you, for your own sake, listen to them."

Hephaestion motioned to one of his guards to bring forth three of the Theban elders, each of whom bore bruises, and whose clothes were torn and stained with blood, dirt and soot.

"You," he said, pointing to the man closest to him. "What is your name again?"

"Cleadas, my lord," the old man said humbly.

"Good Cleadas, tell the king what you told me."

"Noble King Alexander," began Cleadas nervously. "Please spare what is left of my city, and of my people."

"Why should I show such mercy to traitors?" Alexander replied hoarsely.

"But we are not traitors, sire, no."

"Oh? Then how do you explain this...this...this rebellion?" Alexander shot back, his temper uncooled and his anger rising.

"We were not disloyal, sire," Cleadas said nervously, spreading out his hands before him. "We were...well...we were just gullible?"

"Gullible? Gullible? What do you mean, gullible?" asked Alexander, truly surprised by this line of argument.

"We were told you were dead, you see, my King," the old man pleaded, the others with him nodding in agreement as he did so. "So we were not rising up against you, but only against those whom we believed would succeed you. And we have paid the price for that gullibility. We have more than paid the price," he continued, tears in his eyes, his voice trembling. "Our beautiful city is a smoldering ruin, our young men dead on the field of battle, and there are bodies in the very streets of Thebes. Our women disgraced, our children homeless and fatherless, we have paid enough for our mistakes. I beg you, in the name of the city where your father, in his youth, was educated, to spare what little remains."

As Cleades and the other Theban elders fell to their knees, groveling and weeping at his feet, Alexander began to take pity on them. He motioned for the guards to escort them away, took a deep breath, and turned to his friend.

"What would you have me do?"

"Only what is right and what is honorable. If this old man has not moved you, then there is another who, I believe, will."

Hephaestion once again motioned to a guard who, in response, brought forward a young woman. Her face bruised, her hair disheveled and, beneath the Macedonian military cloak a soldier had draped about the woman, her dress torn to the point of immodesty, she knelt before Alexander.

"And who is this, Hephaestion?"

"My name is Timokleia, your majesty, youngest sister of Theagenes."

"The general who led the army against us at Chaeronea?" asked Alexander, incredulously.

"The same, Majesty. His bones are still out there, along with those of the Sacred Band, and others who fought for the liberty and freedom of Greece," she replied, with as much pride as she could muster in her condition.

Although Alexander bristled at her remarks, he nevertheless was impressed by her courage. "A brave and honorable soldier was your brother. He was a true taktikos, a worthy opponent who knew how to marshal men on the field of battle. He fought well. Many Thebans earned my respect that day, but none more than he."

"Then in his name I ask for justice," responded Timokleia, a tremor in her voice. "For me, and for my children, the nieces and nephews of Theagenes."

"How so, good woman?" asked Alexander.

"For my children, that they be released from captivity. They have been taken by the slavers who follow your army."

"It will be done, you have my word," said Alexander. "And for yourself?"

"That I may be allowed to live, so that I may care for my children."

"Has someone threatened your life, Timokleia?"

Hephaestion answered for her. "The Thracians, my lord. They were about to cut off her head when I came upon her."

"Why would they do that?" asked Alexander.

"Because I killed one of their officers" responded Timokleia without a hint of regret.

"Why? How?" asked Alexander, his curiosity piqued.

"Because he raped me, and when he was done, demanded I give him all of my gold, and silver, and jewelry."

"And did you?"

"In a manner of speaking, yes. I showed him the well in our garden where I told him I had hidden my family's treasure. When he leaned over the side to get a better look, I pushed him over, down into the well. Then I threw rocks and stones from our garden down at him, until I was sure he was dead."

Alexander, taken aback at her story, did not know how to respond. Instead, he turned to Hephaestion once more, and ordered that she be escorted to where the slavers were encamped, and, once she had found her children, that she and they be escorted back to their home, and a guard placed to keep them safe.

"It is too late to save the city, Hephaestion," Alexander continued, once Timokleia had been dismissed. "Too late to call the men back. They are drunk with victory. They won a war up north and, with barely a pause to cheer, were force marched 250 miles south in two weeks, only to fight another battle – a battle they did not seek; a truly unnecessary war. They are like hungry wolves turned loose among a flock of sheep. The feeding frenzy will not stop until their appetites – all of their appetites – are sated."

"But surely you can still save something of Thebes?" pleaded Hephaestion. "You showed mercy to this brave woman, why stop with her? Would you have it said that you desecrated the birthplace of Heracles, or his temple? What of the tomb of Antigone? My noble cavalry, your own Companions, are still around you, still in their ranks. At least send some of them to protect what yet can be protected. No soldier will defy them; they respect and fear the Companions too much, as they respect, and fear, and love you."

"What would you have me save," sighed Alexander, weary and exasperated; "what is there left to save?"

"Some of the temples, perhaps, or the homes of those Thebans who remained true to us. Or the house of that Theban poet Aristotle so often praised in our school days."

"You mean Pindar? Yes, I suppose that would only be right. That is what Aristotle would surely advise, were he with the army. See to it, Hephaestion, see to it that the temples, the House of Pindar and all who dwell within are safe. Take some of the guard and make it so yourself. I depend upon you to salvage what is left of Thebes, if only for the sake of our old teacher."

"We can always blame the Plateans and the Phoceans for all of this, I suppose," mumbled Hephaestion.

"True," nodded Alexander. "Send a message to our ambassador at the League of Corinth. Tell him to organize a vote by the members to condemn Thebes for breaking the common peace. Furthermore, I want them to demand the city be razed, in punishment for violating the peace now, and for what Thebes did as an ally of the Persians in the past."

Hephaestion, stunned, stammered "but if we show some mercy..."

"Mercy?" chortled Alexander. "No, not mercy – for a few, maybe, like that brave woman, or those old men, or a few temples and fewer homes, but no more than that. A little terror,that is what we need here. Mercy is quickly forgotten, but terror is always remembered. Thebes will be an example. The rest of Greece will think twice before defying me, lest their cities suffer the same fate. The Persians, too, will hear of this – and it will make them tremble, knowing that they will be the next to feel such wrath."

Hephaestion gave up. He knew there would be no sense arguing with Alexander anymore on this point. Once the young king had made up his mind, nothing and no one, not even his cherished Hephaestion, could make him change his mind.

"I want these walls torn down, so that there is no stone left standing upon another. But," added Alexander in afterthought, "I will spare the temples, the homes of our allies and that of Pindar, as you propose, dear Hephaestion, if it is not too late."

Hephaestion saluted and made his preparations to restore order. As he quickly gathered his troop, he dispatched another group of armed men to the House of Pindar.

Just as so many other soldiers had broken ranks to see to the safety of their families once it was apparent that the city was lost, so, too, did Captain Dimitrios in despair race to his own home. He hoped it was not too late to save his brother, Klemes the physician, and his best friend and shieldmate, Ari, who was recuperating in Klemes' care, and what others of the family still lived.

The way home was a hard one. Smoke obscured the otherwise familiar streets, many of which were blocked by open fires, collapsed walls, or gangs of drunken, brutal looters – not all of them foreigners. Several thousand of the city's slaves and many of its poor were taking vengeance of their own, seeking to grab whatever they could make off with of from the homes of the oligarchs – or any who were even the least bit wealthy. These, too, did Dimitrios, still carrying his battered shield, try to avoid as he made his way home.

"My King," General Antipatros said in reporting to Alexander the next morning. "The city is secure. The worst of the fires have burned themselves out for lack of fuel. What areas are still afire we have isolated and contained, and expect they, too, will extinguish themselves for want of anything to feed the flames."

As Antipatros was concluding his report, forward came yet another of the many commanders of the army, Antigonos, known to his soldiers, for obvious reasons, as Monophthalmos, or One-Eye.

"We estimate that about 6,000 Thebans have been killed, some in battle, most in what followed. The slavers have rounded up the rest of the population, nearly 30,000, more than two-thirds of them women and children, my King," he smiled cheerfully. "We have penned them in outside the Proitides Gate. The prettier ones, of course, will be bought by the officers before we let the slavers march them away. I've taken a few of the choice ones for myself, although I will gladly give you first pick of the lot, should you desire," he added with a wink and a smile. "The rest seem fairly strong and healthy and will fetch a good price on the markets. More than enough to cover the costs of this southern diversion from your purpose."

"And our losses?" asked the king.

"Some 500 dead. I have already taken the liberty of ordering the priests to prepare a funeral. As for the Thebans..."

"A deep pit will do for them, General," spat Alexander. "All the closer to hell, as they deserve."

"And the army, my King, shall I make preparations to return to Macedonia?"

"We are not done here in the south, yet, General," said Alexander grimly, paying little notice to the commander's report concerning slaves – or his offer to pick one for his bed. "We have to dig out the roots of this conspiracy, and eliminate the source of the poison that caused Thebes to rise up against us. I give you three days to get the army into marching order."

"Aye, then we go back north, and then across the Hellespont into Asia as we planned?" asked Antipatros.

"No, not yet," replied Alexander. "The time has come to silence that worm-tongued Demosthenes. We will put an end to this division among Greeks once and for all. Leave a brigade here to finish the destruction of the city. And by destruction, I mean total destruction. Make of it an *abaton* – a place of 'no go.' Hephaestion," he added, turning to his friend, "tell the Phoceans and the rest of the cities of Boetia to lay claim to what Theban farms and orchards they want. The rest they can leave to the thistles and tamarisk trees to take over. I want no city to sprout back up here to vex me. Oh, and as for the rest of army; tomorrow, we march...to Athens."

10

Pindar's House

AMIDST THE RUINS OF THEBES

The orgy of rapine, slaughter, looting, and arson that is part of the sack of any city taken by storm, would normally have abated once the baser instincts of the victorious soldiery had been sated, or at least once exhaustion set in. At Thebes, however, another and even more powerful force drove the victors: revenge.

Macedonians felt betrayed. They wanted to make the Thebans pay for what they had done to the commanders of the garrison of the Cadmea fortress. Phoceans and Plateans, however, had older – generations older – scores to settle. For nearly two centuries, young children in those cities had been frightened into obedience by being told that the Thebans would come for naughty young boys and girls at night. Now it was their turn to come for the Thebans.

For farther back than any in their rebuilt cities could remember, horror stories of what the Thebans had done to their ancestors had been told around the hearth and the camp fire. It was the Thebans, after all, who had ignited the spark that started the 30-year war between Athens and Sparta, when they had bribed a traitor to open the gates of Plateai and tried to seize the city by coup de main – and without a declaration of war! And even before that, it was Thebes that had taken Persian gold and opened the way through Boetia to Athens for the Great King's ravaging hordes. Never mind that in living memory the Thebans had overthrown the oligarchs who had done such deeds and later freed Greece from the nail-shod boots of Sparta's red-cloaked killers; the list of betrayals from a century or more ago were more deeply written in the hearts of Thebes' neighbors.

In Phocea and Plateai, hate had been kept alive for decades by such stories – and in the sacking of Thebes that hate was unleashed in its full and horrific fury. Scores, fresh and ancient, needed settling, or so the victors told themselves to excuse their savagery. Alexander's acquiescence only emboldened them in their near total destruction of once proud Thebes.

Captain Dimitrios witnessed the fury and ferocity as he made his way back through the smoke-clouded, rubble-strewn streets of his dying city. At the little temple near the Cadmea, where he had so often found peace, for example, the stone benches had been smashed, the fountain broken and even the young laurel trees that had been growing out of the stones cut down.

As he came into the Street of the Tanners, Dimitrios stumbled upon a trio of soldiers who were taking turns raping a woman and her young girls. Two others were piling up plunder from her home and the workshops nearby. Alone and with only his sword and a broken spear, Dimitrios knew that to charge in to try and save the family would be suicide – but it was the honorable thing to do. Better to take a chance now and even die than live with the guilt of having done nothing.

As he flipped his spear to bring its bronze-sheathed butt to the fore, he tried to decide how best to take on the rapists and looters. Just rushing in headlong would certainly lead to a glorious death, thought Dimitrios, of which warriors from before the time of Achilles and Hector were said to dream. It would also mean that he would surely die, and to no purpose. There was no poet around to sing of such a sacrifice, and not even the slightest chance that such a sacrifice would save the woman or her girls.

Although it tore at his heart and his sense of self, Dimitrios realized that there was quite literally nothing he could do, except at best, take one or two of those men down with him. It would also mean that any chance he had of saving his own friends and family would be forfeit. With tears of shame creating little rivulets through the blood and dirt which covered his face, the hoplites captain turned away from the brutal scene. He crept through the debris that littered the street, and ran down an alley, an alley he knew would at least lead him toward his goal: home.

Back in that home, his brother Klemes was attending to those citizens of Thebes who had sought refuge in the House of Pindar. The building itself was no palace, and was certainly no fortress, as the poet had eschewed riches. Still people saw it as a place of hope amidst the horror. If Klemes had learned anything from his studies at Hippocrates academy on the island of Cos, it was that a physician should encourage such feelings of hope among those in his charge. Hope, as his teachers had hammered into him, can perform miracles, and miracles far beyond the skills of even the most learned of physicians.

What hope those who clustered within the House of Pindar had, however, sank when a pair of Platean hoplites kicked in the door. Their smoke and blood smudged faces and maniacal smiles evoked screams of fear from the children cowering in the corners. Had their mothers any tears left, they would have wept in anticipation of what tortures these devils would inflict upon them and their children.

Klemes, however, was neither frightened nor worried. He was simply annoyed.

"Don't just stand there, you two," he spoke in a commanding tone to the two intruders, "go fetch me some water from the well down the street. There are many injured and hurt here, and others, too, in need of water to slake their thirsts and wash clean their wounds. So, go on, go on I said!" he continued in his most imperious voice. "Why are you still lolling about? Go! You will find buckets in the courtyard. Go!"

Shocked and stupefied by the physician's demeanor, the two soldiers forgot why they had come into the house. Lives spent following orders from their elders, their betters, and their officers, the pair reacted automatically to being told what to do. With the women, and children, and wounded in the House of Pindar looking on incredulously, the enemy soldiers bowed, tugged at their helmets, turned around, and grabbed a bucket in each hand as they went outside.

Dimitrios had been sneaking up behind the pair when he heard his brother's command and saw the two soldiers obey Klemes, as if it was the most natural and expected thing to do. As they all but ran out to do his brother's bidding, Dimitrios walked past them, into the house and slumped, exhausted, against the door jam. Klemes turned away from splinting the broken arm of a young boy to see who now had come to interfere with his work, but only for a moment. As he went back to treating the child, Klemes said simply "well, brother. It is about time you showed up."

Hephaestion's guards had done the impossible. By mid-day they had restored order to what had been an orgy of butchery, carnage, slaughter, looting, and arson. Unfortunately, however, they had been able to secure only a handful of temples and other key buildings that the king had grudgingly agreed to spare, the House of Pindar among them. Dimitrios and Aristophanes chafed at knowing they had to thank Hephaestion's Companions for their lives, but Klemes did not care. All he cared about was that there would be no more interruptions.

"What happens next, Dimitrios," asked Ari of his friend and captain. "What are we going to do?"

"We are going to keep fighting, my friend."

"How, and with what?" Ari responded incredulously. "There is nothing and no one left to fight with. Thebes is dead – as are our comrades."

"But we're not dead, not yet, Ari," replied the captain, grimly. "There will be others who will stand for Greece; others who will fight for freedom. We will find them – and offer them our swords."

"Brave words, Dimitrios," interrupted Klemes. "But your friend Ari isn't going anywhere, at least not soon. Nor am I, not while there are sick and wounded who need my help."

"Who said anything about you coming with us, brother? What do you know of war?"

"I know every bit as much of war as you do, brother," Klemes shot back angrily. "It is here, all around us, just as it was three years ago at Chaeronea. The blood, the broken bones, the hacked-off limbs, the entrails spewing out, and the corpses. This is what war is all about, brother," he said, with a particular emphasis on the last word. "Wherever you go to fight and whomever you fight alongside, there will be more of...this" the physician added, sweeping his hand to indicate his patients. "They will need attending to, as may you. It is not only those who stand in the phalanx who fight, brother. Others also serve. So," said Klemes, taking a breath, "like Ari was asking, where do we go from here?"

PART II

Athens

SOUTHERN GREECE

YEAR TWO OF THE REIGN OF ALEXANDER OF MACEDONIA

11

The House of Demades

ATHENS

News of the razing of Thebes spread quickly throughout Greece, as Alexander had anticipated. Rightly fearing that Athens was next, the city leaders sent a delegation in great haste, to intercept the Macedonians and to seek an audience with the king. Demosthenes, having lost all support for a confrontation with Alexander, cast about for the right man to send out to meet the young king. The choice was obvious. Of the eight most important and most influential men in the city, only one had argued against Demosthenes. Only one considered himself a friend of Macedonia, and, more importantly, he was also the only one Alexander would also consider a friend: Demades.

Once a sailor in the fleet, Demades, like so many of the poorest class of Athenians, had managed through hard work and perseverance to become a man of some property. When Athens joined the alliance against Macedonia three years earlier, he had marched with the army to stand alongside the Thebans at Chaeronea. When Philip had spared his life and that of the other Athenian prisoners of war, however, Demades had decided that cooperation, not confrontation, was the best way to secure Athens' future in a Greece dominated by Macedonia. He soon let the Macedonians know of his willingness to speak for them, and became a conduit for Macedonian gold into the city. With such largess his to distribute, Demades grew in popularity, became the voice of Macedonia, and the leader of the pro-Macedonian peace party in Athens.

It was to such a man that Demosthenes, much to his chagrin, was forced to turn as the army of Macedonia appeared outside the city.

"He will want my head, will he not, this young lion of Macedonia," asked Demosthenes of his rival.

"I expect so, Demosthenes. Can you blame him?"

The elder statesman nodded in agreement, adjusted his robes and, composing himself, came right to the point of his meeting with Demades. "What will it take to change his mind? To get him to accept, how shall I say, a lesser sacrifice in my stead?"

Demades smiled knowingly and responded, as Demosthenes had expected. "It is not a matter of what it will take, but how much it will take."

"By which of course you mean how much you will take of my money to convince this boy to leave my head on my shoulders."

"Yes, Demosthenes. Exactly. I think ten talents would do – five for me, and five to grease some very important and very grasping Macedonian hands."

"Ten! Ten talents!" Demosthenes all but screamed. "That would keep ten triremes and 2,000 crewmen at sea for a month! That is twice what I sent to put steel in the Thebans to rise up and go to war!"

"Yes, it is," smiled Demades gloatingly. "But you see what only five talents got you. If you want to share the fate of those Thebans you roused into rebellion, then five talents will surely suffice. Should you want to survive, however..."

"All right, all right," scowled Demosthenes. "Ten talents it is then. But I want more than to just survive, Demades. I am not going into exile, not if I impoverish myself so. For that kind of money I want you to guarantee that I will remain in Athens – and that my voice will still be heard."

"You ask a lot for a measly ten talents, my dear Demosthenes," chortled Demades. "For that, it will take another couple of talents –

and a promise of your support and that of your clique in matters political."

"It is a high price you ask, Demades..."

"No, Demosthenes, it is merely the price of defeat."

True to his word, Demades asked for leniency for his city and for Demosthenes. He explained to the king, as Cleades had said of the Thebans, that Athenians too, had been "gullible." That they had been duped by Demosthenes into believing that the young king had met his demise in the north. Demosthenes, Demades pointed out, had even brought before the assembly a soldier who claimed to have seen the king fall. That he had a seemingly bottomless barrel of gold to throw about, only further convinced many to support him. Most if not all of that, the Athenian envoy admitted, apparently had come from Persia. Rumors were that the Great King had given Demosthenes 300 talents with which to raise his rebellion. Not enough to sustain an army, but plenty to bribe others to raise one.

For his scheming and dishonesty, Demades told Alexander, Demosthenes had been reprimanded. Although Alexander had demanded that the orator and seven other politicians in his clique be handed over to face royal judgment, the delegate in his obsequiousness had convinced the king to rescind that demand and accept a single scapegoat – a minor associate of Demosthenes named Charidemos. Alexander agreed, but in return, however, he demanded money, ships and men for his war with Persia.

The Athenian was ready with an argument to counter that demand, just as he had been ready to argue against turning over Demosthenes and his cronies to the Macedonians. Charidemos, in the meantime, had been warned that, unless he was willing to become a sacrificial scape-goat, he would better exile himself. He had agreed, thanked Demades for the warning, and fled to Persia, where he found refuge in the court of Darius.

"The Great King can marshal armies that drink rivers dry and take weeks to pass by," the Athenian delegate said in arguing against starting such a war. "What will you send against these innumerable hordes of Asia? You have at most 20,000 men."

"No," smirked Alexander. "I have 20,000 Macedonians, soldiers all. The Great King has no soldiers – only slaves. My men are hard, hill-born herdsmen, with fire in their veins. The Persians are soft city-dwellers and farmers, spoiled by the lush, fertile fields of the lowlands and floodplains of Asia. They are feeble, and live only to please their king."

Demades and the other Athenian delegates shuffled their feet nervously, adjusted their robes, and seemed not only unconvinced but also embarrassed by the young king's diatribe. The unease of the Athenians at being lectured was evident, but Alexander noticed that a few seemed to nod slightly in agreement. Others were whispering among themselves, as if acknowledging there was some kernel of truth in what he was saying. Alexander could see the doubt in their demeanor starting to dissipate, which only spurred him on.

"My tutor, Aristotle, had the measure of the Persians. 'Natural slaves,' he called them. Did not Herodotos observe that while we, Greeks, labor for ourselves, the Persians work only to serve and please their masters? And those masters are not the noble warriors of old that Herodotos met when he was collecting material for his history some 100 years ago. They have become effeminate from overindulgence in luxuries, immoral from easy living, corrupt, cowardly, and lacking in both faith and honor. None such as they can stand against us. How many times did we, Greeks, and especially you, Athenians, defeat their hosts? By Zeus, their officers used whips at Marathon and Plateai to keep their men in line. Whips! Can you imagine anyone taking a whip to a phalanx of Greeks?"

That remark drew laughter and other signs of approval and agreement from the Athenians. Sensing he was beginning to sway them, Alexander continued.

"The Persians of today will fare no better against a Greek army. Just look at how Xenophon and his men marched into the heart of

Persia and back out again, swatting aside the Persians like so many flies."

That remark, like the last, also caused many of the Athenians to laugh or at least smile. Feeling that perhaps now he had them, Alexander decided the time had come to drive his point home.

"Our Greek lands can no longer support our people. Our cities are crowded, our soil rocky, and our people poor. Think of the lush farmland of Asia, of the vast expanses where we could found more colonies, settle our teeming masses, and put an end to their poverty. And then, of course, there is one more reason to march east. One that overrides them all: revenge. Did not the Persians burn your city, golden Athens, to the ground while your people huddled on the island of Salamis? True, you recovered your lands after defeating the Persians in the epic naval victory you won by its shores, but would you not like to repay the Persians in kind for what they did to your beloved city? Would you not like to help burn their cities, tear down their temples and see them humbled? Then come with me, support me, and we shall make these Persians pay for the wrongs and sacrileges their ancestors committed on the sacred soil of Greece!"

"And what exactly does Macedonia demand of us, if we are to join in this endeavor?" challenged one of the delegates. "Why should we fight against one king if only to become subjects to another? We are free men, citizens of Athens, not base-born barbarians who grovel before some potentate."

Alexander angered visibly at this insult, but Demades quickly intervened in an effort to bring peace and calm to the room. "What he means, King Alexander..."

"I know very well what he means, Demades. I am no simpleton. I know an insult when I hear one," Alexander shot back angrily. "Within your city walls you may do what you want, and remain 'citizens' of Athens," he added, with a sneer as he mouthed that particular word. "But outside of those walls, you will do as I command, for I need subjects who obey orders if I am to defeat the Persians, not citizens who debate my commands."

The Athenian delegates, even Demades and others of his pro-

Macedonian clique, bristled at Alexander's remarks. Demades, however, knew that after what had happened at Thebes, there was no question as to if Athens would do the king's bidding, but only what obedience to him would cost.

"King Alexander," interjected Demades soothingly, "let us not quibble or engage in a debate over semantics. You have agreed to spare our city. I am sure we can convince the people that accepting your terms is the prudent course. Now just tell us exactly what you want from us in return."

"A few thousand of your best hoplites, and some light infantry and cavalry as well," replied Alexander. "And two squadrons of your fleet. That and money, as Athens must pay its fair share of the common cost of the war. And one thing more," added the young king. "Peace at home, and by that I mean an end to the backstabbing, in word or deed, by Demosthenes and his crowd. Do that and I would be satisfied. Do that," he added, with a wry smile, "and you will have my gratitude and not just in word, but in more, shall we say, tangible ways."

"Like what, my King," asked Demades, his demeanor showing he had accepted Alexander's bargain, and was merely haggling over the price tag.

"Like a garrison of Macedonians on the isthmus of Corinth, between Athens and Sparta," replied Alexander. "A garrison from where, if you needed it, my soldiers could be in Athens in a few days," responded Alexander. "And, of course," he added, "I would continue the stipend my father gave you and your party in gratitude for your support of our cause."

"I accept your generous offer, King Alexander," said Demades with a broad smile. "I cannot but wait to tell Demosthenes of our arrangement. He will not be pleased – which in itself will be a joy to me. Although humbled, though, he will surely be relieved to keep his head."

12

The Port of Piraeus

ATHENS

A lexander and his advance guard were not the only visitors to come to Athens from the north. Several hundred refugees from Thebes had also gone south. These fugitives managed to escape the slavers by tagging along at the very rear end of the train of camp followers, wagons and herds of live animals that followed the army of Alexander. Hidden in the clouds of dust kicked up by the army, the emigres hoped to find a welcome, or at least some succor, in the great city.

Among this innumerable rabble were a trio of men for whom Athens was not a final destination but only a way-station on a longer journey: a journey of revenge, a journey of justice, and a journey of freedom. One, a former wine merchant and captain of the citizen soldiery of Thebes, walked at the front of a tumbledown, creaking oxcart. He did his best to keep the sullen, sluggish ox moving, while another man, a physician, walked alongside, keeping constant watch on a third man who, like the first, had also stood in the ranks with other hoplites of his now defunct city-state. Each bump, each rut and each stone in the road jostled the cart and jarred him as he alternately sat or lay down in the thick piles of straw in its bed. Beneath that straw the men had hidden what little money they had been able to scrape together, as well as the physician's medicines and the captain's armor, helmet, shield and sword.

"How much longer do you think it will take us to get to Athens?" asked the man in the bed of the cart, his speech involuntarily punctuated with muffled groans and other noises that spoke of his discomfort.

"The city proper is just over that next rise. You'll be able to see the acropolis when we crest this slight hill," responded the former captain. "But don't start feeling all comfortable when you do, because we aren't stopping in Athens – we don't dare, as it will be lousy with Alexander's soldiers."

"Dimitrios," interjected the physician, "we must find a place to hole up, and soon. All of this has been hard on Ari; his leg is only starting to mend, and each time you hit a hole in the road isn't helping matters."

"How much worse do you think his leg would get if some Macedonian sergeant started poking around under the straw or began asking questions about how Ari got that wound? It doesn't take a physician or a philosopher to recognize a gash from a spear. Alexander may have spared our house, but he also made it very clear that descendants of our illustrious ancestor were safe only so long as they stayed within its confines. That protection disappeared the moment we left that jail – for jail it was, if a comfortable and a familiar one. I don't want any of us to wind up as slaves, or worse, which is what has happened to every other soldier of Thebes who didn't already die on the battlefield."

"If we aren't going into the city, then just where the hell are we going?" asked Aristophanes.

"Piraeus. The port on the other side of the city," responded Dimitrios. "Athens, you know, isn't on the water. It is inland. Its port is about six miles past Athens proper. I have friends there we can stay with for a few days– and some goods in a storehouse that should have come in by sea a few weeks ago. I can sell or trade them for passage for us on an outbound ship. We talked about this before we left Thebes, remember?"

Too exhausted from all of the jostling to respond, Ari just groaned and laid back upon the bed of straw in the back of the cart, while

Klemes continued to trudge on ahead, one weary step after another. Ari soon fell asleep – or passed out from the pain, Klemes was not sure which – but either way, he decided that such rest was more important to his patient than seeing what sights of Athens he would see as they traveled through the crowded, dirty and stinking streets.

Dimitrios' worries of being stopped, questioned and searched by Macedonian troopers, it seemed, were for naught. As chance would have it, the trio had arrived in Athens just as the celebrations of the Eleusinian Mysteries had begun. The streets were mobbed by revelers making merry. What soldiers there were about could not be bothered to look for unwanted strangers or fugitives. Most were themselves swept up in the drunken bacchanal. Others succumbed to the enticements of those celebrating the "goddess of the poppy" or fell under the spell of the drugs made from the flower associated with Demeter, the fertility deity to whom the worshipers and merrymakers paid homage to in their carousing.

Initiates to the Greater Mysteries were given cups of kykeon to drink down, and encouraged to share with the priests the revelations made to them by the gods while in a drug-induced trance. Those who thought they were being offered the traditional poor-man's drink of water and barley flavored with mint soon discovered their vision blurred, their speech slurred and their mind a maelstrom of sights and colors. As the additives were but herbs provided by the bounty of the gods, the revelers explained to those whose faculties remained sharp enough to ask, what harm could there be in imbibing them?

While these and even more serious and more elaborate rituals went on behind the closed doors of temples, other priests went into the fields with farmers to pour libations from sacred vessels into the ground to seek Demeter's blessing for the seeds they would be sowing. After that began the feasting, dancing and other pleasures associated with honoring the goddess of fertility; these would last all through the night.

As tempted as Dimitrios was to participate in this wild and bois-terous public party, he eschewed such temptations and worked his way through the crowds to the far side of the city. As little if any business would be done today, the road between the pair of long walls that connected Athens to its port were all but empty. Razed by the Spartans after their victory a century ago, the walls had been quietly rebuilt during the Corinthian war, and provided a safe and secure passage from the city to its main port of Piraeus.

Unlike the muddled, twisting streets of the main city, Piraeus had been built on a plan. The architect, Hippodamos of Miletos, had laid out a logical grid system and had divided areas into public, private, sacred, commercial and industrial spaces. He had also carved out a place for a central market, the Agora, and even a pair of theaters. His real genius, however, was that all of this was designed to support the three separate harbors that made Piraeus the most important naval base, shipyard and merchant marine spot not only in the entirety of the Hellenic world – but of the entire known world itself.

While Athens was a warren of curving, zig-zagging streets and back alleys, through which Dimitrios had great difficulty navigating, especially with an oxcart, Piraeus was a pleasure to traverse. All of the streets and even the alleys were straight. All main streets were 45 feet wide, all of the lesser streets 25 feet wide and all of the alleys 15 feet wide. Only a fool or a complete stranger could get lost in Piraeus, and Dimitrios was neither. By dusk, when the Athenians in the big city were just getting serious about their partying, Dimitrios reached the one house in Piraeus where he knew people would still be sober and at home: that of Solomon the Jew.

Situated in the area reserved for foreign merchants to reside, the house of Solomon was very ordinary and plain looking, at least from the outside. Its austere outward appearance, however, was a facade – an intentional mask to conceal the very well-appointed, almost luxurious living quarters inside. Dimitrios knocked quietly on the door, as he had little energy left to do more.

The wooden door opened a crack, and a hushed voice asked in heavily accented Greek who would seek entrance at such a late hour, on such a day where no business would be conducted. "Tell your master," Dimitrios replied wearily but respectfully, "that a wine merchant from Thebes asks if he is still welcome at an old friend's seder."

The doorkeeper said he would pass on the request and bid Dimitrios wait. Within moments, a loud voice within boomed an excited command in a mysterious tongue. The door opened wide and its frame was almost filled with a large, heavy set, balding man with a full beard and a blue and white prayer shawl draped about him. As he threw open the door, he stretched out his arms and joyously shouted Dimitrios' name.

"Dimitrios!" he exclaimed as he hugged him so tight the Greek could barely breathe, "you are alive! After the stories they tell in the agora about what happened at Thebes...I...how...who...."

"Those stories and worse are all true, old friend," sighed Dimitrios. "You see before you three of the lucky few to have escaped death or slavery. As for the rest of my..."

The Greek captain could not continue. For the first time in the weeks since the sacking of his city, the Theban soldier broke down and cried. Sobbing with sadness for what had been lost, and in relief for finally reaching a place where he could let his guard down and breathe without fear, Dimitrios could not find the words to express his emotions. His brother, however, had no such difficulty, as he offered their host a simple bow, and introduced himself and the man in the bed of the cart behind him.

"You are welcome here, and you will be safe here. You have my word upon that," Solomon responded. "Under this roof there are no Greeks, no Athenians, no Thebans, no Macedonians and no Jews. Under this roof, there are only friends."

13

The Port of Piraeus
ATHENS: (THE NEXT DAY)

"Forgive me, Dimitrios, for the humble fare we put before you last night," Solomon told his friend the day after the Thebans had shown up at his doorstep. "I shall more than make up for that tonight. I am going to the fish market myself to choose the best, the freshest and the most succulent delights of the sea that Athens has to offer," he added jovially, his own appetite already piqued with anticipation of the evening meal.

"My brother, my friend and I appreciate your hospitality, Solomon," said the captain with a nod, "but after the events of the last few weeks, just being able to sit quietly and safely, with some bread, some cheese and some olives and a bit of salted sprats, well, that felt like a feast."

"Salted sprats! Bah!" said Solomon with evident disgust. "They are only fit for the poor – or the traveler. I am ashamed that there was nothing better to offer you than food from the servants' larder. Tonight, however," he smiled broadly, "you will wish you had the neck of a crane!"

"What? The neck of a crane?" said a puzzled Dimitrios. "I don't follow..."

Solomon let out a deep, hearty laugh from the bottom of his ample belly. "Because cranes have very long necks, and you will want to savor the delicacies my cooks will present tonight, all the way down."

Still laughing at his own witticism, Solomon trundled off to the fish market, a trio of servants in tow, each carrying a large, empty basket. "Now, remember what I told you," he said over his shoulder to his entourage. "Just because the fish is wet doesn't mean it is fresh. Despite the laws against it, there are some who still manage to douse their wares with water when no one is looking."

Dimitrios, weary though he still was from his long march from Thebes, tagged along. Solomon had promised they would visit the warehouse where Dimitrios had wines in storage, including amphorae from Lesbos, Chios, and other islands in the Aegean and Ionian Seas famed for their vintages. Solomon offered to broker the contents of the warehouse, and to take over its lease. It was all decided but for the haggling, for Dimitrios knew that, while his friend would offer a fair price, he would not be denied the joy of bargaining. That bargaining would be done in daylight, while both men were stone cold sober, for once the wine was mixed in the krater, it would simply not do to mix business with drink.

Dimitrios followed Solomon from street to street and from stall to stall, taking in all the sights and sounds and smells of the busy market. He heard vendors crying out about their fish, some from as far away as Sicily or the sea beyond the Dardanelles, as well as dogfish from Rhodes and even eels from his own Lake Copais, near where he had stood with the phalanx against Alexander's horsemen. Although there would be few diners at the meal that evening, Solomon was selecting delights for each of the many, many courses he planned to offer his guests, and to savor himself.

"How about we truly treat ourselves, Dimitrios," asked Solomon cheerily. "Perhaps some barracuda or sea bass or...or some gilt-heads!"

"At those prices, wouldn't they be a little hard to swallow"" chided Dimitrios, smiling at making a pun. "No need to spend that kind of money on me, Solomon. Even some grey mullets or octopus would be more than a treat."

"Grey mullet! Octopus! What are we, shopkeepers and laborers?"

said Solomon with a startled look upon his face. "I feed my servants better than that, Dimitrios! What kind of a host would I be if I served my guests such common fare. No, my friend, we will have a proper meal, and one that you will remember! Now, how about a nice, piping hot slice of tuna from that stall over there?"

Seeing that Solomon was determined to have his way, Dimitrios nodded in acceptance, and joined his friend at the tuna-seller's cart. A few slices of hot fish did much to lighten his mood and restore his energy, but afterwards, while passing one fishmonger's stall, he caught his reflection in the tub of water in which some live eels were still wriggling. The wretched apparition that greeted his gaze was enough to make Dimitrios look for the closest barber, as would any sailor fresh off the boat from weeks at sea. With his long hair, Dimitrios worried he might be mistaken for a Spartan – or, worse, with his longish, scraggly beard, a philosopher.

Piraeus had almost as many barbers as tavern keepers – and whores – and when Dimitrios signaled to Solomon his intent to visit one of the first, the merchant responded with an understanding and relieved look. "I did not wish to offend you last night or this morning," Solomon explained, "by remarking on your rather disheveled if not wild appearance. Go get your hair curled or cropped, whichever your preference, and by all means have your beard trimmed – perhaps to a neat point," added Solomon. Then you will look a proper gentleman. Oh, and by the way, a little dye would help, too," he jibed, "for you are getting as gray as a goat in places."

Barbers being as talkative a lot in Athens as anywhere else in the world where he had traveled, Dimitrios soon found himself bombarded with gossip, and in the center of a debate among the barber and his waiting customers as to which tavern nearby offered the best wine, the most edible food, the most honest gaming tables and the most comforting companions. The talk, however, as is also common to barbershops everywhere, turned to politics, and at the center of that, what Alexander's coming meant for Greece – and for Athens. Dimitrios longed to break into their argument but held his tongue, for such discussions often ended in fights or stabbings, and as he had a greater purpose – and others dependent upon him – he clamped his lips and his jaw tight shut.

When it came to be his turn, and the barber asked him the usual question "how would you like your hair cut?" Dimitrios responded curtly: "In silence."

Afterwards, Dimitrios found himself sorely in need of a drink. He eschewed the wine cart outside the barber's, as he did not think it proper to drink in the street, and passed up as well a few taverns whose customers were already boisterous, even though the sun had yet to reach its zenith for the day. Men who have a thirst as well as a temper to quench, however, soon give in to their desires, as did Dimitrios upon reaching the end of the street, which, as is so often the case, had a tavern on the corner.

Elbowing his way inside, Dimitrios found a stool in the corner, away from the larger, common tables. "Wine," he called out as a man in a wine-stained smock carrying empty cups brushed past. "A cup of wine, and be quick about it," Dimitrios added in a tone that was as surly as it was impatient.

"Wine? Wine?" the man said as he stopped abruptly in his tracks and turned about to face Dimitrios. "You some Spartan who cut his hair just to look human," he chided Dimitrios. "Only a Spartan or a drunk would so insult me. Or perhaps you are a Thracian. They are infamous for swilling cheap wine, for they care nothing of its texture, aroma or even taste. Why not just drink beer like some barbarian if you are just looking to get drunk or quench a thirst. In the kapeleion of Sarambus one does not simply just ask for 'wine,' good man. For I do not serve 'wine.' Nor do I serve it in a 'cup' like some street vendor."

Taken aback at this unexpected diatribe, Dimitrios rather curtly replied: "Well, if you don't sell wine, what's in those jars over there?"

"Those 'jars' as you call them," the man replied rather snootily, "contain the nectar of the gods. The finest Mendean, Chian and Thasian wines you will find in all of Athens. And I, sir, do not 'sell' wine; I prepare it. I am exact in my measurements: two parts wine to five parts water; no more, no less. One does not ask merely for a drink in my establishment," the man continued, "but must first tell me why he wants a bowl, and if he does not know what kind of wine he wants, as most do not, I divine it. You, sir, for example, seem to need something to chase away a bad odor that has spoiled your disposition. Either that or you have lost someone or something that mattered to you. For that I would suggest the Thasian, with its lovely apple smell – a perfume sure to waft up your nose and into your head while it trickles down your throat and warms the belly."

Dimitrios did not take offense at this scolding schooling. An importer of wines since his late father brought him into the family trade, he knew a kindred spirit when he met one.

"Not the Thasian, thank you. You wouldn't happen to have any Magnesian, by chance? I long for its smooth, generous body, and that little touch of sweetness that can make anyone's day just a little bit, well, sweeter."

The man raised his eyebrows, nodded his head and changed his tone at that remark. "Forgive my impertinence, good man," he said with a slight bow. "I see you know your wines, and no one who does so can possibly be of low character, as, forgive me, I mistook you for being. I apologize, too, for inferring that you were a Spartan or a Thracian or worse. Someone with your understanding of wine could never force down some cheap, common swill that so many establishments around here serve and call 'wine.' I can offer you a nice Magnesian – but for someone who seems to know his wines, perhaps you would like to sample a wonderful Mendean I have been carefully tending. It has just come into full bloom, and is nearly at its peak."

"That would be welcome, friend," replied Dimitrios. "It is easy to miss the peak with the Mendean, for it soon begins to tire and then decline once it does."

The man smiled again, obviously impressed at his customer's knowledge of fine vintages, and hurried off to prepare, as he had put it, a proper and expertly mixed krater of fine Mendean. Dimitrios watched in approval as the man added wine to the water, rather than the other way around. This method flavored the water more than watered down the wine, and showed Dimitrios that the man was as he had described himself, a preparer of wine as opposed to a mere tavern keeper.

"It is a pleasure to have someone in my establishment who can talk intelligently about the glory of the grape," the man said when he returned with the wine for Dimitrios. "So, are you just a lover of wine, or is your knowledge, how shall I put it, based on something more than just one too many nights drinking? You're not one of those idle rich who flit about from symposium to symposium, getting stinking drunk with politicians, philosophers and others of a similarly useless lot, are you?"

Dimitrios smiled, took a sip of the deep, dark Mendean wine and, after nodding appreciatively, answered the man's question, and added one of his own. "I would not be a very good importer of wine if I could not tell good wine from bad, or which wines would be best purchased with the intent to let them turn to vinegar rather than try to pass of as something worth drinking."

"Ah," reacted the man with a knowing smile. "Well, as one purveyor of fine wines to another, then, let me properly introduce myself. My name is Sarambos, as was my father's and his father's before him and, if the gods so ordain, will be the name I will give to the child now growing in my wife's belly, should it be a boy, of course. This is more than just a tavern, as someone with your experience I am sure has already figured out. I provide the wine to some of the finest homes in the city. Should you be invited to one of the better of the symposia I was talking about, just ask from whom the host purchased his wine for the evening. My name, most certainly, will be his answer."

Dimitrios realized that he had not stumbled into this particular tavern purely by chance, but had been directed there by the gods. "Sarambos, how would you like to meet my friend Solomon?"

"Why?" replied the tavern keeper, "is he in the wine trade as well?"

"Sort of. I have a warehouse full of the best wine you could ever hope to find, and he is prepared to act as my broker. I would, of course, instruct him to make a special deal for you..."

"There is, methinks, some urgency to your disposing of the contents of this warehouse," Sarambos interrupted. "Since you do not have the look or demeanor of a pirate or smuggler about you, might I guess that you are in a hurry to dispose of your wares as you need money, and quickly, for some new venture....or because you are planning to leave Athens and quickly?"

"Not just Athens, my friend," replied Dimitrios, "but Greece. And yes, I need the money for a new venture."

"And may I ask what that venture might be?" said Sarambos in a conspiratorial whisper.

"To go fight against Alexander."

14

Piraeus

TWO WEEKS LATER...

Т he hospitality of Solomon, two weeks of solid rest in his home, and the profits from the deal with Sarambos, did much to restore the health and spirits of Dimitrios, Klemes, and Aristophanes, whose wounds, although not fully healed, showed much improvement. So, too, did they find comfort in the arms of the flute girls and other female companions for hire that frequently graced their after-dinner drinking bouts in Solomon's home. While Klemes preferred to spend his time discussing science and medicine with one of the more mature, more intelligent (and more expensive) hetaira, Aristophanes took full advantage of the healing powers of one of the younger girls. Dimitrios, however, like their host, found sufficient enjoyment and distraction in the music, dancing and other little performances put on by the women.

"I find as I get older, my dear," sighed Solomon one night while a girl tried her best to entice him to come to bed, "that I am more than likely to disappoint you, and hence myself, in these matters. So, let us save each other the embarrassment and the mutual let down when I am unable to perform. Just looking at you and feeling your warmth and inhaling your lovely scent will have to suffice. If you want something more, then perhaps my friend the captain here..."

"No thank you, Solomon," replied Dimitrios. "I am more than entertained as it is."

"Oh, but surely, Dimitrios," Solomon argued, "a young man such as yourself..."

"I am not that young, not anymore," laughed Dimitrios lightly.

"You are younger than I," Solomon pointed out.

"As are most men," Dimitrios replied with a little laugh. "No, it is not age or the lack of ability to perform, but something else."

"I can hire a pretty boy or two next time if you would..."

"No," laughed Dimitrios quite loudly, "that is not what I mean. It is just that, well, my wife...well, when we came together it was because we both wanted to, and that has rather spoiled the other women for me, if you know what I mean."

"Of course," said Solomon, "I understand that, and all too well. The plague took my wife, just as the fever took yours. It has been many years now but, still..."

"Then, my friend, let two old widowers raise a cup in memory of their late wives, and find what consolation we can in the more modest of the entertainments these lovely ladies can provide."

Such frivolities, although appreciated, were mere distractions, especially for Dimitrios. The Athenians had breathed a collective sigh of relief when Alexander returned north, but Dimitrios knew Alexander was not going home to rest. He would mobilize more soldiers and make preparations to join the Macedonians already across the Hellespont. That Alexander himself would soon be taking the field again, only added to the urgency Dimitrios felt about leaving Athens. The Macedonians were already fighting the Persians, and if Dimitrios was going to be part of that fight, he had to cross the wine dark sea to Asia – and soon.

Finding a ship to go east was not difficult. It was not yet the end of the rowing season, although once the Pleiades vanished from the evening sky, there would be precious few captains willing to risk a crossing to Asia. The cranes were already beginning to migrate south to Egypt. Every sailor knew that meant winter was coming, and soon it would be time to pull up the ships into their sheds or onto solid ground, so their hulls could dry out and their bottoms be scraped. Dimitrios had made the journey by sea often enough before, but this time it would not be in search of wine to import. It would be a one-way passage, at least for the foreseeable future, if not forever.

Solomon knew better than to try to talk Dimitrios out of his quest, and decided that if the captain was going to war, then he should go in style.

"Dimitrios," he told him one evening, "you need look for a ship to the east no longer. I have found you a berth on the finest ship in Athens, and at no cost. The captain is willing to make room for your brother and your friend, as well."

"And what lumbering hulk is it that you have procured passage for us in," laughed Dimitrios. "If they are willing to take passengers aboard at no cost, does that mean they plan on making up for it by robbing us blind or selling us into slavery – or dropping us into the sea as a sacrifice to Poseidon?"

Solomon drew himself up to his full height, standing as tall and as straight as Mount Olympus itself. "The 'lumbering hulk' as you call it, is the *Paralos*. And it is captained by the treasurer of Athens, who has no need of whatever paltry sums you three would command in the slave markets."

Dimitrios was taken aback, and it showed. "That is impossible, Solomon. That is the ship of state – the flagship of the Athenian navy!"

"Only in time of war, my friend," corrected Solomon. "We are still at peace, even if we are to send other ships and men to serve in Alexander's war with Persia. He is carrying a delegation of priests and ambassadors on a circuit of the island city states of the Cyclades and the Ionian shore."

"'He?' What do you mean 'he'..."

"You Theban landlubber. 'He' is the *Paralos*. It is the only ship anyone has ever heard of that is not named after a woman or a female goddess. As it is named after Poseidon's son, we can hardly refer to the ship as 'she.' Tell your brother and your friend that, too, so none of you risk insulting the *Paraloi*."

"The who?"

"Damn it, Dimitrios," sighed Solomon, shaking his head back and forth. "The *Paraloi* – that is what the crewmen of the *Paralos* call themselves. Oh, and don't make the mistake of calling the captain a trierarch. He is simply one of the Paraloi, too. Every other ship in the navy may have been built by one of those rich men or their sons, but the *Paralos* was built by the city. It is our ship – more than that, even. It is a symbol of how our dear Athens is married to the sea, with *Paralos* acting as the groom and Athens the bride."

"So how did you manage..."

"Never mind that, Dimitrios. Let us say that the treasurer owes me a few favors for making up some alleged shortfall when the treasury was audited, and leave it at that. All that matters is that you get where you are going, and get there safely. There is no better ship in the world, nor a more experienced crew than those that sail aboard the *Paralos*."

"How can I ever repay you for this, and for all of your other kindnesses, Solomon. I don't know..."

"Do not worry about that," said Solomon, gesturing with his hand for the captain to be silent. "If you can in any way take that spoiled Macedonian brat down a peg, then it will be repayment enough. And while you are at it, perhaps you would mutter my name when you take out a few of those Macedonian bastards."

The evening before boarding the *Paralos*, Dimitrios tried to talk his brother and his friend out of going with him. "Why not stay here, with Solomon?" he suggested. "He can surely find more patients for you, Klemes, as well as work for you, Ari. You could both make a good life here, in Athens."

"So, my brother," replied Klemes sternly, "you think you are the only one who can stop Alexander? The only one who wants revenge for what that barbarian did to Thebes?"

"No, no, brother, that is not what I..."

"Well, that is exactly what it sounds like, Dimitrios," jumped in Aristophanes. "We didn't follow you this far just to escape a dead city, or to hide ourselves away as if the past did not matter. No, my friend, that is not why we followed you. We are not staying behind while you go off and have all the fun."

"Fun? Fun?" laughed Dimitrios. "You've only been in a couple of battles, Ari, but they should have been enough to show you that war is anything but 'fun.'"

"I know that, and know it all too well, as does your brother," said Ari, pointing to his bandages for emphasis. "I have no illusions, and if ever I did, what happened to our home took care of that."

"But you know you can't stand in the line with that leg, or even keep up on a march..."

"Yeah, but like Klemes and I told you back in Thebes before we set out, there are other ways to fight a war than to just hold a spear and shield. At the very least you will need a friend, someone to help keep camp, or to clerk for whatever company you lead. And Klemes..."

"...can speak for himself, thank you Ari," interjected the physician. "My services will be needed even more than yours, Ari, or even my brother's. Soldiers only fight battles; physicians clean up afterward, and there are damn few of us as it is even here in Greece, let alone out there, and most won't go anywhere near a battlefield. So shut your mouth, dear brother. We are coming with you – or, maybe it is you who are coming with us," Klemes added with a bit of smirk. "Maybe it is you who should be trying to talk Ari and me into taking you with us."

That, of course, was something he did not have to do, for Klemes and Ari both knew that the former captain would have no trouble finding employment. Although a wine merchant by education, tradition and trade, Dimitrios had trained and served as a citizen soldier his entire life. As a veteran captain, a well-educated man and an experienced traveler, Dimitrios was just the sort of man who would rise up the ranks in one of the numerous companies of Greek mercenaries. Those soldiers for hire formed the heavy infantry core of the private armies of the Persian governors, or satraps as they were known, in Asia.

"Oh? Really? Well, Klemes, Solomon says the satraps are all looking for experienced soldiers. Arsites, the governor of Hellespontine Phrygia, is already engaged with the Macedonians over in the Troad. Spithridates of Ionia will no doubt march to join him. Those two are the first line of defense for the Persian empire. Sure, they can field hordes of levy infantry, but such troops are poorly armed, rarely armored and of questionable value. They will run if given any excuse – or opportunity."

"Surely there is more to the Persian army than a bunch of peasant rabble," remarked Klemes, whose knowledge of military affairs was only slightly greater than that of agriculture.

No," replied Dimitrios. "The satraps can also call upon large numbers of tribal light cavalry to scout and harry the enemy as they advance, but they, too, will not prevail against a Macedonian line of battle. They serve a purpose. They plink and pluck away at the edges of an enemy formation, but that is all. When it comes to actual hitting power, the Persian governors rely on men of their own class: the local nobility.

"Those magnificent horsemen are a sight to see," Dimitrios continued. "They are fabulously wealthy, and each rides to war encased in armor and armed with bow, sword and mace. As valiant as these men of privilege and breeding are known to be, however, they are warriors, not soldiers. They seek out single combat. They yell their own name and shout a challenge as they charge. They are terrifying, but they fight on their own or as groups of individuals, rather than as formed units. The Macedonians, however, are a machine – and they will spit them on their long pikes and roast them for breakfast."

Klemes grew a bit paler with every sentence Dimitrios spoke and with every point he made in what had become something of a lecture. "So the Persians are already doomed, then?" he asked with a tremble in his voice.

"No, not by a long shot," continued the captain. "This swirling mass of light and heavy cavalry needs a base to maneuver from, that's all. It needs a solid, staunch block of hard men to stand firm and hold their ground. Something to encourage the reluctant levies to stand and fight. The satraps need heavy infantry to anchor their armies. For that they rely on the Greek mercenaries, in solid phalanxes. Veteran soldiers, like me."

Klemes seemed uneasy with these answers, and while still resolved to follow his brother wherever he led, found his doubts as to the wisdom of this enterprise beginning to take root. "I recall what our father said about mercenaries, if you don't, brother. He had a very low opinion of their worth as soldiers – or even as men. You know..."

"Yes, I know what father used to say, but things are different in Persia. We Greeks prefer to fight our own battles, and as such are suspicious of hirelings or those paid to stand in the ranks where men of quality should otherwise stand. But Persian governors and kings have been hiring such mercenaries for as long as anyone can remember. Herodotus writes of it, so does the Athenian Xenophon. He was a general of such mercenaries in the years immediately following the Peloponnesian War. Xenophon's written account of his experiences fighting first for one Persian on the losing side of a civil war and then of fighting his way home back across Persia may have been meant as a cautionary tale, but it has instead only inspired other Greeks to take up the mercenary trade. That book is also said to be one of Alexander's favorites, and he supposedly often cites it in support of his arguments that no Persian army could stand up to Greek heavy infantry, let alone the Macedonian pike formations that had defeated them. 'For if Xenophon's hoplites had cut their way from the Aegean coast to Babylon and back,' he has been rumored to say, 'then how could the Persians hope to stand against Macedonia's even more superior army?'"

"And yet it is just such a 'superior army' you intend to go up against – again?"

"Yes, Klemes. I have to. And I am not alone. There are many who have left Greece for Persia, ready to fight the next battle against the little tyrant. Solomon knows of a number of Athenians of note in

Ephesus in particular, who are getting ready to fight, and so that is where I intend to go."

"All right," shrugged Klemes. "I guess I should have known you would have it all figured out. But," and he said this quite sternly, "you also should have known better than to try to talk me or Ari out of coming with you."

"Well, I suppose I do," replied Dimitrios a bit sheepishly, "but I had to try. You know that I would be lost without you two to look after me, right?" added Dimitrios with a grin.

"And me without you," replied Klemes.

"Same goes for me, too," added Aristophanes. "Which is why I brought along these," he continued, as he reached inside his cloak to pull out three small iron bars, none much longer than a hand's breadth.

"What are those for?" asked Klemes.

"For the oath, of course," Ari responded.

"What oath?" asked Dimitrios.

"Our oath to remain together, no matter what happens, and that none of us will leave either of the others behind...or without seeing their corpse receives the proper rites, should it come to that."

Klemes and Dimitrios both nodded in agreement. "That doesn't need to be said, I hope you know," said Dimitrios to Ari.

"True," replied Ari, "but it somehow feels right to make it all formal and legally binding."

"Okay, but what do those little iron rods have to do with that?" asked Klemes.

"It is something I read once, about how to seal a treaty two kings each tossed an iron bar into the sea," replied Ari. "They said that they would keep their oaths until the iron would rise up from the sea and float upon the waves."

"Ari," sighed Dimitrios, "you know iron doesn't float."

"Exactly."

PART III

Ephesos

ON THE COAST OF ASIA MINOR

Year Three of the Reign of Alexander of Macedon

15

Ephesos

THE TEMPLE OF ARTEMIS

The journey across the wine dark sea had been a lengthy one, as the Athenian ship of state on which Dimitrios, Klemes and Aristophanes had taken passage stopped at every major island on the way from Athens to Ephesos. The ship had made a circuit of the Cyclades, stopping at Ceos, Siphnos, Melos, Paros, Naxos, Mykonos, and many even smaller islands in between before lurching east to Icaria. From there, they went on to Samos before finally reaching the great port city of Ephesos. Since its founding by Greek colonists over six centuries ago, the city had grown into a key center for traders seeking access to the markets of Asia. It also attracted thousands of pilgrims who came to honor and ask the blessings of the goddess Artemis, whose temple, legend had it, was built by the son of the river god Caystrus.

A true wonder of the world, it was praised in poetry and song as the nearest thing man could create to rival the glorious marvels of Olympus. And like that home of the gods, it mounted to the clouds, and when touched by the sun, its brilliancy was beyond anything else on earth.

Even grander and larger than the Parthenon, the temple was more than a place of worship or a tribute to the gods. The temple was both the very heart and the pride of the city – both of which suffered greatly when it was looted by raiders, ravaged by floods and destroyed for a third time when the city fell to the Lydian king, Croesus. Each time, however, like the fertility goddess for whom it was built, the temple rose again from the earth, reborn. It was at the feet of this thrice-risen holy place that Dimitrios, Aristophanes and Klemes came to give thanks for their safe passage across the sea and to ask a blessing for their coming endeavors.

"I do not see how making a sacrifice to Artemis is going to help us very much," said Klemes to his brother. "After all, she is a goddess of fertility, not war. Just look at her statue – and what are those, breasts or eggs on her chest, I can't quite make out?"

"You're the physician, Klemes," chided Dimitrios. "If you can't tell an egg from a breast then perhaps you should go back to Cos for further study. It isn't that far from here, you know, maybe another week at sea down the coast, if that."

"I have had enough of ships and voyages at sea, thank you, brother," said Klemes. "And of sleeping on rocky beaches, night after night..."

"You know the sailors won't spend the night at sea, Klemes," piped in Aristophanes. "They can't see where they are going in the dark, and they don't want to wind up crashed on some rocks or stuck on a sand bar. Besides," he added, "it wasn't every night. There were a few nights when the moon was full and if the sail wasn't filled by the Etesian Winds they would row at night, their way lit up by the phosphorescent glow on the sea, or that weird, greenish white light that seemed to emanate from the mast."

"So, a few weeks at sea and all of a sudden you're an old salt?" joked Klemes. "Pshaw; you'd never even seen a ship, let alone set foot on one, until we got to Piraeus. This was not my first crossing of the sea, you know, so I think I know more about what I am talking about than you do!"

"Shhhh, that's enough you two. Show some respect; we're in a temple after all..."

"Yeah, but a temple to a fertility goddess..."

"Who is also the goddess of the hunt, might I remind you, dear brother, or didn't they teach you that at that fancy academy for hypocrites..."

"Hippocrates, brother. The academy of Hippocrates, not hypo..."

"I know, I know. But what I said still stands. Besides, this is the biggest temple any of us have ever seen or that has ever been built, so that says something about Artemis. Praying to her must get results, otherwise why would anybody build such a thing..."

"Yeah, well it seems not everyone had their prayers answered. Look at the scorch marks. Somebody tried to burn this place down not long ago..." remarked Aristophanes as he pointed to the extensive and as still yet unrepaired damage.

"That was over 20 years ago," Dimitrios replied, "at least that is what I heard a priest outside telling some worshippers. I heard that Alexander believes the fire was caused by Zeus, hurling lightning bolts on the night Alexander was born to celebrate the birth of his half-human, half-god son."

"Is Alexander still prattling on about being of divine origin?" remarked Klemes. "I doubt this fire was sent from the heavens. More likely some madman or someone whose prayers were not answered...."

"Or the answer he got was 'no,'" interjected Ari.

"Either way," remarked Dimitrios, "I am sure that arsonist is in Hades, probably suffering from a different kind of fire, if there is any justice in religion, anyway. Besides, you can see they are working at repairing that damage – and adding on to the temple. So what I said still holds. There must be something to this goddess."

"Well, since we are not asking for help making babies then what is it that we need from the goddess of the hunt," said Klemes. "After all, what or who is it that we are hunting, Dimitrios?"

16

Ephesos

THE PALESTRA

With its magnificent temple, vast marketplaces and immense harbor, Ephesos was the brightest star in the glittering constellation of Greek colonies that bejeweled the shores of the Aegean Sea. As it was a gateway for people and trade coming into or exiting Asia Minor, so was Ephesos also a conduit for news and information about what was happening in the world, and especially events of importance playing out in the cities of Greece and the Persian Empire. The wealth of information, however, was in itself a problem, for rumor and gossip too often contradicted, confused and suborned the truth. Among the best places to gather, sift through and corroborate that information were, as in all cities, the bathhouses and taverns.

Finding the taverns where those who truly knew what they were talking about as opposed to just spewing forth their opinions or speculations, however, was the real challenge. Men in their cups rarely told tales without bias, while those seeking someone to stand them a drink would say whatever they thought their patron wanted to hear. While Dimitrios made his way from tavern to tavern where, with his knowledge of the wine trade, he could hob-knob with the wealthier and more worldly merchants and tavern keepers, Klemes and Aristophanes made the rounds of the best bathhouses.

"My teachers claimed that water has many healing properties," Klemes told his young friend as they strolled down Curetes Way, from the Gate of Hercules toward the center of the city.

"Didn't do much for Agamemnon, thought, did it," joked Aristophanes.

"That he was murdered in his bath by his wife upon returning home from Troy in no way diminishes, let alone contradicts, what I was talking about, Ari. Remember, Odysseus is said to have bathed frequently while a guest of Calypso, and the last thing he did before leaving her island was to bathe."

"It is not bathing I object to, Klemes. It is bathing in public, especially in my condition."

"Ari, you have nothing to be ashamed about. You are a strong, fine-looking young man. Your scars were won in honorable battle, and just because you need assistance with your ablutions..."

"But in the palestra with its wrestlers, and the adjacent gymnasium with all those athletes and others showing off their muscles and talents at sport..."

"As you once did, if what Dimitrios told me is true, and as I am sure you will again, once you have healed properly."

"But will I? Will I ever heal 'properly,' as you put it? Back in Thebes you said I would never again be able to stand in the phalanx or march..."

"Yes," nodded the physician, "and, sadly, I still believe that. But I also said you might someday be able to ride a horse, and that you could do many other things besides being a soldier. You also have a brain – and a healthy and a smart one at that, young man. You can read and write and do your numbers, and you know at least a little of the sciences, thanks to that father of yours. Any fool can bear a shield, wield a spear and get himself killed. That's my brother's game, but it does not have to be yours. Ah, here we are," said Klemes, who had kept the conversation going as Ari hobbled down the stone street. "Now see, you did that long walk all by yourself, with only a walking stick to help keep you steady. You are getting better, Ari, and will continue to do so, if you let yourself, that is. Now, let us go inside. We have work to do."

The "work" to which Klemes referred was to discover, as Dimitrios was trying to find out in the taverns, if there were any mercenary companies recruiting or expected to be passing through the city. One did not simply just set up a stall in the agora and call for men to take up arms, as Dimitrios had explained, and to walk into the citadel and ask its commander would not do either. That could get one escorted from the city, thrown in jail or impressed into the garrison, none of which were what Dimitrios, Ari and Klemes had in mind when they braved the seas to reach Asia. Mercenaries were a type that most people and cities knew of and needed, but of which they were also suspicious, and as history had shown too often, with good reason. Even finding a mercenary company that was enlisting would not be enough; it had to be the right company, a gathering of professional soldiers who would fight not just for pay but for honor. Even better would be one that also had a cause to fight for.

"Exiles dine on dreams," Dimitrios had explained to Klemes and Ari. "We just need to find some fellow exiles who share our dreams of standing up to Alexander."

"And of revenge. Don't forget about that," Aristophanes had reminded his friend and the physician at the time they had that discussion. "We have 30,000 dead and enslaved Thebans whose souls cry out for justice against that murdering monster."

As they entered the palestra, Klemes and Aristophanes were impressed by the number of wrestlers practicing their sport. The gymnasium alongside was also packed with young men hard at work at their exercises. That the clientele was drawn from the best families was even more evident from the public bath which served the wrestling school and the sporting arena. Its size, beauty and cleanliness also spoke of the wealth of this patrons.

There were several similar complexes in Ephesos, but this particular public bath was very popular among the city's more exclusive athletic clubs, as Dimitrios had learned while scouting the taverns.

Where such men congregated, Dimitrios had explained to Klemes, there were certain to be those who knew something of war. It was in this environment they might learn of preparations being made to fight the war that Alexander's advance forces had already begun up north.

With his leg not yet completely healed, Ari dared not ask to participate in a wrestling match and could not physically join those running around the track. There were other ways to stretch his muscles, of course, and once Ari had disrobed and begun his exercises, he saw that several of the other men also bore scars, some of which, he imagined, had been gained on the field of battle.

While Ari joined in and began to mingle with his fellow athletes, Klemes sought out the areas where older men, all modestly clothed rather than nude like the athletes, were discussing matters of the mind, rather than of the body. He moved about on the fringes of each of several of these groups. As he was disinclined to argue philosophy and even less interested in debating the merits of one poet or dramatist versus another, Klemes moved on from one to the next, until he overheard one man speaking about the merits of gymnastic exercises in regards to keeping the mind and body healthy.

"I tell you, friends," the man said in addressing a quartet of rather well-attired men who were seated on a circular bench, "there is a correlation between regular exercise and the ability to move without pain as we get older. I think it lubricates the joints and gets the bodily fluids flowing. It even helps keep the mind sharp. You, sir," the man added, motioning to Klemes to come closer, "you look like a man of learning. Do you not agree?"

Klemes, never shy about offering his opinion even when it was not asked for, did not hesitate to respond.

"I do agree. Just because we get older doesn't mean we should stop coming to the gymnasium," he added. "If anything, I think that it is when we stop coming to the gymnasium that we truly get old, not just older."

As Klemes became drawn into their conversation, he learned that he was amongst fellow physicians, two of whom had also studied at the academy of Hippocrates in Cos. He was soon drawn into their camaraderie, and not only lost track of the time but would have forgotten his purpose in coming to the wrestling school, gymnasium and baths had not one of the men suggested the time had come when a good soak would do them all well.

Aristophanes had, similarly, fallen in with a group of young athletes who showed him equal welcome. Just as exercising the mind brings men closer together, so too does exercising the body, and once such common ground is found, guards are let down and talk on one subject inevitably leads to another, and another. By the time that Ari and Klemes had each finished bathing, they had each gathered bits and pieces of the kind of information that Dimitrios was seeking. It seemed that one general of note, Memnon of Rhodes, was gathering forces at Miletos, a city not far down the coast from Ephesos. Although Memnon was a Rhodian Greek himself, Klemes learned, he had married well into the Persian nobility, and was committed to the defense of the empire. Even more important, however, as Aristophanes had heard, was that he had once been a hostage of King Phillip's in Macedonia, where he had come to know and loathe a particular prince of the royal house.

That prince, one of the wrestlers had told Ari, was now king of Macedonia.

17

Miletos

THE THEATER

With so many small vessels plying the Ionian and Carian coast, Dimitrios, Klemes and Aristophanes had little trouble procuring passage on a southbound ship. Just as Ephesos was the great harbor of Ionia, so was Miletos, the principal roadstead of Caria. Both were Greek cities. Both had at one time or another risen up against the Persian empire. Both now once again sported the winged Ahurumazda above their gates, as both had come to realize that resistance to the empire was useless. Both, however, had also learned that the empire preferred to discipline rather than destroy. Both thus had been spared, after a ceremonial sacking, of course, yet each also had been treated more like disobedient children than treasonous rebels. Both now once again prospered as centers of trade – of which the imperial governors took a hefty bite.

Miletos was rich in history and lore, as the great Herodotos himself had remarked and written. Originally from the comparatively nearby city of Halicarnasos, Herodotos was raised on stories of the glory of Miletos, for in his day it was the greatest of all of the Greek cities of Asia. This city at the mouth of the Meander was the mother of three score colonies ranging from the shores of the Euxine Sea to the coasts of Sicily – and perhaps beyond. Its ancient glory was reflected and kept alive on the stage of its massive outdoor theater, upon whose stage annual performances of Phyrnichos' "The Capture of Miletos," (or, variously, "The Sack of Miletos") were sponsored by the satrap as a not-so-subtle reminder of the futility of rebelling against the empire. Today, however, a rather different kind of dramatic performance was being staged in the great amphitheater.

"Who is that plumed peacock upon the stage," Klemes asked his brother as they entered the vast arena. "I have never seen such an over-sized crest on a helmet before. If the weight of it doesn't pull him down, I imagine a gust of wind would fill it like a sail and topple him to the ground."

"Shhh!" Shushed a stranger, who grabbed the physician by the arm. "That is Ephialtes of Athens, commander of the garrison and a general in the armies of the Great King. He is a warrior of great renown and..." the man added much more quietly..."he has many guards about the theater. So I would mind your tongue, traveler."

While Klemes was being scolded, and warned by the stranger, Dimitrios was busy looking about the theater. Its stone benches were filled with every assortment of fighting man he had ever heard about, and more. Young men, old men, men of middle age. Many bore scars, although whether these were gained from battling or brawling, Dimitrios was uncertain. Probably from a bit of both, he thought. Most wore some bits and pieces of battle gear, although much of it appeared even more battered and worn then the men themselves.

There were a few accoutered head to foot in bright, shiny armor, from brilliant bronze breastplates that reflected the glare of the hot Carian sun to equally shiny greaves and helmets. These, laughed Dimitrios to Aristophanes, were "not real soldiers, but only rich youngsters playing at soldier."

"But they do look the part of some hero of Homer's," replied Aristophanes. "See how they sparkle and gleam, and how tall and strong they stand."

"They are nothing but bored young men of privilege seeking to find adventure and glory," remarked Dimitrios. "Oh, some, perhaps, might not be too bad, but most I imagine are just seeking to escape from the tedium of a life where every want and need and wish was immediately fulfilled, and fulfilled by simply waving about their hand to a servant or their purse to some eager merchant or willing woman. Such men make for very bad soldiers, Ari..."

"And why is that?" asked Aristophanes.

"Because they are the kind that get other men killed, either because they cannot hold their place in the line or because some other well-meaning fool will try to save them in the midst of battle – at the cost of his own life. Don't look to them, Ari, but to the men over there, in the back rows. Those are fighting men – or at least they were."

"You mean those seedy-looking, scruffy men stretched out on the benches? Ugliest bunch of brutes I've ever seen."

"Ari," said Dimitrios with a bit of a laugh. "The uglier the soldier, the better. It means they've been in a fight – and stayed until it was finished, and were still standing when it was over."

"But look at them," continued Ari. "No two are dressed alike. You've got men in open-faced pot helmets, and others in ancient helmets with noseplates and cheek guards. There are men wearing cheap armor that hasn't been hammered and fitted properly, and others whose gear looks like it was handed down from their grandfathers. And that bunch over there," he added, pointing at a particularly dirty bunch, "all they've got are hides and felt caps, like mountain men."

"And don't miss those boys over there, with the boiled leather armor or with linen shirts," added Klemes mockingly.

"Those linen shirts have several layers, glued together, with metal plates in between," interjected Dimitrios. "They're flexible, light and will stop just about anything other than a direct thrust. We should talk to some of them," continued Dimitrios, "they will know what is really going on here at this muster."

Dimitrios and Ari made their way through the crowd, looking for a space to sit. Although Ari's leg had healed fairly well, he could still only walk for relatively short periods, and it had been a long trek from the port through the heart of the city to the great theater.

"Sit here and rest a bit, my friend," Dimitrios said as he pointed to a space at the end of a row. I'm going to ask around and see what's up."

"Isn't that fellow up there, on the stage, Memnon, the general you wanted to meet and offer your sword to?"

"Apparently not," interrupted Klemes, who had followed a few steps behind his brother and Ari. "But he is raising mercenaries for Memnon, as that fellow I met in Ephesos told me. That other lad who accosted me as we came into the theater confirmed it. He put out the call for soldiers, and they answered. Some of these men are so desperate, it seems they will sign up just to get a hot meal and a new cloak. It seems many of them are so poor they have been living in caves, or have been reduced to playing highwaymen or have become common thieves."

"What?" gasped Ari in disbelief. "How could anyone hire men such as that and think they would fight?"

"Those are exactly the kind of men who would fight – and fight hard, at least as long as they are properly led," said Dimitrios. "Men like that know what it means to be hungry, tired, cold and with only a friend or two to watch their back. This is not like the militia at Thebes, Ari," added Dimitrios. "We were in our beds in the morning, in the field at noon and back home before nightfall, or knew we would be in a few days at most. Most of these men have no homes, let alone beds. They know little of comfort. No, Ari, these are just the kind of men the Great King needs – and just the kind we are looking to join up with."

"Yeah, if you say so," replied Ari. "But if these are the men this Memnon fellow needs, why did he send this old goat to blather on about things. Just where the hell is this Memnon?"

"Memnon, it seems," interjected Klemes, "is already on the march. As that man I was conversing with told me. Alexander sent his father's old general Parmenion back into Asia to set up a base for an invasion up north. Memnon beat Parmenion once before, back when Philip sent his favorite general over here two years ago. Memnon beat him then on the banks of the Skamandros River, up in the Troad. He was too late to stop the Macedonians from swallowing up a few small cities, but he soon made them spit most of their conquests out and run for the coast."

"How do you know so much about that?" asked a perplexed and surprised Aristophanes.

"Because I listen," sighed Klemes. "The gods made us with two ears and only one mouth for a reason. And when I do open my mouth to speak, it is to ask questions, so that I might learn something. You would do well to do the same yourself."

"Well," snapped Ari, "I did learn something today. That general has an unlucky name."

"Yes," sighed the physician, "I know. Ever since that goat herd Ephialtes betrayed Leonidas and his 300 Spartans by showing the Persians the way around the pass at the Hot Gates, that name has been anathema to all Greeks. But then again, for a man to bear the burden of that name, and hope that by his courage and accomplishments to restore its honor, well, that takes a special kind of confidence, a special kind of courage...."

"...and maybe a special kind of hubris...or...madness," quipped Ari.

"That's enough of that, lads," said Dimitrios. "If that fellow up on the stage is hiring men for Memnon, then we are in the right place. After all, if Memnon is the one who beat Philip's best general two years ago, then he is surely the one the Great King and his satraps will turn to stop Alexander. They'd be fools to do otherwise."

18

Dascylion

PALACE OF THE SATRAP

"You forget your place, Memnon," said the man in the glittering silk robes, as he pointed one of his ring-bedecked fingers at the Greek general's face. "You may be married to a Persian princess, and a proven and loyal servant of the empire," he said as he rose from his heavily cushioned chair, "but a servant you are, and nothing more. It is we, the satraps and our nobles who will say how this war will be fought, not some...some hireling Greek!"

Arsites, satrap of Hellespontine Phrygia, had refused to come to Sardis, the administrative capital of the satrapies of Asia Minor. His province to the northwest, along the shores of the Hellespont, was already crawling with Macedonians, although most had stayed close to the coast, rather than move inland. What few raiding parties Parmenion had sent inland had been quickly, easily and bloodily dealt with by Arsites' cavalry, of which he had thousands at his command. Instead of going to Sardis, he sent word for all of the other satraps, high-ranking nobles, chieftains and great landowners to gather at his own palace in Dascylion, not far from where the cavalry of both sides were engaged in their sanguinary, teasing dance.

Dascylion had been built as a pleasure pavilion on Lake Manyas, and was lavish to the point of gaudy as its rich décor attested. On one side of the palace was the lake, upon which a few small fishing boats bobbed and a handful of female bathers frolicked behind a long, tall silk curtain that was raised to keep out prying eyes. On the other, inland side was the paradeiza – the meticulously planned and lovingly maintained garden, in which a hundred species of flowers and as many of small trees, ferns and bushes thrived and were maintained by the care of a small army of gardeners. Clear, clean paths of glazed brick guided visitors and guests as they recreated themselves upon its walks, all to the sound of gurgling fountains and songbirds – whose wings had been clipped so they could not leave this paradise in which they were imprisoned.

Despite its sublime grace and rich furnishings, for the governor this paradise was much more than an indulgence. It was his satrapial palace, and behind its light and glistening exterior were thick walls of brick and stone, with massive wooden gates that could be shut and barred to keep those inside safe and secure from any unwanted guests. Like the Persian Empire itself, Dascylion appeared to be an inviting place of dazzling, delicate and undefended beauty, ripe for the picking, but, at its core, it was strong, powerful, dominating and, when its master was provoked, deadly.

Into this glorious death trap Memnon marched, attired in his most splendid and gleaming armor, cape flowing behind, horsehair plumed helmet of shimmering bronze in hand and heavy leather boots pounding. Sycophantic attendants of the satrap ran to meet him, seeking to slow him down so that they might see to his needs, relieve him of his burdensome war gear and sit him somewhere to take refreshment while waiting to be announced. Memnon would have none of that, and parted his way through them with no more effort than if they had been branches of ferns blocking his path on the paradeiza's bricks.

The number of attendants thickened before him, but then slunk away before his bull-like demeanor, unable and now unwilling to slow, let alone halt, his steady march. The general knew the way into the heart of Dascylion almost as well as he knew the corridors of the many imperial palaces of his friend and liege, Darius, and without ceremony or pause burst through the silken drapes that separated the satrap's private audience chamber from the great hall.

Inside were a gaggle of perfumed, silken-robed men with rouge on their cheeks, kohl around their eyes and exquisitely coiffed and oiled hair and beards. To the unknowing eye these effeminate sybarites appeared to pose just the opposite of a threat. But as Memnon so well knew, their attire, just like the gardens and silk drapes of the palace, were but a show. For behind the rich clothes and gaudy makeup were men of iron and steel, elite horsemen who built and ruled an empire, and who were as ferocious as lions and as dangerous as panthers.

"Ah, the king's pet Greek soldier has finally made his appearance," said the host, Arsites, in a slithering tone that managed to not only insult Memnon but was meant to show him — and the others - who was really in charge. "Come join us around the map. I was just explaining where we will meet this upstart barbarian kinglet in battle, and how we will drive this brazen pup back into the sea from which he came."

"But that is not your decision to make, nor do you have the authority to make such a plan, let alone give such orders," said Memnon angrily as he slammed his helmet down upon the map, making the little wooden models of soldiers and horses jump. "The Great King himself gave me the responsibility of protecting the empire against the Macedonians..."

"Yes, Memnon. He did. Two years ago, when he put you at the head of 5,000 of your fellow Greek hirelings," said Arsites with a snake-like slither to his voice. "And you still have command of them — but only of them," he added, the timbre of his voice gradually changing from soothing insult to one of unchallengeable command. "You have no authority over our soldiers, our subjects... or us!"

Memnon gritted his teeth. Though Greeks born in Rhodes, he and his brother had risen fast in the empire. That brother, Mentor, had married well and won many battles for Persia – then threw it all away when he backed the power-play by his father-in-law Artabazus, at the time satrap of the same province of Hellespontine Phrygia,that Arsites now ruled. It was after that failed revolt they had taken refuge in Macedonia, and where he had met King Philip, his frightening if stunningly beautiful Queen Olympias and their spoiled brat of a son, Alexander.

As Arsites continued to prattle on in his insulting manner, Memnon's ears tuned him out and his mind wandered to that time in Macedonia.

Memnon remembered how he had at first liked the boy. Alexander had an inquisitive mind. He had asked Memnon question after question about what things were like in the empire. How they lived, how they fought, how they governed. Alexander had learned much from his tutor, the scholar Aristotle, but much of what the man had taught the prince was so biased and wrong that it not only poisoned the lad against Persia but somehow made the young Macedonian believe that Greeks as a race were superior to the Persians. Memnon had tried to convince Alexander otherwise, but to no avail, such was the hold Aristotle and, especially, the queen had on him that he believed himself the son of a god, and destined to rule the world. There is no talking to someone once they buy into such drivel, and Memnon was glad when his brother convinced the Great King to pardon the family so they could return to the empire.

Mentor had earned that pardon by doing what the brothers did best – and had recovered a rebellious Egypt for the empire. Sadly, his brother had since died, but Mentor had left him his lands in the Troad, his fortune and, perhaps most important of all, his wife, Barsine. Memnon had fallen in love with her the moment he saw her, such was her beauty, her grace and her gentle heart. That she was also one of the few women he had ever met who could out-ride, out-think and out-argue his brother, or himself for that matter, only deepened his love. Had she been married to anyone else but his brother, he would have stolen her away or fought a duel to win her. But Memnon had remained true to his brother, despite the burning hunger that ate away at him for so many years. Mentor knew of his suffering, but also of his loyalty, so upon his death bed he had asked Memnon to take care of and to marry Barsine, if she would have him.

"Memnon? Memnon! Did you hear what I asked?" spat Arsites, who was obviously annoyed at having to ask twice. "Were you off dreaming of your Barsine, again," he jibed, "or are you plotting once more to betray the empire, as your brother did not so many years ago?"

Those remarks drew a laughter from the other governors and generals, especially Spithridates, the satrap of Sparda, the domain that included Caria, Ionia, Lydia and Lycia, and in whose palace in Sardis they had been supposed to meet – until Arsites ordered a change of venue. "Could you blame him, Arsites? We have all seen the lovely Barsine. She is a rare beauty, and is fit not only for a royal bed but a royal throne..."

"...and as such is wasted on this Rhodian Greek soldier of fortune," snarled Arsames, who had come the farthest, from distant Tarsus, capital of his satrapy of Cilicia, to attend the war council. It was not that Arsames had any reason to be jealous of Memnon because of Barsine, for his own wife was also famed for the beauty of her face and figure, as well as for her political acumen and influential ties to the imperial court. Arsames looked down upon all Greeks as inferiors, and, as such, unworthy of marrying a woman of pure Persian blood like Barsine.

The trio of satraps, three of the most powerful men in the Persian empire, were not the only ones present with Memnon at this council of war. Several of the lesser nobility hovered about, as well as two men who avoided the gaze of their betters and stood in the shadows in the corner. Each represented their masters, the officials known respectively as the Eye of the King and the Ear of the King. Expert gatherers of intelligence who fed information to the palace and ferreted out disloyalty, they said nothing, were asked nothing, but were denied nothing. A whisper from either of them could ruin a career – or end a life, even that of a satrap, let alone a hired general. Memnon shuddered at the very thought of them, for while he knew he was loyal to Darius, the new King of Kings, he also knew that he would always be suspect because of his brother's rebellious past.

Spithradates, a blood relative of the Great King, Memnon knew, was especially wary of giving him command of a large army. Besides, Spithradates, just like the other two, wanted the credit for vanquishing Alexander once the young Macedonian landed. Each of the three satraps, and each of the lesser nobles, boasted of how they would seek out Alexander for personal combat. Each described in great if fanciful detail how they would be the one to cut off the boy king's head, which they would then present to the Great King on a silver platter.

Memnon had no such delusions. He had no time for them. There was simply too much else to do and to worry about, if Alexander was to be stopped, let alone sent packing back across the straits.

"We should gather the Persian fleet, my lords, and blockade the Hellespont," suggested Memnon. "We have twice the number of ships they do, and we are united in command and in our cause. The Macedonian fleet itself is small, and is augmented by squadrons from many other cities. Most of those cities hate and distrust each other and all resent being bullied into taking orders from a Macedonian admiral. We close the Hellespont and this war is over before it begins. Alexander won't be able to cross into Asia, and we can mop up the advance guard up at Abydos at leisure."

Arsames barely let Memnon finish speaking before making known his opposition to that plan. "Do you know what it costs to put even a single trireme or quadrireme into the water, or keep it on station for a month or two or three?" he asked in a way that ensured all knew his question was put rhetorically. "Why incur such an expense to prevent a Greek landing? That won't end this war. It would just mean spending hundreds of talents to keep a fleet in the water, and for months or even years. No, let him come across. Let Alexander and his whole army come over to our shores. It will be like letting a herd of sheep march themselves into the butcher's yard."

All of the other Persians in the room, except for the two in the shadows, shouted their support for Arsames and seconded his view.

"Yes, let him come. We shall teach this Macedonian boy what war is all about," boasted Spithradates.

"That boy already knows more of war than you do, Spithradates, or any of you," objected Memnon. "He has spent his whole life learning about, training for and preparing for war – for this war. He was still but a boy on the day he won victory for Philip at Chaeronea, and did it leading from the front. He beat tribe after tribe in the north, then marched south and took Thebes when it revolted. He razed it to the ground and cowed the rest of Greece into submission. Alexander knows about war, and has no need of being schooled in it by amateurs like you."

"You sound like you are afraid of this beardless boy, Memnon," chided Arsites. "Don't tell me that the 'great' Memnon who beat Philip's best general only a year ago is quaking in his boots because he must face this beardless boy? Don't worry," Arsites continued, smiling an oily smile and raising a hand to stop Memnon from replying, "we will take care of him. Be grateful we are letting you come along to watch."

The satraps and nobles then competed with each other in boasting of how brave and strong they were, of who could bring the greater and better forces to the field, and of how short and easy would this campaign be. Memnon steamed and simmered for as long as he could bear it, then blurted out "stop this blabbering! This is a council of war, not a drinking party. Prance and primp and pride yourselves all you like when back home in your lavish palaces, but..."

"But I am home, and this is my 'lavish palace,'" interrupted Arsites rather snootily. "And I and my guests are free to speak as they wish, especially when it is the truth."

"But it is not the truth – only fantasy," objected Memnon. "None of you have fought or even seen a Macedonian phalanx. It is a walking fortress – and one with sharp teeth and claws that reach out twice the length of your longest lance...."

"So?" said Arsites. "They are still only infantry, and peasant infantry at that. We shall ride rings around them with our cavalry. Our arrows, javelins and darts will decimate them from well outside the reach of those pikes, and then when they are weakened, we shall charge with our armored horse into their midst, split them apart and cut them down."

"You forgot, my brave Arsites, that the Macedonians have cavalry – and fine cavalry at that. The Companions, the Thessalian lancers, the Thracian..."

"Pshaw!" said Arsames. "One Persian noble is worth three Macedonians, and we have twice, even three times their numbers of horse. What can they field, maybe four or five thousand mounted men – and half of them on those shaggy little mountain ponies? I have 2,000 cavalry of my own with me – each mounted on a mighty charger raised from the finest horse stock in the world! Spithradates," asked Arsames as he turned to his comrade, "how many horse can you field?"

"As many as you, Arsames. My Hyrcanians are the finest horsemen in the empire."

"And I can bring as many as both of you combined," boasted Arsites, not to be outdone. "A thousand Phrygian horse and thrice that many from Paphlagonia."

"Do not forget my cataphrachts!" chimed in Rhoesaces, Spithradates' brother, a lord of vast estates of his own. "I need but stamp my foot and up will rise a thousand fully armored men, each mounted on an equally armored horse."

"And don't forget about my Cappadocians!" shouted another noble.

"Or my Bactrians!" added yet another. The chorus of competition ended in a heady cheer as the satraps and nobles assured themselves of a short war and its certain and glorious outcome. Only three men in the room kept a sober countenance. Memnon was one; the secretive men in the corner were the other two.

"Now, you see, Memnon," chided Arsites. "There is nothing to worry about. And you have, what, about five hundred of your Greeks on horseback? They can come along for the ride – if they can stay on their horses, that is. I am sure we will find a place in the line of battle for them, on the far left, of course - if they are up for it?"

"Lords," sighed Memnon. "If you won't stop Alexander from landing, and if you want to use your cavalry, then use it properly. Use them to get around and behind the Macedonians. Cut their supply lines. Raid their camps. Burn everything in their path. Make a dessert out of the areas where they invade. Starve them, harry them, lure them deep into a dead country - and then bring them to battle when they are weakened and most desperate."

"What!" Arsites shouted, rising so quickly from his chair as to knock it over, its cushions falling about the floor. "Burn my own lands?

These are MY lands, Memnon. You want to burn farms, burn your own – oh, I forgot, yours are well to the south, down by Miletos. Well, the Macedonians won't get anywhere near them, but if you are so keen to see smoke and fire, go burn those. Unlike you, I'd rather fight to defend my land than burn it!"

Only the quick intervention of Spithradates prevented Memnon and Arsites from coming to blows, although others goaded the northern satrap to do just that.

"I think we are done here, gentlemen," said Spithradates. "We are agreed. We will marshal our cavalry and march north. Arsites, I presume you will call up the local levies as well? Not that we will need them, of course...and, oh, Memnon, do bring along your Greek infantry. Those indolent mercenaries of yours might be of some use – perhaps they can guard the camp and the baggage train?" he said half-joking, half-insulting. "By the way, just where are your vaunted Greek infantry lazing about these days?"

19

The Meander River

ON THE ROAD TO SARDIS

"You mean we have to *walk* all the way to Sardis...and maybe to the Hellespont? Damn it, Dimitrios, I'm a physician, not an Olympic runner!"

"I said *march*, not just walk, and definitely not run, brother," Dimitrios replied with a laugh. "Besides, Ari has found a wagon to carry my gear, and anything else that needs carrying. We wouldn't get far loaded down with armor, helmets, spears, swords and shields now, would we? I am sure you can hitch a ride with him."

Klemes chuffed and, a bit embarrassed, mumbled an "Oh. Well, thank you," which made his brother Dimitrios laugh even more. "After all, as a captain of one hundred, I merit a wagon or at least a cart of my own, and a small staff."

"So, that is what I am reduced to, is it," said the physician haughtily, raising himself to his full height in an effort to be able to look down upon his brother. "Mere 'staff?'"

"No, brother dear, not at all," said Dimitrios reassuringly. "Every company commander has been given a stipend over and above his pay to hire what we call 'extra-ordinaries.' Some of the captains pocket the money or use it to hire on a private whore for the duration, but most of us know better. Investing in a physician, a cook, and an aide to help with the paperwork saves a lot in the long run. So, you, of course, are the physician – and not just for me, but for the company as well..."

"Surely Ari isn't going to be the cook, is he? Man can't boil an egg let alone..."

"No, Klemes. I would not inflict that on either of us. There are plenty of women who will be following along behind us, along with sutlers, farriers, bakers, blacksmiths and peddlers of all sorts. We will have no shortage of opportunities to hire what we need as we need it...or of propositions to decline...or accept," he added with a wink.

"Such a child you still are, Dimitrios," Klemes commented with a brotherly scowl. "You act like you are going off on a jaunt for some fun, rather than marching to war. Bah!"

"No, I'm not," replied Dimitrios quite seriously. "I know what is at stake, and what is coming – more than you do, Klemes. Trust me, I am not taking any of this lightly. It is not some lark in the park we are about, but it is also not a funeral parade..."

"Well it is, for some of us..."

"Yes, sadly, it is. But, hopefully, not for you or me or Ari. So let yourself smile a bit, okay, brother. You do remember how to smile, don't you? You just lift the ends of your mouth up like this..." he added as he used his fingers to force Klemes face into something akin to a smile.

"If you say so, Dimitrios. But tell me once again, how is it that you were chosen to be a captain?"

"Pure luck, Klemes – or perhaps fate. I was standing in one of the lines to sign up when Ephialtes himself came strutting along, looking over the shoulders of his clerks to see how they were coming along, and damn it if he didn't recognize my shield."

"Why were you carrying your shield in line, brother?" asked the doctor.

"Because it has the symbol of our city – the club of Heracles – emblazoned on it. I thought if there were any of our other fellow Thebans about they might see it and come over..."

"And did they?" Klemes asked quite somberly.

"No," replied Dimitrios quietly. "If there are any of our people about, either they did not see my shield or just ignored it."

"But Ephialtes didn't ignore it, did he?"

"No, brother. He didn't. The general came over and asked me if I was truly from Thebes or if I had just found or stolen the shield. That's when he invited me to his tent."

Dimitrios then related what had happened in his meeting with Ephialtes, the man responsible for raising the mercenary corps at Miletos.

"Were you in Thebes when Alexander attacked it," Ephialtes asked Dimitrios.

"Yes. I led my company of hoplites against him, just as I had two years before that."

"So that means you were at Chaeronea?" Ephialtes asked.

"Aye"

"I was there, too. With the Athenian contingent. Sad, brutal, bloody day. So, let me guess, you came here to get even with Alexander?"

"Something like that, general."

"So two thumpings by the Macedonian imp weren't enough for you? You looking for a third?"

"No, general. This time I want to do the thumping. Me and my brother, and my friend."

"Oh, so there are three of you then," smiled Ephialtes. "I've heard the tale of seven against Thebes, but so, what, now we've got 'three for Thebes' is it?"

"I wish there were seven of us, or seven hundred, general," replied Dimitrios. "And of the three of us, I am the only one capable of bearing arms. My friend still limps and suffers from a wound he got fighting the Macedonians outside the city, and my brother, well, he is a physician, and took some sort of oath as he calls it to do no harm to others or something like that."

"Well, I can use all the good men I can get," nodded the general. "And if you look around," he said, gesturing with his hand to the mob of soldiers lining up to make their mark with the clerks, "there don't seem to be a lot of 'good' men around. I could use someone who could mold at least some of them into something resembling a fighting unit. You say you were a captain of Thebes? Well, now you are a captain of Persia – or at least of Memnon's mercenaries. Pays four times what the common soldiers get, plus a bit on the side."

"Thank you, general, I won't let you down!" Dimitrios replied enthusiastically and with gratitude.

"See that you don't, Theban. See that you don't."

"Four times what a common soldier makes, eh?" said Ari as he approached his brother and the physician. "And just what does a common soldier make in this army, anyway?"

"About five obols a day, or whatever that is in Persian coin. And out of that you have to buy food and drink and whatever else you need, for the empire doesn't provide rations for free. Although at least there is a supply train, with wagons full of grain and olives and salted fish, so if there isn't a local town to sell food, we can buy it from the wagon train."

"I guess I can get by on five obols a day, after all, I didn't come here to get rich," chimed in Klemes.

"Yes, well, Klemes," said Dimitrios, looking down at his feet and shuffling about in the dirt, "you aren't going to get five obols a day. You're not a soldier, so you don't work for Ephialtes or for Memnon, or the empire."

"Then who do I work for," the physician shot back. "Please don't tell me that..."

"Yes, brother," smiled Dimitrios. "You work for me."

20

The Hellespont

ALEXANDER'S CAMP AT SESTOS

W hile Persian satraps, nobles and generals conferred on how and where to fight Alexander when he came across into Asia, the young Macedonian king was already preparing to do just that.

Alexander had spent the winter in Macedonia, holding feasts, hosting games, making sacrifices and, of course, marshalling his forces. He had amassed over 30,000 infantry and 5,000 cavalry for the invasion of Asia. His trusted, veteran Macedonians, Thessalians and Thracians, however, accounted for fewer than half their number. About a third were made up of assorted barbarian and other mercenary forces. While not all of the Greeks who made up the remainder were as enthusiastic for the crossing as either the Macedonians or the mercenaries, there was little overt dissension in the ranks. What grumblings there were of being dragged north from their cities, Alexander calmed with promises of loot and glory – especially the later, although it was playing to their lust for the former that proved the more effective means of maintaining morale.

Olympias had tried but failed to convince her son to allow her to accompany him into Asia, for despite the power she held over him and had infused into him on his deathbed in Illyria, the young king was still very much his own man – and his earthly father's son. Rebuffed by her son in that direction, she used her wiles to suggest that she, as queen, rule over Macedonia and its Greek conquests in his stead. While Alexander proved less able at refusing her this request than the former, his generals were stronger at resisting her charms, spells, promises, bribes – and threats. No one general could ever hope to stand up against Olympias, but united they were able to weather the storm of her rage and to convince Alexander to leave one of their number in charge.

A military man, they argued, would be better able than any woman, let alone Olympias whose grasp of martial affairs was so far from the practical that it bordered on the fantastical, to put down any insurrections, such as had occurred in Thebes. Although Alexander was loath to part with any of his father's veteran commanders, he settled on General Antipatros to guard his base in Greece and Macedonia. For that purpose he raised a second army of 12,000 infantry and 1,500 loyal cavalry to ensure that his orders would be obeyed – and that Athens, and his mother, would be held in check.

From Macedon Alexander marched his army east across the mouth of the River Strymon, and after three weeks on the road he entered the camp at Sestos, on the European side of the Hellespont across from Parmenion's stronghold at Abydos. The crossing of the main army he entrusted to Parmenion and to Admiral Nearchos, who had mustered eight-score warships and innumerable merchant vessels to carry them across the straits. Too impatient to sit and watch, let alone deal with the petty details of moving over 35,000 men from one shore to the other, Alexander directed his sailing master, Menoetios, to prepare the royal trireme for a separate journey. Menoetios would take him across the straits and down the coast a bit to make landfall not with the army, but on a beach beneath the ruins of ancient Troy.

"Why don't we just go over with the rest of the army," Alexander's beloved friend and companion Hephaestion asked. "That is our proper station."

"Nonsense, Hephaestion," replied Alexander, giddy with excitement. "Old Parmenion can handle that. He is good with the details, and what's more, he likes that sort of thing. Like when he moves blocks or toy soldiers around a map when he talks strategy. The crossing will be just like that – only with real men and real ships. Leave him to it. We have more important business to attend to, you and I."

"What could possibly be more important than invading Asia?" asked Hephaestion incredulously.

"Troy," replied Alexander rather matter of factly.

"Troy? Troy?" Hephaestion queried. "There's nothing there but ruins. You of all people should know that, you read that damned book every night, over and over and over..."

"Precisely. And that is why it is so important that we go there, to the tomb of Achilles, the hero of that war. We're related, you know..."

"Alexander," sighed Hephaestion. "You know that is just something your mother made up, right? There is absolutely no way anyone can be certain that they are descended from somebody who lived what, 800 years ago, if he lived at all. Homer could have just..."

"What? Made him up?" responded Alexander with genuine shock and disbelief in his voice – and in his eyes, which had gone wild with the talk of Troy and Achilles and Homer. "The Trojan War was real, everyone knows that, and so was Achilles. Everybody knows that, too. And that hero's blood runs in my veins. I am Achilles reborn – and you are my Patroclos!"

"Hmmm, Alexander, you know that neither of them came through that story alive, don't you? And that Achille's friend Patroclos died first..."

"Yes, Hephaestion! And he gave him such a funeral, with a great pyre, and games and..."

"Well if it's all the same to you, Alexander, couldn't we be somebody else from the story. You know, like somebody that survived the war and came home to tell about it? That Odysseus fellow, well, he was pretty heroic, and noble, and smart, coming up with the wooden horse and all that and..."

"And then he died of old age," said Alexander rather sourly. "Is that what you want for us? No, my friend, we are like Achilles and Patroclos. Our lives will be like theirs; stars that burn briefly and brightly and then fall into the sea, remembered forever for their great deeds, forever young..."

"He do go on a bit, don't he," the sailing master remarked under his breath to Hephaestion. "You know there is no nay saying him, not when he gets his blood up like that. It's all her doing, but you knows that. You knows that better than most I suspects."

"But I don't really want to die young, even if it means I do get a nice funeral," Hephaestion replied, speaking low so Alexander wouldn't hear. Not that the young king was listening anyway, as he was off in a world of his own, spouting verses from Homer. "After all," mumbled on Hephaestion, "what good is somebody holding a celebration in your honor if you can't come?"

Alexander, of course, got his way – as he always had his entire life, and especially now that he was king. Menoetios watched as the king and his friend and some of their Companions built a small stone altar on the European shore, then as instructed set a course across for the Troad. Alexander did not wait for the ship to reach the shore. As they came close to making a landing, the king hurled a javelin off the bow and then leapt overboard into the surf. All the way to the beach he kept shouting something about Achilles, and how he would take the hero's sacred armor from its resting place and wear it as his own. And then there was something about claiming Asia with his spear, but Menoetios could not make out most of the words, as they were drowned out by the crashing of the waves onto the shore. Hephaestion shrugged his shoulders, pulled up the ends of his cloak and dutifully followed. After all, what else could he do?

"Can't very well let Achilles go off on his own, now, can I?" he said as he got off the ship. "What kind of Patroclos would I be if I did?"

21

The River Granicos

EPHIALTES' COMMAND TENT

Being once again among a fellowship of hoplites, Dimitrios felt almost at home, or at least more at home than he had been at any time since, well, he had been home. That home, of course, was no more, and if he was to ever return to Thebes and rebuild it, then the man who had torn it down would have to be defeated, humiliated and, if the gods allowed, killed. Dimitrios prayed every night that the gods would grant him that pleasure, or to at least allow him to be there when Alexander was brought down. With a company of 100 trained, disciplined soldiers to command, Dimitrios believed that if his prayers had not yet been answered, at least they had been heard. All the more so when Ephialtes asked for a volunteer to lead a scouting mission across the river.

"The Persian scouts have told us where the Macedonians are encamped, and how many of them there are. What they have not been able to confirm is whether Alexander himself is with the army. They could not get close enough to see if the young king is there yet. Furthermore, their reports as to the lay of the land between us and the Macedonians are a bit lacking. Perhaps that is because they rode around the enemy camp, and saw things only from the perspective of men on horseback. You, Dimitrios, are a foot soldier like me. I want you to scout out the terrain from a foot soldier's perspective. I need to know where my phalanxes can maneuver and where they cannot. Oh, and one thing more..."

"Yes, General?"

"I want you to go where no Persian, let alone a Persian on a horse can go. I want you to go into that camp, mingle with our fellow Greeks and find out everything you can about them. Will they truly fight for a king who oppresses their cities? How dependable and how loyal are they, really?"

Dimitrios hesitated a moment to let the general's words truly sink in. Then he drew himself up as straight as a spear, nodded his head slightly and offered a formal salute as he replied "You can count on me, General. When do you want me to go?"

"Around dusk, Captain. So you will have enough light to find your way out of our camp and to the outskirts of theirs. Once it is dark, you can find a way to get among them, but I want you back here in the morning, a little after dawn. That way you will have enough light to see the river from their side as well as ours."

"Yes, sir. Anything else?"

"Yes. Don't get yourself killed. You are to be my eyes and ears tonight, not my sword arm. You will get a chance to be that soon enough."

"We're going to go where and do what!" exclaimed Ari. "Does your brother know about this?"

"First of all, Ari, this is not a 'we' but a 'me' – well at least me and a couple of the other men in the company. You and Klemes are to stay here, and that's an order."

"And do what, primp and paint ourselves like some damn Persian noble?" said Klemes as he entered the tent he shared with his brother and Ari. "Or shall I grab a jar of olive oil and a cloth and oil up your shield, so the blazon shines? We came this far together, and what, at the first sign of any real trouble you think we're going to let you face it alone?" he said, adding a dismissive and intentionally unpleasant sound that was something less than a laugh yet more than a curse.

"Klemes, my brother. This is reconnaissance mission. A purely military matter, not a medical one. I don't need to put you at risk."

Klemes glowered at his brother, giving him a look that was both a sign of disagreement and disapproval. "We've all been at risk since that day Alexander came to Thebes, so don't give me that nonsense. Besides, if you are going to sneak into a camp and try to get soldiers to talk, what makes you think they will talk to some soldier they don't know. Now, a physician, well, everybody talks to a physician. Everybody has something they think is wrong with them. A blister to pop, a boil to lance...you know soldiers. Now you, of course, they would be immediately suspicious of, asking questions about this and that. But me, well, I'm just a simple medical man, a kindly old physician trying to make a few coins plying my trade, so why would I be interested in the bigger picture?"

"And me, Dimitrios, I can be very helpful as well," chimed in Ari. "With my limp everyone will know I am not a soldier, so I can just wander about like a servant. Give me a couple of jugs of water and wine and I can go just about anywhere and no one will notice me, or think twice about me even if they do."

"But...but..."

"No 'buts' about it Dimitrios," said Klemes sternly. "It is settled. We are going with you and that is that."

As the sun began to set, Dimitrios, Klemes, Ari and four hoplites from their company set out from their camp behind the long hill on the eastern side of the Granicos River. None wore armor, carried shield or spear, or were otherwise encumbered. Each carried a short sword or small knife, some bread and cheese and a few olives, and not much else. The four common soldiers were there primarily for support, and to set up a position where Ari, Klemes and Dimitrios could fall back to once their mission inside the camp was complete. At worst, they would be a rear guard to buy the others time to get back to the Persian side of the river, should there be any trouble.

As they passed the Persian lines, the men struggled to scramble down the bank of the river. The bank on their side, although only about neck-high, was fairly steep, and had they been in full battle kit would have presented a formidable obstacle to go down, let alone climb up. Dimitrios made note of that in his head, as he did also of the lay of the river itself. While not deep enough to do more than slow down a horse, in most places it was thigh or waist high to a man on foot. The river bottom, moreover, was sandy and littered with stones, which made for difficult footing.

"I know this is not much of a river – I've fished in streams bigger than this" jibbed one of the four soldiers. "Still, though, I wouldn't want to try to keep formation marching through this and up that bank, let alone if someone was waiting for me on the other side with a forest of spears,"

Dimitrios nodded in agreement. This was the kind of thing the Persian cavalry scouts had missed as they casually splashed through it on horseback. It was the kind of information that battle plans are made of, and just the sort of small detail that Ephialtes would appreciate.

The seven men – a lucky number for a Theban, as Dimitrios intended when he decided on the size of the scouting party – reached the western bank with less difficulty, as it was lower and less difficult to climb than that on the Persian side. Again, thought Dimitrios, this would put the Macedonians at yet another disadvantage if they did come across the river. The Persians would have the higher ground.

As darkness fell, the seven found themselves guided to the Macedonian line by its campfires. The picket lines, however, had not quite yet been set. Leaving his four soldiers behind a low rise just outside the lines, Dimitrios, Ari and Klemes scattered and fell in with some of the foraging parties who were returning to the camp with wood, water and whatever else of use they had scrounged from the nearby farms and countryside. Few of the men in those parties paid any notice, weary and burdened as they were. Most were thinking about what they would eat for dinner and how long before they could tuck in under a blanket or cloak for the night.

For many of those men, however, there would be little rest. Dimitrios right away recognized the signs of a camp on the eve of battle. The Macedonians and their allies were furiously at work sharpening the blades of their pikes, long spears, swords and javelins. Others were repairing and oiling up the leather straps for their shields and other gear. Officers and file leaders were busy inspecting their progress and offering encouraging words – and issuing threats they hoped they would never have to make good upon to those who might be slack in their duties or show a lack of courage in the coming fight.

After moving about for an hour or so, Dimitrios was certain he had learned what he had been sent to find out. It was time to go, time to get his information back to the general, who would have precious few hours as it was to make their own army ready. Dimitrios looked around for Klemes and Ari. Surely they, too, would realize that they would have far less time to mingle, to listen to complaints or otherwise discern the mood of the troops, than Ephialtes had thought they might have. The answers to his questions were obvious.

Alexander, moreover, must surely be here, for why else would the camp be in such a state of readiness? Parmenion would not attack on his own, not after having had his wrist slapped last week by the Persian cavalry, which had chased the Macedonian's advanced guard back almost into their own tents. That was at another river, one of the many annoying watercourses the Macedonians had to ford on their march from their landing beaches inland. The Granicos, however, would be even more difficult to pass, thought Dimitrios, especially with an entire army defending the far bank.

But coming forward they would be, and a lot sooner than Ephialtes thought. The general needed to know for certain if the Macedonians would be coming in the morning, and from what he saw after only a few minutes, it was more than apparent that this army was not only going to fight for Alexander, but was actually eager to do so. Just from picking up bits of conversations here and there as he walked about the outskirts of the camp, he could gauge the mood and the morale of the soldiers, Greek, Macedonian and others. Their mood was almost festive, as they boasted a little of the glory they would win, and a lot about the riches they would loot in what they believed would be an easy victory.

"The Persians not only dress and paint their faces like women," he heard one soldier joke, "but they fight like them, too. Scuttling about on their pretty ponies, plinking their little toy bows to shoot arrows at us rather than stand and fight like men, in a shield wall."

"Those Persian nobles bring their harems to war!" another laughed. "Think of all of those women, and of all of the silks and jewels and gold in their tents! We'll go back home rich as satraps and with harems of our own!"

This, thought Dimitrios, is an army drunk not on wine but on a headier brew – greed. So certain were they of victory that they were already counting the treasures they would scoop up. Alexander and his officers had done their work well. Even if they might have their doubts about winning, they had made certain that their soldiers had no fear of defeat, only of not getting their fair share of the booty there would be to grab.

Dimitrios spied Klemes at a nearby campfire, administering to the blisters of one rather large soldier whom, by his look, appeared to be from Boetia, not far from his own native Thebes. Klemes saw him as well, and acknowledged his brother's signal that they should make their way back to their meeting point. All he needed to do now was to find Ari...whom he saw kneeling on the ground with some others, rolling dice out of a cup onto a cloak they had spread out on the ground. Ari, it seemed, was not only gambling, but winning. That, Dimitrios knew instinctively, was going to be a problem.

"Put up your money, me lads, or make room for those who can!" shouted Ari as he picked up the cup and shook the dice with glee. "Last man to plunk down a coin is a Spartan!" he joked, which got a big laugh for, as everyone knew, there were no Spartans in this army. They had stayed home, pleading that old excuse about religious festivals and ephors and oracles and all that. Not that they were the great warriors they had boasted of old; Thebes and its General Epaminondas has put the lid to that old legend in their grandfathers' time.

"Read 'em and weep, men," chortled Ari, as he gathered up his winnings yet again. "Read 'em and weep."

Even before he reached the scene Dimitrios knew what was about to happen. One of the gamblers all but jumped to his feet, fists clenched and uttered the demand that every loser at dice since the days when savages first threw the knucklebones of dead animals and enemies across the dirt floor of a cave had uttered before:

"Let me see them dice!"

Ari, never known for having the coolest of heads, responded just as predictably. Rising from his knees, he socked the big man in the gut, and from there things went really bad. Dimitrios knew there was no time to calm things down, especially as the rapidly escalating altercation had attracted the attention of a pair of what, from their dress, were obviously officers. Even if he could quiet things down, there were surely questions that would be asked and answers that would be demanded. None of that would work out well for him or Ari, even if they had the time to try. So, Dimitrios did what had to be done. He hurled himself into the fray, bowled over a couple of the gamblers, one of whom fell into the fire with a loud scream, and grabbed Ari by the scruff of his tunic.

"The money!" he screamed at Ari. "Throw it up into the air!"

"What!" said Ari in surprise. "Are you crazy? There's a small fortune here, and I won it fair and square!"

"Not with those dice, you didn't, Ari," replied Dimitrios. "I told you a long time ago to get rid of those!"

Ari smiled a bit sheepishly, and then did as his friend had asked – he threw his winnings up into the air with both hands, and shouted "here you go, men! I've gotta be going!"

After which he and Dimitrios turned about and headed for the picket lines at as best a run Ari could manage. Klemes saw them take off and followed, albeit at a bit more leisurely of a pace. "Well, well," he said to himself. "I must be a better physician than I thought. Ari moves pretty damn fast for a man with a bad leg."

But not quite fast enough, Klemes realized, as a gang of angry soldiers tumbled into Ari and Dimitrios. Fortunately, many of the soldiers were not exactly sure who was angry at whom, only that there was money on the ground to grab and a brawl to join. As the officers Dimitrios had spied earlier motioned for some armed guards to come with them to break up the rapidly expanding fight, Klemes looked around for some way to create a distraction, anything that would force the officers to respond to something more dangerous than a soldiers' free-for-all.

He was not alone in that thought, as the four men Dimitrios had left outside the camp took it upon their own initiative to do just that. Each had made their way into the camp and, while so many others were drawn inward to the tussling gamblers and scattered coins, each had picked up a burning brand from a fire and had tossed it into a pile of dry fodder, an empty tent or, in one case, a cart packed with jars of oil – which went up very nicely and very quickly. The four then began running about the camp, pretending panic, and crying the alarm.

With their tents, carts and supplies ablaze, the battling soldiers quickly forgot about the fight and what or who started it, and scurried back to save what they could from the flames. One man, however, the big fellow Ari had punched in the stomach, was too enraged and too focused on the man he thought had cheated him at dice to care about the fire. Dimitrios tried to pull him off of Ari, but the man was as big as a bull – and just as strong, and just as fierce. He threw Dimitrios off as if he were naught but a cat that had landed on his shoulders, and delivered a blow to Ari's head that nearly separated it from his neck. Bellowing and howling like a mad animal, the angry gambler was so fixated on his two opponents that he did not see Klemes come up behind him – or the log the physician swung to smash into his skull.

"Come on, you two, get up. We're leaving this party and fast!" yelled Klemes, not that he needed to, for Dimitrios and Ari were already stumbling away from the flaming camp and heading for the safety of the darkness. While almost every other soldier in the camp was now concerned with the fire, there were guards on the picket line who were disciplined enough to stay at their post. They saw Klemes, Dimitrios and Ari running away from the fire while everyone else ran towards it. Backlit by the flames, they were easily noticeable to the guards, two of whom leveled their spears and moved toward the fleeing Greeks.

What they did not see or even think to look for were four other men who came at the guards from the dark – four men with knives and short swords. An unequal contest though it was against men in armor, Dimitrios' four soldiers hurled themselves at the guards, doing their duty as their captain had feared they might be need to do. The guards went down, but not without a fight – and shouts that alerted others on guard that intruders had been in the camp, and were escaping.

A chase ensued that was part flight, part running fight, as pairs of soldiers left the picket line to run after Dimitrios and his party, none of which, to their credit, were willing to leave the slowest member of the group behind. Even with Ari's limp, however, the scouting party was able to gain ground on the guards, who, weighed down with armor, helmet, shield and weapons, soon began to tire, especially after a few tumbles and missteps in the dark.

Battered, bruised, and bearing cuts and other light wounds, the seven Greeks eventually outdistanced their pursuers and reached the Granicos. Allowing themselves only a moment to dive in, Dimitrios and his men waded as quickly as they could bring themselves through the river, all the while calling out for help to the Persian guards who patrolled on their bank. Three or four of the Macedonian camp guards reached the river just as Dimitrios and his men were crossing, but a few flights of arrows from the Persian horse archers sent them scurrying back into the protection of the darkness, their way home guided by the blazing Macedonian camp.

22

The River Granicos

MEMNON'S COMMAND TENT

“I don't like it, Memnon. I don't like it one bit.”

“I don't much care for this battle plan either, Ephialtes,” sighed Memnon, “especially not after what your scouts reported. By the way, that young officer...”

“Dimitrios, a Theban,” Ephialtes answered the question his commander was about to ask. “Good man.”

“Yes, indeed. If we ever get out of this battle alive, have him report to me. We are going to need good officers – good, solid, Greek officers, if we are to have any hope of defeating this spoiled Macedonian kinglet.”

“Then you really don't have any faith in this battle plan, do you, Memnon?”

“No, but, like you, I have to obey orders. And it is not so much that it is a bad plan...”

“Yes, it is, and you know it, Memnon. That river out there is not very wide or very deep, and while it is a bastard to cross, it can and will be crossed. My men – our men – should be there at the top of the bank when the Macedonians try to claw their way up it. Those massive phalanxes of theirs will be nothing more than disorganized mobs. Imagine trying to stay upright on those slippery rocks and shifting, wet sands while holding heavy, 12 to 18 foot pikes! Keep them in the river and they're at our mercy. Just think of it. A solid line of shields and spears at the top of the bank, while the Persian archers on horseback behind us darken the sky with arrows. It will be a massacre – and payback for every defeat, every insult, Philip and his brat ever inflicted on us."

"Yes, Ephialtes, that is how we should deploy, but our masters have other ideas. They want to line the banks with their cavalry, so they can fire directly into the Macedonians as they cross."

"All right, I can see some wisdom in that," mumbled Ephialtes. "Then once the Macedonians get close, the Persians will ride off to the sides, like curtains being pulled, to reveal my hoplites. We take a few steps forward and there we are, as I recommended. That could work."

"Yes," said Memnon, "it could. That is how it should happen, and I have put that idea forward...but that is not how it is going to happen."

"Why not?" exclaimed Ephialtes.

"Because while the light horse on the far ends of this two-mile-long line will do that, the nobles and their retainers who will be in the center will not. They won't retire – they think that would be cowardly. No, they will fire and fire away with their bows until their quivers are empty, and then they will hurl their javelins when the Macedonians get closer. Then they will draw their swords, their axes and their maces, and scream their own names to tell the gods and the Macedonians who it is who will come to kill them."

Ephialtes stared at Memnon, his mouth open in disbelief, his shoulders hunched and his hands balled into fists as they rested on the map. "That is ridiculous. That is insane. Cavalry, standing still on a river bank against infantry? Cavalry are supposed to charge across open ground, not hold the line. Worse, they'll only get in the way of my hoplites."

"No, they won't," said Memnon shaking his head. "You see, your hoplites won't be there."

"What? Then where exactly will they be?" grimaced Ephialtes.

"Back, way back, up on that hill there. Between the river and the camp."

"And just what in Hades are we supposed to do there? Sit and watch?"

"Yes, Ephialtes. Watch. Watch the nobles gain glory and honor. They believe they can do it all on their own, and do not wish to share the credit -or the presumed rewards- with...us."

"Memnon..."

"Do not say it. I know what you are thinking. I tried to object. I tried to pull rank, even to waving the staff of command that came directly from the hand of Darius to me. Well, maybe not directly, but at least by his orders. But Darius is far, far away, out to the east, quelling some tribal uprisings or some other nonsense. Despite my warnings he thinks of the Macedonians as if they were just another barbarian incursion on the fringes of the empire. He has even less regard for any Greek, enemy or ally, subject or mercenary. The satraps share that, it seems. Arsites says we are 'a little people, a petulant people, who squabble among ourselves like spoiled children.' How do I enforce my will upon such men as those?"

Ephialtes laughed. Not a hearty, happy laugh, but one that showed his disdain and disgust.

"Do they not recall Salamis, or Marathon, or Plateai or Thermopylae? Do they not remember when our forefathers sent them packing, with their tails between their legs?"

"No, Ephialtes, they are familiar with those battles, but they have, how can I put it," Memnon paused, trying to find a diplomatic way of saying what was on his mind, "re-interpreted those events."

"Re-interpreted? How do you re-interpret a defeat, let alone a series of defeats? Have they learned nothing?"

Memnon grinned at his old friend, moved to the side of the tent to take up a cup and pour himself some watered-down wine from a beaker. He offered to do the same for Ephialtes, but the white-haired veteran demurred. Memnon nodded, took a long swallow from the cup, wiped his mouth with his sleeve and shook his head.

"At the court of Darius such defeats are thought of differently. Thermopylae, as they see it, was a triumph. A victory in which an upstart king and his army was defeated, and after which they were able to capture, loot and burn Athens. The Athenians so feared them that did not even man the walls – although one small band did try to hold the Acropolis, of course..."

"Against orders, if you remember your history," interjected Ephialtes.

"Yes, true, but the court historians and the king's advisers are correct in both cases, at least technically. As for Salamis, they blame the foolhardiness, cowardice and even treachery of the captains of the Phoenician squadrons for that – and note, quite rightly, that the other half of the fleet did return safely to the ports in Asia Minor."

Ephialtes shook his head. "Return? You mean fled! And then Xerxes and the rest of the army ran for home as well. It was only because Themistocles didn't follow up his victory and sail to the Helle-spont to burn their bridges that they got away!"

"A decision he made, I believe, in order to ensure that Xerxes did leave – as he knew the great king must. After all, how long can the king of an empire that reaches the four corners of the world remain on the outermost fringes of that empire? Themistocles wanted Xerxes to go home – and to take his army with him. He knew the Greeks could never raise an army large enough to defeat Xerxes and his host of 100,000, but the garrison he knew the king would leave behind to hold those areas of Greece which had fallen to him, well, that was a force the Greeks could deal with..."

"And they did! At Plateai!" said Ephialtes proudly. "And that is something I will drink to!" he added, as he also went to the table to pour himself some wine.

"But that, dear friend, was 150 years ago, and the Persians like most men prefer to embellish their victories and play down their defeats. They also remember that after Plateai, as you know, we fell out among ourselves, as we always do. Spartans against Athenians, Thebans against Spartans, Corinthians against whomever they felt was insulting them that year...and each time, in each conflict, one or more of us would go to the Persians, looking for money or ships or..."

"Yes, yes, I know," grumbled Ephialtes. "That is exactly how I came to be here, as you know, and how your family, too, eventually came to serve the empire."

"When the Athenians dominated the seas, my family's fortunes in Rhodes fell, and we looked east. My brother, Mentor, and I won regard first as scouts and then as surveyors, mapping so much of Asia Minor for the old Great King, Artaxerxes. He was particularly fond of Mentor, so much so that he gave him a small army and sent him to make trouble for the rebels in Egypt. Damn if my brother didn't turn a raid into a victory. For that he warded with the hand of the beautiful Barsine, daughter of Artabazus, who was then satrap here."

"I did not know your brother well, but heard naught but good of him."

"Would that he were here today, Ephialtes. He was a far better general than I could ever be. He wouldn't have just given Parmenion a bloody nose at the Scamandros River – he would have thrown him all the way back into the Hellespont, and then swept across the water to snatch up Alexander to boot."

"It is well that you honor his memory in your heart, and that you took his widow into your household, Memnon. Both do credit to you."

"Ha!" laughed Memnon. "Marrying my brother's widow may be a custom among the Persians, but I deserve no praise for that. I loved her from the moment I saw her, and still do. Sometimes I feel guilty, though. She would not be mine if my brother were still alive..."

"Well, I say we are just as fortunate to have you as our commander, Memnon. If only you could get the Persians to understand what we are up against."

"I have tried but, you see, my old friend, because of the way the Persians remember history, the great king does not take a threat of invasion from Greece seriously. That is why he is happy to leave the matter to the local governors and his mercenary generals. And that is also why," Memnon sighed, "the satraps have no respect for you or me or those 7,000 hoplites you brought to fight for them. That is why they do not want you up in the front line. They think they do not need you. They feel you and your men are worthy only to guard the camp, and to keep the levy infantry from running away."

Memnon leaned over the camp table and toyed with the little wooden figurines that marked the position of each command for the coming fight. "Not that that rabble of farmers is good for anything anyway. But it cheers the satraps so to see the peasants where they can keep an eye on them – and where they can see their betters in action. All the better to remind their subjects what they would have to deal with should they even think to rise up. Besides, the nobles want you out of the way. They don't want to have to share their glory with a bunch of Greek hirelings."

"That is Arsites talking, not you" said Ephialtes, finally understanding that the battle would, indeed, most likely be lost. "Have you told them that what they are facing is something more than the Greek city state forces their fathers faced and dealt with? That this army is different from anything they have seen or had to fight? That the Macedonians are not just soldiers, but cogs in a giant, monstrous machine – a machine that eats up, grinds down and spits out entire armies, and which dines on cities for dinner?"

"Arsites did not want to hear about that. He knows what he knows and that is all that he wants to know. And it is not just him, but the other satraps and the lesser nobles..."

"You mean those who have never actually fought in a battle before. Surely the veteran commanders..."

"I would have thought they would have talked some sense into these firebrands," added Memnon with a deep sigh, "but you know how the nobles are. Once someone even hints at a suggestion that things might not go their way, he is derided as defeatist, or coward – or even a traitor. Nothing is as predictable as a Persian once he thinks he has been insulted, or that his honor or abilities are being questioned. No, their pride, it gets in the way."

"And as the playwrights tell us," said Ephialtes sadly, "pride will be their undoing. So, I am just supposed to watch from a hill while the Persians allow themselves to be slaughtered? Then what do I do when the Macedonians form up on the plain between my hill and the river?"

"Nothing, Ephialtes, nothing. Because you won't be there, old friend. You'll be long gone from this field."

Ephialtes, who in his youth had often been referred to as a giant of a man, both for his height and build as well as his strength and courage, began to turn red with anger.

"I am no coward to leave the field of battle and abandon my men. Nor am I some old woman who needs to be sent away, or is that how you now see me, you by whose side I have stood in many an..."

"No, no, Ephialtes, not that. No. On the contrary," said Memnon soothingly, and in as friendly and as calm a manner as he could muster. "I need you out of here so you can prepare for the next battle. Omares has been given command of all of the infantry – your men and the Persian levies. He knows the value of your men, even if the other Persian nobles won't let him make the best use of them. Let your second in command, Clearchos, take charge of the men. I will even send my nephew, Thymondas, and my own sons, Agathon and Xenocrates to help him and Omares hold the line. Perhaps they can convince some of the nobles to pull back once things start to go wrong. And go wrong, I fear, it will."

"All the more reason why we should be out there in front..."

"Yes, but at least with your men standing on this hill, maybe they can give the Persians who survive the first part of the battle something to fall back to. A place to get away to, to rally behind, and to fight another day. It is for that other day that I need your help. Go back to the coastal cities. Raise and train new troops. Put their defenses in order. If we lose here at the Granicos tomorrow, as I fear we will, we will at least have Sardis, Miletos and even Halicarnassos to fall back to. Those long pikes of the Macedonians may be hell on a battlefield, but they will be of no use against the stone walls of those cities. Cities you must turn into fortresses, impregnable fortresses. We will wear him out before their walls, and force him to expend time and men laying siege to each one. If those cities are properly fortified, we can slow him down, keep him busy for years – and maybe even stop him cold, or at least exhaust him enough to negotiate a peace. And if that does not do it, those cities may keep him so busy that I can slip into Greece or even Macedonia with the fleet and an army."

"You always did see the big picture, Memnon," acknowledged

Ephialtes. "I am a simple soldier. I see an enemy across the field, but you look beyond. I fight battles, but you, you fight wars."

Memnon took the compliment with a gracious nod. "So, rather than die gloriously on the field of a battle that is lost before it begins, will you live and help me win a war? Will you do that? If not for Persia, where we have made a home, or for your beloved Athens, which has had to bow its noble head to the Macedonians, will you swallow your pride and do what I ask, what I need, for our families...and for an old friend?"

Memnon could not tell if the tears he saw welling up in Ephialtes' eyes were tears of disappointment or shame from not being allowed to stand and fight, or of some deeper emotional response. Either way, the old general nodded in acceptance of his orders. Words, however, failed him. So choked with emotion was Ephialtes, that all he could do was come forward and briefly embrace his old friend, and commander. Pulling back almost immediately, Ephialtes brought himself to parade-ground attention, struck his chest with his fist in a salute so powerful that the bronze of his breastplate sang as if it had been struck by an armorer's hammer.

"As you command, General Memnon, so it shall be. I ask but one boon of you."

"If it is in my power to grant, considered it already given. Of what do you ask of me?"

Ephialtes looked his friend directly in the eyes, and with a slight but knowing smile, replied simply: "Don't die tomorrow. Just don't fucking die."

23

The River Granicos

THE MERCENARY LINE

From his position in the center of the Greek mercenary line atop the long hill to the east of the Granicos, Dimitrios had an unimpeded view of the arena in which the battle he longed for would be fought.

To his left and right were the serried ranks of hoplites in the Great King's service. Here were thousands of soldiers-of-fortune, freebooters, adventurers, hired thugs, exiles, refugees with nowhere else to go and men with no other prospects but to fight for pay. These men from mainland Greece and her colonies among the islands of the Aegean and the shores of Asia Minor had little in common with each other, save that they had chosen to be here this day. Their loyalty bought with Persian gold, they bound their lives and honor not to a crown or to a cause, but only to each other. True, there were a few who, like Dimitrios, had a score to settle, a thirst for revenge that could only be quenched in Macedonian blood. But for most in that armored line nearly 7,000 strong, they were there because this was the only place they believed they could be, doing the only job they felt they were suited for, or able to get.

Behind them were the gaudy, gilded and carpeted tents of the Persian aristocracy, most of whom had actually never been to the

Aryan homelands of the king of kings they served. They, and even their fathers and grandfathers, had been born in Asia Minor. Descendants of conquerors rather than conquerors themselves, few had ever borne bow or lance except in the hunt, or swung a sword or mace, except in practice. Proud, arrogant and boastful of the deeds they believed they would do, these noble warriors and their household retainers had ridden out from their lavish tents that morning to line the east bank of the meandering, curving Granicos.

Dimitrios already knew most of their leaders and provinces of origin from studying their banners and the manner of their equipment. Immediately to his front, in the center of that two-mile-long line of 20,000 horsemen, were those local nobles, clad in layers of linen and silk, and armed with an assortment of swords, scimitars, maces, battle axes, hammers, javelins, darts and, as with all of the Persian cavalry, bows. To their right were horse archers from Bactria, and wild horsemen from the distant steppes, the later led by one Rheomithres. To the left of the nobles were the Hyrcanians, mounted mercenaries from the shores of the sea of the same name, under the prideful Spithridates, satrap of Ionia. Rumor had it in the camp that Spithridates had boasted that he would seek out Alexander for single combat, and that he could take off his head with a single stroke of his blade.

To the left of Spithridates stood the Paphlagonian heavy cavalry of Arsites – the Phrygian satrap who had stolen command of the army from Memnon. Even though it had been by the order of Darius himself, king of kings, that the Greek general be given responsibility for the defense of the empire against the Macedonians, Arsites and his fellow satraps had bristled at this insult, as they saw it. No one of the true blood should ever have to take orders from some Greek, and a mercenary Greek at that.

Although still in titular overall command, Memnon could issue no order that Spithridates, Arsites or Arsames would follow unless they perceived it as being their idea. Arsames, with his Cilicians, claimed that part of the line to the left of Arsites. They relegated Memnon and the 500 mounted Greek colonists from the cities of Asia Minor to the far left of the line – a vantage point from which he could neither view nor direct the course of any unit but his own.

Back on the hill where Dimitrios and his company were placed, Dimitrios could see the last, more numerous and least-valued troops in the army. Nearly 20,000 levy infantry lolled about just behind the Greeks. Untrained, armed with an assortment of weapons and farm implements, these men accounted for more than half of the numbers in the army. Disdained even by the nobles who called them to arms, they were the least willing combatants on either side. Called up by satraps, nobles and landowners who purely for pride's sake competed to show who could bring the greater numbers to the field, no one, least of all those nobles, expected them to actually fight. In that at least, thought Dimitrios, Arsites and Memnon were of one mind.

As Ephialtes and Memnon had already determined, the deployment of the army did not make best use of either the heavy mercenary infantry or the fast, mobile, missile-armed cavalry. Still, if handled properly, with the cavalry eventually drawing back to the flanks of the Greek infantry, all could be saved. Steadfast on the hill, their flanks secured by the Persian horse, the Greeks would be an immovable object, a wall of iron and bronze against which the Macedonians would not only butt their heads, but have to struggle out of a river and uphill to do so. Then, at the right moment, the Greeks could charge downhill while the cavalry swept in from the sides, a combination that would rudely shove the Macedonians back over the steep banks and into the slippery waters of the Granicos. That was where the real slaughtering would be done.

Unfortunately, however, as Memnon and Ephialtes knew, no such order would or could be given, or would be obeyed even if it were. The Persian nobles in their unwavering pride were determined to fight and win on their own, with the infantry serving merely as an audience to cheer them on and applaud their inevitable victory.

The Persian commanders had needed all day to move their men into position. The army thus had risen just before dawn, with most units given little or no time to cook breakfast. For hours upon hours the host of men and horses had stood in the full heat of the day, waiting for the Macedonians. Finally, as the day turned to evening, their opponents arrived upon the field.

As a citizen-soldier who had spent many a day on the drill field at Thebes, Dimitrios could appreciate the way Alexander moved and deployed his army. Most armies would set up camp, but Alexander instead directed his formations to move from a single column of march into a battle line. The head of the column divided in two; with the Greek allied, Thracian and Thessalian horse marching out in a column to their left and the Companion and Paeonian cavalry, light infantry and archers splitting off to their right. Once the head of each of these had reached the spot opposite the ends of the Persian line, they simply halted and turned to face their foes. While these fast-moving troops spread out, up into the center came the solid mass of heavy infantry – the Macedonian phalanxes – six massive blocks of pikemen. These also peeled off to either side, with the regiment of Shield-bearers, the Hypaspistes, at the far right of the infantry line. They would be the unbreakable link between the heavy infantry center and the cavalry of the Macedonian right. They would form the base for the maneuvers of the Royal Squadron and the Companion cavalry, whom everyone knew Alexander himself would lead into battle.

This time, however, rather than have the Companions to their right, Alexander had inserted the elite of his light cavalry between the Shield-bearers and the Companions. The Thracians, at whose hands Dimitrios and his company had suffered during Alexander's approach to Thebes, and the Prodromoi, another crack band of light horsemen, took position in this part of the line. Dimitrios thought this highly unusual, for such light horse never stood in the main line of battle, but operated on the wings, where their speed could allow them to capitalize on an enemy mistake – or get out of trouble if things went wrong.

At first Dimitrios thought that this was just for show. A martial display meant to match and overawe the Persians. He, Ari and Klemes had covered the ten miles from the Macedonian camp back to the Granicos last night, but without any armor or weapons to weigh them down. Alexander's men had to make that trip in the heat of the afternoon, and burdened with full kit. This late in the day any other army surely would normally stop, set up camp, and then retire to it, to cook an evening meal and rest up for battle in the morning. That is the way it had always been done, by the book and by common practice. What general would be so foolish as to tire out an army by marching all day and then send them directly into battle? It simply was not done. It simply was not possible.

Yet that is exactly what happened.

Standing on a low hill to the west and south, Alexander watched as his army moved with precision from line of march to line of battle. His most senior general, Parmenion, beamed with pride, for it was he and his friend, the late King Philip, who had trained these men. Their movements going into and out of formations had been choreographed and practiced over and over and over again for years.

"Splendid, are they not my king?" His statement more exclamatory than interrogatory, Parmenion nevertheless longed to hear some words of praise from Alexander.

"Yes, splendid indeed," murmured Alexander in reply. "But we don't have many hours of light left, so we had each better get to our posts for the attack."

"Pardon me, my king," asked Parmenion, "but what do you mean 'attack.' They have been marching all day. They are hungry, thirsty and tired, and will not be at their best. Now that we have shown the Persians what a real army is like, let the fear of it creep into their minds and souls – such souls as they have. I would let our soldiers make camp and attack in the morning, when they are fresh, fed and well-rested. Besides, why fight our way across a river when we can go around it. I would go downstream in the morning, and maneuver them out of their position – and get them while they are on the hop."

"Yes, that is what you would do – and what I would do, if I were Parmenion," said the young king with a smile as he reached for his helmet. "But I am not Parmenion. I am Alexander," he added with a little laugh. "After all, if I did not hesitate to cross the stormy waters of the Hellespont, why should I let that little trickling stream slow me down? To allow the Granicos to do so would but cast dishonor on the Hellespont, would it not?" the young king added with an impish grin. "Besides, the enemy are here, now. Today they offer us battle, whereas tomorrow they might move off – then we'd have to chase them down. So come now, Parmenion, to your station on the left, as always, while I go to the right."

"Lord," Parmenion said as he moved to block Alexander from the king's beloved steed, Bucephalos, "should we not make a plan, first. Do I just attack straight across the river?"

"No, at least not until I give the signal. As for a plan, leave that to me. I have it clear in my mind what to do, and will not waste any more of the light in explaining it. Just wait for my order."

"And if this plan you are keeping to yourself doesn't play out?" asked the old general.

"Then I will come up with a new one that will."

The king gave Parmenion no time to respond. He laughed and glee-fully leaped up onto the back of his massive stallion. After whispering something into Bucephalus's ear off they rode, leaving Parmenion and the other generals to watch his dust. "Well then," sighed Parmenion, "you heard him; off to your posts."

"Who is that fool with all of the white plumes on his helmet?" Clearchos asked as he saw a lone rider on a big black horse leave the hill on the far side of the river.

"That, my general, would be Alexander," said Dimitrios, whose company stood at the general's back in the center of the line.

"Are your eyes that sharp, captain?" said the general in chiding disbelief.

"No, but I recognize that horse, and that armor. I've seen it before," replied the captain.

"Oh, yes, Ephialtes mentioned something about you being at

Thebes or whatnot," said Clearchos as he peered harder to make out the man on horseback.

"Yes, general," replied Dimitrios. "I saw him up close."

"Obviously not close enough," harrumphed the general, "or at least not close enough to skewer the little bully with your spear. Would that you had been, then we would not be in this mess."

Dimitrios knew that to respond to the general's comment would serve no purpose, only to further agitate him. That Clearchos saw the same flaws in the Persian plan as he himself had observed increased the esteem in which he held his general – but only made his own concerns worse.

"I have a very bad feeling about this," mumbled Clearchos, kicking a clod of earth with his boot. "A very bad feeling. If they are coming across the river today, now, it is we who should be down there to meet them, not these perfumed Persian peacocks on their pretty prancing ponies."

Dimitrios and many of the other officers and even some of the men in the ranks allowed themselves a grin or a little laugh at the general's remark, but immediately realized their mistake in doing so when Clearchos angrily spun about to face them.

"You think this is funny? Do let me in on the joke then, why don't you?"

None of the officers replied. Most, like Dimitrios, just looked down at their feet, or to the side, too embarrassed to look their general in the eyes, let alone further spark his ire.

"I thought not," said the general sternly. "Let us do our duty and maintain ourselves in readiness, just in case someone in charge has the good sense to let us do what we were paid to do."

The Macedonians did not charge headlong into the river, at least not everywhere, as the Persians had somehow and naively thought they would. Most of the Macedonian army just stood their ground, on their side of the river, just out of range of the short bows of the mounted

Persians. Dimitrios noticed that Alexander continued to spread out to the flanks, even halving his usual 16-rank deep pike formations to files of only eight men. With a marsh to the north and another river feeding into the Granicos from the south, Alexander filled that space so that there was no opportunity for the Persians to try their usual trick of sending out horse archers to harry the flanks.

The Macedonians cheered and jeered and made a lot of noise, but only in one spot did they attack – and not with pike-carrying infantry or heavy cavalry, but with the light horse and some peltastes – lightly armed, fast infantry trained to fight alongside the horsemen. Alexander sent his Thracian and Prodromoi light cavalry and the peltastes into the river at a spot just to the left of the Persian center. The Persians happily met this band of horsemen and the light infantry that had come along with them with a hail of arrows. Flight after flight of these deadly projectiles rained down on the Macedonians as they entered and began to cross the river. The closer they got to the Persian side, the heavier became the storm, as the Persian nobles lowered their bows to fire directly at the oncoming Macedonians. As Alexander's men kept coming forward, the Persians shifted to javelins, causing even more casualties among the advancing enemy.

Undeterred by this shower of missiles, Alexander's light horsemen came on – but found little footing for their horses where the water met the steep and muddy bank. After a few minutes of this punishment, the Thracians and Prodromi, who were not trained for such close action, began to fall back, although in moderately good order. Rather than hold their superior, commanding position at the top of the bank, however, the Persian nobles did just what Alexander – and Memnon, and Ephialtes and even a lowly captain like Dimitrios – knew they would do. They left the high ground and gave chase.

Down the bank and into the river the Cilician and Paphlagonian cavalry streamed. Their blood up, they were crying shouts of victory and calling out their own names, the better so that their opponents and the gods above would know to whom the glory should accrue.

That was when Alexander struck.

This was the opening Alexander had planned, waited and wished for. He led the Companion cavalry down into the river, turned them to face upstream, and charged, lances lowered, straight into the left flank of the Persian horse. Those Persians in the river did not have a chance. They were either bowled over or swept away. As they fled, Alexander and his Companions gained the spot at the top of the bank that the headstrong Persians had abandoned. Memnon tried to shift his men to reform the line, but by now Alexander's right wing of mixed horse and foot were crossing in support of the king, drawing Memnon's own squadrons into the fray. Then Mithridates, one of the many son-in-laws of King Darius and commander of several squadrons of Cilicians, hurled his men into a headlong and disorganized charge. So did Spithridates, both of them blindly drawn forward by the white plumes of Alexander's helmet.

All pretense of formation soon fell apart, as the nobles vied with each other to kill the king. Mithdridates got there first, having bulled his way to the front. Alexander got the better of him, and thrusting his lance into the noble's face unhorsed Mithridates, breaking his own lance in the process. At that moment Rhoesaces, brother to Mithridates and an honored knight of the regally-named "One Thousand Kinsmen of the King," took a mighty swing at Alexander. His heavy, Damascene steel saber came down hard, denting Alexander's helmet and slicing off one of its white plumes. Partially stunned, and with blood streaming down from where the helmet had been struck into his forehead, Alexander wavered – but only for a moment. Taking in hand a spear tossed to him by a bodyguard, the Macedonian king thrust it mightily into Rhoesaces' chest. Alexander put such force behind it that it penetrated his target's breast armor and down Rhoesaces went, clutching the king's spear as he died.

The king's ordeal was not over, far from it. Like a magnet attracting splinters of metal, Alexander drew the Persians toward him. In the heat of the melee, Spithridates burst forward, his long, bright, curved scimitar glistening. A mere sword stroke away was Alexander, now disarmed and unaware of the threat. As the Persian satrap raised himself from his saddle and lifted his arm for the killing blow, a big, burly Macedonian named Cleitos the Black charged up and with a single stroke severed Spithridates' arm at the shoulder. Behind Cleitos came the Royal Guard, adding fresh impetus to the charge of the Companions.

Now effectively leaderless and in increasing disarray, the Persian horse facing Alexander and the Companions broke. As they fled, they exposed the flank of the center line of cavalry. The Macedonians plowed into them, causing the entire Persian center to shudder. Parmenion took note of this, and he knew, instinctively, that this was his moment. Without waiting for an order from the king, Parmenion gave the signal, and with a shout the entire Macedonian line charged into the river. The Persians opposite them, unnerved at having their line broken and with Macedonians now to the front as well as on their flank, fell to pieces. Rather than fall back and retire in good order as Memnon and Ephialtes had hoped against hope that they would, the cavalrymen broke ranks and raced each other to the rear.

"Damn, them, damn them to Hades," growled Clearchos, as he watched the Persian front line unravel. Only on the extreme left, where Memnon and the Ionian Greek horse were locked in combat, did any part of the front line continue to hold its ground. Thousands of panicked horses and their even more panicked riders scattered seeking safety. Many tried to break through the hoplites line in an effort to take the most direct route away from the Macedonians, but Clearchos would not let them through.

"Hold the line! Hold the line!" he shouted, his commands echoed by Dimitrios and other captains up and down the wall of shields and spears. And hold the line did, as frightened Persian horsemen and herds of now riderless horses flowed down the front of the hoplites line and off to the sides. The horses and riders raced each other to put ground between themselves and the enemy they had recently boasted they would destroy.

As the horsemen fled, so did panic set in among the levy infantry. Held there only by fear of what their landlords and masters would do if they ran, once they saw those same lords and masters in flight what little discipline they had evaporated. Twenty thousand levy infantry threw down their arms and took to their heels, running as fast as they could to follow the example of their fleeing nobles.

There was not only no hope of rallying them or the cavalry – there was noone to rally them. Most of the key Persian commanders were already dead, as they had sought combat one-on-one with the Macedonians, and had not survived. As for the high command, Spithridates was down, Memnon was pinned fighting for his very survival and Arsites was carried away in the tide of fleeing horsemen – or at least so he would claim later when stories of this epic defeat were told. Within the space of half an hour or so, not a single Persian horseman remained to stop the Macedonian advance.

As the dust of the fleeing horses settled, the Macedonians emerged victorious from the river, shouting cries of triumph and jeers at the Persians who had fled before them. Over 30,000 Macedonian pikemen, sword and shield bearers and battle-tested cavalry reformed the line, without a word being given, as if they had practiced this move on the parade ground.

And there, before them, at the top of a gentle slope of rising ground, stood 7,000 Greeks. Dimitrios and his company stood front and center. Riding up and down before them was a rider wildly racing about on a big black horse, the remaining white plumes on his dented helmet wet, dirty and drooping...and the sword in his visibly shaking hand dripping blood.

24

The Long Hill

CLEARCHOS

From his position at the center of the long hill, Dimitrios had an unobstructed, panoramic view of the disintegration and flight of the Persian cavalry. Horsemen from a dozen nations scattered in panic, taking the host of levy infantry with them. What had once been an army of over 50,000 was now reduced to barely 7,000 – all of them Greeks of one sort or another. As the dust and noise of their flight settled, a lone rider approached the hill from the south and east.

Although obviously a Greek from his dress and armor, he carried a Persian banner, its long serpentine tail fluttering behind. The horseman rode at full gallop up to the center of the hill, rearing up and came to a bone-jarring halt only steps away from Clearchos. He dropped the battered banner down into the dust before the general's feet. Without a word and without dismounting he stretched out his hand and shoved the scroll he had been carrying in his pouch in the direction of the mercenary general. Clearchos did not move forward or speak, but merely motioned to Dimitrios, the officer nearest to the rider other than himself. The Theban captain stepped forward and the instant his fingers touched the scroll, the rider, who seemed as frightened as he was relieved to have delivered the message, kicked his heels into the horse's flanks and galloped off as if his life depended on it – which, of course, it did.

"I fear I know what it says, Captain Dimitrios," said Clearchos calmly, with a sense of resignation in his voice, "but if you would please read it out loud."

"General Clearchos, as you are no doubt aware..."

"Louder, Captain," barked the Greek mercenary commander. "I want all of my officers assembled here to hear every word of this message."

Dimitrios swallowed hard, cleared his throat and read out the message in a booming voice: "General Clearchos, as you are no doubt aware, the Persian cavalry have been defeated and have been scattered. Much of my own cavalry force was borne away in their flight. What numbers I have left are such that I cannot offer you any support, or hope. The day is lost. If you can retreat, do so. If not, then in the name of the great king I release you and your men from royal service. Do not throw away your lives uselessly. You have my permission – even my encouragement – to accept whatever terms of surrender King Alexander sees fit to offer. Memnon."

"Here, let me have that, Captain," said the general, offering his hand, palm up to take the scroll. The general perused it briefly, and carefully rolled it up. Clearchos took a deep breath, muttered a vile, angry curse and then suddenly hurled the scroll to the ground. With obvious effort he drew himself up and motioned for Dimitrios to come closer.

"Well, Captain, you heard the orders. Go see if you can find a large olive branch or something else to identify you as a herald. When you do, take a couple of men and march that way," he added, pointing to the west, where the Macedonian army was reforming. "You've been able to pick out their king earlier this day. So go and find him again. Tell him I wish to parlay. If he presses you as to why, tell him that there is no need for more blood, especially Greek blood, to be shed on this field. Tell him I am willing...willing," he said, pausing as he forced himself to say those words no general, no Greek and certainly no Spartan like himself ever thought he would have to utter, "willing to discuss terms of our surrender."

Even though Dimitrios understood what Clearchos was ordering him to do, the thought of crossing the plain and begging Alexander for mercy made him shudder to his core. "Begging your pardon, General," replied Dimitrios, "but I did not surrender when that tyrant burned my city and razed it to the ground, and I will not surrender to him now. My spear has not tasted blood this day, and she is very thirsty."

Clearchos glowered at the young Theban captain. Marshalling his very considerable authority, the mercenary general stared at him, his eyes ablaze with a cold fire beyond anger.

"Captain Dimitrios. Are you a soldier, or are you not?"

"Yes...yes General, of course, General," said Dimitrios, taken aback by the question.

"Then do as your general commands," he roared. And then, in a quieter voice, almost to himself but just loud enough for Dimitrios to hear, "as I, too, have been ordered."

"But General, sir, we have 7,000 good men here..."

"No, Captain. It is not 'we' who have 7,000 good men here. It is I, and I alone, who have men here. I am responsible for them, and Memnon has made it known that I am now solely responsible for them. My first duty is no longer to Memnon or to the Persian king, but to these men – my men. As Memnon has rightly written, and by the rules of war, the time for battle is over. Much as I would like to go home dead in glory on my shield rather than carrying it back in disgrace, this is not Thermopylae, I am not Leonidas, and these are not my personal bodyguard. I will not order, or even ask, these men to die for nothing.

"Look out there, at the Macedonians and their long pikes, their mass of heavy cavalry, and their Greek and Thracian hirelings. They outnumber us five to one, and I will not sentence these men to certain death. So, Captain, will you be a soldier for at least another hour or so, and obey my command? Or do I need to find someone else to do so?"

Conflicting emotions warred within the mind and heart of Dimitrios. The citizen-soldier in him was conditioned to obey orders. The Theban exile, however, wanted revenge – and to both, the warrior and the expatriate, the thought of surrender was anathema.

"Well, Captain?" asked the general one more time, his patience obviously wearing thin.

"As you command, my General, so shall I obey," Dimitrios found himself responding. He was not aware of the words coming out of his mouth until he heard them with his own ears, but of course once he had said them, there was no taking them back. He offered the general his salute and then marched back over the hill to the camp. There he would surely find an olive branch or something suitable, as the general had directed. By the time he had returned, a scribe had written down the general's reply and sealed it. Clearchos had told Dimitrios to take a pair of men with him, making him the leader of a delegation rather than a mere messenger. Dimitrios could think of no better men to have at his side to bolster his courage for this mission than his brother and his best friend.

The Macedonian officer who rode out to meet Dimitrios, Klemes and Aristophanes as they crossed the plain was obviously an aristocrat, and not just because of the ornate and obviously expensive trappings of his horse or the gleaming bronze of his well-oiled armor. He rode high, his back stiff as a spear and his knees tightly gripping the body of his horse, a horse that pranced as if on a parade ground rather than one directed to walk across a battlefield. After listening to Dimitrios' request to be taken to the king, he refused to do so until the captain first spoke that message to him. Satisfied, the officer and horse each gave a dismissive snort and turned about. Without looking back over his shoulder, the officer lazily waved his hand in a signal that obviously meant "follow me."

Silently, the trio complied. Klemes lowered the branch – not that of an olive tree but at least something with green leaves. Dimitrios strode forward, forcing himself to remain calm and dignified, as if, like the officer's horse, he, too, was on parade. Aristophanes limped along behind, not really sure why he was there, other than that Dimitrios had said he needed two volunteers as the general had directed. Klemes and Aristophanes did not volunteer; they did not have too. As soon as Dimitrios told them his orders, they just automatically fell in behind him.

As the officer moved forward, the files of the phalanx before him parted, opening to the sides like drapes to reveal a narrow corridor, a corridor down which he rode haughtily, with the three Greeks falling in step behind. The Macedonians had reformed into their traditional 16-deep files, Dimitrios noted, as they no longer needed to worry about covering a wide front or wading through a river. Slaves moved about the lines, offering chunks of bread or some wine to the soldiers, which he noted they poured into the cupped hands of the men, who drank greedily. The men, he also noted, were still in a battle formation, not a marching one, as they had not set down their pikes, set aside their shields or removed their helmets or other gear. These men were getting ready for another battle, and they wanted the mercenaries on the hill to know it.

"Where are they taking us?" Aristophanes whispered to Dimitrios. "Aren't we going to see the king?"

"I doubt it," Klemes answered for his brother. "We are merely message bearers. We'll probably talk to some minor official from the king's court, or maybe one of the lesser generals."

Klemes, however, was wrong. As the last of the pikemen parted, the trio came face to face with a burly, bald, and obviously battle-hardened soldier. He was obviously a high-ranking officer at that, as his dented, dirty but still very high quality armor, flowing cape and plumed helmet in his hand gave evidence. Dimitrios halted a few steps from the officer, gave a formal and respectful salute, and handed him the scroll.

The officer directed a man on his right, who appeared to be of similar rank to Dimitrios, to take the scroll. The officer unrolled it and read it, first silently, and then aloud. The senior officer nodded, and with a very little yet very satisfied smile, looked Dimitrios in the eye.

"My officer, here, will see to you. I regret we cannot offer you any comforts, or even some shade in which to rest, but we will have some watered wine and bread brought to you while you rest. It should only be a short wait, as I will take your general's offer directly to the king. The decision is his, of course, but, personally, I commend your general on his good sense. When you return with the king's answer, you can tell him that I for one am glad that no more Greek or Macedonian blood need be spilled today."

As the general departed and the junior officer escorted them behind the line, Aristophanes asked of him: "Sir, who was that officer? Is he anyone of note?"

"You could say that, soldier, you could say that," the young officer laughed. "That was the grizzled old lion of Macedonia himself. That was Parmenion."

25

Behind the Macedonian Line

THE LION STANDARD

P armenion was beaming with a triumphant joyfulness as he strode to the makeshift headquarters that Hephaestion had set up for the king. While grooms attended to the king's charger, Bucephalus, Alexander, obviously agitated, nervously paced back and forth, mumbling something in some language none around him could quite make out. As Parmenion approached, however, the king took note and called out angrily:

"What is the delay, Parmenion! Why have we stopped moving forward! The day is not yet ours and the light is fading! We have to kill them, kill them now, before they get away!"

Parmenion recoiled briefly in shock and surprise, as the king's face was covered with blood, some still oozing from a clotting but obviously deep cut across his forehead. But it was not the blood as much as the eyes that struck Parmenion – they were wild. Still, he did not let the king's strange look, bloody face or furious words diminish his own joy. "We have stopped to dress ranks and reorder the troops, Lord. And the day is indeed ours. The Persian cavalry has fled, their levies have run off and those men on the hill..."

"Yes! Yes! Exactly!" Alexander screamed madly, his eyes wide and wild and furious and staring off into space. "Why are they still there? Kill them! Kill them all, Parmenion!"

"We do not have to waste men to do that," said Parmenion, forcing a smile in an effort to calm the king. "They want to surrender. They have asked for terms. Here, see for yourself..." he said with a smile as he reached out to give the king Clearchos' scroll.

"Terms! They want terms! They shall have no terms, Parmenion! I do not bargain with traitors! Kill them! Kill them now, Parmenion, now!!!"

Parmenion was once again taken aback by the intensity and fury of the king's words – not to mention his look, which was that of a crazed, irrational creature the likes of which he had never seen before. And the eyes – the eyes were not, well, not quite...human. They looked like those of a snake – and a snake about to devour its prey.

Hephaestion moved between the general and Alexander, who continued to rage about traitors and Zeus and blood and other things that were hard to follow. He put his palm on Parmenion's shoulder, and with the other hand raised a finger to the old general's lips, to indicate that he should hold his tongue.

"Alexander, my King, my friend, my brother," began Hephaestion as he turned slowly from Parmenion toward the king. "The enemy is defeated. Those that remain wish to supplicate themselves before you, and seek your pardon and your forgiveness. Your victory is complete. The day is yours, the glory is yours, oh great lord."

"Aye, lad," interjected Parmenion. "Your father would be proud. King Philip could not have done better himself!"

Hephaestion glared over his shoulder at Parmenion, indicating by the look in his eyes and his raised eyebrows that the general had said exactly the wrong thing.

"My father is Zeus! I am the son of a god! Time and time again I have told you this, yet again you chide me and taunt me with the name of that drunken, one-eyed gimp who sat on the throne! He was nothing, nothing, you hear me! He was not my father! Zeus is my father, and like my heavenly father I can hurl thunderbolts, earthly thunderbolts at my enemies, do you hear me? Do you!"

Parmenion was about to speak but Hephaestion quickly moved to silence him.

"What Parmenion surely meant, my lord, is that the late king could not have won a more complete victory, and that you have this day indeed surpassed him – again. As for casting thunderbolts, there is no need, for what few of our enemies remain on the field have placed themselves at your mercy."

"Mercy? Mercy?" Alexander screamed, more agitated, more emotional and angrier than before. "They shall have no mercy, Hephaestion! My father will not allow it! Any Greek who takes up arms against me, takes up arms against all Greece, against the entire Hellenic world, and against my father and the other gods! They had their chance, Hephaestion, they had their chance! I sent messages to all of the Greek cities of Asia Minor, telling them of their coming liberation! And how, and how..." sputtered Alexander, his face purpling with fury, "how did they answer me! They took up arms against me! Against me! No, Hephaestion, they are traitors. They had their chance! They shall have no mercy!"

"But they are soldiers, like us," said Parmenion, again hoping to calm the young king. "They were merely doing their duty, and now, now they have seen they were on the wrong side. Now they want to surrender – why, their general has even offered his men to us, to fight alongside us for hire..."

"What! He wants us to pay them to serve me!" shouted Alexander, his rage unbounded. "No! I want no hirelings, no paid..."

"But we already have mercenaries from Thrace and..."

"No! Parmenion! No! Kill them, kill them all, and kill them now!"

Alexander continued to spit and sputter and gesticulate wildly, not at Parmenion or Hephaestion, or at anyone in particular, but at someone or something that he, and only he, could see.

"But, my King..." Parmenion started, only to once again be cautioned into silence by Hephaestion. His look of resignation told Parmenion that there would be nothing to gained – and much to be lost – if he spoke further to the king.

"This is not the first time he has been like this," Hephaestion said quietly beneath his breath, so that only Parmenion could hear. "Ever since that night at Pelium..."

"You mean when that witch, his mother...with the snakes..."

"Exactly. Something...strange...happened in that tent, the night we thought Alexander was going to die..."

"What! What is that you are saying?" screamed Alexander, striding forward, his eyes ablaze. "Why are you all just standing around! I gave an order! Attack, attack! Kill them, kill them all!"

"You heard his majesty," said Hephaestion sadly and with deep regret in his voice. "Ready the infantry, Parmenion. I need some time to send our cavalry around the flanks and rear of the hill. That way when you begin the assault, Clearchos and his men will have nowhere to run and," he then added with a whisper, "maybe by then, Alexander will have become himself again."

Parmenion was stunned, but while he officially outranked Hephaestion, a youth who was no older than his own son, Parmenion saw that the king's best friend was right. This was not the time to challenge Alexander.

"All right. But give it half an hour. I want that officer from Clearchos to have time to get back to his general. I will not have it said that Parmenion does not respect the rules of war, or the sacred inviolable role of a herald, let alone one who came bearing an offer of surrender. Perhaps once we start up that hill they will throw down their spears and shields, and maybe by then the king's blood will have cooled."

"I hope so, Parmenion, I truly hope so," sighed Hephaestion.

Dimitrios was both surprised and honored by the professional respect Parmenion showed him, but also stunned by his words. Part of him indeed longed for a chance to fight the hated Macedonians, to sate his vengeance for his lost city, but he understood the decision of Clearchos to surrender, or to even allow any of his men who wished to seek service with the king to do so. To stand and die on this day would change nothing. There would be another day, there had to be another day – or so he had rationalized things while walking towards the Macedonian lines with Clearchos' offer. Now, however, it seemed that today would be the day to fight, for the Macedonian king would see the Greeks on the hill lying dead rather than kneeling before him. Well, said Dimitrios to himself as he marched steadily across the plain and back up the hill to where his own general stood waiting, if I am to die today, at least it will be while fighting Alexander, and fighting in good company.

If Clearchos was surprised by the refusal to discuss terms of surrender, he did not show it. Not even when Omares, whose Persian infantry had run off, rode up to ask if he had been given terms by Alexander.

"It is against all of the rules and conventions of war to refuse quarter to an enemy," said Omares angrily. "Is there any way you can retreat?"

"No, sir," Clearchos sighed in response to the Persian commander. "If we try to march away they will ride us down. Better that we stand here, on this good ground, and give as good an account of ourselves as we can. If we blood them enough, Alexander might call them off and reconsider. If not, well, we will at least make him pay a stiff price for his pride."

Omares was visibly moved by the old general's grit. "Well, then," he said as he dismounted his richly caparisoned stallion, "if you are going to stand and fight, then allow at least one Persian to stand with you this day."

"There is no need, Omares," Clearchos replied. "Go while you can. Ride away. One more corpse will not change things."

"No," laughed Omares as he shrugged off his cape and drew his sword from its sheath, "but one more sword might. And if not, well, at least you and your men will know that there is at least one Persian who did not abandon you this day."

Clearchos, visibly moved, clasped Omares by the shoulder, and nodded in wordless recognition of the Persian commander's courage and nobility. As the Macedonians beat their drums and blew their horns in preparation for their advance, Clearchos called his commanders to his side. To Memnon's sons, Agathon, Thymondas and Xenocrates, he gave orders to ride to freedom, and to their father, while there was still time. Omares seconded that command. The Macedonian light cavalry had already begun to stir, and it would be a quarter of an hour at most before they completed their maneuver to get behind the Greek line. That gave the trio at least a head start on their flight. He even gave Agathon his own horse, for the young man's steed had gone lame. Agathon had bravely offered to stay and fight, as had his brothers, but Clearchos would not be moved. Agathon tried to refuse the general's offer to take his mount, but again, Clearchos would not take 'no' for an answer.

"Please. Take her," the general said, a tear in his eye as he stroked his mare's face and tugged at her mane. "She has served me well, and has earned her rest, and her freedom. I would take it as a great, personal favor if you see her safely away from here, and give her a green pasture in which to live out her days. Remember me to your father, lads. Tell him I tried to do as he asked, but that the Macedonian king would not even discuss terms. At least we will blood them a little when they come. That much, at least, I can do."

Thymondas and Xenocrates protested again, but Clearchos warned that he would tie them to their horses and see them led away if they continued to refuse his order. Sullen, they rode off – but at least, as the general said to himself, they did ride off, and that meant they might just get out of this alive. That, he sighed, was more than anyone else on this hill could hope for.

26

The Hill

THE HOPLITES LINE

"Give him his due, Captain, Parmenion knows his craft," remarked Clearchos as he watched the six Macedonian pike blocks march in lockstep toward the hill. At sixteen-men deep, that central portion of the Macedonian line was twice the depth of the usual hoplites line, and twice again that of Clearchos' formations. The Spartan general had to thin the lines and spread out in order to cover the flanks and rear of the hill as the Macedonians spread around to encircle him. Not only were his lines stretched taught in the face of the massive formations, but the pikes the Macedonians carried were twice as long as the spears held by his own men.

"At least they only have those little shields, no bigger than cooking pans, and only among the front ranks," mumbled Clearchos, "while our men have real shields – shields that cover them from neck to knee, along with the shoulder of the man next to them. But you have met these lads before, or so I'm told, Captain. So, any suggestions?"

Generals do not ask lesser officers for tactical advice, but Clearchos, who had only been given the command when Ephialtes left at Memnon's request, had never faced a Macedonian pike phalanx before. A veteran soldier of the Spartan warrior class, Clearchos was well-versed in traditional hoplites warfare, and could count the number of times he had stood in a shield wall by the number of scars he bore. He had fought wild barbarian horsemen, pirate raiders from the sea, ax-wielding hill tribes and numerous Greek enemies, sometimes in the name of Sparta, but more often merely for pay. These formations he saw coming toward the hill were not something new – but they were something new to him.

"Parmenion knows I cannot hold the entire crest of the hill without spreading out. It is just too much ground to cover. But the high ground is our only advantage, small enough as it is. Now, if some of the Persian cavalry had stayed around to protect my flanks, perhaps I could have strengthened the line...but not now. See, Captain, they are keeping us focused on the pikes while their shock cavalry moves to our flanks, and their light horse and light infantry filter about our rear. I had hoped they might be distracted by the army's camps, but it seems Parmenion has trained them well – or he has put the fear of the gods in them to keep them from breaking off to loot the tents."

Dimitrios did not know why the general was saying such things, for in his experience generals usually pranced about behind the lines, giving orders and looking confident. This man, this Spartan, had not only given away his horse, but had planted himself here, spear in hand, front and center – right where the fighting would be heaviest.

"Pardon me, General, but since you asked, those pikes are not invulnerable."

"Go on, Captain..."

"Those men are very well-trained," Dimitrios admitted out of respect for his enemy, "but even they must be tired. I was in their camp last night, and even then some were complaining of how long Alexander had kept them on their feet, and at a crippling pace. They marched all day today, fought their way across a slippery river and up a steep bank, and, well, those pikes are heavy and unwieldy as it is. Now they have to hold them at an angle as they come uphill towards us, which will test even their training and endurance. And the slope is uneven – which means that forest of pikes will have gaps in it. We can make those gaps wider if we send a few men into them, and have others use their shields to push the pikes aside from within the gaps.

Then, when they are disorganized, we come rushing downhill. We will have the advantage of ground..."

"...and of surprise, as they seem to think we will just stand here and wait to be butchered," Clearchos responded, as he nodded his head at the captain's suggestion, and looked about at his own line.

"A nice idea in theory, but these men do not know how to fight like that. That is not what they are trained for," he said sourly.

"Begging your pardon, General," Aristophanes, who was standing behind Dimitrios and holding the captain's shield and spear, interjected. "Haven't you seen soldiers brawl when they are off duty? When we argue over a woman, or dice, or because we drink too much wine, we don't don our kits and strap on our shields. No, we grab whatever is handy. We know knife and sword every bit as well as spear and shield. Not every battle has to be by the rules – we know how to fight dirty; we do it all the time."

"Who is this fellow, Captain? Does he not know his place?" said Clearchos testily, obviously insulted by this affront offered by a common soldier.

"Excuse me, General, he is my friend. He, too, has fought the Macedonians before – and while he should know better than to blurt out like that," Dimitrios added, with a stern look over his shoulder at Ari, "he is right. We don't always fight in a shield wall."

"All right, Captain. I did ask, and we have nothing – quite literally – nothing else to lose, as I doubt any of us will get off this hill alive anyway. We still have a few minutes. Explain your tactics to my staff officers and they will pass the word as quickly as they can."

As the staff officers moved down either side of the line, small bands of men moved out of the shield wall to crouch about a dozen yards down the hill, towards the Macedonians. Although they tried to march machine-like toward the Greeks, the pikemen in their tightly packed phalanxes began to stumble, slip and falter here and there as they struggled to keep ranks in the broken ground. What had been an ordered, unbroken, bristling hedgehog of sharp pikes became less and less organized as it advanced. While still a very formidable and menacing sight, it became a bit less so with every step. Seeing their chance, the small groups of Greeks made their move.

The Macedonians were taken by surprise, but although their forward motion was stopped, they did not take a single step backward. Many of the Greeks did get under and inside the reach of the front ranks of pikemen, a number of whom had no choice but to drop their long pikes and reach for the knives and short swords they wore about their waists. The Greeks did have an advantage at first – from the sheer audacity of their attack and from hitting the phalanxes while they were still stumbling about – but it did not last long. The Macedonians were just too well-disciplined to crack, let along break and run. Still, Clearchos saw there was an opportunity to rock them back, and he took it.

The Spartan general took three steps forward out of the shield wall, turned to face his men and raised his spear as high as he could. Looking first to the right, then to the left, he turned about, leveled his spear at the enemy, screamed the Spartan war cry "Au Au!" and took off at a run downhill. A moment later, the rest of the Greek infantry did the same, some shouting the piercing "Alala" or booming "Eleleu," or some variation specific to their home city.

"Hear me, Alala," prayed Klemes out loud, echoing the opening words of a verse from his ancestor, Pindar as he watched Dimitrios lead his company into the fray. "Hear me, Alala, daughter of Ares, prelude of the spears, you to whom men fall as offerings for their homeland in death's holy sacrifice."

Perhaps the goddess heard the words Pindar had crafted so long ago, for, if not her spirit, then something else bolstered the courage of the men on that hill. From a grim band waiting for death to come to them, they had suddenly become the bringers of death themselves – and death they did bring at the point of their knives, swords and spears.

"What is happening? What is happening?" shouted Alexander, who had finally agreed to allow his physicians to cleanse the blood from his face and stitch up his head wound.

"It seems the mercenaries have counter-attacked, Majesty," one of the king's young aides reported. "They have come charging down the hill and into our pikes."

Furious at the Greeks for having the effrontery to do something other than wait patiently to be massacred, Alexander shot up from his camp stool, knocked aside the physician and scattered his instruments about the ground. Woozy from the loss of blood and leaning on the pole that bore his lion standard for balance, Alexander swayed about – but waved off the aides who sought to steady him.

"Bring me Buchephalus and a lance!" the king shouted at no one in particular.

"But, Majesty," begged the physician who had been treating him, "you are in no condition to..."

Alexander slapped the man with a blow that sent him reeling. "Do not tell me what I can or can't do! I am the King! I am the son of Zeus, and my father will give me strength! Now," he added, still in an agitated state, "where is my horse!"

Dimitrios had not been among the first wave of skirmishers, though he had longed to be, but such was not the place for a captain of a hundred. That place, that proper place, was in the center of the phalanx, where as many men as possible could see him. Lead from the front, Epaminondas had famously said and done, and lead from the front he would, as had the legendary Theban general before him.

Down the hill he charged, his men screaming their war cries, and headlong they spilled into the disorganized mass of skirmishers and pikes. Pushing and shoving pikes aside, they struggled to close with the Macedonians. So close they could smell the wine on their enemy's breath, the mercenaries jabbed and struck with their spears, and when those spears broke, out came their swords. Then their knives, and finally their fists and even teeth. If the Macedonians were going to treat the Greeks as savages unworthy of mercy, then savages they would be...and savages they became.

Brave and desperate though they be, the 7,000 mercenaries were outnumbered, and outnumbered five to one. Surrounded, their flank and rear companies bombarded by Cretan archers, Agrianian javelineers, Rhodian slingers and the missiles of the Thracian and other light cavalry, the 7,000 soon became the 5,000, then the 4,000 and, as the sun set, the 3,000. Still, as the world darkened, they kept on fighting.

"My King, call an end to this slaughter," begged Parmenion, who reigned in his horse as he reached Alexander's side. "There is no point to this."

"Yes there is, Parmenion," growled the king. "Yes there is. Do you see these stains on my clothing? Those are blood stains. My blood. The blood of more than 30 of my Companions – 30! Men I have known since childhood, now dead. Dead because of these..."

"But sire," pleaded Parmenion, "it was Persians who shed their blood, and we have made the Persians pay. These are just mercenaries, Greeks, not unlike others in our army. Call off the attack, I beg of you."

"You may be a great, old soldier, Parmenion," seethed Alexander, "but I am your King, and the son of a god. To dispute what a king commands is sedition," he said angrily, "but to dispute what a god commands is blasphemy! Take care, old man," he concluded with a threatening gesture, "for you are this close to being guilty of both!"

"But, sire," continued Parmenion, who bristled at the insult but, like the veteran soldier he was, refused to back down, "this must end. Besides, it is already getting so dark that we cannot tell friend from foe, and our men are killing each other in the confusion."

"Then bring up torches, yes, that's it! Bring up torches!" shouted Alexander. "Hephaestion, have the archers shoot flaming arrows to light up the field! Fire! I will have fire to see my enemies! Zeus, send us your lightning so we can kill the traitors! Parmenion," he added, his face so close that the old general could smell his hot breath, "I will not say this again: kill them, kill them all!"

Despite the king's harangue, and the light from a hundred blazing torches and impromptu bonfires, the pace of the battle slowed, and finally sputtered out. Men too weary to fight collapsed where they stood, some too weak to put up any resistance when a death blow came. More numerous, better disciplined, and winning, even the Macedonians began to waiver. As mercenary after mercenary fell to their knees, weak from wounds or simply exhausted from the fighting, so did the bloodlust of the Macedonian foot soldiers lessen. To kill a foe in close combat was one thing, but to murder a man on his knees took a special kind of hate...a hate the common Macedonian soldiers simply did not have, or at least could no longer sustain.

Even Alexander himself began to tire, his body pushed far beyond the limit of any mortal man. Hoarse and barely able to maintain his seat upon his stallion, Alexander did not so much order a halt in the fighting as he simply let it come to an end.

Over the next hour or so, men who had only moments before been at each other's throats now began to help each other to their feet. Greek and Macedonian alike, many hard to tell from one another in the sputtering torchlight, so covered in blood and dust and worse were they, walked and crawled and dragged themselves toward the fires, seeking a spot of ground free of corpses to stretch out upon.

Physicians and slaves began to make their way about, bringing water, bandaging wounds, or giving some comfort to the dying. For Klemes, this was his time – the time he hated most, but the time when he was most needed. Although he helped each man he came across, there were two he most sought to aid, if he could only find them.

27

Slavery

"We count the prisoners at around 2,000, give or take perhaps a hundred or so, who are unlikely to live out the day," the staff officer said in his report to the king. "We have taken their shields and armor and weapons, and the men are raising a trophy made out of the captured arms up on the hill."

As they had done for centuries, perhaps as early as the Trojan War if Homer was to be believed, victorious Greek soldiers had raised a temporary monument to mark their triumph on a field of battle. Akin to a tree made of spears, decorated with the shields and helmets of the fallen, the trophy was a sacred and revered symbol of their victory. It also served as a tribute to their comrades who had fallen and as a salute to the valor of the vanquished. At the foot of this trophy, moreover, the Macedonians had laid out their own dead, and set them in neat rows, as if in formation.

Alexander wept and wept openly as he slowly walked the line of corpses. To those whose names and faces he had known, he bent low to touch their cheek, to place a hand on their shoulder, or to kneel and deliver a kiss on their forehead.

"I want each of these brave men to be remembered!" said Alexander tearfully to his officers. "I want artists brought forward, to draw their faces so that sculptors and bronze-workers can create statues of them. Those statues I will have set in a garden back home, so that they and their sacrifice shall never be forgotten!"

Perplexed staff officers looked about, wondering where to find such artists on a bloody battlefield 20 miles deep into Persian territory, but to their credit, such men were, somehow, found. When Alexander – or any king – made a wish it was the same as if he had issued an order, and that meant it must be made so.

"As for the Persian dead," said Alexander as he turned away from the Macedonians who had fallen in his service that day, "find some local holy men so that they may bury their nobles with the rites befitting their station. But first," he added wryly, "strip them of anything of value – if the men have not done so already. I want their armor, however, even if that means buying bits and pieces back from our own soldiers who have beaten us to it. Send every city in Greece a fine suit of this armor, so they can put it on display for all to see. But, for Athens," he added with a rather sly grin, "send 300 suits – all as offerings to the goddess Athena, in recompense for the burning of her temple by the Persians so many years ago."

"That will tweak their sharp noses a bit," Parmenion laughed.

"As I intend."

"May I make a suggestion," interrupted Hephaestion. "Perhaps we could be a bit more diplomatic about that and still accomplish the same thing?"

"And how would you go about that, my dear Hephaestion?" asked Alexander.

"Send the armor back, but with it displayed on wooden crosses, as if the armor was being worn, and in formation. And then have them mounted on large carts, on each of which we inscribe these words: 'Alexander, son of Philip and the Greeks (except the Lacedaemonians) dedicates these spoils, taken from the Persians who dwell in Asia.'"

Alexander nodded his head in agreement and, smiling, added "very good, Hephaestion. We remind the Athenians of our cause, and let the Spartans stew in their own juice. They wouldn't even let a corporal's guard leave their precious Laconia to join us, and so they shall be reminded that they have no share in this glory. Parmenion," the king added, "when I said send armor to every city in Greece, make it every city save Sparta."

"Yes, my King," replied the old general. "And what of the prisoners, Lord King," asked Parmenion, "shall we send them home with the captured armors as well?"

"No," the king replied sternly. "The prisoners are all dead men – at least dead to me, to their families, to their home cities – and to all Greeks. You should not have allowed them to surrender. I told you to kill them all."

"My King, do not ask me to kill unarmed men – men who have surrendered. I gave them my word that..."

"Yes, you gave them your word – and disobeyed mine by letting them surrender. But I shall not make you break your word – again. They may live, but on my terms. They have dishonored us all, and so they shall work to cleanse themselves of that stain. Theirs shall be a never ending task, like Sisyphus, that they shall die trying to accomplish. As Sisyphus labored in Hades, so shall I send them to the closest place like that on earth – the mines. They can rot there for all I care."

"But Lord," objected Parmenion, "these men fought honorably. At least let us ransom them back to their families and cities."

"No!" said Alexander sharply. "They would only be an embarrassment to their relations and neighbors. To send them home or even to sell them back would only encourage others to take Persian gold Darics to march against us – and to rise up to strike at our backs as we drive into the empire.

"Parmenion," added Alexander sternly, "since you care so much for these traitors, I leave them to you. Place them in shackles, and stake the shackles to the ground. Feed and water them, or do not, that I leave to you."

"Sire," sighed Parmenion, "where am I to find shackles for 2,000 men?"

Alexander did not bother to respond, but stalked off toward his tent, calling loudly for wine.

The men of Parmenion's brigade were not happy with their assignment to shackle, tie up, guard, and care for the prisoners. They had marched all morning and afternoon, had drunk no more than a few handfuls – literally handfuls – of wine, and that while waiting for the battle to start. They had then waded their way across a river, climbed a rugged bank, run across a plain, and then charged up a hill, all the while under fire from arrows, javelins, slingers' bullets, and then had fought a bitter hand-to-hand combat against the Greek mercenaries. While others in the army celebrated by looting the Persian dead and their camps, getting drunk or gorging on captured provisions or simply falling asleep, exhausted, the men of Parmenion's brigade had been given one last task to do...and they took out their resentment on their charges.

Even Parmenion was too exhausted to oversee the treatment of the prisoners of war whom he had tried to save. An old man – some said the oldest in the army – Parmenion was even more worn out than his men, and left it to his senior officers to see to the captives. They, in turn, passed that duty on to the junior officers, who in turn did the same to the sergeants and so on. The treatment of the mercenaries in their charge was as haphazard and as careless as it was wholly inadequate and often unnecessarily cruel. It was a cruelty not born of malice but of bitterness – a bitterness the Macedonian soldiers had for the task, more than for the men they were to guard.

Dimitrios had been one of the lucky ones. One of the 2,000 who were allowed to surrender rather than be butchered in their serried ranks. So, too, had been Aristophanes, who had stayed close to his friend throughout the fight. Both had suffered cuts and bruises and a number of other minor wounds, which were made only worse as they were roped in strings of 20 along with the other mercenaries. As Parmenion had explained to Alexander, there was no way to find enough shackles for even a tenth of the captives, so he had his men make do with ropes to tie them up, and then stake the ropes to the ground with tent pegs. Although here and there a small camp fire burned to warm the guards, most of the captives were left lying about in the dark, virtually unattended.

"Halt. Who goes there?" said a rather bored, very tired and barely caring sentry, as a tall man in a long robe came into the light of his fire.

"Just a physician," said Klemes. "An officer told me to see to the prisoners," he added with an intended grumble. "Just when I was about to enjoy some wine and a bit of supper," he added in an obviously unhappy tone. "Damn officers – can't let us have a moment's peace, am I right?"

"Aye," agreed the sentry, in an equally unhappy voice. "As if it's not enough to fight and beat these damn mercenaries, now we have to guard them..."

"...and play nursemaid to them," the physician added, holding up a bag which by his motion the guard understood to be packed with surgical instruments, salves, and whatever other medicines an army physician would need. Alexander's army had hundreds of such men in the baggage train, back with the sutlers, farriers, armorers, army wives, whores and other camp followers. So did the Persian army and especially its Greek mercenary corps, but as Klemes was obviously a Greek, the sentry just assumed he was one of their physicians.

"Go ahead, sawbones, do what you can for the prisoners, not that it will matter much. You won't be doing them any favors."

"How's that?" replied Klemes.

"Because rumor has it that they are to be marched off back to Macedonia, to the mines, to work off their treason as slaves. If it was me, I think I would rather be left here to bleed out than suffer that fate. Almost makes me feel sorry for them – almost," he added with a slight grin.

Klemes was shocked to hear of the plan to send the prisoners as slaves to the mines, but kept that shock to himself. Waving to the guard, he picked up a brand from the fire and with some cloth torn from his robe made himself a torch so as to light his away among the field of captive Greeks. Lest he draw the attention or suspicions of the guards, he stopped here and there to treat a wounded man, or at least make him more comfortable. Each time he did, however, he asked of that man and those nearby if any knew of his brother, and if he had even survived. After about six or seven stops, one of the men responded in the positive.

"Yes, I know him," said the man, whose broken arm Klemes was attempting to set in a sling made from straps. "He was by the general when Clearchos laid down his spear in surrender, as was I. Clearchos is somewhere over there, in the middle of this field, I think. If your brother does still live, he will be there, with the general."

Klemes made his way toward the center of the field, as the man with the broken arm had indicated. He stopped twice more to help injured and wounded men, as he knew it might look odd to a guard if he went directly to that spot. When he did get there, Klemes did indeed find the general – and his brother, who was cradling Clearchos' head in his lap.

"Klemes! Thank the gods you live!" said Dimitrios in surprise and joy, a joy which quickly turned to worry as he added "but why in Hades are you here? Why didn't you flee with the others while you had a chance?"

"What, and leave my little brother behind?" said Klemes kindly. "At the very least I had to see if you were dead, to give you a proper burial. The gods know this Macedonian king wouldn't."

"Well," Dimitrios responded, "as you can see I do not need burying. So get yourself out of here while you can."

"I will not leave you, brother," said Klemes reassuringly. "Where you go, I go...and with a little luck you can go free."

"How? They have some of us chained up, although me, they only tied my foot to a stake in the ground, so I could at least tend to the general here. He's in a pretty bad way, I'm afraid, the old coot. He is too old for this kind of thing."

"His injuries don't look all that bad," said Klemes, as he did a cursory inspection. "Nothing a few stitches, some ointment and clean bandages won't take care of."

"I think it is more than that, brother," replied Dimitrios. "I think having to surrender broke something inside him, as did seeing so many of our men cut down. The weight of that has taken a heavy toll. He would rather have gone down fighting than yield, but he also knew that his was the only voice that Alexander's generals would respect – or at least listen to. It cost him a lot to beg for mercy from them."

"But in so doing at least some of you were spared," interjected Klemes. "Thanks to him I am not winding a funeral shroud around you, but only a bandage around his leg."

"Speaking of legs, have you found Ari? The last I saw of him he was trying to hold a shield over one of the wounded, hoping to save him from a frenzied Macedonian."

"No, Dimitrios, I have not. Let me cut your bonds and together we can go look for him."

"But what about the general?"

At that, Clearchos stirred, opened his eyes, moaned and mumbled something.

"What did he say?" asked Klemes.

"I said," coughed the general, "I said do not worry about me. Go find your friend and if you can escape from here, do so, by any means."

"But, General..."

"Think of that as an order, Captain. It is the last I will ever give – and definitely the last as a free man."

"General, I cannot leave you here. At least come with us..."

"No, Captain. I am old. I am tired. I would only slow you down. Besides, I must remain with the men. They are still my men. Whatever fate they must face, I shall face with them. I could not bear to be free while they labor as slaves, if that indeed is what Alexander has in store for them. No, Captain," he said even more forcefully, or with as much force as he could muster, when Dimitrios started to object, "do not press me further. Go. We Spartans do not like to repeat ourselves. Such is not in our nature. I have already talked far too much for one of my kind. Perhaps," he paused to cough, "perhaps I have been around you Thebans and other foreigners for too long, that I forget my training, my upbringing, and that laconic form of speech for which my countrymen are famed – or chided," he continued with a smile, which ended with another fit of coughing. "Go. Find your friend. Then find Memnon.

Tell him how we fought. Tell him where we are to go. And most of all, I charge you," he said emphatically, punctuating his speech with another fit of coughing. "I charge you to tell him of the courage and nobility of Omares. He should know that at least one Persian stood with us to the very end, though it cost him his life. Perhaps when the heat of battle has cooled and the flush of victory has ebbed, Alexander may see reason – or at least accept a ransom, if Memnon offers it."

"General, if I can get free, where should I go to find Memnon?"

"Alexander will surely head for Sardis; it is the key to this and the other satrapies. Memnon will go there. But I doubt he can organize enough of an army to hold the city. He will go there first, however, before heading for the coast. Alexander will want to sweep up the coastal cities. He must do so if only to guard his back. He surely also expects to find supplies and recruits in those cities. By taking them he will also secure the naval bases, thus forcing our fleet to fall back. If there is anywhere on the coast that can be held it is Ephesus. Memnon knows that. I am sure that is where he will make his stand."

"Then to Ephesus it is, General," sighed Dimitrios, "but after I find my friend."

28

Alexander Moves South

ON THE ROAD TO SARDIS

"The governors of half a dozen cities have offered to open their gates and welcome the army," Hephaestion announced to Alexander as they rode south. "All they ask is that we pledge to restrain the men from looting, pillaging and taking other pleasures by force, or at least keep such activities to a minimum. We are receiving similar offers from a dozen other cities, large and small. Almost all of Lydia is falling over itself to welcome us," he added.

"You see, Parmenion," Alexander said addressing the old general who rode on his right. "They were longing to be liberated, just like Aristotle used to say. The people of Asia will abandon Darius and invite me to be their lord. They know my cause is just and our mission is a sacred one."

"It's because they know when they are beaten," snorted Parmenion gruffly. "Cowardly lickspittles the lot," he chortled in disdain. "Don't let yourself be fooled by their eastern obsequiousness..."

"That's quite a big word for you, Parmenion, isn't it" chided Hephaestion. "Where did you learn that one? You haven't been slacking off and, well, reading, have you?"

"Keep it up, Hephaestion," growled Parmenion, "keep it up. The day is coming when you will push me too far...and Alexander won't be around to protect you."

"Enough, you two, enough," laughed Alexander. "I will not let you spoil my mood. Now, Hephaestion, have your scouts told you what has become of the Persian army...or what is left of it?"

"Most of the levies of course dispersed and went home, and as for the Greek mercenary corps, well, those who are not dead are in shackles heading back to Macedonia."

"But what of the remaining nobles and their cavalry?"

"In full retreat, my King. They are moving so fast that our scouts can barely keep up with them. They appear to be heading for the Taurus Mountains. Perhaps they plan to make a stand at the Cilician Gates."

"That would make sense," Parmenion interrupted. "They could block the passage with a wall, line the hillsides with archers, and make us pay for every foot of ground. And they would have their fleet to anchor their seaward flank, so there would be nothing for us to do but bash our way forward. It will be bloody work, but, well, of course my men will be up to the task."

"Of that I have no doubt, dear Parmenion," said Alexander with sincerity. "But first we need to secure Sardis, free the Greek cities of Ionia, and take a port for our own ships – and by doing so drive their navy farther to the east."

"That means Ephesos, Miletos..." mused Parmenion.

"And then Halicarnassos, especially Halicarnassos," added Hephaestion.

"Yes, Halicarnassos," nodded Alexander. "That is the key. That is their biggest naval base, and the biggest and most famed city in this part of Asia."

The three rode on in silence, the army in a long column stretching out for nearly five miles behind them, with other columns, mostly of cavalry and light troops to either flank. After a few moments, Alexander spoke up, and asked Hephaestion "have your scouts reported if Memnon went with the Persians to the Tarsus Mountains? It would be damn odd if he did..."

"Why is that?" asked Hephaestion.

"Because his roots are here. He is from Rhodes, but counts himself an Ionian Greek. He told me that himself when he was in exile at my father's court years ago. His estates are here, just outside Ephesos. His family is here. His..."

"His heart is here," Hephaestion interrupted.

"Exactly," agreed Alexander.

"Which means he will not run away to the east and abandon it..."

"No, Hephaestion. He will not give up this land without another fight."

"But what will he fight with," laughed Parmenion. "His mercenaries are in chains, his noble cavalry dead or in flight and the local levies dispersed. The cities are coming over to us one by one. Where will he find an army?"

"There are still a lot of mercenaries looking for work," answered Hephaestion.

"Ha!" laughed Parmenion. "And what will he pay them with? We grabbed his army's war chest on the field...or what was left of it after his own men filled their sacks with all they could carry."

"All he needs is one satrap to back him, and he will have plenty of money," replied Hephaestion. He doesn't need Darius' "golden archers," he added, referring to the gold coins issued by the royal mint. "The satraps are allowed to coin silver as they need in order to provide for their defense. Memnon will get someone to mint money, or he will borrow it on his own lands, or he will simply squeeze the nobles and cities as he can. He will have money, and that means he will have an army."

"If he does, it won't be a very good one," harrumphed the old general.

"He doesn't need a 'good' army, just one that can stand behind a stone wall. The question is, where will he make that stand?"

"Halicarnassos," said Alexander in a whisper, first to himself, and then again, louder, so that his generals could hear him. "That is where Memnon will make his stand. He may try to delay us at Ephesos and

Miletos, but those will fall, and he knows it. No, it is Halicarnassos where he will make a final stand."

"The citadel there is particularly well built," Parmenion noted. "We cannot take that by storm. We would need siege engines. Those take time – and planning. Are you certain he will find a willing patron there?"

Alexander nodded in the affirmative. "The satrap there, Orontobates, is a slimy bastard, and a greedy one. He all but stole the post from the last satrap. He will do whatever Memnon tells him to do."

"That will put us deep into enemy territory," Hephaestion noted. "We will need allies..."

"We have one," replied Alexander. "The queen there, Ada, is old, but she is of an ancient line of warrior queens. Her sister, Artemesia, was named after the queen who led a squadron for Xerxes at Salamis. She is a fighter, I hear, just like her ancestor. And it was her brother who was satrap before Orontobates. She has a score to settle, and has already sent word that if we agree to put her on the throne, she will help us. Ada holds the fortress of Alinda, and that controls the road to Halicarnassos. It will make a fine base to prepare the siege.

"Yes, that is where Memnon will make his stand. Halicarnassos. Hephaestion," he said, turning to his friend, "but first thing's first. We need Ephesos. Send word to our navarch Nicanor to move the fleet down the coast, and to set up a blockade there. And Parmenion," he added as he turned to the old general, "you asked me last night where we should go next? Well, now you have your answer. After we parade through Sardis, we head southwest, for Ephesos, Miletos, Alinda, Halicarnassos...and Memnon."

29

The Slave March

WEST TOWARD THE HELLESPONT

Despite Klemes' urging that he and Dimitrios should take advantage of the confusion and exhaustion of the guards the night after the battle to escape, Dimitrios had refused to leave without Ari. Klemes grudgingly agreed, and using his status as a healer to wander among the enslaved former mercenaries, did his best to find their lost comrade. Dimitrios, however, did not enjoy such freedom. Like the rest of the Greeks captured on the Granicos, he was forced to march along as they made their way back to the Hellespont, and the ships that would take them to their new lives in Macedonia – as slaves.

Although Alexander had ordered the Greeks shackled, as Parmenion had pointed out there were just not enough chains and other metal bindings to go around, not for 2,000 men. Dimitrios was fortunately one of those whose bonds were limited to ropes that bound him to ten other men. His hands, too, were bound, and his legs hobbled by yet more rope, tied just loose enough to allow him to march, but tight enough to prevent him from running. Only three things made the march bearable. The first was his brother's ability to sneak some extra food and water to Dimitrios and the others with him at night. The second was the fading but still persistent hope of finding Aristophanes, and the third was his dream of escaping, not to go home, but so that he could once again stand and fight against Alexander.

A few days into the march, Klemes finally found Aristophanes. It was his limp that caught Klemes' eye. It had taken many days to work his way through the long lines of men in search of Ari. It was not a simple task, for he had to make sure he did not rouse the suspicion of the guards. Several times he saw other men staggering along that looked a bit like Ari, but this time he was sure. Klemes continued to make his rounds. He did what he could to help men who had fallen get back up onto their feet, or to convince the guards to let him take a man out of the line to tend to an obvious injury, or staunch the bleeding on a reopened wound. He was never left alone, however, as at least one guard would always be about to make sure the man condemned to slavery would resume the march – or to cut his throat if he could not.

This was a grim business, and a very difficult one for a man who had given his life and his soul to the healing arts. But Klemes soldiered on, as it were, sustained by the hope that he could help Ari and his brother break free one night.

That chance came two days later, just as they reached the coast. A long line of ships had been pulled up onto the beach, to let their timbers dry out and their crews cook a meal, stretch out and get some rest. As the sun began to sink, the guards ordered the men to sit, and for a little food and water to be distributed. Nobody was going anywhere, not in the night. As the guards had done their duty in delivering their charges to the masters of the cargo ships, they were more lax than at any time since that first night. Their job all but done, they ate and drank freely, so much so that even those men who went to relieve their comrades on guard duty arrived at their post quite well lubricated with strong drink.

"This is our chance," Klemes said to his brother quietly, all the while drawing out a small knife to cut his bonds.

"What about the others?" Dimitrios whispered.

"You want me to cut their bonds, too?" answered Klemes. "That is not about to go unnoticed you know, not even with the state the guards are in."

"Don't worry. I've talked with these men," he said, waving his hand to encompass the other nine men in his string, men who had been roped together with him like they were a string of ponies. "They will wait, and one by one they will slink off into the night. A few have friends out here they want to find, just as you found Ari. But I have their word that nobody will do anything foolish or rash, at least not for a little while yet. By then, anyway, Klemes, we may be grateful for anything that distracts the guards, eh?"

Klemes grumbled something about his brother being the soldier and he being just a simple physician, but he understood the risks, and knew they had few other options – if any. The ropes cut, their hands and legs now free, Dimitrios nodded to the others and made his way with Klemes off into the dark, where they made their way around the edges of the camp until they came to where Ari was sitting.

Themistocles of Pella held himself to be a good soldier, and a pious, steadfast, strong-willed sort of a man. To remain such, he had promised his mother long, long ago, the only wine he ever drank was so thoroughly cut with water or vinegar as to bear only the slightest resemblance to wine. Themistocles had been drunk only once, as a boy, and he did not like how it made him act, what it made him do, or how it made him feel the next day.

As luck would have it, Themistocles of Pella was the one guard among all of those set to guard the slaves who was not at least a little drunk that night. He was also the one who was posted just opposite the clump of slaves at the far edge of the camp, right where Ari was sitting.

"Can you take him, brother?" Klemes whispered to Dimitrios as they crouched behind a rock, not far from the sober guard.

"Not head on, and not without making so much noise that it will rouse the camp. Perhaps if you go chat him up and distract him...

"What do you mean 'chat him up?'" responded Klemes rather indignantly. "What am I supposed to say, 'hi, soldier, new in town?'"

"You always have something to say, brother, about everything and anything. So what, now you are suddenly at a loss for words?"

"Damn it, Dimitrios, I'm a physician not a philosopher! I have opinions, yes, and I am always ready to share them, but you know I am not good at starting a conversation. I need...well, you know, I need somebody else to start it so that I can, well, jump in with some witty retort or thoughtful point."

"So you are saying that I should go talk to him? I'm in rags, covered in dirt and dried blood, and with rope burns around my wrists and legs. I'm the very kind of person he is supposed to be guarding, the kind he is supposed to make sure stays tied up!"

"All right, all right," grumbled Klemes. "Wait here. I'll think of something to say to him, but I suspect I won't be able to keep up the conversation for long, considering who I will be talking to..."

"Don't worry, Klemes, as soon as it looks like you have his full attention, I will sneak up and jump him. But be ready to help me. He's a big one, that lad, and he's in full kit, sword, spear, shield, and all. And the best thing I could find to use as a weapon is a rock. You're gonna have to pitch in."

"With what?" replied Klemes somewhat taken aback.

"How about that knife you used to cut our bonds?"

"Damn it, Dimitrios, I'm a physician not a butcher! I took an oath to save lives, not to take them!"

"That again...All right, give me the knife," grumbled Dimitrios. You hit him with your fists, or kick him with your feet or, I don't know, use your teeth if you have to."

"You want me to bite him?" asked Klemes incredulously.

"If you get the chance, sure," replied Dimitrios. "I am sure you'll think of something when the time comes...and that time is about now. Get out there!" he added, giving his brother a shove.

As Klemes stumbled from behind the rock, trying to get his

balance, he made quite a bit of noise – noise that attracted the attention of the guard.

"Halt! Who goes there," said Themistocles, in the words that every guard in history or history yet to be made has used or would use in the future when surprised at his post.

"Good afternoon to you, soldier," responded Klemes a bit nervously. "It's just me, Klemes, the physician, making the rounds of the camp. Must make sure the chattel – or are they cattle – are healthy enough to bother taking aboard the ships. Can't be wasting precious cargo space on men who are about to die, can we?" he added, words just stumbling out of his mouth as he slowly advanced on the guard.

"Oye, I've seen you about," replied Themistocles, starting to let down his guard. "The lads all get a good laugh out of you, jumping about to bandage a man here, give a bit of water to a man there...seems a waste of time, if you ask me. These men are all gonna die in the mines anyway."

"The mines?" asked Klemes.

"Yeah, so I hear. They're all to be sent to the mines. Some might get lucky and go to the quarries; at least those will be able to die in the sunlight, and not in some dark, dank tunnel underground. Serves them right, though, if you ask me," he added as he spat to punctuate his opinion. "Traitors to the cause, money-grubbing mercenaries, the lot of them. We should have just killed them all at the Granicos. Then me and my mates, we'd be with the king and the army. Meanwhile those that are with him are getting all the spoils, while we just shepherd these lambs to the slaughter."

So preoccupied with making his point that he was, Themistocles did not see Dimitrios sneaking up behind him – or at least he didn't see him until just before Dimitrios raised his arm to strike. Klemes knew in a flash that his brother would not get in the first blow, as the guard was already leveling his spear to skewer him. To do so, however, the guard had to turn away from Klemes – who, with an unthinking leap, jumped upon the soldier's back, causing him to stagger to keep to his feet. That was just the opening Dimitrios needed. He charged forward, smashing the rock into the guard's face with one hand, and grabbing his spear with the other.

The scuffle did get the attention of the slaves nearby, but it was all over in seconds. The sound of the scuffle and the movement among the slaves, however, were enough to arouse the suspicions of guards to either side, and as they came stumbling forward, their shouts woke other guards from their stupor. Within minutes the camp was in an uproar. It was just the sort of thing that Dimitrios had hoped to avoid.

30

Sardis

THE CITADEL

"What do you mean you sent an offer to Alexander to surrender the city!" Memnon shouted, his stupefaction at the news outweighed only by his anger.

"What other choice do I have?" shrugged Mithrines, a veteran soldier whom Memnon had placed in command of the garrison at this key city. "You and Spithradates took the best men I had, and where are they now? All you left me with were those too old or too sick to march, and the town watch. That's not enough to hold the citadel, let alone man the walls or put up any kind of fight."

"Mithrines," said Memnon in as calm a voice as he could manage, "I know you can't hold Sardis against Alexander, but if you could just slow him down for a few days..."

"And if I do, what becomes of this city, and her people? You know the rules of war better than any man I know. If I so much as close the gates and fire a single arrow, I give Alexander cause to loot, pillage, rape, and burn the city. Surrender is the only way to spare these people from that. It is the only way I can defend them."

Memnon knew that what the governor of the citadel said was true. He also knew that he could offer no immediate help to bolster the defense, or even provide hope of succor if Mithrines did fight. Still, he had a greater duty to the empire that went beyond saving one city, especially one that was doomed to fall to the advancing Macedonians.

"Could you at least hole up in the citadel and deny him that for a few days? You could open the gates to the city and give him Sardis in return for sparing its people, yet still retain your honor as a soldier and perform your duty as a soldier of the empire."

"And you would march to my relief?" asked Mithrines, knowing the answer would be negative.

Memnon sighed, sat down on the stone bench beside the fountain where Mithrines had received him, and lightly shook his head.

"So I thought, old friend," said Mithrines knowingly. "So I thought."

"Then at least come with me, Mithrines, you and those strong enough to march. I need all the veteran soldiers I can gather."

Mithrines drew himself up, clasped his hands firmly behind him to further straighten his stance and looked down at Memnon. "To do so would be to abandon my post, Memnon. Somebody has to offer terms to Alexander, and somebody has to take responsibility for the people. I will not run away. This is my city. My family is here. If I stay, perhaps I can keep them safe."

"I understand. You are a good man; a man of honor. If my family were here..."

"Look," said Mithrines quietly, gently. "I know you are a solid old soldier and all that, but after how the satraps treated you at the river battle...well, do you think maybe you should just...you know...go home?"

"Home?" replied Memnon in surprise.

"Yes, old friend. Home. To that lovely wife of yours, and your children. Go bundle her up in your arms and get her and the rest of your family away from here. Away from this war. After all, you've done your share of fighting. By the gods, you've done my share as well, and more than most of the satraps. Most of whom, by the way, are falling all over one another to see who can be the first to render proskynesis..."

"And you think I should do the same?"

"No! No! I know better than to even think let alone say that! You are too proud, anyway. All I am saying is that this ship is sinking – so go leap overboard and swim ashore. Let the rest of these miserable slaves fawn and grovel. You go get your lady. Then go away some-place safe. Or at the very least, take her to safety and go tell Darius what is really going on out here."

"Part of me wants to do just that," sighed Memnon. "I long for her every day...and every night," he sighed. "But Darius..."

"Look," Mithrines said, putting his hand on his friend's rather broad but slumped over shoulders, "I know Darius gave you an order..."

"No!" Memnon shot back, suddenly rising to his feet. "The king did not give me an order - he gave me a command! And I don't just mean that he commanded me to defend this part of Asia – he put me in charge..."

"But didn't the satraps ignore that order? Didn't they supersede – even outright steal your 'command?' You've done your job..."

"No. I haven't," replied Memnon forcefully. "And even if the satraps desert the king, I can still fight. I will still fight."

Mithrines sighed, but nodded in understanding. "Then you must do what you must do. Me, well..."

"I know, old friend, I know. Well then, can you at least spare me a string of fresh horses, and let me ask for volunteers from the garrison to go south with me?"

"Of course. Where are you going next?"

"Ephesos. There are two companies of solid, Greek, heavy infantry there."

"They won't be nearly enough to hold the town," observed Mithrines.

"No, but there are a lot of exiles from Greece, and even from Macedonia, there. And it is a port, a good one. I have sent word for the fleet to gather there. Besides, Ephialtes is already there, training men and strengthening the fortifications. Once I get there I can raise more money to hire more troops, and I will, even if I have to strip the gold from the Temple of Artemis!"

"Well, good luck with that, my friend. I will try to buy you a little time – not by fighting, of course, but perhaps by feasting Alexander and his generals. I understand they like to drink, and I will offer them enough wine to drown them and their whole army. Maybe if the Macedonians go on a three-day drunk it will give you a better head start," he added with a smirk.

"That would help," said Memnon gratefully as he stood up, adjusted his armored, and gathered up his cloak. "And at this point, any help would be appreciated."

Memnon and his small entourage galloped out of one end of the city as Mithrines rode north to make his offer to Alexander. The governor and several of the town fathers accompanying him were intercepted by Alexander's scouts, who escorted them back to where the king was riding, about eight or nine miles from the city. The governor, to his surprise, was welcomed and welcomed warmly, once he had made the intention of his mission known. Mithrines had hoped to buy Memnon time by dragging out the negotiations, but Alexander would have none of that. He talked as they rode south. It was not until they reached the Hermus River, about an hour's quick march from the city, that Alexander called a halt. Mithrines had convinced him that the Macedonian king would be welcomed as a liberator, and if he and the army were to parade through its streets, a pause was needed to allow the long marching columns to form up in proper array. Alexander made good use of the time to dictate messages to his scribes. He appointed governors and garrison commanders to areas which he had conquered or which were in the process of submitting to his rule as he drove deeper into the empire. He examined reports of supplies, unit strengths, and the progress made by his deputies at home as well as information gathered by his agents abroad.

Rest did not come easy to Alexander, nor did he need as much as most men. Whether driven by his spirit, his pride, his ambition, or the demons his mother had called upon to resurrect (or at least revive) him at Pelion, Alexander was almost perpetually in motion. The young Macedonian king was a machine that came to a stop only when absolute exhaustion – or absolute intoxication – forced such a stop upon him. Thus, after a few hours of pacing back and forth and dealing with administrative details, he grew impatient with the halt at the river.

Mithrines may have given up the city, but he was still able to find ways to detain and distract the young conqueror, as he had promised Memnon. He personally conducted Alexander on a tour of the city, and then escorted him through the gates of the triple-walled citadel and up to the top of its battlements. Alexander was so impressed with the majesty of the fortress atop the city's acropolis that he began to talk about building an altar there to commemorate his victory and to give thanks to his father.

"It would indeed be fitting to raise an altar here in honor to your father," agreed Mithrines, who sought any opening that would keep Alexander occupied. "I believe we have some coins with King Philip's likeness on them that we could use as a model for..."

"Not Philip!" said Alexander angrily. "I said it was to honor my father – Zeus, the king of the gods!"

As if on cue, the sky suddenly grew dark, and with a rumble of thunder and a flash of lightning, the heavens opened up.

"There! You see!" yelled a delighted Alexander, "my father is pleased!"

"My mistake, Lord King," said Mithrines, bowing deeply to hide the amused look on his face. "It is indeed a sign that Zeus, of course, is your father. Well, we have some excellent artisans here in Sardis, and if your majesty would give me a few days I am sure I could gather them together so that you could instruct them on..."

"Yes, yes, of course," said Alexander somewhat distractedly, "see to it at once. Oh, and I will need you to arrange for quarters and supplies for the new garrison. I intend to leave a battalion of Argives here to secure the city. Pausanias will be in charge once I leave, and Nicias will collect the tribute..."

"Tribute, my King?"

"Yes, Mithrines, tribute. Liberation does not come without a price, and we have a war to fund – and an altar to build! Don't worry, I am not greedy, nor is my father, Zeus. We will take some of that tribute in kind – provisions, weapons, armor, horses, and the like. I expect you to give my officers every assistance possible and, oh, by the way," said Alexander, barely taking a breath, "there is one building in the city that I am particularly eager to see, and which I believe you have forgotten to point out in our tour of Sardis."

"And what building is that?" asked a perplexed Mithrines.

"Why, the treasury, of course."

31

The Hellespont

TO THE SHIPS

The little scuffle with Klemes, Dimitrios, and the burly guard, was the spark that ignited the fire. The more guards that came running, the more prisoners rose up to get in their way. Knives came out. Swords were wrestled from the soldiers. Bonds were cut. Burning brands from the campfires became weapons – as did rocks, sticks, fists, feet, and teeth. It was a battle the captives knew they could not win – but days of mistreatment, abuse, and the anger at being treated as slaves rather than prisoners of war, fueled an explosion of violence – and one made more intense by the knowledge that, being sentenced to die as slaves, they had nothing to lose.

While the guards were hardly the cream of Alexander's army -they were more like a less desirable substance that also floats to the top- they were still soldiers. Armed, armored -at least in part- and almost equally unhappy about being where they were, the guards matched the prisoners in their exasperation and violence. Over the course of an hour scores of men went down, most for good, until the officers and a detachment of cavalry were able to restore order.

That hour was spent well by Dimitrios and Klemes, who made an ally of the confusion to free Ari, dash off to the shoreline, and find their way down the coast to a small fishing village. Stealing a boat was easy enough, and while neither Klemes nor Ari were of much use, Dimitrios, at least, had some inkling of what he was doing.

"I am no sailor," he admitted, "but I have spent enough time crossing back and forth across the sea, buying and selling wine, that I was able to pick up a thing or two. You two can make yourselves useful on the oars while I handle the tiller."

"Row? Row? Row your boat?" objected his brother. "The damn thing has a sail, so why the hell do we have to row?"

"Because if we raise the sail, it will be too easy to spot us. Dark night, white sail – you figure it out," responded Dimitrios.

"Yeah, that," agreed Ari, "and the fact that you do not know how to actually, well, sail."

"I'll figure it out," grumbled Dimitrios, acknowledging that his friend was right.

"Oh, great," said Klemes, straining at the oars. "It's dark, we don't know where we are or where we are going, and the man at the tiller has no idea how to sail the ship. What could possibly go wrong?"

"There doesn't seem to be any food or water here, either," added Ari, "so you can add that to your list."

"We'll manage, we'll manage...somehow," said Dimitrios, who tried to be reassuring, but came off as something quite the opposite.

"Well, we know that Asia is on our left," interrupted Ari. "So if we keep Asia to our left, we will eventually get somewhere down the coast where we can find a friendly garrison and a proper ship, right? Alexander probably hasn't been able to gobble up all of the ports yet, right?"

"Let us hope so, Ari," said Klemes, "let us hope so, or this is going to be the briefest escape in history."

After about three days of rowing and sailing down the coast, the three friends spotted a pair of warships coming up from the south. As that was the direction of the Persian controlled ports, Dimitrios assumed they would be Persian, and he was at least partly right. As they were brought aboard the lead vessel, Dimitrios learned that the ships were manned by Phoenicians, who made up the majority of the crews of the Persian fleet.

"What can you tell us of the Macedonians," the commander of the vessel asked his new guests. "Are there many ships of theirs up ahead?"

"A small fleet, Captain," replied Dimitrios. "Mostly transports and a few supply ships."

"Any warships?" the Phoenician officer asked.

"Not that I saw," replied Dimitrios, "but then again, it was dark and, frankly, I wasn't counting ships – just trying to get away from them."

"Well," the Phoenician captain said thoughtfully, rubbing his chin, "perhaps we should go have a look then?"

"What! We just came from back there!" Klemes groaned. "We need to put as much water as we can between us and them. We need to go in the other direction, to a friendly port."

"Oh, and you will, my friend, you will. I promise," said the officer reassuringly. "We are based at Ephesos. We will be rejoining the squadron there...but first, we go back up the coast. Those are my orders. The squadron commander wants to know where the Macedonian fleet is, and where it is heading. So until we find it, we keep going north."

The two Persian warships did just that for the rest of the day and into the next, stopping only at night to beach the vessels and rest the crews. About midday on the second day, Aristophanes thought he spotted a bank of clouds on the horizon.

"Those aren't clouds," a Phoenician sailor who overheard him said. "Those are sails. Lots and lots of sails...and I don't think they are ours."

Dimitrios looked in the direction his friend and the sailor were pointing, and made his way aft.

"Commander," he said as he found the officer in charge. "You know how you said you would head north until you found the enemy fleet?"

"Yes," he answered.

"Well," Dimitrios said as he pointed to what Ari had thought were clouds, "I think you've found them."

32

Ephesos

BLOOD IN THE STREETS

lood quite literally flowed through the streets of Ephesos. The Greek exiles who had been running the city for years were never beloved, and their treatment of the natives of Greek heritage as some kind of second-class Hellenes did not endear them to the general populace, nor did their reputation for corruption. The news of Alexander's victory at the Granicos encouraged some elements of the oppressed citizenry to rise up, a decision further encouraged by Alexander's agents and the gold they funneled to the opposition leaders. Government officials, wealthy exiles, and anyone against whom common folk carried a grudge were ambushed on the streets or dragged from their homes by gangs of toughs. Mobs gathered to ransack businesses and government offices, and then scattered as soldiers arrived to restore order. Instead of a fortress set to withstand the might of the Macedonian armies, Memnon found a city in turmoil, and one ready, and even eager, to open its gates to welcome Alexander.

Ephialtes had done his best, but with only two companies of veteran hoplites and the city watch at his command, it was all he could do to keep the navy yard and citadel secure. His frustration and anger were eclipsed only by his humiliation at having failed to do as his commander, Memnon, had ordered.

"I relied on you, Ephialtes. I needed you to strengthen this place for a siege, and instead what do I find? Chaos!" shouted Memnon angrily as he met with Ephialtes in the citadel. "Utter and complete chaos! Do you know that my escort had to fight its way through the streets to get me here?"

Ephialtes, visibly shaken and thoroughly chastised, did not offer any excuses. "I am sorry, General. I have failed the empire, and I have failed you. That you yourself were at risk in the streets only...only..."

"Enough of that. We need to regain control of the city. How many men have you mustered?"

"Not enough, lord," admitted Ephialtes gloomily. "I offered a rich bounty, but for every Daric I offered someone else offered two. No sooner would I arm and equip a man that off he would run at night, taking his weapons with him. I even tried locking men into their barracks at night...but in the morning all I would have would be broken down doors and beaten up guards to show for it. Memnon, I do not know what to do. This city is lost, and I do not know how to get it back."

Memnon was speechless. Was this the proud Athenian general who had fought at Chaeronea? Who had accepted exile in Persia rather than take a knee to Alexander? The man who had offered to stand and die at the Granicos, even knowing defeat and death were all but certain?

"Perhaps if I had more men..."

"There are none," grumbled Memnon.

"What of Thymondas, at Miletos. Last I heard, he had gathered nearly a thousand men."

"...and they are needed there," Memnon replied. "Especially now, especially if we are not going to be able to defend Ephesos as we had planned."

"It is all my fault, lord," said Ephialtes, who drew his sword and handed it, hilt first, to the general. "I have failed you. I have no option but to lay down my command. I ask only that I be allowed to march in the ranks, as a simple soldier, so that I may at least in some small way retain my honor."

"Damn it, man, put away your sword!" said Memnon angrily.

"There is no time for this sort of thing. There is no time for such theatrics, Ephialtes. You Athenians," he sighed, "it is always about the drama with you, isn't it. You were once a city of soldiers and sailors, but now it seems you are all just philosophers and playwrights. I don't need some grand gesture fit for the stage, Ephialtes. I need an officer I can depend upon."

"I fear I am no longer that man..."

"Oh, by the gods, stop it, stop it Ephialtes! There are damn few men whom I can rely on as it is. I thought you were one of them. If you truly believe this city is lost, then lost it is. We'll just have to salvage what we can. Can you help me with that? Can you?"

"Yes, I suppose so, lord..."

"You suppose so or you can? Which is it, Ephialtes?"

"I can...try. I can at least try. What would you have me do?"

"If you can't keep order in the city, then at least make sure you keep secure the port and the citadel. Admiral Autophradates is bringing the fleet here," Memnon explained. "When he arrives, have him strip the arsenals of everything he can load aboard his ships. Whatever he can't, he is to burn or dump into the sea. Surely you can hold things together long enough for him to do that, can't you?"

"I will, or I will die trying," said Ephialtes, recovering his composure a bit.

"I don't want you to die, and not for that," sighed Memnon, once again impatient at the Athenian's dramatics. "Do your duty. Hold out long enough to let Autophradates do as I said, and then get the hell out of here. I want you on the last boat out of town – and by that I mean the very last boat- and alive, and with whatever men you can take with you."

"And then what?" asked Ephialtes.

"Miletos. Tell Autophradates to shift his fleet to there. I will meet the both of you at Miletos. The governor there, Hegesistratos, is a mouse of a man but he is my mouse, and a capable if fidgety rodent at that. I need a day and a night at my estates to the east of here, enough time to get my wife and children to safety, and then I will ride hellbent for Miletos. See if you can buy me some time, any time at all, to put that place in order. Can I depend upon you, Ephialtes? Will you buy me the time to get my wife and children away?"

"Yes, my General," said Ephialtes, raising himself to his full height, back straight as a spear and chest out proudly. "I will."

If Memnon had all but given up on Ephesos, it still remained the goal for Dimitrios, Klemes, and Ari – and for the captains and crews of the two Persian vessels they had encountered while fleeing the slave camp. Getting there, however, was becoming less and less certain.

The Phoenician officer in command of the Persian scout vessel was sparing no effort to go there, but a squadron of Alexander's ships was not far behind – and was closing. The officer, Abibaal, had raised the sail in order to give his exhausted rowers a chance to rest. The wind, however, was not cooperating. The breeze was steady but not strong, and it was all he had to work with. His oarsmen were professionals, veteran sailors all, yet they were only human, and could only be driven so far without a break. Klemes joined two others of the crew who moved about the rowing benches, handing out cups of sour, watered-down wine, chunks of stale bread and handfuls of wrinkled olives. It was not much, although it was all that could be done aboard the cramped wooden warship.

"Captain Abibaal," asked Dimitrios as the two peered out over the stern at the oncoming Greeks, "is there no way to increase our speed? Can't you throw your supplies or something overboard to lighten our vessel and allow us to go faster?"

Abibaal laughed at the soldier's suggestion. "What cargo? Other than a few skins of wine, there is nothing to throw. We are a scout ship, not a merchant man or even a trireme. We don't even have a ram!" he added with a knowing laugh. "We are built for speed as it is. That is our only real weapon. We are meant to find the enemy and then race back to the flagship with our news. The only extra weight we are carrying is, well...you, and your friends. Are you offering to jump overboard?" he added with a smirk.

"No, I guess not," replied Dimitrios. "But perhaps I could relieve one of your oarsmen?"

That really made Abibaal laugh.

"What's so funny?" asked Dimitrios, offended and puzzled.

"That would only slow us down even more. My dear soldier, my men work as one. They move as one. They live for their oars. To substitute you for one of them would only throw the others off their timing and pace. Besides, I don't care how good you are at carrying a spear and a shield, for even the strongest soldier would falter after a quarter of an hour at the bench. It is not just a matter of muscle, but of stamina – and of timing," he explained, then added, with a smile, "but thank you for offering. I am sure you meant to help."

"Is there nothing, then, that I can do?" asked Dimitrios.

"Well," said Abibaal, "if you have an in with Poseidon, now would be the time to petition him with prayer."

"But you cannot petition the lord of the sea with prayer."

"That is not how we sailors see things. So, since there is quite literally nothing more you can do, and as you are, frankly, becoming a distraction, how about you humor me and go pray, or at least go through the motions. After all, it couldn't hurt."

Dimitrios, having nothing else to do, began to do as the sailor had asked. Within a quarter of an hour the sky began to darken, and the wind began to pick up. As the clouds gathered, the rumble of thunder and the flash of lightning announced the storm. Most of the pursuing Greek squadron turned about and headed for the shore, but three of the lighter vessels kept coming ahead, despite the wind, and the rain, and the lightning.

"Well now, that is something," Abibaal whistled as he looked first at the clouds, then at Dimitrios. "I thought I was only joking, but I guess you do indeed have an in with Poseidon. But hang on, soldier," he added with another laugh, "there are still three of them after us, and with this wind, well, hang on, because it is going to be a bumpy ride!"

33

Ephesos

CHAOS

E phialtes did his best to comply with Memnon's orders, but the harder he cracked down, the wider and deeper the cracks became. The arrival of the fleet brought temporary solace, but once the navy began to pull out, all hell broke loose – among his own men. Fearful of being abandoned, Ephialtes' Greek mercenaries abandoned their posts and made a rush for the port. They seized a pair of merchantmen and forced the captains of those ships to take them to safety. There was no question of following the fleet, not after such an insurrection, as they would be treated as deserters and worse. Where they went from Ephesus, no one knew...but wherever they went, they would be of no use to Memnon.

Ephialtes had tried to hold his men together, promising that he would get them to safety, but when the fleet began to pull out, panic set in. When the mercenaries ran, the city watch melted away. With no more than a squad of men still loyal, and the mob running rampant throughout the city, Ephialtes decided that he could follow at least one of his orders – that to stay alive. With a grim visage and a weary stride, Ephialtes and his small band made their way to the stables, and with a string of spare horses in tow, rode out of the city, hoping to reach Miletos before Alexander's own cavalry blocked the way.

"They're still gaining on us, Captain Abibaal," said Dimitrios. "I guess my prayers didn't work as well as we needed them to," he added with a strained laugh. "Is there nothing else we can do? Can our rowers pick up the pace?"

"They are about dead at their oars as it is, my friend," replied Abibaal with a concerned sigh.

"Well, their rowers can't be any better off. They must be just as tired as our men."

"Not if they are Athenians, as I am beginning to suspect they are," the Phoenician officer responded. "Alexander demanded Athens supply him with a squadron of their best and fastest ships. Those may be some of them."

"Aye," agreed Dimitrios. "Athens has always had the best oarsmen. They serve their fleet at the rowing bench the way men of property serve as hoplites. I met such men when I was in their city, before coming to Asia."

"Then you know what we are up against, my friend. I would bet on my crew over any other ship in our fleet, or in that of any of the Greek states – except Athens. In a race on the water, my father told me, if Athenians are involved, always bet on Athens."

"Then why don't we just raise the sail – the wind will be equal for us both."

Captain Abibaal laughed. "Well, it is a good thing that I am in the navy and not you, soldier. The wind is coming from our southwest quarter. It would only drive us back toward them. So, no sails. To raise sails means capture and slavery, or worse. If we row well, we live. If not..."

Despite the wind, the waves and the rain, the ships giving chase did not falter. Every hour they came just a few ship lengths closer, and if the enemy were indeed Athenians, the Phoenician captain knew that he and his crew could only delay the inevitable, not prevent it.

As the waves got stronger, the rowing became even more difficult. Dimitrios saw how a crashing wave would put the oarsmen off their timing. Some were nearly washed overboard and had to grab on to their comrades or their benches, and whenever even one oarsmen did so, all of the others on his bench and those behind and in front of him would falter and have to reset.

"Captain," he said as he wiped the rain and spray from his face, "you said you did not want me at the oars because it would upset the timing of the rowers."

"Yes, I did," said Abibaal.

"Well then, how about if we do something to upset the timing of their rowers?"

"I would love to," grunted Abibaal, "but how? I don't have any way of doing that."

"But I do...or, should I say, my friend does."

"What do you mean," the Phoenician officer asked, trying to puzzle out what magic one of the Greeks might possess to hinder their pursuers.

"Do you have any bows on board?"

"Yes, of course. That's about the only weapon we have besides our speed. Why do you ask?"

"My friend Ari, he is an accomplished archer. He won prizes at home, and ever since he was wounded in the leg, he has tried to become even better with a bow. Since he cannot stand in a shield wall with his injury, he can stand behind it and provide covering fire. If he could pick off a few of their rowers, that would break up their timing, wouldn't it? I mean they'd have to help a wounded man or move a dead one from their bench, or try to take cover..."

"It would never work," Captain Abibaal sighed. "We are still too far away. We are well out of bow range."

"Then let them come closer."

"What?" said the Phoenician officer in alarm.

"Yes, slow the pace of our rowers so that the Athenians can close the distance. That will give your men at least a little break. Once in bow range, Ari can pick them off one at a time. There is nowhere for them to hide..."

"Dimitrios," scowled the naval officer. "If we get close enough to fire arrows at them, don't you think that they might just have a couple of archers who could do the same?"

"No, not at all," said Dimitrios with confidence. "They would be shooting into the wind. Ari would have the wind behind him. Trust me, Captain Abibaal. This is the kind of thing a soldier knows, and knows from experience. We just have to find the right distance where we can hit them and they cannot hit us."

"And how do we do that?" asked Abibaal, suddenly very interested in the Greek officer's idea.

"Leave that to my friend," replied Dimitrios. "That is not something for a hoplites or a sailor, but for an archer to figure out. Ari!" he said as he turned and shouted for his friend, "Ari. Get up here...and grab a bow."

PART IV

Miletos

WESTERN COAST OF ASIA MINOR

Year Three of the Reign of Alexander of Macedonia

34

Miletos

MEMNON TAKES CHARGE

s Ephialtes was fighting a losing battle to bring order to and bolster the defenses of Ephesos, Memnon reached Miletos, and prepared to ready that city for war. That, unfortunately for Memnon and the Persian empire, was not to be an easy task.

As Alexander walked into Sardis, he sent out flying columns in every direction to secure the towns and smaller cities of Ionia, and to clear his own path into Ephesos. What Memnon had hoped to have been a roadblock to the Macedonian advance instead became a welcoming, if somewhat disorderly base. The Macedonians may not have had to fight to take Ephesos, but they did have some difficulty in restoring order in the troubled city. Even while the Macedonians were taking possession of the urban center and the docks, its angry populace dragged many a wealthy man from their homes, and stoned them to death while they ransacked their possessions, raped their women, and herded their children off to the slave pens – or worse. The fires set by arsonists, looters, and the departing Persian fleet alike, also took time and manpower to get under control, but by the time Alexander himself was ready to enter, things were calm enough for his victory march.

As Alexander gathered supplies in preparation for his move south to his next target, Miletos, Memnon struggled to make the city ready to oppose him. That was a job made all the more difficult by the governor of Miletos, a rather corpulent and oily bureaucrat named Hegisistratos.

"So you're telling me that you, too, have already written to Alexander with an offer to open the gates to him without a fight, just like Sardis?" roared Memnon as he slammed his helmet down upon the governor's desk.

"Yes, of course. What else was I supposed to do?" the man said, cringing behind the desk as if it were a fortification that could protect him from the general's wrath.

"You could do your duty, and prepare to defend this place as Darius has entrusted you to do," bellowed Memnon. "The outer defenses are in such decrepit shape as to be unworthy of the name – and there is not a man on station to guard them! Just where is your garrison, governor?"

Hegisistratos cringed again, raised his arms as if to ward off a blow and replied "Here. In the city proper."

"And just what are they doing in here when the war is coming from out there?"

"Keep...keeping order, General," mumbled the oily haired man in the silken robe. "They are protecting the treasury."

"You mean they are protecting you," said Memnon in disgust. "You and the wealth you have made skimming off the taxes and tribute to his majesty. Well, at least we will have money enough to pay the workmen to shore up the walls, and to hire men to hold them."

"You mean to fight the Macedonians, and here?" asked the governor in dismay and fear. "Why, why, the city will be ruined. All will be destroyed. All will be lost..."

"Yes, probably," said Memnon rather matter-of-factly. "This city will not withstand the Macedonians, not for long."

"Then why fight?" asked the governor incredulously. "Why fight if they are going to win anyway?"

"To buy time, that is why. To bleed them, to make them pay in blood, and treasure, and, most of all, in time. Time is our ally, not theirs. The more time we can give the empire, the more forces can be raised to come here and stop Alexander."

"But...but...but where does that leave me...I mean us..."

"No, Governor, you meant 'me,' as in what is to become of you as we defy the young king."

"Yes...yes...exactly..."

"Well, Hegisistratos," laughed Memnon slyly, "it means you must become a hero. Or at least look like one."

Through the power of his name and the force of his will, Memnon was able to convince the commanders of the local Persian and mercenary forces in the city to do as he ordered – albeit for a handsome price. He drew upon the authority given him by Darius to issue commands, and to delve into the city coffers to convince them with gold where words failed. His promise that the Persian fleet would be arriving soon instilled some hope in them as well. It also instilled in them the fear that if they did not do as Memnon bid, the fleet would enforce his orders, and do so with the kind of severity for which the empire was too well known.

When a forest of sails appeared on the horizon a week later, those officers, as well as Hegisistratos, realized that they had made the correct choice in doing their duty. The Macedonian army, according to the scouts Memnon had sent out, was still many days march away. Now at least they could proclaim, and with surety, to the admiral that they were good, loyal subjects of the empire. At least that is what they were about to do, until they saw the designs on the sails.

A fleet had indeed arrived, as Memnon had predicted. But it was the wrong fleet.

While Admiral Nicanor and the advance squadrons of Macedonia and a dozen Greek allied cities set up their blockade of Miletos, a trio of scout ships continued their pursuit of a lone Phoenician vessel farther to the north. And they were closing in on their prey.

"Are they in range yet?" Captain Abibaal asked of Dimitrios and Ari.

"Let us see," said Ari calmly as he drew back on the bow, raised it high, and let loose an arrow. The arrow splashed into the sea about a ship's length ahead of the pursuing Athenian vessel, whose officers did not appear to have noticed the single arrow coming down through the storm of sea and rain.

"Almost," said Ari, as he notched another arrow and counted quietly and slowly to ten before launching it at his target. This time the arrow struck the enemy ship – but only in the prow. Again, the Athenians seemed oblivious, neither noticing nor even suspecting that they were now the quarry of those they hunted.

Again, Ari notched an arrow, counted to ten and let fly. This one caught an Athenian rower in the shoulder. As he slumped forward his oar shot up out of the sea, slightly throwing off the pace of those of his fellow oarsmen who had seen their comrade fall over. Ari fired three more times, twice hitting rowers, before the Athenians sent one of their own men with a bow onto the prow. Ari shot him before the man could take aim. Two more men tried to take the place of the fallen archer, but again, they too fell to Ari's fire. Unable to protect his crewmen, the captain of the lead Athenian pursuit ship did the only thing he could do – he stopped, backed oars, and tried to get out of range of the archer who was decimating his crew.

"That should keep them out of our hair at least for a little while," laughed Ari. "It will at least force them to keep their distance."

"Well done, young Theban," said Captain Abibaal with appreciation and respect. "But I think you should go and find someplace to sit down and rope yourself in."

"Why is that?" asked Ari.

"Because the storm is about to get a lot worse."

"Aren't you going to put in to shore, then?" asked Dimitrios as he looked to the southwest at the darkening sky and the rising waves.

"Nope," said Abibaal. "If we go to shore, the Athenians will just come and take us.

"You don't mean you're going into that?" asked Dimitrios in a near panic.

"Of course. It's our only hope. Besides, if we are to die, let it be at sea, battling the storm. We are sailors," he added as he looked Dimitrios in the eye, "and if we are to die, we will die as sailors, not as slaves."

The captain of the Athenian squadron decided otherwise. He signaled the other vessels to come about and head for shore. There was no sense risking their ships. What they had failed to do, the storm would do for them. That Persian ship was as good as lost already, and her crew were dead men – or soon would be in that storm.

35

Miletos

THE SACRED WAY

A s Ephialtes rode up the Sacred Way into Miletos, he was surprised to see how few soldiers there were, manning the outer walls. Neither the area around the Necropolis, on the rising ground below the city, nor the Old Citadel Hill, just to the south of the tombs, showed any signs of military activity. He knew both positions were the key to defending Miletos, as they controlled the base of the peninsula upon which the city was built.

Ephialtes and his small escort were dusty, bone-weary and barely able to sit their horses, such was their exhaustion. They had had to ride long and hard to keep ahead of the Prodromoi, the elite force of light cavalry Alexander sent ahead of his armies to scout the territory. It had been a close-run thing to escape capture or death from these small but fierce bands of enemy horsemen – unlike that bunch of mounted infantry which protected Ephialtes. There were many times when Ephialtes and his men could see the Macedonian horsemen on a far hill or across a valley, but they knew better than to try to engage them, for where there was one band of enemy cavalry, others would surely be nearby.

The gate where the Sacred Way entered the city was wide open.

While there were sentries on station, they showed little interest in the Greek general and his party. The guards seemed both distracted and agitated. Those were clear signs of what Ephialtes knew from his recent experience indicated that the guards were more ready to bolt than to stand their ground. These were not determined sentinels, he realized, but restless conscripts only looking for an excuse, or an opportunity, to flee.

Ephialtes knew Miletos quite well. Even if he had not, he needed no guide to point the way to the citadel. From its position on the rocky hill at the tip of the peninsula, the citadel was visible from every point in the city. As he rode through the South Agora, past the Nymphaion and the Delphinion, and up through the narrow streets, he saw few signs of martial preparedness. To the contrary, he saw other signs, clear signs of a people who, like the guards at the gate, had not resistance but surrender – or flight – on their minds.

As he neared the fortress, the old general took some heart that at least the guards at the citadel appeared to be doing their duty properly. Even though the Captain of the guard detail recognized Ephialtes, the fellow mercenary officer went through the proper motions of asking him to identify himself, his purpose in coming to the citadel, and whom he wished to see there. The crisp, serious, and steadfast way in which the officer performed his duty earned him a smile from Ephialtes, along with a paternal pat on the shoulder.

"It is good to see that there is at least one proper soldier left in Miletos," he added with as much of a smile as the weary general could manage. "I need to see General Memnon immediately, but I would appreciate it greatly if you could see to the quartering of my escort and the stabling of their horses. They have had a hard ride from Ephesos."

"As have you, General, begging your pardon," the young officer said with concern, dropping the formalities for a moment. "I can direct someone to show you where to clean up, have a meal, and perhaps a short rest before taking you to see General Memnon."

"That is very kind of you, Captain," replied Ephialtes with a nod, "but there will be time for that later – not much time, I am afraid, but time enough. I thank you for your concern and for your kindness, but I must see Memnon, and see him now."

The young officer turned command of the guard over to a sergeant and personally escorted the old general into the citadel. Ephialtes, to his shame, began to shudder, involuntarily, for the change in temperature from the hot, sunny street to the cool interior of the stone fortress came as a sudden shock, and all the more so as he was hot, sweaty, and bone-tired from his long ride. The officer did not remark upon the general's state, but simply undid the fasteners on his cloak and offered it to Ephialtes, who accepted it with equal graciousness and with a nod of gratitude. It would not do to appear before his commander in chief as a shivering, dirty, and beaten old man. The cloak helped ease the shivering, covered the dust, and gave him a semblance of dignity as he entered the audience hall where Memnon had set up his headquarters.

Memnon was moving toy soldiers and models of ships about on a scale model of the city and its defenses that was laid out upon a large table. The officers to whom he was explaining his plan, at first did not appear to notice Ephialtes, but did so once the young officer escorting him stamped his heavy boots on the stone floor, came to attention, saluted, and announced his arrival to Memnon's aide de camp.

Upon hearing his friend's name, Memnon suddenly stopped what he was doing and glowered at Ephialtes.

"What the hell are you doing here, Ephialtes? You should be in Ephesos, where I left you, holding the city against Alexander."

"There was nothing left to hold, General," Ephialtes said with a penitent bow. "The garrison fled, the city watch deserted, and the mob ruled the streets. I know I have failed you, General, but please understand that there was nothing I could do. My staff and I barely escaped with our lives, and have ridden hard to get here to make the situation known to you. I felt that it was my duty to report my failure to you, in person, and as soon as possible."

In a fit of anger, Memnon smashed his fist down on the table, sending some of the toy soldiers and wooden model buildings clattering off onto the floor. "Then that means Alexander will be here soon – and a lot sooner than I want him to be. As you may have noticed when you rode in, Ephialtes, this city is in no way ready to withstand a siege."

"Yes, General," said Ephialtes in agreement. "There don't seem to be many men on guard, and no sign of anyone building new fortifications."

"That's because there are no men to do so," muttered Memnon.

"But what of Thymondas and his men? That's a thousand good men, men you said you would need here and thus could not spare for Ephesos," asked Ephialtes. "If they are not here, where are they?"

"That, my old friend, is a damn good question. The earth seems to have swallowed them up. I've had scouts out looking for Thymondas for the last three days. I need him and his command here, and even sooner than I had thought. Without them, we have no hope of putting up even a token defense of the city, let alone holding out against a siege. I truly needed you to buy me some time at Ephesos. Didn't the Admiral lend you men to secure the city?"

"No, sir, he did not," said Ephialtes, swallowing hard. "He could do nothing, such was the state of things. The best he could manage was to load what supplies and naval stores he could take aboard his ships, but there was no sense to remaining in the harbor. The marines he landed were barely able to hold the port long enough for him to set fire to the remaining stores and sheds before heading back out to sea."

"Well," said Memnon still quite angry, "if the fleet is not in Ephesos, and it is not here, then just where the hell is it?"

The storm had scattered the Persian fleet, and with the winds coming hard from the southwest there was little chance of making for Miletos as Admiral Autophradates had planned. So he did the next best thing he could think of, to seek the shelter of the straights between the island of Samos and the mainland, near the Mycale Peninsula. Any vessels sailing south for Miletos would normally pass through these straights, rather than waste time sailing around the big island, or so the Admiral believed. With a good, sheltered beach and plenty of fresh water nearby, Mycale would make for a good place to reconstitute and reorganize the fleet, and to still support Miletos from the north.

Nicanor also knew of the straights, and for the very reasons that his Persian counterpart Autophradates went to Mycale, he avoided them. He had landed troops on Samos, where they had been welcomed as liberators by the mostly Greek inhabitants. With the island as a base, he managed to get most of his navy around Samos and into the bay of Miletos, without having to fight his way through the straights of Mycale. His fleet was now between the Persian navy and its bases, and well situated to set up a blockade of Miletos.

It was not just Memnon who was surprised his fleet was no longer at Ephesos. That came as quite a shock to Captain Abibaal as well, as his battered ship and her exhausted crew saw Macedonian banners wafting from its battlements. Before any of the warships in the harbor raised sail, the Captain quickly turned his vessel about and headed down the coast to the south.

"Where are we going now, Captain," asked Dimitrios.

"South. Since Ephesos has clearly fallen to Alexander, our fleet must be somewhere to the south. Miletos, most likely. That is the next major port – unless they've kept on going all the way to the big naval base at Halicarnassos. Either way, we'll head for Miletos first. I can set you and your friends off there if you'd like, even if I have to keep heading south."

"Is that where you think we might find Memnon?" asked Dimitrios.

"That is where I would go," said Abibaal, "but then again, I'm a sailor, not a soldier, let alone a high and mighty General like Memnon. You should at least be able to find out his whereabouts from someone there. But relax, Dimitrios. We still have many days and nights to go – and I have to get this ship up on a beach and dry her out for a day. She is already feeling sluggish, having taken on so much water."

"I wouldn't do it too close to Ephesos, not with the Macedonians already there."

"Don't worry, soldier boy," Captain Abibaal said with a little laugh. "I know this coast much better than they do. I know lots of little coves and inlets where we can hide out for a day or two. So don't worry.

You're as safe aboard Captain Abibaal's ship as you would be in your own home!"

"That's of little comfort, Abibaal," sighed Dimitrios.

"Why is that?" asked the Phoenician Captain, suitably perplexed.

"Because I don't have a home any more. Alexander burned my city to the ground."

Miletos

IN THE SHADOW OF THE OLD CITADEL HILL

I f there was a race to see whose army and navy would reach Miletos in strength first, Alexander was winning it. His admiral, the Navarch Nicanor, and the fleet were already there, and had established a forward base in the bay, on the island of Lade. A squadron of Prodromoi scout cavalry had already taken possession of the Old Citadel Hill, from whose heights they could look down upon the city. If anyone so much as moved about the city, let alone set about building fortifications, the scouts would see them – and would let Alexander know about it.

No one was more conscious of this than Glaucippos, a close friend and benefactor of Governor Hegisistratos, and one of the richest and most influential merchants in Miletos.

"He is going to get us all killed," said Glaucippos in a hushed voice.

"Who is?" said his dinner guest, Hegisistratos, playfully.

"Memnon, that's who!" answered his host. "We are all going to die! All of our goods will be taken from us and our children sold into slavery. We cannot defend our city against this Macedonian."

"I already sent word to Alexander that I was willing to surrender the city," said Hegisistratos with a shrug as he took another sip of wine.

"But then Memnon showed up. He does not have many men, but they do control the citadel, so what can I do?"

"You can do plenty. Look," said the corpulent merchant, pointing his greasy finger at the governor, "you still have some men who are loyal to you, and only you, and there are others whose loyalty can be bought, or at least rented."

"Go on," said the governor, this time taking a lengthy drink from his wine cup.

"I will go to see Alexander myself. Me, and a few of the other more worthy citizens of the town," explained Glaucippos. "We will tell him ours is an open city, a peaceful city, a neutral city. Greeks, Persians, Macedonians, anyone, can come and go as they please. They can trade at the port, repair in the harbor, buy and sell in the agora, and have anything they want. Of course there will be a price to be paid, but I am sure we can come to some arrangement. After all," added Glaucippos, "isn't having a friendly city in his rear worth more than one he has to attack and garrison? All he has to do is agree to honor our status as an open city and he will have just that. Then we will all be safe and well...and so will our goods."

"Why should Alexander agree, when he can have the place for the asking," laughed the governor. "Spilling a little blood doesn't seem to bother this young king, or any king. And Memnon, well, Memnon," said Hegisistratos with a chortle, "why should he agree, either? Maybe he doesn't have enough men to hold the city, but he can hold the citadel, and deny it as well as the port to Alexander. He'd never agree to an open city. Besides, what's in it for him if he does? And don't say gold, because this is one general who can't be bribed. With his wealth, and estates, and family connection, the only thing that could sway him would be glory – which he will not get by turning over the city to that nasty little Macedonian pup."

"That's where you come in, my friend," said the merchant to the governor quietly. "While I am off making my presentation to Alexander, you and a few of your loyal men...well...you know..."

"You want me to kill Memnon? Kill the man whose authority came from the hand of Darius himself?"

"Oh no, no, no...nothing of the sort, nothing like that," Glaucippos assured the governor rather coyly. "Just, well, keep him out of the way for a day or so...Keep him occupied, or detain him somewhere where he can't interfere. Or bundle him off to a ship and send him off somewhere. You don't have to kill him, no, no, no, nothing like that, no, no...well, unless, you know..." he added with a wry smile.

The governor looked down into his wine cup, swirled the contents, and took a long, deep drink. "You think Alexander would agree?" he asked. "If he does, the price I will be paying for my...err...services...will be very high..."

"...but imagine what it would cost you, and all of us, if he storms the city and turns it over to his men to sack," replied Glaucippos. "Saving the city – and our personal fortunes – would be more than payment enough in itself, don't you agree?"

Later that night, long after the governor and his wealthy host had collapsed in a congratulatory and drunken stupor, a long, narrow column of men quietly marched along the coast and up to the city. They took great care to be as silent as possible, even wrapping cloth about their feet to muffle the sound of their tread. The main gate was open and waiting for them, their coming having been made known to only a select few in the city. With as little sound as possible, they marched into Miletos. The column made its way deep within the city, squads and companies peeling off to the left and right as per the plan. Three of the men, however, kept on going to the citadel. The gate was open, and they were ushered inside without ceremony or challenge by an officer who had been told they were coming.

That officer was Memnon. He shook the hand of the first of the three men to enter the citadel. That man was his nephew, Thymondas, and he had brought with him a thousand sturdy, veteran, and, most important of all, loyal fighting men.

As Captain Abibaal's ship passed through the straits between Samos and the mainland, he was relieved to finally see a few friendly ships on the water. Scout ships, like his own, as well as a thickening collection of merchant vessels, increasingly crowded the sea lane as he sailed south. The storm had passed, and the winds had turned fresh and favorable. His oarsmen welcomed the restful boredom as the few hands who tended the sails did their job. That boredom lasted only until they turned the headland in the shadow of Mount Mycale, as the mighty precipice cut off the winds that had filled the sails. Hands to the oars, they drove the ship forward to an easy beat, and into the roads where hundreds of warships and other vessels of every size and description were either at anchor or drawn up on the narrow beach.

Dimitrios tried to count the ships but finally gave up. There were hundreds of triremes and scores of the big four-decker quadriremes. Towering above them all, however, were a dozen of the massive quinquiremes – huge battleships with crews of 400 or more, each ship mounting naval artillery and with upwards of 100 archers and other marines aboard. Captain Abibaal's tiny scout ship was dwarfed by these sea monsters, a point brought home as he rowed to and tied up alongside a majestic leviathan, what Dimitrios could only assume was the flagship of the Persian fleet.

Too big and heavy to beach, the quinquiremes stayed on the water until they could be towed inside the giant ship sheds at major naval bases – and Mycale was not such a base. It was little more than a supply port in a harbor protected from storms by the peninsula and the mountain that loomed above it. Captain Abibaal climbed aboard the flagship, made his report to the Admiral, and was back aboard his own ship in short order.

"Well, Captain, how did the Admiral take your report?" asked Dimitrios. "Did he say why the navy is here rather than at Miletos, like you thought?"

The Phoenician captain wiped the sweat from his brow, adjusted his tunic and called for his other officers to attend him. When they were assembled, he responded to the Greek soldier's question so all could hear.

"I did not tell the Admiral anything he did not already know. Seems the fleet had to leave Ephesos when the mob took control of the city and welcomed in the Macedonians. As for the ships we met, well, that, too, was old news to the Admiral – or, rather to his aide, to whom I reported. The Greeks slipped around Samos in the storm and beat us to Miletos. They have about 160 warships there, based on the island of Lade which commands the approach to the harbor."

"Well, then they have trapped themselves," said one of the officers gleefully. "There must be easily twice as many ships here – so when do we head south to sweep them from the sea?"

"The aide did not confide in me the plans of the Admiral," Abibaal grinned. "It is obvious that the fleet took some damage from the storm and is doing what it can to refit, make repairs and revictualize. That will take another few days, I guess, as there are far too many ships for this place to handle."

"Well, we'll get our turn soon enough, I imagine," the officer said, nodding his head in understanding. The other officers muttered their agreement, and looked relieved at the prospect of some rest, some time to stretch their legs and to perhaps buy and cook a proper meal ashore.

"Unfortunately, no," the captain responded. "Too many scout ships were either lost or so badly damaged in the storm that the Admiral needs us to go back to sea. We are, after all, the eyes and ears of the fleet," he added with pride. "As soon as we can take on fresh water and some rations, we are to head due south, to scout the enemy around Miletos, and to make contact with the garrison. The Admiral wants to let them know that we are coming. He also needs to learn from them their situation, and anything they can tell us about the Macedonians. That," he said turning to Dimitrios, "should be welcome news to you and your friends."

"How's so?" asked Dimitrios.

"The Admiral's aide says Memnon is already in Miletos. You wanted to get back into the fight, well, come along with us and we'll make your wish come true."

37

Miletos

ALEXANDER ON THE MARCH

lexander's journey south to Miletos was not so much a military march as a pleasant saunter – an unhurried victory parade with delegations from cities and towns either side of the route stumbling over each other to shower praises upon and assure their conquerors that they would be good, loyal subjects.

There was even music to add to the triumphant atmosphere. Flutes and pipes, horns and drums, and voices of men singing their rude marching tunes, joined in with the trampling of hooves, the creak of leather, the jingling of bronze, the tread of hob-nailed boots, the slapping of sandals, the creaking of wheels – and the joking, and cursing, and catcalling of voices from a score of Greek and Asian dialects. All of this was quite literally music to the ears – especially to the ears of the supremely confident victor of the Granicos, Alexander.

The two flying columns, each of 5,000 men, that swept through the Aeloian and Ionian towns, were greeted with flowers rather than arrows, and with gifts of amphorae of local wines, rather than tubs of burning oil hurled from their battlements. Some of the locals did indeed welcome Alexander as something of a liberator, but most simply understood that resistance was futile. Better to make the best of the situation and give willingly, rather than to lose all by trying to fight back.

It was the same logic that drove Glaucippos to make his proposal to Hegisistratos about opening the gates of Miletos to Alexander. As Thymondas and his troops quietly entered the main gate, Glaucippos and a few of the more adventuresome of the city fathers had slipped out of Miletos through a lesser gate. Hegisistratos had made sure that it was his men on duty there that night, so that the plotters could go out unnoticed. They were almost immediately intercepted by some of the Macedonian scouts based on the Old Citadel Hill, who, after having been well-rewarded for not killing them outright, agreed to escort the party north. The next day, they encountered the outriders of the main army, and after another bag of silver changed hands, were escorted to the king's tent.

"What is all of that commotion out there?" Alexander asked of Parmenion as they viewed a sketch of Miletos that had been prepared by their staff.

"Probably just another gaggle of 'grateful' citizens from some dirt water town or another wishing to offer their thanks and praises – and to plead that we spare their jumble of huts from the excesses of our army. They appear to like being 'liberated,' provided we don't 'liberate' them of their goods."

The staff officers allowed themselves a little laugh at Parmenion's jibe, but Alexander did not seem amused. To the contrary, he bid Parmenion to have them enter. "It has been hours since anyone bowed and scraped and kissed my boot," he said in a tone his staff was not certain was joking. "It has been a long day, and I can do with some refreshment of this sort."

With little ceremony, the guards ushered Glaucippos and his party into the royal presence, as they had done with dozens of similar delegations for the last few days. The merchant and his friends nearly stumbled over one another in their eagerness to supplicate themselves before the king. Alexander let them go on singing his praises and humbling themselves for a few minutes longer than he knew they would be comfortable doing (as he found himself enjoying the adulation) but eventually bid them rise.

"So, you have come to surrender Miletos to me, then?"

"Yes, honored lord, yes. By all means, yes," blathered Glaucippos. "The city is yours to enter. We welcome all visitors to our fair city, Greek, Macedonian, Persian, all."

While Alexander was smiling as Glaucippos began his little speech, by the end of the second sentence he began to frown.

"Excuse me...what is your name, and just who are you, again?" the king asked.

"My name is Glaucippos, my King. I represent the merchants and city fathers of Miletos, if it pleases your grace," he said, fawning and scraping in his best interpretation of a worshipful subject.

"Then tell me, Glaucippos," the king said slowly and warily, "are you here to surrender the city or not?"

"Well, yes...and no...maybe" said the fat merchant, swallowing hard between each jumble of words.

"Yes? No? Maybe?" Alexander responded testily. "You are either here to surrender the city or not. There is no 'maybe' about it."

"Well, sort of, you see, great King," said Glaucippos haltingly, "we mean that you are of course welcome to visit our city and to enjoy our hospitality. Should you or your army require anything, we of course would be more than accommodating, and would give you the best prices...even a discount...and of course if you yourself, well..."

"Enough!" shouted Alexander, suddenly angry. "You blithering, greasy, slimy little idiot. Do you presume to put conditions on your surrender? With a wave of my hand I could raze your city to the ground and sell you and your families into slavery. I could erase all evidence of your petty little city's existence! Just as I did with Thebes! While Thebes will live on in the histories, I will see to it that yours does not. The very name of your city will be erased and forgotten. So," he added loudly, putting his face so close to that of the merchant that their sweat and breath were as one, "would you care to rephrase that little speech of yours?"

"I...I...I...meant...surrender, of course, surrender," the merchant managed to say with great difficulty. "Surrender. Complete surrender. We throw ourselves at your mercy...your mercy for which you are renowned..."

"Mercy? Mercy is for friends," said Alexander with growing disdain and evident impatience.

It was at this point that Hephaestion joined the conversation, and moved to place himself between the King and the merchant.

"Tell me, good man," said Hephaestion with grace, respect and in a calm voice, "are you in a position to surrender Miletos? We had a missive last week from the governor, one Hegis...Hegis..."

"Hegisistratos, lord," said Glaucippos, relieved for the respite from the king's ire. "I have conferred with him, yes, and we are of the same mind."

"Ah, good, then," said Hephaestion, smiling his most diplomatic smile, and looking back and forth between the merchant and the king. "See, it was just a little misunderstanding. So, dear Glau...Glau..."

"Glaucippos, lord. Glaucippos."

"Yes, quite," said Hephaestion, clearing his throat gently. "Glaucippos. What of the garrison? They are ready to march out and lay down their arms, are they not?"

"Well..." replied Glaucippos hesitantly. "Almost."

"Almost? What do you mean by 'almost'?" asked Hephaestion, who had not expected any answer other than a totally affirmative one.

"It is just a small matter, really. I mean, our city militia, of course, they are more than willing to do anything you ask, but..."

"But what?"

"Well, you see, it is a bit delicate of course," mumbled Glaucippos. "There is a small matter, just a minor hiccup, nothing really..."

"Spit it out you idiot!" the king interrupted.

"Memnon." said Glaucippos quietly, his head down and his eyes averted.

"What?"

"Memnon," said Glaucippos a bit louder.

"Is Memnon in Miletos?" Alexander asked excitedly.

"Yes. Yes he is," said Glaucippos. "But don't worry, your worship, the governor and I, we have a plan to..."

"Oh shut up you fool!" interrupted the king. "Did you hear that Hephaestion? Parmenion? We have him! At last! Quick, break camp – and I mean break camp now! Parmenion, seal off the peninsula. No one gets out of Miletos! And send a messenger to the engineers, I want the siege train up here, and now! Clear the roads of anything between the advance guard and them – I want those siege engines up front, assembled and ready for action by tonight, and if they are not, someone will pay for it. Someone will have their head catapulted into the city if those engines are not ready!"

"But, sire, but..." Glaucippos all but screamed.

"I said shut up, you sniveling little worm of a man," spat Alexander in disgust. "You dare insult my intelligence by pretending that you can surrender a city defended by Memnon? He would never surrender. And I would not want him to. Go back to Miletos. Go tell your people to prepare to defend themselves. And do not waste any time, for when the dawn comes, our siege engines will begin their bombardment. Go back to your little city, you worm. Oh, and one other thing..."

"Yes...yes...Lord" said Glaucippos, a large wet spot now evident on his robe just below the waist, "what...what is it?"

"Tell Memnon I am coming."

38

The Island of Lades

CAPTAIN ABIBAAL MAKES HIS RUN

Captain Abibaal knew the waters off Miletos like he knew the back of his hand. Unfortunately, the night was so dark that he could not see the back of his hand, or much of anything else for that matter. What little moon there had been, was now shrouded in a thick blanket of clouds. If not for the small lamps aboard the Greek patrol galleys that were strung across the harbor entrance, he would have most assuredly rammed into one of them by accident in the darkness.

"Well, at least we know the Greek fleet is still here," muttered Klemes from his place on deck by his brother, their friend and the captain.

"Where else did you think they would be?" quipped Captain Abibaal. "The Admiral knows they are here; what he wants to know is how many ships are here and how they are deployed. My guess is that they have made a base over there, on the island of Lade, just to the west of the city. That seems to be where their patrol line starts."

"How can you tell in this darkness?" asked Dimitrios.

"The last light over there, see," replied the captain. "Past that ship everything is dark. That is right about where Lade is, as best as I can tell, considering the city is over there," he added, pointing due south. "The lights stretch from there to...there, which is about where the beach should be."

"So, what do we do, now?" asked Dimitrios. "You can't sail through that line?"

"No, but I can sail around it."

"How? In the dark?"

"It won't be that hard. We'll just stay about this distance away from the lights, sail parallel to them and then keep on going until we clear Lade."

"Captain, how will you see the island?"

"Easy. Where the lights stop, the island starts. As we pass the island, it will block out the lights of the city. I know the size of the island...approximately."

"What do you mean, 'approximately,'" asked Klemes with a worried tone in his voice.

"I know about how long it should take at this speed to pass it by, and when we're there, I will turn us to the south, and we can slip into Miletos from the seawall side. The Greeks won't expect us to come from that direction."

"And if your approximation is wrong?" asked the physician.

"We'll hit some rocks and start to sink," Abibaal explained in a mock serious voice. "You can all swim, can't you?"

With a fresh wind blowing from the land, Captain Abibaal was able to keep his sails full and his oars shipped. That made for a quiet journey, one made all the more quiet by his orders to the crew to keep silent and to make as little noise as possible. There were twenty Greek patrol ships in that line, each with a small lamp at its fore and aft. Those ensured that they would not run into each other, and also let them keep their station as well as their distance from one another. As they sailed down the line, Dimitrios quietly counted to himself how many patrol ships they had passed. All went well until he counted "nineteen," at which point the silence of the night was broken by a loud clatter. Klemes had gotten up from his spot aft to take a leak over the side. He had become entangled in some ropes and took a tumble, knocking into some of the rowers, knocking their shipped oars into one another.

The lamps on the patrol ships began to brighten and shine in their direction. Up and down the line more lamps were lit, and shouts of alarm were passed from ship to ship. Beacons soon flared on Lade, as the night watch came to life on the island.

"What the hell is wrong with you?" Captain Abibaal whispered angrily at Klemes. "I told you to stay put and be quiet! Now look what you've done!"

"Damn it, Captain," answered Klemes as he struggled to untangle himself from the ropes and oars, "I'm a physician, not a sailor."

"Then it's lucky for both of us that I am!" the Phoenician officer barked back.

"Captain, they're hailing us and demanding to know what ship we are and from where," the first mate interrupted. "What should I tell them?"

"Tell them nothing. We're not going to play 'pretend' with them. They aren't that stupid," he replied. "Oars! Out!" shouted the captain turning to amidships. "Row, damn you all, row! Fool speed as soon as you can!" he added as he turned to the coxswain.

"Did he just say 'fool speed?" Ari asked Klemes. "What the hell is 'fool' speed?"

"It's the same as 'full speed,'" remarked a nearby rower, "but with more desperation."

"So the jig is up and we're turning back, then?" remarked Dimitrios.

"Hell, no, my Theban friend. We're going west – straight past Lade, around and then down into Miletos."

"But that's insane!" Klemes cried out. "Didn't you say their whole fleet is at Lade?"

"Yes, I did," smiled the captain. "And all of those big ships will be beached or at anchor, and their crews snug and warm ashore. They're not going to scramble the squadrons, not at night, and not to catch one ship. They'd wreck the fleet if they tried -and like I said, they're not that stupid."

The Phoenician oarsmen put their backs into it, pulling harder and faster as the boatswain set the beat to keep them rowing in unison. The Greek patrol ships were slow to give chase, as it took time for their captains to sort it out among themselves who should keep station and who should follow the unknown craft. Give chase, however, two of them did, although to little avail, as Captain Abibaal had a strong lead on his pursuers.

As they rowed furiously past the island, Dimitrios could make out small, flickering camp fires beyond the alarm beacons. Around them, he imagined, thousands of Athenians, Corinthians, and other Greeks from a dozen cities were telling stories, swapping yarns, sharing boasts of their prowess with the ladies, and arguing over whose city was better at what. Not so many years ago he would have been in among them, and he might be even now, had Alexander spared Thebes. But, he had not, and so tonight Dimitrios found himself not among his fellow Greeks but instead fleeing from them, his hopes for escape wagered on the backs of 50 foreign oarsmen, half a dozen Phoenician sailors, and their strange and mysterious captain.

"Faster, damn it, faster!" shouted that captain to the boatswain, whose skin was already damp with sweat from beating his drum. "I want to put the island between us and those patrol boats, and I want to do it now! Not later, not tomorrow, but now!"

His ship's lead continued to lengthen, but just as they cleared the island and prepared to swing south, two more ships came into view. Both were rounding the tip of the island from the south, just as Abibaal was about to change his heading to that direction.

"I thought you said they weren't so stupid as to scramble the fleet!" yelped Klemes.

"They aren't, and they haven't," he replied. "They must have sent a signal across the island to the guard ships on this side of Lade. I didn't think there would be many or even any here. Damn it!"

"So now what?" asked Dimitrios. "We can't turn back and we can't go ahead – so what do we do now?"

"Well, my Greek friend. I'm heading for the open sea. They won't follow too far from their station."

"But what about me? What about getting me, my brother, and Ari into Miletos?"

"Well, Dimitrios," the captain said as he spat over the side. "You have two choices."

"What are they?"

"Well," he replied as he looked to the open sea, "you can either stay with us and go back to the fleet or..."

"Or what?"

"Well, that depends," the Phoenician captain said with a laugh.

"Depends on what?" asked Dimitrios.

"On how well you can swim!"

The guards on the seaward walls of Miletos had noticed the movement of the Greek guard ships and had sent a message up through the chain of command. Ephialtes, Thymondas, and Memnon were in council, planning their defense of the city when they were interrupted by the captain of the guard.

"Excuse me, General," the young officer said as he entered the council chamber. "There is something unusual going on just outside the harbor, and I thought I should bring it to your attention."

"What do you mean by 'unusual,' young man," said Ephialtes, addressing the officer.

"It's the Greek patrol ships. Some of them have moved off station, and the beacon fires on the island are now lit."

"Could it be our fleet trying to break through?" asked Thymondas, looking at Memnon.

"It shouldn't be," he answered calmly and thoughtfully, as he rubbed his chin. "I can't imagine Admiral Autophradates would try something so stupid as a night action. He'd lose most of the fleet in the confusion."

"Well, there is something stirring about out there," replied Thymondas.

"Maybe the Greek sailors are seeing mermaids or sea serpents – it is awfully dark and scary out there" said Ephialtes with a mocking laugh.

"Perhaps," replied Memnon with a little laugh of his own, "but whatever it is, it would be best to know about it. Soldier," said the General to the young man who had brought the message, "go down to the docks and find the naval officer on duty. Miletos has a few ships of its own. Tell the officer there to put a couple of patrol ships out into the harbor to take a look. Tell him that he is just to take a quick look and then get back. After all, only a fool tries to fight on the sea at night."

Captain Abibaal's plan to head out to the open sea turned out to be a non-starter. No sooner had he made his decision to do so than several more lights appeared from that quarter.

"Are those ships out there?" asked Dimitrios.

"Well, they're not sea monsters," Abibaal sighed. "They must be part of an outer line of patrol ships. Nicanor, it seems, is very thorough – or very frightened – of our fleet."

"So what do we do now?" asked Dimitrios. "There are Greek ships behind us, Greek ships ahead of us, and now Greek ships off our starboard side out to sea, and they're all converging on us."

"There's only one thing to do..." said the Phoenician captain.

"Ship oars and surrender?" interrupted Klemes.

"Never!" growled the Phoenician. "We never give up. We never surrender. My people have been sailors since before any Greek ever got their feet wet in salt water."

"Well, okay then," said Klemes suitably chastised. "But you still haven't answered my brother's question: what do we do now?"

"Don't worry, I've got a cunning plan."

"Good. What is it?" asked Klemes.

"You'll see soon enough," barked the captain back at the physician.

"So, you don't really have a plan yet, then, do you?" scoffed Klemes. "I knew it. He's just making things up as he goes along. We're all going to die."

39

Miletos Harbor

MIDNIGHT

Of the 160-plus ships of Alexander's fleet, all but about a score of lighter patrol ships were anchored in the shallows or had been hauled up onto the beaches of the Island of Lade. The island itself stood guard over the sea routes to Miletos, with its watchtowers and warning beacons set to look out for and give the alert should hostile warships approach. Lade and its small local garrison of watchers served their city well – or at least they had done so until a few days ago. That was when Admiral Nicanor and his grand fleet had arrived. Nicanor easily drove the small squadron based at Miletos back to the security of its sheds and moorings in the inner harbor. Since then, Lade had served Nicanor as his forward base.

It was to get past this base that Captain Abibaal and his crew were striving with all of their might. While there was little threat from the grand fleet itself, the Greek patrol ships were closing in from fore and aft, and even starboard. There were not many of them – four, five at most – but they were more than enough to catch the Phoenician scout ship in their net.

Abibaal was certain his men could outrow the pursuers coming up behind them, but the faster they rowed to get away from the ships aft, the closer they came to those coming from the other directions. Ari's skills as an archer had saved them once before – but that was from the threat of stern chase, and in daylight. In the nearly moonless dark, even as accomplished an archer as Aristophanes of Thebes would have little chance of seeing his target, let alone hitting it.

With no better plan in his head, Abibaal could do nothing more than trust in the sinews of the half a hundred men who sat the rowing benches to get them to the only safe haven available: Miletos harbor. Unfortunately, however, these veteran oarsmen were only human, and were nearing the end of their strength.

To keep them going a bit longer, Ari, Dimitrios, Klemes and two of the sailors went about the benches with bowls of bread soaked in wine and flasks of well-watered wine. The rowers could not pause to take any refreshment with their hands, so the others had to serve them, popping small bits of the bread into their open mouths and pouring the wine into their mouths. Another sailor splashed water on the rowers to cool the sweat-soaked, overheated oarsmen.

"We need more speed!" the captain yelled to the boatswain, who was also beginning to show serious signs of fatigue from constantly beating the cadence on his drum. "Pick up the beat!"

"These men are giving all they've got, Captain," the boatswain yelled back in reply. "They can't take any more!"

"They have to!" bellowed the captain, "and they will! Isn't that right lads!"

Abibaal knew his men could not spare the energy or break concentration to cheer or sing out in agreement, but he could see from their faces that they were indeed digging deep within themselves to find something, anything they had not already drawn on. He also knew that whatever they could find, that would be all that was left. Abibaal could see the lamps on the Greek ships to his fore and starboard get brighter and brighter as they got closer and closer, and he knew they were losing the race. There was only one thing more that could be done, and it was an order no captain wanted to give.

"Dimitrios!" the captain roared. "The mast. It has to go! Now!"

Before a galley went into battle, its mast, sails, block and tackle, and other sailing gear would be taken down and stored in port, or on a beach. Captain Abibaal had not done so, as he had bet on his sail to get him to Miletos and let him slip quietly into the harbor. While rowing, however, the heavy timber mast only weighed them down and, worse, slowed them down. To heave it overboard was as difficult a maneuver as it was a painful choice – but he knew it was their only hope.

The captain turned the tiller over to his first mate and, axe in hand, began chopping away at the mast. There was no time to go through the laborious task of shipping the mast as they would were they to store it on shore. It had to go, and go now, and since it did have to go, the captain decided that he should be the one to do the deed.

Dimitrios put down the bowl and flask and moved amidships to help him. As Abibaal chopped, Dimitrious pushed the mast, hoping to use its own weight against itself. One of the sailors went about cutting the yards while another began tossing blocks and tackle and rope overboard. Yet another grabbed anything else that could be thrown out to lighten the ship. Water casks, loose gear, anything that was not battened down – or which could be unbattened, went.

This sacrifice gained them ground in their race with the Greek ships to their starboard and aft – but only brought them closer to the one ship that was coming straight at them. The lighter Abibaal's ship became, the faster it bolt, and that meant that the speed at which his vessel and the Greek patrol ship dead ahead would collide would be all the greater. To ram her, however, was out of the question. Abibaal's scout vessel did not have a bronze ram, for that was not its purpose. The Greek vessel, however, might be so equipped. In the dark, Abibaal had no way of knowing, nor could he see beneath the water as the Greek's prow cut the waves, to get even a glimpse of bronze. To ram the Greek ship would bring him to a dead stop, and probably break the back of both small vessels. But there was one trick left – one last trick that could see them to safety, if it worked.

As the mast went down, Abibaal tossed the axe overboard and raced aft. He grabbed the tiller from his first mate and turned his ship to aim dead on for the oncoming Greek patrol ship – the last barrier to finding safety in Miletos. Would the Greek captain take up the challenge in this game of nautical chicken, or would he sheer off – and if so, which way – to port, or starboard?

Faster and faster they closed, leaving the ships to the aft and starboard of the Phoenician vessel farther and farther behind. As the clouds parted briefly, Abibaal could see the enemy captain on his deck in the moonlight. There was no panic in him, that was clear. Like the Phoenician, his visage was grim and warlike, and there was no sign of fear in his body or his face. Seconds before the two ships would crash bow to bow, Abibaal swung the tiller, first hard to port, then quickly back hard to starboard. The Phoenician ship leaped to his touch – and as he screamed the command "Up oars!" his men did so, and at once. Their oars straight up, the ship drove forward like a missile – and sheered and splintered the oars on the starboard side of the oncoming Greek warship.

Their momentum carried the two ships away from each other, and as soon as his vessel was clear, Abibaal gave the order for his men to put their oars back into the water and to row hard. He spared but a moment to glance over his shoulder, where the Greek warship floundered, its crew as bloodied and battered from the splintered oars as their ship itself. Abibaal had turned their own oars against the Greeks, and left their ship awash in blood as men had been torn apart by the shattering of the oars in their hands.

That was the scene aft. Ahead were the lights of Miletos, and a pair of local galleys that were coming to escort them in.

40

Miletos Harbor

AFTER MIDNIGHT

As the Phoenician ship glided into the port, Dimitrios expected that the crew, and especially the oarsmen, would collapse. To his amazement, they did just the opposite. Such was the pride they had in each other, their ship, and their captain, these men who had been sweating blood only moments before sat up and rowed in unison to the much slower but still steady beat of the boatswain's drum. When the captain gave the command to "Ship, oars!", they did so with a precision and style that left the hoplites captain speechless.

Once they docked, however, the exhaustion overcame them all. Some men slumped at the bench, while others collapsed and slid or fell off onto the deck. The adrenalin rush having subsided, even the captain had difficulty staying on his feet.

"Well, my Theban friend," said Abibaal in a raspy whisper in between taking hard breaths, "I promised I would get you and your friends to Miletos, did I not? Well, then, in the name of the Royal Navy, welcome to Miletos. It may not be the jewel of the empire, but it will be a hard gem for Alexander to crack."

"Thank you, Captain," Dimitrios replied, offering a sharp salute to show his gratitude and his respect, one professional to another. "I owe you a debt. I used to be in the wine trade, and maybe one day, when this war is over, we can take a different kind of sea voyage together, and one that will be easier, more enjoyable and, of course, profitable."

Captain Abibaal offered his shaking hand along with a weary smile, in acknowledgment of the Theban's offer. "Perhaps I will take you up on that one day," he replied with a grin. "After all, my men and I were simple merchant seamen before we were sailors of the king, and, hopefully, we will be so again."

"What will you do, now, Captain?" Dimitrios asked.

"We will rest and refit – and then go back to sea. Don't forget, my mission is to scout the Greek fleet and then report what I saw to the admiral. I'm only half-way done, as I see it."

"But how will you get out past the Greek blockade?"

"Well, I got in, didn't I?" he said with a little laugh. "Don't worry. I'll figure out something. And you, my friend, I imagine you will find some fellow exiles to join up with and get back to the fight as well? Best of luck to you, as I think you may need it."

With a nod and a wave, Dimitrios, Klemes, and Aristophanes marched down the gangplank and onto the dock – where a very officious looking fellow in very crisp, clean clothes and with two impeccably kitted out soldiers to either side, awaited them.

"Hold on there, the three of you. Just who do you think you are and where do you think you're going?"

Despite his incredible fatigue, Dimitrios drew himself to attention and, with his best parade-ground manner, shot the official a stiff salute. "I am Dimitrios of Thebes, captain of one hundred in the army of Ephialtes, and a survivor of the battle on the Granicos. I have urgent business with General Memnon, if you would be so kind to escort me to him. As for these two, one is my brother, a physician in the army, and the other is my friend, a soldier of my company."

So much information and such an attitude were not what the dock officer was expecting. That these scruffy, grimy looking fellows in their torn, dirty, and bloodied rags were soldiers in the army and not beggars or simple seamen, had not occurred to him. Nor did he expect one of them to be an officer, let alone one known to the great Memnon himself. Although his first instinct had been to drag these vagrants off to the garrison for questioning, the officer quickly changed his mind. If this man was someone Memnon wanted to see, then any officer who so delivered him to the general's presence might be rewarded, or at least recognized for having done the great man such a service.

"All right, come with me. I'll send word to the citadel and see if General Memnon knows you and wants to see you. In the meantime, let me find you something more presentable and, ahem, some soap and water. You men, frankly, stink, and are in desperate need of a bath."

"But I have urgent..."

The officer cut off Dimitrios with a simple hand gesture. "I understand. I will, I assure you, pass you up the line if what you say is true, but not until I am sure you are at least clean and presentable enough. In your current state, your smell would knock a pig off a pile of manure."

Half an hour later, a much cleaner, less pungent, Dimitrios stood at attention before the three generals who were charged with the defense of Miletos. Ephialtes was as surprised and as happy to see Dimitrios as the captain was to once again clasp hands with the mercenary commander. Thymondas, already informed of the young officer's method of arrival in the city, was suitably impressed, but it was Memnon whose attitude most surprised Dimitrios.

"I honor your courage and resourcefulness, Captain," said the general with respect, "and applaud your loyalty. I also wish to express my regret at the loss of so many of your comrades, and your commander. I never expected that Alexander would refuse you all honors of war, let alone that he would refuse to offer terms, and slaughter so many fine and honorable soldiers. It is against all of the rules of civilized warfare. It is what his barbarian ancestors might have done, but I thought he had grown beyond that and become more civilized. I see, however, that I was wrong. I will forever bear the burden of having abandoned so many good men to his mercy – or lack of it."

"It was not your fault, General," replied Dimitrios, still at attention.

"The Alexander you may have known when you were in Macedonia so many years ago is a different person now. I have looked into his face twice, first at Thebes and again at the Granicos. He is neither king nor man, but something...something..."

"Something, what?" asked Memnon quizzically.

"Something dark. Something frightening. Something not altogether...human."

Dimitrios did not have to explain further. All three generals felt the horror that Dimitrios had felt and seen, so striking and convincing was his demeanor. It was not just what Dimitrios said but how he said it, and how he seemed to tremble with revulsion at the very mention of Alexander. The three said nothing, so lost were they in reflection upon the moment. Finally, Dimitrios himself broke the silence.

"I would like to get back into the fight, General, if I may. Me and my comrades."

"Haven't you had enough of war," asked Thymondas quietly and gently.

"In some ways, more than enough," sighed Dimitrios honestly.

"Then why not go home..."

"Because, Thymondas," Ephialtes interrupted, "he has no home. Alexander saw to that."

"Well, General, technically," Dimitrios said with a cough, "my home, well, rather, my house, is still there. For some reason Alexander spared it, as it is the house of my ancestor, Pindar."

"The poet?"

"Yes, General Thymondas. Apparently Alexander has some regard for my ancestor's poetry. It is about the only building he left standing in the city. Thebes is a dead city – and a city of the dead. There is nothing there to go back to...other than painful memories of the glory that was once Thebes, and the graveyard Alexander made of it."

"Ephialtes," said Memnon, "could surely find you a place in the ranks if you wish..."

"I do, General, most assuredly, I do..."

"Yes, I am sure, but Captain, I have many good men who can stand in the line of battle, and officers, good officers aplenty, to lead them.

What I do not have, however, are men whose honor and loyalty I can trust – present company excepted, of course, gentlemen. In this empire, loyalty is a currency worth more, and more rare, than gold. I want you by my side, on my staff."

"But General, I am a combat soldier..."

"Yes, but also a man of learning – and of commerce, if what Ephialtes has told me of you is true. You understand the art of the deal, are exceptionally observant, and have a talent for survival. You are courageous, and resourceful, and true to your comrades. Those are each in themselves rare qualities, and they are in short supply not just here, but everywhere, in the empire and beyond."

"But I want to fight, your honor, and not..."

Memnon raised his hand gently in a signal that Dimitrios was to stop talking and listen. "Oh, have no worries on that score, my Theban friend. There is much fighting to be done and you, lad, will be in the thick of it."

41

The Necropolis

ALEXANDER STORMS MILETOS

s dawn broke, the guards on the still yet unfinished outer defenses heard a strange muffled rumble to the south. It came from the direction of the outer city, that area beyond the defenses which had fallen to Alexander during the night, without a blow. The sound came from within the mist that had yet to burn off. It grew steadily louder, but was still indistinct. One guard thought it sounded like the pounding of the waves – but those would have come from the three seaward sides of the peninsula, not from the landside. As that soldier turned to ask the corporal of the guard if they should report this to the officer of the watch, a flight of arrows suddenly exploded from the mist, puncturing the necks and shoulders of the guards, or piercing the eyes of those who had the misfortune to look up as the rain of arrows fell.

A second, then a third flight followed, and with them out of the mist came a loud shout and the sound of singing. That served to announce the serried ranks of Macedonian infantry who burst out of the fog, first at a walk, and then at a dead run. Many carried ladders, ropes with grappling hooks, and bundles of sticks to fill ditches. Others carried logs, which could also be used to fill or bridge ditches or be placed against the low wall to help the attackers climb up the ramparts.

The surprise attack had indeed been a surprise, and had caught the defenders quite literally napping – but not for long. The sounds of battle washed over the walls, through the camps, and into the town itself. Within moments these sounds were answered by the blaring of trumpets, the banging of signal drums, and the shouting or orders by sergeants and officers who hurried to get their men up to the battlements.

"Alexander's attacking!" shouted Dimitrios as he burst into Memnon's quarters in the citadel.

"Of course he is," agreed the general, whose knowledge of the attack as well as his calm demeanor both came as a surprise to the young officer.

"How did you know, General?"

"Because I'm not deaf," he replied with a little laugh. "I also knew he couldn't long resist the chance to capture the outer walls, which, as anyone on his side of them could see, are very lightly held – and incomplete. What general could resist such a temptation, eh?" he added with a grin. "Certainly not someone as impetuous and certain of himself as our young Macedonian kinglet, right?"

"You knew he'd attack this morning?" asked Dimitrios, quite perplexed by the general's reaction.

"This morning. Tomorrow morning. One morning next week...I knew he'd take the bait eventually," replied the general as he calmly splashed water on his face and grabbed a towel. "It was just a matter of time."

"Take the bait?"

"Yes, Captain, the bait. That ancient outer wall was in such disrepair that we'd have had to tear it down in order to build a proper one. So I let it serve another purpose...and it has. It has lured Alexander into attacking prematurely. He thinks that I am lazy or didn't have time to repair those ruins of the old, outer city. His men will take them – but that will break up their formations and weaken their command structure. Instead of advancing on the city as an army in a solid line of battle, they will rush forward in groups, each isolated from the other. We can pick them off one at time that way. Understand? Good. Now, help me with my armor. We've a battle to fight."

The thinly manned defense line did not delay Alexander's attack very long. It didn't have to. The broken ground and ditch in front of it, and the jagged, jumbled rocks, stones and timbers of the incomplete works proved more of an obstacle than did those guarding it. In their excitement and certainty of an easy victory, Alexander's men poured up, over and through every gap they could find. They were in such a rush to be the first into the city, that none of the units took the time to halt, dress ranks, and put themselves in proper order. Not that it would have been easy to do so, not in the mess and muck of what was basically a construction site.

The thin screen of defenders there, put up a short but sharp fight. When the trumpets blared a second time, they fell back upon each other to form small islands of resistance at key points in the line. Those portions of the defense were much more complete than most of the line, and intentionally so. Secure in these posts which offered protection, a fighting platform, and all-around security, the guards let the Macedonians flood past. Few of the attackers wanted to peel off to take on these isolated posts, lest others in the first wave get into the city before them and thus get the pick of booty and women. Besides, they knew there were more soldiers following, and their thought, when they had one, was to let those fellows do the dirty work of mopping up the strongholds they were bypassing.

From the citadel to the main town wall was barely a kilometer, and Memnon and Dimitrios covered the ground quickly at the jog. They climbed the steps two at a time to the top of these much sturdier, far more daunting, and thoroughly complete ramparts. When they reached the rampart they were treated to a panoramic view of Alexander's attack force. It stretched the width of the peninsula. It was an awe-inspiring sight, so many thousands of men all but tripping over themselves in rush to reach the city.

"Ever seen such a sight, Captain?" chuckled Memnon. "By the

gods, I've never seen ten thousand men in a race before. Thymondas," he said, turning to his nephew who had been waiting for them as they topped the wall, "now's your time."

Thymondas raised an arm, looked to the left, then to right, and then made a sudden, violent chopping motion. At that signal banners rose, trumpets blared, and a barrage of bolts, rocks, and arrows erupted from the walls, as every piece of artillery and every archer fired into the tumultuous mass of Macedonians below. Below the walls, among the gravestones, monuments and altars of the Necropolis – the burial ground between the main walls and outer fortifications – more archers along with slingers and javelinmen rose to add their missiles to the shower of death from above. Between the large headstones and tombs, groups of spearmen with shields as tall as a man formed defensive hedgehogs to protect the light troops. Hundreds of the bravest, most impetuous, or most ignorant of the Macedonians charged forward, pushed from behind by thousands more, only to impale themselves on those spears.

What had begun as a mad, headstrong, and irresistible rush suddenly collapsed into a confused, disorganized, and impossible to lead muddle. Barred from going forward by the spears, assailed from above by a storm of missiles, and canalized by the defensive islands, the Macedonians found themselves caught in a trap – and a muddy one, and one into which more and more men unwittingly poured. The one-sided slaughter went on far longer than it should have, as none of the Macedonian officers were able to bring any order out of the chaos. They simply just could not be heard above the screams, shouts, and cries of surprise and pain.

From his observation post high above it all on the Old Citadel Hill that dominated the peninsula upon which Miletos was built, Alexander watched in helpless fury as his surprise coup de main collapsed into a bloody disaster. In his rage he tore off his helmet and hurled it at one of his young aides, beaning him soundly and knocking him off his feet. Whatever curses or commands Alexander was spewing were soaked up by the thunderous clamor from below. As he hurried down the path from the tall hill, pebbles and dirt scattering as he ran, his aides and the other generals on the hill soon got the message that they needed to follow the king, wherever he was going.

As he tumbled to the bottom he called for his horse, which had been adorned with its best trappings in preparation for what Alexander assumed would be a triumphal procession into the city. Such plans, he now realized, had been quite premature. Instead of riding calmly in a victory parade, the helmetless king kicked his horse's sides violently, as he raced to restore order to his men caught in Memnon's abattoir.

He need not have bothered, for by the time he reached the open ground on the Macedonian side of the front line, his men were already rushing back in panic. Hundreds of soldiers raced past their king, having thrown away their weapons, shields, and even helmets so as not to slow themselves down in their flight. The wave that had crashed so violently over the outer defenses now receded with equal if not greater force, and even Alexander and his mighty warhorse, Bucephalus, could not go against that human tide.

As the Macedonians fled, the defenders followed, but in an orderly, steady, and determined manner. When they reached the outer works they stopped, lined its uneven ramparts, and continued to plink away at the routing enemy. Those Macedonians who had been wounded, separated from their units or otherwise left behind were put to the sword by the Persian soldiers and Greek mercenaries as they scoured the slaughter pen between the main and outer walls. Despite the urging of Thymondas and Ephialtes to go over those walls and pursue the Macedonians, Memnon ordered his men to halt at the outer wall.

"But surely we should keep going," pleaded Ephialtes. "We have them on the run! We could follow them right up into the camp, burn their tents, maybe even nab Alexander himself!"

Thymondas seconded the opinion of the old Greek general, and offered to put himself at the head of the pursuit.

"Alexander took the bait and made a mistake," said Memnon as he again refused their advice. "Let us not make the same mistake, and in doing so snatch defeat from the jaws of this victory. Our losses appear to have been light, and our men have seen that they can not only with-stand but defeat Alexander. The myth of invincibility that he has been carrying and spreading about since even before the Granicos, has been shown to be just that – a myth. That makes this a double, even triple victory. Let us savor it," Memnon added, "and let Alexander choke on it."

Ephialtes grumbled his unhappy acceptance of Memnon's decision. Thymondas, although his blood was still up, held back from further argument. Memnon had made up his mind, and that was that.

"Don't worry, my valiant Thymondas and loyal Ephialtes, there will come another day, and soon, when you can kill as many Macedo-nians as you like."

"You think he'll try again, after this?" asked Thymondas.

"Of course," replied Memnon, "for three reasons. First, Miletos is second only to Halicarnassos in importance to anyone who seeks to control the coast of Asia Minor and the seas around it. Both are major cities, with important harbors. Both are key bases for our navy, and both are heavily fortified. To advance on the second, however, Alexander needs to take the first. He cannot leave Miletos threaten his rear as he advances into the Persian Empire."

"Can't he just seal off with a siege and a blockade and move on?" asked Ephialtes.

"No," replied Memnon. "His fleet cannot stay here forever, and especially not with our navy nearby. As for the land side, well, he'd have to leave half of his army here to maintain a siege – and even that would not be enough to prevent us from breaking out and then hitting him in the rear. He also needs this as a base for supplies – and needs to deny it to us as well. That is why he will try to take this place."

"And the second reason?" asked Thymondas.

"The second reason is because his pride has been stung. We taught him a lesson today, and he does not like being schooled. He cannot abide defeat, let alone humiliation, and today, today," he laughed broadly, "today we have humiliated him. He will be back, and when he does, this will be the rock upon which I will break him."

"Excuse me, General," Dimitrios interrupted. "You said Alexander would attack for three reasons. What's the third?"

"Me," chuckled Memnon. "He'll attack because I'm here. He wants me, and now he wants me bad."

42

Old Citadel Hill

PARMENION AND THE EAGLE

As Alexander's battered battalions limped back to their camps, Parmenion climbed the slope of the Old Citadel Hill. The panoramic view from the old acropolis of Miletos was stunningly beautiful, but it was not for the pleasure of such a sight that he made the rugged trek. From there Parmenion could look down upon the battleground and into the city, the port, the island of Lade, and beyond. He could see the layout of its defenses, even the deployment of its troops, and the placement of its artillery – or at least as much as Memnon allowed him to see. Looking out due north, past the city, he could see the broad bay, with the island of Lade and the Greek fleet to his left, and the headland of Mount Mycale in the distance beyond that. He could not pick out individual ships with any certainty, but he could see the Persian fleet was still there. Why it had not come from Mycale to engage the smaller Greek fleet at Lade, he believed was due to simple cowardice. The Persians, as he saw them, were no better than women, and sought solace in numbers to compensate for their legacy of defeat at Salamis and in many other sea battles with the Greeks over the last century.

Parmenion's grasp of history was as biased as it was incomplete, but it gave him comfort and stoked his confidence. Both needed stoking after today's debacle. He fumed at how his men had been tricked, massacred and, worst of all as he saw it, humiliated by those effeminate Persian soldiers, who painted their faces, coiffed their hair in greasy ringlets and, most disgusting of all, wore pants- and baggy pants at that. Such dress was meant for clowns and actors, not men, and certainly not soldiers. Yet despite their effeminate ways, the Persians had won the day over the true men of Macedonia. That had never happened before, or at least not on such a scale, and, he vowed, it would never happen again, at least not on his watch.

As he alternately fumed and raged, Parmenion suddenly spotted an eagle flying down from the clouds. The huge, majestic bird was bigger and grander than any he had ever seen before. It circled high above the camp, then flew twice around the city and out toward Lade, where it found a perch on a large rock near one of the Greek ships that was drawn up on the beach. Parmenion's heart leaped in his chest, and all of his anger, fears, and humiliation washed away. This was an omen, an omen of certain victory, an unmistakable message from the gods, no, from Zeus himself, that the Macedonians would triumph after all. All they had to do to make it so, Parmenion believed, was that they do as the message so clearly directed them to do – fight the Persians at sea!

Parmenion almost fell several times as he raced down the hill toward the camp. He was moving so unusually fast that his young aides struggled to keep up with the old man, whose limp from an ancient wound for once did not seem to slow him down. Getting down the hill was quick and easy, however, compared to making his way through the madhouse that was the camp. Shattered, wounded men were lying about everywhere, their comrades either trying to help them, find help for them or carry them to someone who could help them. Others were racing about, trying to organize a defense of the camp, even though Memnon had shown no sign of coming out from behind his defenses. Then there was the king himself, his rage not only unabated but getting worse, as he struck out in anger at everything and everyone he could reach. Although Parmenion would normally have walked the other way and kept quiet when the king was in the midst of one of his frequent tantrums, this time he did not. Out of breath, his faced flushed, and his legs shaking, he nevertheless burst into the king's tent and shouted out so all could hear: "Victory! Victory my King! The gods have sent us a promise of victory!"

Everyone in the tent froze, even the king. The assembled generals, aides, servants and guards were sure that Alexander would explode in redoubled anger and hurl something heavy, sharp or equally deadly at his father's old friend and comrade. But he did not. His eyes blazed and his mouth opened wide – but then, as if someone had pulled a lever, he calmed down. Perhaps it was Parmenion's mention of the gods, or of victory, or just the sheer unexpected explosion of Parmenion onto the scene and in such a state, but whatever it was, it worked.

Alexander blinked twice, as if to clear the fog from his eyes, and stretched out his hands – one to clasp Parmenion on the shoulder, the other to take his hand. He drew the old general close, looked him in the eye and smiled.

"So, Parmenion, what is this about the gods, and a promise of victory?"

Parmenion had yet to calm down, or to regain his breath let alone his composure, and excitedly relayed all he had seen about the eagle, and what he was sure it meant.

"...and...and you see, my King. Isn't it obvious? We aren't meant to take Miletos by land – but by sea! The eagle flew around the camp without pause, flew over the city and then came to rest alongside our ships. Could the gods be more clear? They are saying 'use your navy, Alexander, if you want to win.' Now, you know me, Alexander, I'm a soldier, and I've never thought much of sailors and, frankly, dread stepping foot on a boat even when it's in dry-dock, let alone afloat...but even I can see what this means. Perhaps that is why the gods showed this sign to me – because if there is anyone in the camp less likely to put his faith in the fleet than me, well, I don't know who that could be."

Alexander smiled, patted the old man on his cheek, and called for his servants to bring wine – and stools for him and the old man to sit upon, as every other piece of furniture in the tent had been reduced to a pile of broken sticks because of the king's rage.

"Parmenion, my brave, stone-headed, dear Parmenion. We have but 160 ships – and the 20 best of them are crewed by Athenians, and you know how they think of me. How Admiral Nicanor keeps these sailors of a dozen cities who hate each other almost as much as they hate me, from killing one another, I do not know. How they would fight in a battle, or even if they would fight, is something, frankly, I do not know."

"But...but the eagle..."

"Yes, Parmenion. The eagle. That was one eagle. The Persians have close to 400 ships over there just across the bay in Mycale. You can see them from that hill you came tumbling down from. They have just as many more they can bring up – from Halicarnassos, Tyra, Sidon, Byblos, Cyprus and, of course, from Egypt. We cannot come close to matching them at sea..."

"My King! When have numbers meant anything to Macedonians...or Greeks for that matter? The Athenians were outnumbered six to one at Salamis. Greek navies have triumphed every time they have met the Persians at sea, no matter the size of their fleet! Surely..."

"Parmenion. The Greeks did not win every battle at sea against Persians, and even if I had a fleet that was bound to me like that of Athens was to Themistocles when he fought Xerxes at Salamis, I would do the same. Admiral Nicanor's fleet is all illusion. It is not a fleet but merely a collection of ships meant to give the Persians pause. Frankly, I am surprised they have not called my bluff and swept the lot from the sea – not that it would take much."

Parmenion's adrenaline rush came crashing down while the king was speaking. He suddenly felt his age, his exhaustion, and his aches and pains. Crestfallen and confused, he sighed a very deep, deep sigh, looked the king straight in the eye and asked, pleadingly, "then what the hell does that bit with the eagle mean? Surely it was a message from the gods? It couldn't just be..."

"The random actions of some bird of prey? No, Parmenion, I don't think so. Like you, I believe it is a sign from my father – my real father, not the man you knew as such, but my father in the heavens, Zeus almighty. You've just misinterpreted it, that's all," he added with a fatherly smile – to the man who was, indeed, old enough to have been his father – or even grandfather.

"Persia has command of the sea. We cannot challenge them on the waves. To do so would be to invite defeat. We cannot risk that, especially not after today. One more day like today and my enemies would rise up all over Greece. We'd be cut off from home, alone, and with no way back. No, Parmenion, the gods would not tell me to fight at sea, as they know all of this. Now think again, Parmenion. This eagle, where exactly did it land?"

"By the ships..."

"But not on a ship, right?"

"No...no, Majesty, not exactly."

"You said it landed beside a ship, on the beach, on land, on dry land, right?"

"Yes...yes, now that you mention it."

"Well, there you have it," said Alexander, rising slowly, slapping his muscular thighs with his hands. "The eagle came to rest on land, not on a ship. Zeus is telling me to put my faith on a battle on land. And that is what we will do, but this time, we will do it properly."

43

Miletos Acropolis

THE VIEW FROM THE CITADEL

J ust as the view from the Old Citadel Hill at the foot of the peninsula afforded the Macedonians a panoramic and detailed view of Miletos, so did the citadel on Miletos Hill at the very tip of the peninsula. It overlooked the city's impressive Lion Harbor, the protected anchorage that poked into the city like a finger. Behind the massive chain and forts that defended the seaport were forty warships – the Miletos Squadron of the Persian royal navy. If the Greeks made any move with their fleet to attack the city, those ships could quickly explode out from their haven to oppose them. The several score fat merchant vessels riding high in the commercial harbor, their holds empty, were more vulnerable to attack, but the artillery atop the turrets overlooking the seawall were there to deter, if not defeat, any attempt to sink or cut them out.

From the pinnacle of the citadel, the Greek fleet at Lade and even the Persian one across the bay at Mycale could be seen in great detail. So could the expanse of the town below, with its two main markets, its half dozen large and several score smaller temples, and its theater and other public buildings. Also apparent was the perfect gridplan designed by Hippodamos, the architect who, a century and a half ago, had worked out an urban plan that not only made sense, but also made navigating the city very easy. Hippodamos had loved his city so that he could not bear for it to be anything but perfect, or so the city legend went. Dimitrios, however, thought perhaps Hippodamos had some issues with the rambling layout of the old city, and making everything precise and orderly must have been some kind of an obsession for him. Perhaps that is why after the old city was destroyed that, rather than waste time and resources just rebuilding it, Hippodamos instead saw in that destruction an opportunity to design a more modern and more thoughtfully laid out city to replace it.

Although Miletos Hill was not as high as its opposite twin, the addition of the ramparts, battlements and towers of the citadel built upon it meant that a man standing at the top of the very highest tower could look directly across into the eyes of someone atop the far hill some 2,000 meters away as the crow flies – if, of course, they could focus at such a distance.

That is precisely where Memnon stood – with Dimitrios beside him. From their high perch they could see their own troops and defenses, and with some detail the Macedonian camp at the base of the Old Citadel Hill and the Sacred Way, the road that led off toward Prience and Didyma in the interior. That something was stirring inside that camp was obvious, for the Macedonians were buzzing like bees in a hive – and agitated bees at that.

"What do you think they are doing, General?"

"What they should have done when they first got here. They are gathering tools for a proper siege. They will raise earthworks across the base of the peninsula, with appropriate gaps, and will build siege engines – battering rams, towers, mantelets and the like – to come through those gaps. I imagine they are building other siege engines, the kind that can hurl great stones or firepots as well. Alexander's generals are not used to sieges, as neither the king nor his father ever had enough patience to conduct one by the book. Especially not this book," he laughed, waving about the scroll in his hand.

"And what book is that?" asked Dimitrios.

"*Poliorketika*," replied Memnon, "by Aeneas Tacticos, a general of

the Arcadian League, from around Stymphalos, down in the Pelo-
ponnesos."

"Never heard of him," said Dimitrios with a shrug.

"Not many people have," replied Memnon, "and I'm counting on
that."

"So, what's in this book that is so critical," asked the captain.

"It is pretty much a treatise on how to defend a city, as well as how
to properly besiege, and then assault one. It offers insights into how to
fight a battle in an urban area, after the enemy has breached the walls,
and how to conduct such a fight from the attacker's point of view as
well. That's where I got the idea for that little trap we just set out
among the tombs. That, and of course your story the other night, about
the battle at Thebes."

"You paid attention to what I said?" asked the captain with
disbelief.

"As would any good soldier worth his salt," Memnon replied. "If
you want to know how to defeat an enemy, it pays to listen to men who
have fought against him."

"But each time I have, I have been on the losing side," sighed
Dimitrios.

"One learns more from defeat than from victory – or at least they
should," said the general. "This Aeneas Tacticos was as often on the
losing side as on the winning side. It was only by learning from the
former that he discovered how to be on the later. Take our situation, for
example," continued the general. "As defenders, we have to be on
guard for internal treachery as much as for the external threat. We have
mercenaries whom we have to keep in check so they don't go bossing
about and abusing the locals, or else the people will turn on them – and
us, and see the enemy outside as their rescuers."

Dimitrios nodded in agreement, being well aware of the low character and voracious appetites of the mercenaries he had served amongst
at the Granicos.

"And then we have the city itself. It has strong points and weak
points. Anybody can hold a strong point, but the weak points, well, that

is where you really need to focus. But you don't put your best soldiers there..."

"No? Why not? Isn't it obvious..."

"Ah, Captain," smiled the general, "you see? Of course it is obvious to most people that you put your best men at the most vulnerable spot. But in this case the 'best men' are not necessarily the best soldiers, but those who have the most to lose if the wall is breached. You put the people who live there to the job of defending what is theirs, along with others who may have a personal, religious or financial stake there. You can count on them to be vigilant, and not succumb to the tedium or temptations of garrison duty."

"I would never have thought of that," said Dimitrios. "So, what other tricks does this old general have up his sleeve?"

"Well, he's not that old – I mean, yes, he's dead now, but not dead long. He fought alongside Xenophon, and survived the battle of Mantinea – and that was fought barely 30 years ago. Aristotle took it from the general's own hand."

"How do you know that?" asked Dimitrios.

"Remember," instructed Memnon. "I was a guest – or hostage, or whatever you want to call it – in the Macedonian court for a few years. I had little to do except read – and read I did. I read everything I could get my hands on, and when I ran out of books I went to Alexander's tutor, Aristotle, and asked to borrow from his personal library. That's where I found this book."

"But you still have it? You never returned it?"

"No. It opened my eyes and made me look at city warfare in an entirely new light. I figured this would be useful to me someday, and as Philip was already boasting about marching on Persia, I thought to myself, why should I let him in on its secrets and insights. Like the trick we used to set a golden path for Alexander the other day, to lure him in...and then smash him."

"And that was all there, in this book? What was it called?..."

"*Poliorketika*," replied Memnon. "Yes, or at least the inspiration for it. And there's more, like instructing people to go up to their roof and throw tiles down at an invader in the streets – ever seen how big some of those tiles can be? Not even the best helmet is much use against that. Or how easy it is for people to get weapons – from the tool markets, construction sites or even temples. Which means we post guards to make sure undesirable elements can't arm themselves to turn on us, and then, if the enemy is about to breach the walls, to distribute these weapons to people we can count upon. He even came up with a rather novel system to pass on messages through a hydraulic semaphore system, which I've ordered to be set up in the citadel and several of the taller towers."

"General, you have a lot in common with my brother, Klemes. I mean, he's a physician, not a soldier, but he's always telling me: 'I read, therefore I know things.'"

"Wise man, your brother," said Memnon with a nod. "Wiser than mine, I think," he added sadly, remembering how his brother had picked the wrong side in a dynastic dispute. "Wiser than mine."

The two men were silent for a bit, until Dimitrios felt it was up to him to break the mood.

"Well, General," he said with a laugh. "I guess they will have to learn to read over there, especially after the schooling you gave them the other day."

"Don't get cocky, my young friend," said Memnon in reproach, "that was Alexander's mistake. And he won't make it again. Alexander is bold, rash, headstrong – but he learns, and he learns quickly. After all, he had Aristotle for a teacher, and Aristotle does not suffer fools, nor produces them."

"So, General, what do we do in the meantime?"

"We wait," said Memnon. "We wait, and make ready. Get out your little wax tablet and scratch this down: I want all officers at the inner and outer wall to prepare bags of dirt, piles of stone, whatever timbers they can strip from houses, and buckets of water and sand. If Alexander batters a wall, we shore it up, repair it or build a second wall just behind it. If he sets fire to the wall, we douse the flames with water and sand. The commanders of each section of the wall are to report to the quartermaster to receive their allocation of shovels, axes, wheelbarrows and other tools. Got that, Dimitrios?"

"Yes, sir."

"Good," the general said as he again took in the view. "Give that to one of the scribes and have him make copies to distribute. And while you are at it, have a copy sent to the governor."

"Hegisistratos?"

"Yes, he is still governor, after all, the little worm. It is only correct that we should keep him informed about the defense of his city – even if he tried to surrender it to Alexander. Oh, and before I forget," Memnon added, "add this to the copy you send him: he is to draft slaves, craftsmen, and any other workmen he can find to assist our soldiers in this task. My men can't both stand watch and build walls, or at least they shouldn't have to do it alone."

"He'll find some excuse not to..."

"Yes, Captain, he will make some excuse why he cannot do as I ask. When he does, I'll offer to ask the king on his behalf to defray the tribute for a few years. That will get him off his ass."

"And if it doesn't?"

"Dimitrios, are you that new to the workings of this empire, or the world? He's a greedy little bastard, but he's my greedy little bastard. He turned this decaying, dilapidated backwater harbor town into the greatest metropolis this side of Damascus. He knows how to get things done, and how to make a profit on the side when he does. Never under-estimate the power of greed – or of a little bribe. Not in this empire."

"He is very frightened, my General," Dimitrios replied. "That might still not be enough to get him off his ass."

"If it doesn't, well you can pull him to his feet, and make him bend over so I can put my boot up that puckered plump behind of his," said the general laughing. "In the meantime, go have those messages copied and sent. Then go get yourself something to eat and a bit of rest. And here, take the book. Better yet, take it to your brother the book lover and ask him to read it for you. Have him let me know if I've missed something important. But I'll want you back at headquarters after sundown. There's something else I will need doing then. Well, what are you waiting for, get going!"

After doing as the general had ordered, Dimitrios went to find Ari and Klemes, hoping the two would join him for a meal and a drink. Never one to turn down a plate or a cup, especially if someone else was buying, Aristophanes was happy to oblige. Klemes, grumbling as usual, demurred, explaining that he had a meeting with some other physician or magician or crackpot who wanted to show him some special herbs that would help him expand his mind or something or other. He did, however, gladly accept the book, and assured Dimitrios that he would indeed read it – as soon as he could find the time.

"At least this general you so admire not only can read but actually does read," observed Klemes. "If what he learns in those books can put an end to his madness sooner and save lives, or at least the lives of our men, all the better," added the physician. "The gods know there are enough generals in this world who care little for the butcher's bill, just as long as they get a statue raised to mark their own glorious victory. I have just about had enough of trying to set broken bones, sew up wounds and push intestines back into men who have had their bellies ripped open..."

Aristophanes and the captain left Klemes to his own devices and walked the length of the city. They started at the barracks by the citadel at the base of the Acropolis of Miletos and passed the Delphinion, the Nymphaion, and other shrines, temples, and religious buildings. All were packed with worried citizens making sacrifices, burning incense, placing offerings on altars or giving gold or other gifts to the priests.

Despite the repulse of the Macedonians only days before, the citizens of Miletos were frightened of what was to come next. While some put their faith in the gods, others, Aristophanes remarked, put that faith in Memnon, and by extension, Dimitrios and the rest of the army.

Just past the Nymphaion, the two came upon the Southern Agora, the larger of the two markets in the city. The Southern Agora was not really on the south side, but more accurately the east side of the city. While the city's other market, on the opposite side of the peninsula, was appropriately called the Western Agora, somehow this one on the east had gotten a different name.

"Maybe they call it the 'Southern Agora' because it is south of the citadel" suggested Aristophanes. "Or just 'south' of wherever they were coming from."

"Your leaps of logic never cease to astound me, Ari," jibed the captain.

"Ah, well, such is the curse of a classical education, eh?"

"I had all the education I needed at home and in my father's business, thank you very much, Ari. The world was my school. While you were sitting on your ass under some damned tree in Thebes, I was off and about seeing the cities and islands where my father made deals for the wine he brokered. And my father, well, he made sure I learned to read the great books. You know, Homer and all that."

"Well, did this grand tour of yours teach you where to find a good meal?" Ari joked. "We've been walking around for an hour or more and I was famished before we started. You promised me a meal and a drink, so come on now, enough sightseeing. I'm hungry."

There were many stalls, and shops, and carts offering fresh or prepared foods throughout the agora. One shop that was particularly crowded drew Ari's attention – and with good reason, as he and Dimitrios soon found out. The man there was selling fish that had been rolled in some kind of coating and quick fried in oil. His customers were so insistent and demanding that he did not even have time to wrap the fish up, but tossed it by the chunk to the next man in line. For a few obols more he would place it on a plate and pour some spicy sauce over it, which Ari insisted they try after each had a few handfuls of the hot, fried fish.

A few stalls down there were others selling olives, and cheese, and flat bread, all of which went quite well with some cheap, watery but still pleasant wine from another vendor. A few honey cakes and a couple of pieces of fruit from other stalls also tempted the two as they ate their way through the agora. Ari spotted an unusual building with a crude drawing of a woman's charms, and as he was trying to convince Dimitrios to go in with him – and give him some coins to pay for the entertainment – the agora went silent. Thousands of voices hushed almost at the same time, for up in the sky to the south, a massive ball of fire climbed up, hovered for a breath, and then came hurling down with the speed of a thunderbolt, to slam into the lower town. The earth shook, people screamed, and clouds of smoke, dust, and flames exploded into the air.

The bombardment of Miletos had begun.

44

Miletos

THE OUTER WALL

The first fireball was the signal for a dozen other siege weapons to begin their long range bombardment. For the rest of the day, a steady staccato of flaming pots of oil and boulders rained down upon the city and its outer wall. Memnon's instructions had come too late for the defenders on that part of the city to comply, and they were too busy ducking the incoming fire to do so, even if the tools and materials Memnon ordered had been at hand. So many fires had been started by the flaming pots that the city remained illuminated throughout the night – thus making it easier for Alexander's artillery crews to maintain a steady and fairly accurate bombardment. By the next morning, the already unfinished outworks were in such a sorry state as to be nearly unrecognizable from the rubble around them.

When Alexander's attack came, it did not come with wild shouts and screams like the former one, but with a steady drumbeat, to which the advancing infantry kept time. The Macedonians advanced in grim silence, a silence punctuated only by the creaking of the wheels of the rolling wooden walls, or mantelets, and tower shields behind which their archers took cover. Alexander's siege masters walked their bombardment forward, lengthening the range of their fire with each volley, so that their stones, rocks and firepots fell not on the front line, but behind it, into the Necropolis where most of the last assault had floundered. There was no question of reinforcements from the city coming out to bolster the defense, not through that rain of death. Some soldiers on the outer wall did attempt to flee to the presumed safety of the city, but they, too, became casualties in the middle ground. The heavy boulders that fell in that area smashed men and tombstones alike, turning the graves and monuments of the Necropolis into rubble.

Unable to flee, the men on the outer line had only two options: surrender or fight to the death. As the Macedonians had clearly shown their disinclination to offer quarter, that left the defenders no option at all. Fight, and fight hard, they did – but to no avail.

As the Macedonians reached the ditch at the outer works, their line of tall tower shields and mantelets parted to allow unarmed men carrying bundles of sticks and armloads of other debris to rush forward, dump their burdens in the ditch and then scurry back for more. Others dragged forward wooden ramps to bridge the gap. Once those bridges were down and the ditch at least partially filled, the Macedonian infantry began their paean, the death song that was meant to bolster their courage and sap that of their enemies.

Then the attack went in, and the slaughter began.

"The outer works have fallen, General," Governor Hegistratos said as he confronted Memnon at his headquarters in the citadel. "By the rules of war we still have time to ask for terms – for an honorable surrender. Once the Macedonians breach the main town wall it will be too late – they will rush in and rape, pillage and loot the city, and kill us all."

Memnon looked up from his map of the city, slowly strode over to the governor – and slapped him hard on the cheek.

"You've wanted to surrender since before the Macedonians even reached your gates, you sniveling coward!" barked Memnon. "You've profited and profited obscenely for years as governor of this city, you little worm, and now the time has come to pay your dues. You even mention the word 'surrender' or anything like that again and I will so help me by the gods chain you to a post on the wall and let the Macedonians use you for target practice. And just to be sure that you keep your mouth shut about this, I'm assigning you a bodyguard – and not to guard your body but to prevent you from committing treason. Captain Dimitrios!" he shouted over his shoulder, "find the biggest, meanest, foulest-tempered Greek in the mercenary corps, and tell him he has a new job. He's to be the governor's nanny, and he has my permission – no, my insistence – that he take any disciplinary action he thinks fit if this man steps out of line again. Do you hear me?"

"Yes, General!" replied the captain, clicking the heels of his boots together and saluting with parade-ground perfection. "I have just the man for the job!"

"You want me to do what?" asked Ari incredulously. "You want me to babysit the governor?"

"Somebody has to do it," said Dimitrios with a shrug, "and it has to be someone he can't bribe, or threaten, or coerce, or otherwise corrupt. You may not be the biggest, meanest soldier in the force, like the general asked for, but you are one I can trust – and that is far more important. Besides, even with your gammy leg you can still outrun that fat bastard."

Aristophanes simmered. "I want to fight, god damn it, not hide behind the line and squire around some lazy bureaucrat. You're going to need every man you've got when Alexander comes across the Necropolis. You know how good I am with a bow. Any luck and I can plink an arrow into one of his beady little eyes. You know how easy it is to spot him – he's always at the front, like he was at the Granicos."

Dimitrios sighed, put a hand on his friend's shoulder and said "I know. Don't worry. You will get your chance. Memnon will insist the governor be on the wall, if only to show the populace and the soldiers his commitment to the cause..."

"Yeah, with me holding a dagger at his bum, right?"

"If that is what it takes. You can take a couple of men from the ranks to help out. Try to take some of the walking wounded, you know, those who are fit enough to hold a sword but still not ready to stand in the line of battle. It'll be your first command," he added with a smile. "Who knows, maybe someday you'll even make corporal?"

The next few days were fairly quiet ones for Miletos and its defenders and inhabitants. Alexander's engineers needed those days to clear away rubble and flatten the ground enough to allow for the siege engines to be brought forward. What had been the outer works defending the city now became the forward line from which to besiege it. From his perch on the Miletos Acropolis, Memnon had a bird's eye view of those preparations. It was a view of which he intended to make good use.

"Men," Memnon said to his leading officers as they gathered around his map table, "as you can see, I have marked the position of Alexander's heavy artillery with these little wooden blocks. Each has a number, and that number marks the target for each group of workmen in your assault parties to attack. We will send three columns of men from each of the gates and sally points on the town wall. I will command the middle column. Thymondas you have the left. Anyone have any suggestions for who should lead the third – and no, Ephialtes, not you."

"Why not, sir?" grumbled the old general, his pride obviously hurt.

"Because I need you to watch our backs. You will command the city, provide covering fire and, most of all, make sure nobody shuts the gates behind us."

That last remark sparked a little laugh among the other officers, but Memnon cut that short with a stern glare.

"I am serious. There are elements in this city who have already tried to make a deal with Alexander," he said, glaring at the governor, "and they will try again. Ephialtes," he said turning from the governor and looking directly into the old general's eyes, "I am giving you the city because I know I won't have to worry or keep looking over my shoulder if you are here. Besides, if I fall..."

Memnon did not continue on that track, but returned to the battle plan. "In addition to the three main columns, we will send a few groups by small boat on both flanks. As you can see," he added, slapping his palm down on the map and spreading his fingers wide, "our attack will look like a hand reaching out to claw at Alexander's line. Your soldiers are to seize control of the outer wall at those five points, and hold them..."

"Hold them? For how long?" asked Thymondas. "As soon as we attack, the Macedonians will put every man in motion to drive us back. We shall be horribly outnumbered, and they can bring up men faster than we can bring more out of the city."

"You don't need to hold out for very long – just long enough for the work parties to do their job. It will take the Macedonians time to form up for a counterattack – and that should be long enough to see this through. Once the engines are destroyed or at least put out of action, you can start to withdraw. Ephialtes, here, will provide covering fire from the town walls, first with the bolt-throwers and stone-throwers and then, as you come back closer to the gates, with the archers. Governor Hegisistratos," he added, pointing to the well-dressed but quivering official "will be on the walls himself, to give our men added courage. Isn't that right, governor?" he added with a wry smile.

Aristophanes poked the governor in the back with the hilt of his sword, and Hegisistratos jumped a bit, but did respond, if grudgingly, in the affirmative.

"What makes you think you will fare any better going through the Necropolis than Alexander did the other day," asked the governor. "You trapped him there – won't he do the same to you?"

Thymondas, Ephialtes and other officers all began talking at once, with the old general muttering something about Hegisistratos being of conjectural progeny and dubious antecedents, but Memnon cut them off with a sharp slashing motion of his hand across his throat.

"The governor has a valid question," said Memnon calmly and respectfully, much to the surprise of his officers. "Believe me, I have gone over that very possibility in my mind over and over again. It could go wrong, it could go terribly wrong. But unlike Alexander's attack that time, ours has a plan, a purpose, and a timetable. Also, we will go at night – which I know makes things a lot more difficult to control, but our attack is more focused than his. It is not as ambitious, and if it does go wrong, I'll call it off, and Ephialtes will cover our withdrawal."

"And if you get killed or wounded, who then will call things off? inquired Ephialtes. "And while we are on the subject, why in the name of Hades are you going out there, risking yourself in the middle of all of this, if I may ask?"

Memnon looked up and replied simply and silently with a broad grin.

"As I thought," sighed the old Greek officer. "You want to be out there, don't you?"

"Of course I do," said Memnon rather matter-of-factually. "A general's place is at the head of his troops. Can't very well ask men to do something I wouldn't do, now, can I? Besides, what happened there the other day has shaken them up a bit. Undid all we gained from trapping Alexander's first mad rush. Do them a bit of good to see the brass out there in the muck with them, eh what? Besides, Ephialtes," he added with a laugh, "I'm not going to let the young men have all the fun!"

The "fun" began about two hours after midnight. The naval assault parties climbed into their small boats to paddle along either side of the peninsula. Advance pathfinders slipped out through the sally ports and main gate to mark the way forward through the treacherous and tortuous tombstones of the Necropolis. Every 20 paces they set small earthenware pots with holes knocked through one side – the side facing the city. Each held a cup of oil, and each was set alight to provide a tiny beacon visible only from the city. After the pathfinders had marked the first four parts of the path, the attack parties followed out slowly and as quietly as possible. The workmen would follow, but none would enter the Necropolis itself until the fighting men took control of the positions where Alexander had placed his siege engines.

As he watched the men slip out of the city, Aristophanes so wished to be out there with them, rather than be stuck up on the wall with the governor. Klemes was safely tucked away in the rear with the other healers, but Ari did not envy him what was sure to come. He had been on the receiving end of Macedonian weapons – and of physicians' treatments, and did not wish for a repeat of either experience. Still, he bristled at remaining behind – and made his distaste known to the governor by his demeanor. His post as the governor's minder, however, did give him a good view of the action as it was unfolding. He could see the progress of the silent bands of soldiers by noting as they passed the lights, which would seem to wink out as each body came between the little oil pots and the city. Although he could not make out individuals, he could see the "hand" of Memnon stretched out to claw at the Macedonians.

The question was, would the claw grab the prize, or be caught in a bear trap.

45

Memnon's Claw

THE OUTER WALL

imitrios kept close to Memnon as the middle finger of his "claw" crept silently through the Necropolis. He could make out shadows of the men following behind them and moving to either side, but even with the little lights from the pots that marked the path, he could not make out their faces, or that of his general. Most of the men, he imagined, were, like himself, as nervous as they were determined. None were used to fighting in the dark – or going into battle without horns blaring, drums beating and other men singing their battle song. This slow, quiet advance in the darkness was unsettling, for every man felt alone, even though he knew his comrades were nearby.

The tension proved too much for one man, who stumbled and fell on a broken tombstone in the battle-damaged cemetery. The clatter of his spear as it fell and bounced from tomb to tomb, and the clang clang clanging as he dropped his shield and when his helmet tumbled off his head, resounded through the otherwise silent night, as if someone had banged a gong or clashed cymbals together. The noise drew the attention of the Macedonian pickets who huddled at protected posts just ahead of the outer wall, at the southern end of the Necropolis, and they went scurrying back to the main line, shouting the alarm.

"Well, that's it then," grumbled Memnon. "At least we got this far. All right, now that they know we are here, let us make some real noise!"

Memnon gave a great bellowing roar, like a lion uncaged, jumped up upon a monument, and bellowed a war cry – which a thousand voices echoed as the men of the attacking columns eagerly shed the blanket of silence under which they had moved for the last hour. Horns blared, drums banged, and shouts and screams came from both sides of the Macedonian line, as Memnon's three main columns rushed forward with a blood-curdling yell, all pretense of secrecy and silence abandoned.

The adrenaline rush of the charge exploded in their hearts and propelled the soldiers in the columns to go up and over the barricades. The few defenders on that line were quickly overborne by numbers, and the exhilaration of the charge carried the Persians and their Greek mercenaries deep into the Macedonian position...but not deep enough.

The Macedonians had not been caught entirely wrong-footed. Alexander had kept some of his best units under arms in shifts, just in case should such a sortie occur – or should the besieged try a break out. The Agrianians, Alexander's crack light infantry drawn from the tribe of the same name, were the first to respond. They had more stake in holding the line than almost any other unit in the army. After all, it was they, along with some squadrons of Thracian horse and the Companions, who had seized the outermost part of the city in a lightning dash, before even the rest of the army arrived. They had no desire to give up ground they had already paid for, and their javelins hit true, especially at such close ranges as they were now engaged.

They did not have to fight on their own for long, as other units of the light infantry came flooding out of the camp to join them. This was their kind of fight – in and out of the shadows, using cover to their advantage, and fighting in a wild, disorganized melée, rather than in the formal linear style of the heavy infantry. There was no space here for the men of the phalanx to wield their 12 and 18 foot long pikes, but there were plenty of other men perfectly equipped to fight in this kind of battle. The sword and shield men of the elite Hypaspistes regiment, the cloud of peltastes and other lightly equipped javelinmen, slingers, and even a few archers, came quickly to the fray. In this kind of fight there was no need to form up, count heads, and deploy into a mathematically correct and precise formation. This was a dog fight; a wild, confusing, horrific struggle where bare hands and short blades were of more use than large shields and long spears.

And Memnon was in the thick of it. He was the biggest dog in this dog fight, and Dimitrios was right there alongside him – quite literally guarding his back. Memnon was no longer giving any commands because there were none to give – and no one could have heard them if there were. This fight had neither organization nor formality, nor even sense to it. Three fingers of men pushed forward into an ever thickening mass of bodies, while two more tried to come in from the sea around their flanks. What Memnon had envisioned as a hand clawing its way through sand into the heart of the Macedonian line became a hand stuck in mud, and mud that was becoming increasingly deep and rapidly gummy.

Memnon had kept the attacking force deliberately small for purposes of surprise, but as more and more men piled out of the Macedonian camp, the attackers became the attacked. Try as they might, none of the men in the three main columns could take possession of any of the siege weapons. The group led by Memnon himself came the closest. Dimitrios saw a man in front of him put his hand on the brace of a bolt thrower – only to have it nailed to the beam by a broken javelin another thrust through his hand. As for the groups of boatmen to either side of the peninsula, most never even came ashore. Under heavy missile fire, they either turned their boats around and rowed quickly back to the harbor, or just jumped overboard and tried to swim for it. With the fingers of his claw being broken, nibbled at, or even snapped off, Memnon tried to gather as many men to himself as he could for one last, desperate and focused strike.

And that is when Memnon went down.

Dimitrios rushed to cover the general's body with his own. "Help! Help the general!" he called to any around him who could hear above the din and screams of battle. "Help the general!"

Three workmen came forward in response. All of the others who had followed the columns out of the city with the intention of smashing the siege engines had long ago fled back to Miletus. These three were about to do so when they heard Dimitrios' cry for help. They stashed their tools back into their belts, and pushed their way through the tangled mass of dead and dying bodies to grab at the unconscious general's arms and legs. As they began to drag him back out of the front line, word of Memnon's fate spread and spread quickly. Without their general to lead them, the already wavering attack columns began to recede. Many men threw down their tools and weapons and just ran for the city.

A few stout lads, however, coalesced around the general and those carrying him. Slowly they fell back, giving ground grudgingly, but giving it up none the less. The farther they fell back, however, the bolder the Macedonians became. Like hyenas sensing fear and a bloodied prey, Alexander's warriors lurched forward in a tide of their own, and one that threatened to engulf the wounded Memnon and those seeking to save him.

From his post on the wall, Ephialtes could see very little of the battle on the far side of the Necropolis. All he did know was that there was a battle on the line of outerworks – and that groups of workmen and soldiers were streaming back in panic toward the city. "The general's attack must have stalled," he said to an aide. "Send out a scouting party to find General Memnon, and ask if he needs reinforcements or has any other instruction for me."

The aide saluted and ran off, down the steps, motioning for a group of soldiers to join him on his way out of the main gate, which remained partly open, as it had been when Memnon passed through it an hour or so ago. Ephialtes followed their progress as far as he could see, then suddenly saw the officer running back as fast he could. The young aide came rushing through the half-open gate and turned up the stairs to the battlements, which is where Ephialtes met him. "It's the general..." the aide said, panting and struggling to both get his breath and calm his panic. "He's been wounded. They're carrying him back now."

Ephialtes turned about and raced back up the steps to the battlement. He shouted for runners to attend him. "Go to each of the towers," he told the couriers. "Tell them to fire some small fireballs as far and as high as possible. Distance is the key here. We need them to fly far, hang high and light up the Necropolis. Then tell them to prepare to provide long-range covering fire. Our men are coming back, and I think they are going to need help if they are to get back inside the walls...alive."

Hegisistratos could not help but overhear Ephialtes give those orders. Half-smirking, and at least partially pleased with himself, he asked the old Greek officer a question to which he already knew the answers.

"So, the surprise attack, the 'claw' that was supposed to be our salvation, has failed," the governor stated more than asked. "And what of our glorious general?" he added, twirling one of the oily ringlets that had fallen out from beneath his gold-trimmed cap.

"It appears he may have been hurt. I'm not certain and don't have all of the details."

"Tsk, tsk. What a pity," hummed the governor. "Well then, I suppose command revolves back to me, does it not? After all, I am the highest ranking Persian official in the city, now that Memnon is, shall we say, incapacitated. Or at least indisposed?"

The smarmy tone rankled Ephialtes to his very core. "No sir, the general left me as his second in command. Not you," the old professional soldier replied sharply.

"Oh? Well, we shall see about that, won't we. You are, after all, nothing more than a foreign hireling, when it comes down to it. Surely you can't expect to have any authority over those of us of noble blood? You are but a barbarous Greek..."

"Memnon, I will remind you sir, is also a Greek!"

"Perhaps, technically, General," replied the governor, his self-confidence and self-worth returning, "but he has at least married into a noble family of the blood, and has sired children who carry that blood, even if it is diluted with his own. Besides, his authority came straight from Darius himself. Your contact with the emperor, correct me if I am wrong, is limited to seeing his face on the gold Darics with which you are paid?"

"Hegisistratos, I have no time for your Persian riddles and games. There is a battle going on and I have a part to play in it. So until it is over do me the kindness of butting out – and of going to hell or wherever it is your kind slithers off to at night."

If Ephialtes expected the governor to argue, or to run off in a huff, he was disappointed. Hegisistratos was enjoying himself and made no attempt to hide it.

"Well, then, 'General,'" he replied with a taunting emphasis on Ephialtes' rank, "if you wish me to leave the wall, I will do so. As governor of Miletos I have much more pressing and important duties to attend to than to just stand here and watch Memnon's retreat."

Hegistratos made an obscenely slow, deep, and mocking bow, gathered his hands inside his robe's flowing sleeves, and began to walk down the stairs. Aristophanes, who had been present as ordered, did not follow.

"Aren't you supposed to stick with him, lad?" Ephialtes asked.

"Yes, General, but, well..."

"What is it?"

"My friend, Captain Dimitrios, he's out there with Memnon," replied Ari nervously and with deep respect.

"Yes, I know," sighed Ephialtes.

"No, I mean with him. Right with him. If the general is hurt, Dimitrios will be guarding him. Unless, unless Dimitrios..."

"Yes, yes. I quite understand," muttered Ephialtes. "Then go on, go out there. See if you can find him – or at least help bring Memnon back into the city. I'd go myself, but..."

Aristophanes did not wait for the explanation. He just saluted and raced down the steps, taking them two or three at a time, and ran for the gate. He thought highly of Memnon, but it was not the general he was out to save.

46

Miletos

THE MAIN GATE

Dimitrios struggled to keep his shield high to protect the body of his general, but doing so while falling back, through the dark, and with the Macedonians closing in was no simple task. Many a stone or lead bullet from enemy slingers banged off his shield, and a few others clanged off his helmet, but at least he managed to keep the commander safe. A few men gathered around him to add their shields to the protective barrier, but several of them quite literally took an arrow or a javelin meant for Memnon. Sometimes stumbling over the gravestones, and the rubble, as well as over the dead and dying, the small party made agonizingly slow progress is getting the unconscious general back to the main gate of Miletos.

The attack had not only faltered, it had fallen apart. Only small pockets of men were still engaged in a fighting retreat; most of the rest had either run away or were bleeding out on the field. Memnon's effort to destroy Alexander's siege weapons had failed, and failed miserably. A fact the Macedonian king made even clearer by having those engines open fire on the ground over which Memnon's force was trying to retreat, and upon the wall – its main gate – to which they were heading.

The battle, however, was not entirely one-sided. With their own troops no longer engaged on the outer works, the defenders of Miletos were able to conduct a counter-bombardment of their own. Although only the largest of those weapons had the range to hit Alexander's siege engines, others were well placed to pound, skewer, and set afire the Macedonian troops who were in pursuit of the retreating Persian force. It was under cover of that fire that Ephialtes had organized a company of Greek mercenaries into a turtle formation – where all but the front rank held their shields above their heads – to head out of the main gate in hopes of finding, protecting, and escorting back their general. This was not a fighting formation, and Aristophanes attached himself to that group, where he and a few other archers and slingers flitted about to protect them should any Macedonian troopers come at them.

The clatter of stones and arrows that fell from above would have unnerved all but the heartiest of hearts, yet still they advanced, slowly and in step, with a sergeant at the front calling cadence as they did. All went well until a large fire pot landed on their shields, broke open and spewed flaming pitch and oil on their shields and down amongst them. That proved too much to bear, and the turtle shell cracked open, with some men screaming in pain as they tried to roll on the rocky ground to put out the fire that was burning their clothes and their skin.

Aristophanes, however, kept on going. He was but singed by the fire, and otherwise unhurt. Although his bad leg still hurt and left him with a limp, he kept moving forward, scrambling his way through the dead and the debris. There was no use to call out for Dimitrios, for he could not have heard his name being called above the hellish din of battle and bombardment. Not that Ari had enough breath to yell, even if he could have screamed loud enough to make himself heard. Instead, he trusted his eyes and moved ahead to what appeared to be the thickest clump of soldiers still in some kind of formation. In the midst of that, he found his friend.

"What the hell are you doing out here?" Dimitrios yelled in surprise when Ari placed his hand upon the captain's shoulder. "You're supposed to be back on the wall, with the governor!"

"Screw the governor," spat Ari. "You're a lot more important to me, and so is Memnon."

Dimitrios was too exhausted and too frightened to argue, and just decided to accept whatever help he could get from any quarter. "All right, then. Grab a shield and help me keep the general safe."

"What's wrong with him, is he dead?"

"No, he's still breathing, he's just out cold. Something clocked him really good in the helmet, and he went down. We're trying to get him back to the city," he added, as another shower of stones, bullets and arrows rained down upon them. Two men, one to either side, fell, but those carrying the general kept on moving, hoping that others would aid their fallen comrades. Dimitrios was in a race to get back to the city before Alexander's counterattack beat him to it or cut him off from the gates. A hundred paces or so from the city gate, he lost that race.

What resistance there had been to his left and right collapsed, and collapsed completely. The few men who had been falling back in good order had finally had enough. Once they saw the open gate, they bolted for it. They dropped weapons and shields, tore off helmets and armor and ran for it. Many overly eager Macedonians followed, striking them down as they ran. Others stopped to loot the dead or dying, while others themselves fell, targets of the archers on the wall. Still other Macedonians, however, swept around through the routing troops to get behind the one, shrinking body of Persian troops on the field: the band of men shepherding the wounded Memnon.

"Circle up! Circle up!" shouted Dimitrios, as there was no longer any point in heading for the gate. There were just too many Macedonians between them and the city. Those who were helping him protect Memnon, fortunately, were the bravest of the brave. Persian and Greek alike, they closed ranks in a tight circle about their general, ready to die with him rather than give up his body.

"Surrender and live!" a young Macedonian officer with two feathers on his bronze helmet shouted above the din. Standing on a broken monument, the officer shouted "give us your general's body and you will live!"

Dimitrios caught a glimpse of the face of the man, and it sent both a chill and then a fire through him. The Macedonian officer was their king: Alexander himself. If there had been even a small chance that

Dimitrios would have accepted the offer, that put an end to it. He had come too far to give in to Alexander.

"You want him!" Dimitrios shouted over his shield, "come and take him!"

Despite their exhaustion, or perhaps because of it, Ari and the others around him gave a cheer, and yelled curses of their own at the Macedonians who were closing in about them. Just as all seemed lost, a loud trumpet blast split the air, and out from the open gates charged a dozen armored horsemen, swinging axes and swords, hurling javelins and screaming their own battle cry. The shock and surprise of that charge scattered the Macedonians who had come between Memnon and the city. As the cavalry spread to the left and right to make secure their flanks, the small band of men carrying the general made a run for it, or at least ran as fast as they could while holding him above the ground. Minutes later, they entered the safety of the city, followed by two horsemen – the only two of the twelve brave souls who had charged out to survive their glorious, if doomed, charge.

Klemes was there to meet them as they came in, along with a dozen stretcher bearers and two large carts with their mules and drovers.

"Quickly now, place the general in that cart," he said, after a cursory look at the stricken commander. "Get him to the hospital. I'll be right behind you," Klemes added, pausing only to be sure that his brother and their friend were alive.

"You two, go along with the general. Looks like you could both use some patching up."

"Memnon...Memnon..." said Dimitrios, panting and dropping unsteadily to one knee.

"Don't worry, brother," said Klemes reassuringly. "I'll do everything I can to save your general. You need to worry about yourself, now," he added with a bit of command to his voice. "You don't look too bad...or too good for that matter," the usually stoic physician managed to say with a little smile. "Best get yourself looked at. My helpers will see to you, and to our gimpy friend here..." he added, turning to Ari. "And what, pray tell, made you limp out into a battlefield?"

Aristophanes did not reply with words, but with a wide, almost silly grin, as he nodded his head and pointed his thumb to Dimitrios.

"All right then, the two of you, get on to the hospital," Klemes groaned. The physician followed, muttering as he went. "Boys will be boys. Still playing at war, at their age!"

While the battle outside still raged, Hegisistratos, no longer shadowed by Ari, had slipped away from the wall and made his way to a quite well-to-do house in the center of the lower city. It was a house he knew very well, and one in which he was also very well known. The slave at the door did not dare pause to halt him, and knew he did not need to announce the governor as he entered. For there, waiting for him, was the owner of the house and half a dozen other richly attired, over-weight, and concerned citizens.

"Ah, governor, so glad you could shake off your minder and come meet with us," said the owner of the house, Glaucippos. "How goes the war?"

"Badly, very badly – at least from a certain point of view," he replied as he reached for a cup of wine that a scantily dressed boy handed him.

"And whose point of view would that be?" asked Glaucippos slyly.

"Not ours, I assure you," said Hegisistratos with a smile. "Memnon's attempt to destroy Alexander's siege engines failed, as I warned him it would. But would he listen to me? Of course not!" he added with a dramatic gesture to his forehead. "And not only did it fail – it was a disaster. Hundreds of men dead, hundreds more wounded – and Memnon among them!"

"Memnon?" said Glaucippos excitedly and with glee. "Dead? Wounded? Which is it? Is the big man truly down?"

"I am not sure, Glaucippos," replied the governor as he drained his cup and held it out for more. "He was carried in from the field, uncon-scious. What matters most is that he cannot wield command at present. That opens a window for us to try once again to negotiate with Alexander. Now that the king has seen how hard and expensive a nut this is to crack, perhaps he will be more...how shall I say it...amenable to reason, for a price."

"I agree. Despite having been insulted when I last tried – perhaps the young Macedonian will now be more reasonable. You said Memnon was down, but did not answer my question. Is Memnon dead or not?"

"Frankly," sighed Hegisistratos as he drained his second cup and held it out again for a refill, "I could not tell if he was living or dead. I did not have time to wait around and see, lest that smelly Greek soldier that has been following me around came back. All I know is that he was carried in, and that he has been taken to the hospital by the Southern Agora, the one that insufferable physician from Thebes has set up."

"Well, then," said Glaucippos thoughtfully, "perhaps we should send a man to make sure."

"Make sure of what?" asked the governor as he made his way down to a couch to rest and enjoy his third cup of wine.

"To make sure he is dead," smiled Glaucippos with a hungry look, "or that he soon will be."

47

Miletos

ALEXANDER'S CAMP

"I saw him, I tell you Hephaestion, I saw him!" screamed Alexander through gritted teeth as he hurled his helmet across the tent, knocking over cups and bowls and everything else that was on the shelf he hit. "I had him right there, almost in the palm of my hand," he added angrily, stretching out his hand and then closing it tightly.

"Who? Who did you almost have?" Hephaestion asked.

"Memnon! Memnon, that's who! He was right there, no farther than the other end of this tent from me. There were only a handful of men with him. Some were carrying him, the others were trying to protect him with their shields. Greek shields, too, damn them!"

"What happened?"

"A troop of Persian cavalry burst out of the main gate at the last moment, and I was forced to stop and defend myself. The usual way, you know, with them calling out their own names in challenge...what could I do?"

"Yes, yes, of course, what could you do?" said Hephaestion with just a careful hint of mockery in his voice. "It is not as if you could have let, say, one of a hundred Royal Companions step in between you and them and answer the challenge for you, so you could have charged after Memnon."

"Are you making fun of me, Hephaestion?" Alexander shot back, his anger and ardor still hot from the battlefield. "Are you?"

"Never, my King," said Hephaestion soothingly as he came closer and rubbed the back of his hand across the king's sweaty cheek. "Never," he cooed softly, as he repeated the gesture.

"Well, you had better not. Not you, Hephaestion," sighed the king, visibly calmer and suddenly sweeter, "I could not bear it, you know. I could not bear it."

"Of course, I understand...Alexander," replied Hephaestion, genuinely sorry he had been a bit catty with the king. "But you may have already 'got him,' in a way," he added.

"What do you mean?"

"Well, you said he was being carried. That means he was either dead or wounded, and if the later, perhaps it is a fatal wound. Even so, dead or alive, hurt or hearty, he's penned up tight in that city, and he's not going anywhere."

"No, he's not," said Alexander as he again gritted his teeth. "No, he's not," he added as he walked quickly over to where he had thrown his helmet, retrieved it and placed it firmly back on his head. "Come on, Hephaestion, we've got work to do."

Hephaestion knew better than to ask. It wouldn't matter anyway, because where Alexander went, Hephaestion always followed... eventually if not sooner.

"Parmenion!" Alexander shouted as he stormed out of his tent, Hephaestion in tow. "Parmenion! Somebody get me Parmenion!"

"Here I am, my King," said the old general, hurrying as best as he could through the mud.

"Parmenion," Alexander said sternly as he walked over to meet the old soldier and put his hand on the general's shoulder. "I don't hear the siege weapons firing. Why is that, Parmenion? Why do I not hear the 'whoosh' of fireballs, the 'zap' of giant bolt being shot across the field, or the 'thud' of the stone-throwers when their arm hits the padded bar and they let loose their boulders upon the city? Why not, Parmenion? Why do I not hear such things?"

The old general looked genuinely puzzled, yet took care to give a reasoned and measured response. "It is still night, majesty, and it is a waste of time to try to bombard what the crews cannot see. Besides, there was a battle in the way, as you well know," he added with a grin. "And congratulations, by the way. Nice work, chasing Memnon off as you did."

The mere mention of Memnon's name felt like a stab in the side to Alexander, and did nothing to soothe his growing impatience.

"What do you mean they cannot shoot at what they cannot see, Parmenion? It's a city. A big city. It stretches the whole width of this peninsula and thousands of paces back from that. They don't have to 'see' anything. All they have to do is make sure their weapons are pointed in the right direction and fire. Their weapons are pointed in the right direction, are they not?"

"Yes, my King," nodded Parmenion.

"Good. Well then, rouse them from their warm beds, pull the blankets off them and their whores if you have to, but get them to their engines. It will be dawn soon, and if I don't hear the siege engines firing before then, I will load them myself – with the bodies of the crewmen themselves. Tell them that, Parmenion. That should light a fire under them. Oh, and one more thing..." he added as he spun about, heading back for his tent.

"Yes, my King," asked the old general.

"They are to keep firing, all day. And all night, and all day tomorrow and so on. Work them in shifts, draft men from the baggage train or the regiments if you need to, but keep them firing. Memnon thought he could burn my siege engines, did he? Well," he added, rubbing his hands together with glee, "let us remind him, and his soldiers, and the citizens of Miletos that he failed, and that failure has consequences. Pour it on them, Parmenion, pour it on them. And don't stop until those walls start to crumble."

The steady rain of rocks, stones, bolts, fire pots, and fire balls that Alexander unleashed did drive home the point of how Memnon's attack had failed. Those inside the city it did not dishearten or frighten were few. Even the most steadfast defenders began to cringe and cower when they heard the missiles coming. It was a reflex motion, and one once learned, hard to put aside. In the hospital where Klemes and the other physicians labored, the bombardment took another toll – as many of the feverish and wounded cried out in fear when they heard the smashing of the big stones upon the walls, or the unmistakable crash of a house collapsing from the boulders. Those whose courage was still strong were nonetheless affected, as they were the ones putting out the fires, or dragging the injured to the hospital, or freeing those trapped in the rubble. They were weary, so weary that they could no longer feel fear. Rather than seek cover when they heard or saw the missiles coming, they sought them out, trying to track them to see where the big stones and fire pots hit.

One small group inside the city, however, took a small pleasure from the bombardment. Glaucippos, Hegisistratos and their small clique of wealthy merchants, officious bureaucrats, and haughty temple priests believed that each rock that fell, each house that was smashed, and each body that was broken moved the mood of the populace one step closer to accepting the surrender they planned to broker. True, Alexander had spurned that offer once, but now they planned to sweeten the pot, and sweeten it with the one treat they were certain Alexander could not resist: Memnon.

"How is the 'great man?'" Glaucippos asked Hegisistratos. "Has he resumed consciousness yet?"

"No, not entirely. My informers in the hospital say he wakes from sleep once in a while, but only to shake or mumble something incoherent, and then falls back on his bed, not to stir again for hours."

"Is he wounded?"

"In a manner of speaking, apparently so. It seems a bullet shot out from some slinger struck him just here," the governor said, pointing to the bridge of his nose. It left a dent and a mighty nasty bruise – his whole face is bruised, I might add. Pity, I suppose. He never was a terribly beautiful man, but he was at least a bit dashing. Now I doubt his own wife would be able to look upon him without shuddering," he added with a sly laugh.

"Ah, yes, the beautiful Barsine. Well, she was widowed once already," said Glaucippos smacking his lips, "and it seems like she will be again, and soon. Perhaps when this is all over I should pay her a visit..."

"As if she would deign to admit you to her presence," laughed Hegisistratos. "She is not only painfully beautiful and serenely haughty, she knows her value. A princess of the true blood, that one. She fears no one, needs no one, and her favors cannot be bought – only taken, except, of course, if she gives herself willingly..."

"As she did to Memnon, and to his brother, her late husband, before him?"

"Yes, Glaucippos. And you, if you will forgive my honesty, are not the strapping handsome hero type she goes for. Your vast riches mean nothing to one of the blood. Besides, we are being a bit premature, aren't we? Her husband is only mostly dead...and mostly dead is not yet entirely dead."

"I can arrange for that..." said Glaucippos with an evil, lascivious grin.

"You can, but you will not," said Hegisistratos as he waved a cautionary finger at his fat co-conspirator. "If you want to truly make Alexander an offer he won't refuse, we need to keep Memnon alive."

"But why?"

"Because if you give Alexander a corpse, he will moan and groan and lament the foul murder of a hero, or go on about how great a foe Memnon was. That lunatic will hold funeral games and make a bonfire to send his body to the gods – and he won't send it alone, mind you. Not Alexander. He's read too much Homer, and is too fond of drama. No, we need to give him a live Memnon. One he can show off as a trophy, or challenge to single combat...like a Persian Hector to his Achilles."

"A who to his what?" asked a puzzled Glaucippos.

Hegisistratos gave a deep, purposeful sigh to show his annoyance at the fat merchant's ignorance. "You really should read more, you know, Glaucippos – and something besides your account books or those erotic scrolls your agents sneak in from Egypt. Hector. Achilles. They are heroes from that book Alexander keeps beneath his pillow. He is so taken by it that he has made himself believe he is a descendant of Achilles. His mother, that witch Olympias, has encouraged that belief – along with the claim that her boy was sired by Zeus."

"But how can anyone be descended from some character in a book that someone made up?" replied the fat merchant. "And as for being fathered by Zeus, well, as beautiful as Olympias may have been, why would the gods come down and sleep with mortal women when they have all of those lucsious goddesses and nubile nymphs wandering about half-clothed up there among the clouds?" he added with a puzzled sigh. "Anyway, it is all just stories and legends and what not, isn't it? I'm not an unlearned boor, although you may think I am...I do read, you know. Why, I've even sponsored plays for the theater..."

"Where you make a tidy profit from selling food and wine and little trinkets, and take a cut from the prostitutes who ply their trade outside. Yes, I know. Such a thespian you are, such a muse you must be to the poets," grinned the governor.

"Well, you've never turned down your share of the profits, if memory serves me right, my dear Governor, or any other share of anything. You be careful how you treat me, Hegisistratos. After all, I have the money, so why do I need you to make a deal with Alexander? What exactly is it that you bring to the table, hmmm?"

"Why, gravitas, my fat friend, gravitas."

"And what the hell is that?" asked the merchant.

"It's a word I picked up from a scholar who had toured Sicily and the lands to the north of it, Latium or some place. It is a word they use to denote a person who deserves respect, whose intellect and bearing are of the highest caliber, and whose words should be taken seriously. In other words, my fleshy, flaccid fellow...me."

48

Miletos

THE HOSPITAL

"I wish I knew more about this type of injury," said Klemes to his friends, Ari and Dimitrios, as he examined the still unconscious Memnon.

"How about the other physicians and men of learning in Miletos, have you asked for their advice?" Dimitrios asked his brother.

"Pshaw! Charlatans and butchers, with a few soothsayers and priests thrown in for good measure, that's all they are. I have been advised to bleed him, pack him in ice, throw him in a cold bath, poke needles into his head and every other conceivable part of his anatomy, including places I would never, ever stick a sharp object. And, oh, my favorite, was to bring in a couple of flute girls – both to play the flute and then, ahem," said Klemes with a bit of embarrassment, "play his flute, if you know what I mean."

"And the priests?"

"That was the idea of the priests," explained Klemes. "In this city it seems the flute girls work for the temple. Men are actually encouraged to go to the temple, meet with the girls, consummate their visit on holy ground, and then make an offering to the gods – which, of course, means to the priests. Quite a racket, if you ask me, but I guess it fills the temple with warm bodies."

"Very warm, I would suspect," laughed Aristophanes. "Sure beats burning incense or sacrificing doves," the young man giggled. "I have a sudden urge to 'pray,'" he added. "Either of you feeling particularly religious, today?"

Klemes chose to ignore Ari's playful comments, and continued with his description of the cure he had tried and had been advised to try. "There is one thing I saw on Cos during my studies, but I am reluctant to try it."

"What is that, Klemes? If it is something that might cure the..."

"It means drilling a hole in his skull," Klemes said, interrupting his brother. "I've never done it myself. I'm not even sure where to drill, or how deep to go. The oath I took at Cos warns physicians about this sort of thing. 'First, do no harm,' is how it goes. He could just wake up on his own, you know. The body has ways of healing itself that we've yet to understand."

Dimitrios placed his hand on his brother's shoulder, looked him straight in the eye and said "I trust you. Do what you think best."

"Even if that is to do nothing?"

"Even so, brother. But," he added, "if he doesn't wake up soon, all will be lost."

"How so? Isn't Ephialtes in charge for now? He's an able general, isn't he?"

"The trouble with Ephialtes," explained Dimitrios, "is that he is a Greek. Not a Greek like Memnon, who comes from Rhodes and who has married into Persian royalty, but a Greek from Greece, and a mercenary at that. The Persians won't follow him, and the people have no confidence in letting a foreigner decide their fate."

"Then Thymondas," argued Klemes. "He's Memnon's nephew, born to a Persian mother. Surely he would do?"

"He's young, not much older than Ari, here. Thymondas is brave and a good soldier, but face it, brother, he has his rank because of who his father was and who his uncle is. The Persians know that. No, they need someone they can look up to, someone they can believe in, someone whom they can see as..."

"A hero? A savior? Is that what they need, Dimitrios?"

"Yes," said Dimitrios with a sigh. "That, or a miracle."

That miracle the people of Miletos hoped for came the next morning. The Persian fleet left its anchorage across the bay and began making for Miletos. People from all over the city rushed to the seaward-facing walls and to the harbor to see the parade of some 400 ships coming toward them. Among those on the wall were Ephialtes and his staff, along with Dimitrios and Aristophanes.

"Are they coming to save us?" asked Ari hopefully.

"I think they mean business this time. Look," said the general. "There's not a single sail in sight."

"Why is that?" asked Ari.

"That's because they've taken down the sails and stored them and everything else that is unnecessary on shore. They're manning the oars, not the sails. They've come decked out for battle, not for show."

"Will the Greeks go to meet them?" asked Dimitrios.

"We shall see," said the general. "We shall see."

The Persian fleet kept on coming, in pristine battle array. Not a ship was out of place, or out of line. The highly trained Rhodian, Cypriot and Phoenician captains and crews maintained their formation and their steady speed, slowly coming closer and closer. As for the Greeks, Admiral Nicanor deployed his fleet – but to the far side of the island of Lade, and he kept it there. If the Persians wanted a battle, they would have to come to him. To do so they had to either go around Lade, or come between the island and the city, or split the fleet and do both. What Nicanor lacked in numbers, he hoped to make up for with Lade.

That large island to the west of Miletos provided cover from the weather to both of the city's main harbors – the commercial and the military, which were on that side of the peninsula. The small stone castle on the island was packed with artillery and archers – and defended by over 4,000 of Alexander's foreign mercenaries. That made it too strong to attack from the sea. Any force trying to land would be cut down before they could clear the surf and form up. The castle provided a formidable base of fire that could rain destruction down on the flanks of any ships that tried to row past it. That point was made painfully clear to the advance squadron of Persian warships that tried to do just that.

The Persian move was no more than a feint, a ruse meant to invite, taunt or otherwise lure Nicanor out from under the protection of Lade. It didn't work. The cagey admiral refused to be baited. Besides, Alexander had issued strict orders not to engage the Persians at sea unless the odds favored the Greeks. They would only do so if the Persian admiral came at them, and in doing so subjected his fleet to the artillery on Lade.

"Why have they stopped?" asked Ari. "Our fleet has just...stopped."

"That's because they want Nicanor to attack them, out in the bay, where their numbers can swallow him up. But he's not that stupid," Dimitrios replied.

"Then why don't they just go straight at the Greeks?"

"Because, my young friend," Ephialtes chimed in, "only a fool takes wooden ships against a stone fortress. Our admiral may not be exceedingly brave, but he's also no fool. And he is doing his duty...look, to the right, there. He is running some ships to the beach, on the landward side."

On the landward or eastern side of the peninsula were two much smaller islands, each of which were still in the hands of the Persians. They guarded a channel that led to the beach on that side of the peninsula, a beach used by the city's fishermen and any boats that were too small to need the docks in the commercial harbor on the Lade side. As the main fleets continued their standoff, about a dozen Persian ships pulled up to that beach. Each disgorged a handful of soldiers, and each carried a sack. When the first dozen were finished unloading, they pushed off – and a second dozen came in, then a third and a fourth.

"Dimitrios, go welcome our navy friends. Seems they have brought us some reinforcements and supplies. I know they can't bring in many men or a great deal of cargo, not in those ships, but any help is welcome. Besides, it will mean a great deal to the morale of the garrison and the citizenry. Get me an inventory of the supplies, and find out who is in charge of the reinforcements, and bring him to me."

The shuttling of men and supplies continued all day, which is how long it took, as the beach where they could unload was short and narrow. And, as Ephialtes had observed, the ships the Persian admiral detailed for this service were not cargo ships or troop carriers, but were meant for other, more martial tasks. The vast majority of his 400 ships, moreover, he kept squared off against the Greeks, just in case Nicanor became impatient and accepted his challenge – which, of course, he did not.

As the day lengthened, the shuttle service slowed and the Persians began to peel off back to Mycale. Although the blockade of the city had not been lifted – the main harbors were both still closed off by the Greeks – at least the people of Miletos had seen that they were not forgotten, were not alone, and were not beaten – not yet.

Not everyone in Miletos, of course, was happy with this minor miracle, especially not Governor Hegisistratos or his merchant friend, Glaucippos.

"This is an unwelcome turn of events, governor. It will make our job all that much harder – and expensive, if you know what I mean. Bribing hungry, frightened guards sunk in despair is easy and cheap – but after today, the cost is going to go up – way up."

Hegisistratos agreed. Frustrated, a little angry, but also a little proud of the admiral for what he had done, the Persian governor was not deterred from his plan. "This changes nothing in the long run," he said to Glaucippos, "it just means we need to act much sooner and more decisively, before anything like this occurs again – and it probably will. Can your men be ready tonight?"

"Of course," nodded the fat merchant. "And I have a fisherman who's more than willing to take on some passengers for a short trip to the Macedonian side of the lines. He's actually a bit angry about what happened today."

"How's so?" asked a puzzled Hegisistratos.

"Says he wasn't able to bring in his catch, not with all of the warships coming and going on the beach. That cost him dear – and he spent a day on his boat in the hot sun, knee deep in dead fish. You can imagine the smell..." explained the merchant, holding his nose and making a sour face to punctuate his point.

"Well then," laughed Hegisistratos, "perhaps I should send him a vial of perfume. That and another bag of silver coins should remove the stink, eh?"

Alexander was another who was not pleased with the flow of troops and supplies that came into the city that day, even if it had been a mere trickle and not a flood. He saw it all as he stood on the Old Citadel Hill, and with each relay of boats he got angrier and angrier.

"Shall I signal Nicanor to attack?" asked Parmenion.

"No," said Alexander through gritted teeth. "We've already gone over that. The chance of victory is small and the consequences of loss too great. As long as we have a fleet in being, and the fortified island of Lade supporting it, the threat to Miletos remains. And the Persian fleet has to either sit it out on the beaches below Mount Mycale or sail away..." he continued, his initial anger and frustration giving way to an idea, and then a smile.

"Is Philotas still chomping at the bit as his cavalry has nothing more to do than forage for the army?" he asked Parmenion.

"Yes, poor lad," said Parmenion with a little laugh. "He so wants to get into this fight – but I told him, a siege is no place for cavalry; can't storm a wall or ride through a breach on horseback."

"No, of course not. Those dozen or so nobles who charged out of the main gate learned that – even if they did buy time for their general to get inside. Only one or two of them made it back into the city, right?"

"That is right, my King," said Hephaestion. "Our men saw to that. They did well enough against us on the flat in front of the city, but as soon as they reached the Necropolis, well, that was that. The rocks and tombstones and monuments there are hard enough for one man on a horse to navigate, let alone charge through."

"Well, Hephaestion," replied Alexander, "tell Philotas I have a job for him after all – a way for his cavalry to take a much more active part in this siege beyond scavenging for food and fodder."

"He will be very pleased to hear that," the king's friend responded with a puzzled look on his face. "What do you have in mind?"

Alexander grinned. "The Persian fleet. It is too big, too strong, too well trained and equipped for us to attack with our navy. So we will attack them with our cavalry."

Parmenion and Hephaestion both gave Alexander a questioning look, as they were not quite sure they heard him correctly. "Pardon me, my King," said Hephaestion. "Cavalry against warships? You can lead a horse to water but you can't make him walk on it."

"No," laughed Alexander. "And maybe you can't make him drink it either, isn't that what Aristotle used to say? But that is the key to winning the naval battle. The Persian fleet is unbeatable on the water, but not at the water."

"At the water?"

"Yes, Hephaestion, but not the water their ships sit upon, but at the water their crews drink. There are more men on those 400 ships than there are in our entire army – and you know how much water our men drink. Cut the Persian sailors off from their source of drinking water, and they will either have to sail off or die of thirst. The old 'water, water everywhere but not a drop to drink,' yes," said Alexander glee-fully, "that's the way we'll do it!"

Later that day, the Thessalonian scouts made their report to the king. The Persian fleet was drawing its fresh water from the Meander River, the chief of scouts explained, a river Alexander had crossed on a bridge of seven boats his engineers had constructed. The river flowed down to the sea, near where the Persian fleet was beached, its waters fed by streams from Mount Mycale. Hundreds of men were involved in bringing water from there to the fleet in a never-ending, continuously moving effort, he added as he drew a circle with his finger on Alexander's map table to better explain the process.

"And they have guards? Men on watch?" asked Alexander.

"A few score, no more," the chief of scouts added, "and they are not proper infantry, just marines from the fleet. Men who know how to fight from the deck of a ship," he smiled broadly, "but have little experience of fighting on land, and even less of facing cavalry."

That was exactly what Alexander suspected, and was thrilled to have confirmed.

"Philotas," he said to the cavalry officer who had dispatched the scout and accompanied him back to the king's tent, "I heard you have been grumbling about being left out of the fight. Something about being little more than green grocers and game hunters? Well, here's some game for you to hunt. Take all of the light cavalry, all except enough pickets to keep watch at our back, and scatter those water carriers at the Meander. Hephaestion will follow up with the Companions – including the Royal Squadron – just in case you meet any formed resistance..."

"I won't need the heavy cavalry, my King," replied Philotas. "My lads will do. They'll run down those water bearers and marines and cut them down before they can reach the safety of their ships!"

"Yes, of course," acknowledged Alexander, "but they have set up a barricade inland, around the beach. Hephaestion and the heavies will make certain they do not even think twice about coming out to chase your light horse away. Nothing like a mass of big men on big horses, bronze helmets shining, to keep them behind their palisade. And no need to storm it. Thirst will do the rest."

49

Mycale

THE MEANDER RIVER

I t was Captain Abibaal and his crew's turn to bring water from the Meander back for the squadron on the beach. Their own ship was still blockaded inside the harbor of Miletos, where they had made their run to bring Dimitrios, Klemes and Aristophanes into the city, but sailors need to be on the sea, not in a city. So when the small boats brought in food and reinforcements to Miletos on the Mycale side, Abibaal was there to meet them. In return for help unloading their cargo, the captains of the small ships agreed to take Abibaal and his men back to the fleet. Out of deference to his long and honorable career, the admiral had given Abibaal a choice.

"I have no ship for you, Abibaal," the Persian admiral explained, "and do not expect to have one anytime soon. I do have ships that need officers and crew, and if you agree and your men wish, they can fill in as replacements. I know you are a captain, but unless you want to serve as the first mate on another ship, I have nothing for you, at least not now. Of course, however, it would be a shame to break up such a well-trained crew as yours, so..."

"Yes," a suddenly hopeful Abibaal responded. "Anything. We'll take anything. Do anything. Just let me keep my crew together."

"Well," the admiral chuffed, "I do need someone to take charge of bringing fresh water from the Meander to the fleet. You will have wagons instead of a ship, but, if you do this, it will spare the crews of the other ships the hard work – and that would be of great service to the fleet – and to me. Besides, it is either that or split you all up. So, what do you say?"

Captain Abibaal did not hesitate to accept the offer. He was an old enough salt to know that even when an admiral asks, it is really just a more polite way of issuing a command. Only someone whom the admiral respected would be given the opportunity to say 'no;' not that any officer who wished to see the sea again would give such an answer. Besides, the good admirals rarely forget those who do their bidding willingly, and Autophradates was among the very best.

"Very good then, Captain," said the admiral, who expected that Abibaal would agree to his request. "If you do as good a job on land as you have done on the sea, you will get another ship as soon as the opportunity arises. Of course you might get your own ship back again, should the Greeks grow tired of their blockade. But, in the meantime," the admiral said with a little smile, "do keep track of the water wagons, and try not to leave any of them behind."

"Put your backs into it!" Abibaal shouted to his crewmen who were loading the water wagons at the Meander. "There are thousands of thirsty lads back on the beach, and they can't very well drink sea water now, can they?"

The work was backbreaking – even for men who made their living at the oars. Hard as it was, it was better than lolling about in Miletos, where idle minds and idle hands were too easily tempted to get into mischief – or worse. Besides, at least this way they were all together, working as the team they had worked so hard to become. The oarsmen and sailors did the heavy lifting, while the oar master kept them all working in unison, just as he had when he drummed out the beat for the oars aboard their ship. That still left plenty for the officers to do –

someone had to keep the tally sheets, and keep track of to which squadron the drivers were to make their deliveries. Keeping 400 crews from getting thirsty was a monumental task, and one that was about to get a lot more difficult.

"Captain," said a marine who had come down from the watch tower the sailors had built beside the river, "you had better come see this. I think we are about to have company."

Abibaal followed the marine back to the tower, climbed the rope ladder to the platform and looked in the direction the marine pointed.

"All I see is a cloud of dust," Abibaal told the marine. "I can't even tell where it is coming from, let alone what it is."

"It came from the right, either just inland of Miletos or from the city," said the marine. "I have been following the dust clouds for some time now."

"Well, if it is from the interior, it could be almost anyone. Reinforcements for Alexander..."

"Or a relief column from the satraps?" asked the marine hopefully.

"Perhaps," replied Abibaal, "but I would not get your hopes up. And if it is from the city, it would be from Alexander's camp outside Miletos."

"But if so," asked the marine, "then where are they going? There's nothing of interest to them out here, is there?"

Captain Abibaal peered as hard as he could, trying to pick out figures from the dust cloud, but it was still too far distant. Then it struck him.

"There is something of interest to them out here, marine," said Abibaal with a knowing sigh. "Us. We're out here – or more correctly, our fresh water is out here, and beyond that, the anchorage. You had better tell your officer to get his men in battle order...he may soon have a fight on his hands."

With that, the marine and the captain raced down the rope ladder. The marine went to find his officer, while Abibaal hurried to the river.

"That's enough for now, lads," he called out, signaling his crew to stop working and to gather about.

"But we've lots more wagons to load," said the oarmaster, "and the daylight is already starting to fade. There is so much to..."

"We're done with that for today, lads. Something is coming around the bay that does not bode well. I think the Macedonians are coming for us. I think they mean to knock us back from the river and attack the anchorage. We need to get aboard the wagons and get back to the beach. If we are caught outside of the palisade, the admiral will be very upset."

"I didn't know he cared about us that much," one of the men jeered.

"He doesn't," said Abibaal harshly. "It's not you but the water wagons that concern him," Abibaal told the crew. "And he told me not to lose any of them," he added to himself as he turned his back on his men and went to gather the tally sheets.

Wagons, especially wagons loaded down with large amphorae of water, do not move much faster than a man can walk – not march, but just walk. Having the men board them would have only made them go even slower. Abibaal knew he was in a race to get his men and their wagons back to the relative safety of the palisade that had been raised to guard the camp where the sailors of the fleet slept and took their meals, but he also knew it was not a fair race. If that was indeed part of Alexander's army inside that dust cloud, there would be cavalry, and he had no hope of outrunning them. He only hoped that they would stop at the river either to water their horses, or to wait for their infantry to catch up. If they did not, the only protection his men had would be the small troop of marines who were acting as their rear guard.

The Thessalian horse did stop at the river – but only to look around to make sure it was safe for the rest of the column to follow. Philotas knew better than to let his horses drink for more than a few minutes. An overheated horse and a river of cool water do not go well together, and there would be time enough later to water the horses properly. After detaching a few riders back to the heavy cavalry that were coming up from the rear and sending out scouts and flankers to ensure that all was safe, Philotas pushed on. The Thessalians were only lightly armed, but Philotas did not expect to encounter anything or anyone they could not handle.

Try as they might, the drovers could not make the oxen pulling their wagons and carts go any faster. Neither the big, four wheel wagons or the smaller two-wheeled carts, which were little more than chariots with wicker sides on them to keep their cargo from falling off, could hope to outrun men on horses.

And they didn't.

The only weapons the 50 oarsmen and the dozen sailors and officers had with them were their knives. The marine guard had helmets, shields, throwing spears and swords, but nothing that could pose much of a serious threat to the Thessalian horse. Still, they tried. The marine officer formed his men into a shield wall, and made a very respectable attempt at a fighting withdrawal. Trained to fight aboard ship, they were not in their element, but they were brave men, professionals.

And they died that way. Each selling his life trying to buy more time for Abibaal and his wagons and men to keep going.

Philotas never could resist torturing a wounded animal, or taunting a beast at bay. The slow murder of the marines – for that was what it was, murder, not battle – was a sport to him. He surrounded the marines and made a competition out of it, offering prizes to the men that could skewer a marine with a javelin thrown from horseback. Philotas did not send in all of his men at once, but in pairs, allowing the others to take a bit of rest while they cheered their comrades on and took bets as to who would hit a marine, who would rack up the most number of hits or kills and the like. As for the wagons, they did not interest Philotas. They posed no challenge, offered no more sport than hunting sheep and offered no loot. But this, this dancing around the slowly shrinking circle of marines, this was fun – and after so many dreary days of foraging, and scouting, and patrolling for the army, his men needed some fun, as did he.

Philotas did send a pair of horsemen to follow the wagons, mostly as a precaution against having a column from the naval camp surprise him and interrupt the new sport of "pin the javelin on the marine" he had invented. They kept their distance, but were still close enough to taunt the sailors, and make crude and lewd comments as to what they would do to them should any fall behind. Abibaal fumed, but did not want to do anything that might send them scurrying back for reinforcements. To do so would only risk the lives of his men – and rob the marines' sacrifice of meaning.

Abibaal had sent his fastest runner – or at least the man everyone said was the fastest, for they rarely spent enough time on land to be sure – ahead to the camp. He doubted the man would get there quickly enough to allow the admiral to send out a major rescue party, but at least the fleet would not be caught napping. The fellow, however, had been fleet of foot enough to do just that. And he got through soon enough for the officer of the guard to send out a small patrol to escort the wagons in for the last few thousand yards. Those marines reached the wagons just as Philotas and his advance guard rounded the bend to their rear.

"Look, lads!" shouted Philotas with unbridled glee. "More meat! Have at'em!"

The handful of marines formed up, as they knew they would be cut down if they tried to run. Their officer, young and brave as he was, encouraged them – and yelled back to Abibaal to make a run for it.

"Forget the damned wagons!" he screamed, "just go...go...go!"

Even the drovers knew they could not escape if they stayed with the wagons, and took off into the foothills of Mount Mycale, knowing it would be difficult for the enemy cavalry to follow up those steep slopes and into the broken ground. Abibaal at first thought to follow them, but instead ordered his men to leave the lumbering wagons and run to the camp – not that he needed to encourage them to do so, as their instincts for survival got the better of them.

The marine detachment that had come from the camp died as well as those who had formed the rear guard, and as they died, one by one to the laughing Thessalian horsemen, Abibaal and his three score crewman sprinted flat out for the palisade.

As the gate opened, he allowed himself a little cheer, as he knew his men would live.

But, damn it, he grumbled. He'd lost the wagons.

50

Miletos

THE HOUSE OF GLAUCIPPOS

K lemes had tried everything he could think of to revive the general. Ephialtes had hoped to keep Memnon's condition secret, but the governor and his cabal made sure that everyone in the city and its garrison knew the truth – or at least the truth as they inflated it. The drop in morale, the fear of defeat, and the feeling of being abandoned by the fleet, only made it easier for Hegisistratos to spread his own poison among the populace. A sense of gloom and despair now permeated Miletos. As the people looked about for a new savior, the governor's backers were only too happy to present their man not only as the man of the hour, but one whose rightful position had been usurped by a dangerous adventurer.

While Dimitrios saw little of this at the high command, Aristophanes could not get away from it. Out in the streets, in the taverns, and even in the barracks, there was evidence that the defenders were beginning to crack. Whenever anyone said anything gloomy, there were others quick to second the sentiment, and none to rebut it. Soldiers always grouse and grumble, as Aristophanes knew well, but there was much more to this than men just bitching about the usual things. The air was thick with the smell of defeat and the stink of impending treachery.

Those odors emanated from two places in the city in particular. The first was the governor's own office. The message from there was subtle, well-crafted, and designed to discourage the people rather than make them despair. That task belonged to Glaucippos and his clique. Even before the siege began, even before Hegisistratos had contemplated seeking terms with Alexander, Glaucippos and other wealthy merchants had tried to make a deal with Alexander. Although their offer to open the gates and surrender the city in return for a promise to spare their property had been rudely and sternly rebuffed, Glaucippos and his gaggle of upper class worthies believed they could still make a deal with the young Macedonian. If anything, he explained to his cronies, the staunch defense of the city to date had only increased the value of what they had to offer. All they had to do, Glaucippos told them, was to sweeten the deal.

Memnon, he continued, was that sweet. They only had to walk into the hospital, grab the unconscious general, and spirit him out of the city.

"What could be easier?" Glaucippos said with a smile, as he opened a small chest a slave had placed before him. "Here are four bags. The first contains copper coins – they should be sufficient to bribe the guards at the hospital," the merchant explained, as he tossed it to a rather nasty looking soldier of the governor's household. "The second is full of silver – and that is to bribe the gatekeepers at the Mycale-side beach gate," he said as he passed the heavy bag to a shadowy figure known to hold sway with certain criminal gangs in the city. "And the third," he said as he reached in and pulled out a pile of shimmering coins, "is full of gold, for the fisherman who will row the boat to take Memnon's unconscious body from the beach to the Macedonian lines."

"And the fourth?" a wealthy wine merchant asked. "What is in the fourth bag?"

"Why, see for yourself," said Glaucippos as he dipped his fat hand into the bag and pulled out an emerald as large as an egg.

"And who is that for?" another of his conspirators asked rather greedily.

"This and everything else in this bag are for the men who distribute the contents of the other three bags, and deliver Memnon to Alexander. Now, do I have any volunteers?"

Glaucippos had not expected any of the merchants, landowners, temple priests or other of the city's elite to participate in this little enterprise themselves, nor did he want them to do so. He knew they all had their own retainers, or clients who had the skills, the cunning, and the courage needed to undertake this mission. As they argued amongst themselves as to whose people were best suited to accomplish this abduction, Glaucippos sat down on a well-cushioned couch, called for a servant to bring him wine, and enjoyed the show. Men who had been worried, nervous, uncertain or even so frightened as to think of pulling out of the plan, now practically fell over one another in their eagerness for the enterprise. Each knew there were risks involved should their men fail and be caught; Memnon's officers still held authority enough to arrest, torture and execute enemies of the state – and of Memnon. They still had the Greek mercenary corps and the Persian regulars who came from other parts of the empire. The city militia, the governor's household troops and their own private gangs of thugs and bodyguards were no match for those professionals in a real battle – but in a street fight, they would likely prevail. On the other hand, most of these lesser-trained troops were as likely to bolt and melt away into the back streets rather than defend their patrons against Greek hoplites infantry and Persian noble cavalry. If they were to turn on these professionals, they would have to be certain that the Macedonians were coming – and coming as their new masters, not their conquerors.

Glaucippos took a certain delight in watching his guests argue and make deals over whose man or men would go on this little expedition. Each knew the risks, but also the value of the return on this investment of flesh and blood. After a second cup of wine, Glaucippos found himself more bored than amused, and by the time he finished the third, too impatient to wait any longer.

"Enough!" he shouted, seeking to get their attention. "So, who is it going to be who leads this venture?" he said, with a rude burp for punctuation.

"My acolytes will ensure that Memnon is removed from the hospital," said one of the temple priests.

"And my lads will then escort him through the beach gate," added the hooded figure in the back of the room, the man whose name everyone knew but did not dare speak aloud, lest one day as they walked the streets their journey would come to a sudden, violent, and final end.

"Well, then," said Glaucippos. "That sounds more like a relay race than a kidnapping, but I rather like it. And who will arrange the fishermen and their boat?"

"That would be my fellows," said the wine merchant proudly. "There are a few we employ on a regular basis to, ah, well..."

"Smuggle in a bit of wine on the side, besides that which you pay the tax on and dock fees for?" laughed Glaucippos.

The wine merchant did not reply verbally. He simply shrugged his shoulders, looked down at the dregs of wine in his cup, swirled it about and then allowed himself a little smile as he took a sip.

"Well then," said Glaucippos, "that only leaves the men who will share the reward from the fourth bag. And who shall have that pleasure?"

"Me," said the governor's man, who stepped forward and opened his cloak just far enough so that the others could see he was armed and armored. "The governor would insist, if he were here," he added in a stern manner that let the others know he would not be contradicted.

"Well then," nodded Glaucippos respectfully, "it is settled. I wish you all good hunting and good luck," he added, as he motioned for his slave to bring in wine for everyone.

"When do we go?" asked the governor's guard.

"Tomorrow night. That should be enough time for you all to make the necessary arrangements, right?" said Glaucippos. "After all, it's really little more than a simple kidnapping, isn't it?"

The guards at the hospital were not the best nor most attentive to their duty, for they believed they had little reason to be. After all, nobody had ever tried to break into a hospital – and few of those inside were in any shape to break out. True, Memnon was a patient, and as such his rank dictated that he should always have guards about, but that was part formality, part courtesy. After the heavy losses during the general's ill-fated sortie, however, there were few enough good men left to man the walls as it was, and to waste them on what was little more than a ceremonial post seemed nonsensical. Each unit in the army and garrison had their assigned sections of the wall and the city to protect, and the hospital, as it was as far from the enemy as any place in the city could be, was not a priority, even if one of its patients was the commanding general.

As it was deep inside the city, it only seemed right that the duty of guarding the hospital should fall to the city militia. Learning which men in particular would be on duty that night was a simple enough task for the temple priest, and a visit to their homes earlier that day was arranged just as easily. The priest did not even have to spend any of the copper coins in the bag that Glaucippos had set aside for the task. A simple promise to the guards that, should they excuse themselves for a short time, they would be rewarded by the gods – and incur their wrath if they did not - sufficed. When his acolytes arrived at the hospital a little after midnight, there was no one to challenge them. Into the hospital they walked, slowly, quietly, and solemnly, armed only with an excuse that they were here to offer up prayers for Memnon's recovery...that, and the little knives they used when sacrificing small animals in the temple, just in case.

The general had been given a room of his own, but was not alone. Ephialtes had insisted that, as long as Memnon was a patient, at least one of the general's own men be assigned to him at all times. A pious fellow, the bodyguard, although surprised to see four temple acolytes at his general's beside so late at night, was easily convinced of their holy mission. He even accepted their invitation to pray with them, and knelt down – never to rise again.

As the chief acolyte wiped the blood off of his small blade and replaced it in the sheath strapped to his thigh, the others worked quietly to wrap the general up in a pair of sheets, so as to cover Memnon's body and his face. The four then gently placed him upon a litter and, each man taking his place, quietly bore the general out of the hospital.

51

Miletos

THE HOUSE OF HEALERS

Klemes could not sleep. Try as he might, he could not rest, at least not until he found an answer to the puzzle that was Memnon's sorry state. He had scoured the library for clues and had borrowed every scroll he could from those of his fellow healers who actually sought out knowledge rather than merely practiced what they had been taught. So here it was, still several hours before dawn, that he again found himself bleary-eyed, pouring through old medical scrolls – some of which were so faded as to be barely readable.

Fortunately most were in Greek, for after all, Miletos had its own school of medicine, the one founded by Thales 200 years ago. It was also close to the more modern medical school at Cos, where he had learned his craft. Both were founded and still run by Greeks, and were repositories of medical information collected and translated from Egyptian, Babylonian, Jewish and even Chinese texts, the last thanks to missions sent there from Persia by Xerxes a century ago.

To Klemes' way of thinking, the knowledge compiled and transferred to students in these and other schools were the greatest gifts that Greek civilization had given to the world. Even Homer had acknowledged the value of Greek healers. "A physician is a man worth many others," he mumbled to himself, recalling a line from his readings of the *Iliad* so long ago.

The table was heaped with so many works that, when he reached for one, another would roll off onto the floor. He skimmed through texts from the school at Knidos, and from the Neucratis in Egypt and many other medical schools, each of which, like that of Cos and Miletos, were also founded and still staffed largely by Greeks. When picking these up, one from his own school fell off the table and rolled open. As he bent down to pick it up one particular line caught his eye: "the place of the physician is at the bedside of his patient."

"Well, then," he mumbled to himself, "perhaps that is indeed where I should be."

The bombardment of Miletos, which Alexander had ordered to continue day and night, had slackened, as it usually did in the hours before the sunrise. The crews, even working in shifts, were worn out. At this time of night only a few boulders and maybe an occasional fireball or two were fired at the city each hour. Soldiers and citizens had time to place bets as to where they would land, and many had gotten quite expert at predicting which tower, which part of the wall, or which house inside the wall would be struck. Fortunately, the hospital was well out of range of even Alexander's biggest siege machine, but even here people could not escape from the sound of the rocks as they slammed against the defenses or crushed a house.

Despite the steady noise of the bombardment, Klemes was careful to make as little sound as possible. The healer in whose house Klemes had been offered quarters was fast asleep, along with his family and servants, and he took care not to wake them. As he left the house, walked into the street and rounded the corner toward the house of healing, he spied four men carrying a litter. The body upon the litter was wrapped up in what he assumed was a burial shroud, a sight too often seen at the hospital and elsewhere in Miletos these days. The four men stopped suddenly in their surprise at seeing another person out and about at this time of night. Klemes paid them little attention, other than offering a cursory wave of his hand in acknowledgment of their presence and in gratitude for the service they were performing in removing a dead body from the hospital.

When he entered the building, however, he did note that there were no guards about. There was one servant, fast asleep in a chair, but no one else on the ward. He remained quiet, not wishing to wake any of the patients, and slowly made his way to Memnon's room. At first his heart quickened, for there was the general lying not on his back, as he had left him, but on his side. Hope rising in his breast, Klemes put his hand on the body – and then realized that it was not Memnon, but someone else, and that someone was dead, and the body was still warm. It was that of the man he had left to guard the general.

"Those men..." he said aloud, recalling the four men carrying the litter in the street. "They've got the general!"

Klemes stumbled through the hospital, swerving around the beds and litters, calling for the guards – but none answered his cry of alarm. Dozens of patients who had been sleeping were awakened by the clatter of Klemes knocking over bedpans and buckets as he lurched and blundered his way through the hospital maze, but still no guards answered or appeared. A few of the walking wounded struggled to get to their feet in an effort to follow Klemes to rescue their beloved general, but the doctor was out the door, down the steps and into the street long before they could catch up with him.

Normally a very quiet, reserved and studious fellow, it was completely out of character for Klemes to scream and shout, let alone run and panic, even if it was a panic with a purpose. Perhaps it was less because the general had been kidnapped than because a patient in his care had been snatched from a sickbed that got his blood up, but whatever the reason, Klemes was not going to stand by and let this wrong happen. He ran about the streets like a mad man, screaming and yelling the alarm, and behind him a dozen patients who were able to get out of their beds tumbled out of the hospital to add their voices to his cry for help.

The citizens and guards of Miletos had grown used to having their nights disturbed by the irregular bombardment, but this cacophony awakened even those who had grown so accustomed to the crashing and whooshing of rocks and fireballs they were able to drift off into an uneasy slumber. Oil lamps and candles blazed to life in the houses that Klemes and the limping, stumbling patients passed. Soon, most of that quarter of the city was awake and aware that something bad was happening – although exactly what it was that was happening was not exactly clear, as dozens, then scores of voices only added to the confusion. Even the sleepy sentinels at the gate and along the walls were roused from their dull nighttime reverie, and shouts for the corporals and sergeants of the guard to take action rang along the wall from guard post to guard post.

As the city became alert and people and soldiers alike ran about seeking the cause of this alarm, one small group of people stood out from all of the rest: the men scurrying about bearing a litter through the streets. Challenged by sentries on the walls above and questioned by citizens on the street, the acolytes panicked. Instead of walking about in a steady, unhurried pace so as not to arouse suspicion, they tightened their grip on the litter and took off at a run for the postern gate that led to the fishermen's beach. The gate was open and unguarded, as Glaucippos's coins had been more than sufficient to unlock and raise the bars and to see its guardians off to their beds, with the jingling in their purses as their lullaby.

The acolytes' race to the beach, however, did not go unnoticed or unquestioned. Challenges rang out from the walls as the acolytes dashed through the sally port. Archers shot flaming arrows to light up the beach. Slingers fumbled in their pouches for stone bullets and other men hurled javelins, all in an effort to force the runners to halt. Too much in a panic to bar the gate behind them, the acolytes were followed through the wall onto the beach by a jumble of angry guards, shouting civilians, limping hospital patients - and Klemes. As their feet sank into the sand and missiles fell all about them, the acolytes let go of their burden, leaving Memnon to tumble off the litter onto the beach, and ran for the fishing boat that awaited them in the shallows.

They almost made it.

The mixed mob caught them as the fugitives waded into the little waves that were lapping up on to the beach. One dove into the sea in hopes of swimming to the boat, which had already begun to pull away, but as he reached the little boat, one of the fishermen beat him away with an oar, lest he hinder their flight. A slinger's bullet in his shoulder, however, put the sailor down, and a flaming arrow caught the little sail – at which point the fisherman surrendered.

While the sergeants of the guard and a young officer tried to sort out what was going on and just who these men were and what they were up to, others attended Memnon, who had tumbled off the litter and rolled into a puddle, face down. One of those was Klemes, who had come running along in pursuit after giving the alarm at the hospital. As the physician gently turned him about so that he would not drown, Memnon gave a shudder and started to cough, spitting out water and grit. His lips began to move, and as the last of water dribbled down his cheek, he opened his eyes, looked at Klemes and asked in a scratchy, weak voice:

"What...what the hell is going on...and why am I all wet?"

52

Miletos

THE CITADEL

Klemes had no answer as to why Memnon had suddenly awakened from his coma. He suspected that the noise and jostling associated with his abduction, as well as the water from when he had been dumped from the litter, might have had something to do with it. Either that or nature had taken its course. The priests, of course, had tried to take credit for his remarkable and sudden recovery, but as a trained physician, Klemes put little faith in, well, faith. Then again, as he admitted, he was not entirely sure what had brought the injured general back to his senses. Memnon, however, was certain that the physician's care had at least prevented his death – as had, of course, Dimitrios' heroism in dragging him back to the safety of the city walls after the disappointing and failed attack on Alexander's lines.

"Physician," said the general, clasping Klemes by the hand, as he tried to sit up from his bed, "I owe you my life. I owe you and your brother. No, don't try to refuse to take the credit," he added as Klemes and Dimitrios each tried to say something. "When a general offers his gratitude, just shut up and accept it. Having a general think he is in your debt may come in handy sometime," Memnon added with a little smile. "Now, if you will excuse me," he said as he started to rise, "there are other, more pressing matters to which I must attend."

"Not on my watch," said Klemes pointedly. "You may be the general on the battlefield, but here, in this hospital, you're just another patient – and as a physician, I outrank you. Besides, it'll do you some good to spend a few days listening to the screams, cries, ravings, and death rattles of the men you sent into battle. Maybe if a few more generals and kings actually saw such bloody handiwork, they might be a bit less inclined to start their miserable little wars."

Instead of acting shocked or becoming angry, as Klemes had expected, Memnon reacted quite differently to the physician's outburst.

"Believe me, my dear physician," replied Memnon contritely, "if I never had to see another battle or send another man to fight I would be the happiest man alive. I would much rather spend my days walking through my fields and gardens with my wife, my incredibly beautiful and loving wife, teaching my children how to ride and hunt, but," he paused to cough, "some greedy, malicious, bastard either rises up in rebellion or invades the lands of my king."

"And, of course," responded Klemes in a rather unpleasant and insubordinate tone, "there is no one else who can go and fight but you, right? You think you are that indispensable?"

"No," Memnon coughed. "It's just that if I don't go, someone else will go – and that someone might not be as miserly with the lives of his men as I am. You think I find any glory in sending men to their deaths? No, my good physician, my glory comes when my men are victorious – and I can send them home to their wives and children, and with them carrying their shield rather than stretched out in funeral attire upon it."

Klemes reached out to take the general's hand in his. "I know," Klemes said rather sheepishly. "I know you are the best man for this dirty job. My brother says you care about the men – more than any other officer with whom he has served, including Ephialtes. Forgive me my rant. It has been a long day, and there are so many wounded. So many I cannot save. So many..."

"I know," replied Memnon as he sat up and once again started to rise. "And that is precisely why I need to get back to my command post in the citadel."

"General," said Klemes, more gently than before, and with true sincerity, "you still need rest. You should be in your bed."

"If I had the time, physician, I surely would," replied Memnon, "but I don't. Captain Dimitrios," he said turning to the officer, "I would be grateful for your assistance in helping me to my feet."

Although his progress was made slower than normal due to his injuries, the general put on a great show of being up and about, and of making sure that as many people and soldiers as possible saw him as he did so. He waved and saluted and hailed everyone in sight, all the while gritting his teeth to prevent crying out in pain. By the time he reached the citadel he was sweating profusely, but still refused Dimitrios' suggestion that he take some rest before going about his normal duties.

"I will have plenty of time to rest once Alexander is defeated – or if he defeats me," quipped the general. "In the meantime, there is much work to be done, so let us get on with it. Have the guards bring the prisoners before me."

Dimitrios signaled to the soldier at the end of the room, who, after nodding in acknowledgment, opened the doors to the large hall that Memnon had made into his headquarters. As the doors opened, other guards brought forward three bruised and battered men, each chained at the wrist and ankles and linked together by another chain that ran through the iron collars around their necks. Dimitrios and Klemes each barely managed to suppress a gasp of surprise, for they recognized the high priest and the governor among the trio.

"Brave defenders of Miletos," Memnon said to the assembled officers, Ephialtes and Thymondas among them, "regard the vipers in our nest. You see before you three men who have betrayed us. It was these men who were behind the attempt to abduct me, and for the dual purpose of delivering me to Alexander as well as undermining our defense. They and their agents planned to open the gates to the enemy – an action which, as all of you, especially Greeks, know, would result in both the fall of the city – and death or slavery to its defenders."

"Who is the third man?" asked Ephialtes. "I know the governor and the high priest, and presume they made a deal with the Macedonians to retain their power and position, but this third man, the fat little fellow in the back, who is he?"

"That, my friend, is – or was – the richest man in Miletos. His treason is based on greed. He wanted gold, assurances that his estates, mansions, warehouses, and ships would be safe, and that those of his rivals would be given over to his keeping. Well, my three Macedonian whores," he continued as he turned to face the trio in chains, "each of you shall have what you wish, in a manner of speaking."

"What do you mean," exclaimed a puzzled Thymondas.

"Hegistratos, here, wished to stay on the governor's throne, here in Miletos. He shall have his wish. The guards will bind him tightly to his throne – and he shall be burned alive upon it in the city square.

"The high priest wished to retain his exalted position. He shall. He shall be taken to the highest point in the city, where he shall be impaled upon a stake.

"As for Glaucippos. Well, he wanted gold, and gold he shall have. I have ordered the goldsmiths to prepare a bath of molten gold – into which he shall be drowned."

Screams of fear and cries of protest erupted from the three prisoners, along with curses and pleas for mercy. Ephialtes, Thymondas, and the other officers and city officials in the room kept quiet, as did Dimitrios and Klemes. Each knew the punishment for treason was death – and death by means most painful, most foul, and most fitting. As Memnon pronounced judgment, he held above his head the baton given to him by Darius himself. That sign of authority silenced any objections and any questions that the assembled officers and city fathers might be considering. It was a sign that Memnon spoke for the King of Kings, and no one dared question his decision, as it would be the same as if they had objected to the word of Darius.

To his great relief, Dimitrios was spared the task of carrying out the lethal and gruesome punishments of the traitors. Their treason had been exposed by the captured acolytes and fishermen, who had proven eager to give up their masters. For their willingness to confess, each had been given a quick and merciful death. Their heads were lopped off, loaded into the baskets of catapults, and hurled in defiance at the enemy lines. Although no one in the Macedonian camp knew these men, Memnon had ordered clay tablets inscribed with the details of their crime to be stuffed inside their mouths. Thus they would tell their tale, in a manner of speaking, in the event some curious Macedonian took the time to inspect the unusual ammunition with which they had been bombarded.

One such inquisitive soldier did just that. He reported what he found to his corporal, who told his sergeant, who told the first man he could find who could read – the company clerk. Within an hour of its discovery, the head and the clay tablet that had been in its mouth were on a camp table in Alexander's tent. Parmenion, Hephaestion, and the other generals and close companions of the king were shocked and angered by this display, but each grew silent as they heard Alexander chuckle.

"So, Memnon thinks, what, that this will give me pause? Demonstrate his resolve? Show me he is ruthless?" said the king, breaking out into peals of laughter. "Well, nobody can say that Alexander of Macedonia doesn't appreciate a gesture of defiance when he sees it. Hephaestion," he said as he turned to his friend, "how many of those Greeks we took at the Granicos did we keep as camp slaves?"

"About two hundred, my lord King. We put them to digging latrines and hauling away human waste."

"Well, Hephaestion, you will have to find some other slaves to do that dirty work"

Hephaestion shuddered. He dared not ask what Alexander intended for those 200 former mercenaries. He did not have to. Within an hour, their heads were being flung into the city by Alexander's siege engines. They were the opening volley of what Alexander intended to be not only the heaviest, longest, and most destructive of his bombardments of Miletos, but also the last. The king's patience for siege warfare had run out. Tonight he would assault Miletos. Tonight he was determined to take more heads, especially that of Memnon.

53

Miletos

THE WALL

"So, will he come at us today?" Aristophanes asked his friend and captain, as they and Klemes, the physician, stood at the wall of the citadel, watching the Macedonian artillery pound and pummel away at the outer defenses of the city.

"I think so," replied Dimitrios. "This is the heaviest, steadiest, and most directed barrage since the siege began. We knew it would come to this, eventually. Once the wall is breached, he will come – and come in force."

"Do you think we can hold him back?" asked Ari. "They say Miletos is as sound a fortress city as any since the days of Troy."

"And even Troy fell," jibed Klemes. "Although Achilles did not live to see it."

"That is always the one thing that puzzled me about Alexander," remarked Dimitrios. "His mother claims descent from Achilles, who may be merely a character made up by the poets, none of whom, by the way, mention him ever fathering children."

"Actually," interrupted Klemes, "she claims to be descended from Molossos, the son of Pyrrhus, who claimed to have been the grandson of Achilles. It all gets a bit murky, but half of the royal families around the Aegean make the same claim."

"That Achilles must have been one prolific son of a..." laughed Ari.

"Nevertheless," Dimitrios resumed, cutting off Ari before he could finish his remark, "Alexander styles himself as Achilles reborn. He even wears the armor he took from the supposed tomb of Achilles outside of the ruins of what might be Troy, although nobody is certain the city really existed, or if those really are where the legendary city stood. But what really bothers me," the captain continued," is that Achilles died before Troy fell, which means he was, basically, a failure."

"And not just that, if you recall your Homer, which Alexander supposedly reads every night – when he's not too drunk, at least," added Klemes, "his name is not that of a Greek, but of a prince of Troy."

"What? What prince?" asked Aristophanes.

"Alexander, King Priam's son," replied Dimitrios.

"Huh? Never heard of him," Ari replied.

"Yes, you have," interjected Klemes. "Paris' real name was Alexander – or Alexandros, which is the same thing. That is the name he was given when he was born. His sister, Cassandra, had a vision that he would bring death and ruin to the city and the family. So the child was taken from the city as an infant, and left to die of exposure – but the gods intervened. A shepherd found him, gave him the name Paris, and raised him as his own. It wasn't until he was nearly 20 that his true identity was revealed."

"So, let me get this straight," sighed Ari, taking a deep breath. "A man named for a prince of Troy, thinks he is the reincarnation or some-thing of a great warrior, who, even if he did exist, not only failed to take Troy but died in the attempt, right? And he wears that dead warrior's armor as a good luck charm while trying to take a city that is probably far better defended than the one his supposed ancestor or whatever died trying to take?"

"That about sums it up," nodded Dimitrios.

"That doesn't make any sense," replied Ari. "And if he does think it makes sense, then Alexander is either crazy...or mad."

"Actually," said Memnon as he came to the point of the wall where the trio was gathered, "he is a little bit of both."

Dimitrios and Ari immediately came to attention, while Klemes just nodded in an acknowledgment of respect for the general.

"Stand at ease, men. If anybody has earned the right to do so, it is the three of you. You each helped save my life, and it is I who should be saluting you all. So," he said, clearing his throat and changing the subject, "how bad is it? Is the outer wall holding?"

"Yes, my General," responded Dimitrios, "but it won't for long. Our engineers have been shoring it up, and in many places have built an inner wall of wood, then filled up the space in between the two walls with dirt and sand. Eventually, however, it will all come crumbling down."

"And we shall be ready for them, won't we, my Theban friends. This is not my first siege, and it won't be my last. Thymondas has safely kept his archers back from the walls. As soon as the bombardment ends, the Macedonians will come with their ladders and rams and towers...and our bowmen will step up to rain arrows on them, every pace they take."

"Will that be enough to stop them," asked Ari.

"No," said the general. "But it will slow them down, thin out their ranks and make it all the harder for them to take the wall. That is why Ephialtes will be in reserve with our own men – or should I say, your men, captain – your fellow Greeks in Persian service."

"Then that is where I should be, too, General," replied Dimitrios. "I ask for permission to join the ranks of our hoplites."

Not to be outdone, Ari, too, spoke up. "I am not of much use in the shield wall but I am a decent shot with a bow. I would like to join our archers when the time comes."

Memnon replied in the negative to both requests. "No, gentlemen. I need my bodyguards, my good luck charms, about me. You will both have plenty of targets to shoot at and spear through when the time comes. I need men I can trust with my life to guard my back, and you two have shown your worth in that regard."

Klemes gave out a rather unpleasant harrumph, but the general simply turned to him, put his hand on the physician's shoulder and gave him a knowing look. "Do not worry, Klemes, I have not forgotten about you. I owe my life to you even more than I owe it to your brother and his friend. I want you by my side as well."

"No," said Klemes rather brusquely.

"No?" remarked the general, quite taken aback and caught off guard by the unexpected answer.

"No, General," continued Klemes. "I am a physician, a healer. You are not so sick or injured as to require my constant presence and attention, but there are many who are – and many more who will become so. My place is not by your side – but by theirs, in the hospital. Your duty is to defend the city," he added. "Mine is to heal and save the lives of those you risk in doing so. Speaking of which, I believe I have stayed up here, on the wall, overlong. I should attend to my patients, and make ready for the new ones you and Alexander are going to send my way."

With a slight nod of respect, Klemes gathered up the hem of his robe and draped it over one arm, turned and walked down the steps that led to the courtyard of the citadel.

"Well, that was unexpected," said Memnon. "But," he sighed, "the physician is right. We all have our assigned duties, and we all have our part to play in this little drama of Alexander's making. So," he added as he put one hand on a shoulder of each of the two Thebans, "let us take our place on the stage. To the city wall, men, to the city wall."

The city wall of Miletos was the second of the three lines of defense that guarded the city. Alexander had already taken the outermost wall, and from there his artillery were well in range of the main line of defense – the city wall. That wall was pockmarked from the heavy stones thrown by Alexander's siege engines, splattered by the heads of captured Greeks, and singed by the fireballs, all of which had also been fired by the siege artillery. Many of the crenellations along the top had been knocked down or broken by the boulders, and here and there cracks could be seen in the masonry of the main wall itself. Rather than offer the Macedonians easy targets, Memnon had left no more than a handful of men on those battlements – just enough to give Alexander the impression that it was still manned in full by the defenders.

For the rest of the day and well into the night, the battering continued. Just before dawn of the next day the sounds from the bombardment changed – as to the thwang of enemy weapons and bang of boulders hitting the wall was added the sound of falling stones. Whole sections of the wall began to crack, crumble, and finally give way, the debris tumbling down to leave massive gaps in the wall.

That was the sign Alexander's engineers had been watching for. The chief engineer sent a runner to the king's tent to give him the news, and within moments trumpets were blaring all through the camp, calling the men to arms. The time had come to assault the wall.

The tempo of the bombardment increased to a level no one on either side had ever seen before, not even Parmenion or Ephialtes, the two oldest generals on the field. Where walls had been cracked and crumbling, they were now brought down. As the infantry advanced toward those openings, Alexander rode along with them. Every hundred yards he came to a halt and had the men carrying a large red banner unfurl it and wave it with great animation. That was the signal for the siege engineers to increase the elevation of their weapons, to lengthen the distance they would shoot, and to hurl their ammunition not against the wall but over it. The resulting rain of high-arcing fire proved devastating to the defenders – and to Memnon's plan.

The lines of archers and spearmen arrayed behind the now collapsing walls became the victims of this blind fire. Instead of the massive stones used to batter the walls, the Macedonian engineers now let loose with baskets of smaller stones, clay pots stoppered and filled with oil and tar, and compact balls of straw, soaked in oil and set afire a moment before they were launched. The number of casualties caused by this barrage was not great, but its impact on the organization, the morale and the attention of the men under fire was devastating.

Soldiers broke ranks to scatter for cover. Others huddled in tight groups anywhere they could find shelter from the deadly rain. Too many of those who tried to hold their position were struck by the stones or set afire by the bales of straw that ignited the oil pooling on the streets from the broken pots. Officers who tried to get the men back into formation were ignored. As Alexander advanced, the red banner went up again, and again another hundred yards after that. After each such stop, the loads fired by the war engines got smaller and lighter, in order to reach deeper into the city, but no less devastating than their predecessors to the courage of the defenders.

"We have to do something, General," Dimitrios remarked worriedly to Memnon. "The men can't take much more of this – they are starting to waiver..."

"Hell, they're not just starting to waiver, whole groups of them have broken. It's time for me to leave this safe perch and take charge on the ground."

"But General, sir, if you get hit..."

"Dimitrios," Memon said as he strapped on his helmet and motioned for his shield and spear to be brought forward, "there are times when a general has to stop being a commander, and become a fighter. This is that time. Either I lead from the front, or I will have no men left to lead. So, are you up for some exercise? Feel like guarding my back as we go spear some Macedonians?"

Dimitrios nodded and gave a grim smile as he, too, motioned to Ari to hand him his shield and spear. As the two prepared to leave the safety of the citadel, Memnon turned to Ephialtes, who had also begun to gird himself for battle.

"Ephialtes, old friend, stay here."

"What!" boomed the veteran soldier. "Stay here with the old and the lame...no offense, Ari...when there is fighting to be done!"

"There is no need for both of us to go down there," added Memnon. "Besides, if I am down at the breach, who will command the defense of the city? No, Ephialtes, I need you here. If the Macedonians break through somewhere else, it will be up to you to see it and to send reserves to block them. The men need to see me, it may be the only thing that keeps them in the fight, but we all need someone to watch our backs and flanks. That someone, Ephialtes, is you. There is no one else to whom I would entrust the safety of the city – or the life of my soldiers, or myself."

The old general grumbled, hurled his helmet down and then kicked it across the stone floor of the tower from which they were watching the battle. As it banged and clattered, he gave out a growl of reluctant acceptance, and through gritted teeth told Memnon to go.

"Go, go down there and kill enough for both of us. I would rather be down there, by your side, but I will obey your command. Just know that I am not happy about it, but I will do as you order, at least for now."

Memon reached out and clasped Ephialtes by the arm, nodded and strode off, Dimitrios close behind. As they headed off to the fray, Ephialtes turned to Aristophanes and grabbed his shoulder. "I know you want to go and protect your friend, but I need you and your bow here, with me. You should begin to find some targets soon enough, when the Macedonians come through, as I'm not sure even Memnon will be able to hold them back."

As Memnon and Dimitrios ran down the stairs and out into the courtyard, they were met with a rain of stones and fire. The clang and clatter hit the shields they raised over their heads like hailstones on a roof – but with fire at their feet as the barrage of incendiaries only seemed to redouble. Memnon did not scurry for shelter, but instead ran out into the open area immediately behind the crumbling wall and called out to his men.

"It's just a little hard rain," the general said with a loud if forced laugh. "Come out and get wet with me! You can't stop the Macedonians coming through the breach if you are hiding from the rain!" he bellowed.

In ones and twos, and then in small groups, the soldiers came back out into the open. They came slowly. Those with shields held them above their heads. Those without hunched over, all the time looking up at the sky to see what next would fall down upon them. Memnon formed them up and sent them forward, closer to the ruble that had been the main city wall. As Alexander advanced, his engineers again extended the range and increased the arc, this time to fire not in the esplanade behind the wall, but deeper into the city. What had been a bombardment to breach a wall had become a barrage to harry the troops behind it, but no longer. Now the engineers unleashed an onslaught of terror upon the civilian population. As the defenders came forward to face the Macedonian infantry coming through and over the walls, the city behind them would burn – and echo with the screams of the women and children caught in the deluge of fire.

And come up, over and through the walls, the Macedonians did. They hit the wall with the force of a tidal wave – and an angry, bellowing, monstrous wave at that. Like water seeking the path of least resistance, hundreds flowed through the breaches into the city. Hundreds more, unable to find a path and too frenzied and impatient to wait their turn, scrambled up the piles of rubble and tumbled over the ruined defenses, screaming their war cries as they came. The fury and savagery of their charge was enough to unman even the bravest defender, and would have done so had not one man stood in their path.

"Shields, up!" roared Memnon, now in the center of the front rank of defenders set to block the exit from the largest breach. "Spears, out!" he roared again, as nearly a thousand men obeyed, the gleaming, sharp points of their weapons aimed directly at the howling mass hurrying toward them.

"Archers!" cried Memnon, his deep booming voice somehow rising above the hellish din so the line of bowmen behind the ranks of spearmen could hear. "Loose!"

At his signal, five hundred archers lifted their bows and let fly. Each quickly drew another arrow, notched it and shot again, and again, the third arrow being made ready before the first even hit the ground – or a Macedonian at the wall.

Now it was the turn of the Macedonians to be under fire and to feel the fear and terror of death from above. Scores and scores in that rushing mob of men fell with an arrow in their neck, shoulder or chest, but those at the front were ignorant of their loss – or simply too enraged with bloodlust to care. Into Memnon's wall of shields and spears they crashed, bounced, and crashed again. The Macedonians recoiled a second time, but, shoved forward by thousands more coming up from behind, they flowed forward again, many in the front ranks carried forward by the rising swell.

"Hold the line! Hold the line!" roared Memnon, his face and arms smeared with Macedonian blood, his feet seeking steady purchase amidst the gore beneath them. "Hold the line!"

Dimitrios fought hard, too, doing his utmost not just to skewer the attackers but also to use his shield to cover the general. That was no easy task, for Memnon did not simply hold his spot on the line of battle, but kept dashing forward, out of the shield wall, to stab and sweep with his spear, and to be seen by his men as he did so. His example emboldened the Greek mercenary hoplites who held that line, and their steadfastness encouraged the Persian archers behind them. The Macedonians came on, along with their Thracian and Thessalian allies, but as they struck the unyielding line they began to falter. The unexpected courage of the defenders, as well as the bodies piling up from the spears at their front and the arrows falling from above, cooled the bloodlust quickly. The sheer exhaustion of running across the broken ground, scrambling up, and over, and through the rubble, and then fighting for their lives against a determined enemy, also took its toll. Now only the push of the mass of men still coming up from behind could convince the front ranks to go forward, but their fury began to subside under the storm of Persian arrows.

The mercenary line held. The invading tide began to ebb. The city would be safe.

Or so Dimitrios and those about him believed.

But they were wrong...and Aristophanes was the first to realize it.

54

Miletos

THE ISLE OF LADE

lthough he had been promised he would be plinking arrows into the mass of Macedonians from his perch high above them in the citadel, not even as skilled an archer as Aristophanes could draw back his bow far enough to hit a target at that range. Ephialtes was fuming and pacing about, his eyes locked on the life-and-death, back-and-forth struggle at the town wall some 1,500 yards to the south. Ari could not pick out Dimitrios or Memnon from the mass of tiny specks. Nor could he hear the sounds of battle, as the rushing winds and crashing of the waves on the rocks to the north and sides of the tip of the peninsula upon with the citadel was built drowned out the distant noise.

But then he heard a different sound. Something indistinct, but different. Something coming not from the wall, or the city, much of which was now ablaze, but from off to the right, and from the water. If Ephialtes heard it, he did not react, as the general's thoughts and attention were fixed upon the battle at the wall. Yet Ari was curious, a trait for which most of his family and friends had often warned would get him into trouble. So he moved about the citadel to get a better sense of what was making that sound. As he reached the western battlements of the tower, the sound grew louder in his ears, and when he looked down and out into and across the harbor he saw what was making that sound.

Scores of ships, their rowers straining at the oars, were racing across the water from the Island of Lade. While Memnon, Ephialtes and the rest of the defenders were focused on meeting the threat at the town wall, they were unaware of a second, and now even greater threat coming from the sea. Nicanor had loaded up much of the 4,000 man garrison Alexander had sent to protect the fleet anchorage and base at Lade upon his ships – and he was bringing them across the water and towards the city.

As Alexander's attack on the wall had become fiercer and fiercer, more and more of the guards along the other three sides of the peninsula had been recalled from their posts and sucked forward into the maelstrom at the wall. Only a handful of what had already been but a scattering of watchmen remained on guard on the three sides of the city that faced water. Some had already spied the approach of the Macedonian fleet. A few rushed forward, racing to set up some kind of resistance at the points the enemy were about to land. Others ran to raise the alarm - and to look for help.

Aristophanes turned about and moved as fast as his game leg would allow to get back to where Ephialtes was still fuming, the general's attention still solidly locked on the fight he could barely see to the south.

"General! General! Come quick!"

"What are you blathering about, lad. 'Come' where? Don't you see I'm busy...or at least I should be," he added with a grumble.

"It's the harbor! The Macedonian fleet is attacking!"

Ephialtes' jaw dropped as he turned about, stunned by the news. For days he, and Memnon, and everyone else had been focused so tightly on the threat from the south that they had ignored the potential threat from the sea. The Macedonian fleet had done nothing but sit on blockade, hiding behind the Island of Lade, not even daring to take up the challenge of engaging the Persians at sea. Now, of course, that their source of water had been cut off by Hephaestion's raid on the Meander, the Persian fleet of necessity had left their rude base at Mycale, skirted Lade and gone farther south, to Halicarnassos.

Only a handful of scout ships remained, mostly to smuggle in a steady trickle of food and information, and to serve as couriers to maintain contact with the rest of the empire. That left Nicanor with no enemy to face, and left the garrison on the island with nothing to defend against. Alexander had foreseen this, and only a few hours before he launched the infantry assault on the wall, he had sent signal men to the top of the Old Citadel. When they saw the red banners go up in the assault waves, they waved their own red banners from the top of the hill. That was the signal Nicanor had been told to act upon, and act he did.

While his triremes could each carry at most thirty soldiers, he had other ships for cargo and transport available. These he packed with as many men as he could, and launched them as a second wave behind the warships. The triremes and quadriremes would dash into the harbor and disembark their marines, who would secure a landing spot at the docks and jetties. Other warships would demonstrate to keep what few Miletian vessels remained in the harbor from sallying forth to disrupt the landings. Those two forces did their job and did it well. Although three or four Miletian warships did launch, they were too few, and too late, to stop Nicanor from getting his main force into the harbor.

Ephialtes saw them coming, thanks to Aristophanes, but in his heart knew it was too late. Nevertheless, he hurried down the steps of the citadel, bellowing out for runners to alert the reserves.

"My lord General," one young militia officer responded when the grey-haired, grey-bearded Greek came tumbling into his post, "the reserves are gone. Memnon called them to bolster the wall."

"All of them? Surely not all of them went south?" cried the old general, gasping for breath from his run down the stone stairs.

"No, but most of them," replied the officer.

"Well, that means some of them are still around, doesn't it?" grumbled the now angry as well as exasperated general. "So go find them, whoever they are, and have them assemble at the harbor."

"Err, which harbor, my lord? The commercial one or the military one?"

"At the commercial harbor, you idiot. That is where the landings are taking place!"

Miletos, long a naval base, did have two harbors. The military harbor poked deep into the northwestern tip of the peninsula, like a long pointer finger. Its entrance was narrow, however, and well guarded with a chain and strong artillery towers at either side. Nicanor could not have landed there if he tried. But the commercial harbor, that was wide and broad, with many docks and jetties. It had almost no defenses to speak off, except a low sea wall meant more to keep out water than warriors. It was that sea wall which was Nicanor's target, as from there he could drive into the city, cut across the narrow neck of the peninsula and sever Memnon's line of communications to the citadel. From there Nicanor could charge north, through the upper city, past its temples and agoras, to assault the citadel, or south, through the lower city, and hit Memnon's line from the rear. Or he could do both. Whatever Nicanor chose, the city was doomed...unless somebody could hold him at the seawall.

Ephialtes was determined to be that somebody, but the odds were heavily against him. What forces he could muster were few and of little value, being mere militia and the old men and little boys of the militia at that. Still, Ephialtes gloried at the challenge. He would finally get to fight. Now was his chance, his chance to show Memnon and the rest of them that old as he was, this aged veteran had at least one good fight left in him. An army of sheep his cobbled together force might be, but it would be led by a lion.

He prayed it would be enough to save the city, even if it meant it would be his last fight. And if not, thought Ephialtes as he strapped up his shield and grabbed his spear tightly, at least he would die as a soldier should – not in his bed or watching from a tower, but in the line of battle, fighting Alexander.

While Ephialtes ran about urgently trying to muster up enough men to meet Nicanor's landing, Aristophanes fell in with a group of young archers who had answered that call. Although not much more than a boy himself, he was easily the oldest of the half-dozen bowmen by several years. It was evident from their rather poorly-made, old bows and well-worn quivers that these were not trained soldiers, or even members of the city militia. At best, they were country lads used to hunting birds and small game, who had been driven to take shelter in the city when the Macedonians fell upon their farms and villages.

"Stick close to me, boys," Aristophanes said calmly, with an air of command that was as foreign to him as the city in which he found himself. "Your job is not to die for your country, but to make those other poor dumb bastards die for theirs. We are archers, and we have no need to get up close and personal – that is the job for the lads in bronze armor with the pointy sticks and swords. Our duty is to cover them, and to cut into the numbers of Macedonians coming out of the boats. Understand?"

The young boys, each of them eager to prove himself, either mumbled or nodded in agreement. They gave Aristophanes an unqualified respect he had never received, not even from his friends and fellow soldiers back in Thebes. He knew that their illusions about the glory of battle were about to be shattered, if they had not been already, as few in the city remained ignorant or unmoved by the horror of war. In a way Alexander had schooled them all, and class was still in session, as was evident from his current pair of attacks.

Ari and his makeshift squad of archers had some difficulty getting to the harbor. Although the sea breeze drove the smoke from the fires set by Alexander's bombardment of the lower city, many streets had become impassable due to the flaming debris, collapsed buildings and fleeing citizens. Swimming against the tide of panicked refugees, they made little progress. Then one of the boys suggested they get above the crowds, quite literally, by going into a building and from there moving forward by leaping from rooftop to rooftop.

Although Ari was older, bigger and stronger than the boys, this was where they had the advantage over him, and where, because of his game leg and their adolescent agility, he allowed them to take the lead. He struggled to keep up with them, as their exuberance matched their nimbleness, yet they did not move so quickly as to leave him behind. The boys obviously took comfort and strength from the presence of what to them was an "old" soldier.

The rooftop race enabled the small band to reach the harbor much more quickly than had they stayed in the street. They got there long before Ephialtes and whatever force he had organized. As they reached the last row of buildings they could see the harbor laid out before them – and it was a sight to test even the most hardened veteran, let alone a bunch of boyish recruits. Ships were afire or sinking, or both. Sailors were floating, dead or dying, in the water, or struggling to climb aboard a friendly ship or a piece of flotsam as their own vessels went down. Most were merchant crewmen who had tried to get their ships away from the docks and out of the slips into the water in a vain hope of escaping the invaders, lest their ships and with them their livelihoods would be destroyed or lost as prizes of war. Others just wanted to flee what they saw as a dying city. Unfortunately for them, the Macedonians showed no mercy to soldier or sailor, combatant or citizen, and their attempts to escape only hastened them on their journey to Hades.

"We make our stand here, boys," said Ari, huffing and puffing and grimacing in pain from their rooftop run. "Make use of what cover you can find. Pick your targets, take a breath, hold it, aim and fire. Then duck and notch another arrow before standing back up again. Shoot for their necks, or anywhere you can see unguarded flesh. I want live archers, not dead heroes. And you, what's your name," he said, pointing to the shortest and most likely youngest of the boys, "come here. I have a special and very important job for you."

As the others drew arrows from their quivers, Ari could see that these were not war arrows but hunting arrows, good for skewering rabbits or bringing down pigeons, but incapable of penetrating leather vests or thick linen shirts, let alone bronze chestplates.

"Aim at their arms, their faces, or their legs," he shouted. "Your arrows won't do much good anywhere else." He then turned to the young boy he had called to his side. "I asked you what's your name," he said kindly, even gently.

"P-P-Paris, sir," he said nervously, tugging a forelock in respect.

"Well," said Ari with a smile, "you have the perfect name for an archer, don't you? Well, remember, it was Paris of old from Homer's tales who took down the most vicious warrior of his day, and with a single shot – right to the one tiny spot on the giant's body where he was vulnerable, the heel."

"Y-Y-Yes, sir," Paris replied, "or so my father tells me...or, rather," he said, starting to sob, "he used to tell me – before the Macedonians killed him."

Aristophanes felt the boy's pain, and it hit him hard, harder than anything had since the day he had seen Alexander's men burn Thebes to the ground. "Well, I am sure he is watching you now, and that you will do him proud, but not there, with the others," he added, as he pointed to the rest of the boys who were already sending a plunging fire into the enemy boats. "You have the most important job of all. Your job is to guard our backs. I want you to stay at the back of the rooftop, away from the edge facing the sea."

"But how will I shoot any..."

"That is not your job. You stay here, keep an arrow knocked and ready, and keep watch. If any Macedonian comes up the stairs or climbs up onto the roof, you yell out a warning – and then drill him, right between the eyes, okay? Can you do that?"

"Y-Y-Yes, I can," Paris stuttered nervously, "but I want to fight..."

"You will be, and in a very special way. By guarding our backs, the rest of us can fire away, without fear or worry. Believe me, when I say your job is the most important of all, I mean it. Understand?"

The boy nodded, knocked an arrow and stepped back to where he could see the hole in the roof through which someone might climb. From there he could also look down the alleys on either side and to the rear of the two-story building upon whose roof his friends were making their stand. With Paris at his post, Ari took up his own bow, and drew one of his arrows, arrows whose steel tips could bite through all but the thickest bronze armor. Time to kill some Macedonians, he said to himself.

"This one's for Thebes!" he screamed as he let fly his first shaft – which sunk deep into the neck of a Macedonian officer, sending him tumbling from the prow of his trireme and into the murky, bloodied waters with the rest of the dead and dying.

"This one's for my father, you Macedonian bastards!" he cried as he drew and loosed the next arrow into the mass of men coming ashore.

"And this one's for me!"

55

Miletos

ALEXANDER AT THE GATES

Alexander had remained remarkably and unusually calm throughout the early stages of the battle. Rather than leading from the front and racing to become the first man upon the walls of Miletos, he had shown uncharacteristic restraint. Strangely and seemingly detached from the hectic horror of bombardment and slaughter, Alexander had advanced at a measured pace, halting now and again to order the red flags raised, and to watch as his men surged forward into the abattoir that was Miletos. He remained so even after the flags flew from the Old Citadel Hill to order the fleet to begin their invasion into the harbor. Alexander remained unmoved as showers of stones and flaming munitions streamed over his head and into the city, shattering buildings, crushing bones and setting humans and homes alike ablaze. Not the roar of the war engines or the battle cries of his soldiers disturbed his trance-like serenity. It was as if he was above it all, detached from all earthly concerns, and the sounds of war muted almost to silence.

Then something or someone began to intrude upon his tranquility. He heard a noise, no, a voice, and then felt someone's hand on his shoulder, shaking him to get his attention. Still, nothing disturbed his reverie until his face tingled from a slap – a hard, strong, nasty slap delivered by perhaps the only man who would dare to strike the king, let alone live to tell of doing so.

"Parmenion? Parmenion? What the..." he said quizzically, his eyes and thoughts finally coming into focus on the old man in blood-stained armor before him.

"The attack is faltering, Alexander," said Parmenion with great concern and a tinge of exasperation in his voice. "The first three waves are spent, and there are so many dead and dying on the field that our next wave has refused to go forward. Alexander, we have no choice but to fall back and regroup."

"Fall back?" mumbled Alexander, still in a bit of daze. "Regroup? No, no, Parmenion..."

"We must retreat, my King. Our men have done all they can this day. Give the order to pull back. That is what I would do. That is what Philip would do."

If the slap on the face and the shaking of his shoulders had begun to awaken him from his walking slumber, the very mention of his father's name shocked him awake, as if he had been stung by a hot needle.

"I am not Philip," scowled Alexander, petulantly, "nor am I you," he growled. "I am Alexander. I am the son of a god. I am Achilles reborn," he said, his voice rising louder and angrier with each breath. "I do not retreat!"

"Maybe you don't, lord," said Parmenion as he spat a bit of blood, "but your men have to. They can do no more. They are spent. The army is spent."

"We shall see about that," roared Alexander, his eyes suddenly ablaze with an unholy fire. "Where are these cowards who refuse to go forward?" he shouted in anger. "Where are they? Show them to me!" he screamed. "Show them to me!"

Parmenion, too exhausted to argue and too familiar with Alexander to waste what energy he had left in doing so, simply pointed toward the camp. A mass of soldiers, obviously uneasy and visibly hesitating, just milled about at the edge of the battlefield. They moved only to open their ranks to each group of bloody, injured and wounded men who came stumbling back from the front, a front none made any move to go toward, despite the haranguing of their officers.

"Macedonians!" shouted Alexander, as he galloped back to meet them. "Macedonians! Why do you linger here, when your brothers call to you to finish the task they have begun! Will you stay here, idle, cowering in your tents while your comrades gain all of the glory! Will you let them have their pick of women and treasure, and leave none for you to claim!"

Up and down the line he rode, tearing off his helmet so all could see the anger and fury in their king's face. "Who will come with me! Who will come with their King! Soldiers of Macedonia! Who will dine with me in Miletos tonight!"

Whether it was his words or the sheer force with which he delivered them, the Macedonian shirkers heard the call of their king. With shouts and war cries of their own, they surged forward, racing him and each other to see who would be the first of them into the city. The sound of their charge shattered the air, just as the pounding of their feet seemed to shake the very ground. Alexander's men in the breach and at the wall heard it, and felt it, as did Memnon's inside the city.

Their own hearts already fit to burst from the exertion of the struggle, the Greek mercenaries who had held the breach so long began to waiver at the sight and sound of fresh hordes coming up, and over, and through the wall. Even before Alexander and his reserves struck their line, the mercenaries broke. As they fled, they swept the Persian archers along with them. Only a few groups of soldiers kept their shields towards the Macedonians, and even they fell back as they did so.

Dimitrios and those around Memnon were the last among them to retire. Yard by yard they went back, stabbing and slashing at each step. Their stance, however, was futile, as waves of Macedonians swept around them, their minds fixed on the women they would rape, the treasures they would plunder and the slaves they would claim.

"It is no use, General," Dimitrios shouted. "You will only die if you stay here. We have to go, and go now!"

"You're right, Dimitrios," said Memnon with a sigh, his heart now as weary as his limbs from the overlong fight. "Let's make a run for it, back to where the peninsula narrows, between the temples and the South Agora. We'll make our next stand there."

Memnon gave the command. The few men still with him fell back into a nearby alley, turned about and began a weary jog back into the lower city and north, toward the narrows. As they did, small groups of men who had left the line but retained their weapons joined up with Memnon's band. Fortunately there was little pursuit, as Alexander's men thought only of the rewards they could reap now that they were inside the city. Even Alexander had little luck in cajoling his men to chase after the defenders. No words he could shout nor gestures he could make could distract them from their greed, their lust, and their desire to seize their hard-won rewards.

Ever back went Memnon, his ranks not so much swelling as congealing around him. Tired, and battered, and bloodied as they were, the mixed group of Greek mercenaries, Persian archers, and city militia still saw in him a beacon of hope, a rock upon to base their chances for survival, and perhaps even victory.

Their numbers grew as they went north toward the narrows, as did their courage.

And then the Macedonians crashed into them. Not from the south, where they had been fighting them all day, but from the north. From the harbor, where Nicanor had come ashore in all his power.

56

Miletos

TEMPLE OF ATHENA

Aristophanes and his young archers took a severe toll of Nicanor's sailors and the soldiers they landed, but for every man they took down, ten more ran past them, flooding through the streets from the harbor into the city. What few men Ephialtes had sent to block those streets had been swept aside, washed away in a sea of armed men eager for plunder and sport. As the tide of invaders reached deeper into the city, Aristophanes and his bowmen found themselves cut off, their perch on the rooftop an island in the swirling maelstrom of Macedonians.

"I think we've done all we can do here, lads," he said to the youngsters, each of whom were down to their last arrow or two. "It's time for us to be going. You," he added as he pointed to the youngest archer, the one whom he had set to watch their backs, "do you know a way out of here?"

"They've cut us off from the citadel," the little lad replied, trying his best to disguise the fear in his voice. "But I think we can go toward the lower city, into the temple district."

"All right, then. If that is our only way out of here, then that is where we will go," he replied, pausing only to let fly his final shaft. "And since you made the choice of where we run, then you can lead the way. The rest of you," he continued, waving his hand to grab their attention, "follow him."

"Where do we go after we get to the temples?" the youngest asked.

"You go home. You find your families. See if you can keep them safe – or find a way out of the city. You have done more than most citizens of Miletos today – but now it is time to look out for yourselves, and for those you care about."

The boys looked at one another, each afraid to be the first to leave, lest their friends think the less of them, yet each, in their hearts, were more than ready to leave the rooftop. Aristophanes allowed himself a tiny smile, for he recognized what those boys were feeling – which was the same thing he had felt in the battle line at Thebes.

"It's all right, boys. It's all right. Go...go! Before it's too late, go!"

And go they did, except for the youngest.

"I told you to go, boy, and to lead the way for the others."

"I'm staying with you, sir," he replied, with a tremble in his voice. "Besides, the others know the city as well as I do. They'll find their way home."

"And you?"

"I don't have a home here to go to, remember? I told you, the Macedonians burned our farm. We've been living on the streets here, moving about, getting by with odd jobs and handouts. I haven't seen my father or my sisters since yesterday, when the stones and fireballs really started to pound the city. I've nowhere to go, and I wouldn't know where to look for them. So if it is all right by you..."

"Yeah, yeah," nodded Aristophanes. "You can stick with me – or should I say, I need to stick with you. I don't know this city well at all. You're going to have to lead the way – and we better get going now, if there's even still time to make a run for it!"

With that, the little fellow took a few steps back and then ran and launched himself across the space between their rooftop to another. Ari did his best to follow, but unlike the youngster who sailed across the alleyway, Ari was lucky to leap far enough to grab the edge of the next flat-roofed building. He did his best to keep up with the boy, who, at least, had the kindness to stop when he got too far ahead.

After the fifth or sixth such leap of faith, Ari had about had all he could take. His leg was throbbing, his heart was pounding, and he was having difficulty getting a deep breath, but at least the Macedonians did not try to stop him. They weren't looking up at rooftops, but were busy breaking into houses and shops, on the lookout for wine, women, and wealth to grab. A few of the better Macedonian officers were able to keep some discipline, and were thus able to keep at least a few of the soldiers moving forward in some kind of a fighting formation. It was good for them that their officers were able to do so, for as the leading clumps of invaders tumbled out of the warren of streets from the docks, they came upon a wall of shields, out from which poked the deadly spearpoints of those few trained soldiers Ephialtes had been able to rally and shove into the ranks.

The first bands of Macedonians to hit Ephialtes' blocking force paid dearly for their incautious, heady race for spoils. The men coming up behind them, however, who remained under the orders of their officers, fared much better. These were not the phalanx men of the Macedonian pike regiments, but marines, soldiers trained to fight from swaying, slippery decks, not in narrow streets. Still, they were disciplined and as deadly as any body of men in this battle. When the would-be looters were out of the way, the marines had a clear line of sight to Ephialtes' line – a line made up of home guards, members of the city watch, the walking wounded he had culled from the hospital – to Klemes' despair – and any other stout fellow who took up a spear, sword, pointy stick, or club to defend his city.

Their stand was noble – but brief. The marines cut them down in but a few minutes, and without mercy. Ephialtes tried his best to give them courage, but all of his brave words and bold cries were to no avail. The line gave way, and as the defenders broke, they swept Ephialtes away with them.

It was from one of the rooftops above this rout that Ari and his young friend spied Ephialtes. Ari leaped down, along with the boy, and the pair all but tackled the old general, before forcing down a door so the trio could take refuge in a wine shop. The old general was disconsolate, holding his head in his hands as he sat down heavily on a wooden bench.

"It's all over, Ari. I've failed him. I've failed him. The city is lost..."

"You did your best, General. None of us saw this coming – not even the great Memnon," Ari replied with an unkind emphasis on their commander's name. "Speaking of Memnon, Dimitrios should be with him – and we need to find him, or them, before this mad mob sweeps south and hits them in the ass. So, here, General, grab a jug of wine, take a good stiff drink, and let's go and find them – before it is too late for them, or for all of us."

But it was too late. Alexander's foot soldiers streamed through the now undefended breaches, and what few groups remained to stand in their way shattered like a clay pot when struck by the wild mass of Nicanor's men.

"Head for the harbor!" shouted Memnon, seeing their path back to the citadel was blocked. Few other than Dimitrios and those immediately around them heeded his call. Any thoughts of an orderly retreat were swept away by the hordes of wild Macedonians now gushing through the city. Unable to go due north, they turned northwest, toward the harbor. The farther north they went, however, the more of Nicanor's men coming south they met.

"Where can we go, General, we can't go that way!"

"There! Over there!" Memnon pointed with what remained of a spear, its haft broken just below the point. "The Temple of Athena! You can just make it out above the buildings!"

The Temple of Athena was one of the many grand temples in the city. If Miletos was a hand, and the citadel its pointer finger, then the piece of land on which the temple was situated was its thumb, with the commercial harbor in the space between the thumb and fingers. Easily seen from the sea by day, its golden tipped spire shining brightly in the sun, it was a welcome beacon both by day and by night, when fires were lit around it to guide sailors to the harbor. There was no citizen of

Miletos nor any visitor to their city who had not at least seen the temple from a distance. Memnon chose it for his rallying point for that very reason – and because from there he would at least have access to his only escape route – the sea.

The bulk of the Macedonian fleet was so preoccupied with ferrying troops from Lade to the harbor that only a handful remained to maintain the blockade. Even the crews of those ships had their attention drawn toward the city, where fires raged and great plumes of smoke now rose to the sky, to be carried deeper inland by the offshore breeze. Those sailors did not have their mind on their duty, but were agitating their captains to head for the town to get their share of the plunder. As a result, hardly anyone was watching the sea like they were supposed to be doing. Had they done so, they would have spied a few Persian warships that were rowing hard for the coast.

Captain Abibaal had been rewarded by the admiral with yet another scout ship, albeit one that was in rather poor shape, not having been to a proper ship yard in months. Its planks sodden from too much time in the water, it was heavy and slow, but its crew, most of them from his previous ship, worked it hard. There were faster, better ships in the fleet, but the admiral chose this one and a few others to stay back and keep watch on the city while the rest made for the anchorage at Halicarnassos, farther to the south. Abibaal was no soldier, but even he could see that the death knell had sounded for the city and its defenders. There would be men, good men, who needed saving from that catastrophe. If he could pull even a few of them out to fight again another day, then he would have more than earned his pay this month.

Abibaal could see that the harbor was choked with Macedonian ships and that there was a ragged line of blockaders still between him and the anchorage. The beaches near the outer wall and along the lower city were swarming with Macedonians, but there was one rocky beach that still appeared to be vacant – that just below the Temple of Athena. If there was any place people would go to seek solace and sanctuary left in Miletos, it would be there.

And so that is where Captain Abibaal would go.

57

Miletos

TEMPLE OF ATHENA

"Where do we rally, General?" Aristophanes asked the old Theban warrior.

"The Temple of Athena," he answered, breathing hard. "From there we can at least see the harbor, and the agora below it will make a good place to stand our ground. From there, we can try to strike south and join up with Memnon on the town walls...and let him know his back is no longer secure."

"You know the way?" Aristophanes asked the young lad who had refused to leave his side, even after the other boys had done as Ari had commanded to go find their families.

"Of course," laughed the boy. "Everyone knows the way. You really aren't from around here, are you?" he chuckled.

"No, I'm not," replied Ari, "and it doesn't look like I'm going to be around here much longer. This city is dying – and we've got to find a way out of it."

"First thing's first," huffed Ephialtes. "We've got to try to get to Memnon. He has to know..."

Whatever else Ephialtes said was lost in the tumult as yet more fires roared and more people ran screaming through the streets. The blaring of trumpets and shouts of triumph coming from both the harbor behind them and the lower city before them only served to confirm what both Ephialtes and Ari feared. The Macedonians were flooding in from both sides now, which meant that Memnon's line, too, had crumbled.

Still determined to reach the Temple of Athena, the trio pushed on, past and through the fleeing mob of citizens and soldiers who raced about seeking shelter and safety wherever they could find it. As they entered the agora at the foot of the temple, Ari saw a familiar figure on its steps. There was Dimitrios, standing wearily on guard over another man whose visage he had come to know so well – that of the commanding general, Memnon. A handful of soldiers, Greek mercenaries mostly, along with a few Persian archers, clustered about him. A few were trying to form some kind of line of battle across the steps of the temple, but their exhaustion and their sense of defeat was evident. These men, like their general, were beaten, and they knew it. All that remained was to decide how they would die, and how many Macedonians they could take down with them.

"Ephialtes?" said Memnon as he spied the veteran soldier coming across the marketplace, its shops shuttered and its vendors' carts long gone. "Ephialtes!" he cried, as he ran down the steps, arms wide open to embrace his old comrade. "Have you come to rescue us?"

"No, my General," Ephialtes said sadly. "I bear hard tidings. The Macedonians have the harbor. Nicanor brought hundreds, maybe even thousands of soldiers across from Lade. They've cut the city in two from east to west. Our men still hold the citadel, but there is no way for us to get back there. I fear that I have come not to rescue you, but merely to be by your side when the end comes – and that end is nigh."

The roar of battle and destruction rose up once again from the city, to which was added what could only be cheers of victory by the Macedonians. "That sound can mean only one thing," Memnon remarked. "Alexander himself is in the city. I suppose he is looking for me, so he can gloat as I surrender the garrison," the general added, as he drew his sword, "but he'll get no satisfaction from me. I will show him how a general of the Empire dies, and it will be on my feet, sword in hand, cutting my way through his bodyguard."

"Why give him that gift?" said Klemes, who suddenly appeared from inside the temple. "Better to live to fight another day than to throw away your life – and the hopes of your king – in a senseless act of sacrifice. Besides, would you make your Barsine a widow twice-over?"

"Klemes! Brother!" Dimitrios managed to shout. "I never expected to see you again. What are you doing here?"

"Looking for a way out of this bloody city," he replied rather matter-of-factly, "and I've found it."

"What?"

"While the lot of you have been moaning, and groaning, and talking of death, I've spotted some of our ships out there, just off those little islets out to the west. There's not many, but they should be able to take a few of us out of here – including our generals."

Dimitrios dropped his shield and ran up the steps to the top of the temple. Memnon, Ephialtes, and a dozen others, including Aristophanes and his young archer, followed.

"There, over there, do you see them?" Klemes asked, pointing to the few Persian ships in the distance.

"Yes," groaned Memnon, "I do. They are ours, by the looks of them. But we've no way to reach them – and there's no place they can land. Nicanor has the harbor, and those rocks down there will tear the bottom out of any ship that tries to come inshore."

"Spoken like a soldier," Klemes scolded the general. "You're thinking only with your feet, not your head. Look to your shield, general. Look to your big, round, concave shield."

"What about it?" the general replied, genuinely perplexed.

"It is a shallow dish – it will float. It's most wood and leather at its core. You can't sit in it, but you can use it to help you get out to sea, once you take off your armor and drop your weapons, of course. We hold on with our hands, let the outgoing tide take us, and we can probably make it to those little islets out there. I'll bet the ships can take us off from there."

"That's ridiculous," Ephialtes said. "We've not a chance of making it."

"Well we might – or would you rather just let Alexander kill us all?"

"The physician is right," said Memnon. "I was a sailor before I was a soldier, and I learned to swim long before I could sail. After all, I did grow up on an island. We could make it. At least it is worth a try. Anything to deprive Alexander of his glory. I'd rather see Poseidon's smiling face than that Macedonian upstart's triumphant grin any day."

Memnon saw that many of the soldiers were hesitating, not sure what to do, so he took the lead. "Well, Klemes, don't just stand there. Help me off with my armor."

"Damn it, General, I'm a physician, not a valet."

"You are now, physician. As for the rest of you," he said addressing the soldiers in and around the temple, "time to strip off your armor. Grab your shields. We're all going for a little swim."

Memnon and the few dozen men with him did just that, leaving their armor where it fell as they made their way across the temple, down the steps on the far side and to the shore, where a tiny little shrine to Apollo stood by the matter.

"It's a sign from the gods!" shouted Memnon. "See, here's Apollo, and he's riding a dolphin!" he continued, as he pointed to a mural on the wall of the shrine. "So let your shield be your dolphin, say a little prayer to Apollo, and follow me," added the general, as he jumped into the sea.

Dimitrios, Ephialtes, and the others, Greek and Persian alike, followed. Only Ari held back.

"What's wrong, sir?" the young archer who had been at his side all day asked.

"Well, it's just that...well..."

"What?" the boy asked again.

"I'm not that good of a swimmer."

"That's all right," laughed the young lad. "My father used to say I was part fish, because I swam so well. You'll be fine. I'll help you, sir."

Ari, still embarrassed and a bit uncertain, nevertheless grabbed a shield and made for the water's edge, the boy right behind him.

"Drop the sir with me. Just call me Ari," Ari said, turning his head to address the lad. "By the way, I never asked you your name."

"It's Themes," the lad replied. "Short for Themistocles."

"Pleasure to meet you, Themes," said Ari with a nervous laugh. "Now, let's see if you are as much like a fish as your father says."

The men were lucky. Their shields helped them float out with the tide, and most began to kick to propel them a bit faster on their journey. Although weary and wet, most soon reached the group of little islets and rock outcroppings. As he made it to solid ground, Dimitrios stood up, walked to the far side of the tiny island and began waving his arms in hopes that those aboard the ships would see him. Others followed his example, and soon dozens of men were flailing their arms about wildly in an effort to grab the attention of the sailors. All except Ephialtes, that is, who sat rather glumly on a rock, dripping wet.

"Ephialtes, why aren't you waving at the ships like the rest of the men," Klemes asked as he stooped down to examine the veteran soldier.

"I am a General, damnit, not a refugee...or a physician, for that matter," he replied rather testily. "It is not dignified for a General to run about and wave his arms like some madman."

Captain Abibaal could not help but see the men on the islets. He did not know who they were exactly, but he had a good guess. He turned his ship about and ordered the men to begin rowing against the tide, toward the islets. He signaled the other ships around him to do the same. As he drew closer, he could see that scores of other soldiers were in the water between the islands and the city. They had seen Memnon and his group make a swim for it, and they had followed their example. As Abibaal and his ship closed the distance, he saw a few men come wading out. To their mutual surprise, the first face he recognized was that of Dimitrios.

"You look like a drowned rat," Abibaal joked as he called out from the prow.

"Drowning, not drowned," Dimitrios managed to quip with a little laugh. "And we're not all rats. You got room for a general or two?"

Miletos

LION BAY

Alexander's onslaught was unstoppable. He rode the crest of that mighty wave up and over the wall and through the town, until it finally deposited him at the Lion Bay – the great, long, slender military harbor. Some twenty warships were in their sheds – and on fire, as their crews had decided to burn them rather than turn them over to the Macedonians.

"Damn, damn, damn!" cursed Parmenion angrily as he took off his helmet and, as he was want to do in such situations, hurled it to the ground with a loud clang. "We could have used those ships!"

"Let them burn," said Alexander calmly. "We don't need them."

"What?" replied Parmenion. "We're already outnumbered better than two to one at sea. Those ships..."

"Would not have changed that," laughed Alexander. "Besides, I'm disbanding the fleet anyway. So, let them burn."

Parmenion did not immediately reply. He just looked long and hard at Alexander, his surprise and disbelief warring on his face. The later emotion won out. "You can't be serious? Disband the fleet?"

"Why not," replied Alexander. "It costs too much and, frankly, I don't trust most of the captains, especially the Athenian ones. They'd as soon work for the Persians as work for me – and the Persians pay better."

"But it was the fleet that helped us win this victory..."

"You mean my victory?" Alexander replied with an unpleasant, scolding scowl. "They only attacked after I had breached the wall. Nicanor came late to the party, Parmenion. I'd already won by the time his men landed. All Nicanor did was make sure his boys were in for the kill – and to grab their share of the loot. And speaking of loot..."

"Yes, there is a lot of it, Alexander," replied Parmenion with a bit of pride in his voice. "Don't worry, I'll make sure we get a portion of that back. Our war chest is so empty, what few coins left in it just rattle about."

"I want the looting stopped," Alexander said firmly, again taking his father's favorite general by surprise.

"What! The men won't stand for that! They've earned it! The right of conquest is a sacred one. This city had its chance, and when they chose to fight rather than to surrender..."

"True, but some of their citizens did try to surrender the..."

"You mean sell out, Alexander, not surrender..."

"Again, Parmenion, you are technically correct. But nonetheless, I want the looting stopped. Same goes for the rape, arson, and general mayhem. I need this city, Parmenion. Besides, the Persians all but razed it to the ground when they took it from the Greek colonists years ago – or don't you recall your Phrynichos..."

"My what?" replied Parmenion.

"Phrynichos, the playwright," explained Alexander.

"A playwright? What does some pooftah scribbler have to do with anything?"

"He scribbled, as you put it, a play, *The Capture of Miletos*. It is all about the nasty, evil, mean, and godless Persians sacking, burning, and murdering their way through this place when they put down a Greek revolt. I am here as a liberator, Parmenion. How can I do that if I act no better than the Persians?"

"But when you turned down that fat fellow who tried to sell you the keys to the city you said..."

"Oh, that, well," Alexander said as he cleared his throat, "that was all for show. I just wanted to frighten that toad and show him what he was up against. Wonder whatever happened to him? You'll look into that, won't you, Parmenion...after you've put a stop to all of the looting that is."

"Alexander..."

"Enough, Parmenion. Enough. I have told you how it is to be. I need a disciplined, hungry army behind me when we march on Halicarnassos...not some blood-sated, unruly rabble more concerned about how they will spend the shiny trash they've tucked into their sacks than about the next battle."

"So why the hell are we going to Halicarnassos?" asked Parmenion, who was demonstrably angry at yet another surprise command from his youthful king. "It is the most heavily fortified city this side of Babylon. It has three – not one, not two, but three walls. It's defended not by a garrison, like this place, but by an army – and a fleet, as that is where the Persian ships that were off Mycale have gone. We don't need Halicarnassos, Alexander. We can just bypass it and drive inland, like we've planned all along."

"You mean like you planned, or like Philip planned?" Alexander snapped back sharply. "It is just for those very reasons that I need to take Halicarnassos. Miletos was one thing, but Halicarnassos, well, when I take the untakeable, who will dare to stand against me? What city, what fortress will dare keep its gates closed to me, knowing that if I could break down the walls of the mighty Halicarnassos, I could surely do the same to theirs? So no, Parmenion, I will not leave Halicarnassos proud and defiant in my rear. I will take it, and I will make a sacrifice in front of the great Mausoleum there, so all of the world will know that the gods are with me, and that the days of the Persian Empire are numbered. Just as heaven cannot brook two suns, neither can the world have two masters. Taking Halicarnassos will show all Asia who is their real master."

"But..."

"Oh, and because Memnon will go there," added Alexander. "And since you let Memnon escape," Alexander said with a scolding slither, "we have no choice but to follow him...and finish him."

"Why? He is a twice-beaten general, first at the Granicos then here..."

"Thrice if you count his failure to defend Ephesos..." added Alexander pointedly.

"Then all the more reason to ignore him. He is finished. He is discredited. He has no army. So why bother going after him?"

"Because he tasks me, Parmenion, he tasks me. When I was young, he was my instructor while in exile in Macedonia. Now it is he who is the pupil, and I who am the master. I will have him on his knees before me, Parmenion, on his knees!"

Parmenion knew better than to argue any further with Alexander, not once he started making speeches, anyway. It would be of no use, for if the king said they were going to Halicarnassos, then that was where they were going. Even if they were going without a fleet, and with an army of soldiers who were going to be very, very disappointed at being told they had to stop looting the city they had spilled their blood to take.

Memnon stood on the deck of Abibaal's ship as the vessel rowed away from the city. He could see that there were now scores of men on the little islets, like the one he had been rescued from, but there would be no such salvation for those soldiers. The fleet was already far away, berthed at and refitting in the great harbor of Halicarnassos. The handful of ships left on patrol were hard-pressed to take more than a few score of those who had swum out with Memnon. What would become of those men on the rocks, or the city they had fought to defend, he did not know – but even if Alexander decided to show them mercy, he did not know what form that mercy would take.

"So what do we do now, General," Ephialtes, wrapped in a blanket and carrying another for Memnon, asked.

"You and I, we go to Halicarnassos. The satrap there, Orontobates, is an old friend – and the son-in-law of the late king. He has been preparing its defenses for a month."

"So you knew Miletos wouldn't hold?"

"No. I hoped it might, but, as I feared, it did not. No, Ephialtes, I did not sacrifice the city and its garrison, if that was going to be your next question. I thought to wear Alexander out, hoped that his lack of patience would lead him to either make costly mistakes or just grow so tired of a siege that he would go off in another direction. That plan worked, up to a point..."

"Up to the point where the city fell, you mean."

"Yes, I suppose so. But enough of that. On to Halicarnassos. That is the rock upon which Alexander will shatter himself. It was already the strongest fortress in the world, and Miletos gave Orontobates time to make it impregnable."

"So we're going to defend another city under siege," said Dimitrios as he approached the two generals.

"We are, but you are not," Memnon said as he turned about to look his aide in the eye. "I have another job for you – a vital one and, more important, one that is especially important to me. Are you, and your brother, and your friend, up for a little adventure?"

59

Myndos

HALF WAY TO HALICARNASSOS

Captain Abibaal eased his vessel into the jetty at Myndos, a port about half way between Miletos and Halicarnassos, with practiced ease. Compared to his last few berths, this was a welcome respite: no rocky beach to drag the ship upon, no enemy warships to dodge – and this city, unlike the last two he had visited, was not even under attack – at least not yet. Alexander would need time to digest swallowing up Miletos. Restoring order, resting his soldiers, repairing his siege weapons and resupplying his army would take time – not as much time as it would for any ordinary army, or any ordinary commander, but time. Memnon was already pondering how to make the best use of that time, such as it was, and that was where Dimitrios came in. He, his brother, and their friend Ari would take on a task for which Memnon simply did not have enough time to do for himself.

"So tell me again, brother," Klemes asked Dimitrios as they prepared to disembark, "where exactly are we going and what are we supposed to do?"

"We are going into the interior, to one of Memnon's estates. There we are to make sure that the general's wife and children are well, and then escort them to safety in the east."

"And just how far 'east' is it we have to take them?" asked the physician.

"Far enough to be sure that his family are out of harm's way, wherever that is," replied the Greek captain. "It is quite an honor, if you think about it. A man like that, entrusting his family to a comparative stranger."

"A stranger who has been at his side in battle and has saved his life – and more than once" observed Captain Abibaal, who overheard their conversation as he made his way back amidships, having seen the ship docked and tied up to his satisfaction. "I wish I could go with you, my friend," the naval officer added with an audible and exaggerated sigh.

"Why? Getting tired of the sea? Or just tired of fighting?" quipped Dimitrios.

"As to the first – never, and as for the second – well, maybe a little," laughed Abibaal. "No, the reason I wish I was going with you is much simpler than either of those," he said with another deep sigh.

"Well, then, why?" asked Dimitrios with a puzzled look on his face.

"Because," replied Abibaal with a very large and dreamy smile on his face, "because you will get to see the beautiful Barsine."

"Who?" asked Klemes.

"Barsine, my friend," replied Abibaal. "Don't tell me you have never heard of Barsine?" he added incredulously.

"Can't say as I have," responded the physician.

"Barsine," said Abibaal, pausing to take in a deep breath and closing his eyes as if conjuring up a picture in his mind – and a very pleasant picture at that, judging by the look on his face. "Barsine, Memnon's wife. She is said to be the most beautiful woman in the world. A modern Helen of Troy – but far less fickle. She is of the noblest Persian blood. No less than the daughter of Artabazus..."

"The satrap of Phrygia?"

"The same, Dimitrios, the very same. He married a Greek beauty, and together they had a child, a girl of such grace and charm as to beguile Darius himself. He gave her to Memnon's brother, Mentor, as a reward for helping with the reconquest of Egypt from rebels."

"I thought you said she was Memnon's wife, not his brother's," interjected Aristophanes, who had been listening while tightening up the straps on his pack.

"Both, actually," the Phoenician captain replied. "Mentor died but two years after they were married. As you know, it is the custom here for an unmarried brother to take his brother's widow to wife, to see that she is protected, and that she and any children are taken care of."

"Oh, so this was just Memnon doing his duty..."

"No, Klemes, no," said Abibaal. "Far from it. Before Mentor and she were married, Memnon had accompanied Barsine and her father into exile in Macedonia, after her father's own rebellion against the emperor had failed. Memnon fell madly and deeply in love with her, as I believe did Alexander, who was but a stripling at the time, seeing as how she is about eight years older than our little Macedonian kinglet."

"So, he seduced his brother's intended?" asked Ari with a salacious grin.

"No! No! A thousand times no!" Abibaal shot back with an angry shout. "Never! Memnon adored his older brother, and he knew how much Mentor wanted and loved her. No, Memnon was her guardian, her protector, and her companion, and remained so until Mentor's service to the empire restored the honor of both families. It was only later, after his brother died, that he was able to make his true feelings known – and through his love for her heal the wound in his heart that his brother's passing had left. No, my little Greek friend," scolded Abibaal, "this is not one of your Greek comedies, but a true love story, a drama built upon a tragedy."

"And just how is it that you know so much about all of this? Have you ever even seen this fabulous Barsine?" asked Klemes.

"Why, everyone knows of their story, everyone. You've never heard the stories of Barsine and Memnon?"

"No, Captain Abibaal," jibed Klemes. "I guess such gossip never got as far north as Thebes. Or if it did, well, we had other things to occupy our time – like Alexander marching on our city."

"Well," said Abibaal, nodding his head, "I can understand that, I suppose. I swear it, I swear on my mother-in-law's grave."

"I thought you said you weren't married, Abibaal," said Dimitrios.

"I'm not, but I will be someday," said the naval officer, "and when I do, I surely will inherit a mother-in-law along with a bride, and someday we will have to bury her, so..."

The port of Myndos where they docked was half way between Miletos and Halicarnassos. A minor port, especially when compared to its two great neighbors, it was nevertheless an important one. And made more so now, as it was the nearest safe harbor for any army preparing to advance upon and lay siege to the great city of Halicarnassos. Memnon handed Dimitrios letters to give to its governor to instruct him as to that importance, and to outline the preparations needed to put it in a better state of defense. The leather tube in which that letter was to be carried also contained other papers, instructing the governor to provide Dimitrios and his companions with horses, guides, a small escort and whatever provisions and funds the young captain asked for in order to carry out the other part of his duty: seeing to the safety of the general's family.

The governor, as expected, pleaded poverty and argued that he had no men to spare, not with the full power of Macedonia heading his way. Rather than argue, Dimitrios agreed to take but two men from the garrison – a young guide and a rather elderly soldier who, like the nag he rode, had seen better days. As none of the Greeks were experienced horsemen, the governor was also able to pass off on them a trio of old, swaybacked mares for whom this trip into the interior was one last reprieve from the butcher, tanner and glue-maker, each of whom stood ready to do their part in putting an end to the little herd's suffering.

As they left Myndos, Dimitrios was able to get a better look at its walls and defenses, such as they were. Situated between two great cities, Myndos had no reason to expect it would ever need to prepare for war, as it had been inconceivable that either of those mighty fortress cities would ever fall to an invader. Yet now with Miletos gone, Myndos found itself in the unfortunate situation of being directly in the path of an oncoming juggernaut. If Miletos with all of its towers, its walls, and its strong garrison had not been able to resist Alexander, how could little Myndos hope to halt the Macedonian advance? Although the governor did go through the motions of appearing to follow Memnon's orders to strengthen the city's defenses, it was obvious even to Dimitrios that the governor of Myndos was making preparations to see how best the city, and its governor in particular, could best survive and perhaps even prosper under Macedonian rule.

None of that, however, was Dimitrios' concern. He had a job to do, and a mission to perform. While he would much rather be at Memnon's side on the walls of Halicarnassos, he understood that by making the general's family safe, he would be doing a better service to his new employer and far more damage to Alexander than he could do at Halicarnassos. With his mind freed from familial concerns, Memnon would be a much more focused – and even deadlier – adversary.

PART V

Halicarnassos
SOUTHWESTERN COAST OF ASIA MINOR

Year Three of the Reign of Alexander of Macedonia

60

Halicarnassos

THE ROYAL ISLAND

After setting Dimitrios, Klemes, and Aristophanes ashore at Myndos, Captain Abibaal immediately put back out to sea, for he had a precious cargo to deliver to Halicarnassos: Memnon. His men put their backs into it to shoot out of the harbor as fast as possible, exiting which they caught a strong breeze, raised sails and steered a direct course for the mighty city. Halicarnassos was the true jewel of the Persian Empire's Asia Minor holdings, and as well-fortified as Miletos had been, this city was even stronger.

"Halicarnassos is where we shall break this Macedonian pup," Ephialtes said gleefully as he held fast to a rope line that ran along the side of the now racing vessel. "It is impregnable – and the more so now that you will be in charge of its defense," he added with certainty.

"No city is truly impregnable, my friend," replied Memnon thoughtfully. "Who thought Alexander could take Miletos, and do it so quickly – breaking through three layers of walls, blockading and then storming its harbor even when he was outnumbered at sea, and forcing us to flee for our lives. No, Ephialtes, do not tempt the gods by claiming Halicarnassos is impregnable; they are fickle feckless beings who love to play tricks and prove us wrong."

Ephialtes laughed, and laughed so loudly that he could be heard the length and breadth of the ship, despite the sound of the wind and waves. "Has losing Miletos so unmanned you that now you worry about the gods? That is not the Memnon I know. Buck up your spirits, laddie," chided the older man. "Once you see the tall towers of the Tripylon Gate, walk the tall, thick, strong walls, and settle into your headquarters on the Royal Island, you will be your old self again. And this time you will have the fleet in the harbor of the city – with twin citadels to either side, so Nicanor will have no possible way of blockading our navy or invading by sea, not this time. No, Memnon," Ephialtes roared, "as you once told me and I keep reminding you, this is the rock upon which we shall break Alexander."

Memnon's spirits did begin to rise as Captain Abibaal's ship rounded the headlands and Halicarnassos came into view – and what a view it was. The sun reflecting off the polished marble and golden-sheathed peak of the tomb of King Maussolus drew his attention, like the beacon of a great lighthouse. An expensive folly built by a self-absorbed little monarch more as a monument to himself than a final resting place, the Mausoleum, as many now called it, did catch the eye, Memnon had to admit. It was also good for business, as it attracted tourists, and sightseers, and others who came to gawk at its garish splendors, all of whom had to find – and pay for – food and lodging in the city. Maussolus' advisers had cannily suggested he build the tomb immediately adjacent to the agora – the main marketplace – for which the monument served as the perfect advertisement. The king had been touched and warmed by what he felt was the affection the city fathers showed for him by agreeing to the project – but then again King Maussolus was so full of himself that he did not understand their true motive: to make money.

Halicarnassos is all about money, Memnon mused. The biggest, greatest, most vibrant port in all of Asia Minor, it was the perfect crossroads for ships coming up from Egypt and the Levant, across from Rhodes, Cyprus, and even Crete, and down from the Ionian cities.

Trade fleets from here reached across to Greece, Sicily, Italy, and beyond, as far as Carthage and the Pillars of Hercules. Its harbor rivaled even that of the old Phoenician city of Tyre, and was every bit as well-defended.

Memnon, as Ephialtes had predicted, did begin to feel his confidence returning, doubly so when he set foot upon the dock, for there to greet him were two old friends: Orontobates, satrap of Caria, and Autophradates, admiral of the imperial navy. What brought even more joy and certainty of victory to his heart, however, was the tall man who stood behind them. Although Memnon did not know his face, he knew his uniform. It was that of the Immortals – the elite lifeguard of the king of kings, and the only infantry in the Persian Empire who could stand face-to-face against the Macedonians with any certainty of defeating them.

"Excellency, Admiral, I am honored that you came to greet me, whereas it is I who should be seeking an audience with you."

"Nonsense, Memnon, you are the general of all of the armies of the empire, the man hailed by Darius himself as the defender of the realm. It is we who are honored," said the satrap, bowing slightly.

"There has been much ah, confusion, shall we say, in the streets, the agora, and the councils, since Alexander took Miletos. Now that you are here, I am certain all of that will come to a stop. The people, the garrison, and the city fathers will be greatly relieved and inspired, now that you are here to lead and defend us."

Memnon blushed a little at the obsequiousness of it all, but then again, he had been around imperial officials long enough to know it was all part of the game. Frankly, had Orontobates been more serious and less fawning in his welcome, he would have taken it as a sign that his authority had been diminished. Not to be outdone in the sycophantic competition, Autophradates, too, heaped praises upon the storied general. Memnon heard him speak but did not pay attention to his words, instead he looked past him, to the stoic, stone-faced officer of the imperial bodyguard.

"Yes, yes Admiral, all well and good. I trust the navy will do better here than it did at Miletos. I depend upon your skill to keep the supply line by sea open, and to keep Nicanor's fleet at bay – this time."

"That will be an all too easy task," the admiral gloated.

"And why is that?" asked Memnon, puzzled by the naval officer's confidence, especially in light of the navy's poor performance at Miletos.

"Because Nicanor has no fleet," he replied with a massive grin. "Alexander sent it home."

"You're dispersing my fleet!" Nicanor exclaimed in disbelief, a response seconded by Alexander's other top commanders, all of whom he had called together in what had been until recently Memnon's head-quarters in the citadel of Miletos. "Why would you do that? We practi-cally won the battle for this city by..."

Nicanor knew as soon as he started to say it that he had said the wrong thing – and the very thing that would set in stone Alexander's decision to disband the fleet. By even hinting that the glory and respon-sibility for victory was not Alexander's alone, Nicanor doomed the fleet, and his career along with it.

Parmenion tried to come to Nicanor's aid, as did Ptolemy, but Alexander quieted them with a sudden, ferocious look, like a beast warning other predators away from his kill. "First of all, Nicanor, it is not 'your' fleet – it is my fleet; MY fleet. And second, Miletos was my victory – MY victory and MINE alone! MY fleet – under your able command, I grant you – just came in at the end, like beaters at the hunt who come in to complete the kill and divide up the meat when the beast is already skewered, laid out upon and bleeding into the dirt," he added, his tone making it obvious that he felt insulted by his admiral. "Anyway, I have made my decision," he added haughtily. "We cannot afford this fleet – and," he added with self-congratulatory satisfaction, "we don't need it. Not anymore."

"But my King," responded Parmenion. "If we do not blockade the port, then Halicarnassos will never fall. Their fleet can come and go as it pleases, bringing in food and reinforcements at will. No siege can succeed if they do – why, it will be no siege at all!" exclaimed the grizzled old warrior.

"That is correct, my old friend," Alexander replied with a smirk. "There is to be no siege of Halicarnassos."

The gasps of surprise filled the room, followed immediately by a rush of questions and incredulous responses, each of which was lost in the general tumult of words and emotions. Alexander again shot out a hand to silence his generals, each of whom understood that this was not a suggestion, but a royal command – and an impatient one at that.

"We will of course build works at key points around the city, opposite the three gates – the Myndos Gate on the west side, the Mylasa Gate on the west and the Tripylon Gate on the north face of the city. Those will be the location of our camps, and there we will place our siege engines, which will immediately begin to pound the gates opposite them. There will be no siege, per se," Alexander explained, "as I intend to take the city by storm, and storm it as soon as a breach has been made."

"But the navy could..."

"No, Nicanor," said Alexander sharply, "the navy could not help with this. You got lucky at Miletos, but the enemy fleet is already in the harbor – and it is twice the size of yours. They have a citadel at either end of the horseshoe-shaped harbor, and each is well-fortified with great pieces of artillery – artillery which could pound your ships into driftwood in a matter of minutes. So, no, Nicanor, your ships could not help – they would merely be a distraction at best, and one that the Persian fleet and the citadel garrisons on their own could deal with easily."

"But...but even if we are not part of the attack, surely you need my ships to keep the army supplied, to maintain contact with home, to..."

"No, I do not," Alexander replied rather succinctly.

Again the generals, as if playing the part of a chorus in some tragedy, shouted their dismay and disbelief, but once again, Alexander gave the signal for quiet.

"We have no need of lines of supply or communication back to

Greece – or to Macedonia, for that matter. They have nothing to send us, and we have not the means to pay for it anyway. We are adrift here, in Asia Minor, and here we will establish ourselves. We will live off the land – and press the cities we liberate for supplies and manpower as we need. Besides, sending home the fleet will show our men – and the Persians – that there is no going back. We shall be like the sharks, ever moving, constantly feeding on our prey, as we scour the Persians from the coasts of Asia Minor, the Levant...and Egypt. Without bases, their navy will wither and die; so why waste men and money we do not have fighting them at sea? No, my good friends, my generals, my companions – we shall fight and defeat the Persian Navy where we are strongest: on land."

Just as Alexander's generals were caught by surprise by the young king's decision to disband his navy, so, too, was Memnon. At least for Memnon, however, it was a pleasant surprise. It meant one less worry, one less distraction, and one more weight lifted from the Macedonian side of the scale in this war. If Alexander was going to come at him solely from the land side, then so be it. He would be ready for him – as would the weight he would add to the scales, a weight surely to tip them in his favor: the Immortals.

That thought gave Memnon great comfort, a feeling that only grew as he met privately with their commander, Hydarnes. Memnon actually had to look up to the officer, for as unusually tall and strong as the Rhodian commander was, the Persian officer was taller by nearly a head. By the way he held himself, it was obvious to Memnon that Hydarnes was no palace sycophant. True, his trousers and tunic were of unusually fine silk, and woven with golden thread. And his hair and beard were immaculately curled and oiled, but even with the rouge on his cheeks, the kohl around his eyes and the smell of expensive perfume that wafted about him, there was no doubt that he was a fighting man.

That was something that the Greeks, and especially the Macedonians, never understood. From the days of Herodotus, they had mistook what seemed to them marks of feminine preening to mean that the man behind the makeup was something less of a man. Memnon knew it to mean just the opposite. Only a man who had such conviction of his own manliness would go to battle so made up and so attired. What the Greeks dismissed as womanly, the Persians knew to be but fashion: after all, why shouldn't one look and dress their best for what might be their last day on earth?

Hydarnes was just such a man, and Memnon well knew it. No one entered the ranks of the 10,000, let alone rose to command one of its 10 brigades. Nine of those brigades, each of 1,000 men, carried tall, sharp spears with little silver apples at their base. Only one brigade of the ten, the elite of the elite, the best of the best, the bravest of the brave, the noblest of the noble, were different. Their spears rested on an apple not of silver, but of gold. As did that carried by Hydarnes.

"I am honored that the King of Kings should send one of his own bodyguards to serve under my command," Memnon said to Hydarnes with complete and unequivocal respect. "So, tell me, Brave Warrior, favored of the emperor, why did our lord Darius choose you, in particular, for this task?"

"Because I am a soldier – and I am so utterly bored with palace ceremonials," he replied with an ease and honesty that took Memnon completely by surprise. "Do you know just how dull it is to do nothing but walk around the palace day after day after day, inspecting soldiers – and soldiers who are perfect in every respect? There is never a cuirass unpolished, a tunic untucked, or even a hair out of place. They are magnificent, but they are like statues – or toys from a box. I love them all and know them all by name, but..."

"But, as you say, you are a soldier..."

"And a soldier's job, as you have shown us Memnon, is to fight, not stand guard or march in parades."

"But surely, the King of Kings has not sent me his 'golden apples'? Who would guard the palace and the harem and the king's own person?"

"No," Hydarnes said with a sly grin, "he has not sent you his 'golden apples,' as my regiment of the Immortals is known. I turned over my command to my subordinate, who was eager for the honor. Darius allowed me to choose 500 men, drawn from each of the ten brigades, to come with me. They are indeed the finest soldiers you will ever see, General, and better still, each is a volunteer."

"So, that means the Immortals no longer number 10,000?" quipped Memnon with a laugh.

"No, General, there are still 10,000 back at Persepolis. That, after all, is what the title 'Immortals' truly means. When one of us leaves, or falls, another steps in to take his place. Each of my 500 knew this, but in their hearts, and in that of the king, each is still one of the chosen: after all, as it is said, "once an Immortal, always an Immortal."

"And immortal shall we all be, Hydarnes" said Memnon, "when together we send Alexander back to Macedonia..."

"Or to his grave."

Alinda

THE LAIR OF THE ONCE AND FUTURE QUEEN

"The fat old cow wants me to do what?" barked Alexander in astonishment.

"She wants you to accept her as your mother – your adopted mother, or the other way around, or something like that" replied Hephaestion, barely suppressing his glee.

"You know I already have a mother, right?" the young king replied. "And she is trouble enough. I invaded Asia to get away from one mother," continued a bit peevishly, "not to get a second one. Besides, you know how jealous Olympias is of anyone I even smile at...including you...actually, especially you, come to think of it. Imagine her reaction if I accepted Queen Ada as another mother."

Hephaestion could not help but grinning, yet still somehow managed to put forth his case with some seriousness.

"Queen Ada is the key to our being able to lay siege to Halicarnassos. It was, after all, her city and her province before she got kicked out by her brother. She still has followers, Alexander, and she could be of enormous help."

"Enormous is one word for her...have you ever seen a woman that fat? And that smell, what is it?"

"Rose water, Alexander, just simple rose water."

"Well she must bathe in it, drink it and have her clothes washed in it, for I can't stomach getting within a pike's length of her..."

"Which pike? The twelve-footers..."

"No, the eighteen-footers carried by the phalanxes. By all the gods, she smells like a temple after the virgin priestesses have burned their offerings. It is sweet, cloying and, well, it makes me want to vomit."

"Said like a true king, Majesty," smiled Hephaestion. "Well, how about we stick a little strongly scented wax up your nostrils to mask her smell? Could you then manage to get close enough to talk to her, kiss her hand, maybe even allow her a motherly embrace?"

"Not for all the poppies in Persia..."

"Well, if not for the Persian poppies, then how about the currency of Caria. Outside of Halicarnassos she is still revered and honored as queen. With the satrap and his army stuck in the city, the towns and villages will be free to show their loyalty to their rightful queen. They do rather revere her, you know. After all, it was her older brother, King Mausolus who built that gleaming monstrosity of a tomb. It is hideous..."

"As is the queen" snapped Alexander quite snarkily.

"Yes, but each is a wonder of the world in their own right," continued Hephaestion. "Think of what you'd gain. A friendly country-side – and that would be a nice change, wouldn't it? That means Ptolemy can't play his little crucifixion and impalement games, as with her backing he won't have to. For once we'd have farmers willing to sell us their food, workmen happy to build our siege works and, well, even the local ladies might be more conducive to the attentions of our soldiers. Think of what that would do for morale among the troops?"

"Yes, yes, Hephaestion, but...but my mother..."

"Don't worry, Alexander, she knows how the diplomatic game of power is played. She will understand."

"Hephaestion," Alexander asked rather pointedly, "have you met my mother?"

The palace of Queen Ada was not really a palace, nor a fortress, but basically a fortified farmhouse. Her estate at Alinda had been meant as a vacation spot where the royals could escape from the prying eyes of the priests and counselors. A retreat where they could escape the roar and smell of the city and let their hair down – or, in the case of Queen Ada, take it off, for beneath her wig she was as bald as a cucumber. As a place of exile, it was comfortable enough – and close enough so that Pixodoros, who first sent her there, could keep watch on her. Alas, the clever usurper had himself been usurped by his son-in-law, Orontobates, following the former's untimely accidental death. Accidental in that Pixodoros seemed to have accidentally cut himself six times while showing off with the old king's royal sword. Or so the story went.

Orontobates did not pay much heed to old Queen Ada, even after Alexander marched down from Miletos. He did, of course, have her under surveillance. His scouts reported that a number of couriers and rather high-ranking Macedonians had been seen coming and going between the advancing army and the queen's royal retreat. Still, Orontobates did not believe much would or could come of it. After all, he had been around the old bag enough in his younger days to know how she rubbed people the wrong way.

In that, however, he underestimated the diplomatic talents of Hephaestion – who was not only easily the prettiest general of any army in history, but also one of the most silver-tongued. Hephaestion could charm a snake from a jar, a lion from a cave, or Alexander from – or into – his bed. Queen Ada never stood a chance, but then again, she wanted an arrangement with the Macedonians even more than they wanted one with her. For Alexander and Hephaestion an alliance with the old queen made good military sense. While for them it was merely a matter of logistics, for the deposed queen it was something much stronger and sweeter that drove her – the desire for revenge.

Ada did not much care if she ever ruled Caria again, or once more sat her rather plump behind on the throne in Halicarnassos. All she wanted was to make sure that none of those who had played a part in robbing her of her birthright no longer did either. And it wouldn't hurt if they suffered, and not just suffered a little bit.

With Alexander as her adopted son, she could at least have the title and the respect, even if one of the annoying little Macedonian would wield the real power. Let him, she thought. The business of governing is rather tedious anyway, and tended to interfere with her more satisfying pleasures. One of those, she sighed in anticipation, would be seeing Orontobates and his wife humbled. Perhaps she would geld him, cut out her tongue and let them live, the queen mused, as her slaves, for that would really make them suffer.

While Alexander and Hephaestion were being tormented by the rosy odors of Queen Ada, Ptolemy and Parmenion were shepherding the army down the winding roads and through the passes and defiles that led to Halicarnassos. With the Persian fleet having retired to the city's magnificent port, the seas and coasts to the north remained free to what little was left of Nicanor's command. Using the twenty ships left to him for scouting and courier duty, the admiral of the much-reduced fleet was able to scoop up about a dozen merchant ships. Onto them Ptolemy boarded his engineers and their siege equipment, which they dismantled for the purpose of transport. These reached the little port town of Myndos about the same time that Ptolemy's advanced cavalry scouts arrived on its land side. Both Nicanor and Ptolemy were annoyed to find that the town's gates were shut and its walls manned by archers and spearmen. The former seemed especially keen to show off their prowess, picking off individual targets at a far greater range than either Macedonian expected.

This was Orontobates doing, as he had convinced its governor, Hydarnes, that holding the town for at least a little while would buy them time needed to better prepare Halicarnassos for the coming siege. When the town elders demurred, Orontobates sent a detachment of Immortals to stiffen their resolve; a resolve that was further braced with a generous offer from the satrap to evacuate the women and children of the leading families and see them safe behind the walls of the capital city.

This rather stout opposition left Ptolemy in a quandry, as he would have to besiege and then storm the town in order to allow Nicanor's convoy to land, yet the men and the equipment he needed to attack the city were on those very ships. Leaving his Prodromoi scouts and Thessalian horse to watch the city, Ptolemy hurried back up the road down which the main body of the army led by Parmenion was marching. No sense worrying Alexander about this, not when the old drillmaster himself would know what to do.

Little did Ptolemy know just how much Alexander longed for such an excuse to solve a tactical problem. As strategic to his goals as Hephaestion had convinced him these days spent fawning about the fat queen were, he hungered for an excuse, any excuse, to be elsewhere, anywhere. He found his distaste for her attentions such that they could not be assuaged even by the free flow of wine, which was offered in amounts copious even by Macedonian standards. Nor did the companionship of nubile, lithe and willing entertainers of all sexes...for Queen Ada had a taste for the exotic that was not satiable within the usual menu of genders. That was an appetite even she admitted was quite out of the ordinary and very difficult to satisfy but, then again, as she told Alexander as they lounged on the couches for dinner one evening, "sometimes it is good to be queen!"

Despite her proclivity for all things sensual and sexual, Ada was, to Alexander's great relief, decidedly and exclusively motherly in her attentions to him. Alexander, she told him, was the son she never had, the son she had always wished for, prayed for, and made sacrifices to the gods for. With his arrival in Asia she knew that those wishes, prayers, and sacrificial pleas finally had been answered. His coming was thus as much a religious event as a martial one, she told Alexander. While she understood that he intended to march on after taking Halicarnassos, she nevertheless intended to make the most of their time together.

Had Orontobates planned it, he could not have asked for a better, longer or more immersive distraction. Every day Alexander spent drowned in the affections of the plump queen, he and Memnon used to their advantage. Between Queen Ada's captive entertainment and the denial of Myndos to Nicanor, the satrap and the general gained the time they needed to broaden and deepen the ditch that ran along the outer walls of the city, and to bring in supplies and reinforcements by sea. In addition, they used the respite to build strong platforms on the walls for their artillery, and to stake out the ranges for their weapons. Alexander had amassed a great variety of tension and torsion siege weapons that could fire long, sharp, piercing projectiles as well as heavy stones, some as heavy as a man. But while Alexander had to build and haul his weapons forward, the city walls were built with artillery firing platforms, mounts and towers. At each such station stood not only expert, practiced artillerymen but citizens whose militia service consisted of either making sure there was always a plentiful supply of ammunition for their weapon, as well as jars of olive oil to keep it lubricated. There were also more crews and militia than there were weapons, which meant a team could work their piece for an hour, then rest as a relief crew took over.

When Alexander did attack, the men at the catapults, gastraphetes, oxybeles, lithoboloi, and other missile weapons would fire with certainty and accuracy, and without need of ranging shots. Every dart, every bolt, every stone, and every boulder would hit their target – and hit it every time.

All that remained was for the Macedonians to arrive.

62

East of Myndos

IN SEARCH OF BARSINE

"The general should not have waited so long before sending his wife and family out of the war zone," muttered Klemes as he, Ari, and Dimitrios rode north and east from Myndos, into the rich hinterland away from the sea. "And why send us three Greeks, who must travel so far, when he has an entire army at his beck and call?"

"Is all of this griping because of our mission, or is it just because you hate riding so much?" jibed Ari.

"More of the later than the former, but a bit of both, to be honest," admitted Klemes. "Besides, damn it Ari, I'm a physician, not a cavalry scout! I belong in a surgery, in a nice, clean, warm city, and not on a dusty road in the middle of nowhere, bouncing about on some stinking, old flea-bitten nag."

"Tell me what you really think, physician," said Ari jokingly in response to yet more grumbling by his friend's brother. "Nobody forced you to come along, you know. You could surely find some fat old rich ladies who need tending to...or maybe even a queen. I hear that this Ada pays well. Then again, wouldn't that get a bit boring? Grouse all you want, Klemes, but you know that deep down you love this..."

"What!" shouted Klemes. "What do you mean? What is there to love, up to my elbows in bloody intestine or sawing off limbs?"

"It's all in the challenge, and you know it. I've heard you talk about what you do. Where better to learn your craft than on a battlefield? Has to be better than digging up dried out, maggot-filled corpses or looking at drawings of...."

"Quiet, the pair of you," said Dimitrios, turning around on his own horse to address the two. "You may not be cavalry scouts, but Alexander surely has his own out here. And the way you two are going about it, they'd have to be deaf not to hear us. So keep it down. We've got a job to do, and it's an important one."

Klemes scowled at the chastisement from his younger brother, but Ari just smiled, pleased to be on horseback rather than limping about on his bad leg. Although neither he nor Dimitrios were accomplished horsemen, they each had spent more time in the saddle than Klemes. While not the manner of travel to which they were accustomed, even a bumpy ride on a horse beat a long, slow march up country.

And what a country it was – and it was up, both geographically and geologically from the port where they had landed.

"What I don't understand," mumbled Klemes, is why he made us get off that perfectly fine ship back in Myndos. The port is at the far western end of the peninsula, with Halicarnassos to the east and south. We either should have been set down much farther up the main coast, perhaps a little below Miletos, and cut in land from there, or otherwise have gone to the capital with the rest of them, and strike out from there."

Dimitrios sighed, slowed his horse and allowed his brother to catch up before answering.

"We couldn't get off the ship on the coast, because all along the coastline, from Miletos to the south, was already in the hands of the Macedonians. And the general figured if we got to Halicarnassos we'd never get out, for the Macedonians were heading there fast to lay siege. This way we sneak along the back of the peninsula, heading north and east while the Macedonians head south and west. If we're lucky, we should be able to sneak behind them, then shoot out north-northeast into the interior."

"And you know all of this because...why?" asked a doubting Klemes.

"Because, dear brother, I have learned how to read a map."

"And just where did you get that map?" scoffed Klemes.

Dimitrios let out a sigh as started his explanation. "Over the last few years, Memnon has had scouting parties mapping routes all over this part of Asia. He knew the Macedonians were coming, and felt he would have an advantage not only if he knew the ground but also where all the roads lead and how long it takes to get from here to there..."

"...and back again?" Ari interrupted.

"Yes, there and back again, although to be honest," the captain said quite seriously and with a sigh, "once we find Barsine, I doubt we will be heading back southwest to Halicarnassos. After all, by then the entire Macedonian army will be between us and the city. We'll probably have to head farther south, down the coast, and get a ship back to the city."

"Why?" asked Klemes.

"Why what?"

"Why go to Halicarnassos at all? You want us to take a ship into another city that will be under siege? We just escaped from one butcher's yard. We'd just be putting our heads back into a trap."

Dimitrios was about to answer, but Ari did it for him.

"Because your brother, my friend, here, wants the general to know his family is safe. And rather than send a message, he wants to tell him personally. Besides," he added with a smile, "Alexander will be there, too, and if the ultimate purpose of our adventure is all about fighting Alexander, well..."

If "fighting Alexander" – or at least his men – is what Ari sought, he did not have long to wait. A bit after mid-day, they stumbled upon a dismounted pair of Prodromoi, the elite scouts recruited from the finest and smartest of Macedonia's light horsemen. Although they could take up the lance and hold their own against any cavalry in the line of battle, the Prodromoi were better used in other duties, duties that required independent thinking and often even individual initiative. As much mounted spies as mounted scouts, the Prodromoi were rarely caught by surprise – and this was not one of those rare times. The scouts had seen the Greeks coming, and the two that Dimitrios encountered were but the bait meant to lure him and his party into a trap.

Suddenly and without warning, the two Prodromoi he had spied leapt upon their horses, drew their swords and charged. Another, with javelin in hand, burst out of the brush on the right. A fourth came from the trees on the left. Outflanked on both sides and outnumbered as well, any sane soldier would have surrendered – but Dimitrios and Ari had only recently been captives of the Macedonians, and were in no mood to be such again. The scouts would have been most happy to have prisoners to interrogate and to bring back to the main army, and as such were aiming to dismount or disarm the three Greeks, rather than to kill them.

Neither Dimitrios nor Ari suffered from any such limitations: they fought back, and fought back to kill.

As his brother and friend drew their own swords and turned their horses to each face their attackers, Klemes kicked his heels hard into the flanks of his nag, held on with both hands and, together, rider and mount bowled headlong into the first of the Prodromoi. Both men and their horses tumbled to the ground, but as that was Klemes' plan, he was back up on his feet much more quickly than his antagonist. Unarmed except for a small knife he wore at his belt, Klemes grabbed his heavy wooden medical case with both hands and swung it like a bat, knocking his foe back down as he tried to rise. Satisfied that this enemy soldier was down and out, Klemes turned about just as Dimitrios was being pulled from his horse. Klemes ran toward the melee screaming like a harpy and swung his case once more, which shattered, spilling medical instruments and medicines all about while knocking the enemy rider from his mount. At least Dimitrios could now wrestle his single opponent on the ground, and if Klemes knew anyone who could hold his own in such a tussle, it was his brother.

That left just Ari to worry about, and as Klemes, now breathless, turned his attention in that direction, he saw that he need not have been concerned. Ari had stabbed one of the scouts in the side, wounding the fellow so severely that the rider turned his horse about and fled. The young Greek turned about and charged the other rider, who was desperately trying to parry Ari's savage sword strokes. When his badly injured companion rode off, he, too, gave his horse his heels and set off to join his friend in his escape. As for the scouts on the ground, Dimitrios broke the neck of the one he was wrestling, then finished off the other with a slash of his sword to the neck.

Bloodied, gasping for breath and barely able to stand, the three Greeks soon collapsed to the ground.

"We have to get the horses," Ari said between breaths.

"Not until I pick up all the pieces from my medical kit," replied Klemes. "If you are truly determined to put us back in harm's way, well, I'll need my knives, lancets, splints, and medicines."

"Then you two go about that," said Dimitrios as he began to rise up. "You'd only spook the beasts, muttering and scowling and limping about, so I'll go round them up. But hurry, because these scouts are sure to have friends – and are sure to be missed. We need to be far away from here when they come looking for these lads."

63

Halicarnassos

THE PROBE

While Dimitrios was trying to sneak around behind the Macedonians, Alexander and his generals had already set up their war machines around Halicarnassos.

"This is not a proper siege, and cannot be without a navy!" objected Parmenion as Alexander placed little wooden soldiers upon a crude map of the target city. "We have them surrounded on only three sides – which means they can come and go as they like on the fourth: the sea. Let me remind you that it was Nicanor's assault on the harbor and beaches of Miletos that allowed us to break through the city walls from the land side. That is one less toy for you to play with," he added as he angrily swept the wooden pieces from the table.

Had Black Cleitos not placed his frightening bulk between the king and the old general, Alexander most assuredly would have killed his father's longtime comrade. Ptolemy and the general's sons hurriedly escorted the old gentleman from the tent, while Hephaestion worked to cool the king's fiery temper, but with little effect.

"One day he will push me too far," simmered Alexander, "and I will take out his other eye and break his legs, leaving him a cripple to crawl about and beg for his supper – if I let him live at all! Who the hell does he think he is that..."

"He knows exactly who he is, my King," said Cleitos sternly. "He is the senior soldier in the army. Your late father's best friend, closest companion and most trusted adviser. Parmenion has the unwavering respect and admiration of the army, and that," added Cleitos with a broad grin, "is why he thinks he can get away with being an insubordinate old son-of-a-bitch. It is a honor he has earned...and paid for with more than just an eye."

Cleitos' attempt to make his king laugh did just the opposite; Alexander did not simply go into a rage – he erupted into it. Breaking free of Hephastion's calm grip, Alexander thrashed about the tent, kicking, and throwing, and knocking about anything he could – from stools and tables to lamps and servants. A human maelstrom, Alexander became a tempest in human form, as violent and angry as Poseidon on his worst day. His rage unsatisfied, Alexander rushed from the tent, grabbed a spear from one of the guards at its entrance and hurled it with all his might – but fortunately little of his skill – at Parmenion. The old general turned about just as the missile landed at his feet. He shrugged his shoulders and returned the insult with a gesture no less pointed, if somewhat less lethal, than the one hurled at him by the king. His sons in tow, Parmenion mounted a waiting steed and rode off to inspect the lines.

"I am sick and tired of being schooled by that blabbering old shit," spat Alexander, his spittle nearly hitting Cleitos, who again had put himself in the king's path. "I want you to put him under arrest...no, put him in chains, and then chain him to a post in the middle of the camp! Thinks he can instruct me in how to run my war! This is about my destiny! Not his! I swear I will whip him myself until his skin is..."

"Enough!" shouted Cleitos in a tone he used only on the drill field, and one that every recruit knew meant he had had all that he would take. "Go back into your tent and calm yourself down, Alexander," he said sternly, trusting to the habit of obedience he had inculcated in Alexander over the many years of the king's not long past youth. "It is unseemly for you to act this way...and especially in front of the men," he added quietly. "It undermines their confidence to see you two go at it like this, and on the eve of battle at that."

Alexander, his face still bright red, was about to respond and respond quite unpleasantly when he was distracted by a mighty roar of trumpets and drums, and the sight of hundreds of men racing to grab their weapons.

"It's the Persians!" several men shouted as they dashed about in confusion. "They've come out of the city! They're attacking our siege lines!"

"Damn that man!" screamed Alexander in a rage.

"Damn who?" asked Cleitos. "Surely this isn't Parmenion's doing..."

"No, no, no! Not Parmenion you great big dolt!" shouted Alexander as he began to throw yet another tantrum, "Memnon! He's trying to do what he tried at Miletos! He's out to burn our siege engines again! Why can't that man just sit behind his walls and take his medicine like any decent general under siege! Quick, Hephaestion, my armor and my horse!"

As Hephaestion nodded and prepared to comply with Alexander's last order, he said a silent prayer of thanks to whatever god had inspired Memnon to choose this exact moment to attack. Cleitos caught his eye, nodding as if to acknowledge that he, too, was sending a similar missive to the heavens. If nothing else, the attack had at the very least served to distract Alexander and prevent him from doing something that both Hephaestion and Cleitos knew would destroy the army, or at least tear the guts out of it. As Cleitos made to follow and protect the king in battle, he saw that Parmenion and his sons had also heard the trumpets blare, and were marshalling their battalions as if the row with the king had never occurred.

Despite Alexander's curse upon Memnon for again trying what he had tried at Miletos, the king was not entirely correct. Yes, Memnon was once again trying to destroy Alexander's siege engines, but this time he was using a weapon at which the Persians excelled: the cavalry. At Miletos, with the broken ground, outer layers of ruined houses, and the great expanse of tombs, Memnon could never dream of deploying more than a handful of horsemen. But here, with the great, flat open plain between the city and the siege lines, the Persian cavalry could do what they did best: ride fast, shoot fast, race back, and do it all over again. Some hurled javelins, others shot bows, and all raised a cloud of dust that helped hide the second part of the attack force: the thick column of infantry marching out of the Myndos Gate on the western face of the city, a company of Immortals in the lead.

Memnon led the cavalry himself, trusting the infantry assault to Ephialtes with his Greek hoplites and Hydarnes with the Immortals. The cavalry was the smoke to their fire, the distraction – if a deadly one – that would draw the Macedonians to him while his foot soldiers did the real work. Memnon made a particular point of showing himself and shouting challenges in which he referred to himself by name, trusting word would soon reach Alexander of his presence on the battlefield. The cavalry could not leap the trenches and piles of earth the Macedonians had dug to protect their siege engines, at least not as long as the defenders held their line. But they could ride up close enough to force the Macedonians to take cover and keep them occupied on the eastern side of the city – in a sense hitting the Macedonians with a right-handed jab while preparing to swing a much harder blow with their left.

Alexander, his blood still up from his argument with Parmenion, took the bait. Memnon soon spied the king's bright helmet with its twin plumes, along with those of his Royal Companions, as they rushed to the battle line. Alexander had left many places along the line where wagons could be pulled back to expose openings, and where wooden bridges could be quickly laid to allow the besiegers quick and easy access to the open field between them and the city. It was through these openings Alexander was sending his own cavalry – and it was opposite those that, hidden by the cavalry and the dust they kicked up, Memnon had set up blocks of infantry. A line of men with tall tower shields protected two ranks of spearmen, who in turn were backed up by four ranks of archers. Set up in a horseshoe formation opposite each opening, they were set to catch the Macedonians in a deadly cross fire as they crossed those bridges. When the Macedonian horses thundered onto the wooden bridges, the Persian cavalry drew back to the right and left and through a gap left in the horseshoe by their infantry – a gap that the well-drilled Persian foot closed up as if slamming shut a door.

Massacre is perhaps too harsh a word for what happened next, but to say the Macedonian cavalry was decimated is too weak; surprise, slaughter, and stinging rebuke are more appropriate descriptions. Alexander, his initial headstrong and injudicious orders to attack having cost him dearly, was soon sobered by the blood spilled by his precious Companions, who had led those charges. As Parmenion and his sons brought up the battalions of well-ordered pikes, he coolly fed them into the fray. Although the Persian archers took a deadly toll of the lightly armored pikemen, the shieldbearers and spearmen to their front could not hold or even slow down the relentless Macedonian marching machine that bore down upon them. Memnon turned his cavalry to harry them, but that was all they could do, as Parmenion, with practiced care, ordered the files on the left and right of his columns to turn and face the Persian horse – none of whose beasts could be convinced to ride in close to the hedge of spear points that confronted them.

Ephialtes and Hydarnes, too, had fared well at first, but as the Macedonian heavy infantry moved to blunt their attack, they, like the cavalry and archers under Memnon, had to give way. At a signal from Orontobates, whose role had been to act as a coordinator and to pass communications between the wings, the infantry began a steady, orderly withdrawal back toward the city. What small groups of Macedonian horsemen broke into the plain to harass them were quickly convinced to retire, as they came under the fire of the artillery mounted on and set up behind the city walls. That, too, was Orontobates contribution to the attack.

"We almost had them," Ephialtes said later as he and the other commanders met in Memnon's headquarters.

"At least we bled them," added Hydarnes. "Even if Alexander does not show more caution when he next comes at us, I suspect his men and his generals will be a bit less enthusiastic."

"To the contrary," replied Memnon. "The young king will spin this as a victory – and by most measures it is, for we did give up the field. I know him all too well," continued the general. "If anything, he is likely to become even more overconfident, and see in our repulse further evidence of his invincibility, and yet another affirmation of his destiny for greatness. And that," Memnon said with a smile, "that is what I am counting on."

64

Into the Interior

RIDING FOR BARSINE

Dimitrios, Klemes and Ari did not linger long after their narrow victory over the Prodromoi patrol. They paused only as long as it took to loot the bodies and round up the enemy's horses, after which they rode east as hard and as fast as their mounts would allow. They wanted to get as far away as possible from Alexander's army, but after three days of punishing travel the horses gave out. Their hooves were too badly worn to withstand the pavement of the Royal Road, which was still some distance away, let alone carry them across the rugged and often rocky ground overland. To rest the horses until their hooves were ready would mean at least a three or four day break, during which they would be easy as well as suspicious prey for the Macedonian patrols and local bandits.

Neither, however, could they just abandon them and move along on foot. Ari's bad leg and Klemes' worse temperament would severely limit their progress, which would be slow enough even at a marching pace, with only Dimitrios able to sustain. Although none of the trio were much experienced with horses, Klemes, being the physician, offered a possible solution.

"We can't ride the horses, but we can make the ground softer for them," he told his brother.

"And just what kind of magic trick or prayer to the gods will make such a thing happen," Dimitrios responded with a laugh. "I thought you were a physician, not a high priest!"

"Damn it, Dimitrios, I am a physician, and as a physician I am telling you there is a way to make the ground softer for the horses. We take the horse blankets and spare cloaks and clothes we have and we cut them up, make bags and fill them with soft dirt, then wrap and tie them around the hooves of each of the horses. That way when they do walk, their hooves are cushioned – thus making the ground softer for them."

"Then we can ride on?" asked Ari.

"No. I would not suggest it. But we could lead them at a walking pace until we could find someplace where we could trade them or sell them for new mounts. They are too valuable to be left behind, and they can still manage to bear our kit – just not ourselves."

"That will make it fairly slow going for a while," Dimitrios said, thinking out loud, "but it is better than trying to go across country entirely on foot. All right, brother," he decided, "I bow to your medical opinion. So let's get to work..."

After two very slow days in the back country, they came upon a rather large estate on the outskirts of Mylasa, a sizable farming town to the north-north east of Halicarnassos.

"Memnon is well-regarded around these parts," Dimitrios added when outlining his plan on how to approach the estate. "I am sure if I but mention his name, we would find welcome. After all, we could all use a soft bed, a hot meal, and a safe place to rest for a night."

Klemes cleared his throat, and quite noticeably, that being a sure sign that he thought otherwise.

"Now what, dear brother?" asked Dimitrios with a weary sigh.

"These land owners may not be as friendly as you think," answered the physician. "Memnon represents the old order – and he has been chased the length of the land, losing battles and cities to Alexander.

The rich can see which way the wind is blowing, and may not wish to do anything that will put them in the bad graces of the Macedonians – like taking a string of their cavalry horses in trade. They might even pretend to be nice, then sell us out to curry favor with Alexander's crowd...and that crowd is getting bigger every day, and you know it."

"So, you have a better yarn to spin?"

"Why can't we just be three wise men traveling to the east? Better yet...I am a physician, after all, and you, Ari, can be my young servant..."

"And what would that make me?" scowled Dimitrios.

"Why, my bodyguard, of course" Klemes smiled. "That would explain your helmet, armor, weapons, and such. And we can be Ionian Greeks, as there are enough about this area, rather than Thebans, let alone mercenaries in Memnon's pay."

"He's got a point there," chirped in Ari. "Although that means you are going to have to do all of the talking for us, Klemes, and you are not known for being especially charming..."

"Charming! Charming!" huffed Klemes. "I can do 'charming.' Just watch me!"

"Well then," scoffed Ari, "when you get to the big house down there, see if you can charm up some breakfast, because I'm starving...."

As the three men made their way down toward the main house on the estate, several of the field hands ran to tell their master of the approaching strangers. Within minutes, half a dozen armed men came out to greet them. They were not openly hostile nor were they brandishing their weapons, but those weapons were close at hand, close enough to convince Dimitrios that perhaps Klemes' plan was indeed better than his own.

"What do you want, strangers?" the man at the front of the group, and obviously their captain, asked, with more caution than malice.

"We are weary travelers, lord," said Klemes in a far more obsequious manner than Dimitrios had ever heard him speak. "Our horses are healthy and hale, but, alas, spent from so many days on the road. We were hoping to find someone to whom we could trade them for fresh mounts...and, of course, are willing to sweeten the deal with some of the very few coins we carry."

The guards mumbled something amongst each other that the Greeks could not make out, but at least seemed a little less threatened by the strangers.

"Our lord is not here," replied the captain. "But his steward has full authority in these matters. Wait here and I will see if he is amenable.

"Hmmph!" mumbled Klemes. "Such a lack of manners. Man couldn't at least offer us a place in the shade, a cup of water, anything?"

"Now, now, brother," whispered Dimitrios. "They're just wary of strangers, that's all...and at least they haven't drawn their weapons."

"Aye," murmured Ari, "and after what we've been through these last few months, that practically feels like a welcome."

The officer soon returned, along with a young boy and a serving girl, each of whom was carrying a pitcher of water and a ladle.

"The boy here will take your horses and let them graze with ours, while the steward invites you to slake your thirst and refresh yourself out back in our master's paradiso," he spoke directly to Klemes, and to Klemes alone. "As for your servants, they are welcome to sit in the shade. The girl will see to their needs."

Although Dimitrios did not much care to be referred to as a mere servant, it was the role Klemes had created for him, for what was a hired bodyguard but a servant? Then again, it was a relief of sorts for a change, not having to be the one making all of the decisions or putting on his best manners to deal with a stranger. As he sat in the shade, he suddenly realized just how tired he had become, and as such was much happier being offered cool water by a lovely young girl than having to be nice to some gray-haired old steward. Ari, on the other hand, felt his tiredness wash away as the pretty girl gave him a blushing smile.

"I've got a good feeling about this," he said to himself with a smile of his own. "A really good feeling about this."

65

Halicarnassos

ROCKS

A lexander prepared his next assault with the meticulous care to detail of a master builder laying out and constructing a city. He placed and sighted every siege engine personally. He supervised the digging of the advanced works and hand-picked the men and officers for each of the leading assault parties. He drilled them individually and incessantly – and then he changed everything and did it all over again. Twice.

During this week of preparation, the city of Halicarnassos was subjected to a bombardment that was to that of Miletos as a hailstorm was to a summer shower. Memnon and his generals were hard-pressed to shore up and repair the damage. Had it not been for their complete command of the sea that allowed for the evacuation of the wounded and the arrival of replacements, the attrition would have worn them down. As it was, even with the steady stream of reinforcements by sea, the garrison was close to being decimated. If not for the liberal disbursement of extra rations to the troops and to the citizens of Hali-carnassos, all gratis and at the general's expense, morale would have cracked as badly as had the walls.

"When do you think they will come again?" Governor Orontobates asked Memnon.

"Today," replied the general.

"How do you know that for certain?" asked the governor, surprised to the point of incredulousness.

"It's in the wind," Ephialtes jumped in.

"What do you mean 'in the wind?'" said the governor with a disbelieving sneer.

"He means literally 'in the wind,'" answered Memnon. "Can't you smell it?"

"Smell what?"

"The burning meat. The Macedonians are making a sacrifice to the gods. Judging by the smoke and the smell, they must be slaughtering and roasting a whole herd. Probably white bulls, and white steers, and even white cows – that's the kind of thing Alexander thinks pleases the gods most. Makes for quite a show, too," added Memnon. "All that living white mass splattered with blood, and the bright red and yellow flames and the sweet smell of roasting meat..."

"Barbarians," chuffed the governor disapprovingly. "I suppose next you'll tell me they paint themselves with the blood of the slaughtered animals, like some wild men from the hills!"

"No, Governor," Ephialtes laughed. "They drink it – fresh and warm from the slit necks of the living animals. Honors the beast, gets the men used to the taste of blood, and all that."

"Are such things common in Greece – or just in Macedonia, and wherever else from where Alexander recruits his savages?" said the governor rhetorically. "I cannot believe a civilized land such as ours has been unable to repel these repulsive brutes!"

"We will this time, I swear it," said Memnon calmly, as if asking for a little more water for his wine.

"And what, pray tell, makes you so certain?" scoffed the governor. "You've been wrong before – and several times before. Need I remind you of Miletus?"

Memnon reached out and gently put his hands on the governor's shoulders so as to draw him closer and force the Persian to look him directly in the eyes.

"This is not Miletos. I never promised to hold Miletos, merely to hold it long enough to bleed Alexander, and to buy time."

"Time for what!" the governor nearly spat in his face.

"Time for this. For Halicarnassos. This is the rock where I will break Alexander – and tie him to it while the great king brings in an army from the east."

"And what army is that?" the governor replied disbelievingly. "I have heard nothing of any such 'army'."

Memnon took a deep breath, filling his chest and puffing himself out to his full breadth and height, and answered the doubting governor.

"That is because you are just the governor of Halicarnassos, my dear Orontobates. You know as much as you need to know. I, on the other hand, am married to a princess of the imperial house, and where you deal in provinces I deal in empires. I am the strong right arm of the king of kings, and those who serve as his eyes and ears also serve as mine. The king is gathering not just an army, but a host, a great mobilization from all over Persia. He himself is returning from putting down rebellions in the east, and as he comes, Darius is opening his arms to gather up and draw to him bowmen and elephants from India, horse-archers from the steppes, camel-riders from the desert and fierce foot soldiers from the mountains, as well as the armored cavalry of the lords and nobles of pure blood. Even more, he brings with him a new type of soldier – the kardakes – combinations of heavy spearmen and light archers, like the mighty Assyrians of old raised to create their vast empire. And," he added in a particularly strong voice while nodding his head toward the tall imperial guard captain in the corner, "the Immortals. All 10,000 of them."

"Wh...wh...when and where is he bringing this host?" sputtered the satrap, obviously surprised by this news.

"I am not sure exactly when, but as to where, well, that depends."

"Depends on what?" asked the governor.

"On us. On holding Halicarnassos. On tying Alexander to us for weeks, months, maybe even a year. He thinks he has us under siege? The boy king may be a brilliant soldier," said Memnon with a sign of respect for Alexander,"but his focus, while intense, is narrow. He only sees what is directly in front of him. The lad never could read a map, let alone understand just how big of an empire he has invaded. We will teach him."

"And then, what, on into Macedon and even Greece itself?"

"For you, the king and others, perhaps, but for me..." Memnon said with a deep, longing, sigh, "for me it means I may finally get to go home. Home, and my children, and Barsine."

As Ephialtes and Memnon had predicted, Alexander did indeed attack that morning. All along the horseshoe-shaped front, his artillery opened up with as intense a bombardment as had ever been launched in Asia. For two hours his crews kept up a relentless, furious, and well-directed barrage of rocks and stones, fire pots and iron projectiles. The Macedonian crews worked at the double, and at the end of those terrible two hours, as the energy of the siege engine crews finally began to falter, Alexander gave the word for the assault parties to leave their trenches.

Horns blared, drums beat and whistles blew all along the line. A score of tightly packed groups of assault troops went up and over the top and into the open ground between their lines and the smoking, crumbling walls of the city. Behind them rolled massive towers, covered in ox hide and packed with archers and more assault troops. Another wave, the heavy infantry in their formations, formed up ready to follow – to climb the towers and ladders once the advance parties had reached the wall.

It was an amazing, intimidating, and awe-inspiring sight; one designed to instill terror and to squash all hopes of survival, let alone victory, among the garrison. That is what it was designed to do; that is what through his meticulous planning Alexander had intended it to do. And that is what it would have done – had the city been held by any other commander than Memnon. What Alexander had forgotten in his surety of success was that he was using what he had learned of siege warfare against the man who had taught him. A man who had not only taught him about sieges, but who had been attacking and defending cities for two decades – a man who taught his student a great deal about siege warfare, but not everything. Some lessons could only be learned from experience.

Alexander's massive assault was met with an equally massive response. The walls had been reinforced and so absorbed the pounding, and while crenelations crumbled and battlements broke, they did the task they were designed for: to shield the weapons behind the walls and inside the towers. These Memnon had kept silent during the barrage, their crews resting safe in deep tunnels and strong castles inside the city. Only when Alexander's men stepped off into the open did they scramble out of their protected positions to man their weapons. While Alexander's mighty rock-hurlers and bolt-throwers had expended their munitions against stone, Memnon's had a much softer target: men. Men out in the open, many unable to protect themselves with shields as their hands were busy carrying ladders to raise against the walls, bundles of sticks to fill the ditches or wooden ramps to bridge them, or were hauling the great towers and battering rams across the field. Into this mass of moving and quite unprotected flesh Memnon unleashed hell.

Almost every stone, every bolt, every jar of flaming oil or burning pitch found its target. The falling boulders smashed whole platoons like a fist. Storming parties found themselves caught in a storm of Memnon's making, as fire and death rained down upon them. Even the great towers shuddered from the impact of mighty stones, each of which struck with unholy accuracy. The assault, which had been prepared and practiced over and over again for 20 days, collapsed in 20 minutes. Not even Alexander's veterans could take that kind of direct, accurate, and intense fire, especially when it came from an enemy they could not see, let alone strike at. Alexander did not call off the assault – he did not have to; his men simply lost heart – or gave in to their natural desire to live another day.

"How could this happen!" sputtered Alexander, as Hephaestion and

Ptolemy struggled to restrain their friend and king from riding into the maelstrom. "My army turning tail! My men unmanned by a few pebbles and some sharp sticks! Cowards!"

"They are not cowards, my lord," said Parmenion as he rode up, his cloak torn and his horse and armor splattered with dirt and blood. "No man can cross that plain, not against such deadly fire. I have never seen the like. It seems like every projectile finds its mark, as if guided by the hands of the gods to the very spot where it will do the most harm and kill the most men."

Alexander, in a rage, was not calmed by n report. To the contrary, he fell into an apoplectic frenzy – and one so deep and powerful that he could not be restrained. Shaking off the hands of his friends he spurred his horse, drew his sword and screamed a horrific battle cry as he charged into the retreating mass of men.

"Turn around! Turn around! Would you run away while your king goes forward! Turn around, damn you! Turn around and follow me!"

The charismatic king pulled off his helmet so his men could better see him, and whether inspired by his presence or simply shamed by his courage, many of the Macedonians did turn around, grit their teeth, and go back once more into that field – but not for long.

Alexander felt the accuracy of Memnon's fire first hand. Knocked from his mount by the glancing blow from a rock he fell, his shoulder dislocated and in such pain that even the adrenaline that had fueled his rash charge could not assuage. A group of the Companions Cavalry saw him fall and, braving the heavy fire, rode out into the deadly field, the survivors hurtling from their horses to cover the king with their shields and their bodies. Half-swooning from the pain and shock, Alexander could offer no resistance as his guards struggled to carry him from the fray. He was alert enough, however, to notice something quite peculiar as he was taken back to the safety of the siege line.

The rocks. The rocks were painted – but only on the side facing the city. Some were splattered with red paint, others with yellow or white...why? What did it mean? What was it about those rocks?

Outside Mylasa

I HAD A FARM IN ASIA MINOR...

A ri awoke with a start, as he had been certain it had all been a dream, but here he was, in the shade in a grove of fruit trees, with a beautiful serving girl offering him cool water, a plate of olives, and some cheese. Never in his life, and especially not since war had come to Thebes, had anyone waited upon him, let alone anyone so lovely. It was all he could do to remember to thank her, so entranced was he by the softness in her eyes and the gentle way in which she performed such simple tasks. It had been a long time – too long – since Ari had seen a woman who wasn't selling herself to soldiers in a camp or teasing them in a tavern. This was different – this girl was different – and he had no idea what to do next.

Fortunately – or not, depending on whose point of view – Ari was spared the embarrassment of doing or saying the wrong thing (or perhaps doing or saying the right thing) by Klemes.

"Ah, there you are, you lazy little bugger," the physician said as he came through the trees. "I am sorry to interrupt whatever this is, but the captain has been looking for you. You do remember the captain," he added with sly nod, "our traveling companion and, more importantly, our commanding officer? If you can tear yourself away from your...

er... distractions...that is" he added with a knowing smirk and at least one raised eyebrow.

Embarrassed, disappointed, but also a little relieved by Klemes's sudden appearance, the still-groggy young archer struggled to get to his feet. As he began to put his weight on his bad leg, it suddenly buckled, but before Ari fell he found himself caught in the arms of the serving girl. He did not know if he should be ashamed of his infirmity or, in this rare instance, feel happy for it. The unexpected pleasure of her hands upon him just made whatever thoughts and feelings he was having start to swirl about in his head.

Then she smiled at him, and helped him to stand, and all just seemed right with the world – and for the first time in a long, long time. Even Klemes' snarky interruption couldn't take that away from him, not this time.

"I'm coming," Ari said with a sigh, the girl's hands still on his arms as if to steady him. She smiled at Ari again, then released her hold on him, backed away and bent down to retrieve her water jar and the basket of olives and cheese. With a little laugh she scurried away in the direction of the farm house, pausing briefly to look over her shoulder to see if Ari was watching her – which he was, as she knew he would be.

"If you are finished mooning over that little serving girl," Klemes whispered, careful that only Ari could hear, "do you think you could move it along a bit. My brother is waiting, and while I don't mind making him wait for me, I'd rather not have you getting into the same habit. So come along, and remember why we came here. There will be other girls, you know," he added with a sudden and entirely unexpected touch of kindness. "There are always other girls."

By the time Ari and Klemes had reached the main house, Dimitrios was already deep in his conversation with the steward. An older fellow, not yet but on the verge of becoming frail, the steward talked slowly, as if each sentence were a heavy weight that took time, and care, and a great deal of effort to lay out. He spoke in a local dialect that combined bits of Greek, and Persian, and other languages, and Dimitrios was thankful that the steward did speak so slowly, for even so the Theban captain was struggling to keep up with his host.

"What's he saying, Dimitrios?"

"I am not entirely certain of all of the details, but he said something about a great lady and her entourage making their way through the area. Most of the nobles and other great landowners are either with the army in Halicarnassos or have fled to their estates farther east, leaving their lands in the care of stewards like this fellow. He is very concerned for her safety, and for the safety of any who travel about. Since the lords departed, the bandits and raiders they and their retainers had kept in their place are becoming more active. The steward even offered to hire us on as guards, as he fears that these roving bands will try to steal his master's goods and carry off the servants..."

"No! We can't let that happen, Dimitrios! We should take him up on his offer..."

Dimitrios was as taken aback by Ari's unexpected outburst as he was puzzled by his reason for doing so.

"He's just mooning over one of those servants," said Klemes. "Pay no mind to what the lad says. This great lady the steward is talking about, do you think it's...her?" he asked, pausing to catch himself before mentioning Barsine by name.

"Perhaps. He doesn't appear to know the particulars, but from what he has told me, it's a pretty good guess that she's the one we were sent to find. If my Persian were better, I'd be able to find out some more details, but..."

"So...so I guess that means we won't be staying on?" asked Ari, the disappointment evident in his tone.

"No. Hardly. If anything," Dimitrios added, "it means we need to get a move on, and find this woman before she runs afoul of any of those unsavory characters that might be about. As a matter of fact, he said one of his men saw a gang pass by last night, and they were in an awful hurry."

Ari sighed in disappointment, while Klemes just groaned. "I had hoped for a day or two at least to rest," he added as he stretched and cracked his back. "But if as you say..."

"I don't see as how we have much choice, do you? As much as he wants us to stay on as guards, the steward is willing to make a trade for fresh horses. They aren't of the same quality as these mounts, since the lord cleaned out the stables and paddocks to take the best horses with him, but at least it will be better than walking."

"And those ruffians his man says he saw last night, did he mention which way they went?" asked Klemes.

Dimitrios pointed northeast. "He says they went that-away."

Ari looked back every few minutes as they rode away, his mind and heart still back at the farm. Dimitrios didn't notice, being at the head of their small column, and while Klemes did, his backside was already too sore from bouncing on the bony back of his mount to bother saying anything.

"Do you think we'll ever come back here?" Ari asked the physician.

"I doubt it, but who knows?" replied Klemes, annoyed more at his uncomfortable ride than his riding companion. "Those bandits might be going after someone or something other than the 'great lady' the steward told Dimitrios about. Even if she is Barsine, and we do find her, we're supposed to see her safely to the east. And that's the opposite of the direction we just came from, and from your pretty little serving girl," he added, managing a little grin, despite his discomfort.

"A fellow can dream, can't he?" sighed Ari.

"Dream on your own time," grumbled Klemes. "We've got a job to do. I don't want you falling off that sorry excuse for a horse and breaking a leg or your neck, which you keep twisting to get yet one more damn look at...what? Do you think she's going to come running down the road after you?"

"Well, now that you mention it," replied Ari quite perkily, "I'm pretty sure that's her riding that pony back there."

"Well," grumbled Klemes, "I think it is. Damn, just what we don't need; another lovesick child."

67

Outside Halicarnassos

ALEXANDER'S CAMP

"Give them the lash, Ptolemy," Alexander scowled. "Give those prisoners the lash until their backs are raw and the white of their bones begins to show. And if they still haven't talked by then, pour vinegar and salt into their wounds – and whip them again. I want to know how Memnon is able to so effectively target us as we cross that plain."

"Perhaps, sire, it is sorcery...some kind of dark magic?" mumbled Hephaestion. "If that is the case, then whatever these poor souls can tell us won't be of much help."

"I don't care, Hephaestion. I want answers, and I suspect these scouts of his have them. And Ptolemy," said Alexander, turning to his companion, "get those answers. By the way, why am I not hearing them scream? I did not tell you to stop their torture, did I?"

"No, Alex...I mean, no, sire," said Ptolemy more obsequiously than usual.

"Then get back to it, man, get back to it. I want to hear them scream! I want Memnon inside his fortress across the plain to hear them scream! I want every man, woman, and child," Alexander sputtered, "in this camp and inside that city to hear them scream!"

Ptolemy saluted, bringing his fist to his heart, made a slight bow, and backed out of the king's tent. As he exited Alexander heard Ptolemy yell a command – and a curse – to his men to get back to their bloody work.

"Now, Hephaestion," said the king, still scowling in fury and frustration, "about that other matter."

"You mean Memnon's family?"

"Yes. So, what have our scouts and spies been able to find out? Do they know where this precious Barsine and her brood are hiding?"

"Not exactly, my King," Hephaestion said quietly.

"And what does 'not exactly' mean, Hephaestion? You've either found out where they are or not...so which is it?"

Hephaestion took a deep breath, drew himself up to look Alexander in the eye and answered "we are close to finding her, is what I mean, sire – and by that I mean we have discovered that she is on the move, going from one great estate to another. Even better, she is headed this way. Seems she can't bear to be parted from her husband any longer," Hephaestion added with a smile, "so all we have to do is wait for her to come to us – then we'll have her."

Alexander grit his teeth, dug his fingernails into his palms and, barely controlling his anger, slammed his fist onto his map table.

"So that would be a 'no,' then, Hephaestion?"

"Well, in a manner of speaking I suppose..."

"Hephaestion!" the king roared. "Dear, sweet Hephaestion. When I tell you to bring me the wife of Memnon, I mean now. Today. Not whenever she happens to wander into your lap. You say you have information as to her movements? Well, then, go and get her...and this time I mean you go – not your aides, not your lieutenants, not some hapless squadron commander of cavalry, but you. Personally. Find her. Bring her to me – and don't bother coming back until you do. Is that clear?" he added, taking Hephaestion's head between his hands. "Hephaestion," he repeated, this time quietly, almost whispering, but with iron in his voice, "don't disappoint me."

"I never have, Alexander," Hephaestion managed to reply, putting his own hands over those of the king. "And I never will."

"I suppose we should stop for a moment and let her catch up to us," Klemes said as he caught up to his brother and brought his mount to a halt.

"Who?" asked Dimitrios, who had been looking ahead, not back, as they rode.

"That girl," Klemes said pointing the young woman racing toward them on a fast horse. "The one from the farm. The one that was fawning all over our young friend."

"You think she stole the horse just to follow after him?" sighed Dimitrios. "We can't take in some runaway slave; we'll have to take her back."

"You know what Greeks do to escaped slaves, let alone those who steal a horse, don't you, brother? Imagine how much worse the Persians can be," said Klemes, concern for the young woman evident in his demeanor.

"That can't be helped," replied Dimitrios. "We may need to go back to that farm someday, and soon, so we had better send her back. Can't have the locals shutting us out for fear we will harbor runaways."

While the two brothers were discussing what to do with the girl once she caught up with them, Ari had turned his horse around and ridden back to meet her. As they closed the distance between each other, each drew on their reins to bring their mounts to a walk, until they were face to face.

"Take me with you!" the girl asked, breathing hard. "Please, take me with you!"

"You know we can't, as much as I'd love to," Ari replied, though it ached to say no to the girl, for he wanted nothing more in the world than to be in her company. "It's dangerous where we're going," he added. "You wouldn't be safe with us."

"I'd rather take that chance than go back to them," she replied. "You don't know what it's like, being a woman, and a slave."

"And what makes you think we would treat you any better?" said Dimitrios as he rode up.

"I don't know if you would treat me any better – but he would," she said with a big smile as she looked at Ari. "I just know he would."

Klemes let loose an uncharacteristic laugh as he saw Ari blush. "Yes, my dear girl, I dare say he would," he added as he let out another laugh. "What do you say, brother?"

Dimitrios tried to look like he was in charge. He tried very hard to be stern – but he couldn't. Any girl who made Ari blush and Klemes laugh had to be someone special. Still, he thought, this couldn't happen."

"Look, lass," Dimitrios said as kindly yet as steadily as he could, "we're just a pack of rough soldiers and..."

"Speak for yourself, brother! God damn it Dimitrios, I'm a physician, not a soldier! You know, first do no harm and all of that...she'd be perfectly safe with us, or at least with me, and you know it."

"Yes, Dimitrios," added Ari. "After all, who knows what they might do to her, trying to escape and steal a horse..."

"And to us," Dimitrios replied. "They're bound to come after her – or at least the horse – and we've got enough to worry about where we're going."

"Oh, don't worry about that, your honor," said the girl. "They won't be coming after me, or Lemi, here, for that matter," she added as she patted the horse on its neck and gave her a little kiss.

"Of course they will!" Dimitrios shot back. "Don't lie to me, girl. They will surely come after you and your, what did you call her, 'Lemi'?"

"Well, but not today – or tomorrow," she replied.

"And just why not?" asked Dimitrios, as he leaned over to grab her horse's reins.

"Because when I took Lemi, I let the rest of the horses out of the paddock and gave them a good fright. The master took the best horses with him – the others were mostly wild, or only partially broken. And they'll have to be run down and caught by men on foot – and that's going to take time. Speaking of which, we are wasting it sitting around here talking. So, can we please get going?"

"You have no idea where we are going," said Dimitrios.

"Well," she said with a laughter as she clicked her tongue and gave Lemi a little kick with her heels, "it has to be better than where I've been, so let's get going. Yah!" she concluded, as she and Lemi raced down the road in the direction the three men had been riding.

"This is all your fault," Dimitrios said to Klemes.

"How is it my fault, brother?" asked the physician. "It's the boy she's interested in, not me. If anyone's at fault it's Ari..."

"And how is this my fault?" the boy asked.

"Because you've got that...that face of yours," grumbled Dimitrios, "and that stupid, kind, trustworthy kind of face, that's why. This is just like that time with the girl in the tavern in Athens, or back at my father's wine shop in Thebes years ago..."

"No," said Ari, "this time it's different," he added, as he, too kicked his horse to gallop after the girl.

68

East of Mylasa

RIDE, SHE SAID, RIDE

"**G**ive the girl her due, she can ride," Klemes said with grudging respect – and surprise.

"She's obviously a Persian – they're taught to ride before they can walk," replied Dimitrios.

"But the Persians don't enslave their own," remarked Klemes. "Cyrus, the founder of their empire, abolished most forms of slavery 200 years ago."

"Well, maybe she's a debt slave..."

"No," replied Klemes. "Unlike Athens or Thebes, you can't sell yourself or your children into slavery, even temporary slavery, to pay off a debt. The only slaves they allow are those taken in battle from rebels or remote tribes."

"Well," said Dimitrios. "This empire has seen its share of rebels these last few years. Even Memnon and his brother were rebels once; then they won back their lands and ranks by helping the emperor put down a different gang of rebels."

"What are you two blabbering about," said Ari as he caught up with the brothers.

"We're trying to decide just who is this girl who seems so moon-struck by you," replied Dimitrios.

"Why don't you just ask her?" said Ari, rather matter-of-factually.

Klemes and Dimitrios stared blankly at each other, and then turned to give the same look to Ari.

"Well, I suppose one of us could..." said Dimitrios.

"Don't look at me, brother," said Klemes. "I'm a physician, not a match-maker. Besides, it's Ari she likes, so it's obviously Ari who should do the asking."

"I will," agreed Ari, "once I catch up to her. Damn! That girl can ride!"

"Rocks? That's all they said? After all of that torture?" Alexander asked Ptolemy, obviously both perturbed and disappointed in the results of the interrogation of the Persian scouts.

"That's all I could make out, Alexander. You know my Persian isn't very good..."

"But you had an interpreter with you, right? Well, didn't you?"

"Well, part of the time..." mumbled Ptolemy, while uneasily looking down at his own feet. "I mean, they held out a long time, and I didn't think..."

Alexander fought very hard not to lose his temper, but as Ptolemy could easily see, it was a losing battle. If anything, Alexander trying to not become angry was worse than Alexander getting angry. At least when he did scream, or yell, or berate someone, it passed quickly. When he held it in, as Ptolemy knew all too well after 20 years, Alexander tended to get very, very cold – and not a little bit scary.

"What the hell does 'rocks' mean?" the king asked his lieutenant. "The rocks they are shooting at us? Are they somehow different than the rocks we are shooting at them?"

"I can go have the men collect some and we can comp..."

"No! You idiot!" shouted Alexander, his rage near the boiling point out of pure exasperation. "I've seen the rocks they rain down on us. They're just like any other damn rocks. They fall, and tumble, and crush, and..."

The king suddenly paused. His rage giving way to something that was trying to fight its way to his tongue from deep within his memory. Rocks, rocks, rocks. What was it about rocks that he should know, he thought to himself.

"Think hard, think very, very hard," Alexander said, taking Ptolemy by the shoulders and staring directly into his eyes. "They had to say something else besides 'rocks.' Something, anything..."

"Well, now that you mention it..."

"Yes, Ptolemy, come on, what is it," said Alexander slowly, directly and trying to coax out whatever Ptolemy was struggling to recall.

"'Ghermez,' or 'qermez,' and 'sefeed' and some other words I didn't quite catch...or...."

Alexander's eyes lit up, and all trace of anger disappeared from his face. He took his hands from Ptolemy's shoulders and placed them on either side of his face, and then placed a kiss on each cheek.

"You great big oaf. You great, big, silly, beautiful oaf!"

"Huh?" said Ptolemy, completely caught by surprise at Alexander's sudden change in attitude.

"Those words mean 'red' and 'white,' in their language. And I imagine you also heard 'zard' and 'sabz' maybe, am I right?"

"I...I think so," mumbled Ptolemy, still thoroughly puzzled.

"Those are 'yellow' and 'green,' which you'd know if you had paid more attention to Aristotle when we were boys, instead of daydreaming about whatever or whoever you dreamed about back then."

"Frogs."

"What?" said Alexander.

"Frogs," repeated Ptolemy. "I always liked frogs. Wondered how they could jump so high and..."

"Aaargh! Enough about frogs! Ptolemy, you lumbering lummox. Those colors...those are the colors I saw painted on the rocks when we were under fire out in the plain!"

"So?"

"So, the rocks were painted on only one side – the side facing the city," explained Alexander.

"And what has that got to do with..."

"Think! Ptolemy, for once in your life, think! Memnon is using the rocks as aiming points. His men are able to hit us every time because they know exactly how far it is to their targets. I don't know if the different colors are for different ranges, or for different weapons...but that doesn't matter."

"Umm, all right...but how does that help us?"

"Ptolemy, you dear, sweet, thick-skulled bully boy," teased Alexander as he brought him closer again to hug and place a kiss on his cheek. "It helps us because tonight, when the sun goes down, you and your lads are going to sneak out there and move the rocks all about. Move them left, right, forward, back, any which way, I don't care and it doesn't matter – just as long as you move them enough...and switch a few about. Tomorrow we'll launch a probing attack, and then, Ptolemy..."

"Yes, my king?"

"Then we will see just where the rocks fall."

While Alexander was congratulating himself on finding the answer to one puzzle, Ari was working up the courage to ask the questions that would solve another: namely, just who this girl was who had invited herself to join their little group...and how could he convince his friends to let her stay?

They had ridden hard all day, at a pace set by the girl and her horse, Lemi. She had managed to stay ahead of the three men and their mounts, until she decided to rest Lemi at a shady spring by the side of the rough road. The girl knew horses, and not just because she could ride, but also, as Ari noted, because she was careful to let the horse cool down and nibble a little grass before letting her go to the watering hole.

That delay gave Ari time to ride up, dismount, and lead his own horse over to her. It also gave him time to decide how best to ask his questions, hopefully without making the girl angry or alarmed.

"You told us your horse's name," said Ari sheepishly as he walked up to the girl, "but you didn't give us yours."

"It's Halime," she answered without hesitation. "Halime from Mylasa."

"You weren't born a slave then, were you, not if you have a name...and not if you can ride and care for a horse like that."

"No. I was not born a slave – and technically, I am not one now – or at least I wasn't one. More of a prisoner, or a hostage, more correctly."

"A hostage? To whom, and for what?" asked Dimitrios, who had ridden up, dismounted, and led his horse to water just in time to hear Halime's answer.

"To the lord who owns that estate we just left. My father borrowed a great sum of money from him, and I am the, how do you say it, collateral for the loan. Part of the terms of its repayment are that I do whatever his steward would have me do – within the bounds of my and my family's honor, at least. Or at least that is how it is supposed to be, but..." she explained, her words trailing off to allow the men to fill in the rest of the details for themselves.

"I see," said Dimitrios, a bit embarrassed at what images were going through his mind. "So, you were not as well treated as your father had arranged, then?"

"Oh, at first I was," she replied as she used a hand to pull the tangles out of Lemi's lush, blonde main. "But as the weeks and then months dragged on, and there was no word from my father, or from the lord...well, the steward and his chief guard began to say things, and make jokes – although they weren't really jokes, if you take my meaning."

"That is understandable, a pretty young girl like yourself, with your obvious breeding and poise..."

"Men!" she sighed, interrupting Dimitrios' ramblings. "You are all alike, you really are, aren't you. Just because a girl likes to keep herself clean, braid her hair, and change her clothes every day or two, you think it's all for you – all because of you. Well, it isn't," she said, waving a finger at the captain and poking his chest.

"I'd, I'd, I'd never think that," said Ari nervously.

"No, of course you wouldn't," she replied, completely changing her tone and reaching out to brush the hair from his forehead. "I could tell right away that you were different. That's why I ran away with you. I knew the moment I saw you that you were a kind man; one of the good ones. And I was right, wasn't I?" she added with a little laugh and a smile – a smile that struck Ari as hard as if it had been a stone, and as soft and welcoming as if it had been a pillow.

"You said you have not heard from your father or the lord in a while? When did you last hear from them?" asked Dimitrios, trying to bring the conversation back around to where he could find the answers he sought.

"Many months ago. A rider came with a summons for the lord and all of his men to go north, and of course my father, and my brothers, they put on their armor, too, to ride with him. They were to join up with a greater lord. The last I heard, they were going to join the army that the great satrap Spithridates was raising to fight that Macedonian invader. You're soldiers, I can tell. You might have seen them? "

Dimitrios looked first at Ari, then at Klemes, and then back at Halime.

"Yes, Halime, we are soldiers, and, unfortunately, we were with that very army," the captain said quietly. "I think you should sit down. We've got some things to tell you. Have you ever heard of a river called the Granicos?"

69

Halicarnassos

THE QUEEN VISITS HER NEWLY
ADOPTED SON

The unexpected arrival of Queen Ada caused such a disruption in Alexander's camp that all preparations for the next attack were brought to a screeching halt. The army shuddered, much the way a horse about to charge would if its rider suddenly yanked back on its reins or an arrow would fly off wildly if its bowstring broke. The parade – for that is what it was – of Queen Ada threw the camp into complete disorder. Not merely because of its sudden and completely unexpected interruption of the army's routine, but also because of the handfuls of gold and silver coins that the queen's servants showered upon the soldiers as they passed.

No soldier ever has enough money, especially not when they are required to purchase their own food and drink, let alone entertainment from sutlers, itinerant merchants, local farmers, and camp followers. In an army far from home, long on campaign, and bloated with mercenaries, the appetite for coin is only doubled – and in the case of Alexander's army, that appetite had grown into a hunger. As the coins rained down, discipline collapsed, as the men scrambled and fought with each other to get as much as they could grab.

The only way in which the queen's assault on the camp – for in many ways it was indeed an assault, and one every bit as disruptive as if Memnon himself had led a column of elephants on a charge – could have caused even more of tumult was if she had been accompanied by half-naked slave girls who offered the men bowls and skins of wine as they passed through. Which, of course, was exactly what was going on, and all to the accompaniment of the largest and loudest marching band this side of Cathay.

And, of course, there were lions – for lions are noble, along with tigers, and bears, and many other creatures. Some were in cages, others held in check only by strong bare-chested men whose muscles bulged with the strain of holding their leashes. At the center of all of this procession was the queen herself, sitting upon a golden throne inside a bejeweled howdah that itself was perched upon the back of a massive elephant. And that great beast was not one of the comparatively small Indian variety, but a titanic towering tusker whose ivory protuberances were longer than cavalry lances and tipped with gold. Had Zeus himself suddenly dropped in for lunch while tossing thunderbolts out of Apollo's fiery chariot, the impact upon the army and the shattering of its discipline could not have been more complete.

Alexander, needless to say, was not amused.

He was, however, too stunned to express anger, outrage, or any other of the many explosive emotions Hephaestion, Ptolemy and Parmenio expected. The young king simply stood frozen, uncharacter-istically silent, slack jawed, mouth open in astonishment as the moving spectacle snaked through the crowds of scrambling soldiers. It all finally came to a halt at the foot of the small hill upon which his tent stood. With great fanfare that included the pounding of many massive camel-mounted kettle-drums, the clashing of a score of pairs of brass cymbals carried by turbaned men riding white horses and, of course, the blare of many, many trumpets, the queen's elephant came to a dead stop, its tusks nearly tickling the king himself.

As the mighty mammoth knelt, as if paying homage to the young Macedonian, a dozen strong men in silk gauze raced up alongside its now partially supine bulk. They brought forth a set of carpeted steps, which they placed opposite the door to the howdah, and proceeded to assist the corpulent queen in her descent from the grand beastie.

"Ah, there you are, my dear, sweet boy!" she burbled in joy upon seeing the king. "Come, embrace your loving mother!" she added. The buxom matron spread wide her chubby arms in an invitation for Alexander to come and lose himself in her loving clutches. Unused as he was to such displays of affection from his true mother, Alexander hesitated and even began to step back – only to be pursued by the full-bosomed monarch who once again sweetly called upon the king to greet her in the manner of a loving and dutiful offspring.

Alexander had looked death in the eye. He had ridden hell-for-leather into a forest of Theban spears, charged up a muddy river bank to duel with armored Persian nobles, and climbed a ladder, sword in hand, to storm the ramparts of more than one mighty fortress – but this time, the man who never faltered, who never retreated, who never even contemplated defeat, meekly capitulated to the corpulent queen of Caria.

"Oh just wait until Olympias hears about this," Parmenion muttered in glee. "I would not want to be Alexander when she slithers in."

The sound of Ada's parade had quite the opposite effect upon Memnon, Ephialtes, and the other defenders of Halicarnassos, all of whom rushed to arm themselves and raced to mount the ramparts of the city. They were certain that this tumult, and especially the final fanfare, were the signals for an all-out attack, and made the appropriate preparations to respond. Hundreds of archers raced up the steps to the battlements, taking their assigned place at each crenelation, while hundreds more artillerymen scurried to their posts beside the massive stone-throwers, bolt-shooters, and other war engines upon and behind the walls. A thousand Greek mercenaries formed into a phalanx in the open space behind the walls, Ephialtes at their head, while another thousand Persian horsemen, Orontobates in the lead, mounted up and rode into formation to either side of that armored block. First to respond, however, were the Immortals, 400 of whom guarded the gate.

The remaining 100, under the watchful eye of Hydarnes, stood as a reserve of last resort at the citadel by the sea that Memnon had made his command post. Only the navy was slow to react, as it took time for the admiral to harry his sailors from the city taverns and send them to the beaches and berths to launch their warships into the bay.

But no attack came. The music and noise continue to flood across the plain and into the city, carried by an inland breeze that wafted over the walls, through the streets, out into the harbor, and even the bay itself. The defenders stood to arms, teeth gritted, loins girded, and fists clenched for over an hour – but still no man, nor even an arrow came forth from the Macedonian lines.

"What are they doing over there?" Orontobates finally asked Memnon. "Why don't they come at us?"

"I...I think they're...they're having a Dionysian festival," the admiral spoke up, having come to the citadel to ask where Memnon wanted the fleet to deploy so as to best harry the Macedonian assault troops.

"A festival? A festival?" said Hydarnes, first in disbelief, and then with a laugh. "What do they have to celebrate? Is it some god's feast day or time for one of those endless religious celebrations the Greeks use as an excuse for playing games and getting drunk?"

"Not that I am aware of," mumbled Memnon, scratching the stubble on his chin. "Whatever the case, I don't think they are going to be coming at us, not today anyway. Still," he added as an afterthought, "it could be a distraction, meant to put us off our guard. Admiral," he said as he turned, "recall two-thirds of your ships. And Hydarnes, send runners to Ephialtes and the commanders of the archers and artillery. They, too, should stand down two-thirds of their men. The other third, my friends, shall stay on duty, and set up a rotation for the other soldiers and sailors. If Alexander is having a drunken feast, so be it – but if it's just a trick, best we not fall for it."

With help from Ptolemy and Hephaestion, Alexander managed finally to escape from the loving clutches of Queen Ada. Stepping back to gather his breath and his composure, Alexander gave a little bow and motioned for the queen to join him in his tent. She smiled, nodded, and with a tiny flick of her bejeweled pinky her servants removed her portable throne from the howdah and carried it before her into the tent, so that her broad royal behind would have someplace to sit. Once settled in, she waved them back and motioned for Alexander to sit beside her on a cushioned stool those servants had set beside the throne for that purpose.

"Oh, my dear boy, it is so good to see you. I had so wished you would have come back to Alinda to visit your dear mother who loves you so. It is far more comfortable up there, in the mountain, with the cool breezes and cooler streams than it is down here in this hot and dusty plain" she said, wrinkling her nose in an unmistakable gesture of displeasure at the grit and smell of the camp.

"I would have, of course," replied Alexander, whose answer to Hephaestion's surprise actually seemed to ring with sincerity, "but, well, as you can see," he paused, waving an arm in the direction of the tumult outside the tent, "I have been rather busy."

"Yes, yes," said the queen as she opened up a papyrus fan and waved it about to cool herself. "I know, 'war' and all that," she sighed. "Just like my father, and brother, and husband, may the lord of light welcome them to his bosom," she sighed even deeper, her overly ample bosom rising, and falling, and nearly spilling out from her gown. "They, too, liked to play this game. But, you know my dear boy, it really isn't necessary, not all of this," she added, again fanning herself.

"What do you mean?" asked Alexander genuinely perplexed. "Halicarnassos is the most formidable fortress on earth. It is defended by one of the greatest generals of the age, and with their command of the sea, its garrison can never be starved into submission. There is nothing for it than to lay siege, bombard the city, break down its walls, fill in its ditches and then storm it with sword, and spear, and pike. All of that, my dear mother," he added, with a rare sweetness to his voice, "requires preparation. Careful, meticulous, lengthy, and time-consuming attention to the minutest of a million minute details. Otherwise," he added with a smile and a laugh while patting her hand, "I would have flown to your side."

The queen took that hand in both of hers, and drew it to her breast. With sincere motherly love she drew herself close, then closer to Alexander, and said "well then I suppose you can be forgiven, but as I said, it was all so unnecessary to put yourself to such trouble."

"What do you mean?" replied Alexander, thoroughly perplexed.

"What I mean," she said, still holding his hand in hers and then drawing him closer still, "is why go through all of this to take Halicarnassos from the outside, when you can take it from within?"

70

In the Interior

THE EVENING CAMP

Halime did not shed any tears nor become hysterical – nor even sad, when the three Thebans told her the tale of the battle at the Granicos and its aftermath. Instead, she seemed to shrug it all off as if it were of little importance, or as if it were a story about something that happened long ago in another land far, far away.

"Girl, don't you understand?" asked Klemes. "There is a very good chance that your father, your brothers, and all of your male relations and their retainers died in the slaughter that was the Granicos battle."

"Perhaps," Halime responded rather stoically, "but I know my family. We are survivors. My father and brothers are brave, honest, and sensible men. They are experienced warriors, and are neither reckless nor stupid. They would not behave the way you say those nobles did – leaping down into a river on horseback, seeking death or glory, or both," she said with a disdainful laugh. "No," she said, perhaps both to reassure herself and to hammer the point home to the Thebans, "they did not go to war with such foolish notions in their heads. My father is an old campaigner; he trained them in the old ways – ride, shoot, turn your horse away from the enemy, and if he follows, swivel and shoot behind you as your horse keeps on ahead. Their weapon of choice was

– is, rather – the bow. My father always said 'only a fool gets in close enough to use a lance, sword, or mace if he still has an arrow in his quiver.' Even then," she let loose a little laugh, "better to go back to the pack train to get some more than stay there and try to poke people with a pointy stick."

Dimitrios shook his head, for such a method of fighting was not how he was trained – or believed to be particularly honorable. "He might not have had a choice, Halime. Once they broke through the river line, the Macedonians were able to swirl around the flanks and cut off whole groups of our men..."

Again, Halime smiled. "My father found himself in similar situations, and many times. He would tell us that if you ever find yourself trapped and surrounded on three sides, you should ride like hell for that open fourth side."

"So your family were horse archers, with the light cavalry?" asked Ari appreciatively. Now that because or perhaps even thanks to his bad leg he had become a bowman rather than a hoplites, he had come to understand the way missile troops fought.

"Yes," replied Halime. "We are archers and we are horse people. We breed, raise, and train horses for the nobility, and for anyone else who can pay."

"Then you are not of the nobility?" piped in Ari, his hope for an answer in the negative painfully evident to his friends.

Halime stiffened, drew herself up into a solemn, almost royal poise, and gave a disapproving huff. Had her eyes been bows they would have shot sharp arrows at the young Theban, as it was obvious that he had crossed a line with his question.

"We are of pure Persian blood," she stated sternly, forcefully, and with no room for doubt that she felt insulted by Ari's question. "Our family may not be as great and as grand as those of the king or of his satraps, but my family can trace its lineage back to the days of Cyrus the Great...and beyond. My ancestors rode at the side of Cyrus' father, grand-father, and great-grand-father. Most of the so-called nobles out here are latecomers, descendants of the chieftains that Cyrus swept up into his empire as he marched along – with my ancestors at his side."

The three Thebans exchanged wordless, nodding glances at each other. Surprised by her revelation that she was not a servant, let alone a slave, they were astonished at the story she now told of her lineage. They also were taken aback by her unshakable belief that despite the horrors of the war in the north, her father and brothers and others who rode with them might have survived the massacre at the Granicos.

"Well, that explains why you ride so well," observed Klemes.

"And also why you three ride so poorly," teased Halime. "You Greeks are sailors, foot soldiers, and philosophers, or so my father used to say, but when it comes to riding a horse, well..."

Klemes smiled a rare smile. "Yes, my dear girl, you are correct. Then again, Greece is not a horse country. It is all rocks and olive groves, and hardly any place of note is more than a day's walk from the sea – or is already on it. Besides, horses are expensive – and it is hard to find fodder for them, especially when anything that resembles a pasture is already packed from end to end with sheep or goats."

"Well then," Halime smiled, "then I suppose it's not me who needs your help as much as you who need mine. First thing we need to do, is get you some proper horses. Those spavined old fleabags you got from the farm had already been put out to pasture – their riding days are long behind them."

Dimitrios was so angry, he tossed his helmet on the ground and then walked over to kick it.

"Damn it! I knew the steward was being just a bit too nice and helpful, all that fawning over us and playing up his respect for Memnon..."

Halime did not disagree. To the contrary, as she explained in amusement, "the steward could tell you didn't know much about horses and he took great advantage of that. You stink of the cities – and we, country folk, know how to play upon that to our benefit."

"So, what do we do now, Dimitrios?" asked Ari. "Do we go back and show that conniving bastard just what kind of men he is dealing with?"

"That won't do any good," said Halime, before Dimitrios could answer. "They'll be expecting you, and will have called in every thug and farmer with a weapon they can hire, just in case. You'd be dead before you got off your horses – not that any of these would make it back that far anyway."

"So what do you suggest we do, little lady?" asked Dimitrios, his anger unabated.

"We go forward. Into the interior, away from the coast, towards the king's highway. I know people there. That is horse-country, and there are many good and honest ranchers and breeders to be found up there."

"And you say you know them?" asked Klemes.

"I know some, and some will know my father, at least by reputation. Even more important, unlike you, I can tell the good ones from the bad. That goes for both the horse traders and the horses. And don't bother getting on these horses. The best they are good for is to carry your gear, food, and water. It is good you men are more used to walking than to riding."

"And why is that, again?" asked Klemes.

"Because you've got a long walk ahead of you."

While the little Theban band plus one were hiking across country in search of better horses, a great deal was going on back at Halicarnassos. Alexander had gathered all of his key generals together to go over plans for the next attack.

"Tomorrow morning," he explained as he pointed to the rough map before them, "we will send four columns against the city. Ptolemy, you will come at them from the west, towards the Myndos Gate. Parmenion, you will come from the north, against the Tripylon Gate – and yes, I know that is the strongest point in what is reputed to be the strongest fortress in all of the world, but it has to be attacked. Perdiccas," he said, looking at the companion dearest to him in all the world save Hephaestion, "you will attack the demilune...that outcropping of the fortress that outflanks the Tripylon Gate. Co-ordinate closely with Parmenion. As for myself, I will take on the Mylasa Gate, on the eastern side of the city, directly across from our camp. Hephaestion will have the Companions in reserve."

"This attacking all across the front, at four points, will stretch our forces very thin," objected Parmenion. "It means we will be weak everywhere and strong nowhere."

"It also means there will be more targets for the defenders," added Ptolemy. "It means every archer, every weapon they have will have a target – and you remember how accurate their fire can be. It will be a slaughter, just like the last time."

Alexander only smiled. "No, this will not be like the last time. For one thing, last night the scouts went out in small groups and moved around those painted rocks we noticed. The ones they were using to sight in their fire. Now when someone gives the order to fire at a target in the 'white rock' zone, their arrows and rocks and bolts will go somewhere else."

"Surely they will notice that," interjected Parmenion.

"Of course, but not at first," replied the king. "And with us coming at them from all sides, it will take them time to figure that out, and then to readjust. It will confuse them and buy us time."

Perdiccas nodded in approval, but gave out a great sigh.

"And what is it about this plan that bothers you, Perdiccas," asked Alexander, slightly annoyed that his generals did not seem at all enthusiastic, despite his explanation of the plan.

"The bit with jumbling up the rocks is good, but still, that wall is high and bristling with defenders. Every breach we make they repair – or build another wall behind it. There is still the ditch to contend with. Bringing up rams and trying to place ladders on that wall is going to be bloody work. We are going to lose a lot of good men."

Alexander fought back his growing fury, and as calmly as he could, he sought to reassure his generals that this time the assault would work. None appeared mollified, and each exchanged silent glances with the others as if to ask which one of them would speak up next. Hephaestion decided to take on that task.

"My king," the commander of the reserve asked, and asked in a manner that did not obviously challenge Alexander, "surely you intend for three of these attacks to be diversions and the fourth to be the main thrust. Where shall I station the reserves in preparation for a break-through? Which of your four columns will take the city?"

Alexander, as if hoping for such a question, smiled, and smiled broadly. "The fifth column."

The four generals exchanged confused looks and began talking all at once until the king raised his hand to quiet them.

"My lord," said Parmenion, "you have mapped out the targets for four columns. Where is this fifth one?"

"It is already in place."

"Where?" asked Parmenion.

"Here," replied the king, pointing to the part of the map marked with the Mausoleum.

"But that is inside the city," observed Parmenion.

"Exactly," said Alexander with a triumphant smile.

71

In the Interior

NEITHER RAIN NOR SNOW...

Halime spotted the lone rider on his limping horse long before any of her Greek companions. Footsore, worn, and weary from trudging on for three days through the back country east of Mylasa, which itself was back country, the three Thebans were not at their best – or their most alert. Halime, however, never once let her guard down, in part because of how she was raised but also because she did not yet fully trust her escort – for that is how she had come to see and treat them, even if the men still saw her as just some wild farm girl. If they wanted to believe themselves to be her protectors, that was fine for now, thought Halime, but it was she who was now in truth leading them, even if they didn't know it yet.

"There's a rider up ahead," Halime said quite matter-of-factually to Dimitrios, who was struggling to keep up with her through the rocks and scrub. "Looks like an imperial courier."

"Good," said Dimitrios, wearily. "Perhaps he can tell us how to get out of this barren wasteland and find the next town."

"That's what you have me for," laughed Halime. "I keep telling you, over and over again, that I know exactly where we are and exactly where we are going. You just don't seem to understand that every place here in the empire is much farther from any other place than it is where you come from. Your people can practically spit from your city walls and hit those of another city, or a town, at least that is what my father says. Here, you can go for days and not see another soul, let alone a city or a settlement. Here, a person has room to breathe, room to be alone with themselves, or their god."

"I am already sick and tired of all of this 'room' of yours," said Dimitrios as he led his mount turned pack horse through the rough terrain. "I want and need to find a farm, or a proper town, one where we can find fresh horses, buy a decent meal and get a real bath."

"Well, then," laughed Halime, "you're in luck. You see that rider? He's quite a way from his appointed rounds, but with the pass he carries, he can command anyone in the empire to provide him with anything he needs to fulfill his mission. Once you tell him you are traveling under orders from Memnon, I am sure he will be able to help you get what you need. Besides, there's a large group of farms just over the next rise. It's nothing grand like one of your Greek cities, but it will do."

The rider by now had decided that his horse was too badly injured to carry him, and had dismounted so as to give the horse a rest and to better examine her. The sleek, young mare whinnied at the approach of Halime, the Greeks, and their horses, which put the courier on his guard.

"Don't worry," Halime said over her shoulder to Dimitrios, "he's unarmed. The couriers aren't even allowed to carry a dagger, lest even its light weight slow them down." She waved in a similarly reassuring fashion to the courier, who seemed both embarrassed at his situation and relieved that the party approaching him was friendly.

"In the name of the King of Kings," the young man said in an attempt to impress the newcomers as to his importance, "I command you to give me your best horse. I promise that you shall be justly compensated, once you take my poor mount to a courier station."

The rider was younger than either Halime or Ari, beardless, and with only a wisp of a mustache. A slight, slender if wiry fellow, he could not have weighed much more than the girl, thought Dimitrios. This is a young man meant for speed, not for fighting, he determined.

Then again, in a courier service where a message could be relayed the length of the vast Persian empire in under two weeks from end to end, speed was what mattered – speed and endurance, and, of course, a good head on one's shoulders.

"Sorry, my friend, but you are out of luck," replied Dimitrios as they came closer. "Our horses are in worse shape than yours. They're barely able to carry our gear and rations. You'll go farther and get there faster on foot than riding one of these sad beasties."

"Damn!" said the courier. "That means I am going to have to turn back to get another mount. I'm already behind schedule. I should have been at least in Mylasa by now."

"We've just come from there, friend," said Ari as he came up. "You've got three, maybe four days walk."

"Then I will indeed have to turn back. The settlement at Bogdan is at least a day back the way I came, but I'll still make better time getting to Halicarnassos if I do."

"Halicarnassos? Did you say Halicarnassos?" said Klemes, who had also finally caught up with the others. "We've just come from there. There's an entire Macedonian army around the city. You'll never get in – hell, you'll never even get close."

"But...but I must! I have to! I just have to!" said the young man, practically ready to cry. "It's...it's my first mission, and I can't fail...and I'm already behind schedule..."

"There, there, young fellow," said Dimitrios, taking him by the shoulder. "Come along with us to this Bogdan place, and perhaps we can figure something out. By the way, I'm an officer on General Memnon's staff. My name is Dimitrios, Captain Dimitrios. The tall one there is my brother, Klemes, a physician, also in the service of Memnon."

"Ahem," coughed Ari.

"Oh," said Dimitrios to the courier. "The other one's my friend, Ari. He's also in the great general's service. So, what is this message you carry for my general?"

"I'm not at liberty to say," said the young courier, suddenly turning quite serious and formal. "I've already said too much," he added, a little embarrassment showing through his poor attempt at being solemn and soldierly. "I'm...We're not supposed to divulge the intended recipients let alone the contents of the messages we carry. It's part of the code, you know."

"What code?" asked Ari.

"Why, the code of the imperial couriers...like me!" said the lad.

"I read something of that in Herodotus, if I recall," interrupted Klemes. "Something about going at their best speed and not allowing themselves to be hindered...either by snow, or rain, or heat..."

"...or by the darkness of night," said the courier proudly, taking over from Klemes. "Oh, and there's more, if you care to hear it I can..."

"No, no, that's quite enough," said Klemes. "I think we all get the picture here."

"Look, son," said Dimitrios, interrupting the banter between the courier and the physician. "I told you I am on the general's staff...I even have a medallion in my bag to prove it, as well as a letter from the general requiring anyone I meet to obey my requests for assistance as if it were the command of the general himself. Memnon's in Halicarnassos, all right, but you're not going to get anywhere near him, so that makes me your next best bet for completing your mission. So, hand over the message."

"I...I really shouldn't" mumbled the young courier, taking a step back and clutching tightly at the little wallet strapped to his side. "That's against the..."

"I know, I know, against the 'code,' and all that," replied Dimitrios, close to becoming impatient but struggling to remain calm, and civil, and nonthreatening. "But hand it over, I command you. And if it makes you feel any better, I promise to give it back to you once I've read it."

"But it's sealed..."

"By whose hand, that of the king? Of one of his ministers, or a satrap?"

"Err...no," mumbled the courier.

"Then whose seal does this message you carry bear?" asked Dimitrios, quite perplexed.

"That of the lady Barsine..." said the courier while looking down at his feet.

"Memnon's wife?" said the three Thebans all at the same time.

"The very same."

"Well, then, lad," said Dimitrios beaming. "You're doubly in luck. Not only have we come from Memnon on Memnon's business, but that business is to find his wife, deliver a message to her and then escort her to safety far, far from here. So, do you know where she is? Can you take us to her?" continued Dimitrios, suddenly quite excited, quite eager, and quite overwhelming – at least from the courier's point of view.

"Well, I just carry the mail," said the courier. "It's all just a relay race, you know. One rider gets the letter, rides all day, passes it on to the next, who rides all night, and then he passes..."

"We get it, we get it," sighed Dimitrios. "So do you know what link you are in this chain?"

"The second...or maybe the third, I think," said the courier. "We don't have time to ask when one courier hands off to another, but Aleph, the rider who handed it off to me, he might know. Or at least he'd know who gave it to him..."

"So, if we find this Aleph, he might lead us back along the chain where the letter originated?" asked Klemes.

"Most likely," said the courier, "although he's not any more at liberty to say than I am..."

"Enough!" said Dimitrios, finally just grabbing the boy by his uniform and snatching the wallet from him, pulling so hard that the thin strap which attached it to his person broke. "Let me read this damn letter. I need to find Memnon's wife and get her to safety. That's more important than any damn messenger's code..."

"Courier's Code, sir," said the young man, rubbing his aching shoulder where the strap had been.

"Whatever," said Dimitrios, hurriedly breaking the seal and unscrolling the letter. "This is from Barsine, all right. Says she's at some place called Diospolis. You know where that is, right?"

"I do," Halime chimed in. "It's a big horse trading town on the Lycos River."

"Far from here?"

"Twenty parasangs, maybe a little more," replied Halime.

"What the hell is a parasang?" asked Ari.

"About 30 stadia," replied Klemes.

"How do you know that?" asked Dimitrios.

"Herodotus. And Xenophon. I told you brother," said Klemes with a teasing sigh, "it pays to read more. I told you, you can learn a lot from the classics."

"So that means what, at 30 stadia to the parasang and 200 paces to the stadia..."

"What it means is that it is a long walk," said Klemes.

72

Bogdan

TO SEE A MAN ABOUT A HORSE...

Halime charmed the blushing young courier just as she had captivated Ari, disarmed the usually stoic Klemes, and won over the otherwise hard-bitten Dimitrios. She had a natural gift for getting people – and not just men – to like her and to trust her. This gift of Halime's had nothing to do with seducing or enticing men, for, while quite pretty, her beauty was not the kind that drove men wild with lust. Hers was instead of the type which made them smile, feel at ease, relaxed, and somehow happy just to be in her company. Halime had been favored by the gods. And while she knew it and was happy to make use of the blessings they bestowed upon her, she also had the kind of heart that would not allow her to even contemplate abusing that gift. If she always got what she wanted – and she usually did – somehow those who complied with her wishes always seemed to be happy they did so.

It was thus with relative ease that she was able to take charge of the little party without anyone – not even Dimitrios – realizing that she had.

The young courier, who gave his name as Oxycanos – or just "Oxy" as everyone almost immediately referred to him – was eager to please her as he guided the group toward Bogdan. At the same time, however, as he revealed to her, he was worried about how his superiors might chastise him for his many shortcomings. After all, not only had he failed to deliver his message but he also had further broken the courier's code by delivering it to someone other than the person to whom it was addressed.

"You did the right thing, Oxy," Halime said, comfortingly, as they walked over the rough ground toward Bogdan. "If you pressed on, you'd only have gotten yourself killed. At least this way some good will have come from your misfortune," she added with a warm smile. "Besides, you might have even saved lives."

"How's that?" Oxy asked, genuinely intrigued and by now clutching at any straw of hope that he had of being exonerated for his actions.

"Memnon sent Captain Dimitrios to find his wife and to make sure the Lady Barsine and her children are safe. That letter told the general that she was coming to meet him at Halicarnassos. Had that fallen into the hands of the enemy, then the Macedonians would have known she was coming, set a trap, and captured her. Imagine what kind of leverage they would have over Memnon then? They'd force him to choose between surrendering the city and watching his wife and children die – and not in a quick or merciful way, if what these Thebans say about Alexander is true."

"But, still, I..." stammered Oxy, wrestling with his conscience and struggling to find some balance to all of what had happened.

"No 'but still' about it," smiled Halime, working her magic as best she could to put Oxy at ease. "You may turn out to be the real hero in all of this. After all, you may be the key to getting Dimitrios to Barsine in time to save her and her children from becoming pawns, or sacrificial lambs, in this great struggle. You could be the reason why we hold on at Halicarnassos, not to mention how you might indeed be the savior of a great lady."

Oxy slowly began to smile a little, nodding his head in acquiescence to her logic.

"So, you trust these Greeks?" Oxy asked Halime softly, so none of the others who straggled to their rear could hear.

"Well," she said with a wink and a smile, "a little. Although, between we Persians, I still keep a dagger under my blanket at night."

As Halime and Oxy led the Thebans toward Bogdan, fresh horses and, hopefully, the Lady Barsine, back at the front Memnon had more than enough to contend with besides worrying about the safety of his family. From the towers of Halicarnassos, Alexander's four columns could be seen forming up in preparation for the assault. As the Macedonian preparatory bombardment intensified, Memnon strained to find evidence of which of those four columns would be the main attack. Little did he know or even suspect that it would be a fifth column, and one coming from an entirely unforeseen direction.

Alexander started the ball at the Mylasa Gate. His first wave was a long line of mantlets – mobile walls on wheels – behind which his infantry could take cover while light archers darted out and back to fire at any defenders who popped their heads above the battlements. The archery fire was not very accurate, nor was it intended to be. It was more of a nuisance meant to make enemy archers and artillerymen think twice before exposing themselves to shoot. As the mantlets hobbled slowly forward, small groups of unarmed men, most of them slaves, dashed forward to hurl bundles of sticks into the ditch at the base of the wall. Few were able to live long enough for a second such dash, fewer still for a third, but slowly, bundle by bundle, parts of the ditch began to fill.

Memnon watched this slow, meticulous choreography with interest, but did not see any reason yet to commit men from the reserve to the Mylasa Gate. Besides, even before Alexander's mantlets reached midfield, a courier rushed up with a report from Orontobates. The Macedonians were making a similar move on the Myndos Gate, at the exact opposite end of the city. Furthermore, the report stated that the defender's artillery fire was having almost no effect, as most of the shots were way off target. Perplexed at that last bit, Memnon strode down the steps from the tower, mounted a waiting horse, and rode the width of the city to find Orontobates.

"None of the stones we hurl land anywhere near where they are supposed to land," the governor said, quite perplexed.

"Aren't they using the colored rocks as aiming points?"

"Yes, Memnon," replied Orontobates, "but if they are ordered to shoot at a yellow rock it winds up over by a white rock, or a red one."

"Damn," said Memnon quietly. "They've moved the rocks."

"What?" asked Orontobates.

"The Macedonian kinglet is learning from his mistakes. He or someone in their camp must have realized we had painted the rocks to use as aiming points. Alexander's men must have gone out one night and moved the rocks."

"So we just have to adjust, right?" asked Orontobates. "If we want to hit where we see a white rock, we just have to figure out what color it will land on instead, and then we can adjust."

"No," sighed Memnon. "I don't think it will be that simple or that logical. They've moved them all about, and I'll bet there is no rhyme nor reason to how they did it. No, Governor, your men are just going to have to sight their targets anew. Fortunately, most of our artillery is still intact and working properly. I trust you will give them a warm reception, once you get the ranges correct," Memnon said, not in an interrogatory manner but as a command.

Memnon, however, did not have time to judge the effectiveness of Orontobates' response, for another courier came racing, breathlessly, up the stairs to the tower from which the two men were observing Ptolemy's advance.

"What is it?" asked Orontobates as the courier fought to get the words out, his chest still heaving and grasping for air from the run up the steep stairs.

"General Ephialtes...the Tripylon Gate...Macedonians..."

"Come, man, spit it out!" shouted Orontobates.

"No, soldier. Take a moment. Take a deep, slow breath," said

Memnon in a fatherly manner. "Get it right. What exactly does Ephialtes have to report about the Tripylon Gate?"

"Macedonians...thousands of them," said the courier, still struggling for air. "A...a living wall...shields locked, massive towers rolling forward...and a battering ram so massive it could have only been made by Hephaestos in the forge of the gods..."

"Are those your words or those of the general?" inquired Memnon calmly, hoping his own demeanor would help the courier calm down. "Did you see this giant ram for yourself?"

"With my own eyes, lord," said the courier. "And those are General Ephialtes exact words. He made me repeat them twice. And he chose me, he said, because only a fellow Greek could deliver such a report to full effect."

"And why is that?" huffed Orontobates, obviously annoyed and even insulted at the slight to the Persians among the defenders.

"Because," said the courier, "you Persians don't have a god like Hephaestos. He makes all of the armor and weapons of the gods. He even forges the thunderbolts for Zeus to hurl!"

"Well," smiled Memnon, "if anyone is going to be hurling thunderbolts today it will be us. Ride back to Ephialtes, tell him to take heart. He has my full confidence. Besides, the flanking fire from the eastern outcrop will slow that attack."

"But...but sir," replied the courier. "The outcrop, the demilune, the Macedonians are attacking there as well."

"What?" asked Memnon, in genuine surprise. "How?"

"Ladders, sire. Long, long ladders. Hundreds of them. The Macedonians were scrambling up them as I left."

"If they take that outcropping," Orontobates said in alarm to Memnon, "instead of us outflanking their attacks, they will have the entire city laid out before them. They'll see our defenses, and enfilade our positions at both the Tripylon and the Mylasa Gate."

"Well, then, that is where I need to be," said Memnon as he put on his helmet. "And that is where the reserves must go. Young man," he said as he turned to the courier, "do you know who Hydarnes is?"

"The commander of the Immortals, sir? Everybody knows who he is," added the courier with a sense of great respect.

"Good. Then you go to the Mausoleum, you find him, and you give him this," added the general, as he quickly scrawled a message into a wax tablet, closed it and sealed it with his ring. "You tell him to bring the reserves up the road to the Tripylon Gate, and to meet me there. Oh, and one thing more..."

"Yes, General?"

"Tell him to bring the Immortals with him."

73

Bogdan

A LONG AND DUSTY WALK IN THE SUN

Halime led the way to Bogdan with Oxy and Ari at her side, each of the two young men doing their best to outshine the other and gain her favor. Klemes and Dimitrios trudged behind, intentionally staying far enough away as to not have to listen to the verbal duel.

"It is almost charming, isn't it, the way those two lads fawn and follow her around," mumbled the captain to his brother.

"At least it gives them something to take their minds off this dull, weary long march," added the physician. "I know why we are doing what we are doing, but, well, damn it brother, I'm..."

"I know, I know," said Dimitrios quiet exasperated, "you're a physician, not a...what? Soldier? A marathon runner? A..."

"A mule," grumbled Klemes, upset that his brother had stolen his thunder. "A gods-be-damned, flea-bitten, dusty, dirty, stinking mule..."

"Well, Klemes," he answered with a grin, "technically the horse you are leading is the one playing the part of the mule. She's carrying your kit. Your only burden is your anger, your impatience, your grumbling..."

"Oh, shut up," said the physician, as he pulled harder at the reins, clucked his tongue, and managed to get ahead of his brother. "I'd rather listen to their senseless drivel than put up with your insults."

Dimitrios allowed himself a little laugh as Klemes drew ahead of him, and then a sigh of relief. Bringing up the rear meant chewing a bit of dust from the rest of the party, but at least it was quiet back there. Quiet enough to allow him to think, and to try to figure out the next step on their mission. Halime had told him they should reach Bogdan before nightfall. There would be no sense in trying to barter for horses in the evening; so they might as well take advantage of that respite to have a decent meal, a bath, and a night's sleep under a roof or tent, or whatever the inn at the little town had to offer. The next morning they should be able to ride on to Diospolis – and closer to Barsine – which, Oxy said, was less than a day's ride. That of course would be a day's ride at the courier's pace. They would have to go at a more measured pace, not only because their horses would be weighted down with gear, but also because none of the Greeks were anywhere near as experienced or as good with horses as were the Persian girl and the courier.

Dimitrios had managed to get a partial description of both Diospolis and Bogdan out of the courier. Oxy's knowledge of both was rather limited to the stop where he would exchange a tired mount for a fresh one. At least he learned that Aleph, who accepted the message from Barsine to Memnon from her own hand, was likely to be at the courier station. With Oxy's help – and maybe Halime's rather personable charms – he expected Aleph would be convinced to lead them to the great lady. If that did not work, he could always try to pull rank. That had worked, sort of, with Oxy, although if he was honest with himself, the young courier's cooperation was due more to Halime's smile than to Memnon's medallion. Either way, in two or at the most three days he expected to be able to give Barsine the general's own message, and to start the next part of his mission, escorting her to safety to the east.

That, at least, was his plan. Trying to convince a wealthy, privileged, and noble woman of regal lineage to do the exact opposite of what she intended to do, of course, could prove a bit dicey. That, however, was a bridge he would cross when the time came. For now, he just put his head down, put one foot ahead of the other and kept on walking, occasionally giving a tug on the reins of the old horse he was leading.

What Memnon would have given for such a quiet, boring day as Dimitrios was having. The siege of Halicarnassos had become a storm – and a storm on four fronts.

Even with nearly 30,000 men under his command, Memnon was hard-pressed. Each of the four points under attack had to be held; if the defenders gave way at any one point, their positions at the other three would be meaningless. Worse, they would be cut off from each other, vulnerable to their flank and rear, and trapped. Memnon would thus not only again lose a city, but also an army.

The defenders did buckle and falter, and where they did Memnon rushed men from the reserve. At the Mylasa Gate, his nephew Thymondas personally led a group of skirmishers as they sneaked out of a hidden sally port, and hit the Macedonians in the flank. The unexpected attack caused much confusion in the ranks of laborers who were filling in the ditch. The Persians were able to follow them as they stampeded through the line of mantlets and were thus able to set fire to two of the siege towers. Extricating themselves amidst the fire, smoke, shouting, and panic was tricky, but with the Macedonians busy trying to put out the flames on their towers, the archers and catapults on the walls and towers were free to provide covering fire. A small group of cavalry which Hephaestion had sent to intercept the skirmishers came under such blistering fire that even the horses refused to press home their attack. Thymondas emerged with a few cuts and bruises, but the accolades from his troops buoyed not only his morale, but that of all of the defenders at the eastern edge of the city.

On the far side, to the west, at the Myndos Gate, Ptolemy's men fared much better than their comrades on the opposite wall. The elite Hypaspistes swordsmen managed to scramble up and over the wall – only to find that Orontobates had erected a second wall behind it. His archers poured down fire from three sides on the Macedonians. Ptolemy's men made a wall of their small shields, but any attempt to move out from it meant certain and immediate death. Still, the Hypaspistes, veterans all, kept trying to advance – but to no avail. As the day grew long, Ptolemy finally stopped sending men up the ladders into that abattoir, and ordered those who could to climb back down and retire to the safety of their own lines. Some of the Hypaspistes refused to retreat. They died holding up their shields so their brothers could retire. The last Hypaspist on that wall fell where he stood, protecting the body of a comrade who was too badly wounded to move. Despite calls for their death from the victorious defenders, Orontobates intervened with orders to spare them. Arrows protruding from their dying bodies, Orontobates had them carried out of a sally port under an olive branch of truce, their return supervised by heralds from each side.

Parmenion, too, found the going hard. The main entrance on the north side of the city, the Tripylon Gate, so named for its three towers, was famed as the strongest part of the strongest fortress in the world. Parmenion soon learned why. The towers were bristling with all manner of bolt-throwers, belly-bows, and other pieces of light artillery. They also had cranes with claws to catch ladders, and winches that reached out to drop bags of oil onto the attackers – who soon found themselves engulfed in flames. No matter how many times Parmenion placed his towers against the walls there, no matter how many times the ladders went up, Ephialtes managed to meet them with at least equal, and at times overwhelming, force. An old campaigner and one who often had stood in the front rank, Ephialtes took personal command of each counterattack, and in each he fought like a champion. Through his valiant example, and the blood he visibly shed from many small wounds, the veteran commander inspired the defenders to fight on. Parmenion, however, kept throwing more and more men into the fray, and the two were locked like bull elephants fighting for control of the herd.

Parmenion knew this attack was bleeding the Macedonians white, but he had to grab Ephialtes and hold him tight, for there was another assault, a fourth one, that gave him hope. Perdiccas' assault on the promontory to his left could still turn the tide and win the day. The promontory was high and well fortified, but vulnerable, as it was long and narrow, and could be hit from both sides at once – and also at its tip. Macedonian stone and bolt throwers were pummeling it from each of those three sides. Perdiccas did not have them shoot directly ahead, however, but ordered them to intentionally overshoot. Thus the Persians on the wall of the promontory facing west found themselves hit from the east, and vice versa, all while massive rocks and pots of flaming oil fell from the north, down the length of the promontory. Under such a telling crossfire, the Persians could not stand.

As Perdiccas' cheering troops climbed the long ladders and came over the wall, they could see the whole of the city laid out before them. Go east and they would get behind the defenders at the Mylasa Gate. Go west and they would take Ephialtes in the flank and open the Myndos Gate for Parmenion's veterans. Shouting a paean of victory, the Macedonians flowed down to the base of the promontory, ready to outflank both the Tripylon and Mylasa Gates.

And they would have, had it not been for Hydarnes and 400 Immortals.

The Macedonians, bloodied, disorganized, tired yet elated, hit the wall of Immortals like a wave – and like a wave that hits a stone wall, splatters, and recedes. With Memnon at his side, Hydarnes directed his veteran imperial guards with a cool precision that stood in great contrast to the hot and heady flood of Macedonians. Perdiccas' men had come over the wall, and were still coming, but coming in as a disorganized mob – not as a formed body of soldiers. So drunk on the thought of plunder and victory were the Macedonians that what officers still had their heads, could do nothing to bring them to heel. When a handful of men would manage to form up, the wave coming behind them would wash them away, and right into the lowered spears and deadly aim of the Immortals.

Hydarnes had arranged his men in the old way, the way of the

Babylonians and the Assyrians before them. Three ranks of shield-bearing spearmen held the line. The front rank knelt, their spears forward at an angle. The second stood behind them, their spears pointing out at chest level. Behind them, a third rank, to steady the first two and fill in the gap if any before them should fall. This hedgehog of spear points, however, was not meant to kill the Macedonians, but only to stop them. The killing came from the three ranks behind the spears. Every Immortal carried three weapons. A spear, a sword and a bow — and the bow was the primary weapon, and one each Immortal knew how to use to great effect.

"First rank, fire!" shouted Hydarnes. "Second rank, fire! Third rank, fire!" Over and over again he gave the same command, the first rank reloaded and ready as the third fired, and the second already pulling back on the bowstrings as the first let fly. Hydarnes knew his trade, but as a Persian, he also knew that even the strongest archer could only shoot as long as there were arrows in his quiver. That was the job of the servants that followed the Immortals to war. As 250 spearmen held the line and 250 archers let fly, 100 servants kept up a steady flow of quivers to the front. Another 100 brought wine, and water, and bits of bread to revive those archers who faltered from the exertion. Fifty more did the grim task of carrying the dead and wounded from the formation, for the fight was not all one-sided.

While Hydarnes held the Macedonians in check, Memnon pulled together the men who had fled the promontory, and sent them back in small parties along the wall. When they secured a section, Hydarnes would order the spears forward 20 paces, with the archers following after each volley. Ten times Hydarnes and Memnon repeated this maneuver, and by this manner the Persians slowly and steadily regained the promontory.

As the day grew longer, the Macedonian attack grew weaker. Memnon, Orontobates, Ephialtes and Hydarnes had thrown back four columns of attackers.

Then the fifth column struck.

Halicarnassos

THE FIFTH COLUMN

Two days before the big attack, Queen Ada had boasted to her adopted son of how many people in the city would welcome her return.

"There is a faction that loved me – and who always loved me, from the time I was a little princess on my father's knee," she practically giggled in the telling of the tale. "My family, the House of Hecatomnos, made Halicarnassos what it is today – or rather, what it was until my snake of a brother, Pixodaros, betrayed me. Imagine," she burbled as she struggled to speak and chug wine at the same time, "if you will, the splendor and grandeur of my brother's great city..."

"Pixodoros?" asked Cleitos, who, as commander of the bodyguard and personal protector of Alexander, was of course present in the king's tent as Alexander entertained the portly queen.

"No, no, not that brother," said the queen, annoyed at having her story interrupted, "my other brother."

"Idrieos, you mean?" chimed in Hephaestion.

"No, no, you sweet doe-eyed young thing," the queen said, throwing Hephaestion what she thought was a come-hither look. "Idrieos was my husband."

"But wasn't he also your brother?" asked Hephaeston.

"Yes," sighed the queen, "they were all my brothers. Mausolus was the eldest. He was satrap, but was allowed all the respect, authority and trappings of power of a king, as my father, Hecatomnos had been before the satraps' revolt. When he died, my sister – his wife – Artemisia took the throne, such as it was. It was she who completed the great tomb for her dear husband, our brother."

"That would be the Mausoleum," quipped Alexander.

"Yes, my dear boy," the queen said as she put the wine cup out for refilling with one pudgy, bejeweled hand while grabbing a sweet from the table before her with the other. "You are a quick learner, Alexander, as any son of mine should be."

The queen took another lengthy draught of wine, then sucked the honey from the fingers of the hand that had tossed the treat into her mouth, and continued.

"So, that takes care of my dear father, Hecatomnos, my sweet, gentle, adoring brothers Mausolos and Idrieos, and my darling, beautiful and feisty sister, Artemisia. She was named after the Artemisia who led part of the fleet during Xerxes' invasion of Greece, you know..."

"A female admiral?" clucked Cleitos. "A woman on a ship is bad luck, everyone knows that!"

"Perhaps that is why the Persians lost the naval battle at Salamis," chimed in Hephaestion, quite pleased at his jest.

Alexander could see the queen was indeed wounded to the quick by the slur on the name of her ancestor, and very near the point of tears – something Alexander did not want to have to deal with.

"Now, now, my friends. I will suffer no joking at the expense of my adopted mother or her family, and certainly not of the valiant Admiral Artemisia. She led the only part of the Persian fleet to give the Athenians a good fight that day, and it was she who covered the retreat of what remained of Xerxes' armada. Even the great Themistocles spoke quite highly of his valiant little female opponent, as did Thucydides...and who among you will challenge that master historian's assessment? After all, he was a strategos of Athens and led a portion of its fleet in the battles with Sparta, so he knows the value of a fellow sailor and naval officer when he finds one – even if that officer is a woman."

Cleitos and Hephaestion lowered their heads in feigned shame, but also to hide their smiles and better control their urge to laugh. Alexander, for his part, continued to pretend to dote on Ada, and stroked her plump, beringed hand when it reached for yet another sweet.

"Thank you, my boy, oh, thank you," she said, a tear glistening as it slowly made its way down her chubby berouged cheek. "Well, as I was saying before your companions rather rudely interrupted me – an offense for which, were they not your close friends as well as servants, I would demand their heads – or at the very least, their testicles."

That remark did get the attention of Cleitos and Hephaestion, who reflexively placed their hands in a manner as to protect the later of the aforementioned body parts.

"As I was saying," continued the queen. "The people of Halicarnassos loved my father, and they adored me. There were some who were more devoted to my older brother and my sister, his wife, than to me, but my lovely sweet husband-brother Idrieos won their affection once Artemisia passed away. There are many people still who chafe at the way I was treated by my other brother, that snake Pixodaros, whole stole my crown. And then of course there are those whom Orontobates wronged when he took charge from that loathsome, inconsiderate, ungrateful, spoiled, mincing little..."

"I get the point, Mother," said Alexander. "There are a lot of people in the city who are unhappy, but do you really think that they will rise up when you sound the call? I mean, Memnon has near 30,000 men in the city – including not only Greek mercenaries and the garrison, but also some Immortals. Such a force would deter any but the most devoted or suicidal of citizens to take up arms."

The queen quite regally put down her cup, wiped her hands on her gown and brought herself into full royal mode.

"If I tell you that they will rise, then rise they will. All I need do is snap my fingers, thus," she added, although as her fingers were still somewhat sticky, they did not produce much of a snap. "Tell me when to snap, and the city will be yours for the taking."

But Queen Ada's snap had no more effect on the outcome of the attack than it had on the day her sticky fingers failed to make that sound. Oh, there were factions aplenty inside Halicarnassos, and some were very unhappy indeed with the current administration. Unfortunately for the queen and Alexander, however, the only thing they hated more than the government of Halicarnassos was each other. Ada did manage to slip a few messages into the city by the tried and true manner of letters tied to arrows, notes attached to the legs of carrier birds, and even missives carried by divers who braved the rocks and currents to swim into the port at night. The instructions to rise did reach the leaders of those cells whom she honestly believed would rush to open the gates for her, but, unfortunately, the instructions told each of them to gather at the same time and place as the others.

When they did, a riot broke out.

Well, not so much a riot, as a gang fight. A tavern brawl. A knock-down, knife-slashing, club-thumping, fist-striking, neck-choking, pretty much every man for himself donnybrook. This did, as the queen promised, occur at the height of Alexander's attack, but none of the combatants got farther than the agora, and most remained in battle with each other at the rally point – the Mausoleum itself.

The fight was so localized, and so far from the fighting at the walls, as to be of little consequence to the defense of the city. A handful of the city watch and some armed sailors from the fleet sufficed to cordon off and to contain the battle royale, which petered out on its own accord long before the sun set. Even as a distraction, the vaunted fifth column proved a failure. And no one felt that failure more deeply than the woman who had been responsible for it.

When night fell, and not one gate had been forced open, not one section of wall still in their hands, nor one of their men alive, save as a captive, in the city, the Macedonian generals on their own authority called off the attack. Alexander was furious, but no amount of shouts, threats, pleas or promises could make Ptolemy, Perdiccas, or Parmenion send their men back into the fight.

"It is done for today," said Parmenion quite solemnly to the king. "The men have no more to give...nor do I," sighed the old general. "Not if your father himself came back from the grave would I send my men against that wall again..."

"But they are not 'your' men, Parmenion," simmered Alexander. "They are 'my' men. And I say, no, I command you, to renew the assault. The city is ripe for the picking, I can feel it, I can smell it!"

"What you smell, my King," said Parmenion as he took off his helmet and wiped the sweat and dirt from his face, "is the dead. The Persians are burning their dead – and they are burning the bodies of the thousand of Macedonians who died on and inside those walls today. As for the other thousand dead outside the walls," he added as he waved his hand in the direction of the field made bloody with corpses, "those are ours to burn. Or they will be, as soon as the heralds arrange a truce so that we may collect and do honor to the dead and, the gods be merciful, aid any of the fallen who can yet be saved."

75

Bogdan

GARMABEH AND PARAIDAEZA

Despite their mooning over the distracting Halime, Oxy and Ari in effect canceled each other out, thus allowing the Persian girl to direct the party as promised to Bogdan. It was little more than a sheep and horse trading station. It had few buildings save those absolutely necessary for the farriers, tanners, butchers, and others who made their living from the animal trade. As such, it was a bleak, dusty, odoriferous little nowhere on the road to everywhere. What passed for an "inn" was nothing more than a few ragged awnings covering some crude wooden tables, and some flat rooftops with canopies where those passing through could, for a small price, find some shade and a relatively safe place to rest.

"Bit of a let down, isn't it?" said Dimitrios as the group limped down the main street – the only street or, more accurately, the Royal Road.

"I don't know, brother," replied Klemes wearily but in good humor. "After days and days of stadia after stadia, or parasang after parasang, or whatever, on my feet, even this place seems a bit like a *paraideaza*."

"A what?"

"A *paraideaza*, like that lovely garden back at the estate where we met Halime," he replied.

"You could have just said 'garden,' you know," grumbled Dimitrios. "You don't have to always use a five-drachma word when a one-obol word will do."

"Yes, I know, dear brother," smirked the physician as he tied up the reins of his horse to a post by the "inn," and then began dusting himself off. "But it does so rile you when I do. And, besides, how will you every better yourself if you don't expand your vocabulary. You do know what that word..."

"Yes, Klemes," mumbled Dimitrios, equally dusty and in desperate need of a bath, "I do know what that word means. I may not have had the luxury of lying about in the shade listening to pompous old men drone on about such things for hours on end as you did..."

"It's called an education, my over-muscled brother. You should try it sometime. After all, someday you may have the opportunity to go back into the wine business. You don't want to just end up as some worn out old soldier scrambling about the streets begging for drink money, do you?"

Dimitrios shot him an angry glare, but did not respond. He could best his brother in the physical and financial arts, but when it came to bandying words, Klemes was far quicker and far better at that than anyone he ever met. No sense fighting a battle on ground of the enemy's choosing, he thought to himself. Better to retreat, save up strength, and wait for a situation where his talents were of more value than those of his elder, learned and, frankly, often insufferable brother. There are more ways to bully someone than with fists, he grumbled inwardly, and as much as he loved his brother, there were old scores – and a few new ones – that would still have to be settled. Today, however, was not that day. Today, Dimitrios sighed in his mind, today there are much more important matters to attend to – like a bath.

That was something that both brothers – and the others in the party, not just Halime, did share a desire for. If cleanliness is an obsession with Greeks, it is practically a religion with Persians. While Bogdan would not have anything like a real bath house or public baths, there would be somewhere to bathe.

"We call it a *garmabeh*," said Halime when Klemes asked where he might find a place to clean up. "It is nothing grand, like you find in the bigger towns and cities, but it more than serves the purpose. Here it is likely to be nothing more than a tent with good drainage; a place where you can wash yourself from a tub of water heated on a fire, and then cool yourself from a bowl of rose water. I will ask Oxy to inquire at what passes for an inn where we may cleanse ourselves."

"Why don't you just go inside and ask?"

"That would not be proper, Klemes," she said with both a bit of a blush and a haughty manner, as if she had been offended and needed to set things straight. "After all, I am not some serving girl, or a woman of low status seeking to sell her charms, which is the best and worst way any man in there would think of me for even entering that place, let alone asking such a delicate question. No, it is for a man to ask...or, in this case, a boy," she almost giggled.

As rude a place as they found Bogdan to be, it did have the three things the party desired most: a place to bathe, a place to eat and, most important of all for Dimitrios, a place to find horses. Oxy, of course, could take his pick of mounts, and at no charge. All he needed to do was flash his medallion, and any subject of the king of kings had to provide food, shelter, aid, and horses to the courier. Refusal was not an option: not unless they wished to kill the courier, dispose of the body and concoct some story that would satisfy the inevitable inquiry that would follow a courier's disappearance. Such inquiries were undertaken by servants of the Eyes of the King – a shadowy figure whose meticulous and frequently lethal methods always unveiled the truth.

Dimitrios, however, could make no such demand. The owner of the local stables was determined to make up for the expense of outfitting Oxy – who of course chose his finest mount – by fleecing the Greek barbarians as best he could. Halime, a better judge of horseflesh than even Oxy, could only help so much.

"Your brother says that before being a soldier you were a wine merchant?" she asked of Dimitrios rhetorically, for she already knew the answer. "Well, that will be of little help here."

"Why?" he asked, quite perplexed. "A deal is a deal. The rules are the same no matter what you wish to buy or sell."

Halime stifled a little laugh, but her smile gave away her amusement.

"Horses are not amphorae of wine," she replied, still trying not to make Dimitrios think she was making fun of him. "There are procedures that must be followed and customs that must be attended to in the minutest detail. One wrong move and the deal will be off – and blood may flow if you are not careful."

"I understand the art of the deal," replied Dimitrios, taken aback at being lectured to by a mere slip of a girl. "I have been making deals since you were a baby and Zeus was a corporal," he said, drawing himself up to his full height and thumping his chest.

"Well, oh great and powerful Theban wine merchant," she shot back, taking umbrage at his response to her advice. "Unless you want to keep walking all the way to Diospolis or wherever it is you think you are going, or are itching for a knife in the back, please put aside that 'Greek's know best' misplaced manly pride of yours. Let me tell you how we do things here. Remember, my people were born on the back of a horse, and it was on horseback that we built an empire from the shores of the Ganges to the beaches of the wine dark sea. We are very set in our ways, in this perhaps more than anything. So I ask you...no, I beg you," she added coyly, changing her tune from that of instructor to supplicant, "to sit back down and let me explain to you how horse trading works in the Persian empire."

"I hope the horses for sale are better than the food here," grumbled Dimitrios as he grudgingly sat back down.

"Oh, they are, my captain," she replied, "they most certainly are – if you know how to go about it properly."

As a Greek, a Theban, a captain, a merchant, and a hoplites, Dimitrios could not be expected to take the advice of a woman. That went double or even triple when the woman was not only a foreigner, but a Persian, and still, in his eyes, a girl – and a mere slip of a one at that. After all, Dimitrios was a man of the world, schooled in the classrooms of experience in the agora and on the battlefield. In other words, he was too proud to take Halime's advice.

The consequences of which were predictable – or at least what she predicted they would be.

The negotiations went badly from the beginning. Dimitrios had made many a business deal in his career, as had his father and his grandfather before him. The wine business was both literally and figuratively in his blood. Unfortunately, he was not dealing with another wine merchant. Hassan, the horse trader, did not only not play by the same rules as Dimitrios, he did not even play the same game. Worse, Dimitrios had to rely on Halime to translate for him. He had no other choice, for no one else in Bogdan spoke any Greek, and his Persian seemed incomprehensible to a man who spoke this a particular dialect.

Just bringing a woman along to a business transaction made Hassan not only as uneasy as it did Dimitrios; it also made him downright hostile. Already spoiling to find a way to make this foreigner make up Hassan's losses at having given Oxy a mount, he bridled at the presence, let alone involvement, of the girl. Horse trading, after all, was man's work. That this girl seemed to know far too much about horses, and corrected and even contradicted Hassan as to the health and suitability of the horses he was offering to sell the Greek made a bad situation worse.

To recite the litany of offers, counter-offers, claims, corrections, pleas, arguments, heated exchanges, insults, and threats would serve little purpose. Suffice it to say that within half an hour the deciding factors in the making of the deal were not words, handshakes or coins, but knives, cudgels and fists. It was fortunate for Dimitrios that Hassan had few friends in Bogdan, having cheated or at least taken advantage of too many of its citizens, and too often. Otherwise the Thebans would have been overborne by numbers; instead of allies, however, all Hassan had from the people of Bogdan was an audience.

Hassan held back as two of his toughs jumped Dimitrios, pummeling and pounding him with their bare firsts. Ari quickly came to his friend's aid, wielding a heavy stick to bat away the thugs. Hassan signaled for the rest of his men to join in the fray. Two more came forward – the third, and youngest, electing to stay with the horses. When he heard the tumult, Klemes came out from under the tavern's awning. Halime, too, entered the fray to help even the odds. As small and as light as she was, Halime was the only girl in a family of boys, and thus knew from practice how to hold her own in a scuffle.

Had Oxy not already have ridden off to the next courier station, he would most likely have come to their aid but, alas, by now he was hours away. After all, the courier could not be delayed from his appointed rounds, or so demanded his oath.

The unseemly scuffle was finally decided by the inn-keeper. His customers were watching and taking bets on the outcome of the fight, and as such were taking up space under his awnings without ordering food or drink. A bucket of dirty water from the kitchens in hand, he strode forth and splashed the combatants with its contents. Those who kept fighting, he simply clocked on the head with the bucket. Standing like the Colossus of Rhodes, the burly innkeeper put himself firmly between each camp, daring any one from either side to make a move to renew the brawl.

"Hassan!" he bellowed to the horse trader, who had managed to stay behind while his minions did his fighting for him. "Give these Greeks and their girl four of your best horses – not that many of yours are all that valuable. You know the going rate," he spat, scornfully. "Add a tenth to that, and let that be that."

"And as for you, you...Greeks," he said, nodding to Halime to translate. "You will give Hassan your old horses and then pay the price Hassan and I have set, and you will pay it without further discussion. And then you will leave, understand?"

Dimitrios made to respond, but the innkeeper cut him off with a hard look and a stance that made it very clear he was ready to wield the bucket to enforce his demand. Soldier enough to know when time had come to retreat, Dimitrios nodded his head, rose slowly to his feet and held out his bloody, bruised and dirty hand. The innkeeper spat into his free hand, took Dimitrios' outstretched hand, and shook it.

"Now," he said, through a forced smile which did little to hide the threat behind it, "pay the man. Gather your gear – and leave. And take that girl with you. Oh," he added, as Dimitrios started to back away. "Next time listen to her. She might just be able to keep you alive...at least for a little while longer."

76

Diospolis

THE POSTMAN ALWAYS RIDES TWICE

After the dusty scuffle in the dirt in Bogdan, Dimitrios was more eager than ever before to continue his mission. Oxy had suggested that his fellow courier, Aleph, might be able to aid them in their quest to find Barsine. It was Aleph, after all, who had handed off to Oxy the message meant for Memnon in Halicarnassos. Aleph, by Oxy's reasoning, would either have received the letter directly from an agent of the princess, or at least could tell Dimitrios which courier had given it to him. Dimitrios sincerely hoped he would not have to keep backtracking from one courier to the next, but it might be the only way to find Memnon's wife.

"Why couldn't she have just sat still in some nice, comfy palace, keeping cool and cozy in one of those *paraidaezas* of theirs?" grumbled Klemes, whose patience had grown thinner with each passing day on the road.

"This Barsine is not some gentle Athenian woman, who must keep to her house and garden and be seen and not heard," said Halime, who had ridden back to the captain's side after a brief scout ahead. "This is Persia – or at least the Persian Empire. Our women have much more freedom than yours, or so I have been told. We can own property, run a farm, conduct the business affairs of our families..."

"How?" said Dimitrios in surprise. "For all of that you would need an education. You would need to know numbers. You would need to know how to read, and how to write, and..."

"I can read, and write, and calculate numbers – and in three languages," said Halime quite calmly. "My father had tutors for me and my brothers. That is how I know about how you basically imprison your women, keeping them caged up in their homes. Such is not the custom in Persia. Here women are allowed to make their own choices, in at least some matters, that is."

"No wonder the Macedonians think your men weak and easy to conquer," remarked Dimitrios with a laugh. "My family is rare, in that women and girls of the House of Pindar are allowed an education, but that does not mean they have a say in running things, at least not outside of the home. After all, what kind of a man lets a women make her own decisions, let alone for a family?"

"A wise one, Captain," said Halime with a smile, as she gave her horse a little kick and trotted ahead.

"Curious people," mumbled Dimitrios. "Curious people. I hope the king of kings doesn't let his women guide him in his war plans," he grumbled to his brother. "If so, we may find ourselves on the losing end of this war."

"It may surprise you, brother," replied Klemes, "but Darius does listen to his women – or at least to the wisest of them. The queen mother, Sisygambus, is said to have her own network of spies and assassins," added Klemes. "I have heard her described as the spider who sits at the center of a web. A web through which agents from all over the world, and not just the empire, bring her news. She even spies on the imperial spymasters, the men known as the Eyes of the King and as the Ears of the King."

Dimitrios turned and looked directly into his brother's face and asked, quite incredulously, "and just where did you 'hear' such rumors, brother?"

"Back in Ephesos – and again in Miletos," he replied. "While you are busy hacking, and slashing, and strutting about playing the impor-tant soldier, some of us take a little time to listen to what other people are saying. Or, perish the thought, to even ask questions. You know, that method they taught us that Socrates used."

"I know about the Socratic method and all of that," sighed Dimitrios. "You've lectured me on it countless times."

"I don't know why I bother," sighed Klemes. "So," he said, changing the topic, "do you know where we are going?"

"Diospolis. That's where Oxy said we should go to meet the other courier."

"And do you know where that is?"

"Halime does. She says to just follow the brick-lined road."

"Oh?" Klemes said, raising his eyebrows and smiling broadly. "So you are letting a woman tell you where to go? Did she by any chance tell you what lies between here and there?"

Dimitrios lowered his head, looked down at his horse's mane and mumbled in response, "I didn't ask her."

The journey to Diospolis was uneventful – boringly so, perhaps, but Dimitrios had suffered enough delays and distractions already, so he welcomed the boredom. He wondered if Halicarnassos was holding out, or if his commander, patron and, in some ways, friend, Memnon was still alive. All he did know was that he had been given a mission, had made a promise, and had a duty to do as his general asked: find his wife and get her to safety far, far away from the fighting. At least the war had not caught up with him on this road, or not yet, nodded the captain to himself. But, he wondered, how long before it does?

Diospolis was not a great city or even a large town, but compared to Bogdan it was a gleaming metropolis. There was a grid pattern to the streets, few and short as they were, and the place appeared quiet and orderly, yet also very much alive. Today was market day, if the gathering of shoppers and stalls in the marketplace was any indication. While not a grand agora in the manner of the Ionian Greek cities on the coast, there was an arcade for some of the more permanent shops, a caravanserai for traders and travelers and, wonder of wonders, a small public bath fed by a local stream. Even more important, at the end of the main street stood a stable – and a building which flew the banner of the imperial courier service.

"Ari," said Dimitrios to his young friend. "See to the stabling of our mounts. Halime will translate for you if need be. Merchants stop here, so there must be some people here with a working knowledge of Greek. Anyway," he added with a grin, "no sense separating you two at this stage."

The longer they traveled together, the more the archer and the girl had become inseparable – or at least she had become more willing to allow Ari to follow her about.

"Klemes," said Dimitrios, as he dismounted, "Do you think you can manage to find us lodging while I go to the courier post?"

"Well, I'm a physician, not an innkeeper," he grinned, "but I will see what I can do about finding us a bed for the night and a hot meal. As you said, there is probably someone in there with a smattering of our mother tongue – or what passes for it after these Ionian Greeks garble it."

Dimitrios accepted his brother's windy response as a "yes," dismounted, handed the reins to Ari, and made his way to the courier post. It was not a very large or impressive building, but it was a definite mark that signaled clearly that this small town was part of the great Persian empire. The couriers that came and went through here to exchange spent horses for fresh ones, bore missives, news and commands that originated as far away as the Persian trading posts in China to the imperial garrisons along the Aegean coast. It was the one place to find out the real story of what was going on in the world, as compared to the wild and exaggerated rumors that swirled about the taverns and the caravanserais. Not that the couriers read the messages they carried, but at least they passed on what they had heard or seen en route.

As Dimitrios entered the small building, the clerk behind the desk asked him to identify himself and to state his business. He did so in remarkably clear if heavily accented Greek.

"How did you know I was a Greek?" asked Dimitrios.

"The same way I know that you are a man," sighed the clerk. "I looked at you. From your dress, your manner, the shape of your beard – which, by the way, cries out desperately to be trimmed, curled, and oiled and properly so – the only way you could be more obviously a Greek is if you had a sign hanging from your neck that proclaimed: 'Hello, I am a Greek.' So," he added with an impatient clearing of his throat, "state your business. I haven't got all day, you know."

Dimitrios went into great detail as to how he and his friends had come all of this way from Halicarnassos, and of how they had encountered a young courier named Oxy and...

"Will you please stop prattling on and get to the point, soldier, for it is also obvious that such is your profession," interrupted the clerk, who made no attempt to hide his impatience, or his annoyance at having his routine disturbed. "I do not need or want to know the story of your life. I have work to do, so if you want a message to be sent, dictate it to me."

Dimitrios was too tired from the many days on the road to take umbrage at the clerk's officious manner, but neither was he too tired to not finish his story. Eventually, despite the clerk's incessant drumming of his stylus, he got to the point about Oxy, Aleph and the message from Barsine.

"It is highly irregular, I shall have you know," responded the clerk, peering over his long, sharp, pointy nose. "For a courier to disclose the recipient let alone author of a document he carries is just not done. And you say he actually let you read it, as well?" he added, visibly agitated.

"More than that," replied Dimitrios, reaching into the small satchel at his hip, "he gave it to me."

"He did what!" screamed the clerk as he shot up from his desk. "I will have his head for that! That is in direct violation of the postal code, section 17, part three. Wait until I tell my superiors! And you, Greek," he continued, making his displeasure crystal clear, "you will hand over that letter – and at once! At once!"

Dimitrios was not used to being spoken to in such a manner, but, frankly, was too tired, and too weary of all of this to argue.

"I only wanted to know if another of your couriers, one named Aleph, was around or due in anytime soon."

"And why is that?" the clerk asked sharply, his hand still outstretched, palm up, waiting to receive the letter as he had demanded.

"Haven't you listened to a word of what I've been saying," groaned the captain. "Because Oxy thought Aleph may have received the letter directly from the hand of Barsine. Or that he could at least point me to where up the line it may have originated."

"And why is that?" demanded the clerk.

"Because," said Dimitrios with an exhausted sigh, "because she is the wife of my general, and I have urgent business with her."

Unmoved, the clerk once more thrust out his hand, and asked "who is this 'general' of which you speak, and who is this tart of a wife you are prattling on about?"

"My general's name is Memnon, perhaps you've heard of him?" replied Dimitrios, almost too tired to care anymore. Desperately in need of a proper bath, a decent bowl of wine and some hot food, Dimitrios was tired of this game. "And his wife is Barsine. She's a royal princess."

The clerk lowered his hand to his side. He drew himself up to attention, and blinked twice.

"Well," he said with a harrumph to clear his throat, "why didn't you just say so in the first place. And I suppose you have some proof to offer that you come from him?"

Dimitrios did not answer. He fumbled about in his kit bag until he produced the medallion he had been given by the general.

"Let me see it," said the clerk, more respectfully than before. "It appears genuine."

"Well," sighed Dimitrios, "now that we've settled that, can you tell me where I can find this courier? This Aleph fellow?"

"Better than that," the clerk said with a smile, "I can tell you where to find his wife."

77

Halicarnassos

SIEGE

"That bitch!" screamed Alexander. "That stupid, bloated, pompous, lying, royal bitch! No wonder her brother was able to topple Queen Ada from the throne."

"Now, now, my King," said Cleitos, trying to calm the king. "This is, after all, your mother you are speaking of."

"My adopted mother, only my adopted mother – and she did that all on her own. That was none of my doing," grumbled Alexander.

"Well, it did seem like a good idea at the time," sighed Hephaestion. "It also seemed quite logical that there would be people in the city willing to rise up – after all, this is not only Persia, but that part of Persia that has Ionian Greeks, ancient Carians, all sorts of foreign mercenaries, and who knows how many inbred families, if they followed the example of Ada and her lot. That's a heady brew even in peace time, let alone in a besieged city under martial law."

Alexander was pacing around his tent, reaching out for things to throw and smash, and if they did not break when they hit the floor, he started kicking them. All the while he simmered, seethed, and cursed – and drank. Oh, how he drank.

"From all reports," said Hephaestion in as calm a voice as possible, "there was indeed an uprising in the city. Several, in fact. That 'fifth column' you and the queen talked of did rise, in a manner of speaking. Unfortunately, however, it was more like five different columns, each of which, it turns out, hated each other more than they loved Ada. They rose up – and then used that as an excuse and as an opportunity to settle old scores. My spies in the city tell me that the city guard did not so much put down the uprising as contain it. Then they sat back, let it burn itself out, and then just set about cleaning up the debris, like a fire."

Hephaestion's measured and accurate report did little to temper the king's anger. Parmenion, Perdiccas, and Ptolemy, who had also been called to the royal command tent, watched in silence while the king raged on. None knew what to say. Each knew, in their hearts, that their men had given their all. This was not a rebuff, like the last time, when they had been overhasty and overconfident in storming the city, but a defeat – a solid, serious defeat, and one that was felt as such not just by the commanders, but by every man in the Macedonian army. It was a feeling that this ever-victorious army had never felt before, not under Philip, and not under his son.

"So, my King," continued Hephaestion, "the question is, what shall we do next?"

Had any other man in the tent said that, the young king would have taken it as an insult or a jibe, and would have reacted to it violently. As Alexander's closest friend, confidant, and occasional or former lover (or so it was rumored), Hephaestion was the one and only person in the world who had ever been able to soothe him when he got like this. Inseparable in their boyhood (and there were many who made jokes about this being a physical as well as an emotional union), Hephaestion and Alexander had grown even closer as they grew to manhood. Other than his own mother, Olympias, Hephaestion was the only person who dared tell the king the truth, and in such a way that he would believe them. Parmenion, of course, always spoke the truth, but from the old general it always seemed to Alexander more that he was being lectured by an elderly uncle or somehow compared (and found wanting) to his late father. For that reason Alexander's first reaction to anything Parmenion would say was defensive, and his reaction often negative, like a spoiled child reacting to a scolding.

With Hephaestion, however, Alexander, when he did get angry or was made unhappy by his friend's remarks, would then express remorse or even seek comfort in his embrace. This is something Alexander's other boyhood companions, including Ptolemy for one, understood early on – but which Parmenion never learned, or even cared to learn. He prided himself on always speaking his mind. That had been the key to his close relationship with the late king – and the very thing that kept him from having a similar kinship with the son. Put another way, Parmenion did not know when to keep his mouth shut; such is the burden of many who sincerely believe themselves to always be in the right.

"The army's spirit is shattered, Alexander," continued Parmenion. "We need to abandon this siege, fall back, call for reinforcements and regroup. There is a time to press on – and a time to know when to retire and lick one's wounds. In my opinion, this is that time." Parmenion might have been right, and perhaps might have made Alexander see that, had he stopped talking. Parmenion, however, added one of the two phrases that was certain to make the king do just the opposite of what he recommended. The first was "that was what your father would have done." The second was "that is what I would do." In this instance he did not utter just the first, but also the second as well.

If Hephaestion had poured oil on the waters to calm them, Parmenion had tossed in a flaming torch. The ensuing conflagration was predictably violent.

No scribe was present at this meeting, and if one had, he would never have been able to keep up with the flood of comments that flowed from the king's mouth – most of them so rushed and garbled in his sputtering rage as to be almost incoherent. If the exact words were not understandable, however, their meaning was crystal clear – and were made even more so when Alexander grabbed a javelin and hurled it at Parmenion.

The old general had only one good eye, but it was a practiced one. At the very last breath he managed to take a step back out of the path of the deadly missile as it sped past him and tore through the side of the tent. The scream of pain and the solid thump of a body falling down on the far side indicated that if the javelin had not hit its intended target, it had hit someone. While a few in the tent were likely aware that a fellow soldier had been wounded or worse by the king's toss, none said a word. They only looked at their king in disbelief. Even Hephaestion was speechless and unable to react. Cleitos, however, kept his head.

"Friends, I believe this council of war is concluded for now. The king needs his rest, and I believe you should all leave him to it. It has, after all, been a long and taxing day for us all."

No one argued with Black Cleitos – or Cleitos the Dark, whose nickname came as much from his mood as the color of his hair and complexion and his low birth (being the son of Alexander's nursemaid). The strong, brave and powerful bodyguard bowed to no man – not even Alexander, such was his character and proven valor. In saving Alexander's life at the Granicos, Cleitos had more than earned the king's gratitude and respect. As Cleitos ushered the others out, Alexander slunk down to the floor of the tent, his anger and his energy spent like a skin of water with a gash in the side, through which all of its contents have spilled.

Hephaestion was the last to reach the tent flap. He turned to look at the king, but before he could make a move to comfort Alexander, Cleitos shot him a look that would freeze fire. As Hephaestion turned and made his way out of the tent, he heard Parmenion talking in a whisper to the other generals.

"Well, lads," grumbled the old campaigner, "seems like this time we're truly fucked."

"And what are you going to do about it?" asked Hephaestion angrily as he strode forward.

"Me? Me?" laughed Parmenion pointing his thumb at his own chest. "Why, get rip roaring drunk. And then get fucked. Truly, deeply, royally, and repeatedly fucked."

Meanwhile, a very different scene was being acted out in the headquarters in Halicarnassos. Memnon, Ephialtes, Thymondas, Orontobates, and even the dour Hydarnes – along with the admiral of the fleet, celebrated the repulse of the Macedonians with copious bowls of barely watered wine. Much of the populace, baring those that died in the abortive rising, as well as among the garrison (at least those still on their feet) did the same. Although worn and weary from the most intense day of battle that any could recall, even the storied veteran Memnon, the defenders of Halicarnassos partied, and partied hard, or at least partied as long as they could stay on their feet, or awake.

"Surely, the Macedonians will now retreat," said Orontobates cheerfully. "By all of the rules and practices of war, they must do so."

"Aye, we have given them a bloody nose," said Ephialtes as he refilled and then hoisted another bowl of wine. "Like a dog in the street that comes yapping at your heels and runs away yelping after you give it a good kick."

The admiral said nothing, but nodded in agreement as he, too, lifted his bowl.

"General Memnon," said Hydarnes, who had taken only the barest sip of wine, "do you also believe the Macedonians will now depart?"

Memnon allowed himself a moment to down his bowl in one great gulp, wiped his mouth with his sleeve, and replied with a hearty "no."

"What?" said Orontobates in his surprise, echoing what Ephialtes, Thymondas, and the admiral were thinking. "Of course the Macedonians will withdraw. It is inconceivable that they would not. Inconceivable."

"I am not sure you fully understand what that word means," said Memnon quite seriously. "The Macedonians might indeed withdraw – but Alexander will not. He cannot. And as he is the king, no matter the counsel of his generals, or the rules of war, or logic itself, he will stay."

"But why? Why would he, after taking such horrendous losses today? The Macedonians gave it their all," said Ephialtes. "What more do they have to give?"

Hydarnes did not wait for Memnon, but offered a possible explanation. "Alexander is not a mere general. He is a king. A king cannot flee from a battlefield and remain king. Even the great Cyrus himself fought on after being bested by the Scythians..."

"...who took his head in the process," observed Orontobates. "Their damned bitch of a queen sent his head back to Persia..."

"And in a wineskin filled with blood," added Memnon. "Queen Tomyris, or so the legend goes, sent it along with a note saying 'I told you I would quench your thirst for blood'...but then again, that may just be a story."

"Ah, but you know what they say, don't you?" replied Orontobates. "When the legend contradicts the facts, repeat the legend. Makes for a better and more memorable lesson – and a better story."

"Well," chuckled Ephialtes, fumbling with his scabbard, "if Alexander's head needs cutting off, I've the blade for it! And we've already got empty wineskins aplenty."

Hydarnes did not join in the laughter, neither did Memnon, although he could not resist a smile.

"Take care how you speak of the great Cyrus, King of Kings, King of the Four Quarters of the World..." glowered the captain of the Immortals.

"They mean no disrespect, my friend," replied Memnon. "They are so far in their cups...well, you understand."

Hydarnes did not smile or say anything, but simply nodded slightly to the general.

"As Hydarnes was saying – and saying quite rightly – Alexander is a king. And a young king. And an ambitious king but, most of all, a king who believes himself destined for greatness. What's more, he is a king whose mother swears he was sired by Zeus – and has told it so many times to him that he believes it. As a demigod, an Achilles reborn, he cannot contemplate, let alone admit, or accept defeat. He will not retreat," continued Memnon, putting down his bowl, and drawing a line around it in wine with his finger. No, he will dig in his heels, beat his generals with the flat of his sword and do whatever it takes to drive them forward again."

"So, like in one of your Greek tragedies," remarked the admiral, "his pride — his hubris as you call it — will be his undoing? His tragic flaw that will lead to his downfall and defeat?"

"In a word, 'yes,'" replied Memnon.

"Well then," laughed Ephialtes as he downed yet another bowl of wine, this time with both hands, "best we should help that 'hubris' along then. Who's up for a bit of fun?"

78

Diospolis

THE POST MISTRESS

D iospolis was a large enough, prosperous enough, and at least marginally important enough town to merit one of the coveted imperial post's way stations. This was no grand edifice, however, but merely a tidy little building on the outskirts of town with a stable, corral, farrier's shop and a modest residence attached. This was the home for Aleph, the courier, and his wife. While he carried the mail a day's ride in either direction to the next station, she supervised the small squad of workers who kept the remounts ready for the next courier to arrive.

At Halime's suggestion, Dimitrios bought a small vase in the market, as a gift to help ease the way when he would meet with Aleph's wife. Dimitrios had asked Halime to come along, both as an interpreter and to put the woman at ease, lest she be wary of talking to a Greek bearing gifts. No one responded to his knock on her door, but from the sounds he caught in the breeze he surmised that there was a woman out by the corral. She was quite happily humming a tune to herself while soaping down a very dirty, very sweaty horse – one that looked like it had just come in from a long, fast, hard ride.

"Excuse me, good woman," asked Halime. "Are you the wife of the courier named Aleph?"

The woman gave only a quick glance over her shoulder at Halime while continuing washing the courier horse, but in doing so made a little nod to answer in the affirmative. Halime took that as an invitation to come closer, but also waved for the captain to stay back.

"That is a marvelous horse you have there," said Halime, appreciating the beauty of the soaped-up mare Aleph's wife was washing. "It reminds me of one that my oldest brother had while we were growing up."

"So, you know something about horses, then?" said Aleph's wife as she squeezed out the sponge.

"What true Persian woman doesn't?" replied Halime with smile.

"Well, I may know a great deal about horses," said the woman, "but I have never had one of my own – not all of we Persians are as rich as the Achaemenids, after all. I just take care of them for my husband, the courier Aleph, although it seems you already knew that. How can I help you? Has something happened to Aleph?"

"No, no, nothing like that – or at least not that I or my friends know. We met his fellow courier, Oxy, who said Aleph had taken a letter from a great lady, and that he might know where this great lady could be found?"

"Oxy has a big mouth," the woman grinned. "He always talks too much – and especially to pretty girls. I keep telling Aleph that we have to find that young man a wife. Anyway, yes, he was correct, in a manner of speaking."

"How do you mean?"

"Well, first of all, may I ask who wants to know – and why?"

Halime briefly recounted the events of the last few days, the encounter with Oxy, and the mission she was helping the three Greeks to accomplish. The woman listened while continuing to bathe the mare, and Halime kept talking while she led the animal around to dry its coat and graze on some fresh grass. After a while, the young woman motioned for a boy who was bringing in other horses to take charge of the one she was leading. When he did so she motioned for Halime and the captain, who had been standing impatiently in the sun, holding his vase while the women talked, to come into the shade beneath the awning at the side of her house. She bid them take a seat on some rough benches while she went in, and then came back out a few moments later with a jug of cool water.

"I have started a fire to heat some water for tea," the woman remarked. "It is one of the benefits of having a husband in the courier service. Those who take messages to the east often bring back a small pouch of tea leaves. Most barter the leaves for favors, but some simply share them with their families or fellow couriers. Aleph would be angry with me if I did not offer some tea to a visitor, especially one so important as an officer who serves the great general Memnon."

Taking the mention of his commander's name as his cue, Dimitrios asked Halime to inquire of the woman what she knew of the great lady of whom Aleph spoke.

"All I know is that she is indeed a great lady, perhaps even a princess, or at least a noble," the young woman replied. "That at least was the impression we got from the two men who said they came on her behalf to give Aleph the letter that he, and then Oxy, carried for her. More than that he dared not ask, as such was not his place and only for those far beyond his station to know."

Dimitrios sighed a deep, disappointed sigh. He acted as if that was that, but Halime was not ready to give up. She could tell there was more to this story, and that Aleph's wife was eager to tell her, if she would only ask, as she did. With just a little prompting, Aleph's wife described the men and recounted every word of their conversation with Aleph that she could remember hearing. This, of course, took a good deal of time. Aleph's wife was glad for the company, and took great pleasure in entertaining the travelers. As is the custom in her part of the world, a story that can be told in two minutes is best and more frequently told in as many hours. Struggling to follow their conversation, Dimitrios sat silently while the two young women continued to talk. Halime knew what needed to be asked, and rather than slow things down by interrupting, as he so longed to do, Dimitrios trusted her to converse without him.

After taking tea, Halime finally and politely made the expected excuses for their departure. As the pleasantries were observed, she motioned for Dimitrios to stand up and make ready to leave – and to let go of the vase he had been holding all of this time. With little grace but a warm smile, he handed the woman the small gift, bowed, and marched off like a soldier going off duty.

"You couldn't have just asked her one simple question?" he said quietly as they left the courier station area.

"I did, captain, but in Persia there are forms to be observed. Things may be more direct where you come from, but we are a cultured people," she pointed out. "We do not like to rush, to hurry our conversations, or to come straight to the point, as you barbarians appear to demand."

"So," he sighed annoyingly, "did you find out anything important? Anything that at least gives us a hint, a clue, as to where we might go to find the princess?"

Halime let out a little laugh. "Oh, better than that. I know exactly where she is."

"What!" said the captain in surprise.

"Yes, exactly. And if you are very nice to me, and buy me a proper meal, I may just tell you not only where to find the Princess Barsine, but also how to get there. Seems she is at the estate of a noble, less than a day's ride from here. I know it well, as my father provided that noble with horses. Aleph's wife surmises that the princess is waiting there for a reply from Memnon."

"A day's ride? Then what are we waiting for! Let's get Ari and my brother and the horses and..."

"No," said Halime with a haughty, victorious smile. "Not today. It is too late in the day to travel. Even I can get lost in the dark...and besides, there is the matter of that proper meal you are going to buy for me..."

If Dimitrios was impressed with the beauty and layout of the estate where they had first met Halime, such conclusions were wiped clean from his mind when he crested the rise and saw Paradise. Never had he seen a place so aptly named, with its majestic, lush gardens and brilliant fountains, all laid out before him in an extravagant yet welcoming mosaic of flora, fauna, irrigation canals, and stonework. The sight was so breathtaking that at first he did not even see the grand colonnaded house immediately beneath him. Nestled into the curved hillside so as to take advantage of the cool rocks, shade, and prevailing breezes, the house – or more accurately, the palace – was an amazing marriage of art, architecture, and nature. The score or more of horses romping in the nearby meadow, and the smell of bread baking from the kitchens only added to his belief that he had, indeed, wandered into either the Elysium Fields – or the paradise for which the Persians named their gardens.

The peace of that pastoral scene put Dimitrios off his guard, however, and by the time he noticed the half a dozen armored bowmen who popped up from the bushes with their arrows notched and aimed to kill, there was no time to react. All he and the other Greeks could do was to slowly dismount, as the leader of the ambushers motioned for them to do so with his own bow. Only Halime remained mounted...and instead of being frightened or even concerned, was... laughing.

"Burzasp? Burzasp? Isn't that bow a little too big for a boy of your age?" she teased, directing her comments to one of the archers. The bowman slowly turned to face her, and seemed as if he was about to shoot, when two of the men behind him also laughed. The archer's face reddened, and then he slowly lowered his bow and relaxed his stance.

"And I see your big brothers have come out with you to play soldier?" she added with another teasing laugh. "Tell me, are your sisters back there holding your horses, or have you let them come along to play at war with you in the woods?"

No sooner had Halime made her jest than a rustling came from the trees as out stepped two more ambushers – who, even with their faces half covered by black scarves and dressed in men's attire, were obviously young women – or, more accurately, girls. Between the blushing faces of Burzasp and some of the other archers, and the giggling of the horse holders, the commander of the ambush could no longer pretend that his group were threatening anyone. He, too, relaxed his stance. He lowered his bow and made a motion of greeting, which he reinforced with a slight nod of his head toward Dimitrios.

"Well, Halime," he asked, "what brings you and your escort to my father's humble abode? We sent no request for new horses, and it is not like you to come visiting – especially without your father and brothers, let alone in times like these."

"These are truly unusual times," sighed Halime, "and I will be happy to explain why I am here to you, and to your father...and to your honored guest. Tell me," she added with a smile, "is the Princess Barsine well?"

All of a sudden the mood in the clearing changed. Burzasp and his band came on guard, bows up, arrows notched, smiles gone.

"Halime," said Burzasp in a very stern, serious and hostile tone, "get down off of that horse. All of you, and slowly. Keep your hands where I can see them."

"Halime, stay where you are, and translate for me if you please. Sir," said Dimitrios haughtily, remaining in the saddle and with a demeanor to match that of the archer whose arrow was aimed at his chest. "I bear an urgent message for the Lady Barsine from her husband, General Memnon. I am Dimitrios of Thebes, a captain on the general's staff. These two men are my brother, a physician, and my friend, an archer, like you. We have each been at the general's side – at the Granicos, at Miletos, and at Halicarnassos. This young woman is our guide and our interpreter. We were advised that we could find the princess here by couriers of the imperial post. Lower your weapons and take us to her, and immediately. We are, after all," he added with a smile and in a more diplomatic manner, "all on the same side. We are all friends here – or at least we should be."

Burzasp did not move a muscle. He listened to every word the captain spoke, and to Halime's translation. For a breath that seemed like hours, no one moved. No one spoke. Burzasp, it was obvious, was weighing those words and that information very carefully, all the more so because Halime was familiar, and he could not fathom her role in all of this.

"Young man," said Klemes, obviously annoyed and impatient, and, surprisingly, in passing Persian, "either shoot one of us or take us to the princess. Either way you will be doing me a great favor, as I have had it up to my neck with bouncing about this awful country on this damned horse. So either take us somewhere where we can get a cool drink, a hot meal, and a warm bath – or shoot; at this point I don't give a damn either way."

One of the younger archers snickered. Another tried to suppress a laugh. A third did not even try. Finally, Burzasp started to smile.

"All right," he said, lowering his bow once again. "All right. Get off of your horses and lead them down the path. We will be right behind you. Perhaps you are who you say you are. We shall let my father decide – and for Halime's sake, I really hope you are all telling the truth. Oh, and by the way..."

"Yes?" said Klemes.

"We've been following you for quite some time. If it wasn't for her, I'd have shot you all full of arrows an hour ago."

79

Halicarnassos

ALEXANDER TIGHTENS HIS GRASP

"Dig, you lazy sons of bitches! Dig!" said the overseer as he cracked his whip twice. Once to get the attention of the men who were shoveling dirt and moving rocks so the trenches could inch closer to the city; a second time to slice off a bit of skin from the back of one of the workers.

"Press them to it, sergeant," said Ptolemy, who had ridden up to inspect the progress of the siege lines. "The king orders that the new positions for the stone-throwers be ready tonight, so we can move them forward and open fire by dawn.

"Yes, General," said the overseer as he saluted. "Could you spare a few more men for the job? These Persian pups keep collapsing on us. Weak, womanly sods that they are. We need some real muscle if the king wants his artillery moved closer by morning."

"They are Carians, not Persians, to be precise," replied Ptolemy. "Queen Ada has scoured the countryside for men fit enough to dig. There isn't a farmer or laborer within three days march who isn't up here digging dirt, scraping at stones, chopping trees, or hauling away debris."

"Then, sir, begging your pardon," said the overseer, his face blackened with dirt and sweat. "Perhaps the Queen and her lads could go out four or five days march from here to round up some more men. This lot won't last much longer than that, not at this pace."

"You'll just have to make them last – or get more out of them for now," scowled Ptolemy. "And if you don't, you're going to have to get down in the dirt and dig with them."

"Understood, General," said the sergeant, suitably chastised. As he returned to his task, the sergeant gritted his teeth and tightened his grip on the whip. The men in the trenches knew what that meant – and what to expect when he did so.

"We are running short of food," Perdiccas reported to the king. "Every farm, field, orchard, and town has been picked clean – and then picked through again. There aren't enough live animals about for a sacrifice, let alone a feast – or a decent meal."

Alexander received the news with a sullen, simmering look. He had already been pouting over the slow progress with the trenches. Alexander had twice personally flogged messengers who had brought him bad news about supply lines being raided, and troops driven to near mutiny by hunger. The guard on what stores of food remained had been doubled then doubled again – and then replaced and sent to the trenches as punishment for stealing grain.

As if all of this were not enough, reports were trickling in of unrest and agitation in Athens, and of plots to usurp his mother's regency in Macedonia. Then there was the heat; the oppressive, unrelenting sun, and the clouds of flies...even to Alexander it all hardly made it seem worth going to war anymore. Queen Ada did not help matters either. Her constant and increasingly unwelcome attentions were more than Alexander could stomach, let alone endure, and were made only worse by the lack of progress with the siege. There seemed to be no clear end in sight to any of these trials and tribulations. A lengthy siege was trying enough on a man of action, and the king found little relief or comfort among his companions; even Hephaestion was being pissy.

Captain Abibaal, by contrast, found the situation very much to his liking. The Persian fleet enjoyed complete and unchallenged command of the sea. When on patrol, if he did encounter a Greek vessel or an Ionian merchant ship carrying supplies for the Macedonian army, it was a simple and bloodless exercise in confiscation and enrichment. The captain claimed first pick of the prize goods, allowed his men a fair share, and made sure that there was still enough to turn over to the beachmasters and dock supervisors, so they, too, could take a cut before delivering the booty up the chain of command.

Halicarnassos remained well-supplied thanks to regular deliveries by friendly merchant vessels, their cargoes supplemented by what Abibaal and other captains were seizing at sea. If the Macedonians were sick, starving, and suffering from heat stroke, the Persians were by contrast healthy, well-fed, and happily enjoying the shade and sea-breezes of the fortress city. The repeated failures of the Macedonians to take Halicarnassos by storm only reinforced its already high reputation of being an impregnable fortress. As the captain remarked to his first mate one evening, while sitting on the beach drinking from a cool jug of wine waiting for the fish on the skewers above the crackling fire to cook, "this, my friend, is what I thought life in the navy would be like, and finally, it is."

The appearance atop the dune of an officer from the admiral's staff did nothing to alter that mood. Orders from above were part of a sailor's daily life. As much as he enjoyed being his own master on the open sea, there was also some comfort in knowing that there were others who were making the big decisions for him – decisions that, at least since the hell of Miletos, had brought him nothing but adventure, riches, and a comfortable life.

"Captain Abibaal?" the officer called out as he climbed down the dune toward the fire. The captain did not respond verbally, but merely sat up, held up the jug and motioned for the impeccably attired staff officer to approach. The young officer stumbled a bit, his legs getting caught in his own cloak as he struggled to keep his footing in the shifting sand, but managed to regain his composure thanks to a hand from one of the sailors. When finally face to face with the captain, he saluted, fist to breast, and handed him a case, which when opened revealed a wax tablet into which his orders had been inscribed.

"What's it say, Captain?" the first mate asked between sips of wine. "Another patrol? Maybe up the coast to Chios or Lesbos, even? I could do with some fine Chian wine or visit to the girls in Mytilene town..."

"No, nothing that enjoyable, unfortunately," said the captain as he sunk his ring into the wax in acknowledgment of receiving the order. "Seems General Ephialtes wants to go on another one of his little raids. We're to be part of the escort for the transport ships."

"Well, at least we won't be loaded down with hoplites," said the first mate, "it gets crowded enough on board without trying to pack in a dozen or more of those nasty Greek lads with the big shields, long spears, and heavy armor."

"Unfortunately, my friend, that is exactly what it is going to be like tomorrow – and worse."

"Worse? How can it be worse?"

"Because one of those dozen or so hoplites will be Ephialtes himself. Yes, that's right, we've been chosen to be his personal ocean-going taxi."

"Why us?" grumbled the first mate.

"Seems somebody has been telling him tales of our feats of daring do," said the captain with a little laugh.

"Who would do such a thing?" griped the first mate.

"Probably that Theban captain we rescued," replied the captain. "Apparently he has risen quite rapidly in the ranks. Last I heard, he was on General Memnon's staff."

"Yeah, and we all know how those army officers love to talk, don't we?" said the first mate as he took another slug. "Probably made it sound like he rescued us rather than the other way round, I'll wager," he added with a snickering laugh.

"I don't think so, not that Dimitrios fellow," replied Abibaal. "He was quite a stand-up lad. Probably gave credit where credit was due and praised us to the high heavens to the generals."

"Traitorous, ungrateful son-of-a-bitch then," said the first mate as he tossed the empty jug onto the sand. "Couldn't have kept his big mouth shut then, could he? Couldn't let an honest seaman enjoy a comfortable berth. I told you we shouldn't have stopped to fish them out of the drink, didn't I?"

80

Outside Laodikea

A PRINCESS OF PERSIA

Burzasp and Halime walked down the path like two old friends coming back from a day playing in the woods. His archers, however, kept a much more watchful eye on the Thebans who followed the pair, staying both close enough to see and hear what the Greeks might do or say, and far back enough to give them plenty of time to react to any hint of treachery. The *Iliad* and the *Odyssey* were well known in these parts. The lesson to beware of Greeks bearing gifts was well-drilled into those who could read, and who could appreciate that Homer's works were more than just fairy tales about gods and heroes, but offered a clear, deep look into the hearts and minds of Greeks.

The forested path offered many places for an ambush, or where someone could disappear from even the most attentive of watchers. The Thebans, however, did not take advantage of the situation. They instead behaved as the guests-friends they claimed they were – somewhat to the disappointment of at least some of the archers, who obviously ached for a chance to put an arrow through a Greek.

Their hostility was understandable, especially after the events of the last few months. Although many Greeks fought alongside the Persians – most as mercenaries, although some, like Dimitrios, for their own reasons – the Persians remained cautiously distrustful of their hired and allied soldiers of Greek or Ionian Greek origin. After all, to the Persians the Macedonians were just another kind of Greek; only a bit more barbarous. They joked that as painful to their civilized ears as was that barbarian language, that of Macedonians was even worse, for instead of speaking they grunted and barked the tongue of Hellas.

Many of Alexander's soldiers, mercenaries, and city contingents, moreover, were also Greek – of both the mainland and increasingly of the Ionian variety. To the Persians, the later were not only barbarians, but rebels – traitors who deserved the worst and most painful punishment imaginable. And when it came to inflicting pain, the Persians had frequently demonstrated the depths, extent, and inventiveness of their imagination in that regard. No one ever underestimated the value of a Persian education in that regard.

Dimitrios had no wish to test the grudging hospitality of his escort. Although he found himself slightly uncomfortable with the way Burzasp was being so friendly with Halime, he shook it off. Once more, the little horse girl whom they had mistaken for a slave had proved her value. Ari, of course, was smitten with her, as Dimitrios could understand for so many reasons, but what surprised him was that so was Klemes – although not in the same way. While the young Theban archer made cow eyes and smiled almost stupidly whenever she talked to him, Klemes had adopted an almost big brotherly or even paternal affection for the girl. It had been a long time since he had seen his brother so human – or so vulnerable.

As they reached the bottom of the hill and came into the estate itself, Dimitrios could feel the grandeur of the place. Everything was pristine. Somehow even the stable area had an almost pleasant smell to it. Perhaps that was because of the numerous pots and beds of fragrant, flowering plants artfully laid about the stable area. Those scents mingled with the enticing smells coming from the nearby cookhouse which wafted along with the breeze. Everywhere he looked were signs of order, cleanliness, wealth and, most of all, power.

Even the stable hands were dressed in neat, fresh garments instead of the usual torn and grimy tunics of most of those who did the menial tasks that kept horses clean and fed. The straw in the stalls was fresh and clean, and lacked the dusty, musty smell so often found in an army stable or a wagon master's livery.

If the servants were healthy, clean, and relatively well-dressed, the soldiers on guard were even more so. None were attired in battle gear, for to do so would have been unnecessary this far from the front. Each, however, was well-equipped enough to be able to give a good account of himself in a skirmish – and to give his comrades time to retreat and return fully armed and armored, should the need arise. With the marble columns, porcelain fountains and perfect topiary, this estate was quite literally paradise – or at least as close to such a place as he had ever seen.

A paradise, however, is not complete without a god or goddess in residence. And this place indeed had such a deity – for to describe the woman who descended the steps from the palatial residence to which the gardens led as a beautiful, elegant woman would be such an under-statement as to be a lie. The golden jewelry about her hair, neck, wrists, and even toes caught the light of the sun and shot it back out in rays, giving the illusion that they were not reflections but instead emanated from her. The silken coral-colored robes similarly caught the sunlight and glistened, each step causing a rippling wave of fabric and light to dance about her. Some women would dress in such a manner so as to make themselves seem more beautiful than they are; for this woman, however, it was she who adorned and enhanced her jewels and silks, instead of the other way around. Without a second thought, Dimitrios, Ari, Halime, and everyone else in sight either bowed deeply or went down on both knees and prostrated themselves, performing the proskynesis in respect, or out of awe, or both.

Everyone, however, except Klemes. He stood quite still, one hand scratching his chin, and with the other he gave a slight wave and said to the radiant goddess: "Princess Barsine, I presume?"

81

North of Myndos

BY THE SEA, BY THE SEA, BY THE BEAUTIFUL SEA

Gliding across the still waters of the wine dark sea, the squadron of Persian ships rounded Myndos Head then gracefully swung to the east. It was the kind of perfectly choreographed maneuver that would put a troupe of temple dancers to shame. Captain Abibaal's vessel set the pace and led the way as ship after ship slid onto the rocky beach. With barely a pause and while the vessels were still rocking, lightly armored men leaped overboard. Waves lapping at their thighs, the advance guard raced to secure the beachhead. Bare minutes later the rope ladders, gangplanks, and ramps were lowered so that horses, their riders, spearmen, and archers could disembark. Captain Abibaal went ashore with them. So did his chief passenger, an aging Greek general who, despite being weighed down with helmet, shield, breastplate, bronze greaves on his shins, and a long spear, skipped almost gingerly through the water to the beach, giddy as a schoolgirl at being once again on dry land.

"There's no time to waste, Captain Abibaal," said the general. "I'll leave it to you to play the part of beach master and guide the men to the rally points as they disembark. As for me, I'll be with the lads that have already formed up. It's inland we go for a bit of pillage, plunder, and poking about. We'll hit these Macedonian bastards where it hurts them most – their pride – and after we burn their supplies, we'll skip back to the beach and be off before they've so much as dressed their ranks. You just be ready to take us aboard and shove off when we get back. Much as I'd love a pitched battle with those sons of bitches," he added with a great big smile, "that's not what this is all about now, is it?"

"I guess not, General," replied the Phoenician captain, whose long years of service in the imperial Persian navy had taught him the difference between being brave and smart as opposed to being brave and stupid. "A few hundred men wouldn't last long on this beach against an army of thousands..."

"Aye," General Ephialtes nodded, "but even a bee can sting an elephant – and sting him where it hurts."

"Well then," added Abibaal with a laugh, "go lead your little swarm of bees – and sting'em once for me."

With the majority of the Macedonian troops to the west of Halicarnassos busy digging fresh approach trenches and siege weapon positions from which to hammer the Myndos Gate and adjoining wall sections, striking from the beach into their rear was a comparatively easy maneuver. The Persian light troops were experts at finding and taking out guard posts and scouts, and, as Ephialtes had predicted, the Macedonian supply tents were set afire before the defenders could react in strength.

"Don't spare the torches, lads," Ephialtes almost chortled with joy as he directed his men to their task. "Today we are arsonists first and warriors second! So burn'em out, my bonnie ladies, burn'em out!"

With Ptolemy away at the king's tent on the opposite side of the city, command of the Myndos front had fallen on the shoulders of a trio of officers: Moebos, Larriandros and Curlicas. Generals who owed their promotions more to their loyalty and fawning friendship to Ptolemy than to their experience in the field, their ability to react, let alone coordinate their reaction to the Persian landing was as much a comedy as it was a tragedy, depending upon the perspective of the viewer. They bumbled and stumbled into each other as they dashed about the camp, half-dressed in their armor and a bit in their cups. They gave orders which contradicted each other, sent troops right when they should have gone left, and, leading from the rear, were already in a good position to get themselves to a place as far from the point of the spear as they could get.

There were, of course, many fine, brave, smart junior officers who, on their own initiative, pulled together bands of stalwart fighters to stem the Persian tide. But as the tide was already receding by the time they had put their troops in order, there was little for them to do but watch as their camp burned. They were well positioned to stop any move by the Persians to attack the siege lines from the rear – but as Ephialtes had neither the men nor the intention of doing so, were more spectators than players in the game.

The Macedonian light cavalry, however, were led by more aggressive, veteran officers. If the infantry were all but paralyzed and on the defense, these brave horse soldiers raced into action. Trying to lead horses in a cavalry charge through a camp with its jumble of tents, ropes, barrels, and wagons, however, let alone a camp on fire, was not an easy task – or a successful one. More of them were thrown from their horses who balked at the bad footing and worse flames, than fell to Persian arrows. Those who did make it through were easy meat for the spears of the Greek mercenaries who formed the hard core of Ephialtes' raiding force. A few small groups and some individuals did spur their mounts to push ahead, but only to find Ephialtes and a rear guard of 100 hoplites in their path. By the time Ptolemy had learned of the disaster and ridden around the semicircular siege lines back to Myndos, the last of the raiders were boarding their boats and pushing them off into the sea.

The last of those raiders being an aging mercenary Greek hoplites and a somewhat younger but still quite seasoned Phoenician sailor.

533

"Where to, next, General?" asked Abibaal.

"Home. The Macedonians will be on their guard now – that old rascal Parmenion will see to that. 'Fool me once,' as the saying goes, but we'll not pull the wool over his eye twice. After all, he only has one" said Ephialtes as he let loose a deep belly laugh. "Besides, this means they'll be pulling men out of the trenches to double and triple the guard, and they'll need to send more out deep inland to make up for the supplies we burned today."

"So, we just go back into port?" asked Abibaal somewhat glumly. "I am so utterly bored with Halicarnassos...and so are my men. They know every whore and tavern wench by name and long for someone – and something – new."

"Aye, lad, being a garrison soldier is dull work."

"It's even worse for a sailor," replied Abibaal. "Ships need constant upkeep, whether they're on land or at sea – but at least at sea there is the wind in your hair, the sun on your face, and the possibility of something happening at any moment. Life's an adventure at sea, General, even if you're just on a routine patrol. On land, well, on land is where sailors get into trouble...and up to no good."

Holding on tightly with one hand to a rope by the side of the tiller, as the scout ship elegantly plied the waves back to Halicarnassos, and enjoying the cool breeze and the gentle rocking of the sturdy little vessel, General Ephialtes allowed himself a moment's reverie before responding.

"Well, you know, Captain," he said, thoughtfully stroking his chin with the other hand, "I'm sure I could talk Memnon and your admiral into letting you have an adventure – at least a little one, mind you. After all, from what you say, a bit of sport might be just the thing to keep your crew sharp...and out of the wine shops and whorehouses, even if Halicarnassos does have some of the best of both that I have ever seen."

82

Diospolis

THE PRINCESS WILL HAVE IT HER WAY

"I have heard the words my husband commanded you to pass on, good Captain," said the Lady Barsine quite regally but with a hint of a smile, "and I appreciate the perils you and your companions have faced and overcome in order to deliver my lord Memnon's message. That said, however," she added as she slowly rose from her chair, "I find that I am unable to comply with my husband's instructions to retire for safety deep into the empire."

"But my Lady," said the captain, who stood at attention like a free Greek rather than perform the proskynesis of a Persian subject, "the general was quite clear that I am to see you safely away. If I return without having done as he bid, I will not only have failed in my mission, but, if I may be so bold, have failed a friend, for such has the general been to me. Please, Princess, I beg of you, do not put me in such a position – let me accompany you to a place of safety."

Princess Barsine allowed herself a slightly bigger smile, and replied: "Do not worry, Captain. I am not going to send you back to my general, not alone, anyway."

"What do you mean by that, Princess," responded Dimitrios with a puzzled look upon his face.

"What I mean, Captain," she said with what could have been

mistaken almost for a little giggle, were she anyone other than a princess of the blood, "is that instead of sending you back to Memnon, I require that you lead me back to him. After all, a wife's place is at her husband's side..."

"But not in a battle!" said Dimitrios, forgetting his station and coming forward to stand face-to-face with her, or rather her face to his chest, with them each turning their heads to look the other in the eye. "It is far too dangerous! I can't bring a woman into a city under siege!"

"And I am not asking you to bring a 'woman' into a city under siege, but to escort a princess to stand beside her general. I am no ordinary woman, Captain," she said, changing her tone to become more serious, more commanding, more haughty and, well, more royal. "I am Barsine, wife of the marshal of the Persian Empire's forces in Asia, widow of an imperial general, daughter of the satrap of Hellespontine Phrygia and sister of a royal counselor. My mother was a Greek princess and thus the blood of the Achaeans, the Pharnacids, and the Achaemenids runs in my veins. I am, my dear 'Captain' (which she said slowly and quite pointedly so as to remind him of the difference in their rank), a princess – and a princess royal to boot. So, you see, my good Captain, you will not be bringing a woman to a city under siege, but escorting a princess to war."

"Well that went well," said Dimitrios sarcastically as he tossed his helmet across the room to Ari.

"What do you mean, brother?" asked Klemes, who had found a small but rather excellent little library in the villa and was perusing a rare medical scroll he had borrowed from its shelves, when Dimitrios entered.

"The princess doesn't want to go east to safety, as Memnon ordered."

"Well, that is her prerogative, being a woman and a princess at that," mumbled Klemes, turning back to the scroll. "It's not like you can force her to do what the general wants, short of kidnapping her and tying her to a mule – which I think her guards and our hosts would take issue with. You delivered the message; you've done your duty."

"You don't understand, brother," said Dimitrios, fuming. "It's not just that she won't go east. She wants to go to Halicarnassos – and wants me to take here there."

Klemes let out a little laugh, then a bigger one. No longer able to hold on to the scroll due to his laughing, he let it roll up in the middle of the table upon which he had set it.

"Oh, you can't be serious," said the physician, in evident amusement. "This little princess of yours wants to go to what is arguably the single most dangerous place on earth? Which means, not only going back over that awful route we took, but somehow managing to get through an enemy army, and into a city under siege. Really? I hope you told her to pull the other one."

"That is not something one tells a princess," said Dimitrios, gritting his teeth. "Especially not one who is married to your commanding general."

"Well, then, good luck to the little lady and all who travel with her. It is no longer your concern. You did your duty. You delivered the message."

"Didn't you hear me, brother?" asked Dimitrios pointedly. "She wants – no, she orders – us to guide her on this mad adventure."

Klemes laughed again. "Well, I hope you set her straight on that one. I'm not daft enough to go back into that hell, and neither are you, right? There's a lot more to see and do in this world and I intend to do it, and so should you."

Dimitrios gave his brother a look that could not be mistaken for agreement. A glowering, scolding look that without words imparted the notion that he, Dimitrios, had, even against his better judgment and all common sense, agreed to do exactly what the princess demanded – or die trying.

"No," said Klemes, his laughter fading and his uncharacteristically boisterous joviality replaced by a sense of doom and disbelief. "No, you don't mean to say...no, brother. Even you are not that stupid."

The remainder of the very long day was taken up by preparations for the journey. The princess, give her her due, gave no order to anyone to accompany her to Halicarnassos. Instead, she gathered together everyone at the villa. Appearing before them in leather armor and martial traveling attire, sword at her hip and bow and quiver upon her back, she addressed them thus:

"As you all know, my husband, your lord and general, Memnon, is besieged in Halicarnassos. You surely also know by now that this Greek soldier, a captain on my husband's staff, has braved fire and sword, heat and hunger, to bring a message from my beloved. Memnon bids me to take our children and to go east, deep inside the empire, to safety."

Barsine paused a moment to let her words sink in, although she knew that all around her had already at least heard a rumor to the effect of what she had decided to do.

"As much as I appreciate my husband's concern, I have decided that I shall comply with only some of what he wishes. My children left this morning under escort for Damascus. There they will be safe, well cared for, and find comfort in the home of friends of our family. I, on the other hand, intend to join my husband. It is my desire to go west, to find a way through or around the Macedonian siege lines, and to stand by his side upon the battlements of Halicarnassos. That is where the wife of a soldier needs to be."

"Pardon me, great lady," Klemes interrupted, much to Dimitrios' embarrassment, "would it not make more sense to go due south, or south and east, until you reach a friendly port? From there you could take a ship to the city."

"While I am not in the habit of explaining myself," glowered the princess, "I will do so just this once, and in this case, as you are foreigners to our ways – and our geography. Trust me when I say that this is the shortest and quickest route to the city. Besides, can you guarantee I will find a ship willing to sail into a besieged port, let alone a captain who will take a woman, even one of royal standing, aboard?

No, you cannot. So we shall do as I say – and," she said quite regally and sternly (and even a bit threateningly) "we will discuss this no more."

Klemes made to answer, but an imploring and cautionary glare from his brother entreating him to remain silent kept the physician from replying with anything other than a nod of acceptance.

"Then that is settled. As for the dangers, well," she continued bravely and with a smile, "if my husband, a Greek soldier from Rhodes, is willing to give his life to defend the city and people of Hali-carnassos, how can I, a princess of the blood, do anything less?"

Once again, the princess paused for a moment to let her words take root among those she had called together.

"This undertaking is my decision and mine alone. It will be dangerous and difficult, and its outcome is by no means certain. I know that my rank and my blood give me the authority to command each and every one of you to accompany me, to protect me, and to give your lives for me. I have that right," she said quite loudly and with great authority, "but it is a right that I shall not invoke."

Again, she paused, at which point mumbles and murmurs of aston-ishment and confusion rippled through the small crowd before her.

"I know it is not normally our custom, but in this instance, I will not demand that any of you accompany me. Instead, I ask that you do. To those who refuse, rest assured you will face no punishment, nor lose any honor. On the contrary, I will give any who wish to leave a tablet allowing them free passage anywhere in the empire, and a small bag of silver coins to help start a new life. To those who do choose to come with me, on the other hand, I offer nothing but my heartfelt thanks," she added, choking back a little hint of the emotions she felt. "That, and a promise that, whatever may happen, each of you shall be to me not a servant or a soldier, but a brother or a sister, and will remain so to my dying day – a day, which, to be honest, I fear may come long ere we spy the triple towers of Halicarnassos."

"Damn," said Klemes quietly to his brother, "damn, she's good. She's very good." Apparently the two score soldiers, servants, and retainers who heard the princess were of the same mind as Klemes. To a man – and woman – they rushed to pledge themselves to their princess. Some wept, some went down on their knees, and some came forward to kiss her hands, her boots or the fabric of her trousers.

Realizing that no matter what he said or what arguments he could make the princess would be heading west, Dimitrios just gave a great, deep sigh. He did not rush forward, but stood rock still, grudgingly accepting that, while to go with her to perhaps certain death was far from an ideal decision, to refuse to go with her would be worse. If, by some miracle, she got through without him, or was captured or killed trying, it would bring down upon him such dishonor and guilt that he feared he could never raise his head again in soldierly company – or live with himself. While he firmly believed that her chances of success – or even survival – were minimal, he also believed that his presence and experience might improve those chances, at least a little. At worst, he would die with honor defending not just a princess, but the wife of a man for whom he felt not merely the respect due his rank but also the friendship and sense of brotherhood that only those who have faced death together can share.

Klemes, too, was certain this was a bad idea – perhaps the worst idea his brother had ever come up, even worse than this quest to seek revenge for Thebes and their lost friends by fighting Alexander. After all, what had that quest brought? Not riches, nor fame, nor satisfaction. He, his brother and their friend Ari had been stabbed, clubbed, chained, whipped, stuck with arrows, come close to dying of sunstroke and exhaustion, and nearly drowned – and on more than one occasion. Driven to near madness and imminent death from thirst, hunger, wounds, battle, and captivity, neither he nor his brother, let alone their young friend, had anything to show for their exertions. They had not even helped win any battles, instead having been on the losing end at the Granicos and Miletos. While they escaped being besieged at Hali-carnassos, Klemes feared that the three Thebans were now about to add a new entry to their lengthening list of failures.

This quest his brother had undertaken, thought Klemes, may not have been such a good idea as they had all once thought back in Thebes.

Still, just as Dimitrios could not bring himself to abandon the princess, nor could Klemes let his brother commit himself to this task, bad as it was, on his own. Nor could Ari, whose youthful exuberance somehow continued to buoy up his spirits and to whom this all still seemed like some grand adventure. That he was hopelessly in love with Halime, who had been among the first to rush forward to volunteer to accompany the princess, put an end to any discussion in his mind – or heart – as to which direction he would take.

As for Halime, something about the princess spoke to the adventurer in her own soul, and of course to the good, patriotic Persian whom she was. Like Barsine, she too was the daughter of a great warrior and the sister to a pack of soldiers. That her loved ones may have given their lives for the empire only redoubled her own determination to do her part in the war. Brought up to ride before she could walk, to shoot a bow, rope a horse, and track a prey alongside her brothers, Halime was not about to let everyone else have all of the fun – or take on all of the dangers alone. Barsine, seeing something of her younger self in the girl, gave her a look that showed she graciously accepted Halime's offer to serve in her entourage as something more than a mere serving girl or lady in waiting.

Halime was not alone among the Persians at the villa to pledge themselves to Barsine. Burzasp and his brothers, and their family's retainers, also stepped forward. It was but a small step to take when they had already offered her the hospitality and protection of their home.

As for those who lived and worked at the villa, other than some elderly servants, children, and their mothers who had been intentionally excused from the gathering, most took up the other offer of silver and safety. The handful of faithful guards who had accompanied Barsine this far could have taken the money, as she had pointedly offered to release them from her service, however, elected not to take the purse of coins. They, too, agreed to go wherever the princess would lead them. They did not care if it meant they were to go into the jaws of hell or Halicarnassos, between which, as Dimitrios had cautioned, there was little, if any, difference.

83

Halicarnassos

A COMMANDER'S PLANS; A PRINCESS' ACTS

As the princess stepped off on her journey to Halicarnassos, the general she hoped to see and the king she hoped to avoid were busy with their own plans. So, too, were a fat queen, a restless admiral and numerous other actors upon the stage that was western Asia.

Inside Halicarnassos, Memnon and the rest of the Persian high command continued their daily inspections of the damage caused by the Macedonian bombardment. They oversaw repairs and planned and readied minor raids on the coastal areas behind the enemy siege works and the lines of communications beyond. Although they had settled into a routine, no day was dull, no day was without problems, and no day was without challenges. Each rock or flaming pot thrown at the city, and each casualty, chipped away at the morale of the defenders, just as the arrival of each supply ship or the return of a group of victorious raiders bolstered it. Time was not kind, but time was, as Memnon reminded his officers, on their side.

"Every day we hold out," he would conclude each staff meeting, "is a day the army that the King of Kings is raising grows larger. All we need do is hold our ground, and we shall be the anvil upon which the hammer of Darius strikes to flatten the Macedonian invaders."

Across the shored-up battlements, churned-up plain and ever-encroaching siege works, Alexander too met daily with his commanders. He knew time was not on his side – and for more reasons than Memnon gave.

"My mother made a bargain with the gods, not unlike that made by the mother of Achilles," he would routinely remind his officers. "I am like a candle burning bright – but only for so long. I have been given but little time on this earth before I must rejoin my true father on Olympus. I must not squander any more of these precious days left here, in front of this city. So, my dear companions," he would conclude almost every meeting, "it is once again a matter of victory or death and, as I said to you at Miletos, by that I mean my victory...or your death."

The raids by the Persian fleet along the coasts had disrupted Alexander's supplies of food and slaves, both of which he was always in short supply. The siege took on a life of its own, becoming a monster whose appetite was never satiated and which only grew more demanding and more ravenous with each feeding. As the Persian raids grew bolder and more destructive, the farther inland did Alexander's foragers have to go to scavenge for the manpower and victuals that the siege monster devoured in prodigious amounts.

It was one such foraging party that Barsine and her Persian

princess parade came upon as they proceeded on toward Halicarnassos...

It was Halime who first spotted the Macedonians – or, more correctly, as Dimitrios explained after she had quietly called him forward to spy on the enemy, a collection of allied cavalry working for the Macedonians.

"Those outriders there, see, they are the Prodromoi," said Dimitrios as he crouched behind a pile of rocks at the top of the low rise above the valley. Down below, the enemy troops were busy at work gathering supplies – or rather herding men and women into groups to pack and carry food and fodder.

"The lazy ones, sitting on their horses, drinking and laughing, you mean? They're Macedonians, right?"

"No, only a few are from Macedonia. Mostly they are barbarians, recruited from Thrace or Thessaly. They only work for the Macedonians."

"They don't look like they'd be much to take on in a fight," Halime remarked with a little laugh. "Bunch of slothful drunkards who look like they can barely stay on their horses."

"Don't let their idle, drunken behavior fool you into letting your guard down," whispered Dimitrios. "I've fought those bastards too many times before, from a farm outside Thebes to the Granicos and on the way out of Halicarnassos. They are experts with a lance. Each time I have been lucky to escape with my life."

"All right," said Halime, "but then those other horsemen, the ones riding about, whipping the farmers...they're Macedonians, right?"

"Sort of," sighed Dimitrios. "Those are Paeonians. Nasty tribes-men. So nasty the barbarian Thracians call them barbarians. They are experts with the javelin. They race up, throw, turn back, circle around and keep doing that over and over again until they run out of javelins."

"Then what do they do?"

"They go back for more."

Halime was a little confused but was trying to sort it all out when she spied a pair of big, heavily armored men on massive horses. "Now those," she nudged Dimitrios, "those must be real Macedonians."

"Yes, they are. Even worse, however," he added, "they are Companions. From the heavy cavalry, from which Alexander draws his bodyguard and strike force. They must be in charge of this crew."

"So we take them out and the rest, what, all run away?" asked Halime hopefully.

"What do you mean 'take them out,' Halime? We're not here to fight, we're here to scout – to find a way into Halicarnassos without having to fight."

"But we outnumber them!" said Halime, excitedly. "Me, Burzasp and his horse archers, we can knock a dozen of them out of the saddle from here, and then the rest of you can charge in and finish them off!"

"Halime," said Dimitrios as quietly as possible, difficult as that was becoming, "a lot of us are not mounted fighters. We just ride to battle and dismount. Those are trained horsemen – battle-hardened killers. Even if we did kill them – we'd have to kill them all, every one of them, or else they'd ride for reinforcements. And that would put an end to Barsine's Persian princess parade right quick."

"But you've done it before, right?"

"Yes," moaned Dimitrios, "but that was different. Then we had no choice – and they didn't have a pair of Companions with them. Those bastards die hard – real hard. Alexander forms them into flying wedges and leads them into massed formations of enemy cavalry – and infantry – and breaks them, breaks them into little pieces for the rest of the cavalry to gobble up. And I don't feel much like being gobbled up today, thank you very much!"

After Dimitrios finished his rant he heard a sobbing noise. It was Halime.

"What's wrong now?" he asked.

"I...I...I didn't know you were such...such a coward," she managed to mumble between tears. "Or that you were such a bully. You didn't have to speak to me like that...I don't let anyone speak to me like that, except perhaps my father – who would never do so – or my brothers – and then only the ones older than me."

"Halime," said Dimitrios, taken by surprise and immediately sorry for how he spoke to her.

"Well, coward," said Halime, rising to her knees, notching and arrow and drawing her bow. "If you won't fight these bastards, I will!"

Halime's second arrow was in the air before the first even found its target – a Thracian drinking deeply from a wineskin while sitting on his horse. The second struck the shield of a Paeonian, but only because he turned to see why the other horseman was acting so strange. Had he not, it would have struck him in the neck. Within a breath he had grabbed a javelin, given the alarm and spied his target – a young girl on the hill who would have let loose a third arrow –

had not a man in Greek armor tackled her and dragged her out of sight.

The Paeonian horseman kicked his heels into the sides of his mount and raced up the low slope, javelin at the ready, raised above his head, while he scanned the rise for his target. As he went up and over the top, Dimitrios rose up and pulled him from the horse. Halime did not hesitate, and stabbed the enemy soldier repeatedly with her dagger, even while Dimitrios and her target were rolling about in the dirt. Two other riders from the princess' entourage were at the bottom of the hill, holding on to the horses that Dimitrios and Halime had ridden up on. One turned about and raced to the rear to get help, while the other charged up the hill, the reins to the other horses still in one hand.

"Leave him!" shouted the Persian rider. "Mount up! We've got to get out of here!"

Halime ran and jumped up onto her horse, but Dimitrios, being an infantryman at heart, struggled to mount. His horse was skittish, due to all of the activity, and finally, he just gave up. Dimitrios slapped the horse on the rump and then ran after it, racing as fast as he could into the dust that Halime's horse and the others were kicking up. Had he spared a moment to gaze over his shoulder, he would have seen a chilling sight – half a dozen assorted enemy cavalrymen topping the rise and coming at a full gallop – straight for him.

Dimitrios saw the rear end of Halime's horse and those of the other two riders disappear over the next rise. He heard rather than saw the javelins the enemy horsemen tossed in his direction. His lungs about to burst from the exertion, he nevertheless kept on running after Halime. Only moments after she dropped out of sight, however, five riders came boiling back over the top of that hillock. Burzasp and his brothers let fly their arrows as they came up, then expertly, and effortlessly, slung their bows, and drew sword, mace or javelin, each to his own preference. The Persians rushed past Dimitrios, expertly if barely avoiding him, and crashed into the enemy.

The mix of Paeonian and Thracian cavalry had not expected to be confronted by, let alone collide with, an equal number of Persian horsemen. Burzasp and his brothers made quick work of the enemy light cavalry, and then kept on going, back over the rise from which Halime and Dimitrios had first spotted the Macedonian forage party. Dimitrios collapsed to the ground, fighting for breath, as they disappeared from view. Within moments a second group of horsemen – Halime of all people at their head – all but flew over the top of the hillock from where she had ridden but a second ago. She was screaming – no, screeching – a shrill and mindlessly joyful battle cry, waving a sword that was far too big for her, with a dozen assorted Persian riders in tow. Dimitrios just sat there, in the dirt, as Halime and her horde swept past, up, and over the hill toward the Macedonians. Dimitrios heard the sounds of battle, but had no idea what was happening.

As he sat there, still fighting for breath, a shadow fell over him. Dimitrios looked up to see Klemes and Ari sitting astride a pair of tired-looking ponies. Each man had a big grin on his face.

"So, brother," said Klemes, "taking a bit of a rest, are we, while little girls fight your battles?"

84

On the Coast near Halicarnassos

WALKING ON WATER

A s they continued westward, the princess and her party suffered few incidents even remotely as dangerous as their encounter with the enemy cavalry. There were random sightings of scouts, but Burzasp and his brothers either chased them away – or ran them to ground, with fatal consequences for their prey. As it would be impossible to enter the city from the north, due to the siege lines, Dimitrios had recommended driving south, across the base of the peninsula on which the city was set. By staying well to the east, that would bring them to the coast just southeast of Halicarnassos, across from the slender island that paralleled the coast and whose northern-most tip was opposite its harbor.

The princess agreed to this course, trusting that, when they got to the coast, they would be able to spy some fishermen, a trading vessel, or one of the supply ships that fed the city under siege. Even if none of those could offer passage into Halicarnassos, they could at least carry a message to Admiral Autophadrates or even to Memnon himself, either of whom, she was certain, would surely send a ship to pick them up.

Their route took them through or near numerous farms, villas, and villages, but all were devoid of life, human or animal. The people had fled or been enslaved to build the Macedonian siege works. Alexander's foragers had stripped those areas of everything edible, and had carried off all of the livestock. Many of the buildings had either been burned to the ground or, if left partially standing, lacked roofs, as the Macedonian raiding parties had been quite playful and thorough in devastating the area. Every piece of timber that could be carried off had been taken, as the siege works and the army's cooking fires both devoured wood at a prodigious rate. The wild game in the area had also been hunted near to extinction, and even the streams appeared fished out. Having planned to supplement their rations by hunting or purchasing food from these settlements, the princess and her party had brought few rations. As such, they were beginning to feel the first effects, if not of hunger, at least of having to travel on nearly empty stomachs.

It was thus with great relief that a week into their journey Dimitrios caught his first glimpse of the sea. Although no ships were in sight at the moment, the sight of the sea meant this stage of the journey was over. "I may not have gotten the princess to safety as I promised the general," he said to Halime, who continued to serve as interpreter between the captain and Burzasp, "but at least I...or I should say 'we' have seen her safe this far."

"But that is not enough for our princess," replied Burzasp. "She will not rest until she is reunited with her husband. We must contact a ship – any ship – if we are to proceed, and I do not see any, do you?"

"I am a soldier, but I was a wine merchant before Alexander destroyed my city and my livelihood. I understand something of ships and shipping lanes, having traveled on enough of them myself, but I do not know these waters."

"Nor do I, Greek," huffed Burzasp. "Give me a horse and I will ride into hell itself...but of the sea, I know nothing...other than it is ...well, wet, and no place for a horse."

"Ah, yes, as my brother used to say, 'you can lead a horse to water but you can't make it walk on it.'"

"Did I hear someone mention me?" said Klemes, as he rode up to join Dimitrios, Halime, and Burzasp.

"I was just telling Burzasp here that old saying of yours about horses not being able to walk on water..."

"Yes," nodded Klemes, "but they can swim."

"In the sea?" Dimitrios shot back in surprise.

"No, not in the wine dark sea itself, but you see where we are? That long island out there is not far off. A good swimmer could make it easily, and so could a horse. It blocks the waves and the wind, and makes for a calm and shallow channel."

"So you want us to swim our horses across it to that island? To what purpose?"

"Well, Dimitrios, damn it, I'm a physician, not a sailor, but I have seen that island before – and from the other side."

"Huh?"

"To the west of that island lies Cos, where I spent so many years at study. The shipping lanes pass between the two. The water here on this side is too shallow and the rocks too treacherous for passage. Oh, a fisherman might seek shelter here from a storm, but any other captain would beach his ship on the big island – or ride it out in hopes of reaching Cos or Halicarnassos. "

"So what do you recommend," Dimitrios replied with laugh, "you know, speaking as my naval adviser."

Klemes ignored the jibe and replied "we should cross here. We set up a camp and a signal fire in hopes of attracting a ship passing on the lanes. We can also send some riders up the length of the island to a point just opposite the city. There, too, you can set a signal fire. Someone in the city or a ship on patrol is bound to come and investigate."

Dimitrios did not say a word. He was truly speechless, so surprised was he by his brother's detailed answer.

"What? What is it brother?" said Klemes with a very slight smile and a single raised eyebrow. "You may be the only one in this family who can fight his way out of trouble – but you're not the only one who can think his way out of it. Go run along to the princess and tell her my plan...and don't worry, you can let her think this is all your idea. Wouldn't want to burst your bubble or have her pestering me for advice. So, go. What are you waiting for? The sun will set soon and we should be about this if we are to do it today."

"You want me to do what?" Princess Barsine replied in surprise when Dimitrios explained his brother's plan. "Can I not just stay here and make camp while you go swimming to the island? When you find a ship, you can just send it for me."

"Pardon me, Your Highness," replied the captain with a bow. "We have too few fighting men as it is to protect you properly. If we split our forces, that puts you at an increased risk."

"From whom?" the princess said with disdain as she sipped on the last of the wine they had brought with them. "The raiders won't come back – there is nothing of value left to raid."

"But enemy patrols..."

"It has been days since we saw anyone other than a stray scout. Do not worry, Captain, we shall be fine here."

The captain turned to Burzasp, who had accompanied him back to the rough tent that had been set up to offer the princess some shade. The Persian horseman knew that was his cue.

"Highness," he said with as respectful and obsequious a bow as possible without falling to his knees, "the Greek captain is right. The great Cyrus himself warned about dividing forces in the face of the enemy..."

"What enemy?" laughed the princess. "Are you, too, seeing Macedonian faces in every shadow, behind every rock and bush?"

"No, Highness," replied Burzasp, hiding any offense he might have taken from her reply. "But if a scout does show up, we may not have enough riders to chase him away or kill him – or even spot him. And once we set up a signal beacon, they will see it and send out patrols. All it takes is for one to report back about the presence of an unexplained group of riders camped out here and a troop of Macedonian cavalry will be upon you in a thrice. So, please, Highness, for the sake of my honor if not for your own safety, please cross the channel with us. Besides, we will all be much safer on the island."

"But for how long?" she replied, starting to see the reason in the request by Burzasp and Dimitrios that she accompany them over the water.

"Not long, Highness," said Dimitrios. "One of our ships will surely spot the beacon. Besides, we will be on the far side of that island, and thus masked from whatever prying eyes ride along this shore. Even if we are spotted, they will have to cross the channel to get to us...and we will be waiting for them on dry ground on the far shore, arrows notched. And there is little danger of them coming by sea. After all," he added, "Alexander disbanded his fleet, and we, as always, rule the waves."

The princess took a moment to consider the argument. She raised one hand, a signal that none other should speak to interrupt her thoughts. After a few breaths, she lowered her hand, raised her gaze to look Dimitrios directly in the eye, and said "very well then. How do you intend to organize our crossing?"

The plan was a simple one, put forward by Klemes in private to his brother.

"This is the channel," he said, sketching a diagram in the sand. "You should set up three columns of riders. The strongest should be on the outsides, and the princess and her train in the center. That way, should she or any of her women fall from their mount or be swept off their horse, there will be someone to rescue them."

"And where will you be, Klemes?" he asked.

"In the middle, of course. After all, brother..."

"I know, I know, you're a physician, not a swimmer."

85

Halicarnassos

HELL, BY ALEXANDER

"This time the trumpets shall never call retreat. Not again. Never again," said Alexander, raising his voice, slamming his fist on the map table and taking a moment to look directly into the eyes (or, in Parmenion's case, eye) of his generals and companions. "We take the city today, even if it takes us all day, and all night, and into the next," he added with a grim, icy seriousness. "We do not stop, no matter what the cost. Do you understand me?"

Alexander's generals nodded and mumbled variations of "yes, sire," but their lack of enthusiasm was obvious, as was their resolve.

"You don't believe I mean what I am saying about 'no retreat,' is that it? Well, generals, I am serious. Deadly serious. So serious, in fact, that I have ordered the Companion Cavalry to take position behind each of your commands. They have orders to cut down any man who retreats – and by that I do mean any man – regardless of his rank, station, or birth. And if you think they won't do it, well, you know to whom they are devoted," added Alexander with a nasty, vicious smile. "And to further ensure that devotion, I have promised to pay them one of Darius' silver arrow coins for each deserter's head they take. Oh," and he paused to let that sink in, before adding "and a gold one for that of any general who so much as pauses in their assault."

"Sire! That is not only unnecessary and cruel, but also is an insult to our very honor!" roared Parmenion in outrage. "Your father would never treat his soldiers, let alone his generals, in such a manner."

Hephaestion shook his head and rolled his eyes. When will Parmenion learn, he thought to himself. The single most guaranteed way to set Alexander off or to insure you will lose an argument is to compare him unfavorably to Philip. How many times had Parmenion made that mistake? Trying to 'school' Alexander with 'what would Philip do – or do not do,' was the worst of all courses to take. Someday Parmenion would learn that – but today, obviously, was not that day.

Alexander's response, as Hephaestion knew it would be, was swift, violent, and explosive. The king drew his sword and lunged for the old general. Had it not been for Cleitos lurching forward to seize Alexander's wrist with his massive hands, the young king would surely have skewered Parmenion. Even with his great strength and advantage in height, weight, and muscle, Cleitos did not stop the king with ease, as the veins bulging in his neck clearly showed.

Ptolemy, too, acted swiftly, knowing just as Hephaestion did what the king would do in response to Parmenion's taunt. He threw his own not inconsiderable weight into shoving the old general out of the path of the king's blade – and took a deep cut in the arm for his troubles. The other generals stepped back and made to draw their own swords until Hephaestion moved to check them from such folly.

"My lords and generals," said Hephaestion in as loud and as commanding a voice as any the comparatively slight and slender young man had ever used on the parade ground or the battlefield, "my lords and generals!" While a grammatically incomplete sentence, the very phrase was pregnant with caution, and each man in the room – except perhaps the enraged king, the insulted Parmenion, and the bleeding Ptolemy – understood. That shout, plus the general clamor and Ptolemy's scream of pain and surprise, brought in the guards – who, as Hephaestion in his wisdom had ordered, were from his own personal squadron. These were loyal men of the Companion Cavalry – but short of killing the king would do anything – anything – Hephaestion told them to do, and without hesitation, question, or remorse. As such, the commander of the guard looked to Hephaestion for direction as he charged into the tent.

"Guards," said Hephaestion firmly and as calmly as he could manage, "General Ptolemy has injured himself by accident. Please escort him to the surgeon's tent. And take Parmenion along with you, as he appears to be ill. See that both are well cared for, and remain with them until I come to see them."

The officer of the guard understood what Hephaestion was saying, that the one man needed a physician and the other needed watching over – and to be kept secure and isolated, lest Parmenion do something even more foolish than what he had already done. Cleitos, in the meantime, gently wrestled Alexander to a stool, and carefully took the sword from his hand. Hephaestion knelt down beside the king, put his arm around his shoulder and sweetly kissed him on the forehead.

"Why does he always do that!" moaned Alexander, placing his head in his hands, weeping with a mix of rage and embarrassment. "I've burned Thebes, won a great battle at the Granicos, taken Miletos and a dozen other cities and still...still he treats me like a child! I am sick of this, Hephaestion. I am sick of him!"

"There, there, my dear, sweet, and lovely friend," said Hephaestion, all but cooing into the king's ear. "He's just a rough old soldier. He doesn't know when to keep his mouth shut, that's all. You've shown him – and the army, and the world – your mettle. Why let the grumblings of some old limping fart bother you so?"

"If he wasn't such a good soldier I'd have his head," grumbled Alexander, "but I need him, at least for now. You know it, I know it, the army knows it...and, worst of all, he knows it. But not for long, not forever," said the king through gritted teeth. "His days are numbered, Hephaestion, and it is not long before he does something that tips the scales enough to..."

"I know, I know my King," said Hephaestion, taking a cup of watered wine from Cleitos' hand to give to Alexander. "I know. But today...today we need him. Swear, and curse, and spit, and grumble as he will surely do," said Hephaestion with a little laugh, "he will do what you tell him. He will march into hell – and his men will follow him."

"That may be true," replied the king with a nod. "We shall put him to the test, dear Hephaestion, for that is exactly where I am going to order him to go – into hell itself."

Hell is exactly what Parmenion confronted– and Alexander and the rest of his generals and soldiers. Every day Alexander's siege machines had knocked stones from the walls into the 40 foot wide ditch that blocked the path to the towering walls – and every night bands of workmen had come out of the city to clear what they could or to deepen the ditch, parts of which were now more than 20 feet deep. Each of the gates had been battered to splinters, and their towers bombarded mercilessly, yet they still stood – propped up and rein-forced by stones, timber and dirt from behind. In some areas, what appeared to be weak spots from the Macedonian point of view, were actually enticing entry points to a trap. In many ways, despite the ceaseless pounding, the defenses of Halicarnassos were stronger than they had been before the siege began.

What casualties the defenders took – and they took many – were made good by reinforcements brought in by the fleet, whose access to the big, wide harbor remained unhindered. Alexander's foragers had to range farther and farther afield for food and fodder, and even fresh water in the long, hot, dry summer. The countryside stripped bare and its streams drunk dry, his army began to depend more and more on the tenuous lifeline of slow, ponderous, and vulnerable wagon trains and caravans coming down from Miletos and Ephesos. In contrast, the garrison and people of Halicarnassos ate and drank their fill, courtesy of the Persian navy. The supply convoys came with such frequency that the outgoing ships barely had time to clear the quays before the next group of incoming vessels arrived.

In short, two months of siege, assault, and bombardment had taken a heavier toll on the besiegers than on the besieged. Halicarnassos was fast becoming the stone on which Memnon had said he would grind down the Macedonians...and Alexander knew it.

Which is why this attack would be the last – one way or another. It had to be. The Macedonians could not go forward while Memnon and his army and fleet had Halicarnassos as a base to hit their rear; and Alexander could not go back – not if he were to remain king. His treasury was empty, his army nearly as unhappy as his generals, and his rivals back home hungry for an excuse to topple the boy king. Not even Olympias with all of her magic and machinations could keep the wolves at bay much longer. This attack would truly spell victory or death for the Macedonian king. He knew he must take the city or die trying, lest he die later at the hands of an assassin, or mutineers.

Rather than send the same troops against walls they had failed to take in the previous assaults, Alexander shuffled his forces. Parmenion, he sent to the Myndos Gate in the east, while Ptolemy and his troops, along with the Royal Guard, moved from that front to opposite the Tripylon Gate in the north. Perdiccas, he brought from opposite the bastion back to the Mylasa Gate, while Alexander moved from there up to the north, opposite the bastion which poked out like a thumb to the east of the Tripylon. It took a lot of marching and counter-marching to redeploy the troops, but as Alexander explained to Hephaestion "how can men be expected to charge where they have previously met death and failure? To make them relive their nightmares and their disgrace is no way to seize victory from the jaws of defeat. Besides," he added, "fresh eyes may spy openings where those who have too long stared at the same walls for weeks see only strength. And who knows, the challenge of succeeding where other, perhaps in their minds lesser, men failed, may spur them on."

Hephaestion had shrugged his shoulders and nodded his head, having no solid reasons to object to this redeployment, as difficult to arrange as it was. After all, at least it got the men up and moving and out of the rat-infested trenches and shredded tents. A little exercise and a change of scenery, he agreed, couldn't hurt. So forward they went, Alexander watching it all from a spot just north of the Tripylon, his Silver Shields guardsmen and a squadron of the Companions at his back. The advance, timed to hit all three landward sides at the same time, went forward with parade-ground precision. And this time, however, as Alexander had warned at the morning conference, there would be no retreat, no matter the losses.

"They are coming on in the same old way," Ephialtes remarked with a chortle. He, Memnon, and Orontobates watched it all unfold from their headquarters in the citadel of Salmacis on the Royal Island. Situated almost due south of the Mylasa gate, and connected to the city by a causeway, its tall towers provided a secure perch for the high command. Admiral Autophradates had a similarly unobscured and almost panoramic view of Ptolemy's attack from his vantage point atop the castle at Arconnesos, which anchored the opposite end of the harbor from Salmacis and which also served as naval headquarters. From their respective vantage points, the Persian leaders had observed the comings and goings, and back and forth marches of the besiegers for days. After all, there was little the Macedonians could do to surprise the defenders, as from their headquarters the Persians saw every move of every battalion, phalanx, and squadron in the attacking force. But to see them come on all at once, from every direction, and with such determination – that even the Persians had to admit was impressive.

For hour upon endless hour, the Macedonians came forward. Like waves steadily pounding a rock, they rose, crashed, recoiled, and rose again. Unrelenting as they came forward, as courageous and even foolhardy as they fought, none of the attacking columns could as much as gain a toehold on the wall or in a breach, let alone at a gate. Yet no attack faltered, no defenders were given any respite, and losses continued to mount on both sides.

"There must be some point at which they will stop coming on," Ephialtes commented to Memnon as the day wore on and dusk approached. "No soldiers ever born can keep this up, not even your Immortals."

"I agree," nodded Memnon in agreement. "One party did break in but our valiant captain of the Immortals drove them back out, yet even that did not seem to shake their resolve."

"Well, then," said the old soldier, motioning for his helmet and spear, "then let me shake it for them. The Macedonians have been attacking all day – let us see how they like it when we come at them. Let me take the hoplites reserve and sally forth. Those Macedonians won't be expecting it – and they are not formed up to fight against a phalanx. I will sweep them away from the gate and back into their camp – and I won't stop till I've burned their tents, wrecked their siege engines and seized the king's golden tableware as a prize!"

Memnon had learned firsthand of Ephialtes' bravery and skill at command, and knew this to be no mere bit of bluster. If any man could do it, Ephialtes could, and if any men could do it, his Greek hoplites could. The general put a hand on Ephialtes shoulder, gave him his blessing and bid him do as the Greek promised.

"Fare thee well, my friend," said Memnon. "You and your two thousand fellow Greeks have a score of your own to settle."

"Aye," grinned Ephialtes, "and it is time for the little bully to pay the piper."

Ephialtes struck out from the Tripylon Gate in the north just as the sun began to sink, but with so many fires burning in the city and in the Macedonian trenches, there was enough light for the grim work ahead. As the Greek general had predicted, the attack caught the Macedonians on the wrong foot. Ptolemy's weary assault columns were in no condition or formation to stand against the advancing shield wall, which grew in breadth and depth as Ephialtes' Greeks gushed forward from the sally ports and the main gate, which had been opened to allow his attack to hit with the maximum number of men and power.

Ptolemy rallied the Royal Guard – or what remained of it – and counterattacked, but was unable to even blunt, let alone throw back the Greek phalanx. With measured step and cadence kept by pipers, the hoplites moved like a giant scythe, carving a swath through the Macedonians. Soon they were in amongst the Macedonian lines, with small parties from the rear ranks slipping out to set fires to war engines, stores, and tents. The main body, however, continued forward, sweeping aside all resistance as it went, machine like, into the Macedonian camp.

"What is happening? What is happening?" shouted Alexander from his place at the rear of Ptolemy's corps, as groups of wounded men stumbled back from the fray. "I ordered no retreat! I forbid any man to so much as take a step backwards!"

"It can't be helped," said Ptolemy, as he rode up from the chaos, his helmet gone, his armor battered and his arms dripping blood. "Those men are fresh – and they are tough. They are advancing like Spartans!" he added in acknowledgment of the courage and resolve of his enemies.

"Well, Ptolemy, we have met Spartans before," grinned Alexander. "And Thebans, and Athenians, and the rest. I beat them at Chaeronea, and I burned Thebes to the ground! Instead of hiding behind those tall walls they've come out to play. So..." he added cheerfully as he drew his sword and raised it above his head, "let's play!"

With that, Alexander sent the Silver Shields to meet the Greeks head to head. He then struck off with the cavalry to find a weak spot on the flank where he could charge in and disrupt the advancing phalanx.

Alexander's men were brave and tough, and eager for the fight – and unlike Parmenion's pike regiments, the Silver Shields relied on the short spear and the sword, and thus met the Greeks quite literally face to face and breath to breath. The shock of the Macedonian charge brought the Greeks to a halt, and for several long minutes the two lines ground against each other like stone upon stone. Then Ephialtes called for his own surprise – a tall, rolling battle tower that had been built behind the Tripylon Gate. Originally built as a backup defense should the Macedonians break through, Ephialtes had commandeered it for his counterattack. So forward it came, its many levels bristling with archers, who, from their vantage point, rained arrows down into the unprotected ranks of Silver Shields.

The Shields did not break – they were too proud, too stubborn, too professional to crack, but they could no longer push forward. Their rear ranks forced to raise shields overhead to protect themselves and the backs of the front ranks, they could not contribute to the push and shove scrum of shield wall on shield wall. Alexander's veterans began to give ground, rather than take it, and back they went, one very bloody step at a time.

Memnon had ridden forward across the causeway, past the stalemate at the Mylasa Gate and through the city to the Tripylon. He did not, however, come alone. He brought Orontobates along with him, and behind them trotted their last reserve, a small force of Persian heavy cavalry. Memnon ordered them to halt and rest in place as he and the governor dismounted and climbed the crumbling battlements. The fires from the Macedonian artillery and tents that Ephialtes men had set alight allowed him a fair view of the battle taking part below. Seeing the Macedonian Silver Shields begin to fall back, Memnon decided to risk all and throw the dice.

"Orontobates," he said as he turned to the governor, "they will break. I can feel it. If we can make those Silver Shields retreat, there is not a man in their army who will stand against us. Those are the best of their best, and if we defeat them, we defeat Alexander. And I don't just mean we break the siege – we break him, and then we can chase whatever is left of the invaders back to the north, back over the Hellespont, and into Macedonia itself. This is our hour, the hour I was waiting for. Are you with me?"

Orontobates looked up at the general, who was nearly a head taller than him, batted his long lashes and wiped at a tear that was streaking his makeup. "Of course, General, of course...but it is not wise for so many top commanders to be at risk at the same time. Ephialtes, of course, is doing what he does best, and I would not even think of telling you where the proper place is for a general. So, you go out there. Me, well, somebody should be here, in command of the defense. After all, there are two other attacks under way, at the far ends of the city."

"But this is the time, the time we have waited for..."

"And, yes, I see that, but my dear General, this is not my time – it is yours. You are the soldier; I am the politician. You were called upon to fight, and Darius gave you the baton of command to do just that. To me, however, was entrusted this satrapy and this city. It is neither my place nor the best use of my talents to ride out into battle. That is for you, dear General. You go. I shall, what is it you Greeks say, 'have your back?' Go, go my dear boy...go kill that little kinglet. I'll be here when you get back, and I'll be the first to toast at the victory banquet. Oh, and one more thing..."

"What?" asked a very puzzled Memnon.

"Shall we have roast lamb, suckling pig, or a bull on a spit?"

"Huh?"

"For the banquet? Which shall it...oh, never mind, all three...and more. No, go off to your little war...I've much to do. Go, go be off with you..."

Memnon was too confused, too excited, and too geared up to argue. After months of defeat, of being tied down behind walls, first in Miletos and then here in Halicarnassos, he was like a volcano ready to blow. The blood rushed through his veins like lava, and the normally calm, thoughtful, unflappable man of stoicism and logic gave way to the man of action. Like a volcano mantle cracking, he exploded with energy, running down the ramp from the walls, calling for the gates to be opened. Springing on to his horse he screamed at the full force of his mighty lungs just one word: "Charge!"

86

The Island with a View

HELL, AS SEEN FROM ACROSS THE WATER

"Ask the princess to come up here," Dimitrios said to Ari. "She needs to see this."

What Dimitrios wanted her to see was not a pretty sight. Just before dawn, he and Ari, and several others, had ridden from the princess' camp in the middle of the long island to its northern tip. There they set a second signal fire to match that built by the western shore of her camp. By the time they reached the tip, however, the horizon was already bright, lit up not by the rising sun but by the fires blazing in and all around Halicarnassos. Those fires only intensified as they watched, and when dawn finally came, the columns of dense smoke filled the heavens above that hell.

It was not far to the camp and back, and Ari was back within the hour with the princess, along with Halime, Burzasp, and two other riders the Persian officer had detailed to be a royal bodyguard. Princess Barsine did not dismount. She didn't have to. She could see very clearly from horseback what it was that Dimitrios needed to show her.

"My husband...is there?" she asked, rhetorically, trying to control the tremor in her voice as the horror Alexander had unleashed upon the city became apparent. Not even a lifetime of tutors and royal minders had prepared her for how to deal with such a terrifying sight – and one made all the more terrifying from knowing that the man she loved most in the world was caught in the middle of it.

"I am afraid so, Princess," said Dimitrios quietly. He, too, was shaken by what he saw, as was Ari, who mumbled something to the effect of having seen nothing like this since the fall of their native city.

"It is Thebes, all over again," Ari continued.

"Not so, young man," replied the princess, struggling to maintain her composure. "This is different."

"How so, my lady?" asked Ari.

"At Thebes," she said, "you did not have Memnon. Halicarnassos does. He will ensure that Alexander does not make another Thebes of this place. My Memnon," she continued, fighting back the tears and swallowing hard to keep her voice from giving away her fears, "my Memnon will keep the city safe. And I shall be by his side as he does."

"What?" Dimitrios all but screamed in surprise. "Surely you don't mean to go there? Look at that place, Princess. That is what a real war looks like," he added quite strenuously. "Hades himself would not walk into that inferno."

"Yet," she said, as regally and as calmly as she could manage, "that is exactly where I must go. But don't worry, Captain," she said looking down at him from her seat atop her mare, "I do not expect you to take me there. I don't expect any of you to take me there," she continued as she looked at each of her companions. "Just somehow get me aboard a ship, or a boat, or anything that floats and is heading for the harbor," she told them. Then, after a pregnant pause, she added "and once you see to that, I absolve all of you from any further responsibility for my safety. Go where you will. You have all served me and my husband well. The empire has need of such men...and women," she added with a smile as she nodded in Halime's direction. "I would not deprive you of your lives, or the king of kings of your service."

At that she clicked her tongue and gave her horse a slight kick with her heal, and rode back toward the rough camp where she had spent the night.

"Whew," said Ari as she rode off. "Looks like we've dodged that one," he added with a whistle.

"What do you mean, Ari," said Dimitrios in a tone that was part anger, part bitter resolve. "Don't you see what she's done?"

"What? She said we could go," replied Ari.

"Go where?" Dimitrios spat back. "Had she commanded us to go with her, we would have to either obey or mutiny. Had she asked us to go with her, we could have politely refused. But no, she didn't do either of those things, did she, the clever little minx. No," said Dimitrios angrily as he kicked at the sticks they had collected for the beacon, "she put it all on us."

"What do you mean?" asked Ari, perplexed by his friend's remarks. "She said we are free to go."

"No, Ari, that is only what you heard her say. Like my mother, your mother, and every other woman ever born, she knows how to say one thing while meaning quite another. Her words said we could go, but what she meant is that if we do, we are cowards. For what kind of soldiers, or men, or even human beings would we be if we let a lady — and a princess at that," he continued as the pointed to the conflagration across the water, "go into that all alone?"

As Dimitrios and Ari built their signal fire, the one down by the camp was blazing brightly, its plume of smoke rising high in the windless sky.

"I am not sure if anyone is going to see either of our small beacons, my lady," Halime said to the princess. "There is so much smoke coming from the city. These little fires of ours are likely to go unnoticed."

"Well, my dear girl," said Barsine, "now that the sun is up there will soon be a ship going to or coming from the harbor. Their lookout is bound to see it. I just hope they are curious enough to investigate, when they do."

With the battle raging ashore, Admiral Autophradates had stripped his warships of their marines and most of their sailors. He had armed them and sent them to reinforce the city walls, especially those nearest the harbor and in the two citadels that guarded the anchorage. By doing so, he had freed up the infantrymen who had been garrisoning for duty elsewhere along the battlements. One squadron was still at sea, escorting a grain convoy from Egypt, but that was still several days distant. A trio of small scout ships were on patrol to the west, south-west and south. Even though Alexander had disbanded his fleet, and as such was unable to present any viable threat from the sea, the admiral remembered Miletos, and kept up his patrols. Each of the three was still far over the horizon, and unlikely to return until dusk.

While there were no eyes on the water to spy the twin beacons on the long island, there were eyes on the land – and to the east, on the other side of the slender channel that separated the isle from the main-land. Those eyes, however, were not Persian, but Carian – and belonged to one of the scouts who served the corpulent queen, Ada. Curious as to why there were fires – and two of them – on the usually uninhabited island, the scout decided to take a closer look. In doing so he spied a pair of the Persian cavalrymen whom Burzasp had stationed to guard the backdoor to the princess' camp. Their presence was a puzzlement, and as such was worthy of reporting to the officer whose squadron was escorting a caravan from the east toward the queen's mountain retreat.

The officer was most interested in the scout's report. He was also grateful for something, anything that would break up the monotony of escort duty. With the scout's report as an excuse, he left his second in command a trio of soldier with the camel train, and rode off with the rest of the troop to investigate the fires on the island – and the curious riders the scout had seen.

As the day lengthened, the princess' party continued to scour the area for wood to feed the beacon fires, even though no ships were within sight. The princess herself paced restlessly back and forth on the high ground overlooking the beach, straining her eyes to look for sails. She had not returned to the beacon that Dimitrios and Ari were tending, as she could not bear to watch, helplessly, as the battle at Halicarnassos raged. Even from her perch above the beach her mind kept being drawn back to that horror. At least, as long as it was out of sight, she could manage to dampen some of the demons that plagued her thoughts; thoughts filled with fears of what had become or would become of her beloved husband.

Her reverie was interrupted by a man on horseback.

"What is it, Burzasp?" she asked as the rider halted before her.

"We have company, my lady," he replied, battling to catch his breath.

"A ship? You've spotted a ship!" she asked, elated at the rekindling of hope.

"No, my Princess. Riders. On the mainland. They are on the beach and appear to be readying to cross the shallow channel."

"Are they friends of ours?" she asked, hoping against hope that she had misread the concern on his face.

"No, Princess. They are Queen Ada's men, and they are well-mounted and well-armed."

"How many of them are there?" she asked, steeling herself for the answer.

"Too many."

87

Outside The Tripylon Gate

EPHIALTES' HOUR

A s Memnon's soldiers raced to keep pace with their commander on his ride from the citadel to the northern gate, Ephialtes continued his advance from the Tripylon into Alexander's lines. Shield ground against shield as the 2,000 mercenary hoplites shoved and slashed ahead, each step a battle to the death with the Macedonian king's elite Silver Shields. The price paid for each step was high, as the carpet of dead and dying behind the Greeks showed. It was hot, bloody work, but still ahead they pushed, Ephialtes himself front and center, stabbing with his spear and shoving with his shield.

The veteran general, however, was not a young man. He was easily twice the age of most of the men he led, and half again the age of the rest. His short gray beard sopping with sweat, his faced stained with blood – some of it his own – Ephialtes fought like a lion, but even lions grow weary, especially old ones. Each swing of his shield, each thrust of his spear, took more and more effort. Every muscle, especially those in his thighs and arms, was afire with the strain of the long, hard fight. Gasping for breath, the general nevertheless stayed in the fight, encouraging his men with his example as best he could. A body, however, can only take so much. There is only so much that adrenaline can do to keep the fire of battle going in a man, especially when its fuel has been spent. As that fire dimmed, Ephialtes was more carried forward by the crush of the battle than leading it. His jabs grew fewer and less potent. His shield weighed him down more than it protected him.

And that is when the Macedonian's sword found its mark.

Ephialtes screamed as much in surprise as in pain when the short sword stabbed into his neck, just above where he held his shield. The shield should have been there to block the stab, but as his strength faltered, the old general let the heavy shield dip, and dip just enough to give his foe a target. The Silver Shield swordsman who struck the blow did not live to gain any laurels, for the Greeks to the right and left of their general made short and bloody work of him. Others carried Ephialtes back, passing him from one rank to the next of the deep phalanx, until they could safely set him upon the ground he had won.

"The phalanx..." he coughed, as one of the soldiers held his head and another worked to undo his breastplate, "does it go forward still?"

"Yes, my General," one soldier replied. The general, he would later recall, appeared to hear his response, for he smiled at the soldier's answer as he died.

The death of a commander usually unnerves an army so that it will falter, break, and run. Sometimes, however, it only enrages them, and spurs them on as they seek revenge. That is what happened outside the Tripylon Gate. Mercenaries though they might have been, these hoplites drawn from all over the Greek world were Ephialtes' men first and soldiers for hire second. If their general had died fighting for them, they were determined to do no less for him.

And die they did – but they died hard.

Even the vaunted Silver Shields could no longer hold them back. Veterans as devoted to their king as the Greeks were to their general, they were barely able to hold the line – and a receding line at that. Alexander led charge after charge against the flanks of the Greeks, only to be repulsed each time by the disciplined response of these hoplites. Unable to make even a dent in their shield wall from horseback, the king dismounted, put himself at the head of a group of infantrymen and strode into the fight on foot, sword in hand.

Cleitos and the Companions followed suit, struggling to reach their king and protect him with their swords, their shields, and their very bodies. They stopped most but not all of the enemy thrusts. Within minutes the king was bleeding from half a dozen cuts. Worse would have surely followed had not Cleitos with his massive hands physically yanked the comparatively small king out of the line.

Even the presence of the Macedonian king was not enough to defeat the hoplites – but it did slow and finally stop them. Their numbers reduced by hours of combat, outnumbered, and being pushed against to the front, left, and right, the hoplites formed first a semicircle, and then a circle – a defensive orb as the formation was known, with the body of their general at its core. Yet they did not give any ground. They took not a step back, even surrounded now on almost every side.

It was from that side, the side opposite the Tripylon Gate, that Memnon rode forth, a column of Persian lancers at his back. The hoplites managed a ragged cheer at the sight of the commander, and dug in their heels as they awaited relief.

Memnon's column was not alone. As the Persians flooded the field and charged to save the hoplites, another force also appeared on the scene. From within Alexander's camp a cry went up from the walking wounded, the sick, and other veterans who, because of injury, illness, or age had been excused duty. "Philip's men! Philip's men!" cried the old soldiers. "Form up! Form up!"

From one end of the camp to the other, these hoary veterans of King Philip's old army came, wearing whatever armor their broken bodies could bear, and carrying swords, spears, axes, and whatever weapons they could find. A small group even managed to find a stand of sarissas – the 18-foot pikes of the phalanx battalions, and formed up into a small but tight formation eight wide by eight deep. With no general around, they commanded themselves — for so well drilled had they been by the great king that they needed no one to tell them what to do, where to go, or how to fight. In a solid, orderly mass they rose up out of the camp, crossed the siege line and slammed headlong into Memnon's charging column.

When a wave meets a rock, no matter how strong and powerful and fast the wave, the rock wins. Philip's veterans were that rock upon which Memnon's wave broke.

The example set by the old veterans inspired other Macedonian soldiers, including those who had fled the fighting to seek shelter in the camps and trenches, to come back to the fight. Even the artillerymen picked up their tools and strode in to the fight. Alexander, struggling to remain conscious from loss of blood, moved to join them — but was restrained by Cleitos.

"My men...my men need me..." said the young king, half out of his head because of his many wounds."

"No, Majesty," said Cleitos as he gently but firmly held the king. "Besides, those are not your men. Those are your father's men. Those are King Philip's men," said Cleitos, a lump in his throat, "as was I."

As Memnon's men were stopped, driven back, and finally forced to retreat, the hoplites knew their hour had come. While most of the Macedonians gleefully pursued Memnon's routers back through the open gates from whence they had so recently come, the Silver Shields pulled back, reformed, and surrounded the dwindling hoplites circle. The two determined groups of foes wearily faced one another, barely able to stand, as each force was too worn and bloodied to attack the other. Hephaestion, who had come up with his guard as soon as he heard that Alexander had been wounded, advanced slowly and statefully toward the hoplites. The Macedonian formation parted for him, until he and his horse were just behind the front rank.

"Soldiers of Greece!" the handsome young man in brilliant armor, his colorful helmet plumes dancing in the light breeze, called out. "Soldiers of Greece, lay down your arms. Honor has been served, and you have shed so much blood that your courage is beyond question. You have nothing more to prove – or to fight for. The battle is lost. The city is lost. Your general is dead. Lay down your arms, give us his body and I swear on my own king's life that you shall all go free – and can go home."

"Go to hell," came a shout from within the hoplites orb. "And take your bully boy king with you."

Hephaestion expected no less, and responded calmly: "I say again, your honor is served. You may all go home. All you need do is lay down your arms and give us the body of Ephialtes."

A silence fell over the field for a moment. Then, from within the orb, one voice cried out "come and take them." A second voice, then a third repeated those words, and other voices joined them. Within a breath it had become a chant, a defiant chant accompanied by the banging of sword and spear upon shield. Over and over the hoplites repeated their answer, each time louder than the last.

Hephaestion shook his head. "Such a waste," he mumbled, then turned to the aide behind him "I will waste no more of the king's men upon such as these. Silver Shields!" he then shouted in a commanding voice, "part!"

At his command the ranks and rows of men to either side of Hephaestion moved away from the young general, as if they were curtains drawn back from a window. As they did so, they revealed a solid mass of archers, who, at a wave from Hephaestion, darkened the sky with arrows.

"The city is lost, your grace," a minor official on the governor's staff, told Orontobates. "Ephialtes is dead as are his men. Memnon's troops are in rout, and there are Macedonians in the city. They are pouring in through the Tripylon Gate. As they spread through the city, men are abandoning the walls and running, some to find and safeguard their families, others...to who knows where. Anywhere they might escape."

"We are in a city under siege, our backs to the sea," sighed Oronto-bates. "There are only two places to be safe. The twin citadels at either end of the harbor – or aboard the ships. Send for the admiral. It is time to leave this place. Besides," he added, holding a perfumed bit of silk to his nose, "the city reeks of death...and stinks beyond all telling."

Memnon, to his credit, tried to stem the rout, but was carried away by the flood of panicked horses and frightened men, women, and children. There was no rallying the Persian infantry, and even the noble cavalry were riding away as fast as they could. The city guard abandoned their posts as well, their only thought to save their loved ones from enslavement, rape, or slaughter. The already small force of Immortals was much reduced from combat, and carried their noble captain Hydarnes' bloody corpse with them as they fell back to the Royal Island. With four out of five of their comrades dead or dying, the 100 or so remaining Immortals could not save the city – but they could at least keep their commander's body safe from the Macedonians, and the carrion feeders.

Even Memnon's great heart could find no hope, so complete was the defeat. Two months of bitter siege, and a year of seemingly endless war before that, finally caught up with him. His horse shot out from under him by enemy arrows, Memnon stumbled on foot, as if in a daze, going where the fleeing mob would take him. A soldier of the Immortals, recognizing him, drew him to the safety of their ranks. As Halicarnassos burned, they escorted him along with the body of their captain to the causeway that led from the city to the citadel on the Royal Island. Orontobates was there when Memnon arrived.

"Well, my old friend," said the governor, clad in pristine white garments, studded with diamonds, and a jeweled saber dangling from his belt, "it seems we must once again send ill-tidings to our emperor. Come inside. Wash your face. Have a cup of chilled wine – I have had the ice brought in by ship just for such a reason, as I find this season to be beastly hot."

Memnon barely had the strength to look up at Orontobates, let alone to argue with him. He merely nodded, put his head down and followed the servant Orontobates had directed him to follow.

"Prepare my ship," he said to the weaselly bureaucrat who, still shaking with fear, had told him of the death of Ephialtes and the fall of the Tripylon. "Make ready to leave on the tide. And, oh," he added almost as an afterthought, "be sure that Memnon is taken aboard before we set sail. The empire still has need of him."

88

The Long Island off Halicarnassos

A SHORT BATTLE ON A LONG ISLAND

Queen Ada's men had no more difficulty crossing the narrow channel between the mainland and the long island than the princess' party had. A few riders went ahead, but most stuck together in three clumps, each of about half a dozen variously armed and armored men. As the Queen greedily kept the few Carians who had remained loyal close to her side back at her fortress, the men crossing the water were a mixed lot. These were not professionals but hired soldiers, bribed brigands, and refugees who sold themselves into service as a way to feed their families. Only two men in the group were professional soldiers: The commander of this little expedition, and his aide, who had both long served in the Queen's guard. Which means to say they knew a lot about parade ground drill and palace protocol, but damn little about real soldiering.

"Commander," said the aide as they watched the little clumps of men cross the water, "exactly what are you expecting to find on that island?"

"Perhaps a few men willing to take the queen's silver and join her ranks, or, if not, a few slaves to serve her majesty's pleasure – and maybe our own," he added with a wink and a nod. "The scout said he thought he saw some women on the island. So we bribe or capture the men and then buy or take their women. I am so bored of the ones in camp. We could use a little fresh entertainment, don't you think?"

The aide smiled a knowing, lascivious grin, and told the commander "well, then we ought to get going, shouldn't we? Wouldn't want the rank and file to have first pickings or spoil the fun for you and me, now, would we?"

As the two guards' officers waded their horses knee deep into the channel, their main body came out of the water onto the beach across from the mainland. The skirmishers who had gone in first kept going, their horses struggling to climb the rocky landscape. They did not get far, as all three were quickly brought down by very accurate archery fire. Burzasp and his riders had drawn first blood with their bows, but first blood was not enough. They rode down the center of the island, parallel to the channel, firing at the bands of the queen's men on the beach. Surprised at meeting such stiff, deadly, and unexpected resistance, the queen's riders did not seem to know how to react – but the guard commander did – or at least he thought he did.

"Go after them! Go after them, you cowards," shouted the guard commander, his horse splashing through the gentle waves in the channel. "Charge them! Charge them!"

The hired men went forward, but in no fashion resembling anything other than an amorphous mass. Some drew swords, others reached for javelins, and still others notched arrows into their bows, each horseman acting on his own, and not in concert with any others. There was much bumping, and cursing, and neighing of horses, but eventually they all somehow sorted themselves out to at least ride in the same direction. Burzasp and his quartet of riders did not wait to be overrun by a score of men, even a score of such bumblers as these. They let loose another flight and then raced south, hoping to draw the pursuers to the far end of the island, away from the princess.

The princess Barsine paid no attention to that threat. Her eyes, her heart, and her soul were focused only on the fiery inferno to the north. She could almost follow the Macedonian advance into the city by where the next fire broke out. She could see hundreds of people scrambling to the slips, quays, and docks, all pleading for a berth on the warships that were hastily being made ready for sea.

"Do you think my husband is among them?" she asked Dimitrios, who was now arming himself for battle.

"I would like to say 'yes,' your Highness," answered the Greek captain as he fitted his greaves to his shins, "but that would be a lie. If I know your husband, and I think I do by now, he's still trying to hold the city – or at least hold back the Macedonians until others can get to safety."

"Yes, that would be just like him, always being the hero," she sighed, part proud, part disappointed, and all worried. "And here I am, so close yet still so far; unable to help him, or to plead with him to retreat, or...or...to kiss him goodbye."

With what little Dimitrios knew of royalty, he just naturally assumed that they did not cry – or at least did not allow themselves to be seen weeping. The sight of this haughty, proud, princess of imperial blood, with tears streaming down her cheeks and her body shuddering, all but unmanned the soldier. Do I comfort her? He thought to himself. Would that be proper – or even welcome? Had she been just any woman, or even any friend, the answer would be obvious – but with royals, one false move, no matter how well meaning, could cost him his head, just for the impertinence of offering a friendly shoulder to cry on. So Dimitrios, who had fought in the shield wall, stood fast while cities burned about him, and traveled by land and sea, by horse and foot and ship, from the war-torn interior of Greece through embattled Asia Minor, did nothing. It was not that he was paralyzed by fear – but by protocol. He just did not know how to act.

Halime, however, suffered from no such hesitation. She moved to comfort Barsine, who seemed to welcome her soft arms and kind mutterings. Well, Dimitrios said to himself, that's that. She's a girl, and a Persian of good blood – so I guess that's all right.

Dimitrios' musing did not last long, as Ari came limping up, moving as fast as his gimpy leg would allow.

"We've got company; bad company," he told Dimitrios.

"Who? Where?" asked the captain, caught by surprise.

"On the other side of the island. There's got to be close to a score, or maybe two dozen of them," he struggled to say between breaths. "Burzasp nicked a few, and the rest have followed him south, away from us."

"That's not going to work for long," replied Dimitrios. "He's going to simply run out of island. If there's that many of them, they will box him in and force Burzasp to make a stand. We have to help him."

"How?" said Ari. "My bow, your spear, and what, Klemes with his scalpel?"

"Klemes is not much good in a fight..."

"The hell I'm not!" the physician responded to his brother's comment.

"Not in this kind of a fight, brother," answered Dimitrios. "This is going to be against mounted warriors, and we all know how badly you ride a horse. Besides," he grinned, "you'd never get close enough to slice at anyone. This is a fight for spears, javelins, and bows."

"And so what am I supposed to do while you two are off trying to help Burzasp?"

"You stay here, Klemes. Stay with the princess."

"God damn it Dimitrios, I'm a physician, not a nursemaid!"

"Clearly," replied Dimitrios with a smile, "at least not with that kind of bedside manner."

"So, the pair of you are really just going to leave me here alone with Halime and the princess?"

"No, they're not," said Halime. "I'm going with them. I can ride and shoot better than either of these Greek...foot soldiers" she added with a playful sneer.

"Then I'm coming too," said the princess, her tears wiped away and her jaw set with fresh resolve.

"Your Highness, you can't..."

"I can't what, Captain?" the princess shot back, emphasizing the last word. "Do you really think I will just sit here waiting around while the rest of you risk your lives? I am a princess of the blood, and my people are horsemen – and like Halime, I'm much better at that than any of you Greeks."

"Well, you heard the lady," sighed Dimitrios. "But, Princess..."

"Yes?"

"At least stay behind me where I can..."

Dimitrios never finished his sentence, as there was no one to hear it. The princess had leapt upon her mare and slapped it into a full gallop before he could continue. Even Halime had to work at it to catch up, and as for the Greeks...

"Well, so much for being a nursemaid," grumbled Klemes as he struggled to calm his horse enough to mount. "We can't guard her from back here."

At that the three Greeks rode off to save the princess...if they could catch her.

89

Halicarnassos

THE MACEDONIAN WAVE

Memnon would not admit defeat. Nor would he sit and drink iced wine with the governor while the city burned. All logic aside, he allowed the hot passion of his years in Persia to override the cool stoicism of his Greek upbringing. With the remains of the Immortals at his back, Memnon returned to the fray.

To say he fought like a cornered lion would not do him justice; a lion in similar circumstances would be envious of Memnon's ferocity. Whenever a group of Persian soldiers wavered, he was there to bolster their spirits and encourage them to hold their ground. Where a pack of city guards were on the run, he was there to stop them and send them back into the fray.

Yet still, the Macedonians came on. Neighborhood by neighborhood, street by street, temple by temple, building by building they advanced, fighting a hundred battles in as many parts of the city. Many dropped out to snatch up loot, grab women, or find drink, but others kept moving forward. Alexander himself, revived by news of the impending victory, was now in the city. His Companions were spread out behind him, using the flat of their swords or the butt of their spears to round up the stragglers and looters, and shove them forward. Just as Alexander had driven through the Tripylon Gate, so now did Parmenion, and Ptolemy, and the others pour through the Myndos and Mylasa Gates. No longer three battering rams but three crashing waves, the Macedonians washed over the city in an angry tide, one made even more vicious from the months of frustration and hardship of siege. Still, Memnon struggled to hold them back – somewhere. Dashing about from street to street, he sent women and children to the harbor, and grabbed their men who were not already in uniform and gave them a weapon. "If you want your family to get safely away, then you will have to buy them the time to do so," he shouted over and over again as he dragged frightened civilians into the line. "You fight or they die – or worse," he yelled over and over. "Alexander will show them no mercy, nor will his men!"

It was Miletos all over again – but on a broader front. Unlike that disaster, however, at least one side of the city was still secure: the harbor. Flanked by the massive citadels of Salmacis and Arconnesos, and guarded by the Persian fleet, the harbor remained friendly. It was a place to rally, as the Macedonians soon would discover to their extreme discomfort, if the admiral of the king's navy had anything to say about it – and he did.

"Every catapult, every bolt-thrower, every archer on every ship is to be on the lookout for any Macedonians that come near the harbor," Admiral Autophradates told his aides, who sent the message around the fleet. "I know we've left only skeleton crews on the ships, but they will be enough to man the artillery," he added. "I want the naval officers on watch in the twin citadels to make sure the garrisons there do the same. And you two," he added as he pointed to a pair of young marine officers, "each of you take a detachment to the citadels and make sure my orders are obeyed – and that nobody leaves or signals a surrender. Guard the gates from the inside so no one is tempted to leave, and secure the commandant's quarters in each. Now go. Go!"

"But sir," one of the young officers replied, "the governor commands the Royal Citadel. I've seen his servants loading sacks and chests aboard his private barge. I think he's preparing to leave."

Admiral Autophradates scowled at the young marine, with a look so piercing and powerful that the officer trembled from his helmet to his sandals. "Then it is up to you to make sure he doesn't," said the admiral coldly, calmly and with no room for misunderstanding.

"But, sir...Admiral...he's...he's the royal governor...and..."

"Damn it, marine, I don't care if he's keeper of the royal chamber pot, chief eunuch of the harem, or the emperor's personal toenail trimmer! Orontobates must stay and hold that citadel. And if he gives you any lip, well, you have it on my authority to explain it to him."

"But..."

"Look, marine, if you're not up to this, I will find someone else who is. So you go there, and you tell the governor that if I see his barge slip its moorings and head for the sea, I will personally sink it, and I don't care if he's on it when I do. Got it?"

"Yes, sir!" the marine said with gusto as he snapped to attention and gave a perfect salute.

"Then what are you waiting for? Go!" replied the admiral, with just a hint of a smile. The admiral knew the city was lost, but damn it if he wasn't going to make sure Alexander wouldn't be able to enjoy his prize. As long as he could supply those two citadels by sea, there was nothing Alexander could do to take them – especially the royal island. And if Alexander could not take them, he could not use the harbor – or claim the city as his. The navy could not save the city but they could deny its use to Alexander. And the longer they could hold back the Macedonians from the harbor, the more people and soldiers could be evacuated. If they saw their governor leave, however, what little courage or hope the defenders had, they would lose. Orontobates did not know it yet, but he was going to defend the Royal Island to the last. The best way to make sure of that, the admiral grinned to himself, was to make sure he couldn't send his treasure away.

As Memnon, Autophradates, and Orontobates each gave their orders, other officers, who were not in contact with their chiefs, had to fend for themselves. One of those was Captain Abibaal, whose scout ship was escorting a pair of grain ships coming up from Egypt. Although he knew the sea lane by heart, there was no need of his showing the grain ships the way – the plumes of smoke and towers of fire erupting from Halicarnassos were clearer than any beacon. The captains of the grain ships saw the plight of the city from afar, and made to turn away, back toward Egypt. Abibaal sent signals to try to convince them otherwise, but they were adamant. They were not going to risk their ships, their crews, or their cargoes in that conflagration. After all, they were not paid to fight – and doubted the Macedonians would pay them for their grain and allow them to leave.

Abibaal gave the orders to his own crew to follow the grain ships, which he knew he could outrun. His ship lacked the weapons or numbers of fighting men to force the massive grain ships to change course back to the city, but if he could board one, he might convince at least one captain to come to the city with him. After all, the fleet was still in the harbor and fighting was still going on - so maybe all hope was not yet lost, and if it was, those grain ships could carry off a lot of people.

The grain ships turned very slowly. Big, lumbering, heavy laden vessels, they were built for the maximum carrying capacity, not speed. They ran under sail only, as there was no spare room for rowers – and it would have taken hundreds of men to get a ship that big and heavy under way. Abibaal's scout ship, however, was built for speed, and while the grain ships were trying to wear away with the wind, Abibaal lowered sail and sent his men to their benches.

"Row, lads, row! Oar master, beat me out a faster pace!"

As Abibaal turned his ship about, however, he spied another pair of beacons in the distance. One was at the northern tip of the long island opposite the harbor; the other at the center. These were not cooking fires – for no one lived on the long, barren island – but obviously signal fires of some sort. Well, that was something worth checking out – after all, that is just the sort of thing a scout ship is meant to do. Well, perhaps after he caught up with the grain ships...

90

The Long Island

A LITTLE WAR OF HER OWN

I f Dimitrios, Klemes, and Aristophanes thought they were going to save the princess, they were quickly disabused of their dreams of glory. Barsine had more than once told them she could take care of herself, and if they still had any doubts, the trio of dead Carians with arrows in their chests that lie all about her put such thoughts to rest. As they came upon her, she was notching yet another arrow and drawing a bead on a rider who was doing his best to put ground between himself and the princess. He needn't have bothered.

"Ah, Captain, physician, and young archer, I wondered what has been keeping you," the princess said. "So nice to finally show up at my party. A tad unfashionable, being late, in these circumstances, but I forgive you," she commented dryly. "Would you be kind enough to lend me a few arrows? As you can see, my quiver is almost empty, and there are still enemies about. Burzasp and Halime went after them, over that rise. I would have gone with them but these three...no, four...brutes got in my way. No matter, you're here now. Would one of you be so kind as to bring up my horse? She seems to have wandered off during the excitement."

"Klemes," said Dimitrios, "would you and Ari do the honors? I need to have a word alone with the princess."

"You know I'm a physician, not a stable boy, right?" said Klemes. "And that I do not do well with horses – and Ari with his limp would not be my first choice to go chase down a skittish mare...but don't let any of that get in the way of your little chat with her highness," he added sarcastically. "Come on, Ari, let's go find the princess her little pony."

As the physician and the archer stumbled off to chase down the princess' horse, the captain approached Barsine, used both hands to pull off his helmet...and then threw it to the ground where it made a loud "clang" as it hit a rock.

"Why so dramatic, Captain?" remarked the princess, one eyebrow raised in query. "I believe I told you that I did not need your protection – that I could handle myself."

"Gods be damned, your Highness," the captain said in exasperation. "Your husband made me promise to do just that – and to get you away to safety. It was the last order he gave to me, and it was also a request, from one comrade to another. Why must you make this so hard on all of us?"

Princess Barsine smiled. "My dear, noble, naive Greek Captain," she said with a rather sweet lilt to her voice, as if addressing a child. "I am the daughter, widow, and wife of a soldier. I understand your position perfectly. But you should also understand mine. I will not sit in some cushioned cage, somewhere, sipping chilled wine and nibbling on dates while my husband is in danger. And I already told you I could handle myself in a fight. After all, I am a..."

"I know, I know. You are a 'princess of the blood' and a soldier's..."

"And a mother, I may remind you. A mother of three little boys. Compared to them, these Carian mercenaries were a rather timid bunch. You don't have any of your own, do you, Captain?"

"You mean mercenaries?"

"No, silly man, children, and boys at that. I'd rather face enemy soldiers than try to keep three boys under control. Battle is a mere sport, and a relaxing one at that, compared to motherhood. And as I have told you, over and over again, I am no stranger to the field of combat."

While the princess and the captain continued their discussion, a group of riders broke over the top of the rise, their horses lathered up and racing each other as they came charging on. The princess and the captain moved quickly in response. She raised her bow, him reaching for his helmet, but not before the riders were upon them ...and then past them. Dimitrios saw the panic in their eyes as they rode, and when Burzasp and his men came tumbling over the same rise, he could see the reason for their fear. The Persian horsemen had put away their bows and drawn their long, curved, sharp swords. They rode with murder in their eyes, and if there was any mercy in their hearts, there was not so much as a hint of it in their warlike demeanor. Burzasp and his boys were out for blood. This was no longer a battle, but a hunt, and they were determined to bring their prey to ground – and to slaughter them.

As Burzasp and his bloodthirsty band rode away in pursuit, Halime came riding slowly over the crest of the rise. If there was joy in battle for some, Halime showed no signs of it – quite the opposite. Her horse plodded along, and she swayed back and forth with every step the weary mount took. The princess slung her bow over her shoulder and walked with a purpose toward the young girl. When she reached Halime, she took the horse's reins in her own hands to steady the mount, while the captain helped the girl dismount. Once Klemes had seen her ride up, he had left it to Ari to limp after the princess' horse, and turned back to see if he could use his real talents to better effect.

"Is she hurt?" asked the princess with concern.

"Let me be the judge of that," said Klemes as he approached. "Sit her down on the grass, and one of you find some water."

Although the princess was used to giving and not taking orders, she did not argue or take offense. Barsine knew there was some in her pack, and went back to where she had dropped it when she fought her little private war with the raiders. Halime seemed barely conscious. Klemes examined her for wounds and injuries, then with the captain's help stretched her out on the soft dune grass to rest.

"Is she wounded, physician?" asked the princess as she returned and handed Klemes the water bag.

"I don't think so. She has some bruises, as if she was hit by a club or the blunt end of a spear, but I don't see any cuts or blood, or signs of broken bones. The poor girl needs a bit of rest, some water, and some shade. Dimitrios, take some of those javelins and a horse blanket and make her a little open-sided tent. Just to keep the sun off her face. Go," he added quietly, "I'll watch over her. And you, Princess," he ordered, "be so kind as to dampen a bit of cloth to wipe her brow."

If the princess took any offense at being ordered, again, to do a servant's work, she did not show it. Barsine had come to think of Halime as one of her own – if not quite a younger sister, at least a female companion – and her only one in this otherwise men's only club that formed her escort. She showed genuine concern as she helped tend to the young woman; a concern that was not lost on her Greek companions.

"Please, Highness," begged Dimitrios. "Enough of this. Please let us get you away to safety, away from all of this. We are too few as it is, and keep getting fewer. Give up this idea of going to Halicarnassos. It will not end well...for you...or for any of us," he added as he set the little lean-to over Halime's head. "Besides, we don't have a ship, and none have even come to check out our beacons..."

"I'm not so sure of that," said Ari, as he came back riding the princess' horse.

"What do you mean?" asked Dimitrios.

"Look out to sea. I think I can see a sail out there...actually, three..."

91

Halicarnassos

FAREWELL, YE CARIAN LADIES

E ven with Halicarnassos collapsing around his ears, Memnon would not yield the city to Alexander – not without at least one more fight. The Rhodian general had planned from the beginning to use the fortified cities of Minor Asia to slow, wear down, halt, and eventually force back the Macedonian onslaught. As he had told the over-confident satraps long before they mustered their forces to confront Alexander, the Persians could never match the Macedonians in the field. Stone walls, however, robbed Alexander of his two biggest advantages: his unstoppable phalanxes and his powerful Companion cavalry.

At Miletos, Memnon had bled the Macedonians and bought time – time to turn the already imposing fortifications at Halicarnassos into an impenetrable and lethal barrier. When the defenses of Miletos failed to stop Alexander, as Memnon feared they would, he still believed in his overall strategy. Even with its Tripylon towers toppled, its Myndos and Mylasa Gates smashed, the city in flames, and Macedonians, and their allies, and mercenaries running rampant through the rubble, Memnon could not bring himself to admit defeat. He could not even contemplate what had gone wrong – or where he, or his plan, or his army had failed. Defeat was inconceivable.

"I do not think our General or our Admiral fully comprehend the meaning of that word," sighed Orontobates in response to the admiral's command.

"Which word, Governor?" asked the naval courier, panting and out of breath, his skin and linen armor dark with soot.

"Both, actually," said the governor. "You would think that by now he could indeed understand that we can be defeated. It is our third time being bested by Alexander, after all. At this point, I think the only thing that is truly inconceivable is our ability to stop the Macedonian kinglet."

If the courier was shocked by such defeatist talk, he did not show it. If anything, the young officer felt the same. Like so many others, he had put his faith not just in the impenetrable walls of the city, but also in the legendary skills and unshakable courage of their general. No one's morale falls farther and harder than that of a true believer whose beliefs are shattered and proven false. Alexander had done that to the defenders of Halicarnassos – or at least to all but one of them: Memnon.

The general was a whirlwind, rushing about from one end of the shrinking defense perimeter to the other. Directing archers to rally and fire here; grabbing routers by their necks and shoving them back into the line there; but he could not be everywhere at once. The moment he moved on the line would start to waiver. Men would inch back, and then take a step back, and then drop their weapons and run for the docks, hoping for a place on the already crowding ships.

And those ships kept taking on refugees – old men, women, children, the wounded. A few marines of the fleet tried to keep the docks and jetties safe and orderly, or at least as orderly as they could, as more and more people were pushing forward, pleading for a space on the already overburdened ships.

Admiral Autophradates had vowed that his sailors would take off as many people as their ships would carry, but those limits were fast being reached. If he were to take off any of the soldiers, they would have to come now – even if it meant leaving thousands of civilians to suffer the fate of occupation – and worse.

"Ready my barge," the admiral said to his aide as he stood on the deck of his flagship. "And I want four of our biggest, strongest and most loyal men. Not galley slaves, mind you, but professional rowers and sailors. Men of the fleet. Men who call anywhere but here home."

"Yes, Admiral," the aide replied with a salute. As he moved to obey the admiral's order, however, he stopped, turned around and asked: "Pardon me, Admiral, sir. May I ask what you want these men to do?"

The admiral, not used to having his orders questioned, especially by a mere junior officer whose beard was more hope than reality, glowered daggers at the young man. The aide did not ask again, but hurried off, double-time, to see the admiral's command carried out.

Orontobates stared at the map with great intent as men scurried about with boxes, crates, and sacks of valuables. A score of slaves and a few minor officials moved in a steady, constantly cycling chain to load the city's treasures onto Orontobates personal galley: a massive quadrireme. It was one of the first and still rare class of massive "fours" as they were known, as that was the number of tiers of oars that powered them. A Carthaginian innovation which had begun to appear in the fleet of Persia's Rhodian ally, Orontobates' ship was the first of the massive vessels to fly imperial colors, beneath which streamed his own satrapial banner.

"Cos," the governor mumbled as he pointed out the island on the map. "Yes, Cos, that is where we shall take the treasury, Captain," he said to the naval officer standing beside him. "The citadel there is strong, and as Alexander has no navy, it should be as safe if not safer than anywhere else in the empire."

"Pardon me, sire," the officer replied, "but my ship is a man-o-war, not a cargo vessel. She's not built to carry cargo – let alone so many heavy containers as you are loading aboard her. If any of it shifts, we would start to list and then take on water through the rower's ports."

"So?" replied the governor. "Then you had best see to it that it is as evenly distributed as possible and secured firmly. I will...we will need those funds for our next battle with this...this...this Macedonian...boy..." he said with a mixture of contempt, anger, admiration, and fear. "Besides, even if we do capsize and sink, better the treasure goes to the bottom of the sea than into the coffers of that upstart barbarian king."

"Aye, aye, Governor," replied the captain with a little laugh.

"Oh, Captain," said the governor as the naval officer began to withdraw to see to the loading of his magnificent ship, "if my ship does flounder and the treasure winds up beneath the waves..."

"Yes, governor?"

"...understand that you will be there with it."

"Point taken, your Honor," replied the captain with an audible gulp. "I shall see to it personally."

As the captain was racing down the steps of the citadel on the Royal Island where Orontobates had established his headquarters and initially secured the contents of the treasury, he was astonished to meet a familiar face coming up from below.

"Admiral?" asked the captain, somewhat taken aback by the presence of the commander of the fleet.

The admiral hardly paused to acknowledge the captain's presence, other than to shove past him as he hurried up the steps to the top of the citadel. The captain thought to follow him, but quickly set that thought aside, remembering Orontobates' words. Besides, he thought to himself, the admiral was obviously on his way to see the governor, and best to let them short things out.

As the quadrireme commander resumed his downward path, the admiral burst into the governor's map room, his sandals slapping the floor so loudly as to bring thunderclaps to mind.

"Orontobates," said the admiral, "it's time to go. Most of my ships are already at sea, packed to the rails with refugees. The last are at the docks now, and are fast filling up. I've not much room left to take off the soldiers. We need to get Memnon aboard one of them and head out to sea."

Orontobates nodded his agreement. "Yes, Admiral. As you can see, I am loading the treasury upon my own ship. As soon as that is done, I will turn over command of this citadel and the other at the far end of the harbor to a pair of trusted officers. Whatever soldiers we cannot take off and are still capable of resistance should be sent here and there. Both citadels are amply stocked with provisions, and even if we cannot hold the city, we can still deny Alexander use of the harbor – and tie up some of his men here, as he can't afford to leave one fortress, let alone two in his rear if he is to march inland."

"Agreed, Governor. With our command of the sea we can always bring them more supplies – or evacuate them if need be later on. But that is not why I am here. I need your help."

"To do what?" asked the governor, puzzled by the request.

"To get Memnon to leave. We need to get him out of here and to safety, to fight another day."

The governor laughed, and laughed heartily. "I've told him as much several times now. He seems determined to fight on. I am not sure if he still thinks he can win or he just wants to be the last man standing when the end comes. His blood is up, and he is in denial, and denial beyond all hope of reasoning."

"Aye, Governor, that is what I thought you would say."

"Then what do you expect me to do?"

"I need your permission to drag the general off, by force if necessary."

"Ha!," roared the governor with laughter. "You want to drag him off? You and what army?"

"I do not need an army," smiled the admiral, "not when I've got a navy."

At that the admiral spun about and moved with a purpose toward the exit. He raced down the stairs, out the gates to the dock and onto his barge, upon which sat four of the biggest, strongest, toughest looking men to ever wear the colors of the Persian navy.

Orontobates sent runners to spread the word to any officer or group of soldiers they could find to tell them to retreat across the narrow causeway to the citadel on the Royal Island, or to make for the fortress of Salmacis on the opposite side of the harbor. Fortunately for them, the Macedonians had not reached either fortress or any part of the shore of the harbor. Memnon held a thin, narrowing band that peaked at the great Mausoleum and Agora, but which was shrinking fast. It was there, at that magnificent market and monument to a fallen king that Autophradates found the general.

Memnon looked at the admiral as if he was the last man he expected to see. He then issued an order to a group of archers to direct their fire to the far side of the Mausoleum. Then he told a small troop of Greek hoplites to counterattack under cover of their barrage. As he began to move off to give more orders, the admiral grabbed him by the arm. He then spoke to him softly, kindly and with great respect.

"It is over, my friend. It is time to go."

Memnon, his eyes almost crazed with battle lust, blinked. He did not answer with words, but simply blinked, as if the admiral was speaking in a language he could not understand.

"Memnon," the admiral continued, "you have done all you can – and more. There is nothing left to do...but live."

The general again did not seem to understand the admiral's words, and once again made to move off back into the fray. When he tried to break the admiral's hold on his arm, Autophradates tightened his grip with one hand and waved to his oarsmen with the other.

"Come take him, lads," said the admiral with evident sadness. "Be as easy with him as you can – but take him. It's for his own good."

Memnon slowly began to understand what was going on. At first he attempted to resist, but whether it was the sheer exhaustion of the day of battle, or a simple sense of relief, the general collapsed into the strong arms of the four beefy oarsmen. Their charge now barely conscious, each of the big men lifted the general with a gentle touch that seemed entirely at odds with their imposing physicality. They carried him upon their shoulders, reverently, as one would carry the corpse of an honored friend.

"Take him to my barge, my lads. It is time for this one to leave the battlefield. We need to get him somewhere safe, and somewhere from where he can continue the fight."

As he walked beside the men, the admiral reached up and put his hand gently on Memnon's shoulder.

"Rest, old friend. We have a long war ahead of us."

92

The Long Island

...AND THE LITTLE SHIP

Even as the admiral's beefy boys were carrying Memnon onto the flagship, another far smaller ship was approaching the long island south of Halicarnassos. The smoke from what were obviously signal fires sparked Captain Abibaal's curiosity. Besides, after being unable to convince the massive grain haulers to stay on course for the harbor rather than flee, he had little else to do.

"Nice and easy, boys," he called out to the rowers, each of whose name he knew as well as if they were his sons or brothers, "the bottom comes up all of a sudden like in these shallows. Slow it down and let's glide her in nice and easy."

Although there did not seem to be anyone around the signal fire, he could see what looked like bodies on the beach. By their sprawl and how they were spread out he could see they were not merely sleeping, but dead. And obviously not dead for very long, as the fire still smoldered. The closer his vessel came to shore, the more his ears caught sounds of horses neighing, men shouting and swords clashing. That meant at least one side in that fight would be friends of the empire, and if they needed help, well, Abibaal was ready to show them help had arrived.

The captain was the first man over the side, and helped guide the little scout ship to settle gently onto the beach.

"First three pairs, take up swords and shields and follow me," ordered the captain to his oarsmen. "Second three pairs, javelins and bows to stand watch on board. The rest of you, back oars, just enough to keep her free of the sand."

The captain waded ashore, six armed sailors at his back, and walked past the fire. He paused very briefly to kick the bodies on the beach just in case any were alive – they weren't. He then headed for the dunes, crouching low as he neared the crest and motioning for his men to stay back. As he peeked over the top he did not see what he expected. A fight was going on, which he had heard, but the participants were as odd a bunch as any this side of a tavern brawl. Two women, one with a bow, the other a javelin, were struggling to fend off a pair of scruffy-looking horse-herders. A few apparently Persian men were exchanging blows with more heavily armed men – soldiers, but fancy soldiers, by the look of them. And then, off to the side, a man in Greek armor was...

"Dimitrios?" the captain said to himself in disbelief. "What the hell..."

Abibaal stood up, drew his sword and waved his men to the top of the dunes. The captain and his six sailors then stormed down the dunes to join in the battle.

The sudden appearance of a new group which neither side recognized forced a sudden pause in the fighting. Both the queen's soldiers and Persians puzzled over whether these mad, screaming men waving swords were friend or foe. They did not have to puzzle that out for long, as Abibaal and his sailors found their targets and hurled themselves into the fray. The princess and Halime were also caught by surprise, but when the strangers rushed past them to engage the very soldiers they were battling, both raised a cry of joy. Dimitrios was too hotly engaged to chance taking a glance over his shoulder, but when he saw his opponent do so, the Greek captain took full advantage of his foe's distraction – and slashed him right where the neck met the cuirass. As he spun to meet what he thought was a new threat, however, Dimitrios also let down his guard – so surprised was he to see the Phoenician captain standing there, sword shining, face grinning, and a shout of recognition on his lips.

"How many times is that I have saved your life, now, Dimitrios?" laughed the naval officer. "Two, three...or is it four. I've lost count," he added with a broad grin on his face.

"I don't know, Abibaal, but this time it is not just some poor mercenary you've rescued. You see that woman over there?"

"You mean the pretty little one with the javelin?"

"No. I mean the one with the bow."

"Whew!" Abibaal whistled. "You've done well for yourself, Dimitrios. She's stunning...and she's your woman?" he asked, hoping for a negative response as appreciatively lustful thoughts began to push away all notion of further combat.

"No," Dimitrios said, "but she is spoken for."

"Oh? Really?" sighed the Phoenician captain in disappointment. "Then who is the lucky fellow?"

"Memnon."

"What!" exclaimed Abibaal. "You mean she...she..."

"Yes, my friend," said Dimitrios, as he wiped his sword clean with sand and put it back in its scabbard, "that is Barsine, daughter of Artabazus, late satrap of Hellespontine Phrygia, widow of the great general Mentor, princess of the Pharnacids, and wife of the lord commander of the armies of the Achaemenid dynasty."

"She..."

"Yup, Abibaal," he said with a smile. "She's Memnon's wife, and she would dearly appreciate it if you could give her a ride to see her husband."

"Why...why of course..." stuttered Abibaal.

"And when you do, you will have my undying gratitude...for taking her off my hands. That one," Dimitrios added with a sigh, "she has been a lot of trouble."

"Yes," said Abibaal as he looked around at the corpses that littered the dune grass, "I can see that she has."

As Captain Abibaal had very little room to spare for passengers on his small scout ship, he could not accommodate the entirety of the princess' entourage. He offered to sail back toward the harbor to signal a larger and more fitting ship for a royal lady, but Barsine would hear none of that.

"I am going with you and now, Captain. If you have room aboard, I would like to bring the Lady Halime, Captain Dimitrios and his brother, the physician, with me."

"That is quite all right, your Highness," shouted Klemes from where he was tending to one of their wounded comrades. "Leave me here. I have quite enough to keep me busy until the next ship returns. Just make sure they've a physician on board."

Barsine nodded her agreement, turned back to the naval officer and said simply "then it will be just we three. If you will be so kind, please take me to my husband."

Captain Abibaal gulped, looked about, and did not move.

"Well, what are you waiting for?" said the princess quite sternly.

"Begging your pardon, Highness, but I am not sure exactly where he is. I mean, he's somewhere in Halicarnassos, I presume, but where..."

"He will be wherever the fighting is at its fiercest, if I know my husband," the princess sighed. "But perhaps we should start at the Royal Citadel. Someone there will surely know where to find him."

Abibaal was still uneasy about putting so important a person at risk. A warning glance from Dimitrios, who was standing behind the princess, was enough to convince him that it would be better to take his ship and its passengers into a war zone than to refuse the request of so royal a personage...a royal personage who's request, of course, was anything but merely that.

The princess refused the offers of the sailors to carry her to the ship and lift her aboard. Instead, she strode through the surf and hauled herself up and over the rails...then put out a hand to help the injured Halime follow. Abibaal offered her the spartan comforts of his small cabin, but Barsine refused. The princess took herself to the bow and stood there, as if she was the proud figurehead on the prow. It was there she would stand, like a statue, until Abibaal took her where she asked to go: the Royal Citadel of Halicarnassos.

As Abibaal's men backed oars to pull off the beach, the officer, suddenly nervous at making any mistake that might result in royal displeasure being directed his way, called for his men to row, and row hard. It was not far to the harbor, and if he thought his men could have sustained ramming speed all the way there he would have so ordered. But Abibaal was a good captain, one who looked out for the lives and health of his men (unlike some in the fleet whom sailors derisively referred to as "murdering captains.")

At best speed it would take about half an hour, give or take, but with so many ships leaving the harbor and heading out to sea, best speed was not possible – not if they were to be able to avoid being cut in two by some of the big triremes, let alone the governor's giant quadrireme, which he could see was preparing to get underway at the pier on the Royal Island. Abibaal did his best to keep up speed yet avoid collision, and if the princess ever feared otherwise, she did not show it. Motionless and without a word or so much as a sigh passing her lips, she stood there, starring dead ahead at the citadel, wherein she placed all of her hopes of finding her husband.

93

Halicarnassos

THE BIG SHIPS SAIL

Navigating his way into the harbor at Halicarnassos was usually so easy that Abibaal could just about do it with his eyes closed...but not today. The volume of traffic leaving the port was far heavier than he had ever seen. While the navy ships were departing in an orderly fashion, the commercial and private ships were ignoring even the most basic tenets of sailing safety, such was their rush to leave the dying city.

The panic and fear of many of their passengers only made it harder for the sailors to do their job properly, as did the overcrowding of the ships. The occasional fireball or rock that Alexander's siege weapons hurled into the harbor did not help. As the battle for the city moved from the walls into the town, those siege crews that were in range shifted their fire to the twin citadels at either side of the harbor, and at the docks. Most of their shots splashed or fizzled harmlessly into water, but a few unlucky vessels were damaged, set afire or even smashed by the still rather random falling of projectiles.

In short, it was chaos – and chaos with big, overburdened ships packed with panicked people, which included not just the passengers but many of the sailors and their sailing masters. Winding his way through this jumble of vessels, some of which were sinking or afire, took all of the skill Abibaal had learned in a life at sea. He could steer his ship, but he could not control what the other vessels trying to flee the harbor were doing. Most of those ships were also much larger as well as far less maneuverable than his own small scout ship. Should a collision occur, Abibaal knew he would be on the losing end of that game; a game one does not play with a princess on board.

Still, Abibaal knew how to make his little ship dance. He stood to the tiller himself, fearing that, in the split seconds between giving a command to go hard a starboard or turn to port and it being carried out, disaster could strike. As it was, Abibaal came far too close to scraping hulls or smashing oars with outgoing ships for comfort. Through it all, through every twist and turn, and as they rode or cut through the waves from passing ships, the princess stood at the bow, holding on tight and suffering the spray.

Abibaal thread his way through the nautical needle, past transports and barges, and down the outgoing battle line. He even managed to give a salute to the flagship, whose sailors he saw were helping aboard passengers from the admiral's barge, hauling up the sea anchors, and preparing to set sail. Finding a spot on the Royal Island quay, however, was more difficult, what with that big, ugly, hulking monster of a quadrireme moored to the dock. She was massive – but surprisingly low in the water for a warship. Her lower oar ports were sealed and their oars pulled in, so heavy did she sit. With the surface of the sea so close, pulling on the oars would have been both impossible and point-less for the oarsmen – and dangerous, as she would take on water through their open ports. What good is a quadrireme if she only has three banks of oars, he thought to himself. Is she still a "four?"

At least her oars were shipped, so Abibaal could maneuver close by and scoot ahead of her to one of the small jetties nearby. These were used by little ships that carried messages, ferried in prisoners and offi-cials, or delivered catch of the day for the commandant's table. The princess, in her impatience to disembark, did not wait for the sailors to tie up and jumped – and nearly fell into the water between the ship and the jetty.

"Mind the gap!" a wary sailor cried out as she prepared to leap, but that wasn't necessary, as Dimitrios was there to pull her back.

The look the princess gave him when he did was one of shock, surprise, and anger, as well as embarrassment, all rolled into one. The impertinence of Dimitrios' action – to lay hands upon a princess of the blood – could warrant a beheading or at least a whipping and an amputation of the offending hands. Dimitrios thought he saw such thoughts racing behind her eyes, and was just as quick to offer his apologies – and his reasons for taking hold of her. Barsine did not say anything in reply – neither a thank you nor a rebuke. She instead merely gave a nod of her head, then turned about and stepped off the ship onto the jetty as the sailors made the ship secure.

Dimitrios and Halime scrambled after Barsine, who came as close to running down the jetty as she could without appearing to do so, for to run would be unseemly for one of her station. Even when being set upon by Queen Ada's men she had moved at her own measured pace. Navigating through the steady stream of bearers carrying boxes, chests, bags, sacks and amphorae into the already bulging quadrireme was frustrating, but the princess was as nimble as a dancer, and reached the door to the citadel before her companions could catch up. Dimitrios saw the guard raise his hand to tell her to halt and, when that did not work, to try to bar her way with his spear. He felt sorry for the poor lad. Guards never get an even break. If they aren't having their necks slashed from behind in the dark, they're being dressed down by their betters – and just for doing their job. Dimitrios knew what it felt like. He'd been there too often himself.

Barsine's imperious demand to be allowed to pass did not sway the guard, neither did her insistence that he send word to the governor that a royal princess was at his door and demanded an audience.

"If you're a princess," the guard laughed as he gave Barsine in her battle-worn, wet from sea spray clothes, and tousled hair the once over, "then I'm the bleedin' pharaoh of Egypt!"

"If you were, then you'd be dead," said Barsine haughtily. "My first husband killed him, damned upstart incestuous pedophile of a porcine rebel he was. So, unless you'd care to share that fate, I suggest you do your duty. Either let me pass or call an officer."

"You'd better do as the lady says," Dimitrios added as he ran up, huffing, and puffing, and working to gather his breath.

"Oh?" said the guard. "And who might you be? The king emperor of China his self?"

"No. But I am a captain on the staff of this lady's husband – the General Memnon. I presume you've heard of him?"

That reply did take the soldier aback. Derision gave way to contemplation, and the mention of the general's name did give him pause.

"You serious," the guard asked Dimitrios, "one soldier to another?"

"Deadly so. You've done your duty, soldier," he added gently but firmly, "And now it's time to call for an officer."

"Sergeant of the guard, post number four!" the soldier shouted as he kicked open the door. "I need the officer of the day!" he added with a bit of relief. "Tell him there's a pretty lady who needs his attention."

"That's better, soldier," said Dimitrios.

"Aye," he replied. "Begging your pardon sir...and ma'am. Just doing me duty," he added, thinking, but not saying, how relieved he felt she was about to be someone else's problem, whoever she said she was.

Orontobates could not have been more surprised than if one of those angry goddesses the Greeks worshiped had strode into his map room, lightning bolt in one hand, the leash to a beast of war in the other, and a hairdo made of slithering snakes atop her head. Frankly, he would have preferred such an apparition to what he saw coming for him, shabby entourage and all.

"Princess," said the governor with an oily smile and a deep bow, for he had met her before. "Forgive my men for keeping you waiting. I am sure you can understand their suspicion and their caution, this being war and all that. And the chances of a member of the royal family showing up...unannounced...here...and now?"

Barsine waved off the governor's attempt at making excuses, and got right to the point.

"Where is my husband?"

"Not here, Princess," replied Orontobates, gesturing with his hands for her to look about the room.

"He is still in command, is he not?" she asked haughtily.

"In a manner of speaking..."

"Governor. He is either in command or he isn't," Barsine shot back, her restraint already frayed to the snapping point.

"Well, technically..."

"Is he dead?" she asked, leaning in to look the governor directly in the eyes, her patience at an end.

"No, but he is no longer able to carry out the demands of his office," replied the governor, obviously annoyed and impatient to get on with preparations to depart the city.

"What do you mean by that?" asked the princess, with concern evident in her voice. "Is he severely wounded, then?"

"No," replied the governor, anxious for this audience to come to an end yet wary of insulting a princess of the blood. "Not wounded. A few cuts and bruises, the usual," he said with a forced laugh. "You know how he always has to be in the front of things," he added with a weary sigh. "He has collapsed, however. Completely exhausted from the strain of command and days upon days of battle, all without proper rest or sustenance. You know him, lady," the governor said with a shrug and a 'what could I have done to stop him' sort of gesture. "He is not one to take care – or take suggestions, let alone orders, not even when it comes to his own well-being."

"I see," said the princess, a bit shaken with worry yet also relieved, as she had for a moment feared the worst. "Please, Governor," she continued, the energy fast draining from her now that she at least knew her husband lived and was apparently safe, "take me to him." She did not add the "at once" the governor expected, such was her own sudden exhaustion, nor did she pose it in the form of a command – but of a request. It was but the simple request of a woman who longed to be reunited with a beloved husband, a soldier whom she had feared wounded, maimed … or dead.

"I would if I could, Highness," said the governor quite nicely, at least for him. "But he is not here."

"Then where is he?" she asked, becoming exasperated. "Is he still in the city then? Or in the other citadel on the far side of the harbor?" she asked wearily. "Please have your men take me to him."

"I would do so, Princess, were it but in my power. But he is not in the city or the other citadel. He's out there," Orontobates said, pointing to the fleet that was fast scurrying out of the harbor. "The admiral had him carried aboard the flagship. And I will be following them quite soon, once I am...er...finished here."

"You're abandoning your post?" the princess said with disbelief, shock, and evident disdain. "Did you wheedle, and whine, and cheat your way into becoming governor here only to leave at the city's hour of need?"

"Pardon me, Princess," replied the governor, trying to hide his shame behind a mask of pride and with a look that showed he was offended by Barsine's taunt. "There have been a thousand hours of such 'need' since Alexander's army got here, and I have been here to face every one of those. But there is nothing more for me to do here – there is nothing left to govern. The city is lost."

"But the citadels, surely..."

"The citadels, my lady, are under the command of a pair of dedicated – or more accurately fanatic – officers of the Immortals. Sadly, the captain who brought them here, and most of his men, have fallen, but the few Immortals who are left will stay at their posts until the time has come to join their dead comrades. They do not need me, Princess, as I would only get in their way. Besides, the defense of the citadels is a military matter, or it will be once I remove the last symbols of civilian rule."

Dimitrios looked around as more men came in and left, each heavily burdened with such 'symbols' as they exited the room. Most of these symbols sparkled as their gold or bejeweled surface caught the sunlight that came in through the large windows all around the map room.

"Yes, Governor, I see," said Barsine, with even more disdain than before. "Be sure you do not over burden yourself with such 'symbols.' From what I hear, gold does not float particularly well."

The governor cleared his throat uncomfortably. He drew himself up. He tugged at his robes to straighten them and, one hand caressing the ringlets of his well-oiled beard and the other on his hip, inhaled deeply through his nose, as if he had smelled something unpleasant. The look in his eyes was response enough, and as Dimitrios could well see, there was nothing more to be gained – and perhaps much to be lost – if the princess made another comment to impugn the governor's honor, loyalty, courage, or manhood.

"Governor," Dimitrios said, putting himself both verbally and physically between the princess and Orontobates. "Could you at least tell us where the fleet is headed? We have a ship, and if we can't catch up with the flagship, we could at least take the princess to where the admiral is going, and to where he is taking Memnon."

"Cos," said the governor, almost spitting out the word. "The naval base at the city of Cos."

94

Halicarnassos

THE MAUSOLEUM

Alexander was triumphant – but unsatisfied. The fighting was taking too long, and resistance was not the kind he liked to meet. All that was left was a war in shadows and alleys, in the shops and houses, and wherever a small band of defenders could take refuge. There was no honor, no glory, no challenge to be had from such mopping up. But then his eyes brightened, and went wide, and his jaw dropped open with delight and surprise. "There," he said to Hephaestion, "there it is! Now that is something wonderful! That is something worthy of the attention of a king!"

Hephaestion was taken by surprise by Alexander's sudden change in mood – as he often was; but then he saw what had caught the king's eye and he, too, was appreciative of the sight. Fighting was still going on in different parts of the city, but that did not matter to the king, not anymore. For, over to the right, he caught the first glimpse of the great funeral monument and tomb of Mausolus, a true wonder of the world. Not even Hephaestion could change Alexander's mind about leaving the battle to go sight-seeing. The pleas from Ptolemy, Perdiccas, and Parmenion to send some Companions to stop soldiers from looting and raping, and to get back to the business of killing, fell upon deaf ears. Alexander's ardor for battle had been unparalleled when the attack began, and doubly so once the breaches had been made and his men were streaming through the ruined walls and open gates. But once he caught a glance of the sun glinting off the smooth, gleaming white stones of the Mausoleum, his concentration was broken. And then it was refocused, this time on the tomb, to the exclusion of everything else going about him in the war-torn city.

Alexander did not know the way to the tomb, but he didn't need a map or a guide. All he had to do was point his war horse towards it. As tall as a score of men standing on each other's shoulders and perched upon a small hill, the structure was visible from the harbor and from most parts of the town upon which it looked down. Although there were signs of battle all around it – even in the courtyard and on the steps leading up to the platform on which it sat – Alexander did not seem to notice the dead, the dying, or the wounded limping away. All he saw was the beauty above, not the horror below.

"Look at the statuary and the reliefs, Hephaestion," the king said with childlike awe as they rode closer. "What wouldn't Aristotle give to be here with us, to gaze at the sculptures by Leochares, Timotheus, Bryaxis, and Scopas?" he said, his excitement growing. "Remember how he told us of the rivalry among these four to design the tomb, and how Queen Artemesia decided to make a contest of it, by giving each of them one of the four sides to decorate?"

Before Hephaestion could answer, the king was showing him another sight.

"Oh, and the lions! Look at all of the lions," he exclaimed to Hephaestion. He had taken his eyes off the tomb just long enough to regard the row of carved lions that flanked both sides of the staircase that led up to the platform upon which they were standing. "Marvelous, aren't they? I always liked lions. Lions are fierce. Lions are proud. Lions are noble. Lions are – well – like me!" he added all but dancing with glee.

"Sire, they are noble, indeed, as are you," sighed Hephaestion, growing exasperated with his royal friend. "But they have been here for what, four decades now? They'll still be there tomorrow. Mean-while we've got..."

"Oh, shush!" laughed the king, dismissively. "What do I pay my generals for if not for that? I already won the battle for them," he chortled, "let them clean up the mess. They can manage that, can't they, Hephaestion? Even 'pretty boy' Ptolemy or grumpy old 'one eye' can handle what's left of the defenders. This is what I came here for; this is why I wanted Halicarnassos!"

"I thought you wanted it because it was the Persian fleet's biggest port in the area, and because Memnon was here?" replied Hephaestion.

"Yes, yes, all that, of course," the king responded, his eyes still fixed on the sculptures. "But look, look at that, will you!"

"What? Look at what, my King," sighed Hephaestion, taking his helmet off and pouring some water from a gourd over his head.

"The chariot! Look at the chariot!"

Hephaestion hurriedly threw his helmet back on, drew his sword and looked about rapidly, ready to respond to a chariot attack.

"Where! Where is the chariot!" shouted Hephaestion, making ready to defend his friend with his life.

"Up there, silly," laughed the king. "Up there on the tomb. Look, on the roof – at the pinnacle. There it is. A four-horse chariot, with Artemesia and her king at the reins. I think Aristotle said something about Pythos being responsible for that bit of art, eh?"

"Pytheos, not Pythos, Alexander," corrected Hephaestion. "Pythos is the old name for Delphi. Pytheos is the sculptor, not that it matters," mumbled Hephaestion, who finally just resigned himself to the fact that at least for a while they were going to be tourists and sightseers, instead of soldiers or generals.

"So, my King," said Hephaestion, putting on a phony smile and feigning interest, "what is it with all of these depictions of amazons and centaurs wrestling and writhing about – are they battling, dancing, or making love?"

"Perhaps a bit of all three," laughed the king. "After all, there isn't much difference, is there?"

While Alexander was climbing about the four horsemen whose statues guarded the four corners of the tomb, others in the city were still fighting for their lives. As he kept going on and on about the artists, Artemesia, the dead husband she had this raised to honor, and other bits of trivia about the monument, a war was still raging. Those had more pressing things to worry about than to debate the finer points of Greek and Carian architecture.

Although the outcome was no longer in doubt, Ptolemy, Perdiccas, and Parmenion kept shoving troops forward. Each was in a race to see which of them would reach the harbor first. Unknown to their king, the trio had made a wager about which of them would be the first to dip his spear into the sea. They also had a side bet going on as to which would fight, capture, or kill Memnon. Although the king himself had set a price equal to a king's ransom (a lesser king than himself, of course, as all such royals were in his eye) on Memnon's head, the three generals decided to sweeten that already tempting pot with a personal wager. Each was determined to be the one to win both bets, and the king's reward, and as such, what had started out as a well-planned pitched battle, was now nothing more than a free-for-all.

Each of the three generals had a personal bodyguard, and these were the arrows they aimed at the harbor. Most of their other soldiers had melted away to loot, pillage, and have their way with the women of the city. They could not be bothered keeping their men in check – they had their target, and each was damned if they weren't the one to reach it first.

It was Ptolemy who broke through the last, thin crust of armed sailors and marines that the Persian admiral had set up to cover the final withdrawal from the harbor. From his horse, he could see above the clash of shields and spears a group of men carrying a large man onto a big warship. He did not know who the man was, but he was obviously someone important, and that meant someone who would be worth a hefty ransom. Ptolemy hoped against hope that it was Memnon, but even if it wasn't, he thought, this was surely someone who was worth going after.

Ptolemy kicked his horse and kicked him hard. So hard that the stallion reared up and then leaped forward – plunging through the melee and out onto the strand. Ptolemy tried to calm the horse, but it was all he could do to hang on. He even dropped his sword so that he could hold on with both hands. But even that was not enough, as the horse was now so completely spooked, and confused, and unhappy that he bucked and twisted and bucked again – and bucked hard enough to throw Ptolemy from his seat...and into the harbor.

"Well," laughed Perdiccas a few minutes later, as he watched a dripping wet Ptolemy being helped out of the water. "The bet was to be the first to dip their spear in the water – not their ass. And since I see no evidence of your spear anywhere," he added, holding up a spear of his own, water dripping from the tip, "I guess that means I win!"

"Laugh all you want, you little shit," said Ptolemy, with a mixture of embarrassment, anger, and satisfaction. "You may have won the small bet, but you just let the real prize get away!"

"What do you mean?" Perdiccas said with a scowl as he looked from horseback upon the soaking wet general.

"You see that ship, that big one that just left the dock?"

"There are a lot of big ships slopping about in the harbor, Ptolemy. Which one exactly do you mean?

"That one. The one with the admiral's flag on it – you remember what a Persian admiral's flag looks like, right?"

"Yes, of course," grumbled Perdiccas. "Now I see her. So what?"

"Well my dear, dry, droll dumb ass – Memnon's on board. And he's getting away...and there's not a damn thing either of us can do about it."

95

The Royal Citadel

TIME TO GO

arsine rushed to one of the windows of Orontobate's map room which overlooked the harbor. She could see the last of the big ships weighing anchor – last except for the governor's massive quadrireme, that is. Her body language was hard to read, as one moment she seemed almost deliriously happy that her husband had escaped death, while on the other she seemed exasperated to the point of tears at once again having to chase him down.

"Captain Dimitrios," she said as she turned from the window, "run ahead and ask...no, tell...Captain Abibaal that I will once again require the use of his ship. He is to make ready to depart at once – and I do mean 'at once.' We are going to follow the admiral's flagship, even if we have to row all the way to Cos to do it."

"Aye, aye," said Dimitrios, nowhere near as glad as the princess that he would once again stand before his general. After all, technically he had failed in his mission. Yes, he had found Barsine and kept her safe, at least so far, but as far as getting her away east beyond the war zone, well...not so much. As he turned to carry out her command, the governor moved to block his path.

"What is the hurry, Princess," he said in as oily a diplomatic tone as he could muster. As he'd had a lot of practice speaking in this kind of soothing, comforting, and disarming manner, Orontobates' words, as well as his imposing presence in front of the door, brought the captain and the princess to a halt. "After all, why try and race after your husband in some little scout boat when, if you but wait an hour, we can follow them together in luxury, comfort, and style in my own ship. I, too, am going to Cos, where I will happily escort you into the presence of the lord high admiral and see you reunited with your dear husband. Besides, if I may say so, and forgive me if I seem impertinent, but, well, I believe you could use a bath, some clean clothes, and a bit of make-up, not to mention a good meal and some rest before going to see Memnon. You are, and I say this as a friend, a bit worn and scruffy looking at the moment..."

"Scruffy? Who's scruffy?" the princess shot back angrily.

"Well, you are," said the governor a bit sheepishly, gesturing with his hands as he turned about a mirror used for sending signals so that she could see how she appeared.

"I...I see what you mean, Governor," sighed the princess, not quite recognizing herself in the mirror, "but then again that is to be expected considering I've crossed Caria, fought in several running battles, and been nearly half-drowned tossing about in a tiny ship. I doubt you would look any more presentable if you'd been through what I have these last few weeks."

The governor merely smiled, keeping to himself what he would like to say, which is that he, of course, could never contemplate appearing anything less than perfect, regardless of the situation. After all, as a man of culture, breeding, and position, to even imagine himself ever looking so 'scruffy' was simply unthinkable. That is, after all, why one has servants.

"True, your Highness, but all the more reason you should take your time and travel to Cos with me. Wouldn't you rather look your best for your husband rather than appear before him," he added with an expression one would make when they had sniffed a nasty smell or were looking at something rather unpleasant, "...as you are now?"

Dimitrios saw what the governor was up to. Orontobates did not care a jot for how dirty or disheveled the princess appeared. He just wanted to be the one to reunite the couple – and to take the credit for it. It would do much to soothe things between himself and Memnon. It would also let him put in at least some good news to soften the report he would have to send to the emperor about how he had lost the impregnable fortress over which he had ruled. Orontobates could use that to better help him spin things to his advantage, as he could explain how he at least saved a member of the royal clan from a fate worse than death by spiriting her away from the burning city.

Dimitrios saw that the princess understood the same. She did hesitate for a moment, but her sense of urgency and longing to join her husband as soon as possible combined to overrule her vanity.

"I thank you for your offer," she said, in a tone that meant anything but what she said. "But I am afraid I must decline. I need to see my husband as soon as possible, and if you think Memnon will give a rodent's ass about how I look when he sees me, well, then you don't know my husband – or me – at all. So, Governor, good day to you...and," she added as she approached the door and laid a hand on his shoulder, "I wouldn't dally if I were you. The Macedonians will soon find the range to hit your ship at its dock. I think that if you try to place even one more bar of gold or ingot of silver aboard her, she'll sink under the weight."

With that, she and Dimitrios left the map room, raced down the spiral stairs and ran out onto the jetty where Abibaal and his ship were waiting.

Alexander's siege engineers were starting to find the range of the harbor. Now that they had men on the walls to spot for the artillery crews, they could adjust the weapons for distance and angle. The weapons were still too far away to hurl a full-sized load like that which had been used to shatter the walls, but by reducing the size and weight of the projectiles, they were able to fire farther, if with less punch. Then again, it didn't take a very big rock to make a hole in the thin bottom of even the best-built warship, and even a small ball of flaming pitch or a little jar of oil with a wick was enough to start a wooden ship afire.

One of the craftier of the engineers had even managed to haul a couple of smaller catapults and some bolt throwers into the city and set them up where they could see and shoot directly into the harbor. Where there had been fear and confusion before when projectiles fell at random, there was now panic and pandemonium. Ships began taking serious damage. Sailors were killed or wounded at their posts. Refugees, already packed tightly aboard, died or suffered injuries where they stood – and stood helpless, praying only that the sailors would move their vessels to safety before the next round of the increasingly accurate barrage rained down upon them.

The Royal Citadel and the ships docked around it took the brunt of this latest onslaught. These were not only the closest targets for the siege weapons on the eastern side of the city, but also the easiest to aim for. The top of the citadel towered above the harbor, and could be seen even from the siege lines. If the artillerymen missed the towers, they were still fairly likely to hit another part of the citadel, or anything close to it – like ships. The governor's massive quadrireme was the biggest ship in the harbor, and being next to the citadel, was the victim of many of those projectiles that fell around the fort. This would have put any ship at risk – and although the quadrireme was bigger, stronger, and more sturdily built than any other vessel in the harbor, it was also the most heavily burdened. Sitting so low in the water already from the weight of treasure the governor had insisted be loaded aboard her she, to put it simply, did not have as far to go to be driven below the surface of the water.

The captain of Orontobates' quadrireme had already deduced that his chances of survival diminished as each new crate was loaded aboard. Those chances lessened even more as each new round of rocks and fire pots fell and as each moment passed. He had said as much to the governor an hour ago, but finally decided enough was enough. The captain ordered his men to prepare to make way, and stationed marines to prevent anyone from loading anything more aboard his ship. The time had come to leave, and he himself went into the citadel to tell the governor that if they did not leave this instant, they might never leave at all.

Orontobates was about to argue, when a fire pot came flaming in through a window and exploded on the floor of his map room. Several large stones struck the walls of the tower at the same time. The captain's argument made for him by Alexander's artillery crews, Orontobates agreed to leave – pausing only long enough to scoop up whatever jewels he could carry on the way out.

Dimitrios and the princess were way ahead of the governor. Abibaal cast off the instant they jumped aboard. Although Abibaal's was one of the smaller vessels still left in the harbor, even his ship had taken a few glancing flows from the near-misses aimed at the citadel. As he took a quick look behind him, Abibaal could see that his was the last ship to leave the harbor...the last but one, that is.

Orontobates ran up the gangplank behind the captain, who did not even pause to haul it back aboard. He lifted it himself and tossed it into the water as the quadrireme's rowers pushed off and began to pull their oars– and pull them as if their lives depended on it (which, indeed, they did). The ship, however, was slow to respond. So heavily burdened she was that far more power than usual was needed to overcome inertia, and with her lower ports barely above the water line, she had to do so without one of her four banks of oars. That meant a quarter of her oarsmen had nothing to do, and were just quite literally dead weight. Orontobates demanded these extraneous personnel jump overboard, but not a man moved. Many of the men at the oars who heard this order spun about in horror at the governor's command, further diminishing the power needed to move the ship.

"Belay that order!" shouted the captain, who grabbed the governor by his collar and shoved him up against the side. "Listen to me, Governor," he said with an angry, threatening scowl, "another order like that and the men will mutiny and dump you over the side – and maybe me along with it," he added with a whisper. "We need every one of these men to give their all if we are to get out of here alive. And they are not going to do that if we start tossing their friends and comrades into the drink!"

No sooner had the captain said his piece than another rock struck the ship, badly injuring an oarsmen.

"You!" the captain shouted at one of the rowers who had been made extraneous, "help that man. And you!" he added as he looked at another of the unemployed rowers, "take his post. And row, damn, you, row! Row for your lives!"

The Island of Cos

REUNITED LIKE THEY KNEW THEY WOULD

Barsine's eyes never strayed as Abibaal's little scout ship struggled to close the distance with the admiral's great flagship. She did not hear any sound but that of the oars on the water. Not even the crash of rocks on wooden planks, the roar of fire on linen sails, or the screams of terror from refugees and the shouts of sailors could break through her concentration. It was not that she was oblivious to what was going on all about her, but only that she had found a quiet place amidst the maelstrom that was hers -and hers alone.

Abibaal, however, could not afford such a royal luxury. He had a ship to sail and lives to save. He had to be aware of every splash, crack, roar, scream, and shout – and use them as he continually recalculated the chances of getting out of this man-made storm alive. And storm it was, for Alexander's siege weapons had found their range.

Abibaal danced his ship through the splashes and swung a bit to port or starboard to avoid slower vessels – or get out of the way of larger ones, none of whom would change course for his small scout vessel. Many of the captains, it seemed, had forgotten the basic laws of the sea about right of way, such was the panic that was filling sails and driving rowers to the breaking point.

Barsine was actually starting to smile, to let go some of the tension, when she noticed they were no longer on a course toward the flagship, but were instead turning about – back towards the harbor and the Royal Citadel.

"Captain! Captain!" she called out, making her way with difficulty from the prow back aft, struggling to keep her feet on the narrow way between the rowing benches. "Why are we turning back?"

"That's why!" said Abibaal as he pointed toward the dock they had shoved off from only a few minutes before. "It's the governor's ship, it's foundering, and they're signaling for help!"

True enough, the great lumbering quadrireme was indeed foundering. She had been struck several times by large rocks and fire pots. The impact of the stones had rocked the big vessel, causing some of her cargo to shift. Already struggling and far too low in the water for her captain's comfort, that shift was causing her to list. As she did, the quadrireme took on more and more water, thus worsening her list. Fires had broken out in several places, and between fighting the flames, battling the list and dodging the incoming stones, rocks, and fire ports, her captain and crew were hard pressed to keep her afloat, let alone row her out of range of the Macedonian artillery.

Some aboard were already jumping ship. More and more seemed resigned to taking their chances ashore. Most were swimming out into the harbor, calling out and waving as best they could for help. Then came a great cracking noise, as if someone had put their foot through a thin wooden screen. It came from the quadrireme – her back was cracked and she was breaking up. The weight of her cargo of gold, silver, jewels, and other valuables Orontobates had ordered stored aboard, proved too much for the great ship, especially once enemy rocks and stones began to punch holes in her hull. As the ship began to sink beneath the harbor waves, she made a great sucking sound, pulling those in the water near her down to a watery grave. Even with the princess in his charge, Abibaal could not ignore the pleas of those in the water. What sailor could?

There was not much room aboard the tiny scout vessel, as she was built for speed, not for battle or for carrying cargo or ferrying passengers, but room could be made for a dozen or even a score more souls.

He could also throw out a line for others to cling to until Abibaal could swing about and catch up with the big ships. As infuriated as she was about yet another delay in reuniting with her husband, the princess was, after all, human. She left it to the sailors to bring the survivors of the quadrireme aboard. She did what little she could to help settle and comfort the weary, soaking wet, and wretched refugees, one of whom looked uncomfortably familiar.

"Orontobates?" Barsine part asked, part exclaimed as she wrapped a cloak around the shoulders of one particularly distraught looking survivor. The man turned his head slowly to look up at her, and she knew that it was indeed the satrap of Caria, governor of Halicarnassus and richest man in Asia Minor – or at least he had been. His kingdom lost, his city aflame, and his wealth at the bottom of the harbor, Orontobates had lost everything. What he had sought to save was now buried beneath the wreckage of the once-proud quadrireme; his vast wealth entombed with the sailors whose lives were lost as much to his refusal to part with his treasure as to the boulders and flaming pots thrown by the Macedonian artillery.

Something in Barsine took pleasure at seeing the proud, haughty governor brought low. Yet she did not laugh at or taunt him, or even say how it was his own greed that brought him to such a low point. She wanted to and she could have – but Barsine didn't. He was such a pathetic sight that a sense of pity pushed all other emotions to the side. And besides, his defeat was hers as well, for it was her empire that had lost a vital city, her royal family whose prestige was diminished, and her husband who would bear the ultimate responsibility for this defeat. Like it or not, Barsine and the governor were – quite literally – in the same boat, a boat which was now struggling to turn about to bring her, the governor, and all aboard to safety.

The extra weight of rescued survivors and the drag from the score of men holding on to the tow line in the water that she trailed made the oarsmen's job much, much harder. But once Abibaal had fought his ship far enough from shore to be out of missile range, other vessels turned about to rescue the men in the water. The admiral had also signaled to the rag tag fleet of men-of-war and merchant vessels to slow their speed and await orders. He would be damned if his ships would dribble into Cos like flotsam washing in with the tide; they would instead sail in as a fleet. He knew what had been lost, yet also was proud of having fought the good fight. The navy had saved the lives of many citizens and soldiers of the empire – not least of them Memnon, the emperor's friend and general. And so it was, with order and discipline and honor intact, that the Persian Navy's Mediterranean squadron entered the great harbor of the island of Cos as a fleet, with banners waving, colors flying, and drums beating out the rhythm for the rowers.

As the admiral's ship let down its anchor, Abibaal's scout ship pulled up alongside, its sailors calling for the warship to let down a rope ladder. Of all of the people whom the admiral might expect to climb up that ladder, few could have been more of a surprise to him than Barsine. There could be no reason in the world for a princess of the blood to be here, and now, let alone standing upon his deck in dirty, torn, bloodied, and dripping clothing, and those of a soldier, no less. It was only when Memnon, weakened and weary from his wounds as he was, managed to make his way out from the cabin to stand next to him, that the admiral understood why the princess would be here.

"Barsine?" came the voice of Memnon from beside him. The princess somehow heard his trembling voice, and turned to look at her husband. She gave him a smile that shone as brightly as if they were alone, at home, warm, and safe, and dressed in their finest clothes. No matter that they were amongst a crowd of sailors, soldiers, and half-drowned refugees, cold, wet, and dirty aboard a warship a the outer edge of a dying empire. Neither could recall nor imagine ever having been more glad to see the other.

Dimitrios and his brother had come up the ladder behind Barsine, then had reached back down to help Halime and Ari ascend as well. The two Greeks and others had been rescued from the island at Barsine's insistence. Captain Abibaal followed, with Orontobates close behind, Burzasp providing the governor with a shoulder to lean upon. Admiral Autophradates could not believe his eyes at the sight of them, but there they were. A princess, a general, a governor, a mercenary captain, and a physician, plus assorted hangers on, crowded and dripped upon his deck. The admiral stood there, hands upon his hips, his head shaking back and forth in disbelief. As Abibaal came forward and offered a weary yet still proper salute, the admiral gave him a perplexed look and then said, rather quietly, "Captain, you've got some explaining to do."

Epilogue: Cos

AN ISLAND OFF THE WESTERN COAST OF ASIA MINOR

The Island of Cos

PROMISES AND PLANS

Memnon had three reactions when he saw Barsine. The first was surprise, the second was joy, and the third was fury. A fury he directed at Dimitrios. A fury he unleashed even while holding the princess in his arms, on the deck of a warship.

"Captain!" he growled with all of the anger his wounds and weariness would allow, "I sent you on a mission to see my wife safely east. You gave me your word that you would do so. Instead, not only have you disobeyed your orders and broken your word, you have put her at risk by bringing her into a war zone! Guards!" he shouted over his shoulder, nearly doubling up coughing as he spoke – and would have had not the princess held him up. "Guards! Arrest this man!"

Dimitrios's heart sank deep in his chest. It was not as if he did not know that Memnon might react in this manner, but that he had hoped it would at least be tempered by the sight of his wife, safe and sound before him.

"Stop!" shouted the princess in that icy voice of command that comes natural only to generals and those of royal blood. This was the kind of voice that can bring a charging elephant to its knees or cause young officers to fear that their career, and possibly their very life, is about to end.

"Nobody is going to be arrested here today, and certainly not this brave man," said the princess haughtily, without any trace of sentimentality in her speech. "He and his brother, and their friends, did only what I asked – no, what I commanded – them to do! They did try to talk me out of it, as you, my dear husband, would have wanted them to do, but that is as far as they could come to obeying your orders. To obey you, moreover, they would have had to disobey me and, quite frankly, dear husband," she added with a taunting smile, "I outrank you. There are only two men whose orders I cannot override, and as you are neither my father nor my king, my word takes precedence. Far from punishing them, you should reward them...and on second thought, leave that to me. After all," she continued, now looking at him, stroking his hair in as gentle a manner as possible, "I can shower them with favors far greater than anything you can offer."

Memnon tried to object, but knew better than to argue with Barsine. He may be her husband, but theirs was not the typical relationship. She did, indeed, outrank him by virtue of her royal blood, and as she had told him time and time again, "nobody puts a princess in the corner." Such was her way of letting him and others know that a princess does what a princess wants to do...especially if her name is Barsine.

"Captain," she said, turning her head to look at Dimitrios while still holding her husband's hand in one of hers, and pointing to the deck with the other, "kneel."

As Dimitrios did so, Klemes, Ari, Halime, and Hassan gathered behind him. Orontobates, for his part, couldn't care less, and just sat slumped and dripping on a rowing bench nearby and called for wine, dry clothes – and more wine.

The princess let go of Memnon's hand, and with both hands unclasped from around her neck a thin gold chain from which dangled a tiny red jewel. She then bent down, placed it around Dimitrios' neck, clasped it shut. As she stood back up she said "Accept this small token of my gratitude. I give it to you in thanks as a mother and as a wife for seeing me safe through the lands of my enemies and for reuniting me with the father of my children and my husband. And," she continued, while removing a gold band from one of her fingers, "accept this ring, by which I thank and honor you for your service to the royal family. It bears my personal crest, and inside has an inscription. Show this ring to any officer of the empire, and he will give you what you ask, as if the order came from my lips. And," she continued, "should this ring ever be cut from your finger, lost, or stolen, remember the words inscribed on the inside. If spoken along with my name, to any one of high rank or any member of the royal family, they will help you. Now, my dear Captain, you may rise."

Dimitrios, overcome by the receipt of such unexpected honors, rose as commanded. The princess then embraced him gently and lightly, and put her cheek up against his, at which point he began to blush; a blush that cooled and paled when Barsine whispered into his ear.

"You are mine, now, Captain. You belong to me, and only to me."

The princess let go, stepped back and, looking very regal, gave him a nod and a thin, wry smile; a smile that chilled Dimitrios to his very core.

By evening, most of the ships in the fleet had docked or beached, and their crews and passengers come ashore. A rich, cosmopolitan port and center of learning though it was, even Cos struggled to feed, shelter, and offer care for such a sudden wave of humanity. Its harbor could not accommodate so many great ships at once, but at least there were many experienced dock workers, shipwrights, and others upon whom the harbor master could call to aid in the process. The city's shopkeepers and merchants were more than happy to provide food, drink, clothing – and more drink to this unexpected but most welcome influx of customers. They did so at a much higher price than normal; but those who could not pay were still fed, their way paid for with script handed out by a small army of imperial bureaucrats. The empire, as always, took care of its own.

In further acknowledgment of their services to Barsine, the princess insisted that Dimitrios, Halime, and others who had accompanied her so far, be quartered in the governor's palace. She and Memnon, along with Admiral Autophradates, took up residence there, as did Orontobates, who demanded such as his due. His sense of entitlement would not allow him to even think of seeking less prestigious accommodations.

Klemes, however, did not join them. Cos was where he had studied medicine. He sought out one of his old teachers and offered his services as a healer, which, with so many wounded, injured and exhausted soldiers, sailors, and refugees was sorely needed. Even in a city famed for its medical schools, there were just not enough physicians, healers, or other trained personnel to meet the needs of those brought ashore by the fleet.

As the princess had taken a particular liking to Halime, she was invited to stay with her as a lady in waiting, at least for the time being. "I like you, Halime," said the princess when the two were alone in her chambers. "You remind me of...well...me...or at least the me I once was before I was married off to seal a partnership with Mentor's faction. Oh, I did love Memnon's brother, but ours was still primarily a political marriage, as women of my rank are bred for. But as much as I loved Mentor and do love Memnon, part of me longs to be you – to be able to ride, and hunt, and be carefree!"

Halime let out a little sigh, shook her head and replied: "Oh, if only my life were such – but it is not now and never was. When I was younger, I helped my father and brothers on our ranch – raising, caring for, chasing down, and taming horses. I had little time for the pleasures of riding and hunting – except when the time came to find meat for the table. Then, when times were hard, well, my father was forced to leave me as collateral for his debts – although he did not do so without making some conditions, which meant I was a serving girl but not a slave. But the longer I worked for the man he sent me to, the more the lines between the two became blurred. Had it not been for Dimitrios and Ari, I would most certainly be warming the bed of that man, or his sons, or his friends, or maybe all of them. Princess," she added, "trust me, you would never, ever wish to be me."

Halime's candor shocked the princess – but also touched her heart.

"Forgive me," said Barsine as she drew the girl closer, "I did not know. Those of us who live a life of privilege forget – if we ever knew – what so many of our subjects have to go through just to stay alive. I have known pain and heartbreak, but I was always my own person."

"And in that you are fortunate – and blessed," replied Halime. "Would that all of us were so lucky."

Barsine hugged her tightly, then slowly let go and leaned back. "Halime, I am not sure what is next in store for me, but I can promise it will not be lazing about in silks on soft pillows, sipping on iced wines. I would be very grateful if you would accompany me when I leave Cos, wherever it is that I go. Having another woman about in whom I could confide – and also trust in a fight, should it come to that – well, it would be a great comfort to me. I would, of course, see that your family's debts are made good and that you are no longer anyone's property but your own."

Halime hesitated to reply only as long as it took for her to wipe the tears of gratitude from her eyes. "Of course I will go with you. I'd wondered if you'd ask."

As for where Barsine would be going, that was decided in council the next morning; a council at which Memnon, Autophradates, Orontobates, the governor of Cos, and the princess (who insisted upon bringing Halime with her) were present. Dimitrios was also present, although he was unsure as to why, or as what. Was he still an aide on Memnon's staff? Was he now a member of Barsine's household? After the scene Barsine had made on the flagship, he knew he was at least not going to be sent home in disgrace – not that he had a home to go to. And if he were to be sent back into the battle line, why was he ordered to be here, with the movers and shakers of his shrinking universe?

The answer was immediately forthcoming.

"Gentlemen – and my dear wife – it is apparent that neither of my plans to stop, let alone defeat Alexander have succeeded. The first, to scorch the earth ahead of him to deny his army food, fodder, shelter or even drinkable water, was a non-starter..."

"And it is not likely to be accepted by the satraps, nobles and men of property in the provinces now threatened by Alexander," interjected

Orontobates. "We will fight for our land – but we will not destroy it. The land is our past, our present, and our future. We will shed our blood on it and for it – and even breathe out our last breath for it, but destroy it? Never. If you even ask men to do that," sighed Orontobates, "you may as well just give them a Macedonian uniform. They'll fight for whomever promises to keep the land – their land – safe."

The governor of Cos rather meekly nodded in agreement with Orontobates, as Memnon had suspected he would. Even Barsine shrugged in agreement with the two governors, not because she did not see the wisdom of Memnon's plan, but because she knew her class would never implement it.

"Well, then, that leaves us with two options," sighed Memnon. "The first is to try to draw off Alexander's Greek troops."

"And how do you suggest we do that?" asked Orontobates.

"By attacking Greece itself," said Memnon loudly, stabbing a small dagger into the map laid out before him.

"I see you have stuck the dagger into the heart of Athens," teased Orontobates. "Why not into Macedonia itself?"

"Because there is little of value in Macedonia worth taking or defending, let alone threatening. Alexander has left a sizable corps to defend the homeland..."

"Along with his mother," added Autophradates with a grimace.

"Yes, along with his mother," mumbled Memnon in agreement. "She is a force of nature, that one. I came to know her when I was in Macedonia. While I am not sure that she is the witch they say she is, neither am I sure that she isn't. Either way, she is not someone with whom I would care to tangle. Greece, however, is another story. What city states there have sent Alexander men, ships, and money, did so grudgingly. As my Theban friend over there will confirm, there is little love between the Greeks and the Macedonians. Isn't that right, Captain Dimitrios?"

This was not the first time that Memnon had encouraged Dimitrios to speak at a staff meeting, but this was different. He was not asking his opinion – he was demanding he corroborate what Memnon had just said.

"The General is correct. Take me, for instance, and Ephialtes, the gods keep his soul safe, and many other Greeks in your army and navy," continued Dimitrios. "We do not fight just for pay, or to find adventure, like most mercenaries of old. Not this time," he added, pausing for effect. "This time it is different. Most of us have a score to settle with the Macedonians. There are only two things that can unite the many Greek nations, tribes, and cities. The first, as you fellows already learned – and learned twice, is to defend against a Persian invasion."

Orontobates and Autophradates both bristled at that, for every Persian remembered Marathon, Salamis, and Plateai every bit as well as any Greek, but for a much different reason.

"The second, as we showed at Chaeronea," sighed Dimitrios, "is to defy any tyrant who seeks to tell us what to do. Philip was just such a creature, and Alexander is the same. You think of Greeks and Macedonians as one, but we do not. Alexander and his Macedonians are as foreign to us...as, well, as you are."

Memnon nodded a quiet thank you toward Dimitrios, then turned back to the map.

"Alexander has dispersed his fleet. That leaves the seas and coasts of Greece, and her islands, ripe for the picking. The admiral and I will strike out at each of those cities and islands. Not to slash, and pillage, and burn – unless we have to – but to intimidate, cajole, threaten, bribe, and otherwise convince them to abandon their support for Alexander. At the very least they will need to call home the forces they sent to back his invasion, and keep their men, money, and supplies home to defend against us, should we attack. If I cannot scorch the earth ahead of him, then I can at least cut the umbilical cord behind him. And maybe, maybe," he added forcefully, "maybe we can convince enough of those states to join with us in a war of liberation – a war to give Greece back to the Greeks!"

Dimitrios could not have asked for more. This was the very reason why he had taken up the sword against Alexander – that, and of course revenge for the devastation of his home city. Without thinking, he drew his sword, raised it up high and shouted "freedom!" at the top of his lungs.

The others in the room turned about to stare at this curious and loud outburst, making Dimitrios feel something akin to a child who had broken a vase or a puppy who had peed on a rug. Suitably, if silently, chastised, he returned his sword to his scabbard and came to attention.

"And that, gentleman, and my lady," said Memnon with a smile, "is exactly the kind of reaction I hope to inspire among my fellow Greeks."

"You're not really a Greek, dear, you know that, don't you?" teased Barsine. "He's from Rhodes, you know," she said to the others with a laugh.

"But neither is he a Persian, other than by marriage," said Orontobates with a superior slither. "The people of Rhodes are neither fish nor fowl, in the sense that they are neither Persian nor Greek. But they may be Greek enough that the cities on the mainland and on the islands, and in the Greek colonies, may just buy it. It is a risky plan, but it might just work," the governor added in support.

The others did not realize that he did offer his support not so much because he felt it would work as much as he was glad to be rid of Memnon, of whom he felt increasingly jealous. Memnon had lost two key cities to Alexander, but at least he had the wounds to show for his troubles. All Orontobates had to show was some damp robes and empty treasure chests – which he didn't even really have, as those chests were at the bottom of Halicarnassos' harbor.

After the meeting broke up, Memnon and Barsine retired to as private a chamber as could be found inside a palace, where even the walls have ears. Once inside, she closed and locked the door and, quite angrily and with far more strength than one would expect from someone of her station and physique, pushed him hard up against the wall.

"You're not going off on some damn pirate raid, not without me, you're not!" said Barsine quite loudly. "I didn't traipse half way across

Asia Minor, fight off bandits and mercenaries, and nearly drown just to kiss you goodbye again, you know! If you are going, well, husband, I am going with you!"

"No, you will not," interjected the general. "Princess or no princess, there is no place on board any of my ships for a woman – and especially one of royal blood."

The princess shot virtual arrows out of her eyes at Memnon.

"I am, too, going...General," she said, speaking the last word very slowly and deliberately, so as to emphasize that his rank did not give him the authority to push around a princess.

"No, my dear, you are not. You cannot," said Memnon.

"So? Now you think you can tell me what to do?" she added, emphasis on the 'you.' "You don't think I can hold my own with the boys? Did you learn nothing from those long months in Halicarnassos? May I remind you that Halicarnassos is where Queen Artemisia came from? The queen who led the premier squadron of Xerxes fleet when it fought at Salamis?"

"And look what happened to her..." Memnon started to say.

"Yes, look!" said Barsine. "She..."

"She lost most of her ships and used the rest to escort Xerxes' children to safety back home," said Memnon, "and that is what I need you to do. I need you to take our children far, far away from all of this...just as Artemisia did for Xerxes. Besides," he added softly, his voice a verbal caress, "I could not do my duty if you were with me."

"What? What do you mean?" asked the princess, quietly.

"I would not be able to concentrate on the war if you were with me."

"Am I that much of a distraction?" she replied playfully, even coquettishly.

"Well, to be honest...yes," he replied, taking her hands gently into his own. "But more than that. I would always be looking over my shoulder, worrying that something might happen to you..."

"Memnon, haven't I just shown you that I can fight and..."

"Yes, yes my dear, you have...but if you were with me, all of my plans would be clouded by fear of putting you in danger. I would never be able to focus all of my energies, all of my strength on the war or on any battle in which we became engaged. Worrying about you would make me cautious, make me less bold, and make me less of a general. I am and always shall be your husband, but out there," he said, pointing to the sea, "I need to be a general, and not just a general first, but also a general second, third, and fourth. And if anything did happen to you..."

Barsine rarely lost an argument, or had anyone say "no" to her, but as she looked into Memnon's eyes she knew he was right. She put her head close to his, fought back a tear,and somehow managed to say "all right. I will do as you ask. Our children, by the way, are surely in Damascus by now. But that may not be far enough from this Macedonian monster to be safe. I will take them to Susa, or Persepolis, or even Babylon if needs be."

Memnon smiled a great sigh of relief, held her even closer and gave her as passionate a kiss as he could, considering where he was and who was about. As the two parted, Memnon told Barsine: "I am not sending you away only for those reasons, or just to keep you safe, my love. Or even because the children need their mother. I have a mission for you, and it is one that only you can accomplish with any chance of success."

"What?" said the princess in surprise. "What is it that you want me to do?"

"I need you to make a case for me to the King of Kings."

"What case? And why me?"

"My plan of campaign, that's what I want you to explain to him. As for the 'why,' well, that is because he will listen to you. He likes you, he trusts you, and you share the same blood."

Memnon and Barsine were not allowed much of a respite, but were called back to the council chamber by the governor. Dimitrios went along with the pair, as much as a guard as an aide, for the captain did not wholly trust the governor. The council was called again because, as more and more ships came trickling back into the harbor, each with more tales of woe about the fate of Halicarnassos, the governor and even the admiral had become more concerned. They sought reassurance that all would be well. Memnon tried to give that to them by explaining his plan, and how he intended to send his wife to inform Darius of what he intended and proposed.

"Why not send Orontobates?" interrupted the governor. "He is a satrap, after all."

"Yes," interrupted the general, "but he is a satrap without a throne, and without – pardon my candor, Orontobates – without a pot to piss in. Besides," he leaned in close and added in a whisper so only he could hear, "Darius doesn't trust him. He'd do just the opposite of what Orontobates proposed – if he even granted him an audience at all."

"What? What are you saying about me?" asked Orontobates in surprise as he burst into the chamber.

"Nothing much," said Memnon, "just that how much stronger the proposal we wish to put forward to Darius would be if both you and the princess were there to present it to him. My credit, I am sure, is very low with him right now. Only my dear wife, the Princess Barsine, can get close enough to him to explain what has happened, and what I will try to do to set things right."

"And just what is this proposal?" asked Orontobates with a scowl. "What is this idea that is so wonderful that you need a princess of the blood to sell it?"

"Do not worry, Orontobates," replied Barsine with a sigh. "He's explained his strategy to me. Not that I'm agreeing to it, mind you," she added, turning to her husband," as I still don't intend to let you go gallivanting around the Aegean without me, like some randy sailor on leave, or playing at Odysseas..."

That got a laugh from even the dour admiral and sour satrap, and even Dimitrios had to struggle not to do the same.

"My proposal," Memnon explained to the satrap, "as I told my dear, sweet, Barsine, is that our army cannot stand up to the Macedonians, not as it is."

"What!" said Orontobates. "The King of Kings can call up one hundred thousand, two hundred thousand – and more, many more, men, enough to drown that little bugger..."

"Like Alexander almost drowned you?" chortled the admiral.

"Yes, sort of," grimaced Orontobates, "although not in water, but in blood!"

"But not one of them – except maybe the Immortals – can match the Macedonians," continued Memnon. "Our light cavalry are a fickle and finicky mob of marauders. Our noble cavalry is brave but woefully undisciplined, as we saw at the Granicos! Everyone is too proud to take orders from anyone else, let alone let somebody else hog the glory! And our infantry...well...quite honestly...in the open field they're worthless. Remember how the satraps had to chain them to the ground in order to make them stand? And then what did they do? They threw down their arms and begged the Macedonians for mercy..."

"So," sighed Orontobates shaking his head. "Let me get this straight. You want me to tell the King of Kings that the largest army in the world, fielded by the largest empire the world has ever seen, can't stop two score thousand barbarians?"

"Well, not if you put it that way...and that is why I don't want you to be the one explaining this to Darius. My wife will do the talking. After all, you lack, how shall I put it, her special charms."

"Memnon!" the princess shouted in exasperation, folding her arms across her rather ample chest in a pout.

"I am sorry, my dear," Memnon said, "but there is nobody in the world that can hold Darius' attention like you can. He will listen to you, if only to stare into your beautiful...eyes. And what I want you to tell him is that we cannot stop the Macedonians with the army we have. We have to raise a new army – and a new kind of army. An army that is disciplined, equipped, and prepared to fight Alexander. We don't have the time to train a phalanx of pikemen like he has – it takes years to learn how to march without tripping over those long pikes, let alone maneuver or fight with them. Gods, they are 12, 16 or even 18 feet long!"

"So what is this 'new' army of yours about then?" the admiral asked.

"We call up our mountain fighters – men who are hunters, good with both bow and spear. We have them fight the way the Assyrians of old fought. The way the Immortals fight: front ranks spears and shields. Rear ranks bows. The Macedonian infantry fight in deep formations. Massive blocks that make impossible to miss targets, even when they close for hand to hand. The spearmen keep the front ranks of Macedonians at bay while the archers fire volley after volley overhead into the back ranks of the phalanx. It would help if we could train those front rank spearmen to fight like hoplites...and that, Dimitrios, is where you come in," he added, catching the captain by surprise as he motioned for him to approach.

"Me?"

"Yes," said Memnon. "You. I'd give this task to Ephialtes but, as you know..."

"Know what?"

"That he did not escape," Memnon said with a quiver in his voice and tears starting to form in his eyes. "He stayed behind to give the rest of us time to get away. That," he said, choking back his emotion, "and because he told me he would never again retreat. 'I'd rather die on my feet with a thousand wounds than run away from that little bully again,' he told me just before the final assault began. That was the last I saw of him."

Dimitrios was, surprisingly, not stunned by the news of Ephialtes death.

"That is the way he wanted to die," said Dimitrios quietly. "A warrior's death. True, he wanted to win at least one battle against Alexander," the captain added, "but at least he went down fighting Alexander. Did we at least get to recover his body?"

"Sadly, no," replied Memnon. "When he went down there were just too many of the enemy. I was considering sending a herald to the Macedonian camp to ask for his body...or that at least he be given the proper rites."

"No, don't do that," replied Dimitrios.

"Why not?" asked Memnon, genuinely perplexed.

"First of all, because he would not want to be singled out and separated from his men – not even in death. Second, most important, is because Ephialtes never asked Alexander for anything while he was alive, and to ask any favor from the Macedonian king now would only embarrass and anger Ephialtes' shade. Even worse, Alexander, knowing he is dead, might seek out Ephialtes' corpse – and inflict unspeakable horrors on it, just out of spite."

"Yes, you are right – on both counts. Alexander is going to be so angry when he finds out that I have slipped through his grasp again, there is no telling what he might do in his rage. Even as a boy, he had quite a nasty temper. He was the kind of child who would drown small animals and break the wings of birds just to hear them screech. Well, enough of that," he concluded with a mighty harrumph. "So, what of my request? Will you help me raise this new army I propose?"

"I am honored, but I am no Ephialtes," said Dimitrios sadly, remembering the old general whom he admired and, in a way, saw as another father. "As you know, it takes time to train a man to fight in a shield wall. You have to trust the men around you; you have to work together...and you have to have the guts just to stand there and take it...let alone attack."

"And that, my friend, is precisely why you are going along with my wife – to say just that to Darius."

Dimitrios was dumbstruck. He just started shaking his head back and forth in a 'no'...but Memnon grabbed his shoulder and made him look straight into his eyes.

"Dimitrios..."

"General. I can't. I can't stand before the King of Kings and pretend to be something I'm not..."

"You will not be pretending. Dimitrios, you are a soldier, and one of the finest I have ever seen. You might not be so perfect about following orders," he added with a teasing laugh, "but you know how to lead and train men. You've also stood in the battle line against the Macedonians. Believe me, you are more than qualified to tell Darius the truth that he needs to hear. He has enough perfumed sycophants about to tell him how wonderful everything is going to be," he said, casting a quick glance at Orontobates, who responded with a glare. "He needs to hear the truth. And, besides," he added with evident gratitude, "you have shown that you can be trusted to keep my wife safe. She will have need of you. And I need you to do this. I can order you to go, but I do not think I need to pull rank, or do I?"

Dimitrios looked up at the general, who stood half a head taller than he, and then at Barsine, who gave him a knowing look, and back again.

"Ari and Klemes will want to come with us, and I believe the Lady Halime and Lord Burzasp as well, for they have both shown their devotion to the Princess," said Dimitrios as he stood tall. "And after all," he added with a wry smile, "even though I will not be on the front lines with you, I guess in my own way I will still be fighting Alexander."

Join Dimitrios, his friends, the princess and the rest of those who are fighting Alexander as their adventures continue in the next volume of the series, *Throne of Darius II – A Princess of Persia*.

Thank you for taking time to read *Throne of Darius*. If you enjoyed it, please consider telling your friends or posting a short review. Word of mouth is an author's best friend and much appreciated.

Thank you again,
Mark G. McLaughlin

Turn the page for a note from the author.

A Note from the Author...

I have been fascinated by all things ancient for as long as I can remember. Perhaps it all began in earnest when my best friend Nino and I used to spend our Saturday afternoons together watching sword and sandal movies and playing with little plastic Greek hoplites, Roman legionnaires, and so many other assorted toy soldiers. The more we watched and played, the more I wanted to know about the history of that (and other) eras. A voracious reader of history throughout my years in parochial and military schools, I became even more so during my college years at Georgetown – and that hunger to read more and more about the ancient world has yet to abate. To the contrary, my years of painting and wargaming with miniature soldiers (I have over 2,300 from the ancient era alone) and of designing games (of which I have published 24 titles, including *Ancient Civilizations of the Inner Sea* and the upcoming *Ancient Civilizations of the Middle East*) have only drawn me deeper and deeper into those fascinating times.

Although I have been a free-lance journalist (and a prolific one at that) for over 40 years, *Throne of Darius* is only my fourth book – and my second novel. The first two books are historical works, *Battles of the American Civil War* and *The Wild Geese* (about the Irish brigades of France and Spain). The other novel, *Princess Ryan's Star Marines*, is a work of military science fiction, and is based on the board game of the same name, both of which are named in honor of my daughter, Ryan. I am working on no fewer than four games at present (including two more of what will eventually be six in the ***Ancient Civilizations*** series, as well as a novel about Confederate raiders and blockade runners and, of course, the next two – or perhaps it will be three? - in the ***Throne of Darius*** series.

Thank you again for reading my book. I hope you will join me in the further adventures of Captain Dimitrios and company in the forthcoming books in the *Throne of Darius* series.

Connect with me here: markgmclaughlin.com

Visit me on Facebook here: https://www.facebook.com/mark.mclaughlin.357

Acknowledgments

I am of course indebted to the great historians of antiquity, including Plutarch, Arrian, Diodorus, and, especially, Quintus Curtius, all of whom although writing long after Alexander and his empire faded, were still far closer in time to their subject than modern writers. As for those more modern writers, I am equally indebted to a score of famous historians and novelists, from J.F.C. Fuller to Steven Pressfield, from David Grant to Mary Renault, and, of course, to Michael Woods, whose book (and video) *In the Footsteps of Alexander the Great*, were particularly inspiring and edifying.

I would be remiss, however, if I did not mention my editor, Krystallia Papadimitriou for whom Greek is her mother-tongue. Her assistance has been invaluable, not only for her editing talents, but also for her help in making the book more authentic. (We have yet to meet in person but, perhaps someday, she and her family will visit their relatives in America. If and when they do, I will make every effort to be there).

My special thanks also to my great friend and fellow Georgetown grad, Christopher Vorder Bruegge, who spent two months meticulously proofing this work. His comments helped me flesh out parts of the story, and forge better connections between the chapters and characters. Chris and I have been friends for nearly half a century. We have played and co-designed many board games, most notably and most recently *Ancient Civilizations of the Inner Sea* and *Ancient Civilizations of the Middle East*, both of which, by the way, have scenarios that feature Alexander.

Thanks are also in order to Max Sewall, another old gaming friend, for building the website, and to Scott Mitchelson, whose art graces the cover of the novel.

And, finally, a big thanks to Jackie Weger, a professional writer whose patience and advice are both greatly appreciated.

And a special thanks to Charity Chimni for her artistry in formatting this book.

I would most of all like to dedicate this book to my family, especially my ever patient and supportive wife, Cheryl, and our wonderful and equally supportive children: our son, Campbell and our daughter, Ryan. Those who know our daughter will notice that the horse ridden by the girl, Halime, who plays a prominent role in the last third of the novel, bears the name of Ryan's own late, beloved horse, Lemon Twist – or Lemi, as she was affectionately called.

About the Author

Mark G. McLaughlin has been a writer, journalist, author and game-designer for nearly 50 years. His works include two history books, ***The Wild Geese*** and ***Battles of the American Civil War***, and the science fiction novel ***Princess Ryan's Star Marines*** (as well as a board game of the same name). The most recent of his 24 published board games, ***Ancient Civilizations of the Inner Sea***, and its upcoming sequel, ***Ancient Civilizations of the Middle East***, each feature scenarios where players can either be Alexander the Great, or take on the leadership of the Persians (and others) who, like the captain of Thebes in this novel, oppose him.

Mark resides in Peterborough, NH, with the love of his life (and wife of over 40 years), Cheryl. They have two grown children. A son, Campbell, and a daughter, Ryan, the princess for whom a game and novel was named. Mark is an avid miniatures painter and wargamer, and has been fighting out the battles of Alexander and the era for more than half a century.

Connect with me here:
markgmclaughlin.com

facebook.com/mark.mclaughlin.357

What people are saying about
Throne of Darius: A Captain of
Thebes

- Calumnies! Lies! Slander! I am supposed to be the hero and instead I am pictured in this book as a mad and bloodthirsty tyrant! If I ever catch that McLaughlin fellow, I intend to have his body trampled by warhorses and his head chopped off and spitted on a pike!

   - Alexander, King of Macedonia, son of Zeus and Ruler of the World

- A curse upon that libelous scribe that wrote this horrid work! I call upon Zeus, the father of my child, to hurl thunderbolts down upon his head, and urge my ancestor, the great warrior, Achilles, to hunt him down and give him what he gave Hector upon the fields of Ilium.

   - Olympias, Queen of Macedonia, and mother of the demi-god Alexander

- Finally! It is about bloody time that somebody told the truth about that spoiled little bully boy from Macedonia!

   - Memnon of Rhodes, General of the Armies of Persia

- It is touching to know that even after 2,400 years my beauty has not faded... at least not in this author's eyes (oh, won't Helen of Troy be so jealous)!

   - Barsine, Princess of the blood royal of Persia, and wife to Memnon of Rhodes

- Damn it! Mark, I'm a physician not a hero!
  - *Klemes of Thebes, physician*

- War, adventure, romance, courage, cowardice and madness… and all told with a touch of humor. How wonderful to be portrayed as such a hero, and a hero in such a noble cause as that of fighting against Alexander!
  - *Dimitrios of Thebes, captain of a hundred*